New Zealander C. George Muller gave up
world to follow his heart and become a pr
He has a Masters degree in biology, and h
research for the past 8 years – with finding
papers. His travels have taken him across
Alaska, and many places in between. He has worked on projects for the US National Park Service, the New Zealand Department of Conservation, and more than one university. As well as working with seals and cetaceans, He has also worked with four-legged wildlife including wolves, lynx, and grizzly bears – which makes for plenty of interesting stories!

In addition to biology, C. George Muller has experience as a fire-fighter, Search And Rescue team member, martial arts instructor, and soldier.
Echoes in the Blue is his second novel, and was inspired by his experiences on the frontlines of wildlife research and conservation. It was written while living and working in Kaikoura, the whale watching capital of New Zealand.
C. George Muller's first novel won the 2005 Richard Webster Popular Fiction Award.

The Future is in our hands!
George

Echoes in the Blue

C. George Muller

First published in 2006 by Koru Press
Reprinted in 2007 by Koru Press
P.O. Box 51-287, Pakuranga, Auckland, New Zealand

Muller, C. George
Echoes in the Blue

ISBN 978-0-6151-3594-6

This edition printed in New Zealand using sustainable materials and environmentally friendly processes and technologies.

For Laura, who always believed in me.

This book is dedicated to all the wild creatures I have met – and those I have yet to.

Thanks also to the following people who helped make this book a reality: Laura, David, Irene, Anne, Robert, and Lynne for their helpful editing suggestions. Special thanks are also owed to Laura for help with layout and publication, Robert for help with cover and web page design, David for help with all things business and legal, and Dr Simon Childerhouse for review. Thanks also to Larissa Edwards and Andrew Lownie for their positive feedback; a little professional encouragement can go a long way!

Part I – First Blood

Prologue

The Great Whale was suddenly afraid. She hung in the water for a moment, listening. The high-pitched whine seemed to swell around her, echoing through the undersea sound channels. She sensed terrible danger. She hastily called her calf to her, rebuking his playful attempt to engage her in a game. This was not the time. Something was drawing closer. Something terrible.

She called out, a high, piercing song that resonated through the depths of the ocean. She called again, listening desperately for the reassuring call of her kind. But there was no reply in the cold blue emptiness. They were utterly alone…

Her calf had been born nine months before, in the warm embrace of the tepid northern waters. Through the winter she had nursed him, watching him grow from a timid newborn into a playful and mischievous youngster. He was now fat and healthy, but she had used much of her own reserves to produce the rich milk which nourished him, and sustenance was harder to come by in the warm north. They were journeying now to the summer feeding grounds far to the south, in the shadow of the Great White Land. There she would recover her condition, gorging on the plentiful swarms of krill that bloomed in the fertile southern summer. She rumbled in anticipation of the juicy bounty that awaited them, encouraging her little one onwards.

The calf was slow though. His little flukes could not propel him at the speed of a fully-grown adult, and he needed many rest stops on this, his first migration. Their passage was justifiably slow, and they were trailing many days behind the wake of the Herd.

Over their heads, a strong wind was blowing in the World Above. The rolling swells buffeted them each time they rose for their obligatory breath, but the little calf fought bravely, struggling forward with a determination that outweighed his lack of strength. The mother whale was proud. He would grow to be a fine whale one day. Perhaps even a herd bull, a leader among whales.

But she was confused as she hustled her calf onwards.

The history of the whales was long, and their knowledge of the Blue Realm was ancient and intimate. Their kind had been ocean voyagers for countless millennia, a memory stretching perhaps even to the very dawn of the seas. During that time they had amassed a vast knowledge and understanding of life. They were known as great travellers, and undisputed lords of the vast ocean realm. But their rule was peaceful and benign. Rarely did they trouble themselves with the affairs of another kind, living out their long lives simply, content in their own solitude. But lately, in the merest blink of an eye in their timeless history, they had begun sharing the oceans with a new entity; the strange ironclad individuals. They were like whales, large and ponderous, journeying the world's oceans. But the new travellers had no songs, although the harsh noise of their passage filled the waterways just the same. They never responded to a greeting and never deviated from their course, consumed by some vital purpose known only to themselves. So the whales eventually gave up attempts at friendship and learned to ignore the ships that crisscrossed the oceans.

But this ironclad was different. This one was behaving strangely, in a way the mother whale had never seen before. This one had been heading directly towards the duo, brash and aggressive, as if challenging their right to pass by. That was when she began to feel the first prickle of alarm. She had moved aside, changing their course, hustling her weary calf away from the path of the impatient steel monster.

That had not placated it. The whine of the high-speed propellers increased as it swerved towards them again, cutting a wake through the swells as it bore down on the mother and her calf.

Already she could feel the throb of the diesel engines coursing from its hull as it charged towards them. And in a world which held little fear, she was suddenly afraid.

The mother whale was young, and this was her first calf. But the instinct to protect her offspring was strong. As soon as the fear first gripped her, she sounded, calling for him to follow. The calf was confused, still wanting to play in the waves, not understanding the danger. She called again, urgently, and suddenly he recognised the fear in her voice. He came to her at once, a frightened child seeking comfort. But there was no time.

She led him on a shallow dive, aiming to cover as much distance as possible before they would have to surface for another breath. The mother whale forged ahead through the featureless blue, keeping her calf close by where her slipstream would aid his passage. All the while the terrible high-pitched noise reverberated around them. Terror lent speed to the calf's little flukes now, and he swam strongly beside her. But all too soon he began to tire. It was barely a quarter hour later when he veered to the surface for a gasp of air. Though she could have gone on, the mother joined him, determined to protect her baby from whatever danger might lurk above the waves.

She surfaced, a cloud of vapour marking the spot as she exhaled. Beside her, the calf struggled for breath in the rolling sea.

Abruptly, she felt the horrible noise surge all around her as the ironclad accelerated, thundering towards them. In all her life she had never experienced anything like this, but she knew instinctively that this ship threatened mortal danger for both of them.

As if to confirm, a sudden thunderclap brought a whistling projectile her way. It lanced into the water nearby, the steel cable whipping across her back. She panicked at the alien touch, wrenching her body clear in a surge of water. She dived beneath the waves again, the familiar embrace of the Blue World little comfort through her desperation. She knew they had to flee, but where? How could they escape from a hunter that stalked them on the surface? There was no place in the vast ocean they would be safe. Not even the crushing blackness of the Deep could offer them solace. No matter where she led her calf, no matter how far or how fast they swam, eventually the need to breathe would drive them upwards, back to the World of Air where the hunters waited.

Shepherding her calf, she raced on through the empty expanses of blue, fear driving her forward. But the whirring propellers followed her blind rush, and the hunters kept pace above.

Within minutes the youngster was exhausted, and as he clawed for the surface again to breathe, she knew they were done for. She called again, a low mournful sound that would travel the great migration paths, resonating underwater for hundreds of miles. Her voice was frantic, and filled with fear and loneliness. She called for her bull, and the comforting assurance of the Herd.

But no songs came back to her. Only the silence of the Deep.

It was as if the ocean had been emptied of Travellers, and there was no one to share her anguish.

As her calf's narrow back broke the surface, the mother whale knew the Hunters were only moments away. Summoning all her courage she turned to face them, determined to protect her baby. Or die trying.

She thrust aside her natural instinct to flee from the danger and lunged back towards the ship, putting herself between the Hunters and her baby. She rushed straight toward the enemy, hoping to head them off. But her charge was a bluff and the ironclad saw through it. The ship forged ahead without check. At the last moment the mother whale's courage failed her, and as she burst through the crest of a wave toward the ship she veered away to the side, hoping to lure them away instead. In the wild sea she cut directly across the ship's bow, offering them a brief view of her flank before slipping back beneath the churning waves.

But the Hunters refused to be fooled. The ironclad never hesitated from its course, bearing down on the helpless calf like a hunting Mako scenting blood.

The mother whale looked back and saw her baby wallowing weakly in the swells.

Then a thunderclap split the air.

The cruel steel plunged into the calf's tiny back and he squealed in agony as the harpoon tore deep into his flesh. He struggled and thrashed, desperately trying to get free. But he was held fast. With every movement the barbs bit deeper, and his blood soon mixed with the sea. He lay exhausted, whimpering for his mother.

The mother whale was distraught. In whale society she understood and accepted death as a natural progression of life, yet she had no concept of murder. The metallic tang of blood in the water terrified her, heightening her distress. She raced back to his side, trying to comfort him as the life drained from his body. The little calf foundered, too weak to swim. As he sank beneath the waves she lifted him tenderly back to the surface, just as she had done when he was born, helping him take his first breath.

He spluttered weakly as water washed into his blowholes, too weak even to close them.

Then the thunderclap sounded again.

The mother whale felt the shock of the impact as the heavy steel slammed into her side, driving the air from her lungs with a sledgehammer blow. A moment later the pain hit. Waves of searing agony chewed into her flesh like a live thing. She screamed, bucking and thrashing, churning the water to white foam with her struggles. But the barbed harpoon held tight, refusing to relinquish its grip. She shivered at the piercing sting of its touch, tearing at her from the inside. She dived deep into the Blue, trying to escape the pain, but it followed her down. Then the cable came up taught, jerking the cruel steel teeth in her side, stopping her cold. Faint from the pain, and the loss of her lifeblood seeping away into the water, she turned and headed for the surface again. She charged upwards and breached in a shower of spray, launching her entire body into the air. But still she could not escape the harpoon's relentless grip. She crashed back into the sea, and the pain washed over her like waves breaking on a distant shore.

The thunderclap roared again.

The mother whale shuddered as another blow slammed into her back, and a fresh burst of agony tore through her body. But this harpoon was different, and moments later its explosive tip detonated deep within her. The pain was excruciating as the shockwave tore through her body, smashing bone and pulverising her internal organs. She lay on the surface, stunned and broken, unable to command her shattered body to move. Already she could feel the tension on the harpoon cables as she was slowly dragged towards the ship.

The pain seemed far away now. Just a dull ache at the end of a long channel.

The mother whale knew she was dying.

Her last breath was a weak gasp, the vapour cloud as she exhaled was a pink spray of blood.

She moaned softly, trying to comfort her calf to the end. Then she felt the darkness of the Deep rushing up to meet her.

Chapter 1

Richard Major stood at the stern, clutching the railing as the ship swooped down the face of another monstrous swell. Behind lay a vast and featureless tract of ocean, countless miles of heaving green waves topped with foaming white caps. The scenery was repetitive, even monotonous, day after day, mile after mile. Just the wild, empty sea. Always in motion, always changing, but always the same. On all sides the view was identical, except for their narrow wake – the only evidence they had even been here at all. The fleeting white trail stretched behind like an apparition, marking their passage with all the decisiveness of a chalk mark in the rain. Close to the ship the present was enduring – strong white water continually churning out from the stern. But further out the past was short-lived – lasting only until the green expanse claimed it back, wiping away all evidence of their passing. It was as though the ocean presided over everything here. Even destiny.

Richard considered their impertinence, daring to travel so far into a realm where they did not belong. He felt a moment of disquiet, wondering if the ocean might seek to swallow up the insignificant ship as easily as her trail.

Even the sun seemed different in this place. Distant and haughty, offering little in the way of warmth or solace. He found it hard to comprehend the enormity of the sky. Out here, with nothing to break it up, the sky was everywhere, almost as if one could reach up and become part of it. The grey-blue above stretched in an unbroken line as far as the eye could see, challenged only by the deeper blue expanse of the sea below.

Sea and sky. The mighty Southern Ocean. That was his entire world now. And it was not a world to inspire comfort.

Richard shivered inside his bright orange survival suit. The wind was fresh, reddening his cheeks. He tugged absently at the neoprene collar of his jacket. "It'll insulate you against the cold, so make sure you wear it at all times," his brother had warned him. "Since no one knows when they're going to fall overboard it's the only way to be safe!"

Richard's blood ran cold at the thought. Aboard ship the rest of the crew seemed quite cavalier towards the danger though. None of them wore the matching orange gloves and hood that were part of the suit, and most of the time their jackets were unzipped for comfort. Not wanting to look like an idiot, Richard dared to do the same, wearing an old pair of fingerless gloves and a loaned beanie against the cold. He pulled the woollen cap further down on his head. He was glad to have it. Not only did it keep his ears warm, but it covered the bald spot on his head.

Not bald, just thinning, he reminded himself. As if it really mattered. He was only thirty-three years old, but already it seemed like life had passed him by.

Richard dropped his gaze, staring into the churning slipstream behind the stern. The never-ending movement of the ship was the hardest thing to get used to – it was as if the whole world was in perpetual motion, lurching sickeningly every few seconds, this way and that. He couldn't stand properly, let alone walk around anywhere, and it was impossible to sleep. Being crammed into his claustrophobic bunk with a strap to keep him from falling out only made him more aware of the movement. It was like being stuck on a rollercoaster that swooped endlessly around its track, having long ago lost any sense of fun. He knew there were dark circles of weariness under his eyes. He longed for the stability of good solid ground, and the smell of sweet green grass.

Even Richard's journal lay closed and ignored in his cabin. It was usually an evening ritual of his, and a source of comfort as he wrote down the day's events – adding order and meaning to an otherwise confused jumble of experiences. But though his need for it now was even greater than usual, he knew his mutinous stomach simply couldn't cope with the queasiness of trying to write aboard ship.

At least he was able to keep his meals down now. Mostly. The first week at sea had been pure misery, the constant rolling motion sending him running to the rail what seemed like every five minutes. He wondered what the crew thought of him. He had seen them cast sidelong glances at him as they worked, sizing him up. Richard knew he was here only because of his brother, but he hoped the others didn't share that sentiment. He didn't want to be the outsider all the time.

He sighed and looked down at his feet, perched on the precipice. Absently, he read out the name printed on the dark blue stern below him.

Gwendolyn.

The ship was a 44 metre long converted side-trawler. She was a sturdy ocean-going workhorse, designed to handle the worst squalls the North Sea could throw at her – and equally at home here in the wild seas of the Southern Ocean. But with a name like Gwendolyn she sounded more like a frumpy old woman. It was a strange name for a boat, but Richard wasn't about to voice his opinions out loud – and definitely not within earshot of the Skipper. This ship represented the old sea dog's home, entire worldly possessions, and probably even his wife of sorts. Not surprisingly he was a little bit touchy about negative comments. With his bushy black beard and tattooed forearms he looked like a pirate. And you didn't mess with the likes of them.

Richard sighed again. His mind had turned, unbidden, back to his own wife, Gina.

Perhaps the thought had come from his musings about whether the Skipper had a wife. Then again, it was more likely to be a subconscious connection to his thoughts of conflict. Lately it seemed like everything reminded him of his wife Gina. *Ex-wife*, he reminded himself sadly. He just couldn't seem to get her and her infidelity out of his head. And the thoughts gnawed away inside him like a cancer.

"Stand by to lower the boat!"

The shout cut through Richard's daydream.

Oh heck, I'm supposed to be manning the crane!

Richard hurried to the controls, flicking the power switch and winding the cable to take up the slack, just as Cal had shown him. He had no idea why his brother trusted him with an important job like this though.

I'm just an electronics engineer for crying out loud! I design circuit boards!

Richard suspected it was to make him feel valued, but with everyone watching it would be a miracle if he didn't stuff up – and what would the crew think of him then?

"Lower away!"

Cal's shout drifted back over the wind, and Richard took a deep breath and swung the crane out over the side.

Moments later the outboard motor roared, and the Naiad inflatable zoomed away barely an instant after it splashed down, climbing straight up the side of a towering swell before disappearing over the crest.

It really was a tiny boat to brave such huge seas. Richard felt weak at the knees just watching. He had no idea how his little brother managed to handle such a frenetic job, but handle it he did. Blimey, he even seemed to enjoy it!

Cal was kneeling in the bow when the Naiad came into view again, one foot firmly planted on the bright orange pontoon, the crossbow snug against his shoulder.

Suddenly the whale blew again, a blast of air like an escaping steam vent. Even Richard saw it that time – and he suddenly realised it was the first whale he'd ever seen. It was huge. Awesome. A massive dark shadow in the water, perhaps twenty-five feet long, dwarfing the tiny orange inflatable. Its white belly seemed to glow beneath the water, along with the light-coloured band around its fins. Cal had said it was a Minke whale, the smallest of the Great Whales. But to Richard, even watching from the safety of the ship it looked plenty big enough. One flick of its tail could probably overturn the little boat his brother was riding in and send them all to a watery grave.

Richard watched anxiously as the Naiad Team made their preparations. Cal pushed the hood of his survival suit back to clear his vision, and his sun-bleached blonde hair danced in the wind. He put the crossbow stock against his chest and flexed his biceps as he drew the bowstring towards him, showing little effort as he cocked the heavy bow. Richard had tried and failed to draw the bowstring in the calm and composed world of the Gwendolyn's saloon, and that was a far cry from his brother's position balanced on the edge of the rocking pontoon. But then, Cal was always the athlete of the family.

Crouched down behind him was Heath, the Californian. He was a bit of a strange one. His real name was James Heathcliffe but he refused to answer to anything except Heath. Apparently he considered James to be far too bourgeois a name for him. Whatever that meant.

Heath brushed the woolly dreadlocks out of his eyes as he bent over the gear. He took out a tiny dart from the waterproof case and handed it up for Cal to load in the crossbow.

Behind them, Vicki Conner was driving the little inflatable, her dark ponytail flying in the wind. Cal had mentioned she gave up a job offer with a big biotechnology company in Australia to come and work out here instead. Richard was surprised that a woman would want such a physical job as this. Especially a young and pretty woman. But then, what did he know? It seemed gender equality had really come of age for biology. It was just his luck he worked in electronics – no pretty young women were interested in revolutionising that industry!

"Story of my life," he muttered to himself.

He had to admit Vicki was good at what she did though. As soon as the whale spouted she swung the tiller, swerving the speeding boat alongside. No words were spoken, but she expertly lined the Naiad up, keeping it parallel with the surging whale but far enough away not to scare it. Before the creature could even finish its breath Cal was standing up in the bow, lining up his shot. Richard didn't know how his brother could hold his balance so well without using his hands, but his back was straight as a ruler, even as the boat skipped up the side of a massive wall of water. He saw Cal tense, and he held his breath waiting for him to take the shot.

Suddenly, at the last possible moment, another shadow loomed out of the depths. A second back broke the surface and a smaller spout shot up in front of the whale's bulk.

It's a baby!

Richard felt a moment of pleasure at the sight, quickly turning to concern. It was in the way! But he needn't have worried. Cal relaxed his aim, raising his head from behind the sights to watch the little one.

Behind him, Heath also caught sight of the baby whale.

"Nooo," he shouted, lunging at Cal. His shoulder crashed into Cal's side, and he flailed his arms, trying to throw off his aim. He knocked the nose of the crossbow skywards, and it discharged with a loud *thunk*, sending the dart spinning away into the wind. Cal fell over, and Richard held his breath. For a brief moment it looked as though his brother might topple over the side, but Vicki's reaction was lightning-fast. She cut the throttle and swerved the boat back under him. Cal fell against the metal bilge plate with a crash, twisting his body to protect the crossbow as he landed.

Richard exhaled. *That was close!*

Cal jumped up, fury written on his face. Even from that distance Richard could hear the next angry exchange.

"What the hell d'ya think you're doing eh?"

Heath met his glare. "Dude, the baby was in the way."

"I saw it." Cal retorted, his eyes blazing. "Why do you think I didn't shoot?"

Heath seemed to realise he'd over-reacted, but he stubbornly refused to apologise. "I was just ensuring his safety," he persisted, his lip ring making him lisp his 's's. Or perhaps it was his tongue stud.

"What about my safety?" Cal was indignant. "You damn near sent me over the side. Plus you cost me a three hundred dollar VHF tag. You can thank your lucky stars that wasn't a satellite tag you just lost or you wouldn't be here for much longer – but before I put you ashore you'd be going for a swim until you found the bloody thing!"

"Hey man, we're not here to risk these animals' safety any more than we have to," Heath retorted.

"That wild shot was a bigger risk to everyone's safety. What if it punctured the boat? Or hit someone?"

Heath opened his mouth to argue again, but Cal cut him off.

"Listen," he said, his voice surprisingly calm given the circumstances. "I'm in charge here. That means I call the shots." He fixed Heath with a cold stare. "I don't know what you think you're here for, but as long as you are here you'll do things my way. Got it?"

"Spare me your fascist bullshit," Heath muttered under his breath, yanking his floppy hat down over his head as he turned away.

Richard was shocked at the outburst. He abhorred conflict. But then again, he wasn't altogether surprised this had happened. Since he'd first come aboard he'd recognised Heath was a difficult character to get along with; always grumping around, making snide comments about the world, and with a permanent scowl on his face.

Richard's mind went back to the time Heath had been supposed to show him how to do a plankton tow. But as soon as they were out of sight of the bridge he'd left Richard to it and ducked behind a ventilator. There he took out a fat hand-rolled cigarette with what looked like grass clippings sticking out the end. He lit it up and took a deep puff, exhaling luxuriously. "Man, that's good ganja. Really hits the spot. You want some?" Richard looked away, embarrassed and guilty because they were supposed to be working. "N-no thanks," he said.

Heath sneered disdainfully. "Jeez man, you need to lighten up on the servitude front. This stuff'll mellow you out." Richard had looked away, his cheeks colouring.

He cringed at the memory now. It was going to be tough to get accepted by the crew, and not for the first time, he wondered what he was doing here.

Cal and Vicki were the scientists in charge of this research trip, and he, Heath, and Summer were aboard as field assistants to help them. That included not just helping collect data, and analysing it under the microscopes or with computer statistical software, but also running the ship and taking their turns rostered on in the galley, cooking, cleaning, or washing up. It was definitely a different environment to get used to, especially being in such close proximity to your co-workers for such a long stretch – not so easy for someone who preferred to keep to himself. But it was a close-knit environment though, and everyone pulled their weight. The two scientists especially used any spare moment to brainstorm new ideas for their work. That was how Richard had really gotten a feel for what they were doing here. They had explained it to him of course, but it wasn't until he'd seen them discussing their work that he really understood what drove them.

Gathered around the mess table in the corner of the saloon, empty dinner dishes forgotten on the table, Cal and Vicki would bounce ideas off each other until late in the night. They would wave their hands animatedly as they argued some shared problem, scribbling diagrams or equations on the corner of a napkin, their eyes alight as they thought up some new way of collecting data or revealing the answers to the elusive questions they sought.

Cal's work aimed to investigate the population size and distribution of different whale species, using electronic tags to track the animals and computer mapping to plot the results, looking for possible climatic or biological reasons to explain what he saw. Vicki's work was more lab-oriented, looking at genetic variance between sub-populations and among species. She would analyse the DNA samples to see how closely related the individuals were, using it to plot how much contact groups might have with each other, and how recently. Both scientists used the huge photo ID database of known animals they collected to support their findings, and their studies married perfectly together.

Technically, Cal was the senior researcher. It was he who organised and funded the research, hiring the Skipper and his ship on permanent charter, and providing the money and equipment to keep the research going. His post-doctoral research was privately organised and funded, although he retained some ties to the University where he had completed his PhD. Even though Vicki was still working on her PhD, he treated her as an equal and they planned their fieldwork together, working collectively to gather data for each other's research project. It was a professional partnership based on mutual respect.

Richard sighed. He wasn't sure he had much respect amongst the crew. Cal and Vicki were patient with him, but he worried that the others resented his presence here. It was hard to fit in when everyone knew what to do and didn't seem to have time to explain things to a newbie.

He knew he had to make an effort to fit in and be liked though, because there was no getting off the ship and it promised to be a long, lonely cruise if he didn't get on with his new shipmates.

The crew were an international bunch, despite the fact they were based out of New Zealand. He and Cal were Kiwis, of course, but Vicki was an Aussie, and Summer was Canadian – a very attractive one at that! She was from somewhere near Calgary, he thought, but she had sounded evasive and irritated when he plucked up the courage to try asking her. He hadn't succeeded in breaking the ice – if anything she was even more frosty, and he hadn't been brave enough to try again after that.

The other two crew were Americans, although Heath and the Skipper might as well have come from different planets they were so unlike each other. The gruff old captain and the surly animal rights activist seemed destined not to get along with each other, not to mention the rest of the crew.

To Richard, the Skipper was the most frightening of all. Not because he was mean. Just… intimidating. He was probably in his sixties, but he didn't look old at all. It was as though he didn't get older, just more grizzled. His black ponytail was streaked with grey, and his skin looked like a piece of old leather. But he still looked tough enough to take on all comers at a bar-room brawl – and win. His real name was Duke Hayward, but everyone just called him Skipper. Or Skip. Apparently he had fought in Vietnam, with the Navy

SEALs. Apparently he enjoyed it too. Richard didn't have any trouble believing that.

The Skipper didn't say a lot, and when he did you had to listen closely. He'd already made it quite clear he wasn't in favour of coddling anybody, and he certainly wasn't in the habit of repeating himself either. Richard was a nervous wreck from a fortnight of living on edge, listening out for shouted orders and hurrying to obey without making any mistakes. He wasn't about to confuse port and starboard again, not after the last public humiliation in front of the crew.

The Skipper was from somewhere in the South. He had a heavy drawl and his voice was kind of gruff, and it was difficult to understand him with a wad of tobacco always jammed in his cheek. When he did speak he always spoke his mind though. And that included being brutally honest. Richard hadn't forgotten the muttered comment when he'd first stepped aboard.

"That boy looks like he'd blow away in a stiff breeze."

Cal had laughed and cracked a smart remark in reply, treating it as if it had been a joke. But Richard just stared down at his shoes, pretending he hadn't heard.

Richard shuffled his feet now, the embarrassment still fresh in his mind.

Just then the outboard motor revved. He looked up in time to see the Naiad zoom off again in pursuit of the whale. Cal was back in position in the bow, the crossbow already reloaded with another orange dart.

He had designed the little hollow darts himself, and one night in the wardroom he'd shown Richard how they worked, clearly proud of his efforts. The darts were a multi-purpose delivery system that could be loaded with a biopsy punch to get a few millimetres of skin for a DNA sample, or used to insert one of the tracking tags just under the skin. Richard must have looked a bit concerned at the idea, because Cal had been quick to assure him the animals felt practically nothing.

Richard was impressed with the delivery system, but of course the electronics engineer in him was more fascinated by the tiny radio tags – no larger than a ballpoint pen, but able to transmit a radio signal over hundreds of kilometres of ocean for years at a time. He marvelled at the ingenious circuit design that could generate so much potential out of such tiny components.

Apparently in the old days the transmitters used to be almost as big as a paperback book – and had to be manually glued onto the animal's back! Not surprisingly that only worked with dolphins since the animals had to be small enough to be caught and brought aboard a boat to be worked on. Richard stifled a smile. He wouldn't have put it past his crazy brother to try jumping onto a whale's back to give it a go anyway!

The Naiad sped towards the whale, crashing over a wave top in a shower of spray. As he watched Cal standing to attention in the bow, cradling the crossbow, Richard wondered just how much easier this new tag delivery system really was.

Heath seemed to have been forgotten for the moment, crouched in the bottom of the boat, hanging on for dear life as they bounced over the waves.

As the Naiad rapidly closed the gap, the whale blew noisily then pitched forward at a sharp angle. Richard watched as the whole length of her back rolled slowly into view. First the miniature dorsal fin slipped out of the waves, then her tail flukes broke clear of the water.

Cal's shout carried back over the wind. "She's sounding!"

The whale had been at the surface for several minutes, during which she'd spouted several times. It was clear her lungs were now recharged with oxygen and she was finished here, meaning for this dive to last a while.

The inflatable was still about fifty metres behind the disappearing whale though, hurrying to catch up after Heath's over-reaction had delayed them. That was a long way, and the angle was all wrong for the shot. Cal had described what had to happen for the tag to be deployed properly. He needed the dart to fly straight and flat, so it would enter parallel to the surface, slipping just under the top layer of skin like a surgeon's needle. There it would lie flat, with the antenna projecting out flush against the skin, streamlined and out of harm's way.

But at this long range Cal would have to aim the crossbow high in the air to compensate for the dart's falling trajectory. That would have it coming straight down towards the whale's back, arriving end-on like a dart sticking into a dartboard. And that was bad. If that happened the tag couldn't travel deep enough into the thick blubber. It also meant the antenna would be left sticking straight up where it could get damaged, or worse still, the slipstream would catch it as the whale swam and yank the tag out.

Richard held his breath as his brother took aim at the disappearing whale. He would only get one shot, and another lost radio-tag would make this an expensive as well as frustrating day for all of them.

The giant tail flukes tipped forward, rising majestically out of the water.

Like a statue, Cal fought to hold his position in the heaving bow. Suddenly there was a sharp *thwack* as the bow fired. Richard was sure the crossbow was pointed too high, but he trusted Cal knew what he was doing. The orange dart zipped high in the air, scribing an arc across the grey sky. Then it plunged down towards the broad back now sinking vertically into the water. It stuck fast, a bright splash of colour against the dark hide, but appearing as insignificant as an orange tick on the side of an elephant.

Moments later the grey back disappeared from sight into the depths. Richard heard a camera shutter click beside him, then the tail slipped beneath the waves too. The sea closed over it with an air of finality and it was gone. But for the empty dart left bobbing in the swells and the image burned on his memory, the whale might never have been there at all.

"Hey Richard – That's your name isn't it? – I need you over here for a minute."

With a guilty start, Richard remembered his other directives for the day. The voice belonged to Summer Smith, and he was supposed to be helping her. She was the last member of the six-person crew, and definitely the most terrifying.

Without question she was the most beautiful woman he had ever seen, real or computer-generated. And she was far and away the most beautiful woman who had ever spoken to him. Out of the corner of his eye he sneaked a look at her, taking advantage of the fact she was still engrossed with the camera.

She was tall, poised, and stunning. With her blonde tresses tied back in a carefree ponytail, and the 'V' of her half-zipped jacket showing a devilish hint of skin, she was enough to make any man go weak at the knees.

Richard couldn't even look her in the eye without blushing. But that made it even worse. If his gaze shied away from her face then he'd have a sudden panic attack in case she thought he was staring at her chest. And then there was nowhere to look except the floor, while desperately hoping she couldn't feel the heat radiating from his cheeks.

"Today would be nice," she snapped, lowering the camera to fix him with a cold stare.

He could feel the weight of her gaze, evaluating him. "I… uh… sorry," he stammered, hurrying over.

"Here's the data sheet for the Photo ID database," she said, thrusting a clipboard at him. Her Canadian accent was quirky and strangely alluring, like some exotic dessert – not that Richard could really tell the difference though. All North American accents sounded the same to him.

"The frame numbers I took for that female are 389 through 392," she continued. "I'll call out the rest as I go." She tossed her hair and turned back to the camera. "Stapled to the back is the master list of frequencies for the radio tags, and vial numbers for the genetics samples. Fill out the details for each animal. You'll figure it out."

Richard hastened to obey, humming softly and chewing on the pencil as he studied the form. The graphite made a satisfying mark on the shiny greased paper, and he quickly filled a page with his neat handwriting.

It was difficult to keep his mind entirely on the job though, especially with Summer standing so close. The wind blew her hair out in a golden halo, and it seemed to reach out towards him, teasing. Richard closed his eyes, imagining its soft touch brushing his face. Every now and then he fancied he could detect a trace of her perfume on the breeze. He basked in the moment, knowing the chances of being alone with her again on the crowded ship were slim. He knew he should take advantage of this opportunity, but how?

Just talk to her – ask her a question.

Richard swallowed. The very idea made his mouth turn dry. But he knew he had to step outside of his comfort zone. That was why Cal had brought him out here on this trip, wasn't it?

Do it.

His heart began to pound.

Do it!

He took a step forward. "Um…" he stammered. "F-for this box here, do I write the whole six digits for the frequency?"

"No. Just the last three is fine," Summer replied distractedly. "They all start the same." Then she looked over his shoulder at the form and a frown creased her face. "That's not the right frequency! That tag just went in the sea. Cal had to deploy the next tag on the list."

Richard sensed the condescension in her tone and he felt foolish. He had been standing there watching the whole episode, after all.

How could I be so dumb?

Summer wasn't finished yet though. "Don't write so much," she said. "I don't need an essay for each thing. And write bigger. I practically need a microscope to decipher that."

"Um… sorry," he mumbled.

Richard felt his colour rising again. He never had been any good around women.

His thoughts drifted back to Gina again. It was no wonder she'd left him really. Who'd want to stay with a loser like him? And she was right; he had been holding her back socially. It wasn't like he went with her to many of those tennis club functions, and the few times he did go he'd just spend an awkward evening in the corner, looking on while she mingled with all the beautiful people. It was a wonder she'd married him at all. But then, they had both been kind of young, and his new salary had promised the kind of glittering life she craved, even if his social skills hadn't quite been able to match it.

He sighed, wondering how long she'd been fooling around with the tennis coach behind his back. He'd always wondered how he managed to land such a glamorous wife. Now he finally knew the answer. That was the cold hard truth – even when she was his wife, she wasn't really… making a show of being his, while at the same time fooling around behind his back. Richard grimaced. The pain was still fresh, but he was surprised at his own naivety. He should have seen something like that coming. She was far too glitzy for a mouse like him. He didn't deserve her. He knew that in his heart. It was a wonder she hung around as long as she did. Richard's head drooped. That was the cruellest cut of all, knowing the heartache of a failed marriage was only the tip of the iceberg. In the grand scheme of things it was just the ultimate proof; he was a loser.

The break-up had hit Richard badly. Things had gone from bad to worse at work, and the stress piled up along with the workload. As well as his usual work designing circuit board layouts, he'd recently accepted a managerial position which involved a lot more responsibility as he took charge of the whole production process. But suddenly he found he couldn't take it any more. He couldn't concentrate in meetings, his budgets were wrong, and even his circuit boards were filled with stupid errors. And the whole time all he wanted to do was crawl under his desk and cry. He was floundering in the deep end, and it was only a matter of time until he drowned.

He hadn't told anyone about it – his father had always said a man should keep his problems to himself – but Cal had rung out of the blue one day, asking how he was. Richard had tried to put on a brave front, but his brother seemed to know something was wrong. He wouldn't accept Richard's protests that he was fine, and after a little probing Richard ended up pouring his heart out over the phone.

"It's like life doesn't mean anything any more. I don't want to go to work in the morning, but I don't want to come home again at night either. I don't want to do anything. I just feel… empty."

"Bro, I know exactly what you mean," Cal murmured, and Richard was grateful. The last thing he needed then was sympathy, however well-intentioned.

"Tell you what," Cal said thoughtfully. "Why don't you come and help me out for a while? I need another field assistant for my next trip. You could take time off from your work – it'll be like a break to recharge your batteries."

Richard had taken some persuading though. He'd heard plenty of stories about the crazy things Cal did for a living, and he had no desire to get mixed up in that. His brother had earned himself a bit of a reputation as the black sheep of the family over the years. That hadn't always been the case, of course. Cal had once been their parents' pride and joy. He had received good marks at law school and straight out of university he landed a good job with a big firm. He'd had a promising career ahead of him and was looking at buying a house in a nice suburb. He had a pretty girlfriend from a good family, and they were starting to talk about getting married and settling down together. By all measures his life was a success.

But then one day he just quit. Everything. He left the career, the house, the fiancée, his whole life, walking away from everything to become a biologist.

Their Father thought Cal was a fool, a dreamer with his head in the clouds. Richard wasn't sure what to make of it. He still loved his brother though, however mixed up his life choices seemed to be. He preferred to think of Cal as an eccentric – odd but still lovable in his own way. There had to be something self-destructive about the way he'd sabotaged his own career like that though. Who in their right mind would choose to throw away everything to become a virtual drifter, spending his life bouncing from one crazy adventure to the next?

Not Richard. He needed stability in his life. And the last thing he felt like doing was joining Cal on some crazy venture. Let alone at a time when all he wanted to do was crawl into bed and sleep for a hundred years.

But Cal had been insistent.

"Just a month or two. Take some time off. It sounds like you're long overdue for a break. You'll feel better for it – I promise."

So that was how Richard had found himself standing on the dock in Lyttleton, clutching a battered suitcase and wondering what the hell he was getting himself into.

Richard smiled wistfully at the memory. He'd come a long way from that point in two weeks of sailing – and not just the thousands of miles on the chart. He still wasn't sure about Cal's promise he'd feel better, and he remained doubtful he could ever enjoy himself out here… but all the same, for the first time he realised he wasn't exactly missing his other life as an Electronics Project Manager. There was too much going on to feel homesick – especially when home was just an empty house waiting for him.

Suddenly Vicki's shout cut through his thoughts. "Cal," she yelled above the wind. "The calf's about to dive too. I need a genetics sample from him. If you can?"

Cal winked back, laying the crossbow down. "No worries, but he's too little to risk a dart. Can you take us in?"

Vicki grinned in reply. Clearly that was a rhetorical question too.

Cal picked up the sampling pole and began fiddling with the end of it. Richard knew he would be attaching a fresh Velcro pad to the end of it. He'd thought his brother was pulling his leg when he explained how they collected skin cells to do their DNA analysis, but apparently a piece of Velcro on a stick really was the best way.

Cal was lying down on the pontoon now, the pole stretched out at arm's length beside him. Vicki gunned the outboard, edging the speeding Naiad closer. Richard held his breath, wondering if the juvenile whale would see them and flee. Or worse, tip over the boat in his panic.

Under Vicki's expert guidance, the inflatable swooped alongside, within a couple of metres of the swimming calf. Cal leaned out over the rushing green water. Richard swallowed. For a youngster the whale looked enormous, longer than the little orange boat and surely many times heavier. He hoped his brother knew what he was doing.

But the whole operation took less time than a sneeze. Cal leaned out and rubbed the pole along the glistening back. A few seconds later the Naiad pulled away again, and Cal was already sitting on the floor of the boat, holding the tip of the pole out to Heath's gloved hands.

Then the calf flicked his little tail flukes in the air and was gone, leaving them alone on the ocean.

Richard stood transfixed, watching the spot where the whales had disappeared. Those were the first whales he'd ever seen in real life, and now that the excitement was over the enormity of it suddenly began to sink in. They were so impossibly huge, yet so graceful. He stared after them, strangely content, but yearning to see them again.

What must it be like to spend your whole life travelling such a huge ocean?

Richard's other life in Auckland suddenly seemed dull and grey by comparison. That was a world of concrete, mirror glass, and tar seal. Where the largest animal he might see would be a sparrow, or maybe a pigeon. By comparison, the whales seemed almost mystical in their grandeur. Richard was amazed that such massive animals could exist, even more so that he had never felt the urge to see one before. He had lived on this Earth for thirty-three years without ever considering what might lie beyond the city where he lived, or what wonders the world might hold.

But here he was, standing right in the centre of the wild and dangerous Ocean. It was a place of raw power, where nature overshadowed man. A place Richard had never had any desire to visit before, not even in his wildest flights of fancy.

With a sudden start, Richard realised the Naiad was back, bumping its rubber nose against the side of the ship.

Oh blimey…

He hurried to the crane, pressing the winder button and straining to swing the boat back on board. His biceps had always been rather scrawny but he heaved with all his strength, not wanting to appear a weakling.

Cal was still pissed off when he came back on board. Richard could tell by the set of his jaw.

"Good job, Team," he called as he swung his leg over the side, without waiting for Richard to lower the Naiad back on the deck. But his cheeriness was forced, as if through clenched teeth.

Heath followed, looking sullen. He wasn't about to let the matter rest though. "We have no right to physically molest these wonderful beings. Invasive research is almost as bad as whaling," he announced to no one in particular.

"What's his problem?" Richard whispered behind his hand.

Cal shrugged. "He doesn't like some of our research methods. Reckons the dart gun is too invasive." He rolled his eyes.

"Do the whales mind it?" Richard asked.

"Well, it depends what you mean," Cal laughed. "I'm sure they're not over the moon about us driving up to them in the Naiad and sticking them, but that's at the small end of the disturbance scale compared to getting harpooned and butchered, and it's for the greater good. The info we collect adds a great deal to our understanding of the species, including the long-term challenges they face for survival."

"Does the tag hurt them?" Richard asked.

Cal turned to him, deliberately showing his back to the Californian, but talking loud enough for him to hear. "Nah. Pain receptors are mostly found in the lower layers of the skin – just like you could poke a needle into the upper layers of your own skin without feeling much pain. And the big whales have got at least thirty centimetres of blubber above the deep layer where most of the nerve endings are. The tag hurts them a lot less than when you get an injection – more like a sandfly bite. In fact they probably barely notice it."

"But what about the tag under their skin? Doesn't that bother them?"

Cal shook his head. "The plastic sheath is biologically inert, and we're careful to keep it sterile so there's no danger of infection. Apart from that it's so small it's practically insignificant to them – just like when vets put ID microchips under the skin of valuable dogs."

"It's still a violation," Heath muttered. "We forced a change in behaviour on them. What if that baby was traumatised by our actions?"

Cal looked annoyed. "It's a pity that skin scrape didn't hurt the little guy – with the Japanese Fleet around he needs to learn not to trust boats."

Heath stomped off, muttering under his breath.

Richard fidgeted uncomfortably.

Cal laughed. "Don't you worry yourself about him. Sometimes he's just a little bit too radical for his own good, that's all" His eyes twinkled. "At least he didn't ruin my success rate, even if he did cost me a radio tag!"

The Skipper came out of the wheelhouse, a lopsided grin plastered underneath his whiskers – the first time Richard had seen him smile.

"Nice job y'all," he muttered gruffly, but it was clear who most of his praise was directed at. He clapped Cal on the back hard enough to make him wince. "Great shot, Son. Y' could hit the left testicle on an epileptic flea with a shot like that. Mighty fine effort."

Cal laughed off the praise. "My Mum taught me never to brag."

Duke rubbed his beard, looking serious. "Hell son, if you've done it, it ain't braggin'."

Cal laughed again and rolled his eyes. "That would be one for the record books."

Just the same though, Richard noticed he was whistling happily as he secured the inflatable on the deck.

Duke opened his tobacco pouch and casually tucked a wad of the dark leaf under his top lip, then headed for the wheelhouse. Almost as an afterthought he turned back to Cal. "When you're done there's somethin' y' might wanna take a look at inside… While y'all were out playin' I picked up an interesting signal on the hydrophone."

Richard hovered by the doorway as the rest of the crew crowded into the small wheelhouse. He was still flushed with pride that he had managed to operate the crane correctly, recovering the Naiad from the sea's clutches without incident. But no one seemed to have noticed. After it was all over they had rushed straight to the Gwendolyn's bridge, eager to see what the Skipper had found.

Richard stood in the background, trying to see through the wall of parkas that blocked his view, unsure what was happening. Heath was standing in front of him, his tangled dreadlocks blocking his view. Richard wrinkled his nose as the stale smell of body odour wafted into his nostrils.

He manoeuvred himself next to Summer, careful not to stand too close as he looked over her shoulder. She sensed his presence, glancing back with mild annoyance before turning away again. He swallowed nervously, but held his ground. Over the cornsilk of her hair, he could see his brother Cal hunched over the hydrophone, cupping the headphones tightly to his ear as he listened.

"No way," he breathed. "It can't be…"

A buzz of conversation swept through the crowded cabin.

"Shh." Cal held up his free hand for silence, screwing his eyes closed as he concentrated.

Suddenly a huge grin spread across his face. "Hot damn!" he whispered. "I think it is…!"

Chapter 2

Richard Major stood in the doorway to the Gwendolyn's bridge, watching as his brother adjusted the sensitivity dial on the hydrophone, turning it right down towards the lower limits of its range. Someone coughed. The Crew shuffled impatiently. Cal ignored them, refusing to be hurried, a look of delight slowly replacing the concentration on his face.

"It is!" His voice was hushed, almost reverent. "Hot damn, it is!"

Cal leaned across to flick the speaker switch, and the cabin was instantly filled with sound. A deep, echoing song poured out of the speakers. It was a strange unearthly melody that spoke of the mysterious Deep, the timeless oceans, the last wild places on Earth.

The song of a whale.

Richard had never heard such beautiful music. The haunting sounds seemed to emanate from everywhere, and nowhere, as though from the very fibres of the universe itself. He listened, entranced, as the sounds swelled and flowed around him.

"It's beautiful," he breathed.

"It's a Blue whale," Cal whispered back, his eyes shining. "He's calling to his kind."

Richard nodded. He could hear the question in the mournful song, as though searching the vast ocean for a reply. The aching loneliness was almost tangible.

"The sound can be heard for hundreds of kilometres," Cal said. "The low frequency echoes travel through the Deep Scattering Layer of the sea." He fell silent, listening as the whale sang his solo dirge. But there was no answer to the whale's lament. A shadow seemed to cross Cal's face. "The Blues are practically extinct. Who knows how long this guy has been travelling the world's oceans, alone?" He turned away. "His lonely search is a testament to human greed. For tens of millions of years these oceans were filled with the songs of whales. Then in less than a century – barely a blink of an eye in evolutionary terms – we've emptied them."

Richard looked at the floor, waiting for his brother to continue. Presently he did, his voice distant, as though he knew the subject matter backwards but his mind was wandering somewhere far away.

"The Blue is the largest of the Rorquals; the greatest whales of all. The Rorquals were the last whales to be exploited by man. They're fast and strong, living far from the sight of land. For many years they were beyond even our capacity to kill. But then our devious cunning developed high-speed diesel engines, spotter planes, factory ships, and exploding harpoons. In less than a century we have practically exterminated them."

He sighed deeply. "There are barely five hundred Blue whales left in the Southern Ocean now… maybe a few thousand in the whole world, tops. Their numbers are down from a total of nearly 300,000 just a few centuries ago – that's about one percent of their original population!" He shook his head sadly, as though still incredulous. "That would be like culling the worldwide human population to sixty million – about twice Tokyo's size – and wiping out absolutely everyone else. That means getting rid of all the other people in America, Europe, Africa, Asia… even the rest of Japan. Everyone."

Richard swallowed. That was a lot of dead people.

Cal made a face, as if reading his thoughts. "Before you feel too sorry for those few surviving people, remember that even one percent of the current human population would still outnumber Blue whales by 20,000 to one!"

Richard's eyes widened in surprise. "But aren't blue whales recovering now?" he ventured. "Aren't they protected?"

"Blues have been commercially extinct – not even worth the whalers' time looking for – since the 1950's, supposedly protected since 1967, but still they haven't recovered. Their numbers have stayed the same, teetering on the brink, for over half a century. We may already have pushed them too far to ever recover." Cal threw up his hands. "And for what? A bit of oil? Some meat? So some already rich businessmen can make a bit more money?" He muttered a curse under his breath. "What happens when the whales are all gone? What happens when the Earth's natural resources are finished?" He sneered. "The greedy bastards will be rotting in the ground by then. But what are our grandkids supposed to do? What the hell kind of legacy is that to leave for the future?"

No one spoke, each caught up in their own thoughts.

Richard was conflicted. At that moment he began to appreciate what his brother was doing out here – for the first time he thought he finally understood him. But at the same time Cal's angry tone made him instinctively withdraw into himself. Richard looked at the deck. Conflict was not something he dealt with well.

It was Duke who broke through the silence, his gravelly voice sounding surprisingly loud in the enclosed space. Richard jumped, embarrassed in case his thoughts might be evident on his face. But the Skipper was looking at the sonar display.

"He's feedin' now. About ten clicks away," he announced. "As happy as Larry."

Cal seemed to snap out of his trance. "This is a chance in a million," he murmured.

Richard wasn't sure what was going on, but he must have looked puzzled because Cal turned to him to explain. "The Blue whale remains largely a mystery to science. We have so little info on their biology. We don't know how long they live, how far they travel, or where they go when they're not feeding here in the Southern Ocean. No one even knows where they breed." His eyes shone. "Imagine what we could find out if we could get a tag on this guy…"

He snapped into action. "Skip, take us as close as you can. Vicki, prep the Naiad. I'll get the gear ready as we go."

Richard sensed the excitement flash through the Team. Even he had to admit that the prospect of more action made him tingle. It was thrilling stuff – as long as he could watch from safely out of harm's way.

Cal turned to hurry aft. As he ran he nearly bumped into Heath, who still wore a dark scowl on his face.

"Now we're going to harass the greatest spirit of the ocean," he muttered darkly, lisping through his tongue stud.

Cal didn't even pause. "No," he replied matter-of-factly. "You're not."

He called back over his shoulder. "Richard, you'll load for me on this one."

Richard felt his stomach lurch. "W-what?"

"Grab your gear and jump in the Naiad."

"But Cal, I-"

His brother paused, seeing Richard's consternation. He came back and laid a hand on his shoulder, comforting, but at the same time firmly steering him aft. "Don't worry, it'll be ok. Just hand me the gear as I call for it. You'll do fine."

Richard suddenly felt weak at the knees.

The next few minutes passed in a blur, but despite his misgivings Richard somehow found himself sitting in the Naiad, hanging on for dear life as it dangled beneath the derrick. He'd managed to bang his sore elbow again. It was already coming up in a deep purple bruise where he'd fallen off the toilet that morning, tossed against the wall as the ship hit a swell. That particular indignity had been painful and humiliating, but it was nothing compared to how he felt now. He felt his throat tighten as they swung out over the water. The Naiad swayed on the crane and Richard scrabbled for a handhold, too scared to risk looking down. He was utterly petrified.

How did I get myself into this?

He moaned inwardly, but he knew things would only get worse.

With a stomach-dropping lurch, the inflatable began to drop towards the sea. Richard held his breath, staring back at the row of faces that lined the rail.

Duke had cut the throttles while they lowered the boat, and now his bearded face appeared next to the others, watching. His eyes seemed to twinkle with amusement. Richard avoided his gaze, sure the burly Skipper could sense his distress – and was enjoying every minute of it.

He tried to focus on Summer instead. She really was stunning, he reflected. Drop-dead gorgeous. Not to mention light years out of his league. He had no idea where the phrase "drop-dead gorgeous" came from, but if it was possible for the mere sight of a woman to cause a man's heart to stop beating, she would be the one to do it. His heart definitely skipped a beat every time he saw her. He searched her angelic features, knowing even the smallest hint of a smile would boost his spirits. But she wasn't even looking at him, busy fiddling with the camera she would use to try and get a photo ID of the whale.

Richard sneaked a glance at Heath, hunched behind the crane. He was scowling behind his eyebrow stud, his mouth pulled into a tight line. Richard looked away guiltily. He hoped the Californian didn't blame him for this. It wasn't like he'd wanted to take his place. Richard risked a look down, where the dark water swirled hungrily. He shivered and looked away. In fact, he'd happily switch places with anyone in a heartbeat!

Heath's face slowly disappeared from sight as they slid down the navy-blue steel of the ship.

Then with a splash they were down.

"Ropes," Cal called.

Oh heck, that's me.

Richard had to force himself to release his death-grip on the seat. The hook was a fraction too high to reach from where he was sitting, so he took a deep breath and stood shakily.

The boat rocked on the swells.

Richard felt his heart flutter, but forced himself to keep standing. He must have looked like an idiot; hunched over like an old man, arms outstretched for balance, too scared to stand straight or look up in case he toppled over. He tried to block out everything, sure the others would be laughing at him. Somehow he managed to reach up with sightless hands and find the hook, then unclip the ropes without pinching his fingers in the heavy metal clip. Then he collapsed back onto the seat, panting gratefully as he felt its solidness beneath him.

This close to the water he could taste the salty tang in the air. The waves slapped against the hull and the boat lurched alarmingly. Richard lunged for a handhold, thoughts of falling overboard crowding into his head. He gasped out loud, imagining the shock of the cold water as he sank, down, down into the dark depths. Suddenly the fear was no longer a vague nightmare. It was real, substantial, and it threatened to overwhelm him.

This wasn't what he wanted. He didn't mind watching the excitement, but he didn't want to be in the middle of it. This was madness! Dangerous, terrifying madness! He turned, opening his mouth to protest, to demand they let him off. But it was too late.

Vicki saw him and smiled encouragingly, sensing his apprehension. Then she twisted the throttle wide open and the Naiad roared forward.

All of a sudden Richard's heart leaped into his mouth. The roaring of the outboard engine filled his ears, and through his whole body he could feel the thumping vibrations as the sea pounded on the hull. The cold wind whistled past his face, nipping his cheeks and tearing at his clothes. Richard flinched as a burst of spray shot up from the bow. He felt his bowels clench as they dropped down the face of a huge wave. The next one towered over them, threatening to block out the sky. Richard pressed himself against the seat, too terrified to watch, but too mesmerised to close his eyes.

Oh god, this is it. I'm going to die.

Vicki revved the throttle and yanked the tiller over, launching them straight up the face of the wave. The massive wall of water rose to meet them, stretching above like a blue barrier. It seemed impossible that the little boat could make it over the top, but Vicki held her course, aiming them straight up at the curling lip.

For a stomach-churning moment they hung suspended on the top, teetering on the edge of disaster. Richard could barely breathe. At any moment he expected to feel the boat toppling over backwards, ready to be engulfed by the massive wave and pounded into driftwood beneath it. He screwed his eyes shut.

Here it comes…

Then amazingly, the wave fell away beneath them and they were on another dizzying drop to the depths of a trough.

Cal glanced back over his shoulder, an ear-to-ear grin plastered across his face.

"Yeah!" he whooped over the engine. "Ain't this the life, Bro?"

Richard clutched the seat, not trusting himself to answer.

They sped onwards, forging a path through the heaving swells. The cold wind battered them mercilessly. Richard huddled down inside his jacket, trying to pull his collar across his face to shield himself from the wind's bite. He began to feel strangely detached, almost as though this was all a bad dream. Even the screaming engine faded into a dull drone after a while.

"There he is!"

The shout cut through Richard's stupor. He blinked, surprised to find himself still alive. Vicki throttled back and they bobbed on the water, the outboard burbling as they idled in the swells.

With his eyes Richard followed his brother's outstretched arm.

Suddenly he was wide-awake as a huge shape loomed out of the water ahead of them, the broad back topped by a tiny fin nearly three quarters of the way to the huge tail. Richard felt his heart miss a beat. It was absolutely enormous, as long as the 737 he'd flown to Christchurch in! The whale's blowholes were shielded by a high splashguard, looking for all the world like the control tower on the deck of an aircraft carrier. The massive grey-blue back seemed to fill the water as far as he could see, long and broad enough to park several buses on, end to end.

"Holy hell," he whispered, swearing for the first time in his life.

Cal laughed. "You've seen the smallest of the Rorquals… now meet the biggest."

Richard stared, open-mouthed. The whale was easily three times larger than the Minke they'd just tagged.

"The largest living thing to grace the Earth," Cal remarked. "Ever."

As he gaped at the huge form, Richard had no trouble believing that. The whale was absolutely immense, dwarfing their boat like it was a toy. And to think that this massive submarine giant was a living breathing creature was enough to boggle the mind.

"He weighs more than fifty-five elephants, and his brain alone weighs more than a fully-grown man," Cal added. "It's amazing though; for all his huge size he is basically the same as a mouse. Or a human. He has the same body plan, bone structure and internal organs. He breathes air, and he has warm blood, just like all mammals."

Richard just stared, not able to find the words to express what he was feeling.

Cal smiled. "We couldn't last a day in his world. It's amazing to think that a warm-blooded animal can survive in these frigid seas at all. His heart is as big as you to make sure it can pump enough blood to keep him alive, and his arteries are as wide as drainpipes. Just staying alive here is a constant battle against the creeping cold of the ocean."

As he listened to his brother's excited commentary, Richard felt his own heart hammering in his chest. It was a thrilling experience to be so close to such an enormous creature, but it was also terrifying. The whale's sheer size was almost too much to comprehend… The raw strength of the animal was simply awe-inspiring. It was a humbling thought to realise it could crush them like a bug without any effort – perhaps without even noticing them at all! Richard suddenly felt very small and very insignificant. Although they were more than a city block away, the whale was so huge it could have reached them in two flicks of its tail if it wanted to. Thoughts of Jonah and the Whale began dancing in Richard's head.

"C-Cal. Are you sure it's safe?"

His brother nodded, a strange smile fixed on his face. "Yeah, it's ok. He's busy feeding. He hasn't even noticed us yet."

The whale opened his mouth, a huge pink cavern that looked wide enough to swallow an entire rugby team at once. With almost ponderous slowness, the whale closed his mouth again, taking a huge gulp of seawater that could have filled several Olympic-sized pools. The pleats of his throat bulged outwards to accommodate the massive volume of water.

"What does he eat? Will he eat us?"

Cal grinned.

"Don't worry. The largest animal in the ocean feeds only on the smallest. He eats krill… little crustaceans about this long." Cal held up his thumb and forefinger a few centimetres apart to demonstrate. "Did you see the baleen? Long fibres hanging down from the top of his mouth?"

Richard nodded. They looked like bristles on a yard broom – except they were as long as a child.

"They trap the food like a giant sieve. Watch."

With a deep rumble, the whale pushed his mammoth tongue against the roof of his mouth, forcing the water out through the baleen plates in a huge jet. Richard looked on nervously; the rush of water was easily enough to upset their boat.

Cal didn't seem concerned though. "The krill stays behind on the baleen," he explained. "It's probably been over four months since this guy last had a feed. He's heading down from the warm water up north. Somewhere up there he will have spent the winter breeding, and he won't have eaten much that whole time. This is probably his first meal since getting back to the Southern Ocean. He needs to eat a couple of tonnes a day to regain condition, so he'll want to feed down here for several months. We're not far enough south yet to see the really big krill swarms, but look, there's some down there next to the boat."

Richard listened, fascinated, and sensing the unbridled delight in his brother's voice.

"Can we get a sample for dietary analysis?" Vicki asked.

Cal nodded and leaned over the side with the small dip net. He lifted it up and a cascade of water flushed down into the jar attached to the bottom. He carefully unscrewed it and handed it back to Richard.

"Here. Cap this for me will you?"

Richard peered into the jar. Floating inside were several bright orange krill. They looked like short fat crayfish, about as long as his little finger but twice as wide. Much bigger than he'd expected, but still quite small in comparison to a whale. It was strange that something so huge could sustain itself on something so small. Richard's mind wandered – as it often did when he was presented with a novel thought – and not for the first time on this trip. He closed his eyes, imagining what it might be like to be a whale, living out here in this vast blue wilderness.

"What does krill taste like?" he wondered aloud.

Vicki laughed, as though understanding his curiosity perfectly. "Barbecue 'em and they'll taste like shrimp," she replied with a grin, like the question was as sensible as any a marine biologist might be asked.

"Shreemp," Cal repeated, mocking her Aussie accent, then dodged clear as she aimed a playful punch at his arm. Richard smiled happily. Being party to their banter almost made him feel like a member of the close-knit team.

He had wondered at the rather close relationship Cal shared with his spunky Australian colleague, even going so far as to wonder if they were secretly an item. Late one night when he and Vicki were alone in the galley, rostered to clean up together, he had plucked up the courage to ask her about it.

She laughed gaily like it was a great joke. "No, we're just mates." But Richard noticed a brief shadow pass over her eyes as she turned back to the bench. "Cal isn't the settled type. He's well and truly married to his work." She plonked a pile of dishes in the tiny sink. "Besides, there's another girl." Noticing Richard's surprise she waved a dismissive hand. "It was long ago and it didn't work out. She broke his heart… but I know he still carries a torch for her."

Richard waited for her to elaborate but she didn't.

Instead she winked slyly. "That means neither of us is spoken for!"

Richard's throat seemed to close over. He wasn't sure if that comment was directed at him or not, but he felt the colour rising in his cheeks anyway. He hadn't meant to be that informal with her. He had kept his eyes on the floor while he choked out some excuse, then fled the room.

Suddenly the whale rumbled again, a deep resonant sound that seemed to make each individual particle of water tremble. Then its cavernous mouth yawned open, swinging around for another pass through the krill.

Richard gasped at the sight. The dark tunnel was big enough to swallow a car. And it was heading straight for them!

As the gigantic gaping maw surged towards them, they could hear the water rushing into its mouth, gurgling like a giant drain-hole.

Richard held his breath, not sure what to do.

Even Cal and Vicki exchanged a worried glance as the giant bore down on them.

Suddenly the whale seemed to sense their presence. It snapped its mouth shut and veered away in a surge of water. Then its huge pointed rostrum rose straight out of the waves, angled towards the sky, as it studied them.

"Strewth," whispered Vicki in her Aussie twang. "This is a sight I'll take with me to the next life…"

Richard tried to relax, heartened by the others' confidence. He admired the huge beast, watching as rivulets of water ran down the slick blue hide. It was as smooth as polished stone, fading to a soft white hue underneath.

With a sudden start, Richard realised an eye as large as his head was looking back at him. He stared back, transfixed.

The whale hung suspended with its head above the water, watching them with equal curiosity, as if trying to make sense of this strange orange object that had just appeared before it in the middle of the vast and empty ocean.

Looking back into the mysterious depths of that giant eye, Richard suddenly felt moved, as if by some powerful force he had no name for. It was as though he was seeing into the very soul of the creature, and what he saw there seemed to touch his own in return. Its depths burned with a proud fire; the spirit of a survivor born of the last true wilderness. He saw intelligence there, and a great wisdom. Looking into the eye was like looking back in time to a history so intimately entwined with the Earth as to be one with it. But it was also a history tinged with sadness. It was an ancient, almost timeless knowledge of the world – but one which was nearly lost for good. For a brief moment Richard shared that knowledge, and the world he glimpsed through the eyes of the whale was so enthralling it brought a lump to his throat. It was a journey of enlightenment and wonder, of joy and harmony with all the other living creatures – a philosophy so far removed from the ugly contrivance Man had forced upon the order of the world that Richard felt ashamed.

The shared feeling lasted only a moment, but its passing left him with a profound and tragic sense of loss. Almost as though he had been offered a glimpse of Enlightenment, only to have it slip away again.

"Look at that," Cal said, his tone hushed, almost reverent. "He's so big, yet so gentle. Power with restraint. That's such a noble concept, but one which people have yet to grasp." He stared out to sea, as if transfixed. "We could learn so much from whales…" he whispered, as if to himself.

The whale spouted, a huge blast that went off like a steam geyser, shooting vapour straight to the height of a four-storey building. Richard jumped, then recovered himself. "Wow!"

"Take a good look," Cal breathed. "In seven years of research this is only the third Blue I've ever seen."

Richard's curiosity was immediately piqued. "Really? When was the first?"

Cal paused wistfully, as though remembering. "It was seven years ago when I was just starting out with my whale research. She was a young female, just coming into her first breeding season… and she was trapped in an abandoned drift net. It was wrapped so tightly around her tail it cut into her flesh. She couldn't swim properly, and would have taken months to die a slow and lingering death by starvation."

He pursed his lips. "I was already behind schedule, but I couldn't just leave her there. Even so, it wasn't easy. We attached floats to the net to slow her down, but it still took six hours before Vicki could get me close enough to use the boat-hook to cut her free."

He looked slightly self-conscious. "As I watched her swim away I knew I was meant to be a whale biologist. I named her Koru after the Maori word for an uncurling fern frond. It's a sacred symbol of new life. I thought it was fitting since she represented hope, and the future of her kind."

Richard was fascinated. Before this trip he'd had no idea what his brother's work actually entailed. "Who was the second Blue you met?" he asked.

Cal smiled. "Koru had a little calf later that same year."

"What was his name?"

"He was a she." Cal replied, his smile fading. "But she never had a name. She died at only a few weeks old – killed after being run over in a collision with a container ship."

"Oh." Richard hunched his shoulders, embarrassed to see the emotion in his brother's eyes.

Cal blinked back to the present. "It's a rare gift to meet a blue whale," he said quietly. "And to get this close is pretty special…"

Richard nodded, awestruck.

"It's a sight few people have ever seen," Vicki added. "And even fewer might ever get to see again."

It was a sobering thought, and no one wanted to break the mood.

Reluctantly Cal picked up the crossbow and strained to draw it. "We've got a job to do," he mumbled apologetically. "We're not here as tourists to admire the view."

Seeing Richard's disappointment, Vicki smiled at him. "Don't worry, the work we do will help ensure there are always whales."

Richard nodded, a new-found sense of responsibility beginning to form. He bent down to pick up a dart from the gear bag, then reached for the box of radio tags to load in it.

Cal shook his head. "Let's have a Sat-tag."

Richard raised an eyebrow. The satellite tags were an electronic marvel, but a single one cost more than his car back home. "Are you sure? There's only one left."

His brother shrugged. "We deployed six last year and only one is still transmitting. I need some more out there. Besides, what better animal to track than a mature Blue bull?"

With exaggerated care, Richard took out the last Sat-tag and tentatively slid it into the hollow centre of the delivery dart. Handling the dart like it was a baby, he gingerly passed it across to Cal, relieved to transfer the responsibility.

"Good luck," he murmured.

Cal winked before turning away.

"Luck has nothing to do with it," Vicki whispered with a grin, moments before she revved the outboard motor again.

The Naiad zipped across the waves toward the whale, but the old Blue was quicker. He didn't hurry, and there was an almost ponderous grace about him as he dived. The researchers closed rapidly, but were still a few body lengths away when his head slipped back beneath the waves and he raised his massive tail flukes to the sky, trailing streams of water.

Richard gasped. Even from that distance his tail towered into the sky, as broad as the wings of a giant bat swooping overhead. Then the huge flukes slipped into the water with barely a ripple.

"He's sounded already." Vicki's tone was more incredulous than disappointed.

Cal nodded grimly. "He knows what a boat is. I'd say this guy's been hunted before," he muttered.

Richard exhaled, glad of the reprieve. "What do we do now?" As awe-inspiring as the Blue was, he had no desire to get any closer. He'd heard far too many stories of old whaling skiffs being overturned and sunk by their quarry. "Time to go home…?" he offered.

Cal shook his head. "Not a chance. This is the opportunity of a lifetime." He turned to Vicki. "Give me fifteen knots, on the same heading."

Richard swallowed, wondering just how far his crazy brother might be prepared to go to secure his opportunity. He was reminded of Captain Ahab's fatal obsession with Moby Dick, and desperately hoped Cal wasn't about to go to such extreme lengths in pursuit of his own whale. The legendary White Whale had turned and attacked his tormentors, turning the tide on the hunters before seizing the hapless Captain and dragging him to a watery grave. Richard held his breath. This whale was huge. If he decided to attack their tiny boat they wouldn't stand a chance.

As they skimmed across the water, Richard began to feel a familiar tightness in his chest, and his breaths came in short ragged gasps. He knew he needed his asthma inhaler, but he was too petrified to search for it. His white-knuckled grip on the seat was all that was keeping him from being tossed overboard, and he wasn't about to let go.

Cal glanced at his watch, then back at Richard.

"Richard, get on the radio will you? Tell Duke to heave-to and wait where he is. I don't want the Gwendolyn's diesels spooking this whale any more."

"You want them to stop?" Richard tried to swallow. He wasn't sure what terrified him more; knowing he had to let go of the seat to pick up the radio, or knowing that his brother intended for them to follow this gigantic beast alone!

Oh, what am I doing here?

He thought longingly of his desk, wishing he was back amongst his circuit-board diagrams, working blissfully where there was no danger of a sudden and violent death.

"Just press the big button on the side to talk," Cal prompted encouragingly.

Richard felt like crying.

The radio was in a dry bag, attached to the boat on a rubber bungee cord. It was on the floor next to the rest of the gear, but it was out of reach – and with the boat bouncing over the waves it wasn't just a matter of walking over and fetching it.

"Can't we stop?"

Without looking up from his wristwatch, Cal shook his head.

Richard took a deep breath, trying to summon his courage.

"Wait till we're going down the back of a wave," Vicki whispered. "It'll be smoother."

Richard nodded, thankful for the advice, if not the thought behind it.

He waited until he felt the familiar lurch in the pit of his stomach then leaned forward, trying to will the radio towards his outstretched fingers. Suddenly a wave slammed against the hull and he was thrown forward. He flung his hands up in front of his face as he tumbled towards the floorboards. He screwed his eyes shut, waiting for the impact of his head hitting the metal floor. But his fall was broken by the welcome pliability of the gear bag instead.

Gratefully, Richard plucked the radio from it and scrambled back to his seat, trophy in hand. He was wearing his full survival suit, and it was a struggle to work the button through the awkward gloves. But as he clutched the radio to his face, he suddenly hesitated, his heart pattering with a new anxiety.

It's not public speaking, he reminded himself. *It's just the Skipper you're talking to. Just pretend he's right next to you.*

He took a deep breath. "Ah, hello G-Gwendolyn. This is the Naiad. C-come in Gwendolyn. Do you read me?"

Duke's rough voice broke through in a burst of static. "Roger, go ahead Naiad."

All the thoughts in Richard's head suddenly jumbled themselves together, tumbling over each other in their hurry to get out. "Ah, Mr Hayward-," he began. The Skipper interrupted him with an explosive burst of laughter. "Mister Hayward! Mister!" Richard heard him slap his thigh. "Hell, son. I ain't no mister. I work for my living." Duke coughed, making an effort to control his mirth. "Call me Skip, son."

"Ah, ok then Skip…"

Richard gabbled out the rest of the message then lowered the radio dejectedly, embarrassment still colouring his cheeks. The Gwendolyn slipped from sight behind them, only her mast still visible above the heaving swells. The feeling of isolation was strong. Richard hung his head despondently, certain he had just helped seal their fate.

They sped on across the vast blue desert. Mountains of water rose and fell all around them, like giant shifting dunes. The salt spray stung his eyes. Richard looked behind them. The Gwendolyn was lost from sight amongst the towering blue peaks. They were alone on the wild sea, with nothing but blue all the way to the horizon.

Vicki noticed the direction of his gaze and smiled encouragingly. But Richard was beyond simple reassurance. He was wet, cold, and terrified. And right then he'd rather be anywhere else than bouncing over the freezing waves in that tiny orange boat.

He huddled into his jacket, his cheeks numbed by the wind.

Finally, after nearly twenty minutes, Cal held up a hand to stop. He double-checked his dive watch, then nodded to Vicki. "This should be about right."

She cut the engine and they drifted, the silence hemming them in from all sides.

Richard looked around. They were in the middle of nowhere, with the ship waiting somewhere far behind in their wake. He shot a worried look at his brother.

"Don't worry," Cal smiled, "I timed it to the second… He'll swim pretty much in a straight line which should bring him up for his next breath right about here."

Richard gazed down into the hidden blue depths and gulped. "What if he comes up underneath us?"

Cal chuckled, lifting the crossbow to his shoulder. "Then I'd better not miss!"

Feeling his anxiety come flooding back, Richard groped for his asthma inhaler and took an extra-long puff.

Oh, why did I ever let him talk me into this?

Suddenly there was a huge surge in the water behind them, and a giant blue shape burst into view like a breaching submarine.

Richard jumped, nearly dropping his inhaler. The whale spouted, a massive jet of vapour. He was nearly fifty metres away. Richard couldn't help feeling a moment of respect for Cal. In all the empty miles of ocean, his brother had put them within fifty metres of where the whale would appear.

He's a blimmin' magician!

He wanted to offer his congratulations, but Cal was already standing in the bow lining up the crossbow.

It was another long-range shot, but Cal didn't complain. The crossbow was like an extension of himself as he sighted on the target, judging the required trajectory. Richard watched with bated breath as the blue back began to slip from sight again.

Cal stood like a rock, only his finger moving as he calmly pulled the trigger.

Thwack!

Richard held his breath, willing the tiny orange projectile to find its target. The dart flew straight and true, landing right in the centre of the broad back. Moments later the whale dived from sight again, continuing on his long journey south.

Vicki was already motoring slowly over to retrieve the dart with its precious sample. Richard blinked. All that time and effort to get to this spot and it was over already, just like that. Almost like it was easy! He watched his brother packing away the crossbow, beginning to feel a new admiration for him. Despite all the hardships they had to endure out here; long hours, cold, fatigue, and moments of extreme physical danger – Cal was still able to rise to the occasion. For those few vital seconds he was able to put everything to one side and get the job done. Richard knew first hand that was no easy feat, and his respect for his brother was genuine.

Cal picked up the radio and called the Gwendolyn. He was answered by Skip's gravelly voice. "Howdy Naiad. Readin' your new sat-tag loud and clear. Nice job y'all!"

A big grin cracked Cal's face, and he held up his hand for a high-five from Vicki. "Roger that, we're coming home now."

Richard huddled down into his collar for the long cold ride back to where the Gwendolyn waited. The freezing wind stung at his cheeks with needles of ice. It promised to be an uncomfortable journey.

He tried not to focus on the time but they hadn't been going more than ten minutes when he suddenly glimpsed a long white shape on the horizon. He sat up, astonished, but when he looked again it was gone. He rubbed his eyes, but there was only endless green sea.

"Must be seeing things," he muttered to himself, but then a few moments later the phantom appeared amongst the waves again. It was a ship, painted dazzling white. Richard blinked. It was the first ship he'd seen since leaving port nearly two weeks ago, and the first hint there were other people out here. He had been so consumed by the loneliness and desolation of this place he hadn't even considered there could be other people braving the wild sea.

He wondered what they might be doing. More scientists perhaps? It looked like a research ship. Even from that distance he could see the ship was much longer than the Gwendolyn. There could be many people aboard it.

"Look, there's a ship over there!" he pointed excitedly.

"Where?" Cal looked doubtful.

"Over there."

Cal peered toward the horizon. "What kind of a ship?"

"I don't know. It was big and white-."

"White?" Cal interrupted. "Where? Show me!" All of a sudden he looked alarmed.

Richard drew back, startled. "It was over that way, near the horizon…"

Cal snatched up the binoculars and began scanning the waves. "What did it look like?" he demanded. "Did it have three big masts?"

"Um, I dunno. Maybe. Yeah, I think so."

Cal lowered the binoculars and fixed him with a steely gaze. "Did it or not?" he said levelly. "I need you to be sure."

Richard hesitated, a little unnerved by the intensity of his brother's stare. He nodded slowly.

"Son of a bitch!" Cal slammed his fist against the Naiad's rubber pontoon. "That's all we need! Which way was it going?"

Wide-eyed, Richard raised his arm to point south. Cal swore again and lunged for the radio.

Richard recoiled. He hadn't seen his brother this mad since… well, never.

"What's the matter?" he whispered to Vicki. "Is that another research ship?"

She tried to offer a reassuring smile, but it turned into more of a grimace. "Not really," she answered. "The ship you saw is the Kyoeishin-Maru No. 2. They pretend to do research in the Southern Ocean, but it's not real science and their main purpose is definitely not scientific…"

She trailed off, a sad look on her face.

Richard waited for her to continue, worry definitely overtaking his confusion now.

"The Kyoeishin-Maru No. 2 is operated by the Taiyoku Misui Fisheries Company of Japan. They use it as a spotter vessel for the Japanese Pelagic Whaling Fleet."

Richard sat back, Vicki's words still echoing in his head.

Japanese whalers.

Cal was already shouting into the radio. "Skip, we've got company out here. Tell me what you've got on the radar."

The Skipper's voice was distorted by static, but his displeasure was plain to hear.

"Dang thing came outta nowhere… one target to the south-east, cuttin' across your front-."

"That'll be them," Cal murmured.

"Ah've got three more o'the bastards behind that one," he added. "They're east of y'all, truckin' south as fast as they can go."

"Same heading?" Cal demanded, his voice tight with bitterness.

"Yep," came Duke's reply. "They're makin' a bee-line for our whale."

Cal swore and slammed his fist on the pontoon again. When he turned back to face them his face was a mask of anger.

"Vicki, how much gas do we have?"

"About half a tank."

Richard began to feel sick to his stomach. He had a nasty feeling he knew what his brother was planning.

"Might not be enough to make it back to the Gwendolyn," Vicki added.

Cal nodded, his face expressionless. "We could sit tight and wait for Skip to find us when we're done…"

Richard nearly choked. It was dangerous enough chasing whales, but now his crazy brother wanted to take them straight into the very jaws of danger itself – and a one-way trip at that! He hadn't come on this trip to get involved in any fight, especially not while they were unarmed and vulnerable in such a tiny boat.

What the hell is he thinking?

"I don't know about this," Richard ventured. "It doesn't sound very safe."

No one seemed to hear him though. Vicki was staring at Cal, eyes locked on his face.

Suddenly she nodded, and the decision was made. "Let's do it," she whispered.

Richard felt the fear rising in him.

What the hell is going on? Is everyone crazy?

She'd just said there wasn't enough fuel to get back! What were they going to do, just float around out there waiting for a rescue? Were they both mental? What if the Gwendolyn couldn't find them? It could be a long wait out there – and a freezing one.

Richard felt cold at the thought. Death had never seemed so near before.

Cal seemed oblivious. "Take us south Vicki, fast as you can."

Richard was close to panic. "What are you doing Cal? We can't!"

Cal ignored the plea. "Grab something and hang on, Bro."

"But Cal-"

"I'm sorry, Richard, but the only thing necessary for evil to flourish is for good people to stand by and do nothing."

Richard opened his mouth to refuse, to demand they return to the ship. But just then Cal whispered something under his breath. It was meant only for himself, but Richard caught his words before they were lost to the wind; "We could learn so much from whales."

Suddenly an image of the Great Whale's eye sprang into mind. Richard hesitated, something inside making him hold his tongue, and the protest never left his lips.

Cal turned back to him, a strange look in his eyes. "They mean to kill him," he said simply. "And they will. Unless someone stops them."

Chapter 3

Richard shivered as the Naiad pounded over the waves, and the biting wind was only part of the reason. It was easy to feel alone and anxious when contemplating the sheer size of this wild and inhospitable ocean, but everything he'd experienced up until now was just a drop in a bucket compared to this. The windswept and pitching deck of the Gwendolyn suddenly seemed as safe and secure as his little apartment in Auckland by contrast. Hunched down in the speeding inflatable he was only centimetres away from the hungry sea, and every wave that lunged against the hull sent a shower of freezing spray over him. They were right amongst the angry waves and it seemed as though they would be swallowed up at any moment, simply disappearing into the blue depths without a trace.

Richard huddled into his survival suit.

The Gwendolyn was far out of sight behind them now; a tenuous lifeline that was all but severed already. They were taking a huge risk speeding so far from safety, especially when they might not have enough fuel to get back. Richard didn't even want to think about the consequences. It was madness. But worst of all was their destination. Cal was leading them straight into conflict, aiming to steer them right into the middle of the Japanese Fleet's hunt and confront the whalers. His aim was frighteningly clear – disrupt the slaughter. How he proposed to do that, Richard could only guess. But he knew it would be as dangerous as it was difficult. As if being in the water with a frightened or injured sea behemoth wasn't bad enough, now they would have to contend with angry Japanese whalers armed with harpoon cannons and flensing knives too.

Cal hadn't said anything since their pursuit of the white ship began, and his silence worried Richard. He stole a glance at his brother. Cal was perched assertively in the bow, oblivious to the flying spray, brooding. The look on his face was dark, and his jaw was set defiantly. Richard had never seen his brother this angry before, but that only made it all the more concerning.

"Uh, Cal…" he ventured timidly, not even sure what he was going to say to try and break the tension.

Cal turned and fixed his steely gaze on him, but made no reply.

Richard blanched at the intensity of his stare. "A-are you sure we can catch them?" he blurted.

Cal nodded, shouting over the wind. "The Kyoeishin-Maru 2 can hit about fifteen knots. That's under 30 k's an hour, and we're pushing twice that." He smiled briefly but encouragingly. "Don't worry, we'll get them."

Richard gulped, far from reassured. "Are you s-sure they're not doing research?" he asked, desperate to avert the impending confrontation.

Cal shook his head. "That's just a front. They claim to collect age and size data for population studies, but their methodology is flawed, and their motives are far from scientific."

"What do you mean?"

"Scientists can tell everything we need to know about whale populations using non-lethal research. Sure, the Japanese can age a dead whale by counting the rings on its otoliths – inner-ear bones – but knowing that doesn't prove anything unless you know how often they're laid down – and they haven't even tried to find out! You need life history data to corroborate otolith rings if you want to determine an animal's age, at least until you've confirmed your methods. But they're not interested in accuracy. Besides," he added, his voice heavy with sarcasm. "There's heaps of morphometric data left over from the old whaling days that no one's even looked at yet, not to mention the past two decades of illegal Japanese pseudo-science. They sure as hell don't need to go killing any more whales to get their measurements. It's abundantly clear that any data they are collecting is for their own ends. Their research priority is not to learn more about whales, but to come up with something they might be able to use to justify re-commencing commercial whaling – along with anything that'll make the killing more efficient if they do."

Cal looked disgusted. "What use is it to determine the age of a dead whale anyway? What more can you learn about a known-age individual if you've just killed it?"

He sighed. "It's so much more reliable – and sensible – to re-sight known animals and chart their growth and movement that way. You can get years of solid data from just one individual. And genetic studies can tell you far more about reproductive success than just killing a female and counting her ovary scars."

He shook his head incredulously. "How the hell do you work to conserve a population by taking out the breeding females? It's not logical. Killing anything you're trying to save is not logical!" He frowned deeply. "It's pretty plain to me they're only interested in setting up an excuse for killing rather than actually finding out anything."

Richard was confused. "But what about the Southern Ocean Whale Sanctuary? I thought whaling was banned. Why are they allowed to be here hunting?"

Cal laughed, but it came out more of a sarcastic grunt. "That's the million dollar question isn't it?" He sighed again, deeply, hinting at years of personal frustration. "It's a long story, Bro. The Southern Ocean Whale Sanctuary doesn't actually exist in reality. It's just a proposal that was put forward by the government of New Zealand, and other conservation-minded countries."

"So why isn't it real? I thought everyone wanted to save the whales now?"

Cal rolled his eyes. "Unfortunately it's not that simple. Let me start from the beginning. Whaling is supposed to be controlled by the IWC, the International Whaling Commission. It was originally set up back in 1948 by the whalers themselves, and those beginnings are reflected in a lot of its founding principles. In the old days the whale barons used to meet every year and nominate themselves a quota of how many whales they were going to kill. Of course they never gave any thought to how many whales were actually out there, or whether the numbers they were taking were sustainable." He paused for effect. "Hell, they used to kill for fun. Aristotle Onassis had a harpoon gun mounted on the front of his private yacht, just so he could have a bit of sport if he came across a whale during one of his playboy cruises!"

Cal looked regretful. "And when you've got a species that's as long-lived and slow growing as whales, any adults you take out of the population are difficult to replace by normal reproduction – if not impossible. Hence the decline." He shrugged. "The whalers never actually took any notice of their own quotas anyway. It was just open slaughter – based on simple economics of course. If you leave a whale alive someone else will just kill it instead. But if you kill as many as you can, you get the money before anyone else does."

"But that's crazy!" Richard exclaimed. "How can that work?"

"That's the point. It couldn't. At the height of the slaughter the pelagic whaling fleets were killing 60,000 whales a year – that's several hundred every day! The original seven Japanese whaling companies between them fielded 7 factory ships, 86 Hunter-Killers, and over 57 additional support ships – including freighters, refrigerator ships, and tankers – and that was just Japan! Quite an armada eh?"

He curled his lip, his disgust plain. "The pelagic whaling fleets were killing as many whales in a single day as the old sailing ships used to kill in an entire three-year voyage. No population can sustain that. Everyone knew the whales were doomed. But the whalers didn't care about the future. They were making money now, so to hell with tomorrow – even if that meant there were no whales left at all."

"But it's not like that any more is it? They've stopped now, haven't they?"

Cal shook his head slowly. "No. Most countries stopped whaling decades ago, if only because it wasn't profitable to chase the last few whales to the ends of the Earth. But the scarcity of their prey has only made the Japanese more ruthless. Their fleets shrank over the years as costs began to outweigh returns, and one-by-one the unprofitable whaling companies were absorbed by the others until only the largest three remained – led by the massive Taiyoku Misui Fisheries. But whaling has not stopped. It never stopped."

"Why not?" Richard asked. "Why haven't they stopped killing them if everyone knows whales are endangered?"

"That's the problem in a nutshell, Bro. Why indeed?" He looked out to sea for a while before answering. "Being set up originally as a whalers' club, the IWC had certain safeguards built into its rules. It was designed to promote whaling, not to regulate it. You had to have a three-quarter majority to pass any resolution – especially one that was going to reduce quotas. But slowly the old whaling nations woke up to the fact that whales were on the brink of extinction and one by one they changed their stance. But for a long time there were still too many whaling nations for conservationists to get the required three-quarter majority. Japan, Russia, Iceland, Norway, Korea, and Taiwan all voted against any resolution that would cut back on whaling – since they all stood to lose too much money."

Richard was appalled. "That's terrible! But the conservationists won, didn't they?"

Cal nodded. "Technically, yes. It was a long battle though. But eventually they managed to get enough sensible countries to join the IWC and give the conservationists the three-quarter majority they needed to ban whaling. The Whaling Moratorium was finally signed in 1982 although it didn't take effect until 1986 – and it was a long and bitter fight."

"So that was the end of commercial whaling?"

Cal shook his head. "Unfortunately that was only the beginning, and whaling never actually ended. The Japanese whaling commissioner refused to admit defeat, and he wasn't above using the conservationists' tactics against us. Japan persuaded lots of other countries to join the IWC and vote with them. Suddenly there were dozens of little countries – many without even a coastline and with no interest at all in whaling – joining the IWC and voting for whaling to continue… and for their troubles they received handsome kickbacks in foreign aid and trade deals from the Japanese. Japan has handed out over $400 million in bribes so far."

"But that's crazy!" Richard blurted. "Why doesn't someone put a stop to it?"

"If only it was that simple," Cal muttered, almost to himself. "You see, whales live in the open sea where no country has jurisdiction over any other, so the IWC is just a convention – an agreement between countries. And there's no way to hold any country to that agreement, even if they have agreed to abide by it. Back during the height of the slaughter, the whaling countries – in particular the Soviets – wouldn't even tell the truth about how many whales they were killing, let alone sticking to any quota. But even when they exceeded their own arbitrary self-imposed catch limits there were still no repercussions. There was no attempt at regulation or enforcement of any of the IWC's rules, as generous as they already were. And to make matters even worse, because it was a convention rather than a law, a country was only bound by a rule in the first place if they had agreed to it. That's what allowed the Norwegians, Icelanders, and others to keep on killing long after the worldwide Moratorium had finally been voted in – they simply refused to sign the new resolution and carried on killing whales just as they had been."

"But that's stupid!" Richard blurted out.

"You got that right." Cal stared at the horizon. "But the Japanese are the worst of all. They never stopped killing, and their excuse is even more devious… As a kind of lip-service to proper population biology the IWC includes rules saying whalers are supposed to collect population data to ensure sustainability of their catch, so the Japanese just issued themselves 'Scientific Whaling Permits' and carried on killing as many whales as they wanted, claiming it was for research and therefore entirely legal. That's what they say they're doing out here now, science. But every whale they kill for 'research purposes' ends up being cut up and sold in the fish markets back in Japan." He gritted his teeth. "It was the Japanese who kept this whole stupid whaling fight alive over the last twenty years. Every other whaling nation eventually gave up and retired their fleets, but the Japanese kept going, ignoring international outrage and condemnation and refusing to listen to anyone. Their whalemeat market has provided the incentive for other countries – and pirate whaling boats – to keep on killing whales secretly for years. The American Government could have stopped this whole thing for good back in the '80s with trade sanctions, but they chickened out because of Japan's economic clout, and it's only gotten worse since then. Now Japanese whaling is so entrenched they'll never give it up without a fight, and Norway, Iceland, the Faeroe Islands and other whaling nations are copying their stance and coming back to the hunt." He looked annoyed. "The Japanese are demanding a return to large-scale commercial whaling, and they're encouraging as many countries as they can to take up whaling again to support their vote. The War for the Whales is starting up again."

Richard didn't know what to think. He knew about the protests and the 'Save the Whale' campaign of the eighties, but he'd assumed that was old history now. The whales had been saved and the world had moved on, hadn't they? Apparently not.

He could see something needed to be done, but what that was, he wasn't sure.

The thing that bothered him most though, was sticking his own neck on the line. He'd seen those crazy eco-activists on TV before – protesting not only whaling but any other cause that took their fancy – and he had no wish to join their number. They'd always seemed like loud, uncouth trouble-makers, and they certainly weren't shy about antagonising people to get their point across. How could you change anything by making a scene? Their protests were so… confrontational. Getting arrested seemed like their aim most of the time, and it was definitely the best possible outcome from some of the fights they picked.

If you stay away from trouble then it'll stay away from you.

That philosophy had served Richard well over the years. Yet here they were heading straight for trouble at full speed.

Cal was watching him closely, as if his thoughts might be revealed on his face. "Someone has to stop this," he said quietly.

"But Cal, why us?"

"Why not us?" Cal responded. "We're here and we have the ability. Besides, those bastards are ruining my work. I've lost three sat-tagged whales this season alone, costing nearly fifteen thousand dollars apiece! I'm not made of money, and my funding is to study whale population dynamics, not donate expensive electronics for some bloody Japanese fisherman to throw over the side!" His gaze was piercing. "What they're doing is wrong, Richard."

Richard sighed. He didn't know much about right and wrong – not in the sense of having to make such momentous decisions anyway. In the world of electronics there weren't many moral dilemmas. In fact, there wasn't much in the way of mortal danger either. At that moment Richard suddenly felt a long way away from his desk and his nice quiet life.

Richard fell silent as he tried to make sense of the confusion of emotions tumbling through his head. It was a lot to take in.

He followed the direction of Cal's frown as he stared across the waves.

The white ship had grown steadily larger as they sped towards it, and now it loomed ahead of them, blotting out the horizon. There were people moving about on the decks, watching them. But no one waved. The little inflatable was met with a wall of sullen stares.

"Here come the blood-thirsty bastards," Cal muttered, jerking his head to their left. Richard turned to look. Off in the distance were three more ships, shadowing them like grey vultures. They were long and narrow, slicing through the waves as they rapidly overtook the slower spotter ship. They too had a tall mast each, and the sleek grey line of their hulls swept forward to an impossibly tall prow. Richard's eye swept over the towering steel plates of the lead ship's bow, rising almost vertically above the foaming sea. He felt the dread settle over him, the sharp nose of the ship reminding him of an executioner's axe-blade. His eye then fell upon the harpoon gun, mounted atop the bow like a medieval cannon perched on the battlements of a castle. Even from that distance he could see the weapon was massive, its sinister black profile dwarfing the white-hatted crew member standing stiffly next to it.

Richard's fear was suddenly a hard knot in the pit of his stomach.

He looked away.

Cal noticed his concern. "The Kuu-Maru 1," he muttered, his voice tight with resentment. "That's their flagship. The two behind are the Tosho-Maru 25 and Shushu-Maru 1."

"They're fast," Richard whispered.

"Yep. They're the Hunter-Killer boats. They're designed for speed. The Kuu-Maru was re-fitted with new engines in '98, it can top 17 knots now. That's faster than any of its sister ships, faster than the Gwendolyn." He paused. "Faster even than a Blue whale… But not faster than us!" Cal looked back, offering a thin smile that he probably intended to be reassuring.

Richard wasn't convinced.

"Time to show them we mean business," his brother said. He pointed to the padded dive bag that held their gear. "You remember how to work the uplink?"

Richard nodded. Cal had given him a brief lesson one night in the Gwendolyn's wardroom, but that was all he'd needed. Electronics were no problem for him, they were much easier to understand than people.

Luckily the gear bag was close enough to reach this time, so he slid forward off the seat and knelt in front of it, his knees registering every wave that hit the hull. Fighting to keep his balance, he took out the rugged orange field-laptop and opened it up, gripping its armoured rubber sides tightly for balance as he waited for it to start up. The satellite antenna was mounted on a short one-metre mast in the stern, along with the GPS and whip antennas for the radios. Vicki leaned forward and handed him the cable. He smiled shyly back, but she didn't seem to notice. She was too busy scanning the waves ahead.

Richard turned his attention to the keyboard, trying to enable the downlink from the satellite that collected data from their Sat-tags.

"You might have to try the code a couple of times," Cal suggested. "Sometimes the bandwidth is busy. And the bird is quite low in the sky here so it doesn't always pick up the signal first go…"

Richard ignored the advice, fingers flying over the keyboard as he attempted to lock on to the distant satellite. He grinned as rows of numbers began scrolling across the screen.

Bingo!

He was in his element.

"Okay, I've got him," he said, looking through the numbers. "Last reported signal from Mr Blue was fifteen minutes ago." He read out the coordinates.

"Good enough for me!" Cal grinned.

Vicki glanced at the GPS balanced on her knee and the Naiad swerved suddenly as she corrected their course, aiming to pass to starboard of the big white ship in front of them.

Richard watched as the distance to it shrank, the dazzling white superstructure seeming to swell before their eyes, stark against the cold blue of the sea.

Behind them, the Hunter-Killers closed in.

Cal saw the direction of his worried look. "Don't worry, Bro. We're quick enough. We'll get there first."

Richard didn't answer.

He tried to focus on the laptop screen to take his mind off the sick sense of impending doom, but it was virtually impossible not to look.

Suddenly the spotter ship seemed to elongate before his eyes. Richard gawked, jaw hanging open, as a white wall of steel twisted straight towards them, rearing above the waves as the ship swerved to cut them off.

Finally he found his voice. "L-look out! It's turning!"

"Bastard! He's trying to cut us off!" Cal muttered, but he didn't look worried.

Vicki swerved to the right, trying to get around the bow. But the Kyoeishin-Maru 2 continued to turn, presenting itself broadside to block their path.

"Look out! We're not going to make it!"

"Everyone hang on!" Vicki cut the throttle and yanked the tiller back to the left, slamming the speeding inflatable into a high-speed stop, only metres from the steel wall in their path. Richard was flung against the side of the boat, crashing into the pontoon hard enough to drive the breath from his lungs.

He gasped weakly, staring up at the white barrier blocking their way. High above, a crewman stared back over the rail, his black eyes seeming to bore right through him. Richard stared back, rooted to the spot.

"That way!" Cal shouted, gesturing to the left. "Around the stern. Quick!"

Vicki revved the throttle and a surge of white water shot out behind as they sped away again.

Richard could see the Hunter-Killer ships, much closer now and gaining rapidly. They forged relentlessly through the waves, closing in like a pack of hunting wolves.

Vicki made a fast sweeping turn around the broad stern of the Kyoeishin-Maru, then twisted the throttle wide open, sending the Naiad speeding in pursuit of the whale again.

But the delay had been critical. The whalers were right behind them now, led by the charging Kuu-Maru 1. Richard stared up at the bow, grey and threatening, hovering above them like the sword of Damocles.

Even Cal didn't seem quite so confident any more as he eyed it. "Gun it!" he shouted to Vicki. "All the way!"

"It is!" she answered helplessly. "This is as fast as we can go."

Cal swore.

Behind them, the razor-like bow of the whaler sliced through the water only a boat-length away.

Richard held his breath as the Naiad skipped across the waves, beginning to pull ahead, but all of a sudden a line of numbers appeared on his screen. The sat-tag on the whale was transmitting again. "He's surfaced! Dead ahead!"

"Slow down!" Cal ordered.

Vicki throttled back to match the speed of the whale – the last thing they wanted to do was shoot past him, or worse, run straight into him.

Behind, the whaler continued to thunder towards them.

Oh no!

Richard closed his eyes, waiting for the massive grey bow to slice them in two.

Richard cringed as he waited for the inevitable impact. The seconds dragged out.

He felt the Naiad sway as Vicki zig-zagged, and the outboard surged as she juggled the throttle. He could hear the hungry splash of the whaler's bow-wave just over his shoulder, but he was too terrified to look. The seconds ticked by as he waited for it to engulf them.

With a sick feeling he remembered he was supposed to be tracking the whale on the laptop.

Cal gave you one job to do… the voice in his head accused.

Somewhat guiltily he forced himself to open his eyes.

The grey steel monster was still behind, even closer than before. It hadn't slowed or changed course to avoid them but Vicki expertly dodged the scything bow, dancing in and out of the ship's path in a lethal game of chicken, trying to force them off-course.

Richard swallowed and willed himself to concentrate on the flickering screen.

According to the last position report, Old Blue was swimming due south, perhaps hoping to find safety in the frozen seas around Antarctica. Richard felt sad for him. He had a long way to go before he made it that far.

Switching his attention back to the laptop, Richard checked their heading.

"F-five degrees to the right," he called, his voice nearly catching in his throat as he called the course correction to Vicki.

She nodded, still looking over her shoulder, and the Naiad danced back in front of the charging whaleboat.

Richard shuddered and looked away.

Cal glanced at his watch. "He'll be coming back up soon," he muttered. "Eyes open everyone."

As if to confirm, a moment later the whale surfaced just ahead, his spout a tall column of vapour rising into the air before the wind whipped it away. Richard's heart sank. If there had been any doubt the whalers had spotted the fleeing giant yet, it was instantly dispelled. They would have to be blind not to see that. The whale spouted again, a weak blow as if he was gasping for breath.

"He's tiring," Cal muttered. "He can't keep up this speed for much longer."

He put out his hand for the radio, and switched it to channel sixteen, the international emergency frequency. His voice was authoritative as he spoke into it. "Ahoy Japanese whaler Kuu-Maru. This is the tender for the research vessel Gwendolyn. You are interfering with a scientific data collection session. This animal is a marked study animal. Please stop your pursuit and stand down."

Without waiting for acknowledgement he repeated the speech in Japanese.

Richard blinked in surprise. As far as he knew, Cal hadn't studied Japanese since high school, and that was a long time ago now. He himself could barely remember anything of the three years of French he'd learned, perhaps knowing even then it would never prove useful for his chosen career.

The radio sat silently in Cal's hand. Whether they understood the message or not, or if they were even monitoring the radio, Richard couldn't tell. But the whaler never hesitated.

"Japanese whaler Kuu-Maru," Cal commanded. "Stop your engines. This animal is an endangered species, protected under the 1974 CITES convention. I am ordering you to stand down or be in breach of international law."

High on the prow, they could see a crewman standing behind the huge harpoon cannon. Even as they watched, he swivelled the sinister weapon towards the fleeing whale.

"Bastards!" Cal uttered a string of obscenities, shaking his fist towards the bridge. He snatched up the radio again, switching it back to their channel.

"Gwendolyn, Gwendolyn, this is the Naiad."

"Go ahead, Naiad." The Skipper's voice sounded distant amongst the crackle of static.

"We have a situation here. What's your ETA?"

"Fifteen minutes." The Skipper's voice was contrite, as if he knew even fifteen seconds might be too long. "Sorry, Son."

With a sudden burst of speed the grey ship surged forward, the gunner crouched behind his cannon in anticipation.

Cal swore again and tossed the radio in the direction of the gear bag.

"Vicki," he shouted. "They're going for the shot!"

The outboard motor screamed as the plucky Australian twisted the throttle wide open, and the little Naiad shot forward, directly into the harpoon gunner's line of sight. Cal shot a glance at the crossbow lying at his feet, and Richard could almost feel him agonising over the decision.

Don't do it, Cal. They'll kill you!

The crossbow would be no match for the imposing harpoon cannon and Cal seemed to realise that. He turned away, leaving the weapon where it was. He braced his legs against the seat and struggled to his feet in the pitching bow, waving his arms over his head to make himself as tall as possible. He faced backwards, jaw clenched, staring straight down the barrel of the massive cannon, using his own body as a shield. His eyes narrowed, as if daring the gunner to do his worst.

Richard felt his stomach turn.

For several long minutes the standoff dragged on, neither side willing to admit defeat to the other. The whalers were relentless; speeding, swerving, changing direction, continually pressuring the valiant defenders, waiting for the one mistake that would seal the outcome of this pursuit. The Naiad jinked and swayed as Vicki jockeyed for position, battling to keep the little boat where it was needed – directly in harm's way. Cal was resolute in his determination, his face an expressionless mask as he continued to block the gunner's attempts to get a clear shot. Occasionally he would signal to Vicki, indicating a direction, but for the most part their communication was telepathic. Barely anything was said, but Richard could see the implicit understanding that flashed between them without the need for words, just as they were used to working together when studying the whales.

Richard shrank down on the seat. He didn't know how Cal could be so brave. He himself felt sick to his stomach, and he doubted whether he could even manage to stand up, his legs were shaking so much.

As he watched his brother standing tall in the face of danger, Richard suddenly realised he barely knew him at all.

The Cal his family discussed around the dinner table was an oddball and a misfit. A mixed-up individual who didn't really know what he was doing in life. A source of concern and mild disappointment to his parents, wasting his time mucking around instead of buckling down and getting a proper job, working hard, and being successful.

But as Richard watched his brother leading his team, making a stand, fighting for what he believed in, it was as though a light bulb was suddenly switched on inside his head, and he was struck by a revelation.

These people here know my own brother better than I do.

Watching the Team work together like the electronics in a well-tuned circuit board, Richard realised Cal was successful in his own way. His team was more than just a jumble of parts, because when the charge of electricity surged through them they were capable of performing extraordinary feats far greater than the sum of their components.

All of a sudden his little brother wasn't his little brother any more, but the leader of this team. And his leader too. Richard saw him now not as an oddity in the family, but a passionate and caring idealist, and a strong and confident man, fighting for what he knew was right.

This was the real Cal, he realised, and despite what others thought, he was successful. He had chosen a purpose in life. Or maybe it had chosen him? Either way, Cal knew exactly where he was going.

And despite his fears, Richard was beginning to understand too.

***

Hogei Gyofuku, commander of the Japanese Pelagic Whaling Fleet and master of the Kuu-Maru No.1, stood in his bridge. His iron-fisted grip on the wheel was tight enough to make the flesh bulge white on the backs of his hands. The Kuu-Maru 1 slid off the crest of the wave and plunged deep into the trough behind it, shuddering down her length as the bow struggled to burst through the wall of grey water.

The weather was mild for the Southern Ocean at this time of year though, and it definitely wasn't the sea that held his attention. He glared out the windscreen, his temper rising in a crimson wave up the back of his neck.

Those accursed Western protesters are back!

It seemed like barely a season went by these days without some long-haired louts speeding around in their fizz boats, waving their banners, trying to interrupt his hunt – as if they owned the sea and everything in it! He snorted with rage. Who did they think they were anyway, trying to tell him he couldn't fish? Westerners were so narrow-minded. They didn't bat an eyelid at their own fishing industry, and what was a whale if not a big fish? The irony of it was monumental!

Up ahead the whale spouted again, tiring, and he licked his lips in anticipation. He needed this catch. He hadn't caught anything since that measly little Minke and her calf three days ago. The Fleet had found slim pickings so far this trip, searching unsuccessfully, burning up precious fuel.

Until now this entire season had been far from productive. In the old days they used to get ten or even twenty kills a day. Lately the whales were so scarce the Fleet would be lucky to get two or three in a shift, and sometimes they could go for days at a time without getting any. For some reason the whales were getting harder to find…

Gyofuku frowned. He needed this catch to keep his schedule on track. He felt a brief surge of indignation at still being subject to orders from Head Office out here – especially as he knew all the suit-wearing executives in the boardroom who prepared them loved to sneer behind their hands at anyone who went to sea, captain or not.

"We'll see who smells like fish!" he muttered, itching to have those smart-mouthed young braggarts on his crew for just one day! "We'll see whose father was a fish-gutter!"

Gyofuku removed his red plastic helmet and absently scratched the stubble on his head, ignoring the flakes of dandruff raining down.

In reality though, he knew the ass-kissing ladder-climbers of the middle management were the least of his problems. The massive Taiyoku Misui Fisheries empire was run by just one man, and he set the quotas personally. There could be no escaping the master's wishes.

Gyofuku's insubordination quickly evaporated. The last thing he needed was the Old Man on his back. He shuddered involuntarily at the thought of having to return to port and face Amimoto-san without having met his quota. Old man or not, no one dared disappoint Amimoto-san.

Gyofuku replaced his helmet, sitting the hatband on the rolls of his neck.

He glared at the inflatable boat zipping in front of his bow, grinding his teeth with frustration.

So, you try to interrupt my hunt!

As if on cue the radio crackled again, but he ignored their outburst. It was a typical harassment tactic of Greenpeace's from the old days, and one doomed to fail with him. Did they really think he would turn away just because they told him to? He waited for the usual lectures on the evils of killing animals, knowing all that achieved was make him want to run them over!

Gyofuku allowed himself a private smirk. These protesters had initially proved helpful. Indeed, if not for them – and the Kyoeishin-Maru's new military-grade radar that allowed the Fleet to track them over the horizon – he might have had to find this whale the hard way. They had led him straight to a fat blue-back, and the sea-pig was big! Its meat would fetch a fine price at the fish market.

He scratched the skin folds below his receding chin. This would please the Old Man!

The irony was delicious. He almost drooled at the thought of the profit the whale represented.

All that high-grade meat for the price of one harpoon tip!

The promised return for his effort was much too tempting to pass up – illegal or not.

He scowled. Who were the Westerners to decree what was legal or not anyway? His family had been fishermen, and whalers, for generations. Who were these barbarians who tried to lay down the law to him? What right did they have to tell him what he couldn't do?

Japan takes orders from no one!

Clearly the Westerners were waging a deliberate campaign against the Nation of the Rising Sun. Well, he would show the racist troublemakers a thing or two.

"Load the harpoon," he ordered over the telegraph link to the forecastle.

"Not that one!" he shouted, gesticulating angrily as the gunner loaded a penthrite-tipped explosive harpoon. "They are much too expensive to waste. Save it until the pig is already strung on the line."

Through the observation windows he saw the white helmet dip as the man hurried to obey.

"Ready!" The gunner's voice wavered, clearly rattled by the presence of the protesters.

Gyofuku could barely contain his annoyance.

Keep your mind on the job, you useless idiot.

"Prepare to fire!" he ordered. "And don't you miss or I'll demote you to the flensing group. You'll spend the rest of your career aboard the factory ship swabbing the gutting-room floor!"

The gunner hurried to obey, and Gyofuku noted with satisfaction that the man's neck was red with shame beneath his white helmet.

The seconds dragged out, and then the gunner straightened up again, turning uncertainly towards the bridge. "So sorry Captain-san, but the protesters' boat is in the way," he answered back. "They're blocking the shot."

"I know where the boat is," Gyofuku snapped. "Perhaps this will teach them some manners."

"But Captain-san"

"Silence! I said fire the harpoon!"

Chapter 4

Richard held on for dear life as the speeding Naiad pounded across the waves, following the fleeing whale. The flying spray stung his eyes, and sodden strands of hair kept hanging down across his face, obscuring his vision. He didn't dare brush them away though. That would mean letting go his death-grip on the seat. His asthma was back too. He could feel his breathing coming in short, panicked gasps, but he did his best to ignore it. The inhaler was out of reach in his pocket.

Behind them thundered the Kuu-Maru 1. The Japanese Hunter-Killer was relentless, harrying them without pause, alternatively charging forward and swerving to the side in its determination to get past. Yet each time Vicki anticipated the manoeuvre and managed to cut them off, putting the little inflatable directly in the line of fire. Cal stood tall in the bow, a lone figure of defiance, risking his life to protect the Blue whale.

The whale blew again, a weak gasp of vapour, and Richard could see he was tiring from the protracted high-speed pursuit.

Keep swimming, he urged in a silent entreaty. *You have to keep swimming.*

But in his heart he knew the chase was nearly over.

As if to answer his fears, a sudden boom echoed across the heaving green swells. Richard snapped his attention back to the bow of the Kuu-Maru, in time to see the puff of smoke as a harpoon launched itself towards them. He flinched as it shot towards them, the cable whipping behind, filling the air with deadly coils of steel.

Time slowed. He was unable to tear his eyes from it, watching with a pounding heart as the harpoon flew towards them. But at the last moment he realised it wasn't going to hit them and the shot flew wide, splashing into the sea in a fountain of spray.

Cal didn't flinch. "Not even close. That'll piss them off though."

Richard looked back to the deck of the whaler. His brother was right. Already the gunner was hurrying to load another steel lance into the muzzle of the cannon, and on the wind came a strident voice, abusing him in Japanese.

Vicki muttered a curse under her breath, and Richard turned to follow her gaze. With a sinking feeling he saw the other whaling boats had caught up and were already pressing in. They converged from both sides, hemming the whale between their rigid steel hulls.

The Naiad was trapped between them, the grey ships looming so close their shadows darkened the water. There was no way Vicki could block three harpoon guns at once. Feeling sick to his stomach, Richard knew there could be no escape. It was only a matter of time.

High on the prow of the Kuu-Maru the Japanese gunner tightened his finger on the trigger again.

Gritting her teeth, Vicki swerved the Naiad in the way to block his aim, but this time he didn't waver. The chill air was suddenly torn by the hollow blast of the cannon discharging.

Richard felt a sudden burst of adrenaline as he realised the gunner had fired again, and he watched, shocked into helpless immobility as the scene began to play out before him.

With a sinister whistle the harpoon shot directly overhead, trailing its serpent-like steel coils behind it. Moments after the harpoon hit, the line snapped tight behind it. With a crack like a whip the steel cable sliced downwards, directly towards the helpless Naiad and its crew.

Richard's eyes widened as it whistled down on them, and the sound was the scythe of Death itself.

As soon as the cannon fired, Vicki had realised their predicament and reacted in the same instant, yanking the tiller to force the racing Naiad into a high-speed turn to avoid the deadly cable.

But Cal, still standing in the bow, was caught off balance.

As the boat swerved from underneath him he was flung towards the waiting sea, directly into the path of the cable. It was only his lightning-fast reactions that saved him from being tossed overboard, but as he threw himself down, his momentum drove him into the Naiad's rubber side. He had just enough presence of mind to hug the pontoon to keep from sliding over it, but he was balanced precariously on the edge of the boat, feet waving in the air, head over the side as if looking at some fascinating sight in the water – and the force of their turn threatened to tip him over the side at any moment. He was poised on the brink of disaster, the cable flashing towards his neck like a guillotine blade.

Vicki was looking the other way, eyes fixed on the charging Hunter-Killer behind them.

Richard opened his mouth to shout a warning, but no sound came out.

The moments dragged out. Finally, Vicki looked back and saw the danger.

"Cal!" Her scream seemed to hang in the air.

In a flash she let go the tiller, aborting the turn. As the unseen G-forces let go his body, Cal's legs flopped back into the boat. But he was off-balance and stunned, still hanging over the side of the boat, remaining in harm's way as he struggled to rise.

No!

Richard's mind screamed at the danger but his limbs were leaden and he stared helplessly, frozen to the spot as though caught in a waking nightmare. The cable whistled downwards, directly towards the prostrate form of his brother.

Suddenly a red shape flashed past him, launching itself at Cal.

What the…?

With a start, Richard realised it was Vicki, her dark hair streaming behind as she flew through the air. She crashed into Cal like a rugby player, grabbing him around the waist and rolling away from the falling cable. They tumbled into the bottom of the boat in a tangle of arms and legs, milliseconds before the cable whistled through the very spot where his head had been. The steel sliced into the water, just centimetres away from the boat. It hit with the force of an axe blow, sending up a shower of spray that rained back on them. Cal blinked in surprise. "Holy shit!" he managed. "That was close." He turned to Vicki, still pinned beneath him. "You saved my life."

"Don't mention it," she said, sounding somewhat muffled. "Can't have you losing your head."

Cal managed a weak grin, the relief evident on his face. "If I lost my brain d'you think I'd qualify to be an Aussie then?"

She pushed him playfully. "No. It's a well-known fact that Kiwis' brains are located in their backsides. Now how about getting off me before I kick you in the medulla."

The diversion was only temporary though, and as the two biologists picked themselves up any trace of humour evaporated. Their relief at their own narrow escape was instantly tempered by the sight that confronted them, and bobbing on the waves they had an uninterrupted view as the terrible scene played out before them.

Behind them in the boat, Richard looked on as the great whale struggled and bucked at the end of the line, thrashing the water to foam in his desperate attempts to escape. But the harpoon held him fast. It had slammed into the centre of his broad blue back, burying its cruel metal barbs deep into the living flesh. The whale shivered at its awful touch, great spasms that shook his body like an earthquake. Then he cried out, a great mournful bellow of pain. The sound was low and booming yet it tore through Richard's eardrums like a jackhammer, a deep inhuman cry of pain that would haunt his dreams forever.

The Naiad was caught in the centre of a titanic struggle as two giants – one steel, one living – fought each other. One battled for his life, the other fought to take it from him. And between them ran the insidious steel thread that joined the two in their fatal union.

The Blue tried to dive away from the cruel hold the barbs had on his flesh, but each time the line pulled tight and dragged him up short, fresh blood spilling from the ragged harpoon-hole torn in his back.

Minutes passed and the whale's struggles grew weaker, but still he refused to give up.

The Kuu-Maru reversed her engines, white water churning behind the stern, and the cable tightened, pulling the cruel six-inch barbs through his flesh.

Richard felt his heart wrench as the Blue cried out in pain again.

The minutes dragged out. The other whaleboats crowded greedily around, as though anxious not to miss out on the sport. High above the water, the gunners lined up their shots. The Tosho-Maru fired first. The harpoon was untethered, and Richard saw the flash of its sinister orange tip as it flew through the air. The steel shaft drove deeply into the stricken whale, and down at water-level, Richard felt the thud as the grenade head detonated. The concussion squeezed a gasp from his chest, but within the whale the force of the explosion was deadly, driving a shockwave through flesh and bone, pulverising anything in its path. The whale moaned, a low, tortured sound from the depths of his cavernous lungs. It was an alien language, but the message was plain. It was a desperate cry of fear and hurt – and it wrenched at Richard's soul.

The minutes dragged out, as though the whalers weren't quite sure what to do.

The Shushu-Maru fired next, another explosive blast that wracked the shattered body.

Still the great whale did not die.

High on the prow of the Kuu-Maru, Richard watched as the gunner finished reloading the harpoon cannon. He took aim, sighting briefly at the huge blue back wallowing in front of him, then fired again – this time the lance trailing a thick black hose behind it. As the harpoon slammed into the whale's flank, the hiss of gas was clearly audible through the hollow shaft. The Blue screamed in pain as a rush of compressed air flooded into his body, crushing and tearing his internal organs as he was forcibly inflated with air.

"Bastards!" Cal whispered hoarsely. "They do that so he won't sink before they have a chance to cut him up. They could at least wait until he's dead and can't feel it."

The moans of agony weakened as the whale grew weary. His dying cries would travel through a hundred miles of open ocean, but there was nothing that could save him now. The whale rolled over and Richard stared again into his great eye, now dull and clouded with pain. Blood gushed from his blowhole in a crimson spray.

The rest of the world ceased to exist as Richard watched the gentle giant slowly lose his fight for life. Finally, nearly thirty minutes after the first harpoon tore into his back Old Blue gave a final shudder and ceased struggling, his great strength spent. Then the great heart that had beat continually for over half a century, keeping out the creeping cold of the frigid ocean, finally stopped.

Richard was numb. In shocked disbelief, all he could do was stare at the body of the Great Whale, wallowing in the red-tinged swells, the ocean awash with his life-blood. He found it impossible to believe that the majestic creature he'd met that morning was now just a bloated carcass floating in the water. How could it be? He was so huge, so noble. There had been an incredible aura about him, a kind of ageless wisdom that seemed to transcend time. And now suddenly, in a few violent seconds, he was dead. It was like trying to comprehend the death of the Ocean itself.

Vicki's eyes were red. "It's not fair," she whispered. "It's just not fair." She blinked vigorously, trying to hold back her tears. "He was older than any of us, an elder of his kind. He was a herd leader and a dominant male in the gene pool." Her gaze was wistful. "How many new generations did he sire in his doomed species' struggle for survival? How many times did he lead them on their great migration?" She paused, struggling to keep her voice from cracking. "There's no sign of his herd around. Did he sacrifice himself today so the rest of his family could get away…" A single tear escaped and ran down her cheek.

"He was a good leader." She rubbed her face fiercely with her sleeve, as if embarrassed to be seen crying.

"Now he's dead. They killed him. And for what? So some rich Japanese can eat fancy sushi!" Her voice choked then and she turned away, but her shoulders quivered and Richard could tell she was sobbing.

Cal reached up a hand and fiddled absently with the greenstone pendant around his neck, his eyes never leaving the terrible scene. He pursed his lips into a thin tight line, and his hand trembled with rage. His voice, when it came, was surprisingly controlled though.

"We humans think we're so advanced… We always repeat the old saying; 'Nature is red in tooth and claw'." He curled his lip. "We say that as if we're somehow better, more civilised than animals. But animals kill only for survival. No other species kills for pleasure, for sport, or for greed. Of all the creatures on this Earth we have the greatest power over all the others – we alone have the power of life and death over entire species. Yet how do we wield that power?"

He sighed. "We teach our children that we are above nature, better than it, not part of it. As if our intelligence somehow ranks us above all the other beings we share this planet with."

Cal laughed suddenly, but it was a bitter sound without humour. "Humans are obsessed with searching outer space for intelligent life, but why? We've already discovered intelligent beings right here on our own planet, yet how do we treat them? We don't attempt to communicate with them, to learn from them. No, we just butcher them!"

Richard felt it then, a huge sorrow that threatened to overwhelm him. In his mind he could still see the great eye looking back at him, filled with that serene wisdom. Suddenly all the emotion he felt towards the Great Whale seemed to coalesce, and it descended like a great black cloud covering the horizon, nearly sweeping him away with its intensity.

All of his own worries in life suddenly seemed insignificant by comparison – his failed marriage, his dead-end career, the stress – they meant nothing out here. They were lame problems. Pathetic even. With his old life being so far away it had diminished somehow, and since coming out here Richard realised he had begun to feel differently, to see things in a new light. It was as though he had been asleep for his whole life and had only now begun to wake up. The wild ocean was a hostile and unforgiving place, but it was also hauntingly beautiful. Underneath its harsh exterior he had begun to sense a hidden depth, a secret of sorts. And the longer he spent here, the more he began to feel himself waking up to it, as if some unseen thought was calling to him. At first it scared him, but now, deluged by the wave of grief over the death of the mighty whale, everything suddenly became clear. Like the parting of a stormcloud to reveal the sun, Richard realised he had seen what his brother brought him here to see. For the first time in his life he could see past his own narrow world. For the first time in his life he knew what it was like to actually *feel*.

Richard closed his eyes as he felt his own tears coming.

The biologists sat in shocked silence as the Naiad drifted, bobbing aimlessly on the swells. No one spoke for a long time.

They could hear the clunk and rattle of machinery from the Kuu-Maru's decks, and yellow-helmeted sailors bustled around. Richard watched in a daze as the body of the Blue was slowly winched alongside the ship. They looped more cables around his massive tail flukes and pulled his body half clear of the water, lashing him to the side of the ship. A forest of harpoons still stuck out from his back and sides, the wounds bled white by now. They left him suspended there like that, upside-down in undignified humiliation, his head still underwater, somewhere beneath the cold sea.

Then with a growl of diesel engines the Japanese Hunter-Killer began to move off, props churning as it struggled to tow its heavy burden. Flanked by its two sister ships the Kuu-Maru headed for the empty horizon to the northeast.

In the Naiad no one said anything. Their hearts were heavy as they watched the Hunter-Killers leave, and a feeling of bitter failure hung over the little inflatable. Their valiant efforts had been in vain. They had failed.

Richard's mind travelled back to his old life, and this time the feelings were mixed. He had put everything on hold to come out here, but he realised now that he didn't really miss it at all. In truth, he was secretly glad to escape it. His ex was an ulcer waiting to happen! He didn't even want to think about her, so depressing were the thoughts that would envelop him if he let them. His job was stressful and although he enjoyed designing circuit boards, he hated managing projects. Budgets, forecasts, part numbers, and all those interminable meetings!

What's it all for?

That was the big question, after all. He got a good income from his job, but it wasn't like his life was happy or anything as a result. All he did was work, so there wasn't time to spend any money even if he had something to spend it on – which he didn't. Going to work had become his whole purpose for existing. The big picture was ultimately unfulfilling, as though he had an empty void inside him, waiting to be filled. It wasn't something he'd been able to put his finger on before – not until he'd seen the other side. But sitting there, bobbing in the middle of a vast windswept ocean, Richard was suddenly nervous. He could see the direction of his life was at a crossroads, and neither choice was easy. If he went back to his desk job he knew he would die there. It could be literally, many years from now when age finally caught up with him and his useful working life was over, or it could be spiritually, if the pressure got to him first and he burned out, unable to cope any longer – but Richard knew a boring predictable life was all he could aspire to there. Regardless of promotions or pay rises he might be offered along the way, nothing would really change. His job would become his life, and the purpose of his life would be his job.

Ordinarily he wouldn't have blinked at the thought, but being out here gave him a new perspective on things. It was as though the ocean had ignited a little spark inside him, and now the question had been asked he couldn't ignore it.

Is there more to life?

He had been offered a glimpse of a vibrant, exciting life out here, filled with action and danger, but most of all meaning. And purpose was the one thing his life needed most of all.

The life of a wildlife biologist was a risky choice though. It required a bold decision to turn his back not only on his own life, but also the norms of society. And Richard was a cautious man by nature.

Silence descended, and the only sound was the soft slap of waves against the hull. As the Team sat there, wrestling with their own private thoughts, Richard stared at the distant horizon. It was then he noticed a brown smudge in the sky. It was only visible for a moment, then was lost from view as they sank down into the trough of a wave. He sat up, his interest piqued. As they rose again on the next swell, he saw it was a cloud of dark smoke, and below it was a dark shape.

A ship!

Could it be the Gwendolyn, on her way to rescue them? Richard felt the relief flow through him. Getting lost was his worst nightmare and he was still terrified the Skipper might not find them out here, a tiny speck in this vast ocean – especially as the Japanese whalers were rapidly disappearing in the distance. Seeing the ship steaming south towards them was a reassuring sign. Or was it? He was about to cheer out loud, but something made him pause for breath. Richard squinted, trying to make out some detail. Though it was far away, he could see now the ship was big. Much too big to be the Gwendolyn. He watched as a huge black shape slowly materialised on the horizon.

Cal looked up and saw it then, and he inhaled sharply with annoyance. "Bloody vultures have arrived," he muttered.

Richard turned back to him, puzzled.

"That's the Nippon-Maru 1," his brother explained. "Factory ship of the Japanese Pelagic Whaling Fleet."

"Factory ship? What's that?"

Cal made a disgusted noise. "Basically it's a giant mobile slaughterhouse. It shadows the killer boats until they get a whale, then it sails over and they haul the whale aboard up the stern ramp and butcher it right on the deck."

Richard stared at the huge black vessel in the distance. "Why so big?"

"The lower levels contain giant freezers, hundreds of square metres deep. They cut the whale up on deck and send the meat down below where it's put straight on ice. They even package it into cartons ready to sell, right there on the boat." He looked away as though quietly loathing the massive ship dominating the skyline. "The Nippon-Maru is big enough to store the meat from hundreds, even thousands of whales. That means the Whaling Fleet can stay at sea hunting for months on end. They can spend the entire summer season down in the Antarctic, killing whales." His tone was sarcastic. "Very efficient, eh?"

Richard didn't reply, momentarily shocked by the industrial scale of the Japanese whaling.

Cal fell silent too, staring at the ships in the distance as though deep in thought. Suddenly he turned back to look at the others, a strange look in his eyes. "Screw this," he exclaimed. "I'm not about to roll over and give up. We might have lost this one already, but we can damn well make sure they don't win without a fight."

Vicki stared at him, considering. Then she nodded her agreement and without a word, she yanked the starter cord on the outboard. It burst into life, growling angrily in the silence.

"Cal, w-what are we doing?" Richard knew his brother well enough to suspect what he was thinking.

Cal's reply was brisk. "We're going to pick a fight, Bro."

Richard hesitated, a confused swirl of emotions running through his head. His natural instinct was to protest, to run the other way, to avoid danger at all costs. Cal could have been killed by that harpoon, for crying out loud, and now he wanted to go back for more!

What if it's my neck on the line next time?

But before Richard could say anything, a thought occurred to him. This might be his only chance to live, and he wasn't ready to go back to his desk yet. His brother's profession might be dangerous, but his purpose here was undeniable. Richard took a deep breath and made a monumental decision. He decided to go with the flow for a while longer and let Fate decide his destiny.

The Naiad slipped into gear with a clunk, and they were off, speeding towards the Japanese whalers and the Blue whale's giant body. He still gripped the seat tightly as the Naiad bounced across the wave-tops, turning his face away from the wind that whipped at his hair. But for once Richard's mind wasn't on the debilitating fear of danger, or the miserable cold.

The whalers were slow, weighed down by their booty, and the black ship swelled on the horizon as it rapidly advanced. It was the size of a container ship, dwarfing the fast catcher boats as they milled around below its stern like wasps at their nest.

On the Naiad no one spoke, a grim silence settling over them. The whaling fleet was stationary now, and the speeding inflatable bounded across the waves towards them in huge leaps. It was only a few minutes before they were alongside the giant factory ship, passing down the length of it towards the stern.

Richard sucked in his breath and stared up at it with a mixture of fear and awe. The ship was gigantic. Looking at it was like standing on the corner of Auckland's Victoria Street and gazing straight up the length of the Sky Tower. The black hull towered above them, launching itself straight up to a dizzying height, as if to touch the leaden clouds. The superstructure above it reached higher still. It was painted a sickly creamy-yellow colour, and three massive 'n'-shaped cargo cranes rose over the deck like giant soccer goalposts, one ahead of the bridge and two more behind. At the stern, a single tall chimney belched a smoke trail that stretched away towards the horizon. Richard stared, speechless. The Gwendolyn seemed large to him but this ship was three times as long, and the black hull alone stood twice as high without even considering the tall pus-coloured crane girders high atop it. The Nippon-Maru was so huge it was hard to comprehend it was even a ship capable of moving under its own power – the impression it gave was more like a huge, immobile building.

"This is the second Nippon-Maru," Cal said. "And it's even bigger than the one it replaced. They launched this one in 1987 – two years after the

Moratorium on whaling was supposed to take effect. I guess that sums up their attitude eh…"

They rounded the stern and there were the Hunter-Killer ships, crowded close around the whale's body like grey vultures on a kill.

"They're trying to block us out," Cal muttered. Then his tone hardened. "We'll see about that."

He pointed to a narrow gap of clear water, and Vicki nodded. Richard held his breath as she skilfully guided them toward it, and the Naiad zipped between two grey hulls with just metres to spare.

The scene that greeted them inside the circle was dreadfully compelling.

Richard's eye was immediately drawn to the huge stern slipway at the back of the Nippon-Maru. The black hole gaped over three stories high, yawning like a hungry mouth poised to swallow them up. Beyond it was a steep ramp leading up to the deck of the factory ship, high above.

The Kuu-Maru's yellow-helmeted crew hurried to and fro, transferring the cables around the Blue's tail across to their compatriots on the deck of the massive factory ship. In their matching overalls the whalers looked like murderous navy-blue Lilliputians scurrying around next to their huge trophy. Richard stared at the broad blue back, feeling a profound sorrow that the great whale was to meet such a brutal and undignified end as this.

A heavy sigh told him Vicki felt the same way.

Just then a sudden rumble of engines behind them drowned out the shouts and sounds of machinery. Richard jumped around, shocked to see the tall prow of the Tosho-Maru 25 lunging towards them.

"Move!" Cal shouted. "Get us under the stern! Right up next to the whale!"

Vicki twisted the throttle and the little Naiad leaped forward, nimbly avoiding the clumsy attempt to run them down. They sought refuge directly under the shadow of the black ship's stern where there was no room for the Hunter-Killer to follow. Reluctantly the grey ship fell back, growling angrily as it prowled the open water behind them, as if daring them to come out and face it.

Watching fearfully, Richard wondered how long they would be safe here. There was room for one whaling ship at a time to manoeuvre behind the stern, and the Kuu-Maru was already in close. Luckily the little inflatable was shielded for the moment by the carcass of the dead whale, but they wouldn't be safe for long – and the Japanese whalers had shown they were reckless, and becoming increasingly aggressive in their attempts to drive them off.

Suddenly a terrific blow between his shoulder blades sent Richard sprawling. He crashed into the bottom of the boat, dimly aware of a shower of water soaking him.

What the hell was that?

He concentrated on his breathing, convinced he'd just been shot in the back. He was winded, managing only short panicked gasps which set his heart racing in unison.

"Firehoses!" Cal yelled a warning.

Groggily, Richard rolled over and sat up, just in time to see the high-pressure water jet hit his brother. Cal ducked his head down to protect his face, but he didn't flinch as the blast hit his neck and shoulders, cascading in all directions. Vicki swerved to the side and Cal came up gasping.

"Bastards!" he spluttered as water poured off the hood of his survival suit.

The water-cannon was mounted on the stern-rail of the Nippon-Maru, above one corner of the slipway. As Richard watched, another yellow helmet appeared at the other corner and a second water gun burst into life. The two water jets reached out towards them like questing fingers, reminding Richard of searchlight beams tracking a plane, like in the old war movies. Vicki did her best to keep the Naiad clear of the powerful hoses, but with the huge black ship stationary in the water the jets were hard to avoid. All she could do was circle endlessly while the whalers shot down at them like machine gunners in a guard tower.

The hose operators appeared content to keep them busy though, perhaps tolerating the presence of the Naiad as long as the protesters weren't interfering with their operation. Meanwhile their fellow crew members worked feverishly, completing the transfer of cables to the factory ship with military precision.

Richard looked up at the stern. Several crew had appeared at the rail high above, and they raised large signs hand-printed in English.

"Taiyoku Misui Fisheries Company is carrying out legal scientific research," read one. "We're collecting tissue samples," said another. "Stop your illegal interference," read a third.

Cal laughed scornfully as he read them. "Wonder if they believe their own lies?" he muttered.

Just then the rumble of heavy machinery reached their ears, and the cables around the Blue's tail tensed as an unseen winch began tightening its grip. The whale's great eye stared sightlessly at the sky as he was dragged inexorably towards the gaping maw of the slipway.

Cal looked around and Richard recognised the desperation in his eyes. The whalers were about to claim their plunder.

Abruptly, Cal dropped to his knees and yanked the tool-chest from under his seat. He rifled through it then brandished a pair of bolt-cutters, his eyes as cold as a grave.

"Take us in," he ordered. "I'm going to put a stop to this."

***

Captain Hogei Gyofuku raised one ample buttock off the seat and farted loudly. He was well pleased with himself. This sea-pig was big, even for a blue-back. At nearly thirty metres long it would yield plenty of high-grade meat, more than making up for the past few days with nothing.

Not a bad morning's work.

Old Amimoto-san would be pleased with his productivity. Gyofuku still had a way to go to meet his quota for the season, but this kill would keep the Old Goat off his back for a while.

He allowed himself a congratulatory swig from his hip flask, spluttering with pleasure as the fiery liquor hit the back of his throat.

Good saké for a good job!

As he watched his crew transfer the huge carcass across to the slipway, he couldn't help feeling a little deflated though. The big brute just floated there, wallowing in the swells, unmoving. It was a shame really.

"Just like a giant turd," he muttered. It was so much more fulfilling when they were still struggling. True, this one had put up a good fight, but the explosive harpoons had cut the battle short prematurely. The smaller sea-pigs were so much more fun to land. They were manageable on the winch so he didn't have to end his fun so soon. He tensed with delight. There was nothing like the sight of a Minke going up the slipway still struggling, the flensing knives slicing into its hide while it was still alive...

He closed his eyes, feeling the warm glow spreading from his loins.

Next time, he promised himself.

Suddenly a high-pitched engine broke through his thoughts. He sat up, wiping his chin with the back of a chubby hand. It came away wet with drool.

His lip curled into a snarl at the sight of the inflatable. Those damned Westerners were back. Why couldn't they keep their interfering noses out of his business? He ground his teeth. It was time to get rid of them once and for all.

Gyofuku frowned, his eyes disappearing below the folds of his brow. His ship was still tied to the whale though, unable to manoeuvre until they'd completed the transfer to the Nippon-Maru. He deliberated some more. Maybe this was a perfect chance for one of his junior captains to prove himself?

He laughed savagely and picked up the radio. "Tosho-Maru, our annoying pests are back. Crush them like a bug!"

Gyofuku admired the Tosho-Maru's sleek lines as she sliced through the water. Like all his ships, she was a magnificent sight. He watched with mounting excitement as the tall steel bow sliced towards the unsuspecting protestors in their rubber bath-tub.

"Yes," he whispered. "That's it. Just a little more..."

Suddenly the Westerners reacted, eyes round with shock, and the little orange boat managed to swerve clear.

"Iye!" he exclaimed, annoyed as much by the narrowness of their escape as anything.

The Tosho-Maru fell back, foiled.

"Useless fool!" Gyofuku spat. He slammed a meaty fist against the wheel. His thoughts were dark with anger – but then a triumphant grin split his face.

What can they do to stop me?

The sea-pig was already strung on the line. The eco-protesters had failed to stop his hunt. They were as impotent as their hippy ideals they tried to force upon the world.

Let them hang around if they must, they're no more bothersome than a blowfly.

He picked up the radio again. "Attention Nippon-Maru. Prepare to man your water-cannons. It seems we have some filth to hose away."

He cackled with delight as the water jets caught one of the protestors by surprise, knocking him flat on his face.

"On your knees and beg for forgiveness," Gyofuku laughed.

This was turning into an amusing side-show.

The inflatable dodged and weaved, trying to avoid the hoses as it circled below the Nippon-Maru's high stern. Gyofuku heard the slipway winch start and felt the rush of victory.

Let them mill around out there, my catch is practically on the killing deck already.

He wasn't bothered by the barbarians' presence. If circling aimlessly was the worst they could manage, they could do it until the sun went down for all he cared!

But just then the little orange inflatable veered closer, making a beeline for the whale. The fire-hose operators were slow to respond, the high-pressure water jets falling away behind the little boat. It continued unopposed, crashing into the broad bulk of the whale's flank. Suddenly a red form launched itself into the air, landing squarely on the back of the beast.

Gyofuku's eyes bulged with surprise.

A dirty protestor! On the back of my whale!

He stood there a moment, jowls hanging open in shock. But his rage, when it came, was swift and vindictive.

"Nippon-Maru!" he shouted into the radio. "Forget about the boat, concentrate your hoses on that protestor. Knock him off my whale!"

But the hose operators seemed not to have heard him, either that or they couldn't aim straight. The water jets still streamed toward the stationary inflatable, dousing its occupants, but leaving the lout on the whale's back untouched. Gyofuku watched as the man scooted forward towards the base of the giant flukes, knees astride the tail for balance.

What in the name of the Kami gods does he think he's up to?

The protestor leaned forward, straining to reach the cables that bit tightly into the blubber. Gyofuku stared, at the same moment realising what was clutched in the man's hands.

Bolt cutters!

He looked desperately towards the firehoses, but they continued to send a steady deluge of water over the inflatable. His own ship was still blocked by the dead whale.

As he watched impotently, one cable parted, the sudden loss of tension whipping it away. The protestor shielded his face with his arm, then reached towards the next one.

Gyofuku bellowed like an angry bull.

"Imbeciles! I'm surrounded by a bunch of useless imbeciles!"

He slammed the throttle forward, the Kuu-Maru's diesels roaring in response. He spun the wheel hard over to port, aiming dead-centre at the whale's broad back. The bow slammed into the carcass with a sickening crunch, the thud of the impact reverberating through the steel hull. Gyofuku steadied himself against the bulkhead, raising his plastic helmet that had slipped forward over his eyes.

With a surge of triumph he saw the protestor struggling in the water, the loose end of the cable wrapped around his arm. Gyofuku laughed out loud.

The other protestors were in a panic. One was shouting incoherently into a hand-held radio, the other wrestled with the tiller of the boat, trying to manoeuvre it in position to pick up their helpless crew-mate. All the while a stream of water from the firehoses rained down on them.

Gyofuku could see the one in the water was tangled in the cable, floundering helplessly.

How perfect…

The desire to seize this opportunity flared like warm saké in his belly.

He smiled. The inflatable was held at bay by the firehoses, too far away to help the stupid Western dog. But Gyofuku could see the water jets wouldn't match their determination indefinitely, and the Kuu-Maru wouldn't have time to sail around the whale to get to the spluttering protestor. He couldn't afford to give the motherless bastard's colleagues a chance to rescue him. He squinted myopically, sizing up the situation.

There's more than one way to skin a whale!

Gyofuku cackled gleefully as he looked across the motionless blue back that separated them. "Enjoy your swim, Barbarian!"

He reached for the throttle again and poured on the power. The Kuu-Maru's twin screws thrashed the water to foam as the ship shouldered against the dead whale, driving against the immovable object like a sumo wrestler.

For several long seconds nothing happened. Then slowly, inexorably, the carcass began to move. He kept the power on, pushing against it. The huge body hung a moment on the point of balance, as if unsure, teetering agonisingly, then suddenly in a tidal wave of water it upended and rolled over – landing directly on top of the little orange boat.

Gyofuku cackled and peered through the salt-streaked window, searching the choppy water.

The scene that greeted his eyes brought with it immense pleasure. He clapped his hands, laughing delightedly at the sight of the two red-suited bodies clinging to the upturned inflatable.

Of the other protestor in the water, there was no sign.

***

Duke Hayward stood in the Gwendolyn's bridge, a deep frown creasing his weathered features. On the outside he was as unruffled as ever, but the brief radio call still replayed itself in his head. He replaced the radio hand-piece on its hook, concern written on his deeply-furrowed brow. But it was the lack of response now that concerned him much more than the fear he'd heard in the City Slicker's frantic message.

Duke's fist clenched and unclenched. His crew were in trouble. Big trouble. And he was still too far away to help them. At least one of them was already in the frigid water, perhaps all of them by now. And the enemy surrounded them.

Hang tight, y'all. The cavalry's on the way.

But he was worried. Cal's Brother concerned him most of all. He was a little soft to be out here in a man's world. Duke sighed. His gut had told him something like this might happen to him. He'd questioned Cal's decision to bring a landlubber out here, especially one that seemed so wet behind the ears, but the boy had laughed it off. "Don't worry, he's got the same genes as me. He'll do fine." Duke frowned at the recollection. He had spat pointedly over the rail and stomped back to the wheelhouse, annoyed as much at the Kiwi's stubbornness as anything else. Maybe Cal was right though? Richard did seem to be finding his sea-legs well enough at last – for a Townie. He wasn't looking so green around the gills any more and it had been days since he'd been spotted hanging over the rail feeding the fish, despite the big seas. Duke harrumphed. This would set the boy back though. He'd seen grizzled old sea-dogs bawl like babies when facing the prospect of a watery grave with Old Davy. He had little confidence the Townie would be able to save himself, much less any of the others.

He worried about Vicki too. A part of him worried more, although to be honest, a part of him did worry less. She could handle herself – and she had more gumption than a rabbit spittin' in a coyote's face. The Aussie gal had a good head on her shoulders, that was for certain. Duke wasn't sure why a pretty young thing like herself wanted to be out here roughing it in a man's world anyways, but then, it wasn't his place to argue. There was a lot about the world that was different now'a'days, and he couldn't help feeling a little out of touch at times. Even though it was a fellow's responsibility to watch out for a gal out here, in truth she probably didn't need it. Nor would she appreciate it. He grinned briefly as he remembered one time he'd tried to coddle her, and the dressing-down he'd received because of it.

"Just because I don't have any balls doesn't mean I'm a bloody special-needs case," she had yelled. "Got it?"

"Yes Ma'am," he'd answered, not knowing whether to feel chastened or amused.

Yep, Miss Vicki was one tough cookie.

Just the same though, he pushed the Gwendolyn's throttles forward another inch.

His thoughts turned to Cal. Cal would be ok. He could take care of himself – and the others too – so long as he kept his head about him.

He's good man to run a river with, Duke mused. The crazy Kiwi seemed to have no fear, and a determination to stand his ground no matter what. But that could be a bad thing.

Although Duke would never admit it, the boy was like a favourite nephew to him, or perhaps even the son he never had. And he worried for him sometimes. The crew were in good hands with Cal in charge, make no mistake, but the boy was far too headstrong. He was apt to jump quicker'n you could yell *frog*. That had gotten him in strife before. And now it looked like it had again. He was in the water now. They were all in the water.

Those dirty Jappers ran them down.

Duke's grey eyes blazed with a cold fury. He knew it was down to him to save his crew, and he wasn't afraid to open a can'o whoop-ass. He'd fought plenty of gooks before – and won. His hand subconsciously went to the scar at his throat, his mind drifting back to another battle, in another time.

The images came in a blur, but it was a familiar scene – the steamy hot jungle, like a dark green wall surrounding him, silent but for the lazy buzzing of insects. The men creeping forward on silent feet, tense with anticipation, their green tiger stripes blending with the jungle.

Suddenly a nightmare engulfed them.

The flash of gunfire, the heavy crash of AK-47s all around, smoke, the stink of cordite. Men yelling, screaming, the din of battle.

Ambush!

And through it all Duke saw his buddies going down, all around him. Hearing the wet smack of bullets tearing into flesh, the cries of pain, the blood.

Nooo!

Splinters flew out of the tree beside him, and he'd stared, the understanding taking a moment.

Me. They're shooting at me.

Then he saw them, a focus for his anger – glimpses of black pyjamas running through the trees, a straw coolie hat, a curved banana magazine, a star-shaped muzzle flash.

And then the rage took over.

He didn't remember a conscious thought to fire the M-60, but suddenly it was bucking and thrashing in his hands, the bipod dangling pointlessly, miles off the ground. He stood there in the clearing, hosing the trees, forgetting even to take cover. The heavy machine-gun roared as it chewed up the ammo belt, flicking a fountain of empty brass into the air, and spitting a curtain of death into the jungle. He remembered the savage pleasure at seeing bodies fall before it, the crash of the gun mingling with his own hoarse yell.

Duke blinked, surprised to hear how loud his own breathing sounded in the wheelhouse.

As he touched the scar on his neck he felt his blood beginning to boil. He had an old score to settle – and this time no slanty-eyed devils would get his crew.

He held the wheel with one tanned and callused hand, and his grip tightened like a vice as he steered the ship directly toward the danger. With his free hand he reached for the binoculars. The black ship leapt into focus, looming ahead like some foul apparition. Around it he could make out the smaller shapes of the grey catcher boats, clustered conspiratorially around the stern.

"Buzzing around like flies on an outhouse," he muttered, spitting a wad of tobacco juice into the empty bean tin standing next to him.

He held no delusions though. The catchers outnumbered him three-to-one, and any one of them was larger than the Gwendolyn. This wasn't going to be pretty.

"Heathcliffe!" he hollered, deliberately refusing to call the Californian by his preferred name. The little cuss still had too much growing up to do to be paid that kind of respect. "Heathcliffe, git yer ass in here!"

"Yeah what?" The filthy dreadlocks appeared in the doorway, the usual insolent half-smirk plastered across the kid's face. He'd been down in the saloon with that fine-looking blonde Canadian gal, no doubt. Probably trying his luck while there wasn't any competition around.

"Stop trying to get under that skirt and clear the decks for action," Duke growled. "And get the video camera going. We might need t' prove what them Jap sons'a bitches been doing out here."

The Californian turned to go, muttering under his breath. Duke ignored the sullen back-chat and turned back to the bridge.

He grasped the throttle and opened it up to the red-line. The Gwendolyn powered forward, engines roaring in response. Steering with one hand he reached under the bulkhead with his free hand and felt around until it settled on the pistol grip of his 12-gauge Remington 870 shotgun.

"That's my gal," he crooned to the ship. "You can do it." He held the weapon up by the slide and jerked the action, cocking it one-handed.

"We got ourselves some business to take care of."

Chapter 5

Captain Hogei Gyofuku threw back his head and laughed. With the meddling Westerners in the water there was no way they could interfere any more. In fact, his whale was even now on the way up to the killing deck to be flensed. The winch towed it tail-first through the wide stern opening and slowly up the slipway, in a kind of macabre mockery of birth. He delighted at the bright red smear it left on the slipway, hoping the spectacle wasn't lost on the stupid hippies. Gyofuku's extra chin wobbled as he laughed, but his eyes were pitiless black slits. Success felt good, but he wasn't finished yet. Not by a long shot. These meddlesome protestors still needed to learn their lesson.

He gazed thoughtfully at them. They were still in the water, unmissable in their bright red survival suits, clinging helplessly to the upturned inflatable. Helpless as a baby in a pram, in fact.

He slipped the Kuu-Maru into reverse and spun the wheel, swinging the bow clear of the whale's head that still languished in the swells. Laughing maniacally he lined up the little orange boat and slammed the transmission into gear. The Kuu-Maru's props drove the water to foam and it lunged forward hungrily.

The protestors saw him coming and tried to swim away, splashing awkwardly in their bulky clothes. Gyofuku smirked at their pathetic attempts to save themselves – but they weren't going anywhere.

Some time to stew a while will make the anticipation so much sweeter for them!

Savouring the moment, he ignored the swimmers and pointed the whaler's tall bow straight at the silly blow-up toy that was their boat.

After ramming the whale, this impact was barely noticeable. The sharp grey steel tore straight through the side pontoon, slicing through the air bladder which deflated with a sad sigh. There was a brief crunch as the bow drove forward onto the inflatable's rigid hull, then the pathetic little boat was gone, forced deep beneath the Kuu-Maru's keel.

Gyofuku grunted with satisfaction and threw the ship into reverse. As he backed up the wreckage rose to the surface, the crushed ruins of the inflatable barely afloat in the swells, surrounded by a dejected array of flotsam. He bared his teeth in a mirthless smile, then turned his attention towards the fleeing swimmers. With a pang of annoyance he saw that the third protestor – the one who interfered with his whale – had surfaced next to the others. So he hadn't drowned. Yet.

"We'll see about that!" Gyofuku muttered, his smile a cruel grimace. He reached for the throttle again. "You can all pay the price together."

The Kuu-Maru's engines roared again.

Suddenly a dark blue shape swept in from the side, blocking the way with tonnes of steel plate.

A ship!

Gyofuku flinched and swerved away to avoid a collision. As he spun the wheel hard to starboard, the blue bow swished alarmingly close. The new ship's name jumped out at him, lettered in cursive script on the bow. *Gwendolyn.*

Gyofuku snarled as he recognised it.

The protestors' ship! It had been out of sight beyond the horizon when the hunt began. *How did the old tub get here so fast?*

He cursed himself for neglecting to watch the radar. His frustration mounted as he saw what the gai-jin captain intended – while shielding his comrades in the water he threw a cargo net over the side to rescue them. As Gyofuku watched, he saw the first red-suited protestor scramble up it and climb aboard over the far rail.

His sport had been denied him. Gyofuku slammed his fist against the bulkhead.

"Curse you!" he roared. "Curse you all!"

He stared at the blue ship, his features contorted into a mask of hatred.

As he looked on, a long-haired lout came out on the deck, his dirty unwashed dreadlocks blowing in the breeze. Gyofuku wrinkled his nose in disgust at the man's unkempt appearance. He himself showered every other day while at sea, but that hair didn't look like it had seen a bar of soap for years! Did these barbarians enjoy living in filth like apes?

Suddenly his eyes widened as he realised what the man was holding.

A video camera!

Gyofuku swore. That was just like these damned protestors – they loved nothing more than collecting whatever fabrications and falsehoods they could find then running to tattle to their government, or the media. He could see the camera operator carefully filming the entire scene, panning the camera to take in the dead blue-back, the wreckage of their inflatable, and the Kuu-Maru in the centre of it all. Gyofuku frowned. Publicity would cause all kinds of problems for his command. He could only imagine what old Amimoto-san would do to him if news like this got out. He shivered involuntarily, despite his anger. These blasted Westerners could cause no end of trouble for him.

How dare they interfere like this!

The blood pounded in his head, and a red rage gripped him.

"First Officer!" he roared, the veins in his neck standing out. "First Officer, report to me immediately!"

His second-in-command hurried to the bridge, offering a nervous bow from the doorway, as if afraid to enter.

"Assemble a boarding party," Gyofuku ordered.

"A boarding party? Are you sure, Captain?"

"You heard me!" Gyofuku shouted. "Now do it!"

The officer swallowed hesitantly. "Y-you wish me to lead them, Captain?" he stammered.

Gyofuku fixed him with a cold stare. The man could be downright spineless at times. "No," he snapped. "I want you to take command of the ship. I will lead the boarding party myself." Under his breath he added, "I have a personal score to settle with these blasted gai-jin troublemakers."

***

Richard spluttered as a wave slopped him in the face. He gasped for breath, choking as another wave hit him. Even through the survival suit he could feel the terrible bone-chilling cold sapping his strength. It was more than just the temperature that robbed him of his will though. He was shocked at the violence displayed by the Japanese whalers, deliberately running them down like that. The smashed remains of the Naiad floated nearby. He felt weak at the sight of it, remembering his terror as the Kuu-Maru turned and charged straight for them. He looked away, still desperately treading water to stay afloat.

The arrival of the Gwendolyn had been a blessed reprieve. Never had a rusty forty-year-old ex-trawler been such a welcome sight.

Richard felt tears of relief spring to his eyes as she charged in front of the Kuu-Maru, cutting it off and shielding them from the murderous whalers.

But the weary survivors were not safe yet.

High above them, the deck rail beckoned enticingly, but well out of reach. From where they floated, the navy blue hull stretched away above them like a slick steel wall. There was no way they could get up to the safety of the deck.

Richard felt his heart sink. Would the waves claim them yet?

"This way," called Cal, striking out towards the bow. It was then Richard saw the net draped over the side like a gigantic brown cobweb.

"Climb," Cal ordered. "Quick."

Richard gazed up at the net. It was so high and he was exhausted. His limbs felt wooden, as though they no longer belonged to his body. He tried to reach for the net but his arms refused to respond. He groaned wearily. It wouldn't be so bad to give up. He'd just lie back and let the water support him...

"Climb!"

The shout spurred him into action. Richard forced himself hand over hand up the net, though his arms and legs were like jelly. He struggled for grip on the swaying ropes, losing his footing many times and banging his knees and elbows against the side of the ship.

"Come on, Bro," Cal urged from somewhere above. "We're not safe from those bastards until we're standing on the deck."

Richard nodded, willing his aching limbs to obey. He hauled himself up another foot, skinning his knuckles as he lunged for the deck rail. Suddenly a red hood appeared in front of him, and he felt Cal's strong grip under his armpits. The next thing he knew, he was tumbling over the rail. He landed with a thump on the deck, lying in a soaking, bedraggled heap. He breathed deeply, but it almost came out as a sob – a mixture of relief and exhaustion.

I'm still alive!

Richard patted the Gwendolyn's deck, grateful to feel its reassuring solidness beneath him at last. After what he'd just been through, the ship felt as safe as his home.

He turned his head to look for Cal, but his brother was already leaning headfirst over the rail again, assisting Vicki off the net. Heath was at the rail on the other side with the video camera.

Richard closed his eyes and laid his head back, but a sudden blast of water across the deck brought him bolt upright again. It was the firehoses from the Nippon-Maru, he realised, although they were almost out of range. Even so, he'd had quite enough of being a target for them to soak today. He struggled to his feet and began to make his way across the pitching deck, heading for the forward stairway in front of the wheelhouse.

It was then the roaring of big diesel engines made him freeze in shock. He stared across at the sharp prow of the Kuu-Maru, realising with a sick sense of certainty that it was heading straight at him.

Oh no! They're going to ram the Gwendolyn!

Richard looked around in a panic. The stairway was too far away. There was no way he could get below decks in time. He couldn't even make it to the handrail on the side of the saloon. He was marooned in the middle of the deck without even something to grab on to.

He stood there, frozen to the spot, staring up at the prow of the Japanese whaler as it charged toward the side of the Gwendolyn, aiming straight for him.

He felt the rumble beneath his feet as the Skipper threw the engines into reverse, but he could see it wouldn't be enough to get them clear of the inevitable collision.

The massive grey shape loomed overhead, poised like a guillotine blade.

At the last moment it veered away, striking a glancing blow down the side of the Gwendolyn's bow. An instant later the two ships crashed together broadside, the hull shuddering beneath his feet with a resounding *boom*. The force of the impact knocked Richard off his feet and sent him flying, to land heavily on the deck.

He lay there, blinking. The echo of the collision hung in the air, as if the world itself was stunned by the sudden violence of it.

Then he heard shouting, and the thump of feet on the deck.

Richard sat up, eyes widening at the scene in front of him.

While alongside he could see how big the Kuu-Maru really was. The sleek whaler was a third longer and its tall grey bow loomed twice as high as the Gwendolyn's. Half a dozen burly whalers had already jumped down onto her forward deck. They all wore identical blue overalls, and in addition to their white crash helmets, they were armed with long wooden batons.

Richard felt his heart miss a beat.

While the Japanese boarding gang fixed ropes to the Gwendolyn, another whaler jumped down. He was short and stocky, with a thick neck and a belly to match. He wore a red helmet, but that wasn't necessary – it was obvious from his arrogant swagger and the way the other men respectfully lowered their gaze that he was in charge.

Heath was on his knees by the rail, eyes wide with terror. The camera had been knocked out of his hands and was now lying on the deck, several metres away. As Richard watched, the Californian scrambled to his feet, turned, then bolted towards the staircase.

From behind him, Richard heard Cal's desperate shout. "The camera! Get the camera!" But Heath kept running, not hearing, or perhaps not caring.

The head whaler's black eyes flickered beneath his red helmet and he barked an order, gesticulating at the abandoned camera. Two men bowed, then hurried forward towards it.

Richard held his breath, knowing he was too far away to stop them – even if he knew how.

Suddenly he heard running feet behind him and a red shape flashed past.

His first thought was that it was Cal, but the hood was pushed back and he saw the dark ponytail spilling out.

Oh my god, Vicki!

The Japanese were already closer to the camera, but she didn't hesitate, launching herself into a full-length dive across the deck. She slid along the slick metal, snatching the camera from under their noses, then curling into a protective ball as she slammed into the far rail.

She lay there, momentarily stunned, and the whalers stared back at her in surprise.

No one moved. Then a torrent of Japanese cut through the air as the red-helmeted captain ranted and cursed at his men. The whalers abruptly snapped out of their trance, hefting their batons menacingly as they advanced on her.

Richard gasped. Vicki had the camera, but he could see she didn't have time to get away. She would be cornered against the rail where she lay.

Suddenly Cal charged past, fists raised. "Get below!" he exclaimed at Richard, without even glancing down at him.

Richard stared, transfixed, as Cal launched himself at the closest whaler. His fist crashed into the man's ear, just below his helmet. The punch had the momentum of his charge plus the full weight of his body behind it, and the whaler went out like a light. He toppled over and fell heavily to the deck, unconscious even before his face hit the steel.

Cal planted himself in front of Vicki, fists raised, as if daring the rest to approach. One look at the determined set of his jaw was enough to convince Richard his brother meant business!

The other whalers hesitated, clearly afraid of the tall Kiwi who'd just felled their comrade with one hit.

The red-helmeted leader went purple in the face and let loose a torrent of Japanese, shouting and gesticulating at the scientists.

Seizing the reprieve Cal created for her, Vicki jumped to her feet and sprinted aft towards the rear staircase, camera hugged protectively to her chest.

Two whalers tried to follow but Cal stepped forward, grim-faced, blocking their path. Without taking his eyes off them, he stooped over the unconscious sailor and pulled the baton from his limp fingers.

The whalers fanned out around him, their clubs raised threateningly as they advanced.

Richard looked on in horror.

Suddenly Cal looked directly at him, the intensity of his gaze boring right through him. "Run!" he mouthed.

Richard hesitated, partly out of fear, partly out of concern for his brother – although he knew there was nothing he could do to help him.

The leader swaggered up behind his men, knowing he was in control. He tipped his red helmet back out of his eyes, then snapped a curt order.

The men closed in.

"Nooo!" Richard clapped a hand to his mouth, startled at his own bravado.

The leader whipped his head around to eyeball Richard, his eyes narrowing to angry slits in his face. Then he bared his teeth in a sadistic grin, slamming his meaty fist into the palm of his other hand as he leered at Richard. The message was blunt.

Richard ran. As he headed for the rear staircase, the last thing he saw over his shoulder was a ring of flying batons – with Cal's tall form in the centre of it.

Richard ran down the narrow side deck next to the saloon, conscious of booted feet pounding behind him. He passed the outside ladders leading up to the wheelhouse, then the chartroom aft of it. But he ignored them. He didn't want to go up. He needed to go down, into the belly of the ship where he could hide. He risked a glance behind and saw two white helmets running towards him, followed by a red one. There was no sign of Cal.

He sprinted aft, lungs tightening with the exertion.

The crane stood alone at the rear of the ship, the small stern deck empty without the Naiad resting on its cradle. A sudden image of the little boat jumped into his head, lying smashed and broken in the churning swells. Richard pushed down the flood of fear that came with the thought, determined to concentrate on his escape.

The rear companionway faced forwards, so he had to grab the handrail to help him turn. He swung himself around and lunged into the open doorway, feet skidding on the slippery deck. At the top of the steps he paused and sneaked his head around the side of the companionway for a look back towards the bow. The dark blue overalls were thundering down the narrow side deck towards him.

Richard turned his attention back to the rear stairway. It plunged steeply down in front of him, leading to the middle level of the ship. With nothing behind him except the stern crane, there was nowhere else to go.

Richard took a deep breath and hooked his arms over the handrails. He'd seen the crew slide down the staircase like this, but until now had been too scared to try it himself. This was no time to shuffle down backwards taking one rung at a time though!

He lifted his feet clear of the rungs and jumped down the steep staircase, supported only by the handrails under his armpits. It was a terrifying ride, made worse only by the sudden stop at the bottom. He landed heavily on the floor, sprawling onto his hands and knees in the main passageway. Behind him, he could hear his pursuers pounding toward the top of the stairs.

He looked up the length of the corridor and saw Vicki at the far end by the forward staircase, the camera still hugged protectively to her chest. She was almost at the door to the Bio Lab; the room where she ran her genetics profiles to analyse the whale DNA they collected. In her skilled hands the assays were able to provide precise details on the species, age, sex, and life history of each animal – and the ultraviolet-light analysis of the electrophoresis gels required a darkroom in the lab. The perfect place to hide!

She lunged forward toward the door handle.

Suddenly Richard heard the echo of booted feet crashing on the metal rungs of a ladder. His first thought was the ladder behind him, but the sounds came from somewhere ahead. He looked forward apprehensively, hoping it might be one of the crew. His heart sank when he saw dark blue overalls coming down the forward staircase behind Vicki. The look on her face told the same story as she turned. It was clear she couldn't reach the safety of the darkroom in time, and now they'd seen her she wouldn't be safe if trapped in there. She doubled back, heading for the central staircase that led up to the saloon.

Suddenly another set of blue overalls descended down it, cutting off her escape. Richard gasped in horror. Vicki was trapped in the corridor. Only the forward and rear staircases went down to the lower level, but she couldn't get to either. She had nowhere to go.

The whalers guffawed and lumbered towards her from both directions.

Vicki glanced over her shoulder, eyes widening as the gravity of her predicament sank in.

Richard looked around, but there was no sign of anyone else. Heath had disappeared, and Summer was nowhere in sight – not that those two would be much help anyway. The Skipper was still on the bridge, and Cal was still up on deck somewhere. Richard swallowed. He hoped his brother was ok – not least because they needed him here!

He wavered, hands clenching helplessly, not knowing what to do.

The whalers advanced on Vicki.

Suddenly she sprang into action. She looped the camera strap off her neck and made as if to run, but instead she ducked down and launched it along the floor like a ten-pin bowler.

"Richard!" she shouted. "Catch!"

The camera skidded between the legs of a surprised whaler, and before he could do anything it was past him, sailing down the passageway towards Richard.

He bent down to grab it, then instantly regretted his decision as the whalers turned toward him.

Oh hell, what do I do now?

Richard stood rooted to the spot, his mind flashing back to Form One school sports day – the first and last game of rugby he'd ever played. Despite his terror at taking to the field he'd managed to keep himself out of trouble for most of the game – until someone threw the ball to him. He'd surprised himself by catching it – secretly delighted he hadn't embarrassed himself in front of the crowd – then he looked up and saw the whole forward pack of the opposing team thundering down on him like a herd of runaway elephants. Richard's knees sagged as the same sick feeling of dread seized him.

Behind him he could hear his pursuers charging down the ladder already.

Things were rapidly going from bad to worse.

He turned to look back, recoiling from the huge shape blocking the stairway.

Under his red crash helmet, the lead whaler's mouth twisted into a snarl of triumph.

Richard quailed in terror, but the burst of adrenaline finally galvanised his feet into action. He took the camera and fled the only way he could – down the stairs to the lower level.

He landed in a heap at the bottom of the lower companionway, the din of the engine room hammering in his ears. He scrambled to his feet, hands clapped to his ears to block out the throbbing of the diesel engine. He sidled past the long line of noisy pistons, and headed for the door into the main cargo hold. As he wrestled with the heavy bolt, he heard boots coming down the staircase.

Come on, come on!

The heavy door finally swung open, and he burst through it, stumbling over the door lip in his haste. The cargo hold stretched before him, low-ceilinged and dimly lit. The floor and walls curved upwards with the shape of the ship's hull, and reinforcing ribs stuck out from the floor and ceiling like the skeleton of a giant steel creature. He hurried forward into the gloom, the low ceiling pressing down claustrophobically. A faint smell of fish hung in the stale air. No matter how many coats of paint she received, it seemed the Gwendolyn couldn't completely shake off the trappings of her former life – and the cargo hold of a trawler was no place for the queasy. Richard felt his stomach lurch as the ship rolled on a swell, but he forced himself to calm down.

Get a grip, you've got to keep this camera safe. Cal's counting on you!

He hurried towards the forward staircase, knowing only that he had to keep moving.

Suddenly he heard noises up ahead. He skidded to a stop, just as several blue-clad whalers stomped down the forward companionway, cutting off his escape.

Richard looked around, heart beating.

He glanced fearfully at the door behind him and saw the handle begin to move.

Oh no, what do I do now?

Just as the engine room door swung open Richard dived behind a crate. He crouched in the low shadow it cast, trying to control his ragged breathing. But he felt the tendrils of fear coiling up his spine as the footsteps came closer, and it was all he could do not to gasp out loud.

Suddenly a broad shape towered over him.

Richard looked up, heart hammering in his chest. With a sick sense of dismay he saw the red crash helmet of the whaleboat captain.

Richard scrambled to his feet and backed away, holding the camera protectively behind his back – although it was a futile gesture. The hefty Japanese whaler stomped up to him, a vicious smirk plastered across his jowls. The man's squinty eyes were sunken into his face, and his ample chins bristled with dark stubble. He looked mean. The whaler thrust out his hand for the camera, like a gorilla demanding a banana.

The other men sauntered up behind their leader. There was no escape.

Behind his back, Richard fumbled for the cassette eject button, knowing he was already out of time.

The whaler made another impatient grabbing motion, and Richard saw the anger flare in his eyes.

Uh oh, this guy's seriously pissed off.

Richard's mouth went dry. He gulped and brought the camera out from behind his back, not knowing what else to do to avoid a beating.

Suddenly Vicki burst through the circle of whalers, launching herself at the leader. She crashed into him, aiming a clumsy swing at his head. The red crash helmet flew off, tumbling to the floor. The beefy whaler stood there for a moment, blinking, more surprised than hurt. Then he roared like an angry beast and let fly with a vicious backhander. It caught Vicki on the side of the face and lifted her off her feet. She flew backwards and sprawled in a heap on the floor where she lay still.

"Vicki!"

Richard tried to run to her but the whaler stopped him with a meaty palm on his chest. He reached down and snatched the video camera from Richard's hands, a greedy glint in his eyes. Holding it by the strap he swung it over his head and brought it down onto the metal floor. The camera burst open in a shower of flying plastic.

Richard tried to move away but the hand tightened on his shirtfront. The whaler's glare hardened and he drew his baton, leaning in close until his face was just inches away. Richard recoiled as the sour breath enveloped him, and he felt his stomach lurch. He could hear a distant buzzing in his ears, and his knees sagged. The only thing holding him upright was the vice-like grip at his throat.

The whaleboat captain seemed to sense Richard's fear, and his pock-marked face split in a twisted grimace of a smile – revealing a row of dirty and chipped teeth. "I am Hogei Gyofuku, Master of the Taiyoku Misui Fisheries Company's Pelagic Whaling Fleet," he hissed in heavily-accented English. "And you have interfered with my hunt for the last time." He laughed cruelly and raised his baton.

Richard felt a wave of helpless defeat sweep over him. He screwed his eyes closed, waiting for the blow to smash into his skull.

Suddenly a gravelly voice boomed out. "Hey Charlie, why don't you take your hands off my crew and get the fuck off my ship?"

Richard looked up, startled. Relief flooded through him as Duke's bearded face materialised out of the shadows.

Gyofuku growled and dropped him. He turned to face the Skipper, beckoning his men forward. The whalers spread out, batons raised.

Duke didn't waver. The sound of the shotgun pump was unnaturally loud in the confined space, and the effect it had was electrifying. The whalers froze, batons clattering to the floor as they raised their hands. Gyofuku hesitated though, weapon still clenched in his beefy fist, his hooded eyes black with malice.

The Skipper stepped forward and jammed the barrel of the shotgun under his fat chin.

"I said get off my ship. Now move, before I change my mind and pull this trigger."

Gyofuku blanched, suddenly acquiescent, and motioned for his men to back up. But as he turned to leave, some of his bluster returned. "This is not the end," he spat. "We will meet again, stinking Greenpeace dogs. And next time I will have my flensing knife. I will cut me some sashimi, I think."

"Shut yer pie-hole," Duke growled, prodding him towards the rear companionway.

Richard hurried over to check on Vicki. She groaned and sat up, rubbing her head. "Did anyone get the number plate of that truck?"

Richard smiled, relieved to see she was unhurt. "It's ok, he's gone now."

Her face was crestfallen though. "But we lost the video," she murmured. "The bastard won."

Richard couldn't contain his smile. "I don't think so," he grinned, opening his hand to reveal the tiny camcorder tape he'd managed to slip in his pocket.

Vicki stared at it, then a smile burst across her face. "You're full of surprises Richard Major." She leaned up and gave him a hug.

Richard blushed.

The Skipper was about to disappear through the engine room door but at the sound of their laughter he turned back, momentarily puzzled. When he spotted the tape his eyebrows shot up, but his response was typically low-key. "Nice job y'all." He drawled, then nodded to Richard. "You too, Son."

Up on deck the whalers stomped sullenly back aboard their own ship, looking a little worse for wear. The one Cal had punched was still reeling and leaned heavily on a crewmate's shoulder for support, and another was out cold and had to be carried by two others. Yet another was cradling an injured arm to his chest. Richard felt light-headed when he saw the extra bend in the man's forearm, and he looked quickly away. Gyofuku alone was still defiant, his face as dark as a thundercloud as he marched stiffly back to his ship. As the Kuu-Maru pulled away he stood on the bridge, black eyes fixed on the Gwendolyn, watching them like a predator.

Richard averted his eyes, alarmed by the intensity of Gyofuku's stare.

As he looked at the deck, a new thought suddenly occurred to him.

Oh my god, what happened to Cal?

He'd last seen him in a good deal of strife!

Richard broke into a run, heading for the foredeck where he'd left his brother. He burst around the side of the saloon, filled with trepidation at what he might find. He was suddenly guilt-ridden, ashamed of himself for running away and leaving Cal alone and in trouble.

He stumbled to a halt, mouth open, aghast at the sight of his brother. Cal was leaning against the wall, clutching his head in his hands. Richard gasped as he saw blood streaming through his fingers. Lots of blood.

"Cal," he exclaimed. "A-are you ok?"

Cal grinned up at him. "Don't worry, it's just a cut. Head wounds always bleed heaps…"

Richard hesitated, unsure what to do. "Do you need me to get a bandage or something?"

Cal shook his head, sending bright droplets of blood to the deck. "Nah, I'll be ok. Vicki's trained as a vet. She'll stitch me up, good as new."

Cal flashed him another grin. "Thanks for the diversion, Bro."

Richard was confused. "Diversion?"

"Yeah, three of those yobs followed you below, plus the captain." He laughed. "Nice job – there's no way I could have taken on all seven by myself."

Richard stared at his brother, trying to detect any trace of sarcasm in his voice. "But they beat you up. You're bleeding!"

Cal chuckled. "You should see the other guys!"

Richard blinked, picturing the dejected whalers hobbling back to their ship. "You did that to them? By yourself?"

Cal laughed again. "Mum never did approve of me learning kickboxing, but there's certain skills that can come in handy for a field biologist."

Richard stared at the deck. "You're not mad I left you?" he ventured.

Cal grabbed him in a playful headlock and knuckled his damp hair. "What were you gonna do to them eh? Kick them in the shins?" He grinned. "Relax, bro. For your first action you did good." His gaze travelled to the camcorder cassette still clutched in Richard's hand. His eyes widened. "Yep, you did real good."

Suddenly the smile left his face. Richard turned to follow his gaze, his eyes settling on the huge shadow of the Nippon-Maru.

Under a dark and brooding sky, the Japanese had begun their grisly work. The Old Blue had already disappeared through the gaping maw of the slipway, swallowed up by the dark steel monster with its insatiable appetite. A bright red blood smear marked his final passage up the ramp to the deck, high above. Richard could see to the top of his back over the lip of the incline. The great head hung aft, as if yearning for the sea far below. His throat striations sagged against the deck, slumping like a punctured beach ball without the ocean's gentle support.

A crowd of yellow-helmeted whalers swarmed around him, wearing dirty white gumboots and white plastic aprons. They were armed with wicked-looking knives, each with a long handle and hooked at the blade like a hockey stick. As Richard watched, one of them clambered onto the blue back and plunged the knife in up to the hilt of its long handle. With a savage sawing motion he opened a huge flap, walking it the length of the body. The skin and blubber parted with the ease of a child's spoon slicing through a jelly desert.

Steam rose as the last of the Blue's body heat dissipated into the cold air.

A single ray of sun lanced through the clouds, as though to do battle against the creeping darkness of the sky.

The other whalers joined in with gusto, laughing and joking amongst themselves, their long blades flashing under the pale light. Their boots and the fronts of their aprons were quickly smeared with red. They slit the gut cavity open and the huge coils of intestine slithered out, snaking across the deck as though alive. The men waded through them, knee-deep in the softly-steaming piles.

They attacked the blubber, peeling it away in long strips. The naked carcass beneath glistened with a pearly sheen, but it didn't remain so for long. As the knives came down, the garnet-red muscle tissue was revealed, oozing dark blood from the multitude of slashes. Flesh was hacked away from bone until the whale was unceremoniously reduced to a series of bloody piles of meat on the deck.

Richard's eyes widened as the offal was dumped overboard, followed by the blubber.

Cal made a disgusted noise. "Limited freezer space," he explained. "It's more profitable for them if they keep just the best cuts of meat from each whale and dump the rest." He raised his hands in a futile gesture. "People are such strange beings. It's incredible how fickle we are… Whales used to be killed for the oil in their blubber, and all the meat was wasted. Nowadays it's the other way around, they hack off a bit of flesh and dump the rest." He turned away so Richard couldn't see his face, but he sounded sad. "What we consider valuable is constantly changing and so arbitrary. Yet it always comes back to money." His sigh confirmed Richard's suspicions. "Why are people so fixated with making money? What the hell use is money to them anyway? It can't buy anything important. It can't buy you love, purpose, or meaning for your life." He spread his hands wide. "There's so many things money can never buy… a new whale… the un-extinction of a species… a replacement planet to live on when this one is dead." He stared at the horizon. "Chief Seattle once said; All things are connected. Whatever befalls the Earth, befalls the sons and daughters of the Earth. Man did not weave the web of life, he is merely a strand in it. Whatever he does to the web, he does to himself." Cal shook his head sadly. "Wise words, yet no one today seems to comprehend them. Why can't people recognise the value of having a live whale swimming in the ocean – for his sake as well as their own?"

The deck was awash with blood now and the red trickle down the slipway had become a river.

One of the whalers slipped, landing on his backside amidst the blood and gore. His companions laughed uproariously, delighting in the spectacle. They slapped their thighs and mimicked his flailing arms, mocking him. The unfortunate man scrambled to his feet again, cheeks turning the same colour as his stained apron.

Richard turned his head away from their exuberant slaughter, already feeling a lump in his throat.

At the side of the ship he was disturbed to see a bright red fountain gushing from a pipe. The scuppers that drained the deck were overflowing with blood, and the outlet pipe spewed a continuous stream into the ocean. Richard stared in sad fascination as the bloody waterfall twinkled in the narrow shaft of sunlight, vivid against the bile-coloured superstructure of the ship, and the malevolent black hull below. The sea around the stern was already stained bright red.

The sound of grinding machinery reached his ears, and a large shape moved into position at the top of the slipway. Richard stared at it, momentarily confused. The object was the size of a small car. With a start, he realised it was the whale's severed head, hacked from his body by the long knives. The Blue's eyes were cold and lifeless in death, the proud fire within them already extinguished. Richard saw no deep wisdom burning within them now, no spark of intelligence. Just emptiness.

And the stark finality of it was heart-wrenching.

Prodded from behind, the head tumbled and skidded down the steep ramp, already slick with the whale's own blood. It splashed into the sea, landing in the bloody water behind the factory ship. The Blue's head floated for a few moments before it slowly sank from sight, diving into the mysterious blue depths for the last time.

His body was next, an empty skeleton gutted and stripped of meat, tossed out like garbage. It splashed into the swirling red water, a grisly monument to Japanese efficiency. Then the ocean closed over the remains of the Great Whale, reclaiming its own.

Richard blinked as tears pricked his eyes.

Overhead, the clouds drew tighter, blocking out the sun with ominous finality. Richard shivered at the sudden chill in the air.

"Come on." Cal's voice broke through his thoughts.

Richard gazed at him, stricken.

Cal shook his arm gently. "Come on, we have to go now." His eyes softened momentarily, and Richard caught the briefest glimpse of pain behind them. Then Cal was stony-faced again. "I know it hurts. Store it away for when you need an incentive."

Richard allowed himself to be led.

"We need to get underway before the shit hits the fan." Cal urged. He waved up at the Gwendolyn's bridge and motioned urgently to the Skipper. His face was grim as he turned back to Richard. "Good things come to those who wait," he muttered. "And those soulless bastards are about to get what's coming to them."

Richard stared at him, uncomprehending. "Huh?"

Cal offered a brief smile. "Let's just say I left them a little underwater surprise when I went for a swim…"

At that moment a deep rumble reached their ears, and the rear of the Nippon-Maru hummed under the power of its huge engines. The water boiled behind the stern, forced up from deep below the churning props.

Cal turned to watch, an expectant look on his face. Richard glanced at him out of the corner of his eye, not sure what was going on.

Suddenly there was an enormous bang, and the giant black ship seemed to shudder in the water.

Cal laughed. "That should hold 'em for a while."

The faint sound of an alarm bell carried to them, and blue-overalled figures scrambled about the factory ship in a fluster.

"What happened?"

Cal's eyes danced. "The score is Japanese propeller: 0, steel cable: 1."

Richard stared at him. "The cable tangled the propeller? But how?"

Cal grinned back over his shoulder, as though amused by the irony that the whalers' own tow cable was responsible for crippling their ship. "It might have had a little help…"

They hurried up the ladder to the bridge, but as the Gwendolyn pulled away from the Fleet none of the Team's attention was on the disabled factory ship.

"Well done, Son," Duke drawled, slapping Cal on the back. "That was a dandy right hook – way to pole-axe that bastard!"

Cal's laugh was grim. "Let's not hang about here in case they want a rematch."

The Skipper seemed not to have heard him. "That's tellin' 'em how it is!" he chuckled to himself as he opened the throttles. The Gwendolyn responded gamely, throwing herself against the rising white-caps. But Cal was watching the radar out of the corner of his eye, and a minute later he cursed under his breath. Duke followed his gaze. "Dang it. They got the whore going." He gestured at the screen where they could clearly see the large green blob of the Nippon-Maru limping slowly northwards, flanked by its escort of Hunter-Killer boats.

Cal frowned. "The cable must have missed the second prop… Still, they can't stay out here with only one screw, and they'll have to find a port with a dry dock to get it repaired."

"With any luck they'll have to go all the way back to Jap-land to get it fixed," the Skipper growled. "That ought t' put the kibosh on their antics for the season."

Cal allowed a brief smile. "Let's hope so." Then he sighed. "Unfortunately our cruise is over as well. Without the inflatable we can't do much work out here. We'd better make a run for home." He gazed out at the darkening sky. "Looks like there's a big storm on the way too…"

While Vicki got to work bandaging the cut on his head, Cal began to tune the hydrophone, selecting the lowest-frequency sound bands occupied only by whalesong. Whether it was out of habit, or just for something to do, Richard didn't know. But as his brother slowly scanned through the frequencies, no sound came from the speakers except the relentless hiss of static.

Richard was silent. He'd been unable to tear his eyes away from the bridge of the Kuu-Maru until it slowly slipped from sight behind them, and the sight still haunted his thoughts. Through its windscreen he'd glimpsed a red crash helmet, and the pockmarked face beneath it glowered after them with murderous intent.

Part II – Intrigues of the Kuromaku

Chapter 6

Cal Major sat in the window of the café, staring out at the midday traffic crawling past in Colombo Street. Christchurch was small as far as cities went – barely a third of a million people – and pleasant enough to look at with its old stone buildings and English-style gardens. Although this was the main street there were few buildings over two stories high in this part of town, and a pleasing amount of greenery on the horizon… but it was still a city. As he gazed out at the throng, watching with the detachment of an observer, Cal was at best ambivalent about being back. Everyone was in such a rush, constantly in motion but going nowhere, the lunchtime shoppers hurrying past on their errands as though their very lives depended on it. At least the streaked glass shielded him from the stink of exhaust fumes, but he still felt the claustrophobia of the city pressing in around him.

It was more than just the city responsible for his mood though.

He chewed his lip as the usual frustration coursed through him.

How the hell am I supposed to study whales when those bastards are killing them faster than I can even get a tag on them?

The whole purpose of the Southern Ocean Whale Sanctuary was to create an area with no hunting pressure! An area where whales could recover, and science could study a 'normal' population. Yet those bloody whalers treated it like their own private larder to raid! It was almost enough to make him want to give up in despair. It was times like this that he really questioned himself, and even his reasons for doing this at all.

Maybe I should have stuck to being a corporate lawyer?

Cal sighed. He knew he could never go back though. He couldn't give up, no matter how tough the road became. He had sworn an oath to himself that his life was not going to be frittered away in the pursuit of money. He was going to make a difference to the world, regardless of the consequences.

He ran a hand through his blonde hair. His biceps flexed under his tight T-shirt, earning appreciative giggles from two teenaged schoolgirls walking past outside. Cal didn't even notice.

Being shore-bound was even more galling to him. While he was laid up in port with no Naiad, the research season was ticking away. He sipped his water and tried not to let his discontent show. He didn't like cities at the best of times, and after the wide open spaces and the freedom of the Southern Ocean this was like purgatory.

But what he was about to do was even worse.

You're selling out!

Cal did his best to ignore the accusing voice in his head.

He looked at his watch for the millionth time that morning. Aurelia was uncharacteristically late. He wondered if that was deliberate – along with her choice of this venue – but dismissed the thought. She was a born activist, but not that manipulative.

Behind the counter, the waitress smoothed her floral op-shop dress and looked over at him, absently flicking the metal stud in her bottom lip. Cal hunched down in his chair, staring at the bright orange Formica table-top, fervently hoping she would ignore him back. She obliged, tossing her blond dreadlocks and reaching up on a shelf to light an incense stick instead. The pungent-smelling smoke wafted around the room. Somewhat relieved, Cal let his eye wander over the menu board again, trying to decide what seemed the least terrifying. Something nice and safe seemed the best bet – like Nachos. "Everything we serve is GE-free and 100% vegan!" proclaimed the chalk-board, but Cal wasn't sure he could face nachos minus mince, cheese, and sour cream. What did that leave? Nothing on the menu involved any animal product, nor was anything produced in a way that might impinge on the human rights or fair-trading opportunities of any third-world grower. Cal frowned. He didn't know how to take vegans. He could admire their sentiment, not to mention their determination to live life according to their ideals. But at the same time some of their beliefs seemed so pedantic, almost like fixating on what colour to repaint the Titanic's funnel while the whole ship sank around them. While they battled to ensure a South American coffee farmer was paid a decent wage and no cows suffered the indignity of being milked, meanwhile just over the horizon whole species of marine mammals were facing violent and bloody annihilation under the harpoons of the Japanese whalers.

Where are your priorities?

Cal instantly regretted the thought. He didn't doubt that these people would share his outrage at the illegal and immoral slaughter, but at the same time, this was not a problem that outrage alone could fix.

He sure didn't have any answers. He checked his watch and wondered again where Aurelia was – and what had possessed him to agree to this meeting. It would only cause trouble, he knew, to reopen old wounds. Yet at the same time he knew she was the only one who could help him now.

He picked absently at the Formica tabletop with his thumbnail.

He was determined to take the fight to the Japanese, but things hadn't gone according to his plan. He'd broken the story to the media as soon as the Gwendolyn returned to port, but they hadn't taken to it like he'd hoped. The video was too fuzzy to use, the TV stations said, and hence they couldn't confirm his claim a protected species had been killed. The newspapers weren't much better. The journalist took notes, but he seemed bored and disinterested, like he'd rather be somewhere else. They had printed the story but sidestepped any controversial claims. It languished on page four, just a few lines long and easily forgotten. And it looked like it had been. It frustrated Cal that people could be so caught up in their sad little lives that they didn't take any notice of the world around them.

To make matters even worse though, the whole issue was overshadowed by the Japanese Government's response. They made themselves out to be the victims, claiming illegal interference against their vessels and demanding an official investigation. The Team was forced to defend their own actions before they could even get their story told. Cal was still pissed off – about everything – but he knew justice would not come easily. He rubbed his temples and sighed. The whalers might have won this round, but he wasn't beaten yet. There were other ways to get results.

A corner of the tabletop began to lift as he picked at it but he didn't notice. His thoughts were far away.

Aurelia had many contacts. He didn't always agree with the methods they used, but they could get results. At the end of the day it was the result that really mattered. And he was desperate enough to try anything now. He had proven that much just by turning up here to meet with her…

How many times did I vow this day would never come?

It was difficult to admit to himself, but despite everything that had happened between them, deep down there was a part of him that still cared about her. And that was what worried him. He knew he couldn't afford to go through all that all over again.

Suddenly the bell over the door jangled. Cal looked up, straight into Aurelia's sea-green eyes. He felt his heart trip, just as it had the first time he gazed into those mysterious depths.

She wore a bright green top that almost, but not quite drew attention away from her eyes. Her jeans were revealingly tight, and the rips across the thighs showed a seductive glimpse of tanned skin. It was a direct contrast with the cartoon kitten embroidered on one cuff, but that was her to a T. She was an intriguing mix of femininity and fiery authority – and she was still as hot as ever.

"Aurelia Benet," he whispered. She tossed her auburn mane and flashed that dazzling smile of hers and he had to fight the urge to run across the room and throw himself into her arms. He waved to get her attention instead.

"Cal!" she exclaimed, rushing forward to hug him.

He stood and returned her embrace with cool dignity, reminding himself that personal contact was just her way.

Her breasts were pert beneath the thin cotton of her top, and he realised she wasn't wearing a bra. With an effort he kept his eyes from wandering. He didn't know if she'd done it deliberately to taunt him, but he refused to fall for it.

"How have you been?" he asked.

She chuckled huskily. "It's tough managing the troops!"

A sudden image of her sprang to mind, surrounded by adoring hordes of scraggly-bearded male fans. He shook his head, wondering how many starry-eyed hippy lads had signed up to be activists just because she smiled at them. He could imagine them fawning after her like love-struck puppies, hanging on her every word and probably fighting amongst themselves to be the first to carry out her bidding.

He blinked, forcing the thoughts down. However close to the mark they might be, he couldn't afford to let himself care what she did now. He'd already been down that road.

Aurelia took his hand "How are you, Cal?" she gushed.

"Oh, you know," he mumbled. "Working hard."

"Still doing those invasive biopsies?" she challenged, still smiling, but at the same time boring into him with her gaze.

Cal ignored the question, refusing to be drawn. They'd covered that ground too many times before, and getting into another argument now wouldn't help anyone.

"I need your help," he said.

She tossed her long auburn hair, feigning surprise. "I thought you didn't like the way I did things?" she demanded, pouting haughtily.

Cal opened his mouth to deliver a cutting response, then closed it again, knowing that wouldn't help. "This isn't about me," he sighed. "It's about the whales."

He stared at the table and began to explain to her what had happened on the lonely expanse of the Southern Ocean.

Her expression softened as she listened and when he finished she was uncharacteristically silent. He looked up at her and saw her eyes were moist. "That's terrible," she whispered, and he knew her response was heartfelt.

He had wondered if he was doing the right thing here; a scientist asking for help from a Greenpeace leader, but looking into her eyes he knew her heart was still in the right place. They were on the same side – even if they didn't exactly see eye to eye.

Her methods might not be mainstream – unless you were into chaining yourself to stuff – but they were direct, and she knew how to get publicity. He waited without speaking, and sure enough, as soon as the shock had worn off the old 'Aurelia fire' flared in her eyes. "We've got to do something," she announced. "They can't be allowed to get away with this outrage."

He smiled inwardly. Her enthusiasm was contagious, as was her burning passion to right the wrongs of the world. That was what made him fall for her all those years ago, and what still tugged at his heart-strings even now. He forced himself to look away until the moment passed, determined to keep his feelings out of this. He couldn't allow himself to repeat the mistakes of the past. It wouldn't work between them. It couldn't work. Despite their similarities they were just too different.

"We need to bring this to the public attention," she declared. "The people must be informed."

Cal rolled his eyes. "I told you, the media aren't interested. There's no proof, and we don't have good enough evidence to support our side of the story."

She laughed. "There you go again, always thinking like a scientist. You don't need evidence, people will believe whatever we tell them."

Cal bristled, opening his mouth to protest.

She held up a hand to forestall him. "Okay, okay, I take it back. Science isn't all bad. But my way gets results faster. If we generate enough publicity the Government will be forced to investigate."

Cal frowned. "I'm not so sure about that. This is all happening in international waters over the horizon, and out of sight is out of mind." He paused, searching her face. "I think this time we may have to take it to the next level. We may have to shut them down ourselves."

She stared at him for a moment, then a huge grin split across her face. "A call for activism. I knew you'd finally come around one day. I always said you'd make a good protestor."

Cal could see her enthusiasm bubbling to the surface. She was in her element all right. He opened his mouth to object, to tell her that's not what he meant, but she was quicker.

"Ok, here's what we should do." She took out a pen and began scribbling notes on a napkin. "We'll need a three-pronged attack; target the Japanese, lobby the Government, and raise public awareness." She chewed her pen thoughtfully. "Demonstrations outside the Japanese embassy ought to get this campaign started nicely."

Cal cringed. How could she possibly believe that a public disturbance could help their cause? Any reasonable person was likely to be turned off by such a confrontational approach – and that was the support they needed most.

He felt his frustration returning. Getting themselves mired in the old argument wouldn't help.

"I don't think protesting will work so well," he ventured. "Public pressure only works where there's sensitivity to public opinion – and the Japanese Government has already made it abundantly clear they don't give a damn what anyone else thinks. They've been thumbing their noses at the rest of the world for decades over whaling, and they're not going to change their mind because of a few placard-wielding protestors over here in New Zealand. Besides, to get public support you need the public to support you, something I don't think will be so easy in this day and age."

"What are you talking about?" she snapped. "Greenpeace has always been a world-wide driving force in bringing important environmental issues to the public attention."

Cal avoided her gaze. "The world has changed. The fight to protect whales has dragged on for decades. Most people don't even realise it's still an issue. Nor do they care. Society is becoming jaded and disinterested." He looked down at the battered table. "Environmental awareness may have already peaked. Take a look at the world. Models are wearing fur in Europe again, the Canadian harp seal hunt is back in full swing, the Republican government in the US is set to grant mining concessions in Alaska and ignore the Kyoto Protocol, along with dozens of other governments around the world … and commercial whaling is about to resume right under our noses." He felt a rising sense of hopelessness. "Look around you. Life is about consumerism – a 'What can I get from the world?' mentality. We're living in the 'Y' generation now; young people live in an age of instant gratification and diminished personal responsibility. They're not interested in saving the world. Their heroes are all businessmen and billionaires, not scientists or activists. Personal responsibility has given way to personal greed." He clicked his tongue with annoyance. "Hell, after what September 11 did to the collective security paranoia, people are far more likely to view activism as terrorism."

Aurelia's face turned the colour of her hair. "Greenpeace still has a job to do," she snapped. "And as long as we're needed we'll continue to do it. There are still people who support us. There are still people out there who care."

"Not enough of them. Publicity stunts start to lose their appeal when they become commonplace, and public opinion has been overshadowed by the 'War on Terror'. Society is too afraid of Al Qaeda plots to worry about the environment, and when faced with 'Orange Alerts' and continual US scare-mongering, most people are far more worried about supposed threats to their own safety than they are about the environment. It's human nature."

Aurelia was shaking her head vigorously, but Cal could see in her eyes she knew at least some of it was true.

"You must have noticed support for Greenpeace dropping off," he continued. "When was the last time the public really got behind a Greenpeace campaign? Probably not since World Park Antarctica, or the original Save the Whales movement back in the eighties, right?"

She hung her head and her hair swept forward like a red curtain to screen her face. When she spoke, her voice was without its usual warmth. "Alright, so we'll do it without public support. We'll take the fight to where it'll hurt the whalers the most."

Cal leaned forward expectantly.

"The Annual International Whaling Commission meets in Japan in a fortnight," she continued.

Of course! Cal allowed himself a thin smile. An IWC meeting – and in Japan, no less. *Straight into the lion's den. Trust an activist to think of that!*

It was ballsy, but it just might work.

His mind drifted back to the IWC Scientific Committee meetings he had attended in the past. They were smaller than the main Annual Meeting, set up to discuss the science behind population numbers and catch quotas. Cal had laboured there before, struggling to present his research findings until he gave up, disgusted with the Japanese tactics – continually forcing their flawed science to the vote, refusing to abandon their lethal sampling methods, and repeatedly stalling proceedings until all opposition gave in. He shook his head at the memories – it was like beating your head against a wall. Regardless of all the arguments and evidence anyone presented, the Japanese just went right on and did whatever the hell they wanted, and no one could stop them.

Cal felt the glimmer of an idea taking shape though.

At the main IWC meeting things would be different. Unlike the discussions on scientific policy that were attended only by the technically-minded, the Annual Meeting would be attended by the IWC commissioners themselves – direct representatives of their governments. That was where the real power lay, and where there might be a chance to influence things.

Since Japanese Government policy is at the heart of this, we'll have to take our complaints right to the source!

The Annual Meeting took place under the full glare of public scrutiny, and there would be no Japanese side-stepping if they could be cornered there, for all the world to see. It wouldn't be easy though. It would require a determined and resourceful negotiator. One with a legal as well as scientific background…

"Greenpeace is planning demonstrations outside the venue," Aurelia continued. "We were aiming to drum up some publicity, but we could always try to shut them down instead."

Cal waved a hand impatiently. "No, protests won't win this war. We need to beat them at their own game."

She brushed her hair behind her ear and fixed him with her piercing eyes. He could tell she was irritated by his outright dismissal of her idea, but she was also intrigued to hear what he had to say.

"The sessions are closed to the public," he said, musing aloud. "Each government can send only two official representatives." Aurelia leaned forward, staring into his eyes with ill-concealed expectation. "But Non-Government Organisations like Greenpeace can send observers!" he finished triumphantly.

A slight frown creased her forehead. "What good is that? Observers don't have speaking rights."

He grinned lopsidedly, his mind already working overtime. "Don't worry about that. I'll find a way – If you can get us in?"

She nodded. "I think so, yeah." She smiled then, the seductive little half-smile that could bend men around her little finger. "It's good to have you back again. This'll be just like old times, the two of us campaigning together."

Cal hesitated, not sure if she was feeding him a line or not. But as he reached forward to shake the silken-skinned hand she proffered, he couldn't help thinking all his instincts for self-preservation had just gone out the window.

***

Richard sank gratefully into the chair, plain hard plastic though it was. Travelling was hard work and he was exhausted. Although this city was clean and modern he still felt his lungs reacting to the exhaust fumes and pollution. His asthma hadn't bothered him for some time, but he wondered if it was returning again.

Shimonoseki was about the size of Christchurch, but what it lacked in population it made up for in wealth. Richard had been surprised to see such a huge conference chamber and so many five-star hotels in a city with only 300,000 people. Even the nearby streets seemed to shine like the snowy mountain peak in the distance, polished by an army of street sweepers.

"There's a lot of wealth here…" Cal had remarked when they arrived at the brand-new train station.

Richard's head was still spinning with all the sights. This was his first overseas trip and he was still wondering how he really came to be here. Last month was just like any other for him, living the life of an electronics engineer, dutifully bound to his desk while at the same time trying not to crack under the pressure of his wife leaving him. He hadn't thought about Gina for ages, he realised then, although at the time she left him it felt as though his world was falling down around him. Cal was right, the trip had managed to take his mind off his problems. Apart from trying to fend off a breakdown, the previous few months had been no different from any others in his life… but not this month! This month he was travelling the world. In a few short weeks he had seen and done more than in all the years before that. There was an almost dream-like quality about it all, and he wondered – not for the first time – if this whole interlude was really just an elaborate escape fantasy dreamed up by a tortured mind.

It was real though. He knew it in his heart. The cold had been real, and the wind. And the wild isolation of the Southern Ocean. He had nearly drowned under the bows of a Japanese whaler, and seen a giant of the sea slaughtered in cold blood. He had seen all those things.

Now he was at a whaling meeting where his brother was going to put an end to the killing.

Richard looked around him at the conference room, filled with milling delegates toting their briefcases and laptop satchels. All wore suits, and were impeccably dressed. They exuded the kind of oily charm and self-confidence only politicians possessed.

The venue, Shimonoseki, was a small coastal town southwest of Tokyo. It was a world away from the pitching deck of the Gwendolyn. He'd stepped onto solid ground again at the port of Lyttleton, but the fortnight in Christchurch had passed in a blur. His feet had barely touched the ground since – flying out of Christchurch to Auckland, then another twelve hours flight time to Japan, followed by three more hours by bullet train from the heaving metropolis of Tokyo. The Japanese capital was a nightmare, snarled traffic and high rises everywhere, as though the city was bursting at the seams. Like Auckland, the city he'd spent most of his life in, Tokyo sprawled over a huge area – except there were twenty times the number of people crammed into it. Richard found it hard to believe so many people could live in one place, and the grim-faced platform officials who shoved them roughly onto the train seemed to embody the spirit of such a large impersonal city.

Once they had travelled outside its smoggy boundary though, the countryside was pretty. Early snows had dusted some of the taller mountains, but winter hadn't gripped the land just yet. The temperature was a contrast coming straight from a Canterbury spring, but the chill in the air reminded Richard of the Southern Ocean, and he wasn't uncomfortable.

Apparently fishing was big around the coast and Shimonoseki was a prime pro-whaling area, which, according to Cal was why it was chosen as the venue for Japan's hosting of the IWC conference. That and the fact it was the home port of the last remaining pelagic whaling fleet in the world.

"It's an election year in Japan," he muttered. "This is just a bloody vote-buying exercise. The fishing sector here has a lot of money, and a lot of political influence to go with it."

As they walked the short distance from the hotel to the conference venue, they saw the protestors were out in force too. A group from Greenpeace were sitting cross-legged on the pavement, chanting anti-whaling slogans. Surprisingly – to Richard anyway – most of the protestors they'd seen outside the venue were pro-whaling though. He hadn't thought anybody could possibly be able to justify the brutal slaughter of such great, and rare animals. Yet there they were. A host of placards written in Japanese and English proclaimed their views. 'Whaling is our livelihood' read one. 'Moratorium is illegal' read another. The rest were even more contentious. 'Conservationists are selfish and unreasonable!" and 'Greenpeace is racist – Stop denying our culture'. The one that really caught Richard's eye was a long banner that was probably intended to be more moderate though: 'Preserve Japanese Food Culture – Certainly the life of animals is important, but the livelihood of people is more important!'

How can they say that? There are a million other ways to make a living!

Cal walked stiffly past them without comment, but his clenched jaw spoke volumes.

They had passed a Japanese family on the steps of the conference hall, father, mother, and a young child in a pushchair. The youngster was clutching a brightly coloured helium balloon with a picture of a cartoon whale and some Japanese writing underneath.

Cal had pointed it out with a grim expression. "That's the Taiyoku Misui Fisheries Company logo. It says: 'I love nature, support sustainable harvesting'," he explained, his voice heavy with sarcasm. "That's bloody disgusting. That little kid doesn't know he's being used as a political pawn. He's barely even old enough to talk – all he cares about is his free balloon." He shook his head. "This shows the kind of people we're about to go up against," he muttered, half to himself. "Not only will they stoop to any length to continue this fight, they actually seem to believe their own lies. If that gets shown on the news tonight they'll be congratulating themselves for having public support in the streets." Cal looked grim. "As if you can trot out a cheap slogan like; 'We love nature' to whitewash all the dirty business you really get up to."

"Why do the Japanese people believe it then? Why don't they question more?" Richard had ventured. "Why don't they care what's really going on?"

Cal shrugged. "Why don't people anywhere care? Why do they still drive gas-guzzling cars when they know the Greenhouse Effect is going to cook the planet? Why do they still clearfell forests and bulldoze wilderness to build new subdivisions and shopping malls? Why do they allow fishermen to continue strip-mining the oceans when fisheries are collapsing all around the world?" He trailed off. "People are too busy, I guess. Too wrapped up in their own little lives to notice, let alone care."

It was a sobering thought, Richard realised as he took his seat next to Cal, to consider how many people there were in the world – yet how few of them seemed concerned about what kind of a planet they were creating for their children to inherit.

He sat between Cal and Vicki while they waited for the conference to open, trying not to look too hard for Summer in the public gallery. But she wasn't there. There was no way the rest of the Team could have arrived here yet. Even though they had sailed over a week before his flight left, the Gwendolyn wasn't that fast!

He didn't like to admit it, but the past few days without Summer around had been hollow and empty somehow. She wasn't his girlfriend or anything, but dreams were free even so! Just the sight of her smiling face would make his heart sing with joy.

Richard shifted uncomfortably and let his gaze wander over the delegates again. Would this meeting never start?

The IWC Chairman was an overweight man. His jowls sagged and he was red in the face, as though he was out of breath from hurrying up the steps to avoid the demonstrators outside. The Chairman took his seat at a desk in the centre of a large semi-circular amphitheatre. In front of him the delegates were arranged according to their country or organisation. The commissioners sat importantly at their places; each behind a little desk flag and a placard bearing the name of their country. Richard couldn't help noticing that some of them looked bored or annoyed to be here though. One of them was asleep with his head on the fine timber desk – before the meeting had even started!

Cal noticed the direction of Richard's gaze. "The real business is done in all the back-room deals," he explained, his voice sounding strained. "The whaling nations have been busy for months trying to buy support for their agenda. This meeting is just a formality for many of the diplomats here – all they came to do is show up, cast their vote against the Moratorium, then receive their kickback from the Japanese."

Richard looked shocked, but Cal smiled reassuringly. "Don't worry. They might have bought off a lot of countries, but they still won't have enough support to challenge the Moratorium. They need a three-quarter majority, remember?"

In contrast to the bored commissioners, where the two brothers sat with the NGOs, or Non-Government Organisations, the mood was ebullient. The people here came to do a job and they were looking forward to getting started. The NGOs were segregated over to one side, as though they were somehow less important than the official government representatives in the centre. Rather than desks, they got collapsible trestle tables, hung with a pleated cloth skirt to give the passing appearance of professionalism. Richard tapped the table with his knuckles. Underneath the white tablecloth it sounded like plastic.

The Chairman's back was to the rows of plastic chairs laid out for the media and invited public. Reporters waited there, pen and paper poised. TV cameras were banned inside, and the white-gloved police guards at all the doors were zealously searching everyone. Richard felt for the badge on his lapel, checking it hadn't fallen off. No one was allowed in without one, and if you lost it they'd probably throw you out and not let you back in for the rest of the week. With all the protestors outside, they weren't taking any chances with gatecrashers.

The Chairman finally struggled to his feet and began to speak. After a ponderous welcome he began introducing the chief delegates from each country. After the first dozen, Richard felt his mind wandering again.

He sneaked a sideways look at Aurelia, seated on Cal's right. He'd never met her before this trip, although he knew she and Cal had been an item once. Cal never said much about their relationship, although Richard knew his brother had been sad but philosophical that it didn't work out. Despite his rugged good looks, Cal didn't seem to have much luck in love – that was partly the reason Richard had been so chuffed with his own marriage. While he loved his brother too much to be jealous of his looks, it had been a boost to his confidence to snare a bride before his handsome brother did – although his wife hadn't exactly turned out to be a great catch, he admitted woefully. The thought occurred to him then that Cal's seeming indifference to marriage might have been the wiser choice when it came to women.

Aurelia's name came from the Latin word for golden, although she had dyed her hair a much fierier red than nature ever intended it to be. From what little he'd seen of her it matched her demeanour perfectly though. She was a real live wire – attractive, but incredibly feisty. Plus she was an outspoken conservation activist. Far too much of a handful for Richard to contemplate in a woman. She was the kind of woman who could eat ordinary men alive.

But Cal's no ordinary man!

Looking at them now, seated side by side, they did seem to complement each other, despite their differences. Richard wondered what feelings they still had for each other. He tried to read his brother's mood, but Cal's face gave nothing away.

Suddenly Aurelia sucked in her breath. "That's him!" she hissed through her teeth, and Cal stiffened. Richard followed their gaze to where the Japanese Commissioner sat, surrounded by a phalanx of assistants and advisors.

"That's Akogi Yokuke," Aurelia whispered.

Cal's frown registered his disapproval. "I know him. As head of the fisherman's union he's also known as Amimoto-san, or Mr Fish. Quite a fitting description too," he muttered. "Today he's Japan's IWC commissioner, but in real life he's also the Japanese Fisheries Minister, head of the fishermen's union, plus he's a filthy-rich fishing industrialist himself." Cal's sneer was obvious. "How's that for the fox being in charge of the henhouse?"

The chairman introduced Amimoto to the delegation, and he offered a brief bow, smiling condescendingly like a king acknowledging his court.

He was a wiry old man, Richard saw, probably over seventy. His skin was creased and his tidy hair heavily streaked with grey. But despite his shuffling gait he didn't have the air of old age about him. From his expensive tailored suit to his fine leather shoes he held himself with confidence, arrogance even, and his eyes were hard and dangerous.

Suddenly he turned and glared directly at them, his black eyes narrowing to slits. Richard jumped as if he'd been slapped. He looked away hurriedly. Even concentrating on the floor though, he could feel the intensity of the gaze boring into him.

Cal didn't look away. He met the stare head on, and Richard swallowed nervously, marvelling at his brother's confidence but at the same time hoping it wouldn't lead to trouble. It was Amimoto who broke contact first, rising to give his speech.

Cal shifted uneasily in his seat, and Richard could tell the glare had affected his brother too though. "That was strange," Cal remarked, almost to himself. "He definitely looked pissed at us. But he doesn't know who we are. Does he?"

Chapter 7

Richard Major waited until he was sure the Japanese Commissioner wasn't glaring at them any more before he dared to look up. Despite the others sitting around him, he'd felt like that murderous look had been directed at him alone.

As the representative of the host nation, Amimoto stood, bowing stiffly from the waist to welcome the world to his conference.

He spoke in Japanese.

As Richard looked around in consternation, Vicki handed him a pair of headphones, and with a smile, showed him where to plug them in to hear a translator speaking. Cal's headphones remained sealed in their plastic bag however, ignored on the desk. He frowned as he concentrated on the speech, and a strange smile hung at the corner of his mouth. "Amimoto knows English perfectly," he whispered. "It's the language of business, after all. He just refuses to speak it."

The translator spoke English with a Japanese accent, but he couldn't match the power and forcefulness behind Amimoto's speech. Richard couldn't understand a word of the Japanese, but he found himself transfixed by the Commissioner's rhetoric and the imposing presence that seemed to radiate from him. Even the simple welcome was delivered with the intensity of a battle cry.

And it didn't take long for Mr Fish to get down to business.

"The purpose of the IWC is to regulate and manage the hunting of whales," he thundered. "For far too long now this forum has been hijacked by the unreasonable and hysterical demands of conservationist nations. Japan and other legitimate whaling countries have been attacked and vilified from all sides in a shameful display of aggression."

"Hear, hear!" the Norwegian delegate applauded.

Amimoto smiled wolfishly, acknowledging his Scandinavian ally. "The Moratorium on commercial whaling was supposed to be temporary, and I call upon the Commission to lift the ban now, given that whale stocks have recovered and we have the means to sustainably manage a commercial harvest."

"Stocks haven't recovered," yelled a heckler from the public gallery, "but your fleet has been illegally murdering whales in the Southern Ocean for twenty years in total defiance of the IWC's Moratorium! Shame on you!" As the police grabbed him and wrestled him towards the door, Richard thought he recognised the long-haired man as one of the Greenpeace protestors from the sit-on outside.

"As you see, an example of the hysterical attacks we are forced to endure," Amimoto smiled, his voice dripping with honey. "I'm sure I don't need to remind the delegation that the IWC expressly permits the taking of whales for scientific research, therefore our meagre catch is entirely legal. Not only that, but it is both biologically and morally sustainable."

"Bullshit," Cal muttered under his breath. "You'd sell your own grandmother into slavery if you could find a loophole in the law."

"Furthermore, you will also notice that our Fleet is at this moment tied up in port not a mile from where we now sit," Amimoto proclaimed. "It is a gesture of goodwill on our part. A sign that the Japanese are willing to make concessions as we enter these discussions in good faith, and with the hope that the voice of calm reason will finally be able to prevail against the shrill dissenters whose only goal is to hijack the rightful purpose of this conference!"

"He's good," Cal acknowledged grudgingly, as the whaling nations broke into spontaneous applause. "Very good. Except I happen to know his fleet was already in the Southern Ocean for an early start to the killing – and the only reason they're back here is thanks to a certain steel cable."

Beside him, Aurelia said nothing, but her face was flushed with anger.

Amimoto took his seat again, the satisfied look on his face saying everything.

Next, the Chairman struggled back to his feet to announce it was time for opening remarks. Countries would be called in alphabetical order and each delegation was allowed two minutes. Time discipline would be strictly enforced.

First up was Antigua.

Richard watched as the representative from the small Caribbean republic adjusted his tie importantly and puffed out his chest.

"I would like to say that Antigua is very disappointed with the unreasonable stance taken by New Zealand, Australia, and their band of conservationist bullies. They are nothing but arrogant elitists out to hijack the purpose of this organisation."

Cal rolled his eyes. "And so it begins…" he muttered to Richard.

Aurelia's mouth was pursed into a thin line and she spoke through her teeth. "Antigua is just a Japanese puppet. I recognise that brand of eco-terrorism he's parroting." She harrumphed. "There wasn't really any doubt about which way Antigua would vote. And yet they would swear the fact that they just received four million dollars in aid from Japan and a brand new fish processing plant is entirely coincidental!"

"The stupid thing is, Antigua is unlikely to see much benefit from that bribe," Cal added. "Their new factory will be used as a base by the giant Japanese fishing consortiums. Japan will send their trawler fleets to pillage the fish stocks for as long as they hold out. In ten or twenty years time Antigua won't be any better off. The bribe money will be long-spent – lining the present politicians' pockets for retirement – and the Japanese will have sailed away for richer pickings, leaving behind an empty factory… and an empty sea."

Richard nodded. He had no trouble believing that, having already witnessed the Taiyoku Misui Fisheries Company's ruthless efficiency in action.

The Antiguan Commissioner's broad nostrils flared as he worked himself up. "I reject this colonial imperialism! It is the premise of international law that one country cannot tell another what to do, and it is the sovereign right of each country to use their resources as they see fit, without interference from Big Brother!"

Aurelia exclaimed behind her hand. "Yeah, except those whales aren't your resources."

Cal shook his head in agreement. "If they belong to anyone, they belong to the whole world. And if New Zealand wants to make a living from eco-tourism and seeing live whales we can't, because greedy short-sighted countries like that want to kill them all for a quick buck."

Richard was too shocked to say anything. How could anyone try to defend whaling?

The Antiguan Commissioner wasn't finished yet though. He paused as if for emphasis, but Richard noticed he was actually reading off a prompt sheet in front of him. The Commissioner smoothed his tight black curls and adjusted his gold cufflinks, as though preening in front of his own dressing-table mirror.

"There are many species of whales that are not endangered – the Minke whale chief among them – and it is time they were managed properly. Even conservative estimates have put their numbers at over a million animals, and they are not on any endangered species list. There is no reason why a small, sustainable catch should not be granted." He puffed out his chest and raised his voice to harangue the conference. "It is unreasonable to suggest otherwise! The purpose of the IWC is to manage whaling, and the best way to manage whale numbers is to use science. I would like to call upon the committee to vote for the Revised Management Strategy to manage whale stocks sensibly and responsibly."

Cal shook his head wearily. "I wondered how long it would take before they brought that up."

"What is it?" Richard ventured.

Cal sighed. "The RMS is meant to be a scientifically-based system for predicting whale stocks and population growth," he explained in a whisper.

Richard was puzzled. "Isn't that a good thing?"

Cal shook his head. "Nah, if they were really interested in science they'd see that the only guaranteed sustainable catch is zero. They just want to use the RMS as an excuse to start killing whales again."

The commissioner's words echoed around inside Richard's head. "But is what he's saying true? Could Minke whales be harvested sustainably?"

Cal shrugged. "Who knows? Yeah, maybe in theory. But what looks fine on paper often doesn't work in the real world. We simply don't know enough about their biology to be able to say what catch level is sustainable, and by the time we find out it's likely to be too late." He shook his head again. "It's just too risky to allow any hunting on the basis of such flimsy knowledge. Besides, enforcement of the rules is an even bigger problem. How many fishermen do you know who tell the truth about how much they caught and where? Greed always gets in the way of science, and it even overrules common sense. How many fisheries are there around the world that haven't been overfished? You'll be lucky to find one, anywhere. It always happens, it's just a matter of time. People are too greedy, they just can't help themselves." He turned to face Richard, his eyes earnest. "The RMS might sound reasonable, but it's just the thin end of the wedge. If we permit any hunting, if we let them get away with any concessions at all, then one way or another it'll open the door for a return to full-scale commercial whaling."

"Motion tabled," the Chairman announced in a commanding voice. "We will put the RMS to a vote at the end of the week, along with the status of the Moratorium."

"Look at them!" Aurelia hissed. She gestured towards the Scandinavian delegates where the commissioners from Norway and Iceland were congratulating each other, smug self-satisfied expressions plastered across their faces. "The High North Alliance," she mocked, her voice full of scorn. "They're not even trying to hide their glee. Everyone knows the whole RMS plan is their creation, backed by the Japanese of course. They get one of their tame commissioners to present it though, because it sounds more moderate coming from a *neutral* country." The way she spat out the word neutral left no doubt about her real feelings on Antigua. "Just wait!" she promised angrily. "They'll see. We'll defeat it, just like we did last year – and every year before that!"

Cal's expression was grave though. "I'm not so sure," he murmured. "This time it could be close. The High North Alliance has expanded this year. They've got Russia and Denmark on their side now, and they've managed to get Sweden and the Netherlands to vote with them before, along with Ireland. On top of that, the Japanese have been working hard on Korea, India, and China – and they've bought off over two dozen little countries. It could be very close..." His voice trailed away.

The Antiguan Commissioner finished his speech. He smiled self-importantly, nodded towards the Japanese delegation, then took his seat again.

Aurelia glared at the Japanese Commissioner, her eyes blazing with cold fury. Amimoto returned her look with an innocent shrug, as though he had nothing to do with it. The sneer on his face gave him away though, and judging by her gritted teeth it only served to infuriate Aurelia even more.

Richard sat in shock. As the next delegate got to his feet he wasn't even listening as the man began to speak. He didn't know what he'd been expecting from the IWC, but it certainly wasn't this. How could an international organisation tolerate such open corruption?

Do they even care about the whales?

Cal seemed to sense his consternation. "There's not much we can do," he whispered with a shrug. "It's a democracy, along with all the problems that come with it. Every country is entitled to a vote, we just have to hope they're participating for the right reasons."

Richard was silent. From what he'd seen already, many of the reasons were downright suspect to say the least. "Buying votes?" he managed to say. It sounded even more obscene spoken out loud.

Cal shrugged. "There's an old saying, Bro," he whispered. "All's fair in love and war. And this is most definitely a war."

Richard was silent, Cal's words weighing heavily on his thoughts. An image came to mind, a memory of bright red blood staining the ocean. Innocent blood. At that moment he knew his brother was right. This was a war, with all its horrors.

Things still didn't make sense though. "But what's it all for?" he whispered. "Why do they keep doing it? Are whales worth that much money?"

Cal shook his head. "Nope. Even though whalemeat can earn four hundred US dollars a pound in Japan, the fleet technically runs at a loss. Their running costs are huge, and are heavily subsidised by the Japanese Government. If the millions of gallons of fuel they use to sail to Antarctica weren't supplied for free they'd probably go bankrupt. The whole industry is propped up by dodgy politics – that's what keeps them going."

Richard thought about that for a while. If the industry didn't make money then what was the point in continuing? He puzzled over it for a while, but it still didn't make any sense to him.

He tapped his brother on the arm. "So why do the Japanese want to keep whaling?" he whispered.

Cal's sigh was heartfelt. "Who really knows what's going on in their heads?" he admitted. "But it's mostly about saving face now." He held up a hand to forestall Richard's next impatient question. "The thing you have to understand about Japan, is that it's run by the Japanese. They are a very proud people, and also very stubborn. They consider it worse to be shamed than to be dead, so they will never admit defeat. Look at all the soldiers in World War Two who preferred to commit suicide rather than be taken prisoner. The Japanese won't do anything that might cause them to lose face, and that includes bowing to the wishes of someone else. Especially that."

"But why?" Richard persisted. "When the whole world is against them, why don't they just stop?"

"That's exactly the kind of situation where they don't give up! Maybe we were foolish not to realise that at the start," he admitted. "You see, they're fanatics when it comes to succeeding. They don't care what it costs or how long it takes, as long as they are victorious. The Samurai tradition teaches that strategy is the craft of the warrior, and should be applied equally to the sword and the pen. They use that philosophy in war, politics, business, and diplomacy." He ignored the current speaker and his droning monotone, looking right past him to watch the Japanese delegation, his frustration plain. "They're willing to bide their time, while patiently working towards their ultimate goal. They're experts at focusing on the long-haul – not getting discouraged by temporary setbacks, and slowly working around any obstacles in their way, no matter how long it takes." Cal's smile was grim. "Negotiations like this are easy for them because gai-jin – barbarians, as they call us foreigners – don't have nearly the same staying power when it comes to protracted negotiations. The Japanese Commissioner will think nothing of arguing the same point for days at a time, until the opposition simply gives up from exhaustion." Cal laughed sadly. "You'd be amazed how many concessions Mr Fish has won here just because his opposition desperately needed a bathroom break, or simply couldn't force themselves to debate any longer." He shrugged. "Besides, the whole world isn't against them any more. Little by little he's been chipping away. Inviting small countries to join the IWC and support your vote was a trick first used by the conservation movement to get support for the Moratorium, but he's not above using our own strategy against us – although adding bribes is his own touch. Over the last twenty years Amimoto has been slowly courting allies, and now he's ready for the next round of the fight. And he won't stop until he gets a return to full-scale commercial whaling."

"But why. Is pride all it is?" Richard was incredulous. "Why keep going? Just because they don't want to look like they're backing down?"

"It's never quite that simple, Bro. Politics complicates everything." Cal smiled thinly. "You see, the Japanese Fishing Association is controlled by some very wealthy and very influential men. Amimoto is chief among them. He created the Taiyoku Misui Fisheries Company, which owns and runs the Japanese Pelagic Whaling Fleet. It is the largest fishing company in the world, and operates over five hundred ships in dozens of fisheries around the world – including owning controlling interests in the major domestic fishing companies of the US, New Zealand, and Canada. Taiyoku Misui's annual profits run into billions of dollars, more than the combined GDPs of most of the countries where it operates. But it is more than just money that motivates him. It is power. You see, he's also the governor of the local prefecture here, and that gives him a seat in the Diet, the Japanese parliament. His influence then got him a spot in Cabinet, where – no surprise – he secured himself the portfolio of Fisheries Minister."

Cal rolled his eyes, making clear what he thought of it all. "The Japanese Government is elected district by district, regardless of the population size in each area. Get the most prefectures and your party wins, it's that simple!" He gestured out the high windows where a construction crane at the Taiyoku Misui's new processing factory dominated the skyline. "As you know, this is a small coastal prefecture where fishing is a very important election issue. So not only does representing this area give Amimoto influence in the Diet way out of proportion to his actual voter support, but that also translates to an unbalanced drive to support fisheries issues in the Japanese Parliament."

Richard considered that for a while, but things still didn't make sense to him. "But I thought you said the whaling industry wasn't making any money? If that's true why don't they stop?"

"It's not as simple as that." Cal paused a moment, as though reconsidering his words. "Actually it is. The bottom line is that it costs less for them to keep an ailing and unprofitable industry running because it's cheaper than closing it down. Losses can be offset by loans and subsidies from the Government, but if the whaling industry was closed down tomorrow then the fishing companies would have to foot the bill for scrapping or refitting the fleet, and redundancy pay for their workers. There's only a few thousand people employed by the whaling industry, tops," he explained, "Despite what they say. But if each one of them expected half a year's wages or more as severance pay – as they're entitled to under Japan's generous labour laws – the bill would quickly run into hundreds of millions of dollars. It's not hard to see the fishing companies want to avoid that at all costs." He flashed a twisted smile. "No pun intended!"

Richard didn't notice the attempt at humour. He was still struggling to get his head around what his brother was saying. "So this Mr Fish guy, why is he allowed to be the commissioner? If he runs the company that kills the whales – isn't that corrupt?"

Cal sighed and looked up at the ceiling. While Richard waited for him to continue the speaker droned on at the podium, unheard in the background. It was a while before Cal answered. "You have to understand the Japanese do things differently. Their attitude towards corruption is a lot less strict than ours. As well as being a fishing industrialist himself, Amimoto is also a politician. He has a lot of financial support from the fishing industry, support which he considers it his duty to 'repay'." Cal's tone left no doubt what he thought of Mr Fish's conduct though. "His political power-base comes directly from the wealthy fishing industry, whose favour – not to mention the large contributions they make to political campaigns – no Japanese government can afford to ignore either. At every opportunity, Amimoto uses his position in the Diet to advance their causes." Cal grimaced. "Let's just say it was no accident he was appointed Japan's IWC commissioner, and his motives for being here are not hard to see through either."

"But how can he get away with all this? Surely it's illegal?"

"Amimoto has a reputation as a Kuromaku, a puppet-master. Political intrigue is considered an art form in Japan, so they tolerate a high level of backroom dealings. In the West, the same deal-making between business and politics would be considered shamefully corrupt, but over here it creates all the powerful men. Amimoto's network of contacts makes him very influential in the Japanese Government, even though his own prefecture is relatively unimportant. It is well known that Prime Minister Takahashi is a lame duck politician with few ideas of his own – ripe for manipulation by a skilled string-puller. Amimoto isn't just here to kill whales. This is also about power for him. It's his path to the top."

"How do you know so much about him?"

A strange look came over Cal's face and he grimaced. "I'm a cetacean biologist. It's my job to study threats to whale populations."

Richard sat there, his mind reeling. The last month had been a muddle of conflicting emotions, but none more so than now.

He glanced at the public gallery on the off-chance Summer might be there, hoping to find some encouragement. It was depressingly devoid of golden hair. He sighed, feeling lost without her. It was like a revelation when he realised there was a whole other world out there he was missing out on – the real world! But it was also a terrible shock to discover that world was under threat, especially from such naked greed and corruption. Witnessing the violent and bloody death of the Great Whale was bad enough, but meeting the driving force behind it, and learning Mr Fish's true motivations for killing whales was enough to shake his faith in humanity.

For the first time, Richard was beginning to understand the frustration his brother felt. And yes, the anger too. He ran a hand through his thinning hair. Anger was a new emotion for him. Normally he would have shied away from such thoughts, since they invariably led to conflict with other people, and conflict was bad. But something about him was different now, changed, because thinking about conflict no longer filled him with terror. He still felt the familiar surge of adrenaline, and the flight of his racing heart. Only now it wasn't accompanied by panic and the clammy sweat of fear. Rather, his belly burned with the fire of indignation, and anger.

What's gotten into me?

The difference now, he realised, was that his feelings finally had a target. No longer did he need to concern himself with the fear of nameless and faceless criminals who might one day attack or rob him in the street, or even invade his own home. No longer was he haunted by irrational fears of being victimised – a legacy of vicious playground bullying he had never quite managed to outgrow.

Finally his fears had found a face.

As if sensing his thoughts, the Japanese Commissioner glared at him. Richard felt his courage falter as he stared back into those cruel black eyes, but this time he managed to hold his gaze for a second before looking away.

In the whales, Richard had found a kindred spirit. Despite their huge size they were gentle and peaceful creatures, unwilling or unable to fight back, even to save their lives. But their peace-loving nature was not enough to save them. Richard sighed. He knew what it was like to be victimised. The whales needed a defender. As he closed his eyes he felt the protective urge stir within him.

Amimoto was powerful, dangerous, and cunning – the epitome of a bully. But he was also evil and needed to be stopped. That alone was enough to make Richard's mind up.

Cal will do what needs to be done. But if he needs my support then it's the least I can do to help, right?

Richard was so caught up in his thoughts that he missed the New Zealand commissioner's speech, and his clever ploy to use the opening address to table a motion for Non-Government Organisations to be given an opening address at the conference too. He also missed the voting, tense though it was. He only snapped back to reality when Aurelia clapped her hands and laughed out loud. As Richard looked on in surprise, she turned to hug Cal, and planted a victorious kiss on his cheek. "Ha ha," she exclaimed. "I knew we could do it!"

Cal grinned. "It's been a long time coming, hasn't it? This is your moment. Make us proud."

***

Cal Major sneaked a glance at Aurelia as she stood up to speak. She stood with her hands planted on her hips, dainty chin thrust forward defiantly, as though daring someone, anyone, to challenge her right to speak. He couldn't conceal his smile.

Look out IWC, here she comes!

He was happy for her. Not only because this was a huge coup for the conservation of whales, and a monumental step for the IWC – an organisation originally devised as an exclusive 'gentleman's club' for whale hunters only – but also because she had worked so hard to get here. This moment had been such a long time coming, and he felt a sense of pride to be sharing it with her.

Watching her now, standing tall in front of the conference, he felt his heart swell with emotion. This was the woman he'd fallen in love with all those years ago. Passionate, driven, and definitely not about to take any crap from anybody!

Her green eyes flashed as she surveyed the room, ensnaring them all with her gaze. "My fellow delegates," she began, and her voice was clear and strong. "I thank you for the chance to address this meeting today; this is indeed a historic moment in the fight against whaling."

They applauded politely.

She smiled and held up a hand for silence. She always did have a flair for the dramatic, Cal observed. This would be the only chance Greenpeace got to address the conference, and he knew she wouldn't let the opportunity slide without making up for lost time.

Unfortunately, he didn't realise how right he was.

"This conference is a disgrace!" she thundered. "It is patently obvious to even the most dim-witted observer that whales are graceful and intelligent beings, yet here we sit, listening to greedy men trying to persuade us it's right to kill them!" She quivered with rage as she glared at the pro-whaling nations in turn. "You are guilty of murder!" she accused them. "Animals were not put on this Earth for our own selfish gains. They have a right to life, just like every other being in the cosmos, and you have no right to kill them."

As soon as she said that, Cal's heart sank.

This isn't the speech we prepared!

What did she think she was doing, going off at them like that? Regardless of what she believed, it wasn't the way to get things done. He tried to catch her eye, willing her to stop, but she ignored him. She rounded on the delegates, eyes blazing, completely overtaken by her passion.

"Not only is this slaughter morally repugnant, it is also unspeakably cruel! Imagine killing a horse," she challenged the room. "A similarly sensitive and intelligent creature. Now imagine torturing it to death instead. Throwing spears into its belly and forcing it to drag a butcher's cart through the street for an hour, slipping and sliding on its own blood, entrails trailing behind, before it finally succumbs to its injuries and dies on its knees. A painful, protracted, and terrifying death. Well imagine no longer," she shouted, her voice close to cracking. "Because this happens every time a whale is killed – and the IWC sanctions it. This brutal murder is perpetrated in *your* name! Every last one of you is guilty of not putting an end to this crime!"

Cal looked around the room, stricken. Harpooning was definitely not a quick and easy death, but he could see that wasn't the angle to take if they wanted to halt whaling. Arguing against killing animals wouldn't hold any weight here, and even the case for cruelty was difficult to prove. Regardless of what *actually* happened on the high seas – and Cal had seen plenty of whales die a slow and painful death by harpoon – whalers would simply respond with claims the exploding harpoon made death almost instantaneous, just like cattle at a slaughterhouse. And that contradiction of society, more than anything else, would undermine her whole argument against killing animals. You couldn't argue against killing some animals when people considered it normal to kill others. Whatever your personal beliefs, the IWC was not the forum to debate whether it was right to kill animals. It just wouldn't work.

Already he could see delegates tut-tutting and shaking their heads. Even the more ardent conservationists among them were frowning, no doubt anticipating the backlash against their cause.

Why didn't she do it like we planned?

He sighed, lowering his head into his hands. That emotive stuff wasn't going to achieve anything. All it did was alienate people and get them on the defensive, and he knew that for the Moratorium to survive the upcoming vote they would need all the support they could muster. He rubbed his temples.

How many times have I tried to tell her? Why won't she listen?

As if in reply, Aurelia tossed her auburn mane and launched on a new offensive.

"The United States of America is as guilty as those murderers who pull the trigger!" she admonished, waving her finger in the air. "Twenty years ago *you* had the power to end this senseless slaughter once and for all!" She jabbed her finger at the American Commissioner, as though intending to stab him in the heart with it. "The Packwood-Magnusson Amendment to your country's Fisheries Act gave the perfect excuse to impose sanctions against Japan – their repeated violation of IWC rulings should have resulted in a threat to shut down their $500 million tuna fishery within US waters – sanctions that would have closed their $40 million whalemeat market forever, ending this deplorable trade in the butchered remains of our fellow mammals overnight. You alone, among all the nations of the world, had the power to do the right thing and take a stand against this injustice. Instead, you allowed evil to endure!"

Cal rolled his eyes, frantically trying to get her attention.

Not the Americans, they're voting with us!

He signalled her to stop, knowing the United States was only a moderate anti-whaling supporter at the best of times. Due to their own internal politics they needed to allow Inuit hunting of bowhead whales in Alaska – another example of regional politics influencing central government – but it also left them open to blackmail from the pro-whaling countries. Over the years there had been much controversy about American willingness to make deals with the Japanese, securing their hundred bowheads in exchange for supporting an increased Japanese quota of rorquals in the Pacific.

Don't piss the Americans off, we're going to need their vote!

She refused to look at him.

"I charge the United States with being an accomplice to murder! The blood of innocent whales is on your hands too! Shame!"

The American Commissioner's face was beet-red by now, and he looked set to blow a steam valve. Cal hurriedly looked away, in case his stare was taken as an unspoken challenge – although it was already a little late for that, he admitted ruefully

Guess I'm already tarred with the same brush. Guilt by association!

Aurelia finally relented, but the respite was brief. She paused just long enough to take a breath, then turned her attentions towards Mr Fish.

"Japan is the worst offender of all. Your staggering avarice and complete lack of morals or empathy makes me ashamed to call myself a human."

Amimoto stared back, eyes glittering like obsidian. His gaze was like cold steel, lancing toward Aurelia as if to impale her on the spot.

She took no notice though, forging brazenly ahead as though not heeding, or not caring about the consequences.

"Japan has the second largest economy in the world. They have no need nor justification for this senseless slaughter. It is high time Japan faced up to its responsibilities as a world citizen, and if they will not listen to reason then perhaps they will listen to their own greed. I call upon consumers everywhere to boycott all Japanese products until such time as Japan ends this sin against nature. Let's send a message to the government of Japan, that we, the citizens of the world will not tolerate their crimes any longer! Do not buy Japanese computers, electronics, or automobiles! They are tainted with the blood of massacred whales!"

Across the room, Amimoto's eyes blazed.

If anything, it only incensed her even more. "We demand an end to the slaughter! The Moratorium against commercial whaling must be renewed, and it must be strengthened too. A worldwide sanctuary is needed to rid us of the scandalous oxymoron of scientific whaling."

As Aurelia took a breath to continue, the Chairman interrupted her. "Er, thank you, Ma'am, your time is up."

Reluctantly, Aurelia sat down. Cal felt his frustration boiling over. She had wasted their one speaking opportunity at the conference. Her emotive rhetoric had achieved nothing – except alienating more allies. Desperate to seize the rapidly-fading opportunity, Cal jumped to his feet.

"Mr Chairman, I have one last thing!"

The Chairman frowned, then nodded curtly. "Very well, make it quick."

"As is our prerogative, I would like to table a motion for this commission to put to a vote."

The Chairman nodded.

"I move that the IWC refuses to permit Japan's Scientific Whaling Program."

Amimoto inhaled sharply. Despite few outward signs, Cal could see he shook with well-concealed rage. As he watched, the Japanese Commissioner turned and whispered a curt order to his aide.

***

Akogi Yokuke didn't even bother to look up as his order was carried out.

"Mr Chairman," his aide announced, doing his best to mimic the force of his master's presence, and only partially succeeding. "Japan respectfully requests an intermission while we decide how to respond to this scurrilous and scandalous attack on our Government, and our honourable Commissioner."

Nor did Yokuke have to glare at the Chairman to know his request would be granted without hesitation. The fat fool had already been handsomely paid to ensure the meeting proceeded favourably for Japan's interests, and if he'd somehow forgotten that then the promise of a physical reminder should help him remember his orders…

Yokuke grunted to himself as the Chairman announced the fifteen minute break. His appraisal of the man had been correct. The Chairman was a greedy coward after all. He allowed himself a moment of congratulation. Reading the character of men was a skill possessed by a privileged few. But being able to manipulate people for their own ends was a skill reserved for the truly great Kuromaku.

Yokuke turned toward the filthy Greenpeace hippies and his smile was cold and reptilian, the way a snake might regard a cornered mouse.

So, you dare defy me.

His lip curled with distaste as he regarded them. The red-haired woman was ugly to look at. She was pale-skinned, round-eyed, and much too tall. Her breasts were too large as well, half-revealed as they were by her scandalous clothes – but it was more than just a physical aversion he felt towards her. From her shameless attire to her dazzling hair, the colour of red lacquer, she was the antithesis of everything feminine. She was brash and outspoken, nothing like the diminutive, self-effacing women of Japan. Women were supposed to be attentive and obedient to their husbands! Yokuke was too old now to waste time in pursuit of pleasures of the flesh, but when he had, he would never have been attracted to such a shameless display of vulgar, attention-seeking behaviour.

He frowned. This woman was also a crazy troublemaker, that much was obvious. She was one of those environmental agitators who seemed to delight in sabotaging legitimate business to satisfy their own warped ideals.

Yokuke felt his anger beginning to flare.

How dare she question my motives?

Business was about domination – it was the way of the world. Survival of the fittest. The weak were swallowed up by the strong, and the world was better for it.

Yet these unwashed hippies were hell-bent on convincing the world that all business was somehow wrong, as if he, and thousands of other legitimate businessmen like him, didn't have the right to utilise the resources the planet provided.

It was obvious their actions were a shameless attempt at publicity-seeking. Whether they believed their own lies or not, trumpeting them to the world was how they secured their money – donations from the weak-willed and impressionable.

Yokuke felt a moment of anger as his thoughts turned full circle again. What was he to do with these filthy gai-jin who had opposed him?

The protesters had crossed the line from being annoying radicals to becoming a direct threat to him. And his business interests. That could never be tolerated.

With the Nippon-Maru laid up in port for repairs, his profit margin for the season was already stretched thin, and his output was falling behind schedule. He had a business to run, and shareholders to report to. His late father had once taught him that in business, as in life, any loss was intolerable. Accepting preventable losses was the mark of a bad businessman. But Yokuke's responsibilities went deeper than just a balance sheet. His mind strayed briefly to some of the other deals he also had to honour. The wrinkles on his brow deepened. The trade in whalemeat was worth more to him than money, and he knew he could not afford another bad season.

Yet, regardless of the actual losses these Western troublemakers had cost him so far, it was the principle of it that really mattered.

No one crosses me!

He burned at the thought of being challenged by anyone, much less being outmanoeuvred by a bunch of ignorant degenerates. His anger became cold and calculating.

Whatever it took, he would see to it the Fleet returned to the Southern Ocean before the year was out.

Yokuke glared back at the barbarians.

It would appear I also have to put the world right along the way!

He fixed his attention on the blonde gai-jin in the centre.

The Westerner was in his late twenties, and much too young to wield any power worth worrying about. Yet Yokuke sensed he was a dangerous man all the same. He was tall and athletic, brimming with the vigour of youth, but it was his eyes that gave him away. They shone with bravado and assurance, but also confidence in his own abilities. That was a dangerous mix. This was the man Gyofuku had pointed out to him, the protestor with the gall to attack his interests then show up here in person to rub it in.

Yokuke paused for thought. It had been many long years since any man had insulted him so flagrantly, and the others were all dead. His honour demanded no less.

Yet this man has the affront to come here and challenge me directly?

The insult was unforgivable. Yokuke considered his response. It would not do to underestimate an opponent, however young and foolish he appeared to be. Revenge was always best served cold. He wondered if he ought to make an example of his Captain first, as a warning against failing him. Reluctantly, he dismissed the thought. For now, he needed Gyofuku where he was. He might be a foul-mouthed braggart, but he was also the best whaler in the Fleet, and his loyalties weren't outmatched by ambitions.

The fat pig is too dull-witted to think about crossing me, Yokuke observed. *And I need him to catch me more whales.*

Still, it irked him that the Westerner had bested his Fleet Captain so easily.

The attack on the factory ship, the pride of his Fleet, was a direct attack on himself. Yokuke hadn't worked so hard to build Taiyoku Misui Fisheries into one of the most profitable companies in the world to then turn around and let some upstart environmentalists destroy it underneath him.

The question is, what to do about it?

His face never changed, but on the inside Yokuke felt his blood boil at the affront to his honour, and he was surprised at the force of his emotion. A good Kuromaku prided himself on his negotiation skills, and that included staying calm under pressure. Unchecked anger on the inside was a sure path to unchecked anger on the outside – and that was the mark of failure as a Puppet-master. It was a long time since Yokuke had even come close to losing his temper, and this sign of weakness surprised him. He snorted to himself. Then again, that was probably because he was used to doing business in Japan, where his reputation preceded him. These Westerners truly were ignorant barbarians when it came to matters of negotiation. Yokuke allowed himself a moment more to savour his rage before he locked it away. He glared at the blonde New Zealander.

So, my arrogant friend, it appears you need to learn some manners. I shall be happy to arrange a lesson in the finer arts of diplomacy.

As he contemplated, Yokuke was suddenly struck by the symbolism his enemy embodied. The Westerner was very much like a Kajiki. The swordfish was a swift and dangerous predator in the seas, and more than a little arrogant with his strong sword and that fine sail on his back. Yokuke's wrinkled face split into a cold grin at that thought. Regardless of the Westerner's previous successes though, even the strongest Kajiki was no match for a big-game hunter.

I shall enjoy the sport of reeling you in.

Yokuke turned to his aide and hissed an order. "Those two there… the Greenpeace hippies. Have them put under observation. I want to know their every move."

The aide inclined his head. "Yes, Master. Shall I arrange for the local police to arrest them?"

Yokuke shook his head. That would lack finesse. "No. I want them around to bear witness to their own failure."

He bared his teeth in a triumphant grin. "This is the International *Whaling* Commission. It's high time we reclaimed this dysfunctional conference for its rightful purpose. I want a majority on the Moratorium vote this year, and I don't care what it takes. You know which commissioners to target. Make them an offer – one they cannot refuse," he added ominously. "After all, the honour of Japan is at stake here."

***

Dennis Cruikshank sat in the public gallery, his press badge firmly fastened to the lapel of his sports jacket. He twirled his bushy moustache thoughtfully while he listened.

Occasionally, he shifted uncomfortably. He was a big man, with the physique of a bodybuilder – or maybe a heavyweight boxer if he was honest – and the plastic chair had obviously been designed for a smaller, Asian backside.

He was above being concerned about minor physical privations though. Long hours on stakeout had taught him that.

Cruikshank took out his notebook and pretended to take notes, although he was really studying the Greenpeace woman intently. She was a firebrand. He knew the type well.

There was a buzz of excitement from the gallery around him as the woman harangued the delegates, spouting her propaganda.

He snorted to himself. No doubt the reporters could smell a good scandal brewing.

God-damn vultures! All they're interested in is a good story.

He longed for the day when the Press might actually show some responsibility for once. But 'ethics' and 'journalists' were two words that didn't fit in the same sentence, not without adding a big fat 'NONE' afterwards. He cringed inwardly, already imagining the gushing headlines tomorrow, "Feisty young heroine battles the establishment".

He frowned. These kinds of activists shouldn't be encouraged. Most of the time they were deliberately courting publicity, and in order to achieve their moment in the spotlight many of them were prepared to resort to all kinds of means, including illegal.

That was where Special Agent Cruikshank came in.

Another frown creased his forehead. He still wasn't sure about his new title. As far as he was concerned he was – and always would be – a detective.

He rubbed a hand absently over his shiny bald pate. His hair had been thinning lately, his widow's peaks plunging deeper and deeper into his receding hairline. But a year back he'd taken charge. A quick raid with the clippers had seen him go for the 'clean-headed' look. And he thought it fitted him too. With his barrel chest and broken nose, it did complete the look of a prize-fighter, someone people wouldn't want to mess with. And that sat just fine with him. When you dealt with the dregs of society, you couldn't afford to take chances. The less they were tempted to try any funny business the less they needed putting in their place, and the better chance you had of living to collect your retirement pay. A shaved head was also a good way to cover up the grey streaks that had been making their presence felt… Cruikshank quickly squashed any thoughts of aging before they could affect him. The last thing he wanted to advertise was how close he actually was to retirement. Less than a decade to go, and it was starting to catch up with him. This investigation could be his last chance to make Captain – or whatever fancy title the suits could dream up for it in this new outfit.

He glanced around surreptitiously, taking everything in.

He was undercover now, of course, but a man could never lower his guard. You never knew where the crazies would be hiding, or what they might try next.

After all, that was the point of the Intelligence Wing of the new Homeland Security Department, and the reason he was here. He was a detective, and a damn good one.

He grunted to himself. He had been glad to get away on assignment. There were too many collars and ties strutting around back home.

His bushy eyebrow twitched, the only outward sign of the thoughts in his head.

Cruikshank thought the plan of combining spies and cops into one outfit was a damn fool idea, mainly because he hated the CIA's pompous attitude. 9/11 had changed the world in more ways than just the obvious. Of course, it was about time those spooks got a wake-up call to the real world – while they'd been running around playing secret agents with themselves, America had been attacked, right under their noses. Americans had been killed, in their own country! The intelligence agencies' failing was almost as criminal as the crazies who'd carried out the attacks. And if it took a kick up the pants from genuine, honest-to-god beat cops to show these Intel-types how to conduct a proper investigation then so much the better. It just wound Cruikshank up having to be the one to deal with the college-educated idiots though. They pranced around with their expensive suits and fancy theories on how to combat terrorism. Meanwhile, in cities all across America, ordinary cops actually fought terrorism on a daily basis. In the LAPD the enemy wasn't international militants though, but the scourge of street gangs, drug barons, organised crime syndicates, and the like. But the war was no less dangerous, and the cops who fought it were no less skilled.

It was about time someone finally thought to utilise all that home-grown experience in the War on Terror.

Now here he was, in Japan of all places, hunting out enemies of the State before they could do any damage. His bosses were worried about Japanese nationalism breeding some extremists, crazies who might be a threat to friendly Western embassies and diplomatic staff in the region. But Cruikshank also planned to keep an eye on some of the environmental activists and protesters banging their drums over here. 9/11 was definitely a wakeup call for America, and threats to Homeland Security could take many forms. This was the Age of Terrorism, after all.

He twirled his moustache. As a law enforcement officer, he was especially concerned by the blatant anti-US sentiment on display up at the podium right now.

Chapter 8

Cal Major stared at his watch as the next session wore on. It was getting late, and through the high skylights he could see it was already getting dark outside. The shadows deepened overhead, covering the meeting with a sense of foreboding that he found strangely unsettling.

He looked away, irritated with himself, and glanced over at the large wall clock above the public gallery but it confirmed the time. He had initially been surprised to see a clock there – most meeting rooms he'd been in were conveniently absent of all reminders of the world outside, to eliminate distractions and keep people focused – yet now he was forced to admit it was a cunning strategy on Amimoto's part. As the time got ever later and mealtime came and went, the delegates' desire to stay and argue was rapidly fading, reinforced by the relentless reminder of the marching sweep hand.

Cal's thoughts began to wander.

The discussions were interminable, endless politicking to and fro. While each commissioner was entitled to give his two cents worth, most had nothing worthwhile to say, and many were just content to revel in the sound of their own voices.

Cal sighed. He hated meetings.

IWC meetings were particularly frustrating. With two opposing agendas they quickly stagnated into a stalemate. It was the end of the day and they had accomplished nothing – except a lot of empty talk. Any sort of agreement was all but impossible between whalers and conservationists anyway.

The Japanese delaying tactics were working though. Cal could see the fatigue on people's faces. It was plain that Amimoto's strategy was to outlast rather than out-debate his opponents. Even his supporters appeared to have had enough for the day. His was a sound strategy. It might take days, or even years, but eventually people would get sick of his infuriating tactics and give up arguing.

In the interim, Amimoto would continue to exploit his loophole in the rules and keep on killing whales anyway.

As the meeting wore on, Cal's mind drifted to his own strategy. Things looked ominous. The mood of the conference was difficult to judge at the best of times, but the tide of support for conservation was slowly but surely ebbing. During the day's session there were as many words spoken for a resumption of commercial whaling than there were against it. The dedicated conservation countries were still as resolute as ever, but their ranks were thinning. Amongst the rest of delegates, support even for the existing Moratorium was lukewarm at best. A worrying sign. The chances of winning a permanent world-wide whale sanctuary were a fading pipe-dream now.

It was a relief when the Chairman finally struggled to his feet and announced the session would adjourn for the day.

Cal's thoughts were troubled as he stood up though. Across the room, he could see Amimoto deep in conversation with his aides. He knew the Japanese Commissioner well enough to suspect he would stop at nothing to get his own way.

What dirty tactics are you scheming up now?

Cal frowned. This was rapidly shaping up to be the bitterest conference ever, and the outcome hung in the balance.

Things aren't looking good at all…

Cal's stomach growled angrily, reminding him how long the last session had dragged on. He tried to put it all out of his mind for now, allowing Aurelia to take him by the arm and lead him toward the Dining Hall.

Behind them, Vicki and Richard followed, chatting together quietly.

Cal smiled to himself. His brother was finally coming out of his shell. It was good to see him making friends, especially with a good person like Vicki. His smile reached the corners of his mouth. Richard could do a hell of a lot worse than Vicki…

As they walked, Aurelia couldn't keep her huge grin off her face. "What a victory!" she crowed, obviously in good spirits. "Did you see their faces when I finished?" she laughed again, huskily. "Old Amimoto looked like he was going to blow a fuse!"

Cal rolled his eyes at her. "It's not over yet, there's a long way to go. I'm not sure it was such a good idea to go on the offensive so early."

She laughed, unconcerned. "Oh don't fuss. You worry too much."

He felt his frustration mounting. "You pissed a lot of people off with that speech – allies included."

She pulled a face. "So what? This isn't a goddamn publicity contest! I'm here to end whaling, not make friends!"

"That call for a boycott of Japanese products was irresponsible. We discussed that. You know it's unlikely to work – it's too indiscriminate. It'll target the wrong companies and generate a lot of ill-feeling. You could turn public opinion away from the cause."

She tossed her fiery mane. "I don't care who gets pissed off, all companies are guilty of corporate greed anyway. Besides, it's publicity for the cause – and any publicity is good publicity!"

Cal shook his head in exasperation, but said nothing, too tired to argue with her.

Aurelia turned her face towards him, as if surprised at his silence. Suddenly she broke into a huge grin. "You know what, this is almost like old times again… the two of us, out to change the world."

Cal stopped walking and stared at her as if she'd slapped him. He wasn't sure what shocked him more, her words, or the fact they mirrored some hidden recess of his own thoughts. He stood there, a confusion of emotions tumbling through his head. A strand of her hair hung across her face and he looked under it into her eyes, the same colour as the sun-lit ocean. Cal suddenly felt his heart lurch. This was the woman he had fallen in love with all those years ago. Despite everything that had passed between them, he could see she was still the same woman inside. Beautiful, passionate, and determined. A fighter, out to right the wrongs of the world. And he loved her for it. He knew then that no matter what happened, he would always love her. Despite their differences.

He leaned closer, fighting the sudden urge to kiss her.

Once he had believed she was his soul mate. Now? Who knew, perhaps he still did?

She turned her face toward his and gazed up at him, her breath catching suddenly.

It's over. Things are different now.

Cal blinked and straightened up suddenly as the voice of reason stepped in to take control. He couldn't afford to fall for her again – it would only end in more heartache.

He coughed to cover the awkwardness. "Come on, let's get a feed. I'm starving!"

***

Richard stood up as soon as the meeting finished, relieved it was finally over for the day. He sighed out loud, and immediately felt guilty. He knew it was a rare privilege to be able to attend the conference – even if he was only here accompanying his brother – and he'd tried to be diligent and follow the proceedings. But by the end of a day of endless negotiation and counter-negotiation his head was spinning, and he wanted to yell out loud with frustration. He had no idea what the result of the session was – if in fact anything had been resolved. After a full day of deliberations, the conference seemed even further away from reaching a decision than before they started.

Vicki rolled her eyes at him, as if to echo his sentiments. "That was a marathon, wasn't it?" she said with a weary smile.

Richard nodded, grateful to her. "I'm not really sure I follow what's going on…"

Vicki laughed, her dark ponytail dancing merrily. "Don't worry. I don't think half the people in there know what it is they're debating either!" She frowned suddenly, her voice becoming serious. "I know what you mean though. Cal and I normally attend the IWC's Scientific Committee meetings. At least the discussions there are usually rational – except for the Japanese and their pseudo-science, most people are on the same page. Here it's totally different. This is the first time we've attended the main IWC meeting, and I can't say I'm impressed. These discussions are led by politicians and diplomats, most of whom have no scientific background, and know next to nothing about whales." Her frown deepened. "And a lot of them care even less about their purpose here. It's obvious their motivations are political or financial, rather than biological."

She shook her head. "Why these people insist on continuing such criminal destruction is a mystery to me." She looked away. "They'll be the death of all of us one day. And at the rate people are trashing the planet it won't be too long coming either. We're killing the Earth, and once it's dead, humans will die too…"

Coming from anyone else, Richard might have dismissed such a statement as emotive Greenie scare-mongering. Who could say, a few months ago he might still have. But Vicki was not some wacky pot-smoking hippy. She was an intelligent, level-headed scientist, and that made her words all the more foretelling.

Richard was struck by her conviction, the simple but earnest desire to do something good for the world, instead of taking from it like everyone else. It impressed him, although he already knew it was not an easy life to lead. He'd seen that first hand. He stared at her, wondering again why a young, attractive woman would choose such a frustratingly difficult and potentially dangerous lifestyle.

"Why do you do this?" he blurted. "Why not work somewhere safe? Like a shop, or a bank, or something?"

Vicki stared at him, momentarily perplexed. "Somewhere boring, you mean?" Then she laughed, her eyes dancing. "I couldn't work at a desk. I'd never handle the pace!"

She pointed towards the door where Cal's back was rapidly retreating. "Come on, we'd better not let him get too much of a head-start or there won't be any food left for the rest of us!"

Richard grinned and followed his brother down the covered walkway into the adjacent Dining Hall. They each took a plate and stood in the queue for the buffet dinner.

Aurelia was first in line, but she walked right past the first dish, a plate of exquisitely-prepared sushi rolls, with her nose held high. "Raw fish," she sniffed. "They'd better have something vegetarian here because I'm not eating dead flesh."

"Japanese sure love to line up," Vicki observed. "Everything's always so polite and orderly here." She grinned. "I can only imagine the scrum that'd happen if you put this many hungry Aussies so close to food!"

Richard turned to grin at her – and his next step forward took him straight into Cal's back. He hurriedly stepped back, an apology already springing to his lips. A large gap had opened up in the line, centred on Cal. "Hey Cal, you're holding up the line!" he protested.

"Yeah," Vicki added. "We're starving back here."

But Cal didn't answer. He was staring at the plate of sushi. He reached out and picked up a roll, sniffing it suspiciously. He turned it over in his hand, examining it.

"You gonna eat that sushi or just look at it?" Aurelia teased him, but her eyes revealed her disapproval as a vegan.

Cal ignored them, and picking up a knife, he began hacking open the roll. Rice spilled out onto the tablecloth.

Aurelia giggled. "Now he's dissecting his food! What a scientist!"

"Don't eat that," Cal muttered darkly, then without another word he tossed the sushi back onto the serving plate then turned and stormed away.

Startled, Richard turned his head to watch him go. "What's gotten into him?" he murmured.

Vicki didn't answer, but reached over and picked up the sushi. She sniffed it, then a strange look passed over her face. She frowned and looked around. Richard followed her gaze, suddenly aware of the Japanese Commissioner, watching them from across the room. Amimoto's face was impassionate, but the look in his eyes was expectant, almost greedy, like a crocodile waiting for an antelope to test the water. Next to him stood one of his aides, clutching a camera.

Vicki returned the sushi to the plate, wiping her hands on her jeans. "Come along," she whispered. "We're leaving."

"But I'm hungry," Richard protested.

"We'll find food somewhere else. This is a setup."

"What? I don't understand."

Vicki hustled them out of the line and headed for the door, glaring at Amimoto as she passed. As soon as they were out of earshot she muttered, "One bite and we would have been ruined. He would have plastered the picture all over the news tomorrow… It would have destroyed our public credibility, guaranteed."

"What would?" Richard persisted. "What's going on?"

Vicki turned to him, her face grave. "Amimoto was trying to sabotage our campaign. That was whalemeat sushi."

Richard's eyebrows shot up.

"Whalemeat?" he whispered. "Are you sure…?"

Regardless of the political implications, he was appalled at the thought he'd nearly eaten whalemeat – even unwittingly. It would be unthinkable – especially now he'd seen where it came from. An image of the great Blue whale popped into his head, swimming in the vast expanse of the Southern Ocean, graceful and majestic in his own realm. Richard shook his head, still unable to believe someone would want to kill such a magnificent creature at all, let alone for eating. What was the point when there was so much ordinary food available in supermarkets? Rarity wouldn't make whalemeat taste any better than any other kind of meat. Somehow it seemed, well, wrong to eat such a magnificent and intelligent being. Almost like a kind of spiritual or intellectual cannibalism. Everybody needed to eat, but to get some kind of sick gratification from killing and eating whales, that was wrong. Criminal, even, given how endangered they were.

Behind them, Amimoto left the dining hall, his expression unreadable.

Vicki ignored him. "Come on, we'll get some food down the street," she muttered.

Richard shook his head, trying to clear his thoughts. He turned to her. "Uh, if we're going outside I need to get my jacket. I left it on my chair."

"Ok, hurry up. We'll wait for you outside."

Richard hurried back to the debating chamber, his thoughts still dominated by Amimoto's attempted subterfuge.

As he passed one of the function rooms, he noticed one of the movable partitions that walled off the room was slightly askew. From within came the sound of muffled voices. Puzzled, and a little curious, Richard hesitated. Glancing up and down the corridor to make sure no one would see him, he put his head up to the edge of the partition and peeked around it. Inside, the high-ceilinged room was empty – except for a small knot of people over in the far corner. With a start, Richard recognised the grey-haired Japanese Commissioner seated in the centre of the group. He was flanked by two of his aides, and before him stood a young Polynesian man, immaculately dressed in a suit and tie, his black curls slicked tidily down on his head. He looked vaguely familiar. Richard racked his brains trying to remember who the man was. Then it came to him.

The Commissioner of Tuvalu!

He remembered Cal muttering about the man. Tuvalu was a small Pacific Island country and supposedly a conservation-minded nation, yet the Tuvaluan Commissioner was not quite so committed in his views. He was an arrogant self-made businessman, and in Cal's opinion, he was more interested in using his post to further his own ambitions than concerning himself with whaling.

Richard strained his ears to pick up what they were saying, but the echoes in the cavernous room made it impossible.

Just then the Tuvaluan Commissioner laughed confidently, showing a set of strong white teeth. Amimoto smiled too, foxlike, and gestured to one of his aides.

Bowing respectfully to his master, the man withdrew a brown envelope from his jacket and handed it to the Tuvaluan. Richard couldn't see what was in it, but the greedy gleam in the Commissioner's eyes gave a fair idea. The envelope disappeared like magic, and the tall Polynesian strutted from the room, escorted by the Japanese aide.

Richard swallowed, trying to admit to himself what he'd just witnessed.

He was just about to withdraw his head when the aide returned, ushering another Commissioner into the room.

What the hell's going on? Is Amimoto holding court here or something?

This was the Commissioner from Nauru, another small Pacific Island. Unlike the previous visitor, he was wearing traditional garb; a floral shirt and a patterned tapa-cloth around his waist. He was older too, his face creased with the lines of late middle-age. Something about him seemed more regal, and he held himself with a chiefly bearing. Richard could see in his eyes he was uncomfortable though. Whereas the Tuvaluan Commissioner had stood confidently, almost arrogantly, in front of the Japanese, the Nauruan statesman kept his grey head downcast, avoiding meeting Amimoto's steely gaze. Whether out of respect or trepidation, Richard couldn't tell, but it was plain he was here only at Amimoto's behest.

The Japanese Commissioner spoke curtly in his own language, pausing now and then while one of his aides translated into English.

Richard couldn't make out the words, but the meaning was plain.

The Nauruan kept his head down, listening in silence. At one point he glanced towards the door. One of the Japanese aides immediately moved to stand behind his shoulder, as though to restrain him if he thought about leaving prematurely.

At a nod from Amimoto, another brown envelope appeared. The Nauruan Commissioner flinched and shook his head, refusing to look at it. Despite a sharp command from the Japanese he stared at the floor, shaking his head vehemently.

Lip curling into a snarl, Amimoto hissed something that could only be a threat. The Nauruan's face paled under his tan and he swallowed nervously, but continued to shake his head.

With an exclamation of disgust, Amimoto waved a hand to dismiss him and turned away. His aides hustled the shaken Nauruan chief out of the room.

Richard hurriedly withdrew. Head spinning, he hurried away to fetch his coat.

The empty conference hall was shadowy and foreboding in the half-light. Richard thought about switching on the main lights, but elected not to. He didn't know if he was allowed to be here after hours and definitely didn't want to get in any trouble by getting caught sneaking around.

Just get what you need and get out, before anyone sees you!

He walked up to his seat as purposefully as he could manage, his footsteps sounding disconcertingly loud in the silence. Without the delegates and their noisy debate, the room was as quiet as a crypt. Richard shivered. He snatched up his jacket from the back of his chair, and turned to leave. He was about to hurry out when he caught sight of a familiar blonde head by the public gallery at the far end of the conference hall. His shout rang out before he could stop himself.

"Cal!"

Richard hurried over towards his brother, "Hey Cal, I thought you left…"

The words died on his lips as he saw Cal was not alone.

Richard came to a stop, unsure what to do, but it was too late to avoid being seen. He'd already made sure of that!

Cal looked up and smiled at him with weary impatience. He lifted a hand to beckon him forward. Richard bobbed his head and obeyed, embarrassed now to have interrupted a private conversation. As he came closer, he recognised the hawk nose and thinning hair of New Zealand's IWC Commissioner.

"Jim Avery, this is my brother, Richard," Cal explained. "He's working with me."

The Commissioner nodded a greeting, and Richard returned it guiltily.

Cal turned back to their country's Commissioner. "So, what's your answer? Can you help us here?"

Avery looked flustered. "My hands are tied," he protested, wringing them appropriately. "It's not that I don't want to help you…"

"You realise we're in danger of losing this vote," Cal warned, his voice grave.

"I'm sorry, but the country cannot exert diplomatic pressure on other nations, even Pacific Island states we already provide economic aid to."

"Just a word to them-" Cal began, but the Commissioner cut him off.

"I can't do things off my own bat. My job is to represent the will of our government at the IWC and Wellington's directive was plain – economic aid is a separate issue from whaling."

"You know it would get their attention," Cal retorted. It was a statement, not a question.

Avery bristled at the suggestion. "Economic sanctions are inappropriate. That money is to avert poverty, not for use as a bargaining tool."

It was Cal's turn to look annoyed. "I'm not asking you to cut off any aid. And I'm not suggesting any sanctions. All I'm asking is for you to have a quiet word in the ear of these Commissioners. They receive aid from us, and consequently we expect them to uphold certain responsibilities as members of the regional community. Since you're the representative of the New Zealand Government, surely you can make it plain what our country's feelings are on both issues."

Avery looked aggrieved. "That amounts to bullying!" he spluttered. "A democracy cannot conduct itself in such a manner!"

Cal looked annoyed. "Even if the opposition does?" he shot back.

"Especially if the opposition does! We must be fair and open in our dealings at all times. It's up to us to set an example for others to follow."

Cal laughed out loud, but it echoed hollowly in the empty auditorium. "Bullshit. The only example that sets is how not to take on Amimoto. You know he's bought off half the small countries here already."

Avery drew himself up to his full height and looked down his aquiline nose at Cal in what Richard took to be his most condescending manner. "If we abandon the ideals of democracy and fair play then we become no better than what we are trying to fight."

"That's all very well, but the trouble with relying on democracy and fair play is that it loses out to corruption and dirty business dealings every time! Do you think the whales care whether you have moral scruples? Amimoto sure doesn't. Fighting fair and losing is still losing!"

Cal shook his head and turned away. "Come on," he shot back over his shoulder at Richard. "Let's go find the others."

With a parting glance at Avery, Richard hurried after him. As Cal strode down the corridor, Richard could hear him muttering under his breath. He'd heard enough of the exchange to know Cal was pissed off. He swallowed nervously, wanting to say something reassuring, but not knowing the right words. Cal wasn't in a conversational mood, and he didn't want to make things worse.

"This is bullshit," Cal blurted suddenly. He turned to look back, fixing Richard with an intense stare. "We're trying to fight this battle with both hands tied behind our back."

Richard nodded, sharing his brother's frustration, but still not knowing what to say.

They walked a few steps in silence before Cal sighed. "I know it's not Avery's fault," he admitted. "He's just following his orders. But it's just so damn frustrating! Our defence is fractured and far too cautious. Amimoto is running rings around us! We're going to lose this fight!"

He swore under his breath. "The IWC is a joke. It's not the right forum to be discussing whale conservation anyway. I feel like I'm banging my head against a wall trying to get any progress through all this bureaucracy, and even if by some miracle we do manage to hammer out a resolution, it counts for nothing. There's no accountability, and no enforcement of any decisions made here." He shook his head sadly. "Even though we managed to take control of the IWC in the name of conservation – the old Whaler's Club procedures still haven't been changed in nearly sixty years!"

He laughed humourlessly. "It's a perfect delaying tactic; the Japanese maintain the IWC is the only body that should be responsible for regulating whaling, then while everyone is tied up with the IWC bureaucracy they're free to continue killing whales under whatever loophole they're currently exploiting."

Richard frowned, not ready to admit the worst. "But don't we have the majority? Can't we beat them at their own game?"

Cal made a face. "Yeah in theory, and so far we have. But Amimoto will never give up, and one day, through fair means or foul, he'll manage to get the majority back. Then we're screwed. Even during our supposed victory we've been unable to stop the Japanese killing whales, and when they seize control of the IWC again we won't have a hope of stopping them." He knotted his brows. "That Amimoto is a shrewd bastard too. Once he manages to snatch the majority off us, he'll make damn sure we can never get it back again. Guaranteed."

Richard felt a chill pass up his spine, and a mental image of the Japanese Commissioner's private negotiations that afternoon played over and over in his head.

Amimoto can't be allowed to win! But what can we do to stop him?

Richard shook his head vehemently, unable to believe the system would fail them – justice was on their side, after all. "Amimoto won't get the majority back!" he said, with more conviction than he felt. "The world is committed to conservation of whales now… Aren't they?"

Cal looked away, refusing to meet his eye. "For better or for worse, conservation of whales is decided by the IWC. Right now there are sixty-six nations here; 29 are conservationist, 23 pro-whaling, and 14 undecided. Amimoto needs just seven more votes to get a simple majority over us, and ten will give him a clear majority – enough to satisfy his government and convince the world's media."

"I thought he needed a three-quarter majority to resume commercial whaling?"

Cal pulled a face. "In theory he does. But in theory he's not supposed to be killing any whales now, either! Any vote he can win will be enough for him to claim a mandate."

He sighed. "The vote is already closer than it's ever been since the Moratorium was passed – we don't need to lose much support before we're up against the wall. As you know, a large proportion of those fence-sitters are small Pacific, Caribbean and African states, most with no interest in whales – some without even a coastline. Plenty of them have large foreign debts though, and a lack of hard currency." He winked, somehow managing to turn it into a sarcastic gesture. "Everyone needs more money. Who needs whales?"

Richard stared at him, not knowing what to say. This was the first time he'd been exposed to the cold hard reality of what they were up against.

Cal shrugged pessimistically. "What can we do? Each country is free to vote as they choose, and it won't take many pay-offs before Amimoto gets his majority. We've been lucky for many years, but I think our luck has finally run out. And my gut tells me it'll happen sooner rather than later. The future is hanging in the balance."

Richard swallowed. That was a huge responsibility suddenly resting on their shoulders, and all of a sudden he felt the true weight of it. What could they do? The questions that sprang to mind were tinged with desperation.

"Won't anyone help us? How do we stop this?"

Cal looked thoughtful. "I don't know if we can. It is human greed and selfishness that spawned this war against whales, and the Earth itself. Ideally we need to change the world – or at least the human attitude to it – otherwise there will always be another Amimoto waiting to continue the fight."

Change the world?

That was impossible! Everyone knew it. Richard stared at his brother, waiting for him to laugh and admit he was joking. But Cal held his gaze, unblinking. Finally Richard realised he was serious. "Change the world?" he repeated, almost tentatively. "How could we possibly do that?"

Cal shrugged. "Far easier said than done," he admitted. "Top-down control is unlikely to work. As you've seen, lawmakers and politicians are more concerned with economics. If it's likely to cost money, they're not interested. Few think beyond their current term of office. If it's not an issue for the next election then it's not important."

"What do we do then?"

"Ideally, change must come from the bottom up. Individual people must change the way they think. Societies as a whole must demand change from their leaders. Only then will things get done."

Richard blinked, still doubtful. "How can we accomplish that?"

Cal shrugged. "I don't know that we can. People are inherently selfish. They only care about problems that directly affect their life – bills, taxes, mortgages, traffic jams – those kinds of things. Most people have never even seen a whale, so why should they care about them? Our society is based on the premise that the Earth somehow belongs to humans to exploit as we wish, so what impetus is there for people to change the way they do things?" He sighed. "We can't force people to change the way they think, just like we can't force them to care. They need a reason to change their ways, but if they can't see it for themselves already, well, I sure don't know how to show them."

Richard could sense his brother's despondency. "So what's left? Give up?"

Cal gave him a strange smile. "Never underestimate the power of your own convictions, Bro. One man can always make a difference. Who knows what you can accomplish if you put your mind to it?"

Richard wasn't convinced. "Amimoto is so powerful, so well connected. What can *we* possibly do to stop him?"

Cal looked thoughtful. "The IWC is far from perfect, but for now we'll have to do what we can with the mechanisms at our disposal." His eyes glinted. "We need to find ourselves a good lawyer."

Richard stared at him, a million questions suddenly tumbling through his head.

Cal turned away, as if hiding a smile. "Come on, we can't do anything standing here. Let's go find the others."

As they hurried towards the main entranceway of the Convention Centre, Richard could hear a commotion outside. It grew steadily louder as they approached, and as he stepped outside Richard felt as though he'd walked into a wall of noise. The girls were waiting just outside the door, but their attention was fixed on the noisy demonstrations in the square beyond. Vicki looked nervous. "What took you so long?" she demanded. "It's a blimmin' zoo out here!"

Richard stared past her. An isolated knot of Greenpeace protestors was still sitting in the square outside the entrance. In the fading light they sang protest songs and shouted their slogans. "Meat is murder! No more whaling!"

Behind them, a line of police kept an angry crowd at bay – just. Richard could tell the mob were pro-whaling without having to read their signs. Some of them were obviously whalers themselves, dressed in the familiar white gumboots and blue overalls. They shook their fists and hurled obscenities, along with the odd missile. On the street behind, a convoy of large vehicles cruised menacingly up and down. There were trucks, vans and buses, all covered with posters and banners denouncing 'Western Imperialism' and the conservation movement in particular. From loudspeakers mounted on the vehicles, and numerous handheld megaphones in the crowd, an angry barrage of Japanese issued forth, battered the hearing of anyone in earshot.

The Greenpeace protestors sang on, outnumbered and virtually drowned out by the crowd, but seeming unperturbed. Aurelia had a strange gleam in her eye as she watched. Richard wondered if she wanted to go and join them, but he shuddered to think what would happen if the Nationalists broke past the police. They were spoiling for a fight.

"Come on," Cal said, echoing his thoughts. "Let's not hang around here."

As they hurried on, Richard caught the aroma of burned food, wafting from several barbecue grills on the far side of the courtyard. Another group of placard-waving Nationalists stood beside them.

"More whalemeat," Cal observed, his mouth drawn into a thin line. "I expect Amimoto organised this little demonstration too, just to rile us."

Somehow the crowd must have realised the Team were conservationists, because the shouting swelled to a murderous roar as they passed. They sounded to Richard like a pack of dogs baying for blood.

"Don't let them intimidate you," Cal muttered angrily. "That's what they want."

All the same though, he led them quickly across the square and down towards the docks.

As they hurried across the open courtyard, Richard caught sight of another group of Nationalists waiting on the other side of the square, near to the side-street where they were headed. This group was smaller though, and there was something different about them. They weren't shouting slogans and they carried no placards, yet the air of menace surrounding them was unmistakable. With a start, Richard realised they were all wearing white gumboots and blue overalls. Just then, one of them broke away from the group, stepping forward to block their path.

Cal inhaled sharply, just as Richard's mind registered the red plastic helmet on the man's head.

Hogei Gyofuku laughed mockingly as they skidded to a halt in front of him.

Richard glanced about, looking for the police. They were all on the other side of the square, backs to them as they faced off against the noisy crowd.

Gyofuku laughed again. He beckoned Cal forward, challenging.

"Come on, let's get out of here," Vicki urged. Richard could hear the fear in her voice.

Cal stood his ground.

Gyofuku sneered, and behind him, his men shuffled forward threateningly. They outnumbered the Team by a dozen to four. With a sick feeling in his stomach, Richard knew his brother was the only one of the four who could fight. But even Cal wouldn't last long against that many. This was madness!

Cal bunched his hands into fists.

"Cal, come away!" Aurelia shrieked.

"This is the Captain of the Pelagic Fleet," Cal muttered back over his shoulder, although his gaze never wavered from the pockmarked face in front of him. "He's the root of all our problems."

"All the more reason why you should walk away," Aurelia admonished. "Violence never solved anything."

Cal laughed sardonically. "Passive resistance never stopped any atrocities either. I could end this right here, right now…"

"Don't be an idiot! You can't fight them all."

"I can take him though!"

"And what will that accomplish? Absolutely nothing! There's always another thick-headed man waiting to carry on the stupidity!"

Richard glanced at Aurelia. He wasn't positive she was talking solely about the whalers.

"Cal don't! What are you trying to prove?" Aurelia shrieked. "You'll get yourself arrested! How can you stop the hunt if you're in jail?"

Cal hesitated, as though struggling to make his mind up.

"Yeah, you're right," he mumbled finally. He took a step backwards but Gyofuku was unwilling to let things lie. He growled and lumbered forward, a flabby hand reaching for the skinning knife at his belt. Behind him, the whalers closed in, moving to surround the group in the corner of the square.

Cal's head flicked from side to side as he tried to keep them all in view.

Richard gasped. Violence looked inevitable. There was going to be a fight and he was right in the middle of it.

Suddenly he heard the sound of running feet.

Uh oh, here comes more trouble.

Looking around anxiously, he caught sight of the tall form running up a side alley toward them. Moments later the figure burst out into the square and made a beeline towards them.

Richard blanched. "C-Cal," he stammered. "Someone's coming."

"I see him." Cal muttered grimly. "Hold your ground! If we run now this lot'll be on us before we can take two paces."

Richard felt his heart begin to pound. Then the newcomer stepped forward. With a start of surprise, Richard recognised the bushy black pirate beard, and its burly owner.

"Evenin' y'all. You wasn't about to have some fun without invitin' me?" he accused.

"Duke!" Cal exclaimed. "When did you get here?"

"Just cleared Customs and tied up at the dock not one hour ago."

Cal grinned. "Mate, is your ugly mug ever a sight for sore eyes!"

The Skipper grunted. "Looks like I ain't a moment too soon. Y'all appear t' be in a spot of bother here. Reckon it might be time to open a can o'whoop-ass?"

He rolled up his sleeves, revealing his tattooed tree-trunk forearms. With a whiskery sneer he produced a short length of chain from his pocket and began to swing it. It whistled menacingly as it cut through the air. The whalers shuffled uneasily.

Duke gave a satisfied laugh. "Come on then, ya pussies. Who's first?"

"Do you always carry that thing around with you?" Cal laughed, the relief evident in his voice.

The Skipper gave a rare smile. "Only when there might be trouble – and this port is fair crawling with it."

He spat a wad of tobacco juice on the ground and swung his weapon at the head of the nearest whaler. The man's eyes widened in shock and he threw himself backwards in a desperate attempt to avoid the swinging chain. The heavy links whistled though the air only inches from his face, then he tumbled back into the rest of the group, knocking men down like skittles.

Duke threw back his head and laughed his gravelly laugh. "You like that eh? Come on, who wants a piece of me then?"

The whalers backed up, huddled in a nervous group. Despite their numbers, Duke's chain was a great leveller. Richard winced involuntarily at the thought of the damage it could wreak. One direct hit from the heavy metal links would hurl a man to the ground, probably smashing his skull in the process.

Suddenly they heard a shrill whistle blast from across the courtyard. Richard looked back and saw a policeman hurrying towards them.

"Time to make ourselves scarce," Cal warned.

Duke stopped swinging the chain, winding it discretely around his fist.

Seizing the opportunity, a whaler immediately lunged toward him brandishing a club. But if he thought the Skipper had lowered his defences, he was wrong!

Duke's fist shot out and crashed into his jaw, the heavy metal links standing up like a knuckleduster.

The whaler's eyes rolled back in his head and he slumped to the pavement.

The remaining whalers waited, glancing warily at the Skipper, then back to the approaching policeman. Gyofuku snarled in frustration. He snapped a curt order at his men and they began to disperse. Gyofuku backed up after them, but before he turned to follow he gave Cal a vicious parting glare, his shifty eyes glittering with malice. "Your friends not always save you," he muttered in broken English. "One day we have some fun!"

Cal returned his belligerent stare. "Bring it on!" he challenged. "I'm ready any time!"

Richard gasped inwardly at his brother's bravado. He could see no advantage in deliberately antagonising the whalers. They were already surly enough to cause no end of trouble for the Team, and taunting them would only make them madder. Watching the Japanese swagger away Richard felt weak-kneed with relief, but with a sick sense of dread he realised this fight had only been postponed for another time.

"There's a noodle bar just down the street," Aurelia suggested, her authoritative tone indicating she'd already recovered any lost composure. "We can wait there until things quieten down a bit."

"T'hell with that," Duke growled. "I ain't about to eat no goddamn ethnic food. I've no compunction against fixin' chow in muh own galley tonight. The Old Gal is tied up just over yonder…"

"I'll second that," Cal agreed. "It'll be much safer onboard the Gwendolyn. They won't dare follow us there."

Aurelia opened her mouth as if to protest, but Cal shot her a 'Don't argue' look and she reluctantly closed it again.

As they hurried down the narrow street towards the dock, Richard caught sight of a familiar tall fore-mast dominating the skyline. With a sudden smile, he realised it was the Gwendolyn moored at the wharf. Her smooth navy-blue lines looked so stately next to the dirty rusted hulls of the local fishing fleet that he couldn't suppress his happiness, as though he'd just recognised a familiar face in a crowd. Stepping off the wharf onto her stout deck again gave him a feeling of pleasure, a mixture of returning home and being reunited with an old friend.

The field assistants tumbled out of the saloon door to greet them, and there were exuberant "Gidday"s as the Team was reunited again. Richard smiled shyly and mouthed his own greetings. He was pleased to discover even Heath seemed to be in a good mood, his eyes almost friendly below his perpetually grumpy-looking pierced eyebrows. Richard tore his gaze away from the intimidating piercings, and turned his attention towards the blonde vision behind him.

"H-hello Summer."

She nodded vaguely at him, the briefest hint of a smile flickering across her lips before her attention moved on to Cal. "Hello Cal," she purred.

"Hey Guys," Cal responded brightly, grinning at both field assistants. "You two have a nice cruise?"

Heath muttered something, the beginnings of a scowl already forming. He ignored Cal's proffered handshake.

Summer smiled back though, lighting up her whole face.

Richard felt his heart trip, even though it wasn't directed at him. Despite thinking about her almost constantly during the days they'd been apart, seeing her again was like a shock to the senses. It had barely been two weeks, but it was as though time had managed to dull her memory in his subconscious, and the contrast with the real physical form was like comparing diamond and coal. In person, her beauty was positively breathtaking, and an irresistible allure radiated from her, triggering a desire somewhere deep inside him. He stared at her now, trying to etch every nuance of her beauty into his mind. Compared to Gina's plastic artificial beauty – requiring an hour every morning to cake her face in makeup – Summer's beauty was so natural. From her angelic face, framed by her flowing blonde tresses, to her full, kissable lips, she was the personification of the perfect woman. Richard sighed, wondering if a woman like that could ever be interested in someone like him.

His eyes flickered down to her chest, where the twin ovals of her breasts strained provocatively against her cashmere sweater, and he felt almost giddy with desire.

If only I could get a girl like that…

Guiltily, Richard managed to wrench his gaze back to her face. He risked showing a shy smile, but she wasn't looking.

Cal stepped forward and embraced her politely, but Richard could see Summer's hug was stiff and forced. She was already staring past him towards where Aurelia waited.

Duke coughed behind them, clearing his throat. "All this touchy-feely bonding and whatnot is delayin' my supper," he muttered, stomping off in the direction of the galley.

Cal laughed, then turned to introduce Aurelia to his field assistants.

Heath nodded politely as he shook her hand, trying to keep his dopey grin at bay. "You're from Greenpeace!" he gushed, fawning over her. "I've heard about you! You're a legend!"

Aurelia laughed gaily, clearly used to the adulation.

When it was Summer's turn, Richard could have sworn he saw a shadow pass across her lovely features though, and her body language was stiff and forced. He blinked in surprise. Cal didn't seem to have noticed, nor anyone else. Richard had to admit if he hadn't been watching Summer's face he'd probably have missed it too. He had to wonder what that look signified though.

Is she jealous?

He felt a pang of resentment himself at the thought, but managed to dismiss it.

Cal wouldn't do that to me, he assured himself. Besides, it hadn't looked like pure jealousy… more like annoyance.

Richard puzzled over it while the Team caught up on each other's news. He didn't mind standing to one side while they talked, since he was busy with his thoughts anyway. Although he was beginning to feel more like a part of the team now, he still felt a bit shy about speaking up out of turn.

After a few more minutes chatting on the deck, Cal's stomach suddenly growled loudly.

"Uh oh, gotta feed the beast!" he quipped and they all laughed. "Shall we?" He gestured towards the doorway and they trooped down to the galley together.

Richard followed the others below, pleased to find the ship reassuringly stable now that the she wasn't being tossed around at the mercy of the Southern Ocean. It was a relief to be able to walk around without having to stagger drunkenly from one handrail to the next.

They all sat down around the wardroom table that also doubled as the mess. Through the open door to the galley, Richard could hear the Skipper whistling 'Dixie' as he cooked. For once the gimballed stove-top was silent – without its usual incessant squeaking as the ship rocked on the swells.

A short while later Duke staggered out with a huge steaming pot of chilli, which he began ladling onto their plates.

"Mince and beans. My own recipe," he announced proudly. "Genuine South-West cuisine – this'll put hairs on your chest!"

Aurelia looked horrified, but Vicki raised an amused eyebrow at his joke.

Heath's mouth was drawn into a tight line – punctuated only by the ring in his lip. "Enjoy your dead animals," he sneered, eyeing the mince in the meal.

Duke ignored him, turning instead to Aurelia. She was staring at the food with a shocked expression on her face.

"Look at you – starin' at that grub like a calf in front of a new gate. Ain't y' hungry?"

Aurelia fixed him with a steady look, clearly having trouble deciding if she should be embarrassed or angry. "There's meat in it," she said coolly. "I'm a vegetarian."

Duke laughed, slapping his thigh. "Damn! Another one!" He shook his head in mock consternation. "Don't you worry li'l lady, I've got another pot out back for you difficult types. No critters in that'un, guaranteed."

Aurelia politely nodded her thanks, but her eyes blazed – Richard wondered whether she was more annoyed at being called "li'l lady", or being labelled difficult.

Heath stomped out into the kitchen and returned with the second pot which he plonked down on the table for the two vegetarians. His scowl had returned.

Summer paused, spoon half-way to her mouth. She stared at the second pot as if suddenly remembering something. She pushed her bowl away, cheeks colouring slightly. "I, uh... I'm a vegetarian too."

Heath seemed surprised, but handed her a new bowl. Richard gazed at her, wondering where the sudden conversion had come from – as far as he knew she'd happily eaten meat all across the Southern Ocean. Across the table, Cal and Duke exchanged a glance.

Richard shrugged and reached for a hunk of bread. He was too hungry to concentrate right now.

As they ate, Cal addressed the crew.

"Thank you all for sailing up here to meet us. I apologise for the interruption to our schedule, but sometimes these things are unavoidable." His resigned smile of acceptance left no doubt at his own feelings on the matter though. He turned to Summer and Heath, the two hired field assistants. "I'm sorry I was unable to provide any work for you two during the voyage up here and you were left to your own devices for a while, but as you know we had to fly ahead to make it in time for the start of the meeting." He looked down, as if slightly embarrassed at the unforeseen change in plans. "I realise this departure from our schedule means we'll be doing less work in the Antarctic this season, but I'll try and find enough data entry work to keep you busy while we're in port."

They both groaned.

Cal smiled good-naturedly and held up his hands. "I know, I know, it's not as exciting as looking for whales, but I promise you'll receive the same wages, plus a bonus for your patience." He grinned. "And while we're all up this far north I think it would be a good idea to do an acoustic survey down through the tropics on our return journey."

Summer suddenly paused in mid bite. "I want to attend the conference too," she announced, flicking her blonde hair with authority. "Can you get me a pass to the public gallery?"

Cal frowned. "I'm not sure that's such a good idea. We need to keep as low a profile here as possible."

Summer's demeanour hardened. "I didn't come all this way just to sit on a boat in port. I signed up to do research and research is what I'll do – my own, if you have nothing for me!" She crossed her arms across her chest in defiance. Richard's eyes bulged as her breasts nearly popped out of her low-cut top, and he hastily looked away, feeling the colour rise up his cheeks.

Cal didn't seem bothered by her sexuality though. "I'll find something for you to do while we're in port," he promised, trying to defuse the situation. "But we need to be careful about this-"

"I want to go," Summer insisted. "You dragged me all the way up here, and now I can't even go ashore?"

"We'll talk about this tomorrow." Cal's tone was polite, but firm. His eyes flickered towards Duke, and Richard thought he saw a cryptic look pass between them, but it was gone before he could be sure.

Summer pouted and went back to her meal.

Cal wasn't finished though. He surveyed them all with a stern gaze. "This conference has the potential to turn very dangerous for us," he warned. "We can't afford to let our guard down, even for a moment."

He snatched up his spoon, gripping it like a weapon. "Everyone must be alert for trouble at all times. From now on we will maintain a 24 hour watch on the bridge, and no one leaves the ship without my permission. When we're ashore, no one goes anywhere alone, and I do mean anywhere." He punctuated each point by stabbing the air with his spoon. "Aurelia, it's not safe for you to remain in the hotel. I'll find a berth for you onboard."

Heath snorted. "Yeah, in his bunk," he muttered under his breath.

Cal glared at him, but his next words were for all of them.

"Make no mistake about it; our presence in this city is not appreciated. We have powerful enemies arrayed against us and I have no doubt they'll do anything they can to disrupt our plans."

Chapter 9

The next morning, Richard was happy to take his seat in the conference hall. The boredom of the previous day's session was replaced by the sight of Summer sitting in the public gallery, with her brand new security pass pinned to her bosom. Despite Cal's obvious reluctance, she had insisted he allow her to attend, even threatening to quit the crew if she didn't get her way. Richard smiled at the memory of her defiant protest, feet planted and arms crossed provocatively across her chest. Eventually Cal had relented, much to his chagrin – and Richard's joy – although the line had been drawn at her joining their official delegation.

Richard gazed at her now, across the crowded room. The conference hall was centrally heated so she'd taken off her jacket, revealing a tight satiny top with a plunging neckline. With her generous assets and striking blonde hair cascading down over her shoulders she cut an eye-catching figure – and judging by the ill-concealed stares she received, most of the men in the hall had already noticed. Richard felt a quiet glow of satisfaction that she was here with him and the Team.

Sitting up there next to Cal filled him with a sense of importance, like he was set to change the world for the better. Given her insistence on attending the meeting, he felt sure that must be Summer's motivation too. He tried to catch her eye, hoping to share the moment with her. She wasn't looking at him though.

"I pronounce this day's session open," the Chairman announced, his dreary monotone managing to cut through Richard's daydream. "First item on the agenda is the vote to prohibit Japan's Scientific Whaling Program, as mooted by the member from Greenpeace." He inclined his head ever so slightly towards where Cal sat, by way of acknowledgement. Richard noticed the consternation in his brother's eyes. It must be difficult for Cal, he realised, having to align himself with a group of radical activists when he was really a scientist at heart.

Richard looked across and noticed Mr Fish was already staring at them – the look in those cold eyes enough to send frozen icicles of fear down his spine. Richard blinked and quickly lowered his head, trying to concentrate on the Chairman's droning voice instead. He was in the middle of explaining the complexities of the voting procedure. Minor issues usually were decided by a quick show of hands, but due to the possibility of censure of a member state – Japan – if this motion passed, the vote was to be conducted individually. Richard groaned as the Commissioner began calling out country names, starting at the beginning of the alphabet. At this rate it would take half an hour for the vote to be counted! He fidgeted, trying to get comfortable on the hard chair. Next to him, Cal was deep in concentration, carefully scribbling tally marks and quick sums in the margin of his notebook. He would chew the end of his pen, then as each vote was announced he would nod approval, or scowl and mutter under his breath.

The Antiguan Commissioner's vote was first. Not surprisingly, he sided with Mr Fish. In fact, he launched into another explosive diatribe against the "colonial tyranny" of conservationists before the Chairman managed to bring the meeting back to order, huffing with exasperation. Cal's annoyance was plain too. Yet as the voting wore on, his mood became even darker, and the end of his pen more ragged. Richard glanced over and saw far too many tally marks for the Japanese.

The delegates must have sensed it too. The Chairman's voice was strained as he tried to quieten the buzz of speculation that gripped the room, trying to press on with the vote.

"Nauru?"

Richard recognised the Nauruan Commissioner from Amimoto's private meeting the previous night. He watched as the man got uncertainly to his feet. The commissioner was probably a tribal chief back home, but he didn't look like one now. His eyes were downcast, and his grey curls quivered with anxiety. He wrung his callused hands together, before one found its way to the bone carving at his neck, absently caressing the polished surface as if to seek solace from his ancestors. He took a deep breath and opened his mouth to speak… then closed it again.

With exaggerated reluctance, he turned and looked towards the Japanese delegation.

Amimoto glared back at him, the intensity of his gaze hard enough to bore right through the unfortunate chief. Richard quailed at the sight of such animosity – even though it wasn't directed at him. Still holding his gaze, Amimoto gave a small but meaningful shake of his head. It was a subtle gesture, but the meaning was clear.

The Nauruan blanched immediately and tore his gaze away. Looking shaken, he stared at the floor, his shoulders slumping with the air of a defeated man. He took another strangled breath and managed to stammer out a response, "N-Nauru rejects this motion to censure Japan." Then he collapsed back into his chair, still avoiding eye contact with Amimoto.

Richard felt his heart sink.

Another vote against us.

Beside him, Cal pursed his lips with annoyance.

However, as the voting continued his mood lightened again. As if sensing his brother's despair, Cal reached over to pat Richard's arm. "Don't worry, Bro, we're not beaten yet. There are still governments in the world with the courage to stand up for what is right."

As if in response, the Chairman struggled to his feet to call for the next vote. "Seychelles?" he called.

The man who stood up looked European, despite his deep tan. He was tall and handsome, even with the shock of silver hair that marked his age. In fact, Richard decided, rather than making him look old it gave him the bearing of a venerable elder statesman. The man glanced in their direction then, and Richard saw he had a kind face, and compassionate eyes.

"That's Victor Admirante, one of the senior policymakers of the IWC," Cal whispered, his voice hushed with reverence.

At that moment there was a huge crash as a carafe of water toppled off the Japanese Commissioner's desk and shattered on the floor, sending broken glass and spilled water everywhere. Amimoto didn't move, his smirk suggesting it was no accident. There was an instant commotion as several staff hurried over to sweep up the mess.

The Seychelles Commissioner waited patiently. If he suspected it was a delaying tactic, he gave no sign.

Cal leaned over to whisper in Richard's ear. "Commissioner Admirante is a good man, a dedicated conservationist. He was a millionaire businessman once, but he switched to politics to try to do some good for his country, and the world." he nodded thoughtfully to himself, his respect for the man plain. "Admirante was influential in securing the original Moratorium vote back in 1982 – he's the last of the original conservationists who hasn't retired yet." Cal chuckled. "He's been fighting the good fight against this bloody IWC bureaucracy since I was just a kid." His smile faded slightly. "Man, did he piss off the Japanese though! He stood firm against all the bribes they could think of to throw at him. Rumour has it Admirante even laughed in the Japanese Commissioner's face when he tried to threaten him."

Cal glared in the direction of Amimoto, sitting smugly behind his desk. "Needless to say, that didn't go down well with the self-styled samurai lord! Yep, old Mr Fish was furious when this upstart nation in the middle of the Indian Ocean cost him the Moratorium vote. He put a contract on Admirante's life, forcing him into hiding for many years." Cal's grin returned. "But he's back! You can't keep a good man like that down for long!"

With the mess cleaned up, Victor Admirante calmly surveyed the meeting, his presence alone demanding respect. When he spoke, it was with the clear, commanding voice of an orator. "This vote has been a long time coming!" he announced, and a hush descended on the room as they hung on his words, waiting to hear what would come next. "As a long-time participant in this forum, it occurs to me that Japan constantly seeks to impose its agenda on this commission and its members." He smiled, as if sharing a joke with them. "And given that supporting Japan almost invariably requires a prostitution of one's own moral conscience and free will, this situation smacks not of co-operation, but domination – a condition that most definitely runs counter to the spirit of international relations." He surveyed the delegation like a strict but kindly headmaster, a trace of irony tugging the corners of his lips. "The Seychelles is not a client of Japan! The Seychelles is proud to govern itself! I support this motion, and applaud the brave soul who instigated it!"

His last words were almost lost to cheers from the conservationists in the room. Cal heard though, and he blinked in surprise at the praise from such an esteemed source, before blushing bright red as its significance hit home.

Across the room, Amimoto's black eyes glittered with hatred.

The Chairman spluttered with frustration, his jowls swinging like a turkey's wattle as he flapped his arms in a vain attempt to silence the uproar. Eventually he managed to restore order, but his face was still pink from the exertion.

"Tuvalu?" he puffed.

The young Tuvaluan Commissioner jumped to his feet, white teeth shining as he broke into a broad grin. He made a show of checking his suit and straightening his tie, drawing out his moment as the centre of attention. He smiled an oily smile then turned to face the Japanese delegation. He adjusted his gold cufflinks and nodded towards Amimoto. "Tuvalu rejects this motion," he announced. "Japan's Scientific Whaling Program is entirely legal."

The Chairman held up a hand to forestall the indignant mutterings that began to surface.

"United States?"

All eyes turned to watch, and even Cal held his breath as the American Commissioner stood up. He paused dramatically, glaring in their direction. His voice was suffused with petulance as he reluctantly announced his vote; "The United States supports this motion."

Cal's breath hissed through his teeth as he released it. Richard shared his sense of relief, but any good vibe was tempered by the American Commissioner's expression. His parting scowl at Aurelia made it patently obvious he was doing them no favours, and wanted them to know it. He was voting for his own reasons, and was visibly annoyed to find himself voting on the same side as them.

Cal already had his head down though, busily counting up his tally marks. A moment later he cursed under his breath.

"What is it?" Richard craned his neck across, trying to read the result.

Before he could manage, the Chairman began speaking again. "The votes on the motion to prohibit Japan's Scientific Whaling Program have been tallied. The results are as follows: Affirmative: 31 votes, Negative: 27 votes, with 8 abstentions. The motion is passed."

Cal was shaking his head. "That was close. Too close," he muttered.

Richard grinned at him, happy at their success. "But we won! That's the main thing, right?"

Cal didn't return his smile. "I'm not so sure. We've lost most of our majority and all we did is show our hand. The important vote is yet to come, and I suspect we've reached our peak already. This could be the beginning of the conservationists' slide from power…"

Richard blinked, then spoke again, desperately trying to maintain his cheerfulness. "But this was an important vote too. The world just banned scientific whaling!"

Cal shook his head. "No, we only registered our opposition to it. Either way, Mr Fish won't take any notice of what the world thinks – he hasn't for the last twenty years. The Japanese will go right ahead and kill as many whales as they want this year, and every year, just like they've always done."

Richard slumped back in his chair. "So what do we do?"

Cal turned to look at him. "We make damn sure we win the vote to continue the Moratorium against commercial whaling." He looked away, and his voice went quiet. "A vote that's looking shakier for us by the day…" He trailed off, staring into space.

Amimoto stood silently, the air of menace unmistakable as he turned his withering stare upon the conference. Despite the narrow success of the vote to condemn Japan's scientific whaling program, he was allowed a 'right of reply' and the opportunity to defend himself.

The delegates shifted uncomfortably under his cold stare, the anticipation almost as bad as the storm they knew was coming.

Amimoto cleared his throat noisily, then let fly with a torrent of Japanese. His interpreter struggled to keep up with him. "This is an outrage! Scientific Whaling is permitted under the rules of the IWC and all in this room know it! Japan is acting entirely within the law, and in fact, this research is beneficial to further our collective knowledge and assist all the nations of the world."

He glared around the room as if daring anyone to question him. "Not only is our research programme sanctioned by the IWC, but we are doing the nations of the world a service by carrying out this groundbreaking work! Our science has been praised internationally!"

"Bullshit!" Cal muttered under his breath, but loud enough for his voice to carry. "The only evaluation your research program has had is by the same scientists who carried out the research – if they can even be called that!"

He held Amimoto's gaze. "It's not impartial and it's not valid science! The only 'praise' you ever get is from other whaling nations. You never publish anything in reputable peer-reviewed scientific journals – it would never be accepted! The only publication you can get is in your own Japanese fisheries bulletins." Cal laughed disdainfully. "If you have enough money you can buy anything – even legitimacy."

"That's enough!" the Chairman spluttered. "The Commissioner for Japan has the floor. No more interruptions!"

Amimoto's eyes glittered with anger. "This scurrilous attack against us is both cowardly and racist. It is clear that certain factions have hijacked this meeting to force their own agenda of cultural imperialism upon the world. Japanese people are an easy target because the colour of our skin is different."

Richard swallowed and was forced to look down as Amimoto turned the full force of his anger towards them.

Cal returned the stare though. "Skin colour has nothing to do with it," he said quietly. "We're against Japanese whaling, not Japanese people. This is no more racist than our desire to stop the Norwegians killing whales, or the Icelanders. The fact is though, the Japanese are driving this industry; stop them, and we'll stop the whaling."

Amimoto's eyes took on a predatory glint. "These troublemakers pretend to be here at this meeting negotiating in good faith, yet at the same time they are presenting this face to the world they are secretly organising protests and fomenting civil unrest outside this venue, and they are engaging in acts of criminal harassment and piracy against law-abiding fishermen on the High Seas!"

Beside him, Richard heard Cal suck in his breath. This was a new tactic to attack them directly, but Richard knew his brother would have an answer for it. At least, he hoped so. Otherwise the Japanese Commissioner would win this debate.

"Such subversive and criminal behaviour is typical of the anti-whaling lobby," Amimoto continued. "They are selfish, unreasonable, and uncompromising, and their inability to engage in rational debate marks them as dangerous fanatics."

Aurelia's back stiffened ram-rod-straight with anger.

"This New-age mysticism they have thrown up around whales serves only to distract the world from their own selfishness. We Japanese do not seek to impose our cultural beliefs on anyone else. We believe each country should be free to do as it chooses. In my country we consider it ludicrous *not* to hunt whales. It is far more energy-efficient to harness nature's surplus than to submit the land to the inefficient and environmentally-destructive practices of farming sheep and cows. Whaling uses thirty per cent less energy than production of cattle to eat, and therefore is an important industry to create wealth for our nation."

Cal clicked his tongue with annoyance. "Those figures are for coastal whaling," he muttered under his breath. "Everyone knows the Japanese Whaling Industry is bankrupt and their Pelagic Fleet runs at a loss. Their massive fuel bills alone are subsidised to the tune of ten million US dollars every year by The Japanese Government."

Amimoto had paused for effect, but he wasn't finished yet. His eyes glittered as he focused on Cal and his team, as if delighting in taunting them personally. "Whalemeat is also much healthier for our people than Mad-cow beef. The animals themselves are happier too. Free-range whales are spared the prolonged suffering of factory-farmed livestock."

Cal stared back, his face impassionate, refusing to be baited. Aurelia's back quivered with anger though, and she bunched her hands into fists on the table. Cal laid a hand on her arm, as if to restrain her, but she didn't even notice him. All her attention was focused on the Japanese Commissioner, and his inflammatory words.

"You lecture us on 'world opinion'," Amimoto continued, "but who are you to dictate the values of the world? Will you also force your ideals on the Belgians to tell them they cannot eat horsemeat? Or the French their snails? We Japanese consider cows and sheep cute, but we do not tell you not to eat them!"

Richard glanced to his other side. Vicki sat tight-lipped, her blue eyes riveted on Amimoto as he ranted.

"Japan is a coastal nation. We depend on the bounty of the sea to feed our population and provide jobs for our economy. Whaling provides incomes for over 50,000 people. Who are you to take their jobs and force those people to starve?"

Cal pulled a face. "Those are very creative numbers – although that's hardly surprising since Mr Fish came up with them himself."

"Yeah," Vicki added, breaking her angry silence at last. "He's counted not only the whalers, but also their extended families, and every clerk, market trader, or storeman who's ever touched a can of whalemeat in their lives – along with all their extended families too!"

Cal nodded slowly. "The actual employment figure is more like one thousand workers. If that."

Amimoto pressed home his attack. "For thousands of years our ancestors have hunted and eaten whales. Who are you to decree that their descendents cannot? That is the pinnacle of cultural insensitivity! As an enlightened society, the modern world has recognised the importance of cultural traditions amongst indigenous people, and I ask you now to respect Japan's traditions of whaling."

Aurelia coughed and spluttered, as though something was caught in her throat.

Cal nodded grudgingly. "The cunning bastard," he muttered. Richard looked at him, puzzled. "He's trying to beat the system," Cal explained. "In many countries there's widespread support from left-wing politics to allow their native communities to hunt a small number of whales each year. The IWC had to make exceptions to the Moratorium for aboriginal societies who practice subsistence whaling; tribes like the American and Canadian Inuits who hunt whales in order to survive."

Vicki rolled her blue eyes with annoyance. "Amimoto just makes a mockery of that with his claim for Japanese 'cultural whaling' though. Japan doesn't need to hunt whales to survive. Nor have they been doing it for thousands of years."

Cal nodded. "Yeah, the Japanese Pelagic Whaling Fleet was created as recently as 1939, and they didn't hunt for subsistence. They hunted for oil. It was a cheap source of foreign currency to fund their expansionist war against the Chinese in Manchuria."

He raised his voice to ensure he was overheard. "Massive industrial-scale whaling on the open ocean is definitely not a tradition. It only began when whale stocks around Japan became commercially extinct. It was never their tradition to hunt whales 10,000km from home in the waters below New Zealand and Australia."

Across the room, Amimoto glared at them. Richard wondered if he was more annoyed at Cal's show of disrespect by whispering during his speech, or because he realised he was the subject of those whispers.

The Japanese Commissioner slapped the table with a withered hand and angrily launched into his next attack. "Who are you people to force your beliefs onto others? Who are you people to claim it is wrong to kill animals?" Spittle flew from his mouth as he worked himself into a frenzy. "Your culture kills cows and sheep to eat! The Australian Government also sanctions the culling of kangaroos, an animal native to Australia. What is the true reason for that killing?" He rounded on the delegates. They sat meekly while he lectured them, like a rabid teacher chastising naughty schoolchildren. "The reason is because kangaroo numbers have exploded until they reached plague proportions! It is necessary to cull them to protect the grass that is a food supply for many other animals – including human agriculture. Without this control of their numbers, this plague of kangaroos would devour all the food in sight, destroying the landscape for farmers and other animals alike." Amimoto paused to let his words sink in, his head cocked, birdlike atop his scrawny neck as he watched for a reaction. "Our scientific research has shown there is a similar plague in the seas! The quantity of Minke whales greatly outnumbers that of other whales, and through this great weight of numbers they will consume all the food available for other whales. This plague of Minke whales is obviously preventing the recovery of the rare whales, and so they must be culled – just like Australia's kangaroos – in order to safeguard the future of whale stocks! And furthermore, our research has shown this plague of Minke whales is also beginning to decimate stocks of fish, and need to be removed to restore the balance of nature. We must redress the balance of the oceans before it is too late!"

"The cunning bastard…" Cal muttered.

The Australian Commissioner squirmed uncomfortably in his chair and studied the floor, and Vicki, a fellow Aussie, was lost for words.

"That's a complete load of bullshit," Cal hissed. "What kind of logic is that? Minkes are the last un-depleted whale species left, so he says we should slaughter them until they're as rare as the others? Bullshit!" He shook his head in disbelief. "Blaming the last few Great Whales for eating fish stocks is like blaming a woodpecker for deforestation! The total Minke population in the Southern Ocean is claimed to be seven hundred thousand, maybe a million worldwide, tops. How is that a plague? Even a million individuals is not a lot, and that's the world's most common whale – there are more people than that in Auckland, and that's a tiny city by world standards!" He clicked his tongue in annoyance, but he wasn't finished yet. "How can Minkes possibly eat all the food? There were millions more whales in the Ocean just two centuries ago, and they all had enough food then, with plenty of fish left over! I'm sure Taiyoku Misui's massive industrial fishing fleets have nothing to do with the present situation though!"

Richard could feel his brother's outrage as he launched into another angry whisper.

"A plague? How can any whale be classified a plague? There's barely three thousand Blue whales left worldwide – and that's a conservative estimate, there could be as little as a few hundred! Compare that to the six billion people hogging the planet. Each of those few thousand whales is outnumbered two million to one by humans – that's the equivalent of just *two* Blue whales against the entire population of New Zealand." His disgust was plain. "And people are totally responsible for their plight. Whales aren't the only species we've decimated either, not by a long shot. Who's the real plague on this planet?"

Richard sat dumfounded. He was by no means an expert at diplomacy, but even he could see that Amimoto's attack had just torn a swathe through the Conservationists' defence. The non-aligned commissioners were already whispering urgently amongst themselves, discussing the implications of Japan's new 'scientific findings' on Minke whales, no doubt along with the enticing financial opportunities that awaited these whale cullers. The Australian Commissioner was still sitting in embarrassed silence, the mention of his country's controversial kangaroo kill sweeping away any moral high ground he might have had to challenge Mr Fish. Canada and the US both remained silent too, along with any other country whose citizens practised subsistence whaling. They all knew they couldn't speak out against Japan without conceding the advantage on that point. In fact, the New Zealand Commissioner was the only First World representative who voiced his displeasure, and even he didn't look too confident. He was backed up by Victor Admirante from the Seychelles, and a handful of other small countries. But they were in the minority.

Amimoto bared his yellowed teeth in a smile, pausing to admire his handiwork. He was like a vengeful god, delighting in the destruction wrought by the tornado he'd just unleashed. Seizing on the confusion sown amongst the delegates, Amimoto followed it up with his coup de grâce. "The Moratorium against commercial whaling was supposed to be a temporary measure to allow whale stocks to be assessed, prior to a resumption of a commercial hunt. As such, its continued existence runs counter to the letter and spirit of the IWC Convention for the Regulation of Whaling – an entity established to oversee commercial whaling."

His face darkened like a thundercloud and he glared at Cal and his team. "The anti-whaling lobby pretends to engage in talks to foster the appearance of being reasonable, but they are anything but! Their true motive is obvious when they continually delay and make unreasonable demands in an effort to make a future return to whaling practically impossible. Their continued call for whale sanctuaries is a perfect example."

He wagged a bony finger in the air as he continued to harangue the conference. "Sanctuaries are unfair, since they do not distinguish between endangered and non-endangered species. They are racist, since they disregard culture, tradition, and human rights – namely the rights of Japanese fishermen to provide food and livelihood for their families by harvesting whales, as promised under the founding principles of the IWC. Furthermore, whale sanctuaries are redundant under the Revised Management Strategy put forward by my colleagues, since the new management procedures will provide the necessary protection when required."

Amimoto drew himself up to his full height, towering over the delegates with a presence out of all proportion to his wizened and diminutive frame. "Today's vote is a travesty! Japan utterly rejects this attempt to deny us the right to carry out scientific study of whale stocks, as permitted by the IWC rules. Furthermore, it is clear that such tactics are merely an attempt to suppress the truth, since our findings have clearly demonstrated the ability of Minke whales to be commercially harvested. Japan will never submit to these illegal and immoral transgressions of our rights!"

The Norwegian Commissioner began applauding, and was quickly drowned out by cheers from the rest of the High North Alliance members.

Mr Fish held up a liver-spotted hand for silence. "Thank you, my colleagues," he said, "But our battle is far from over. I now call on the signatories of the IWC to heed their obligations. My demands are simple; a dissolution of all Whale Sanctuaries, including those already in force, and a return to full-scale commercial harvesting of certain prolific species. I hereby announce an increased Japanese quota of 100 Humpback whales, 1000 Minke whales, and as many Fin whales as we deem to be sustainable."

Cal's eyes widened in shock. "A hundred Humpbacks!" he spluttered. "But there's only two thousand of them left in the Southern Ocean! …That's the same as taking a quota the size of Christchurch – our third largest city – out of the New Zealand population."

Vicki too was aghast. "Whales aren't fish that can produce hundreds of eggs at a time! They're mammals, just like humans, and they produce just one calf at a time which they have to nurture until adulthood. It'll take them decades to recover from that level of slaughter!"

Amimoto leered at them, as if delighting in their distress. His next words were slow and deliberate, so there could be no mistaking his intent. "These figures represent an *annual* quota to be taken in the southern seas each season. An additional quota of species to be targeted for a North Pacific harvest will be announced in due course. If these rights – as enshrined by the principles of the IWC – are not honoured here, then I call upon all whaling nations to leave this commission and we will form our own body to manage this harvest as we see fit."

He smirked, lowering himself back to his chair amid wild cheers from the High North Alliance.

Richard sat in stunned silence. He had come here to help his brother negotiate an extension to the Moratorium, not to witness its demise. Right now though, diplomacy seemed all but dead. What choice did the responsible nations of the world have left? Let the Japanese restart commercial whaling based on shoddy science, or let them do it totally unregulated. What kind of a choice was that?

It's blackmail, that's what it is!

A spark of anger flared somewhere deep within him. For the first time, he let it burn, surprising even himself. This cause was more important than his own fears. He realised that now. It was more important than any of the Team's problems – and the price of failure was unthinkable.

He glanced at his brother, surprised to see Cal sitting quietly, deep in thought, his head slumped as if defeated.

Richard knew he couldn't allow himself to give up. The Whales couldn't send a representative to this meeting to plead for their own case. He looked about him and saw his feelings mirrored on the faces of his colleagues.

Aurelia was three steps ahead of any of them though. She leaped to her feet, shaking with rage. "This man is a monster!" she shrieked at the conference. "He stands here before you advocating the murder of thousands of innocent whales – a slaughter that is nothing short of a holocaust!"

Amimoto laughed. "Here you can witness a perfect example of the irrationality we face," he interjected, gesturing disdainfully at her. "Perhaps she needs a good husband to settle her down?" he leered, winking suggestively amid loud guffaws from the Scandinavians.

Aurelia was livid. She stood there quivering with rage, temporarily at a loss for words. She clenched and unclenched her fists in abject frustration, her fingers hooked like claws itching to scratch out his eyes.

Amimoto remained in his chair, an infuriating smile plastered across his face. He pressed his bony palms together in a parody of a bow, mocking her.

Aurelia lost it. With a growl like an angry panther she snatched up her glass tumbler of water off the table and wound up like a softball pitcher.

Cal blinked, finally coming to his senses. He jumped up and lunged at her, managing to catch her wrist before she could hurl it. "Wait," he panted, struggling to restrain her. "Aurelia, please."

"Let me go!" she turned her rage onto Cal, battering his forearm with her free fist.

"Aurelia!"

Amimoto's aides reacted, jumping in front of him to create a shield with their bodies, just as a phalanx of security policemen burst into the room. The police made a beeline for the source of the disturbance. Richard could see they meant business. They wouldn't stop to ask any questions and he knew the whole Team was seconds away from being thrown out of the conference – a catastrophe for their cause.

In desperation, Cal swept Aurelia's legs out from under her, planting her squarely back in her chair. "Sit down!" he hissed through clenched teeth.

"We can't let him get away with this!" she insisted. "We have to stop him!"

"Let me handle it," he whispered back. "These commissioners are not vegetarians, and emotive accusations about killing animals won't get us anywhere!"

She opened her mouth to protest.

Cal held a finger against her lips. "I'll handle it. Trust me."

Vicki called anxiously to him. "It'll take more than numbers to convince them… You have to make them understand!"

He nodded. "I'll try."

Richard froze as the white-gloved police swooped on them, batons drawn.

Cal stood up and turned to the Chairman, cool as a cucumber, despite being seconds from disaster. "It's under control now, Mr Chairman. No harm done…"

The Chairman hesitated, considering, then grudgingly waved the police away. They backed off with exaggerated reluctance, as if disappointed at being denied some action. They retreated back to the door where they hovered expectantly, hopeful for a repeat situation.

"Such outbursts will not be tolerated," the Chairman cautioned.

Cal nodded, accepting the rebuke. "Extreme provocation," he smiled, by way of explanation.

The Chairman grunted, neither agreeing nor disagreeing, and turned back to his papers.

Cal did not sit down though. He took a deep breath and drew himself up. "I request a right of reply," he announced.

The Chairman looked up sharply, peering at him through the glasses perched on the end of his nose. "This is highly irregular-" he began.

Mr Fish let loose an angry volley of Japanese. His aide hurriedly jumped to his feet. "Japan objects most strenuously!" he parroted. "According to IWC rules, Non-Governmental Organisations do not enjoy speaking privileges at this meeting!"

Cal ignored the outburst. "According to the IWC rules, the instigator of a vote is allowed the final word if any objections are raised. Since this commission has accepted my motion, and the Commissioner for Japan has just voiced his objections, you must also accept my right of reply."

The Chairman nodded, careful not to meet Amimoto's eye. "Very well, I'll allow it. You have one minute to state your case."

Richard felt a surge of pride as his brother turned to face the delegation… or perhaps it was anticipation!

Cal looked out over the sea of faces and hesitated for a moment. Then another.

Richard gulped. Feeling suddenly alarmed, he wondered if his brother had lost his nerve.

But after a quick breath to marshal his thoughts, Cal's presence returned, as forceful and determined as ever. He launched into the attack, turning to face Mr Fish, as though addressing him alone. "Your attempts to cloud this issue reveal the depths of your desperation. Despite the questionable Australian practice of culling kangaroos, this is not the forum to discuss that issue. Likewise, it is not our concern whether it is right or wrong for a farmer to kill his cows or sheep. We are here to discuss one thing; killing whales, or rather, not killing them. The logic in this case is tragically simple – cows are in no danger of extinction. Whales are. It is in a prudent farmer's interests to take care of his stock, but you cannot claim to be farming the oceans. You neither own nor husband whale stocks, you only plunder them. You are motivated not by sustainable practices, but by greed. That isn't farming, it's strip-mining!"

Amimoto threw up his hands in a show of indignation, turning toward his Scandinavian colleagues for support, but Cal refused to be moved by his show-boating. If anything, the theatrics seemed to goad him on. "The bottom line is simple, a farmer raises and cares for the stock he harvests. You do not. The Southern Ocean is not even local to you. You come all the way down to the waters south of New Zealand and Australia to kill these whales. You attempt to force your selfish beliefs on the rest of the world, and by insisting on carrying out this slaughter you trample the rights of those who would choose to use whales for tourism and other non-extractive uses, or even simply to leave them alone, for the altruistic pleasure of knowing there are a few live whales left in the sea."

Amimoto glowered back across the room, and Richard could tell his anger was real now. He snapped an order to his assistant, but Cal forged ahead, raising his voice to forestall any interruption. "Whales do not belong to you. You have no more claim over them than you do over the Ocean itself." He spread his arms, as if to encompass the room. "My fellow delegates, I urge you to reject Japan's tyranny. You do not have to accept these selfish demands. The RMS is not based on sound science. It is just commercial whaling in disguise, and worse, it would open the door for a return to the slaughter of years gone by. We cannot return to such irresponsible and criminal behaviour. We must not bow down to Japanese threats and bullying. They present us with an ultimatum, but I tell you now, we *always* have another option available!"

Cal's gaze swept slowly over the meeting, as if to connect with each commissioner in turn. "The consequences of our actions will echo down the centuries," he warned. "Who are we to pass judgement over the fate of the whales? What conscience can we claim if we condemn them to the Abyss forever? They will not complain. They will go quietly to meet their fate – a fate we would consign them to for no other reason than our own *greed*!" He spat out the word, as though it left a bitter taste in his mouth.

"How can a society claim to be civilised, which permits such wanton destruction of life? If whales were people, this whole-scale slaughter would be considered genocide. But whales are not people. They look different from us, even if their minds are capable of a similar intelligence as ours."

He spoke softly then, as if his next words were meant only for himself. "Power with restraint. For all our discoveries, we have yet to master that. Who is really the better species…?"

After a brief pause, Cal shook himself, as though waking from a trance. His voice, when it came again, was clear and strong. "Whales are not people, yet they are cursed with having to share this world with us – the only species arrogant enough to treat an entire planet and every living thing on it as our own personal property! The Earth was not created for humans, despite the claims of the religious dogma at the heart of our selfish society. We are but one species out of billions who call this place home, yet we have destroyed countless numbers of them without even noticing their passing."

This time when he stared at them, the commissioners looked down, ashamed to meet his eye.

"Whales are not people, but if there is any justice in the universe they will still be journeying the oceans of the world long after we are gone. Right now, my fellow delegates, their fate rests in your hands. You wield the power of life and death over entire species! Use that power wisely, for history will judge you!"

The delegation sat in stunned silence as Cal took his seat again, just as the second hand on the wall clock finished one revolution.

Richard choked, hurriedly looking down so the others couldn't see his face. He felt as though his heart might burst. He didn't know if it was pride for his brother, guilt inspired by his words, or a stirring conviction to make a difference. Maybe it was a mixture of all three. One thing was certain though, he had never felt like this working at his desk designing electronic circuits.

Around them, the shocked silence endured.

It was broken by Victor Admirante. The Seychelles' Commissioner stood, the first delegate to begin clapping, but followed soon after by Avery from New Zealand. Then it was taken up around the hall, spreading like wildfire.

On the other side of the room, Amimoto's eyes glittered with hatred.

***

Akogi Yokuke felt his anger rising as the thunderous applause echoed around the chamber.

How dare that upstart hijack my meeting? How dare he?

His eyes slitted with malice as he watched the Kajiki showing off like a leaping swordfish, strutting and preening with his false modesty. The delegation's applause continued. The New Zealand Commissioner hurried over to offer his congratulations to the young troublemaker, followed closely by the Australian Commissioner, then all the treacherous anti-whaling lobby in turn.

Yokuke snorted derisively. This ecological movement was a kind of new-age hysteria. The Greenpeace degenerates and their followers were so obsessed with attaining their fanciful ideals they failed to comprehend how the world really worked. They would have people believe the Earth should be permanently locked away in some glass box for fear of disfiguring nature, and people should be unable to hunt the lower animals because all life was somehow sacred.

Yokuke felt his contempt rising. It was obvious such thoughts came from childish and misguided minds, ideas borne out of the luxury and excesses of the West. Such a vision of nature was so laughably unrealistic that it was obviously a product of modern society's distance from nature – and that was the greatest irony of all. After all, the advanced civilisation they enjoyed today was what it was because of the very things they wanted outlawed! Industry and progress *required* the bounty of the Earth to be utilised. Societies prospered because of it – and that very same development fed, clothed, and housed people. Not to mention giving them medical care, cars to drive, and generally raising their standards of living above the level of monkeys in the jungle.

Yet these stupid hippies would have the world believe I'm some kind of criminal against the Earth?

Yokuke felt like laughing out loud at the absurdity of such a suggestion. Only a loose Western society would tolerate such outspoken immaturity and hypocrisy within it. He frowned. In Japan, young people were taught respect for their elders – traditional values that were continually undermined by the spreading culture of decadence espoused by the West. Corrupt Western morals were threatening to engulf the entire world!

His mood darkened. The threat was even more insidious than that though.

The blonde barbarian had made a direct attack on the government of Japan, and therefore on the nation itself. Yokuke puffed out his bony ribs. He had more than just his own political and financial interests to protect now. He also had to lead the defence of his country, nay his people, against such vilification by aggressive and racist foreigners. It would make an old man proud to do his duty for his nation!

How different things would be if Japan led the world, neh?

Yokuke allowed himself a smile at the idea. The Japanese approach to life was so much more sophisticated and pragmatic than those ignorant Western barbarians could even contemplate. He bared his teeth. He had been only a boy in the Second World War, but he vividly remembered when the Empire of the Rising Sun was humbled by the American atrocities on Hiroshima and Nagasaki, and the great Emperor Hirohito was forced to accept the public shame of defeat. What a pity history hadn't turned out differently. Japan's indomitable spirit had helped them do well in a Western-led world nonetheless, but how different things might be if it was the West who was forced to bow to the East instead?

Without such idiotic moral scruples, we Japanese are so much more efficient when it comes to success!

Yokuke burned at the injustice of it. He was careful to nurture his rage where it wouldn't show though. Anger was a good motivator, as long as it was kept in check.

He stared back at the tall New Zealander.

The Kajiki's tactics were good, he admitted. Just like a real swordfish he was not only strong, but also cunning. He had displayed good oratory skills today, and even managed to turn some of the wavering delegates over to his side. At least for now.

"Ignorant fools," Yokuke muttered under his breath. "It will not be long before I bend you back to my will."

For now though, he continued to watch his enemy, searching for some weakness he could exploit. The New Zealander had proven to be a real thorn in his side, both on the water, and now here, at his own meeting. It was true the barbarian had some skills in both ways of the warrior.

With a trace of pleasure Yokuke realised this could shape up to be a genuine Kyokyojitsujitsu – a battle of wills – although it was clearly not an equally-matched contest.

"I shall enjoy finding the fish-hook to destroy you," he promised the blonde head, smiling to himself. The challenge of a dangerous adversary definitely made things interesting. Perhaps he would even enjoy removing this obstacle from his path.

"You may think you are a warrior, but even the best Samurai is no match for the power of a Shogun."

Yokuke's eyes narrowed as the red-haired woman turned to hug her fellow protestor.

Even a blind man could see the look in the Kajiki's eyes as he returned the embrace. Yokuke's lip curled in disgust. The swordfish must be hoping to slip his sword into her sheath. Why else would he hang around, sniffing after her like a dog in heat?

What kind of a man would desire such a physically and emotionally forceful woman?

Yokuke was aghast. Didn't he know his own place? Then again, maybe he did. Allowing such an unchecked challenge to the traditional values of manhood was just another symptom of Western men's weakness.

Imagine allowing his Yang to be emasculated like that!

Yokuke sneered at the very idea. But despite the Westerner's shameful submission to that aggressive woman, he was still a strong and dangerous adversary though. It would not be easy finding a way to hook him, but every man had his price.

Perhaps the proud Kajiki will strike at a similarly tempting lure?

Yokuke smiled as he got to his feet, yet his smile was cold and calculating. He was feeling anything but generous.

He shuffled across the chamber towards the crowd. His aide rushed to support him, but Yokuke slapped his hand away.

"I may be old, but I'm not infirm yet," he hissed venomously.

The Kajiki looked up then and saw him approaching, and his triumph faded from his face. Yokuke glowered at the crowd around his enemy. The other delegates averted their eyes respectfully and melted away, until the two were alone together.

Yokuke sized up his opponent. "You speak Japanese," he said. It was a statement, not a question. The foreigner nodded.

"A fine speech," Yokuke offered, "And well spoken."

The Kajiki inclined his blonde head in thanks, but his eyes were full of suspicion.

"I can see you are a bold and courageous man, and you defend your principles dearly."

The blue eyes continued to watch him warily.

Yokuke showed his yellow teeth in a smile. "It seems the two of us have started out on the wrong foot. I am not a merciless man, nor an unreasonable one, and I have no desire to be the cause of bad karma between two honourable men. To that end, I have a proposition to put to you…"

The Kajiki said nothing. Taking that as a sign of acquiescence, or at least indecision, Yokuke pressed forward. "I apologise for the actions of my underlings which have caused you offence. Your honour has been insulted and you have every right to feel aggrieved. I hope I can make amends for this." He paused, measuring the response. "We are very alike, you and me. We are leaders among ordinary men." He laughed disarmingly. "I can see you are a strong man, and truth be told, I would rather have a strong man as an ally, not an adversary. You are destined for great things, and I can help you achieve them. Join me, and I promise, your success will be assured."

The Kajiki's eyes widened in surprise.

Yokuke continued with a grand flourish. "I will offer you a research grant of two million United States dollars per year, my state-of-the-art research vessel Kyoeishin-Maru, and any other resources you require. All I ask in return is that you conduct your research on behalf of the Japanese Fisheries Agency." Yokuke smiled. "What do you say, my young warrior?"

While he feigned friendliness, Yokuke scrutinised his adversary's face for a reaction. With a surge of triumph he saw hesitation written in the Kajiki's blue eyes.

Chapter 10

Cal Major stared at the Japanese Commissioner, dumfounded.

Amimoto's offer was generous. Exceptionally generous. It was the kind of offer that every scientist dreamed of, the kind of offer that could make a career.

Cal hesitated, pondering the implications.

No more worrying about money!

He chewed his pen absently as he thought. Gone would be the days of applying for funding, and trailing cap-in-hand around big businesses seeking corporate charity. He would never have to write another grant application. Instead, he could devote all his time to research.

And just think of the research!

With a floating research laboratory like the Kyoeishin-Maru at his disposal, state-of-the-art equipment, and no shortage of field assistants, he would be limited only by his imagination. Anything would be possible! He might actually be able to make a real difference!

Cal hesitated just a moment longer, then nodded, his mind made up.

He placed his pen down on the table and stood up, meeting Amimoto's eyes. "Your offer is most generous," he said with a smile.

"Perhaps you need time to think about it?" Amimoto offered. "Please, take as long as you need."

"There is no need. I have an answer for you now."

The Japanese Commissioner leaned forward expectantly, eyes shining with greed.

Cal's smile never faltered. "Your offer is most tempting… But I would rather sell my soul to the devil."

Amimoto's eyes widened in surprise, a reaction swiftly replaced by cold fury.

This time Cal's smile was genuine though. Despite the adrenalin screaming through his veins, it gave him a sense of calm accomplishment to stand up to Mr Fish – the feeling made even more intense by the man's obvious surprise.

What's the matter? First time you met a man with a backbone?

Amimoto's gall was mind-boggling; the presumption that he could buy or bribe his way to whatever he wanted…

Cal resolved then and there to do everything in his power to bring the Japanese commissioner down. "My principles are not for sale!" he said, enunciating deliberately. Despite the inevitable consequences, it felt good to defy the man. Cal's heart thumped with savage pleasure at the cold fury he saw in his adversary's eyes.

"Very well," Amimoto hissed, his voice dripping with venom. "The decision is yours. But know this; I will stop at nothing to avenge this insult. I will destroy you, and everything you care about."

He turned and stormed away, his gait stiff-legged with rage.

Cal watched him go, knowing he had just made a dangerous and powerful enemy.

***

Akogi Yokuke forced himself to remain calm despite the red rage boiling through his shrivelled veins. Could such an insult ever be forgiven?

"Zettai dame desu!" he vowed under his breath. "Absolutely not!"

He waited until the foreigner had left, then doubled back into the conference chamber. He was livid, but determined to have the last say – and his adversary had just made a crucial mistake. He resolved to make the Kajiki pay dearly for it.

Making his way over to the Greenpeace bench, his eye settled on the gai-jin's pen, still damp from being chewed. He bared his teeth in a silent snarl.

Tut tut, how careless! Let's see if I can't find a good use for this!

With a flourish he whipped out a silk handkerchief and swept the object into his pocket.

Then he turned and stormed back to his private quarters, his fury still fresh.

Despite the insult of being voted against – and losing that vote – he knew the result didn't amount to much in the larger scheme of things. He would, of course, ignore the ruling, and continue with his Scientific Whaling Program regardless. The real issue was always the upcoming vote on the continuation of the Moratorium. That was the vote that mattered, and the vote he did not intend to lose, whatever the cost.

Yet it still rankled that the world would dare to challenge him – and that accursed foreigner was at the root of it all.

How dare he defy me?

The Kajiki was proving to be an infuriating hindrance to his plans. Still fresh in Yokuke's memory was the foreigner's response to his gentlemanly and extremely generous offer – the manner of his refusal even more galling than his stubbornness.

How dare he insult me?

Yokuke's thoughts tumbled angrily through his head, clouding his vision so much that he tripped on the sill as he stepped into the elevator. His aide rushed to support him as he stumbled.

"Take your hands off me you clumsy oaf," Yokuke snapped. "I am not nearly as old or infirm as some would prefer to believe. Now, convey me to my suite, I wish to sit down."

The aide bowed deeply from the waist and hastened to obey, keeping his eyes averted as he leaned across to press the elevator button.

Yokuke ignored him and shuffled out of the elevator as soon as it slid open, his mind already far ahead of his painstaking gait. The hotel manager had personally assigned him the Presidential Suite as a mark of respect for his political standing.

Or the depths of his toadying to win my favour.

Yokuke halted outside, gesturing angrily for his aide to hurry up and open the door for him. There were so many sycophants in the world it disgusted him.

As soon as the door was open, Yokuke pushed past him into the room. The aide flattened himself against the wall, head bowed respectfully. Yokuke grunted with satisfaction. His staff knew to keep out of his way when he was in a bad mood, but today it was particularly foul.

The world was a treacherous place. Getting to the top was easy. It was staying there that took uncommon skill. Yokuke's eyebrows lowered in a silent sneer. Great leaders always seemed to attract more than their fair share of attention from ordinary men. Far worse than the grovelling crumb-seekers were the grasping egotists who sought to usurp your success or use it to claw their own way up to the top. They were a constant danger to all successful men. The worst of them were the idealists, men whose irrational principles drove them to ridiculously foolhardy acts when faced with their own defeat. Men like the blonde foreigner downstairs.

Yokuke frowned and looked about the room. The hotel manager had refurnished it especially for him, and his staff had transported some of his own artefacts to decorate it. His gaze travelled across the priceless treasures that had taken a lifetime to gather; antique furniture, art, wall hangings and pottery from the Togukawa era, and his fine collection of Samurai armour and katana swords, each hand-crafted by a master armourer, and steeped in hundreds of years of history. Chief among his loves was his collection of netsukes – Japanese keepsakes – made from everything from wood to precious jade. His favourites though, were the scrimshaw and carved whalebone pieces. Yokuke stared at the glass display case, letting his eye wander over each intricately-carved masterpiece. Each had taken a master carver months or even years of painstaking work to create, the detail so fine one needed a magnifying glass to fully appreciate its craftsmanship. They were resplendent with tiny scenes from an age long past. Most spoke of life in a typical fishing village of the time; fishermen casting their flounder nets, hauling in their catch, spreading out the fish to dry in the sun, and mending their nets by the light of an oil lamp. His favourite netsuke though, was anything but typical. It was carved from a sperm whale jawbone, and the scene on it portrayed a fisherman standing tall in the bow of his skiff, harpoon held high, hunting the largest and most dangerous fish of them all. Yokuke knew such a whaling scene was uncommon, even for that time. Most Japanese villagers never ate whalemeat at all throughout history, and what little they did was far more likely to have come from an occasional beached carcass. That was why he felt such an affinity with this piece. He felt an unspoken bond with the hunter it represented, a leader among men, a rare individual who was prepared to risk his life hunting the most ferocious denizen of the sea – even while his contemporaries were content to drag flatfish from the mud. A faint trace of a smile cracked the corners of Yokuke's mouth.

His mood remained dark, however. Gazing at the treasures of antiquity would not lift his spirits today. His mind was dominated entirely by the problem at hand. The problem of the Kajiki.

Already there were whispers starting within the corridors of power. Prime Minister Takahashi was an incompetent fool easily swayed by a little subtle persuasion, but Yokuke could sense his hold over the man was slipping. This business with the Greenpeace degenerates was a trifling matter, but there were those in Parliament who would seek to use it to their advantage. Yokuke had many enemies, and already they were beginning to move against him. Rumours were spreading through the Diet. Rumours that he was old, senile, and no longer competent. He was used to those, but there were new rumours too, more insidious ones… suggestions that he was leading Japan on a collision course with the rest of the world, a course that would inevitably lead to defeat and shame for Japan.

Yokuke cursed under his breath.

Those are the words of traitorous cowards!

How could they bring themselves to bow to the West like that? It was pitiful to see the psyche of Japan had been so damaged by the defeats of the past that men found themselves unable to strive for victory, even now. It was a tragedy!

I may be an old man, but before I die I will see the honour of Japan restored!

First though, Yokuke knew he needed to consolidate his power.

What was needed was action. Swift and decisive action to remove the seed of doubt before it could fester, silencing those who would use it to bring him down.

Yokuke's mind turned back to the root of the problem. The Kajiki… and what to do with him.

So, my blonde barbarian, you fancy yourself as an idealist?

Yokuke bared his yellow teeth in a smile. There was only one way to deal with the madness of idealism. A slow smile spread across his face.

Let's see just how much you are prepared to sacrifice for your ideals!

Yokuke turned to his aide, hovering by the door. "Servant, has the Enforcer arrived?" It was a rhetorical question. "Bring him to me!" he commanded.

Yokuke settled down on his favourite chair, a carved Japanese maple throne dating back to the thirteenth century. He had had it re-upholstered himself. The pale white leather was soft and cool to the touch. He smiled, pleased with the job his leather-smith had done.

At least I didn't have to cut off his head for disappointing me…

Yokuke sat back, but he didn't have long to wait.

A minute later came a polite but confident knock at the door.

"Enter!" he commanded.

The door swung open and a man strode in.

He was tall for a Japanese, and his short black hair had a trace of arrogant spikiness to it. Beneath his pressed pants and business shirt bulged the muscled physique of a fighter, barely concealed by the thin cotton. Yokuke smiled, pleased by his well-dressed appearance – the epitome of refined strength – unlike some of the man's more uncouth contemporaries.

The Enforcer's eyes were hidden behind the lenses of a pair of mirrored sunglasses, adding to his mysterious aura.

He stopped in the centre of the room and bowed deeply from the waist. He straightened up and, as a mark of respect, removed his sunglasses and tucked them into the pocket of his business shirt. His eyes, now revealed, were black, empty pits. The eyes of a killer. Yokuke met his cold gaze without flinching, searching for any challenge hidden there. There was none.

"Greetings, Kobushi-san," he said.

Kobushi lowered his head in reply, without answering. He stood silently, waiting.

With his glasses off, a healed scar was clearly visible on his temple, just above his left eye. The sharp white line – a sword cut – was stark against his coffee-coloured skin, and served to enhance the air of danger that swirled about him.

Yokuke didn't know the man's real name, nor did he need to. Kobushi was the term for a veteran warrior, a loyal vassal from the feudal era and the time of the Samurai. This was the name Kobushi had chosen for himself, and in him Yokuke was pleased to observe that traditional values were not entirely dead in modern Japan. In the old days, swearing an oath of loyalty to your master was binding on your life.

"I thank you for responding so quickly to my summons," Yokuke continued, knowing full well the Enforcer would have had to drop everything and hurry on the first bullet train from Tokyo to be standing before him so soon after being sent for.

Kobushi inclined his head in acknowledgement, but said nothing.

Yokuke's gaze swept over the man standing before him. Above the crisp white business shirt and the necktie knotted at his throat, Yokuke could see an edge of dark ink lining the Enforcer's skin. There was another glimpse at his wrists, just protruding from the starched white cuffs of his shirt. They were innocuous details, and meaningless to the ignorant. But Yokuke knew they marked the edges of a full-body dragon tattoo, a hallmark of the secret society of the Yakuza.

Although derided by the police as vicious gangsters, the Yakuza were about much more than just organised crime – although they definitely prided themselves on their ruthlessness.

Yokuke smiled to himself. His business connections were based on expedience, not morality, and he found the Yakuza society adept at getting things done. Success was a function of utilising whatever assets were available to you. He nodded to his Enforcer.

"I have a job for you to do."

Kobushi said nothing, merely waiting for his orders.

Yokuke smiled, satisfied. Despite his Yakuza background, Kobushi answered to no one but him now. His gaze moved to the Enforcer's left hand. The pinky finger was missing, amputated at the first knuckle. Yokuke did not find that odd, however, or surprising. In fact, the finger was in his private chambers, preserved in a jar as a reminder of the day Kobushi become his vassal. In the Yakuza tradition, Kobushi had severed the finger himself and presented it to his master as a mark of his loyalty.

Yokuke beckoned his man closer. "Approach!"

The Enforcer lowered his gaze respectfully and stepped forward.

Yokuke reached in his jacket and handed him a Polaroid photograph. "See this man? I want you to take care of him."

Kobushi bowed and reached out to take it.

Yokuke narrowed his eyes at the picture before parting with it. "He has caused me no end of problems," he muttered, a frown creasing his face. "You will see to it that this thorn in my side plagues me no longer. And before he dies I want him to know my wrath. He will know his elimination is by my order. Do you understand?"

Kobushi uttered his first words of the meeting. "Hai, Oyaban! – Yes, Master!"

"Do not fail me," Yokuke warned, waving him away.

Kobushi bowed deeply, then straightened and strode towards the door, replacing his shades as he went.

Yokuke settled back into his chair, conscious of the softness of the white leather. The leather-worker had done a good job, it was true, but it was the quality of the leather that was second-to-none.

He smiled.

He had acquired it himself during his younger days. The hide had been skinned from the aborted foetus of a Blue whale calf – ripped from its mother's womb as she was butchered alive on the flensing deck of his flagship.

Yokuke considered the symbolism of it; the tiny calf had been humbled before getting a chance to grow into a huge and dangerous brute, before even getting a chance to take its first breath. What a beautiful metaphor for man's civilising effect on the raw vulgarity of nature – and a model for how all problems in life should be dealt with!

Yokuke smiled.

His throne was upholstered with the progeny of one of the rarest – and therefore most expensive – animals in the world

How befitting for a man of my stature!

***

The next day, Richard sat bleary-eyed in the debating chamber while the Chairman opened the day's proceedings. He was still groggy having overslept that morning, his internal clock seemingly confused by sleeping in port without the usual motion of the ship to constantly shake him awake. That and lying awake half the night worrying before he'd finally drifted off.

Richard wasn't good at dealing with stress, and the events of the last few days alone were enough to cause a new ulcer.

As the meeting came to order, the Chairman turned straight to the Japanese Commissioner, gesturing for him to take the floor. Richard felt his bowels clench. This had all the hallmarks of a setup, and Mr Fish looked seriously pissed-off. He sprang to his feet, launching into an angry torrent of

Japanese. The interpreter was slow to catch up, but Richard didn't need to wait for a translation to understand the point. Amimoto's vehement expression and stabbing finger in their direction made it quite clear the tirade was directed at them. Richard swallowed and put on his headphones.

"…and I reiterate that our Scientific Whaling program is perfectly legal under the charter of the IWC. Furthermore, Japan is disgusted by these continued attempts to disrupt our programme of legitimate research. Such behaviour is petty and reprehensible in the extreme!"

Amimoto glared at the Team, and Richard was suddenly filled with trepidation. He gulped, sensing the Japanese Commissioner was about to up the stakes. Who knew what form his new attack would take? All Richard knew was it would be swift and deadly. With a sense of fatalism he sat there, like a possum caught in headlights, waiting for the storm to hit.

"It is my sad duty to inform this conference that fraud and deceitfulness lurks in its midst. There is a faction within this room guilty of serious crimes! While they purport to act within the framework of international law and pretend to seek peaceful solutions within the IWC, in reality their behaviour outside this meeting is far from reasonable, or even legal! Rather, they use violence, piracy and vandalism to further their twisted goals!"

Mr Fish rounded on the Team. "There is the guilty party!" he announced, stabbing a bony finger towards Cal. "I speak not only of his perpetual attempts to mislead and waylay the democratic proceedings of this meeting, but also of direct acts of piracy against innocent fishing vessels!"

There were gasps from the delegates, and Cal swore under his breath, knowing he was unable to defend himself under the rules of the conference. "Here we go. The bastard's playing for keeps now!" he muttered.

Amimoto forged ahead, silencing the buzz of speculation that suddenly gripped the conference hall. "This protestor and his accomplices harass innocent fishing vessels and crew with their Zodiac-type speedboats, carrying out dangerous obstruction stunts as they speed around. And as if this continual hot-rodding is not enough, they openly flout the rules of the sea – rules put in place to ensure the safety of all mariners – committing acts of dangerous stupidity where no authorities are around to witness."

Richard watched the delegates. Everyone avoided Mr Fish's gaze as he lectured them – even those who ought to disagree. It was as though he was able to brow-beat the entire room into supporting him – or at least failing to voice their opposition – by sheer force of personality alone.

"These reckless and foolhardy actions were recently the cause of a collision at sea. A collision that involved significant damage to a vessel belonging to the Taiyoku Misui Fisheries Company and injury to several of her crew," he announced, his voice grave.

"What happened?" Cal muttered under his breath. "Did they bruise their egos?"

Richard's mouth hung open, shocked at the injustice of what he'd just heard. "But they ran us over!" he managed to blurt out.

Amimoto glared back at them, but didn't stop. "Such acts of piracy and wanton criminal behaviour endanger the lives of fishermen – men with families! Attacks like this wreak havoc on the innocent crew who fall victim to them. This behaviour is nothing short of terrorism! Such dangerous and reprehensible actions should be condemned in the strongest terms!"

The delegates murmured their agreement, either scandalised by the allegations, or unwilling to speak out against Mr Fish.

All except Victor Admirante. "What a load of rubbish!" the Commissioner for the Seychelles called out. "This is nothing compared to the crimes Japan perpetrates every day in the name of scientific research!"

Amimoto shouted him down, eyes blazing. "This conference is equally guilty of a crime by its inaction!" he warned the room. "The IWC must not shelter the perpetrators of this terrorist attack. While they hide behind the protection of this meeting their crimes go unpunished, and your commitment to the law is called into question! I urge you to censure them in the strongest terms! Deny them the protection of this organisation, so they can be turned over to the Japanese police to face trial. Justice must be done upon them!"

"Hear, hear!" the Norwegian Commissioner applauded. There were calls of assent from around the room.

Amimoto smiled like a fox. "I move that the delegation representing Greenpeace be expelled from this conference, along with any others who support terrorism."

"Wait!" Cal jumped to his feet. "This is outrageous. I must respond to these lies."

"I object!" Mr Fish thundered. "This member has no speaking rights at this conference!"

The Chairman looked flustered.

Cal was not to be silenced that easily however. "According to the rules of this delegation, I formally request a right of reply," he insisted.

The Chairman hesitated. "On what grounds?"

"This man has levelled some very serious allegation against myself and my colleagues," Cal answered. "I respectfully ask this meeting to allow me the chance to reply to them."

"Poppycock!" Amimoto's voice was hoarse with rage. He glared at the Chairman. "This conference must not allow itself to be hijacked by extremists!" His gaze was sharp enough to skewer the unfortunate man.

The Chairman swallowed and lowered his head, as though blinded by Amimoto's threatening stare. He looked like a man on trial, and Richard noticed beads of perspiration standing out on his forehead. Under such intense scrutiny that was hardly surprising though. The last place in the world Richard would have wanted to be right now was in his shoes. The Chairman fumbled a handkerchief from his pocket and dapped at his brow. "I must say, this whole business is highly irregular…" he mumbled.

In response, Cal directed the force of his personality onto the Chairman too. "You know the charter permits me to defend myself against this attack," he replied, careful to keep his voice level. "I am merely asking for my rights to be respected."

The Chairman looked down, avoiding both of them. He shook his head, his jowls flapping nervously. "I must allow it," he said finally. "The rules permit a member to respond to allegations of impropriety, and that must outweigh his lack of speaking privileges." He bowed his head guiltily towards Amimoto, as though begging forgiveness.

The Japanese Commissioner hissed angrily and took his seat. His face was the colour of red-hot lava.

Cal rose in stature as he stepped up to the challenge. His broad shoulders were set with confidence, and his voice was strong and clear as he began to speak. Richard glanced to the side at Vicki and Aurelia and smiled happily, sharing the excited tension he saw on their faces.

Cal's wit flashed like a rapier as he moved smoothly onto the attack, the very essence of a slick trial lawyer dazzling a jury. "The only harassment I know of was carried out by the Taiyoku Misui Fisheries Company. You speak of harassment, but what I know is this: your fleet muscled in on a *legitimate* scientific research program, ruining years of data as well as killing the individual under study – a protected Blue whale."

A buzz of whispered conversation swept through the room. Everyone understood the gravity of the accusation – hunting a protected species was outlawed by the Commission.

Mr Fish exploded like an erupting volcano. "That's a lie! A bare-faced lie! You have no proof my men took a protected species – hearsay is not permitted as evidence," he reminded the conference, before glaring at Cal again. "You were deliberately harassing my crew by hot-rodding around, and you cut right across the bows of my ship – according to the UN Law of the Sea that's a critical navigation failure!"

Cal regarded him with a thin smile. "Your ship was stationary at the time, and my inflatable was on the other side of a whale. Your captain deliberately accelerated and ran us down, taking no steps to avoid the collision, and making no attempt to assist the survivors in the water."

The delegates gasped as one, and urgent whispers flew between them. The debate had just reached a whole new intensity, and no one doubted the potential for these new allegations to result in serious criminal charges.

Amimoto's colour rose. "Lies!" he spluttered, glancing around him. For the briefest moment he looked uncertain, desperate to retain the approval of the conference. Then a thought seemed to occur to him and a sly smirk spread across his face. "So you were there!" he announced triumphantly. "You personally admit to this illegal and immoral harassment of my fleet!" He turned to the conference, appealing to them. "You see? These activists care not for laws when there is no one about to observe them! And this one has just admitted responsibility for his crimes! He drove much too close for my captain to respond in time to take evasive action. He impeded the free passage of a Japanese-flagged vessel, and deliberately obstructed its lawful right to fish in international waters – rights guaranteed under the Law of the Sea!"

"Yes, I was there!" Cal replied confidently. "I was there and I witnessed your Captain board my ship – an act of piracy under those same laws!"

"Lies!" Amimoto challenged him.

Cal smiled again. "Perhaps I should play the videotape of the incident before this conference?" he enquired.

Amimoto back-pedalled, his bony fists clenched white with anger. "That won't be necessary," he replied stiffly, almost conceding the point. "This conference has no need to see any misrepresentation you've managed to concoct!" Abruptly, he launched into a desperate counter-attack. "Regardless, my captain was entitled to board you on account of your illegal interference with our fishing and free passage. Under the UN Law of the Sea our rights are guaranteed, and by violating them you are subject to arrest."

Cal's smile didn't waver. "Only a flagged warship or other government vessel may effect an arrest outside its own territorial waters," he replied confidently, as if quoting straight from a legal textbook. "And only once a prior warrant has been issued against that vessel or its captain." He raised a sarcastic eyebrow at Amimoto. "And since you had neither then your captain's actions constitute an act of deliberate piracy."

Victor Admirante's booming laugh filled the hall, and Amimoto reddened with outrage, first at being outmanoeuvred and secondly at being publicly ridiculed.

Cal nodded his thanks for the Seychelles Commissioner's support. "I think we've listened to enough of the Japanese Commissioner's petty allegations today," he said, "As all here can see they are entirely baseless – If anyone should be censured today it ought to be the Japanese!"

Before Amimoto could respond, Cal turned to the Chairman. "I formally request that the motion to suspend me from this meeting be dropped."

Despite seeming reluctant, the Chairman nodded. "Very well then, the matter will lapse for lack of proven evidence. Do we have any other business for the day…?"

"This man is a criminal!" Amimoto shouted as Cal took his seat again. "He assaulted my crew members! One of them was beaten unconscious by him! This thug must not escape justice!"

Cal smiled back, knowing the Japanese Commissioner was too late with his protest.

Richard looked at his brother with a mixture of pride and surprise. He knew Cal had begun his career as a lawyer, but this was the first time he'd seen him so utterly convincing. Richard smiled, suspecting that passion for the cause was the real reason behind Cal's success today.

"Good job," Richard enthused. "That was awesome!"

Cal screwed up his face though. "A small victory, and temporary. This isn't over and both sides know it." He sighed. "It worked for now but I suspect I've only put ideas into his head. Next time we head south, Amimoto will be sure to arrange for his boats to be deputised and somehow wrangle a warrant for his captain to arrest us. It'll be all on then!"

That night Richard was troubled as they sat around the mess table in the corner of the Gwendolyn's saloon. Cal ate silently, as though deep in thought, and Richard found himself unable to concentrate on his food. He pushed the lentils around his plate, oblivious to the stern look from Aurelia who was in charge of the night's menu.

Richard wasn't even dazzled by Summer, wearing a tight turtle-necked sweater that accentuated her chest. He realised the day's proceedings hadn't gone well, even though Cal managed to come out on top in the debates triggered by Mr Fish. The accusations were becoming more serious, and more personal. Richard could see Amimoto was working up to a grand finale, and without doubt the Japanese Commissioner intended to destroy any opposition before the big Moratorium vote. Richard knew his worries were real. Despite Cal's debating skill, it was sadly true that dirty politics were the most successful. The more mud your opposition threw at you, the more chance some of it would stick – at least in the eyes of the voters. And since Amimoto was certainly not about to give up and go home, that only meant his attacks would intensify.

What's the crafty so-and-so going to hit us with next time?

Richard glanced across the table, but Cal didn't look up. His brother's brooding only confirmed his thoughts were equally pessimistic.

Heath, seated next to him, scowled and forked his meal viciously. He always seemed in a bad mood lately. The vibe was catching though, and soon silence descended over the table.

Cal suddenly spoke up, loud enough to make Richard jump. "We have to do something! The Moratorium vote is coming up tomorrow, and we can't afford to lose. Mr Fish is going to throw everything he has at us between now and then." He frowned. "We need to be pro-active. We need a plan…"

"Publicity!" Aurelia announced. "That's what'll win this. We need to get the world's attention." Her eyes sparkled, as if she was back in her element, and enjoying it immensely. "A publicity stunt should do it. Something big, something that'll make the citizens of the world sit up and take notice!" She smiled. "We'll hold a protest rally, right on the steps of the Convention Centre where the international media can't possibly miss it."

Cal sighed, and Richard thought he detected a note of exasperation. "That's all very well," his brother muttered, "But it isn't the media who are voting tomorrow, or even the citizens of the world. We need something to convince the delegates."

Vicki spoke up. "What about your findings?"

Cal hesitated. "I've been waiting for the ideal moment to maximise their effect, but I guess we're out of time." He lowered his head, seeming to sag momentarily. "I'm not sure it'll be enough though. There are a lot of non-scientific delegates to try and convince using scientific evidence."

"Give yourself some credit!" Vicki admonished him. "You've got seven years of painstaking research there, and your findings are sound. Why would the conference not be convinced?"

Cal shrugged. "People believe what they want to believe. Personal priorities can often outweigh common sense, even when the outcomes are obvious." He stared at the ceiling. "It's too easy for politicians to dismiss or ignore science. I just wish we had something concrete. Something dramatic, and absolutely indisputable."

"What about the videotape?" Richard ventured. "Can we prove the Japanese are hunting protected species?"

All eyes turned towards him, and he looked down at the table, embarrassed.

Richard could feel his brother's eyes still boring through him. "That's a good idea," Cal said, excitement brimming over in his voice. Richard smiled shyly, the praise warming his heart.

Cal rubbed his chin. "Unfortunately the tape isn't clear enough though. We can't prove beyond doubt they killed a Blue."

"What about piracy?" the Skipper growled. "That yellow-bellied captain tried to send y'all to Davy Jones'."

Cal shook his head. "Nah, we covered all that finger-pointing today. It's outside the conference's jurisdiction anyway."

Vicki had been staring at Richard since he spoke, as though transfixed by what he'd said. "Maybe there is a way we can prove what species they killed," she murmured. "We have plenty of equipment right here on the ship."

Cal whipped his head around to look at her, a slow smile spreading over his face. "Of course!" he laughed. "Genetics!"

She nodded. "But how?"

"We could try to lift some blood or tissue samples off one of the ships…" Cal said, thinking aloud.

Vicki pulled a face. "I dunno. The whalers are absolute clean-freaks with their detergent. Any DNA left behind is likely to be pretty degraded. Besides, I don't think they'll let us just wander onto their ship and start snooping around."

"Ayuh," Duke nodded. "That's a fact. Ah've been keepin' an eye on things across the harbour. Their security is tighter'n a virgin."

Cal coughed, partly to interrupt, and partly to cover his laugh.

The Skipper reddened, realising what he'd said. "Sorry Miss," he muttered awkwardly, scratching the back of his neck with embarrassment.

Vicki smiled, enjoying the joke, but neither Summer nor Aurelia looked amused.

Cal smacked his forehead with his palm. "Of course, why didn't I think of it before?" He turned to Vicki, a triumphant grin plastered across his face. "We don't need to creep around to collect evidence, not when it's lying out on public display!"

She smiled, finishing his thought. "The fish markets!"

"The Tsukiji Fish Market in Tokyo is the largest in the world," Cal said thoughtfully. "2,700 tonnes of seafood change hands every day. If it came from the sea you can find it there."

"It's also three hours away by train."

Cal nodded. "The second biggest is the Karato Market in Shimonoseki though, and it's not a mile from where we're sitting. What better place to find whalemeat than in the largest whaling port in the world?"

"Let's do it!" Vicki replied.

"I still think a public protest is the way to go," Aurelia sniffed haughtily.

Cal didn't seem to hear her. "It's settled then. There's only an hour of daylight left, no way we can be back before dark. First thing in the morning will be better." He looked around the expectant faces assembled before him. "A small group will attract less attention," he murmured to himself, deliberating. "Okay, Vicki and Richard, you're with me. The rest of you'll stay here and go to the conference as normal."

Richard felt the familiar fear like a stone in the pit of his stomach. It was dangerous out there – even Cal admitted that. They had to do something though. The consequences of inaction were too dire. For once in his life,

Richard knew he couldn't take the easy way out. He had to do this. No, he *wanted* to do this.

He took a deep breath. "O-k-kay. I'm in."

Inside, he tried to justify the decision to himself. *It's not like we're breaking any laws. We're just going to buy some meat from the market. Besides, Cal will be there if anything goes wrong…*

Cal grinned and clapped him on the back. "Good man!"

Summer hesitated a moment, then stood up. "I'm coming too," she announced, hands planted on her hips.

Cal turned to look at her, a strange, almost quizzical expression on his face. "No, it's too dangerous. Plus we'll need a small group to avoid suspicion."

She faltered as his gaze met hers, blinking rapidly, then averted her eyes. "You promised I could sit in," she finished lamely, addressing the floor.

"No, I said you could sit in on the conference… for the professional experience. This is different."

"But-"

"No buts," Cal said sternly. "Just the three of us. The decision is made." His expression showed he found Summer's insistence a little odd.

She turned and marched out of the room, tossing her hair angrily as she went.

Cal watched her go, the same contemplative expression back on his face.

As Summer passed him, Richard tried to catch her eye. Their eyes met for a moment, but she pulled away immediately. She actually looked relieved, he realised, and he thought he also saw a flash of something else. Guilt maybe? He blinked, sure he must have been mistaken.

Duke was shaking his head, muttering his displeasure.

Cal cocked a quizzical eyebrow at him.

"What if y'all need a hand out there?" the Skipper countered.

Cal shook his head. "Someone needs to watch the Old Girl," he said, patting the bulkhead nearest him. "Besides, if anyone comes looking for trouble they're more likely to start here."

Duke nodded, considering the wisdom of that. "Well, I'll damn-well be waiting for 'em then!" he growled. "No dirty rice-eater is gonna set foot on my boat, and that's a promise!" Richard noticed his brother frown briefly at the xenophobic outburst, but Cal let it pass.

Richard was still thinking about it though, as he stepped outside a few minutes later to clear his head. The next morning's plan was a terrifying proposition. He glanced across the harbour at the whaling fleet, tied up against the far wharf. He stared towards the huge bulk of the Nippon-Maru, the sickly-yellow colour of the superstructure just visible in the last of the light. Its mast lights twinkled on the water, the calm serenity of the scene belying the ships' evil purpose.

It was easy to feel anger towards Mr Fish, and Richard knew the Skipper had good reason for his own animosity, but was it the answer? Regardless, after witnessing the Japanese Commissioner's dirty politics every day it was getting harder to remind himself that not all Japanese were bad people.

That was the least of his worries right now though, when the prospect of mortal danger loomed in the future again. Richard watched as the shadows slowly hid the distant whaling ships. He knew there was no way he was going to get to sleep tonight. He sat down with his back to the mast, staring out over the bay. He zipped up his jacket against the chill of the autumn evening, watching the stars wheel overhead as he settled in for the long wait until morning.

It seemed like only a few minutes later when Cal shook his shoulder gently. "Come on, Bro. It's time."

Richard sat up sleepily. It was still dark, but an air of excitement hung in the cool pre-dawn air.

***

Dennis Cruikshank lowered the binoculars and twirled his moustache thoughtfully.

Now where the hell are those punks off to at this time of the morning?

True, there could be a perfectly reasonable explanation for taking an early-morning stroll, but in Cruikshank's line of work he had learned never to assume anything – and the hour was so early he could practically taste the toothpaste from the night before. He nodded to himself, pleased with his decision to pull an all-nighter to keep these troublemakers under surveillance. Years of experience had taught him if something smelled even vaguely fishy, there was a good chance that somewhere underneath it all there was a fish!

The suspects hurried off through the darkened streets, collars turned up to hide their faces. Cruikshank's eyes glazed with suspicion and he raised the binoculars again to follow them.

His hotel room was on the sixth floor; the elevation giving him a good view of the waterfront and the bay beyond. But he couldn't see through buildings, and it wasn't long before the targets disappeared from view amongst the rabbit warren of warehouses that was the waterfront district.

Cruikshank muttered an oath and panned the binoculars back to the deck of the old trawler. A light burned in the saloon, but there was no sign of activity. He swore again, torn. Reluctantly, he conceded that it was too late to follow the three. They would be miles away by the time he could get downtown. As long as he was manning this stakeout alone, he had to play the law of averages and keep watching the ship. He knew that could mean wasting this opportunity though, and the urge to find out what the shore party was up to burned in him.

Cruikshank's beetle-brows lowered onto his misshapen nose as he frowned.

He didn't trust these activists. They claimed to be representing Greenpeace, but there was something about their manner that didn't ring true. Greenpeace was supposed to be into peaceful non-violent resistance, but this lot had a confrontational air about them – especially that blonde guy who was their main spokesman.

If they're Greenpeace, I'm Mickey-Goddamn-Mouse!

Cruikshank pursed his lips. That blonde guy was definitely one to keep an eye on. A cop learned to trust his intuition, and his had been proven correct at the conference yesterday – he'd found it difficult to maintain his detached disinterest when the accusations began to fly. His heart quickened when he learned of the group's protest at sea, confirming all his suspicions! It was just a short step from protesting to taking it too far, and from the sounds of it there had already been antagonism and incidents of anger-fuelled violence against the Japanese Fleet. From a position like that it was easy for a situation to degenerate further into retaliation and escalation in the future, just like with gang warfare, and directly or indirectly those little stunts could affect US interests. Like a bunch of gang-bangers in a turf war, this group of activists was on the slippery slope to premeditated terrorism. He would bet his career on it.

His frown deepened as he debated what to do about it. These types of militants were often isolated into small cells where they would feed off each other's collective craziness. That made them extremely vulnerable to the group hysteria that characterised gang-related violence, but the close-knit nature of such groups also made it very difficult to expose them. He snorted. For one man to investigate them, the task was next to impossible.

Cruikshank ran a hand over the shaved stubble on his head. Frustration was not an emotion he handled well. He cursed again. First thing in the morning he would send a request to his supervisor, he decided. He knew what the old fart would say though, and his anger flared in anticipation. The one thing more infuriating than having to work along-side spooks was having to report to one. His superior was so wrapped up in his secret-squirrel bullshit that he wouldn't recognise good policing if it bit him on the ass! Cruikshank frowned. How could he justify his request? He had a hunch, that was all. How did you explain you were certain because you had a feeling in your gut? Only a cop would understand, and his supervisor wasn't shy about admitting his contempt for cops. Cruikshank ground his teeth. Understand or not, he would make the bastard listen. There was something fishy going on here, he was sure of it. God only knew what these punks were up to this very moment, but Cruikshank knew damn-well he wouldn't give up until he found out what. And that meant getting the resources to investigate them properly.

I need an undercover agent to get inside their little party!

Chapter 11

Richard kept his hands shoved in his pockets as they walked. The sun wasn't up yet, and the damp mist hanging over the harbour was sharp with an autumn chill. Maybe that was the reason the city seemed cold and unwelcoming, but he still couldn't shake the troubled feeling that hung over him. Despite the presence of the fishing industry in Shimonoseki, or maybe because of it, the waterfront area wasn't exactly the nicest part of town. Fishermen and dock-workers didn't care much for frivolities like urban maintenance or street-sweeping. The atmosphere of the fancy hotel district further up the hill definitely didn't extend this far downtown. Richard peered at the rundown old buildings, with their dark windows watching back from the shadows like eyes. He shivered and hurried to catch up to the others.

Vicki's dark ponytail danced as she turned back to smile encouragement at him. "Nice morning for a walk," she said cheerily, as if sensing his mood.

He stared at her, then noticed the wary flicker of her eyes as she glanced up the street. It was a relief to realise she was on edge too, however hard she tried to conceal it. The reality was simple; Hogei Gyofuku and his pack of thugs could be waiting for them around any of the corners they passed.

"Why do you do this?" Richard blurted out. "Why risk all this danger and discomfort when you could have a nice safe life behind a desk somewhere like everyone else?"

Vicki grinned in reply. "Why not do it? It keeps you on your toes!" Richard didn't smile back though, and a moment later hers faded. She sighed, realising he was serious. "Too many people have taken the Earth for granted for too long, and it's suffering for it. I'm not one of those weird 'spiritual types' who wants to worship nature, but as a scientist I can see a job that needs doing." She shrugged. "Most people don't even see there's a problem, so someone needs to find out how things work, to show people why they need to change their ways, before it's too late." She looked down at her feet, a little embarrassed. "I'm just happy to play my part. There's only one world, and I'd rather spend my life being a positive force on it, not a negative one."

They walked on in silence for a while. Shimonoseki was waking up and all around them locals hurried by on their way to work, heads down, and collars turned up against the cold. As they passed a street vendor's stall, the old proprietor bowed from behind rows of newspapers and cigarettes. Cal nodded politely back, but as soon as they were out of earshot he exclaimed, "This is stupid!" He gestured angrily at the people around them. "Look at these people. Hardly any of them back whaling, yet it's done in their name. The Japanese Government would have you believe its citizens are entirely supportive of whaling, but the truth is far from it. A recent poll in Japan revealed nearly eighty percent *didn't* support whaling, and fewer than one percent regularly eat whalemeat. In fact, hardly anyone under 50 has ever eaten it! That's despite Amimoto's direct attempts to get a new generation hooked on the taste by providing free whalemeat burgers for school lunches, trying to force children to eat it if he can't entice them." He pursed his lips. "At the moment Amimoto doesn't have enough consumers for his product. He deliberately limits the amount of whalemeat going to the restaurants to keep the price high, while he works feverishly to encourage demand. Supplying too much meat to restaurants while demand is low would drive the price down. But do you know what he does with all that excess meat he withholds in the meantime? He sends it to petfood and fertiliser factories! His plan is to market whalemeat as an expensive gourmet delicacy, so wasting meat is better than flooding the market right now!"

Cal shook his head angrily. "All of the claims about cultural practices are a giant smokescreen. This whole thing is just a cynical ploy by Amimoto to line his own pockets!"

He sighed grudgingly. "It's hard to remember sometimes, but the real enemy is not Japan, the Japanese people, or even the whalers themselves. The real enemy is the rapacious whaling policy clung to by a corrupt government."

He kicked a pebble, his annoyance still plain. "Everyone has a part to play though. If the Japanese people put enough pressure on their leaders, change would come quickly enough..."

Richard thought about that. "So why don't they? Surely they care what's going on?"

Cal shrugged. "Another survey back in the eighties showed over three quarters of Japanese thought their country should accept the IWC's Moratorium and give up whaling then. Only seventeen per cent thought they should continue." He scuffed his foot again, taking out his irritation on the stone. "Most Japanese kept their opinions to themselves though, so the Government saw no need to change. These days the voices are even less – on both sides of the debate. By far the greatest numbers of Japanese now are uninformed. They simply have no idea what's going on, or they don't care, leaving Amimoto's misinformation to speak for an entire country."

Richard shook his head, disillusioned and perhaps a little saddened. "Surely the people here couldn't help noticing what's going on?"

Cal's answering shrug was a little more pragmatic. "Well, compare it to the average person on the street back home. Most of them don't know what's going on either. Some of them are ignorant, some are selfish, but most are simply too preoccupied to notice. Their lives are so filled with 'busy details' they don't have time to worry about anything that doesn't affect them directly."

He looked down at the ground. "Even those few people who do care don't usually care enough to do something about it."

Vicki nodded. "Ain't that the truth!"

They walked on in silence for a moment before Richard spoke up. "I care," he said quietly.

Vicki, walking next to him, took his arm and patted it. "And you've earned the respect of your peers for it." Her cheeks dimpled as she smiled at him. "A society grows great when old men plant trees under whose shade they know they will never sit."

Richard blinked as the significance of her words sank in. "Wow, that's profound."

She smiled shyly, still holding onto his arm. "It's an ancient Greek proverb. I memorised it when I was eight years old. My Father wrote it out for me…"

"He must be very proud of you."

She looked away suddenly, but Richard noticed her eyes beginning to mist up. "He died when I was ten," she whispered.

"Oh. I-I'm sorry."

She seemed to droop as she shook her head. "It's ok," she said. A few paces later she spoke again, her voice wistful. "His last words to me were; 'I know you'll make me proud.'" She choked, as if stifling a sob.

"Oh hey, I'm s-sorry," Richard stammered guiltily. He'd only been trying to pay her a compliment, but he realised – too late – that he'd touched on a delicate nerve instead. "I'm sure he is proud of you." He blurted, but realising as soon as he said it that was only likely to make things worse. "I mean, uh, I didn't mean to upset you."

"No, I'm sorry," she muttered, managing a smile. She rubbed her eyes forcefully. "Look at me, crying like a silly girl!"

"It's ok," Richard replied, still startled to see this vulnerable side to her. "Everyone hits a little bump in the road now and then. That's what friends are for."

She smiled gratefully and squeezed his arm.

Richard thought he detected a faint smile on his brother's face, but then Cal quickened his stride until he was walking a few steps ahead, as if to give them some space.

As they walked on, Richard's mind raced. It was out of the question that a confident Action-Girl like Vicki fancied him, and regardless, he wouldn't dream of taking advantage of a woman's distress. But as a friend in need, he was happy to offer her whatever encouragement she needed.

They headed around the bay, past scores of warehouses and fishing boats, towards the colossal bulk of the Nippon-Maru moored in the distance. As they approached, it seemed to Richard that the huge ship swelled in size until it towered overhead, dominating the entire bay. Behind where the whaling fleet lay tied up was a massive factory complex, its tall chimneys belching smoke into the dark dawn sky; a gigantic monument to the industrial-scale whale slaughter. Its bright façade was in stark contrast to the dreary and rundown look of the rest of the waterfront area. The sign over the main building – in Japanese and English – proclaimed it was the shore-based processing plant of the Taiyoku

Misui Fisheries Company. The huge corrugated-steel warehouses alongside it took up two entire blocks. Behind that were the foundations of a half-completed extension to the factory, with scaffolding, blank prefabricated concrete walls, and rows of bare reinforcing-steel rods sticking up like a dead forest.

"Looks like business is good," Vicki commented, eyeing the building site.

Cal nodded. "That's a new whalemeat processing facility." He gazed at the huge expanse of concrete and steel, as though floored by its size. "A construction project this big doesn't come cheap. How much more output will they need just to recoup that investment?" He muttered something under his breath, then added, "I'd say Amimoto plans to kill a lot more whales, regardless of this afternoon's vote."

They carried on, turning up a narrow side street that led away from the harbour. Abruptly, the alley opened out into a huge courtyard behind the factory.

Richard stopped as though he'd run into a wall.

"The Karato Fish Market," Cal announced, with an expansive sweep of his hand.

Richard stared. The first thing that struck him was the sheer scale of the scene, and close behind that was the overwhelming odour of fish. Even at this hour the market bustled with activity. The huge courtyard was packed full of stalls and kiosks, their multicoloured canvas awnings running hundreds of metres in both directions. All of them had huge bins of ice, and all were packed full of fish.

There were fish everywhere. Rows and rows of them. Big ones, small ones, all shapes and colours. From the spot where he stood, Richard could see everything from eels to octopi, flatfish to crabs, not to mention oysters, clams, mussels and dozens of other kinds of fish and shellfish.

"Fish-mongers and restaurants from all over Japan come here to source their fish," Cal explained. "With the fishing port and the Taiyoku Misui Fisheries Company factory based right here, it's the busiest seafood market in the country, even if it's not quite the largest."

Richard looked around, at a loss for words. It seemed like there must be a tray of just about everything in the sea. There were even dead seahorses, and some funny-looking things like fat brown slugs.

"Holothurians," Vicki explained, seeing the direction of his gaze. "Sea-slugs. They're actually related to starfish. An acquired taste, apparently…"

Richard wrinkled his nose. "They eat those things? Ew."

He was forced to jump back out of the way as a man pushing a barrow hurried by. The tails and gaping mouths of half a dozen baby sharks hung over the sides. Richard stared after them as they disappeared into the bustling market. "Lucky this place is open already at this hour," he said.

Cal looked around. "I don't think they ever close."

Another fisherman followed the first, struggling with a heavy cart. On it was a single huge fish, mouth agape as if still gasping for breath. From its pointed nose to the tip of its y-shaped tail it was longer than a man, and rounded like a giant torpedo. Richard stared as it passed. Its fins looked sharp as knives and it had two rows of triangular-shaped spines leading down to its forked tail – shimmering like the scales of a dragon. Its silvery belly darkened to a deep navy blue on top, sparkling with an iridescent sheen. "It's beautiful," he murmured.

"Bluefin tuna," Vicki said. "They spend their whole life hunting in the open ocean, up to a kilometre deep."

"That's a tuna?" Richard was momentarily stunned. "It's so big…"

Cal nodded. "That one probably weighs 250 kilos. Doesn't seem the same when you only see it shredded up in a little can, right?"

Richard nodded, at a loss for words.

Cal sounded sad. "Tuna meat is considered a delicacy here, served as sashimi steaks. A prime specimen could fetch $50,000 each. Not much incentive to leave any swimming around in the ocean is it?"

They went on, heading deeper into the market.

Cal seemed to know what he was doing. He strode confidently past the stalls, scanning the rows of fish with a critical eye, pausing sometimes for a closer inspection. The whole fish were easy to identify, so he focused on the fillets and unidentifiable pieces. He questioned the stall-holders, firing questions at them in their own language. Some joked with him, others bowed apologetically, still others regarded him with suspicion. But always their response was the same; a shake of the head and an "Iye, Gai-jin-san."

Each time Cal nodded his thanks and led the way deeper into the market.

"Maybe it's the wrong time of year?" Vicki offered. "The Whaling Fleet don't normally get back from the Southern Ocean until March."

Cal shook his head. "They were down there hunting whales until we forced them back to port. If those whales they killed are anywhere, they'll be here…"

Gradually, they worked their way down to the end of another row and rounded the corner. Suddenly they came upon a large tent, set slightly apart from the other stalls. On the side was an image of a smiling cartoon cetacean, the logo of the Taiyoku Misui Fisheries Company's Pelagic Whaling Fleet.

"Bingo!" Cal said, but his expression was anything but cheerful. He stepped forward towards the doorway, but his way was immediately blocked by a burly fisherman in a fish-stained apron. Richard had never seen the man before, and he didn't show any sign of recognising Cal, but he scowled suspiciously all the same.

Cal chattered away amiably in Japanese, indicating that he would like to come in.

The fisherman scratched his stubbled chin but shook his head, grunting something in response.

Cal tried again. As he continued arguing with the fisherman, Vicki pulled Richard to the side. "Come on," she whispered.

"What are you doing?" he shot back,

"Come on," she insisted, leading him around the side of the tent. She crouched down by the canvas flap, looking both ways before lifting it up.

"Vicki!" he protested, but she had already ducked underneath. "Holy crap!" Richard stood there, arms flapping as he wrestled with his conscience. There was no way in hell he wanted to go sticking his nose in there, but he couldn't leave Vicki to do it alone. "Bloody hell!" He took a deep breath and followed her into the tent.

He paused inside, waiting for his eyes to adjust to the gloom. He was near the back of the tent, and at the front, a good fifteen metres away, he saw Cal and the fisherman silhouetted in the doorway. In between, the tent was filled with stacks and stacks of cardboard boxes, piled up to eye level. They were stacked on forklift pallets, roughly laid out into narrow rows, with even narrower gaps between them. The atmosphere was thick and heavy with blood, like the smell of a butcher's shop. He wrinkled his nose in distaste. As his eyes adjusted, he saw writing on the stacked boxes. Peering at the nearest one he discovered it was all in Japanese, but the cartoon whale picture stencilled on the side left no doubt as to its contents. This was whalemeat. Hundreds and hundreds of boxes of whalemeat. The corner of the box he was looking at was soaked dark red where blood had pooled in it. He stared in horror at the sight.

"Over here!"

Richard jumped as the harsh whisper interrupted his thoughts.

"Come on!" Vicki beckoned him impatiently from the next row. Richard shot an apprehensive glance at the fisherman still standing in the doorway, then reluctantly crept forward down the narrow row, his heart in his mouth. He would have been the first to admit he didn't have the gumption to be a burglar, yet here he was…

Vicki had already used her pocket knife to cut open the corner of a box, and Richard could see she held a biopsy dart in her other hand. With a sudden stabbing motion she plunged the tip of it inside the box. It came back out with a tiny disc of tissue in the end.

"Put some gloves on and bag for me," she said.

Richard nodded and hurried to comply. He held open the zip-lock bag and carefully dropped the stainless-steel tip inside, complete with its precious sample. Vicki was already reaching into her backpack for a fresh core to fit it to the dart. "Next!" she ordered, giving him a conspiratorial grin.

They moved down the rows, choosing boxes at random to sample. All the while, Richard kept a wary eye on the doorway. Cal was persisting with his efforts to talk, but the fisherman's raised voice indicated he was becoming exasperated trying to get rid of the nosey foreigner.

Vicki and Richard hurried on, working with silent efficiency. As they finished another box, Richard checked the pile of bagged samples in Vicki's backpack, then cast an anxious glance back towards the doorway.

Surely that's enough?

But Vicki wasn't satisfied yet. She crept further down the row they were in, heading deeper into the tent. The pallets had been stacked haphazardly here, and the further back they went, the more the narrow rows converged on each other. The boxes began to lean over too, making it difficult to fit between them. Richard eyed the stacks warily, wondering how much it would take to topple one over and trap them beneath hundreds of kilos of dead meat. "I've got a bad feeling about this," he murmured.

Vicki dropped to a crouch and sidled on.

"Vicki, are you sure this is necessary? Let's get out while we still can."

She didn't answer. Richard sighed and crawled after her.

She stopped near the end of the row, pointing to a battered looking box down the side of a pallet. "That one."

It was right at the bottom of the stack, and the base of the box was soaked with blood, having leaked through the cardboard to form a congealed pool on the concrete floor. Richard wrinkled his nose. "Ew. Why that one?"

She grinned. "Because it's messy. More blood might indicate it came from a bigger animal."

Richard shrugged. It seemed like a long shot to him, but she was in charge.

There wasn't much room to get to it, and the stacks were far too heavy to shift. Vicki lay down and wriggled between the two pallets

The box was half-flattened, crushed by the weight of the stack on top of it. Vicki reached out and tore open the flap. "See how dark the meat is. That's gotta be a different species from the rest."

Suddenly a noise reached their ears. They both froze.

Footsteps!

"Oh crikey! The fisherman's coming back, hurry!"

She stabbed the dart into the meat and yanked it out again. The tip came away dark with blood. "Here, quickly!"

Richard reached for the dart with a gloved hand, and promptly fumbled it.

"Forget the tip," she urged him. "Just bag the whole thing!"

Richard's heart hammered in his chest, and his hands felt like wooden blocks as he battled to cram it into the small bag. The footsteps came closer.

"Quickly!"

"H-here," he spluttered.

Vicki snatched the bag and shoved it into her backpack with the others. "This way, come on!" She scrambled further between the pallets, trying to squeeze through into the next row. Richard followed her into the narrow gap, the stacks pressing against his shoulders from both sides.

A moment later Vicki cursed.

"What is it?"

"I'm stuck!"

Richard felt a spike of alarm. He could hear the fisherman coming down the row already. It was only a matter of moments before they were discovered. Ahead, Vicki cursed again, still struggling to get through the gap.

Richard knew he had to do something, and quickly. His stomach lurched in response, and his heart felt like it would burst right out of his chest. Taking a deep breath, he backed out into the row and stood up. He didn't really have a plan. All he knew was that he had to distract the guard and give Vicki a chance to get away.

The fisherman was closer than Richard had realised. They both jerked to a stop, blinking in surprise. The fisherman shouted something in Japanese, challenging him. Richard swallowed and began to back away. The fisherman advanced, still shouting. Then with a sadistic sneer he began to roll up his sleeves.

Richard felt boxes touch his shoulder. It was the edge of the pallet Vicki was stuck between. If he backed up any further she would be totally unprotected.

I can't leave her!

He looked around, desperately hoping for an alternative. There was none. The burly fisherman took up most of the width of the row. There was no way past him, and if Richard tried to climb over a stack he would be grabbed before he was even halfway up. He glanced about fearfully, desperate for a reprieve.

What can I do?

His mind went blank.

The fisherman cackled and smacked his fist into his palm. It made a meaty slap, and Richard felt his knees buckle. He wanted to be sick.

He closed his eyes and waited for the blow.

There was a huge crash just in front of him and a sudden breeze ruffled his hair. Richard flinched, but surprisingly, nothing happened to him. He opened a cautious eye.

The scene that greeted him was one of utter confusion. The pallet stack across from him was gone, replaced by a gaping hole in the row. The boxes lay in a huge jumble on the ground, blocking the aisle. Underneath them was the fisherman, spread-eagled on the floor, pinned up to his chest by the cardboard-wrapped slabs of meat.

A shadowy figure detached itself from the chaos and stood up, brushing off its pants. Richard stared. "Cal!"

His brother grinned, rubbing his shoulder. "Man, that hurt more than tackling an entire front row!"

The fisherman glowered at him from the ground. As he recovered from the shock, he began hollering like a stuck pig.

Cal jumped over the fallen boxes, heading for the gap in the stacks. "Come on, we've got to go!"

"But Vicki's still back there!"

Cal hesitated. "Vicki, are you there?"

There was no response. From outside the tent they could hear more shouting and running footsteps.

Cal shook his head. "We can't hang around here, Bro. You bought her some time, but now she'll have to take care of herself."

He ducked under the side of the tent, holding the flap up for Richard.

Outside, the scene was even more chaotic. Stallholders were gathering up their wares, hurrying away with their barrows or pulling down the shutters of their kiosks. It was an ominous sign. Suddenly, a gang of blue-overalled whalers burst into the courtyard from the far end, armed with sticks and clubs. Richard recognised the captain, Hogei Gyofuku, at the head of the group.

It was fully light now, and there was nowhere to hide.

"Run!"

Richard obeyed, woodenly, as Cal propelled him in the other direction. The whalers saw them and charged forward, shouting eagerly like a pack of hunting dogs. The brothers ran back through the market, heading towards the factory, and beyond that, the waterfront.

Ahead, they heard the shrill blast of a whistle and a policeman burst into view down the street, blocking their path. Richard slowed down, relieved.

The policeman pointed at them with a white-gloved hand, then raised his whistle to his mouth again.

Cal swore. He grabbed Richard by the arm and pulled him down a side alley. "This way, quick!"

Richard was confused. "That's the police. Won't they protect us?" he blurted.

Cal ignored the question. "Just keep running."

Richard swallowed, feeling a sudden affinity for a hunted fox. "Where to?" he panted. "The Gwendolyn?"

"No," Cal called back. "That's where Vicki needs to go. We don't want to lead them to her. Head for the Convention Centre. Have your pass ready, and let's hope we can lose these bastards when we go through security!"

Richard ran, his breath rasping in his lungs. He tried to concentrate on taking slow, steady breaths, knowing his inhaler was back on the ship. A few blocks later the sun burst over the horizon, sparkling on the harbour like liquid gold. It was a beautiful sight, but Richard wasn't comforted. A nice view counted for little when you were running for your life. Head down, he struggled on.

The sounds of pursuit faded after a while, but still he didn't dare look back. There was no sign of Vicki anywhere, and he felt sick with dread.

***

Cal was on edge as he ushered Richard through the security check and into the conference venue. Their pursuers had fallen way back out of sight, but he wasn't about to let himself relax. He kept his eyes peeled for trouble, but the security police on door duty wore their usual bored expressions. They barely glanced at the brothers' passes before waving them though the door. Cal exhaled with relief. They were safe. For now.

They were early for the start of the meeting, but other delegates were already starting to arrive so they joined the queue and headed to the café to get some coffee. Cal didn't drink the gunk himself, but his brother looked like he could use a perk-up. Richard's face was bright red and he was puffing like a steam train.

Cal could see the anxiety written there too, and it mirrored his own thoughts. He didn't like leaving Vicki on her own, but he knew she could handle herself. "Don't worry, Bro. She'll be fine," he said, meaning it. "She can run faster than a speeding Kangaroo!"

Richard smiled weakly and Cal decided not to mention the thought that was foremost in his mind. If she hadn't escaped, then they were all in serious trouble.

And if she doesn't come up with proof of illegal hunting we can kiss the vote goodbye.

He collected a cup of coffee, frowning at the Styrofoam cup it was served in. The stuff was terrible for the environment. He thrust it at Richard and turned to leave, refusing to let the irony of that get him down.

Remember, as far as Amimoto is concerned, this isn't a conservation conference!

On the way out they passed Jim Avery. The New Zealand Commissioner sat at a table by himself, his thinning hair pointed at the world as he bent forward, engrossed in some reading.

Cal marched up and stopped beside him.

The Commissioner's head jerked up in alarm, then he recognised Cal and visibly relaxed.

Cal nodded a greeting. "It's final voting today. Can the whales count on your support?"

Avery shuffled his papers but didn't answer.

"The Revised Management Strategy…" Cal prompted him.

Avery exhaled like a punctured tyre. "Listen, we can't stop them, Son. The Japanese are going to continue whaling no matter what we do. All we can do now is try to set up some kind of framework to manage it as sustainably as possible."

Cal's jaw tightened. He knew what that meant, and he knew the conservationists couldn't afford to lose any more support. Not this late in the game! He couldn't contain his annoyance. "A sustainable hunt is impossible. You know it's impossible. History has shown it's impossible! The whalers have had their chance to make it work and look what the result was – the Great Whales are on the brink of extinction!"

Avery threw up his hands. "What do you want me to do? I can't work miracles." He sighed. "Face it, Son. The battle is lost. We put up a good fight, but it's over. Now we need to salvage what control we can."

"That's a cop-out and you know it!" Cal's eyes blazed as he fought to control his anger. "Accepting the RMS amounts to tacit acceptance of whaling and it'll open the door for a return to full-scale commercial hunting again!" He took a deep breath. "What about the Moratorium vote?" he said stiffly. "How will the country be voting on that?"

Avery avoided his gaze.

"Do I have your support?" Cal insisted.

Avery shuffled uncomfortably. "My hands are tied. Your proposal to extend the Moratorium to ban all kinds of whaling everywhere amounts to a worldwide sanctuary."

Cal nodded. "Yes, that's the general idea."

Avery ignored his sarcasm. "Although that's nice in theory, you have to understand there are other considerations to take into account…"

Cal folded his arms, looking annoyed.

Avery pretended not to notice. "New Zealand is very small, and our isolation makes overseas trade critical for the country's success."

"What are you getting at?"

Avery smoothed the thinning strands of his comb-over, obviously uncomfortable under the intensity of Cal's gaze. "Japan is a vital export market for the country's agricultural products, and we have much to lose from a trade disruption. Plus our technology industry, economy, and even our standard of living depends on supplies of cars, electronics, and consumer products – all imported from Japan…" He left the statement hanging, but the implication was plain.

Cal knuckled his temples with frustration. The situation was clear enough – for whatever reason, his government was back-pedalling. As a proud Kiwi, Cal was disappointed by that. His country's outspoken support for conservation and environmental issues was well-known on the world stage – even though its opinions were sometimes greater than its size. That agenda worked well enough within Oceania where New Zealand was a regional power, but on the world stage the larger industrial countries often resented being told what to do by a little upstart from the bottom end of the world. And the trouble with being a small isolated island nation was that you were at the mercy of larger countries who felt like pushing you around. And the world was full of bullies.

Cal felt his anger rising. "So what do you propose to do?" he snapped, with more vehemence than was strictly diplomatic.

Avery regarding him down the length of his beak-like nose. "I'm suggesting New Zealand adopts a stance that is in the best interests of the country as a whole."

"But the New Zealand public don't support whaling!" Cal exploded. "They want an end to the slaughter!"

"The New Zealand public also want a stable economy and good diplomatic relations with our neighbours. You can't have everything."

"So you're just going to sell out?"

"It's not selling out. Diplomacy is about compromise. This way we can vote for the status quo and continue to hold on to our integrity as a conservation nation in the eyes of the world, while at the same time maintaining good diplomatic relations with our trading partners."

"It was Amimoto, wasn't it?" Cal sneered. "He's worked on you too."

Avery ignored the jibe. "Son, let go of your ideals for a moment. The status quo is an acceptable compromise. We keep our dignity, and Japan keeps a small scientific whaling quota which will have a negligible effect on the overall population."

"You hope!" Cal exploded. "And you also hope that Mr Fish – as he is so accurately named – won't get any greedier in the future. You're placing an awful lot of trust in a man whose only motivation is to make himself richer and more powerful than he already is!"

Avery studied his fingernails. "The Government feels this is in the best interests of all concerned."

"What about you? What do you feel?"

"That doesn't come into it. My job is to represent the will of the Government."

Cal shook his head. "I pity you," he said sadly.

He turned and walked back to the meeting hall, head bowed in thought. Time was all but up, and the morning's vote looked even more uncertain than ever. It was clear he would get no help from his government.

I guess it's up to me to try to put an end to whaling.

Chapter 12

Richard sipped his coffee, grateful to have it. A morning cup was a long-time habit of his normal working day, and he wasn't about to give it up now. It wasn't that he was addicted or anything, but the caffeine did help soothe his nerves. And today he needed that. His breathing was still a little laboured, although physically he had pretty much recovered from starting the day with a marathon. Mentally however, he still had some catching up to do. It wasn't every morning you had to run for your life!

He cradled his cup like a precious treasure, inhaling the rich, invigorating aroma like a drug.

Aurelia had been waiting for them at their seats, keen to hear how the action went. Richard let Cal fill her in. He still felt light-headed every time he thought what the fishermen might have done had they caught them. He was worried about Vicki too. She was always unfailingly patient with him, always ready with a smile of encouragement. She was a friend, he realised, and he didn't want anything bad to happen to her. He stared into space as he sipped his coffee. Well, maybe he was concerned rather than worried. Cal was right, Vicki was a tough chick who could take care of herself, but Richard wondered if that might not always be enough.

He looked over at the delegates filing through the doorway, hoping to see the reassuring sight of a dark ponytail, or that dimpled pixie-grin of hers.

Suddenly his heart quickened, but it was a different woman he recognised in the crowd. Summer strode confidently through the door, heading for her seat in the public gallery, her golden hair shining like a beacon. She wore a pair of white figure-hugging jeans that accentuated the curve of her hips. Richard couldn't help his smile. He had always had a soft spot in his heart for Canada. To him, it represented a snowy wilderness, a mysterious land of ice hockey, moose, and maple syrup. He'd always found Canadians interesting; they were an intriguing mix of understated British history, and the brash modern culture of North America. And now he had to admit this blonde beauty from the north had stolen his heart.

He couldn't control the happy smile that burst across his face.

She saw him and her lip twitched in return, but her smile was mechanical and without warmth – and gone just as quickly. Richard waved tentatively, but she was already looking away, rolling her eyes as if she found his attentions mildly annoying.

He waited for the Chairman to call the meeting to order, rebuffed but not discouraged.

Several minutes later, the Chairman finally levered himself to his feet and called for silence. "The first business for the day is the vote to adopt the Revised Management Strategy for the administration of whaling, as mooted by the member from Antigua," he announced. The High North Alliance members cheered their support like drunken Vikings, and Amimoto's eyes glittered in anticipation.

Cal was distracted though, ratting around on his desk as he searched for something.

"What is it?" Aurelia hissed, as people turned to glare at the disturbance.

"I can't find my pen. I need it to keep score…"

She tut-tutted like a weary mother. "Here, take mine. But no chewing on it!"

The vote was already underway, and Cal hurried to catch up with his notes, whispering a commentary to Richard as each country was called.

Australia abstained from voting, mainly because they were embarrassed by their kangaroo cull, Cal explained. Richard was glad Vicki wasn't there. She would have been disappointed in her country.

He kept an eye on Cal's figures as the vote progressed. Things were looking very close.

"Kiribati?" The Chairman called.

Cal consulted his notebook. "They've been fence-sitting, but they voted with us last time."

Richard looked up expectantly, but there was no answer.

"Kiribati?" The Chairman repeated. "Where is the Commissioner for Kiribati?"

All eyes turned towards his seat. The chair was empty.

Richard glanced across at Amimoto. The Japanese Commissioner folded his arms across his chest, a smug sneer on his face.

Cal stared at him, muttering a curse under his breath. "That dirty bastard has gotten to another one!"

"Kiribati has withdrawn from the conference," the Chairman declared, crossing the name off his list.

Cal rolled his eyes toward the ceiling. "Damn it! We can't afford to keep losing votes like this!" He turned back to his notebook, looking increasingly concerned as the vote progressed.

"Mongolia?"

The swarthy Asian commissioner stood. "Mongolia supports the RMS," he announced in a thick accent.

Cal rolled his eyes. "Another of Amimoto's foreign aid beneficiaries. It's hard to see what other interest a land-locked country like Mongolia would have in whaling. And the same goes for Mali," he added, jabbing a finger at his notebook.

He sighed. "The system is so messed up. It's so expensive to join the IWC that many smaller countries can't unless their fees are paid for them – something which Amimoto is only too happy to do if they're going to vote his way." He threw up his hands. "Other little nations like Fiji, Tonga, Samoa and the Cook Islands support conservation, but they're too poor to join IWC so their voice doesn't get heard." He shook his head angrily. "There's no reason we can't play that way too, but our government considers it improper to pay the fees for our poorer neighbours since that implies a conflict of interest." He lowered his voice, muttering under his breath about double standards as the Chairman called the next name.

"New Zealand?"

Jim Avery stood stiffly, refusing to look at them as he gave the country's vote – in favour of the RMS.

Cal shook his head, whether out of anger or sadness, Richard couldn't tell. He knew the decision wasn't Avery's fault, or even the New Zealand Government's. Small countries couldn't stand up to large ones, especially when policy was dictated by leaders as aggressive and conniving as Amimoto.

The vote continued, and Cal's notebook showed it was not going well for the conservation countries.

"Seychelles?"

Victor Admirante stood up. "The Seychelles opposes any vote that legitimises the killing of whales," he announced, his voice ringing out through the auditorium. It was a courageous but hollow defiance in the face of such odds though, and even Amimoto wore an amused twist to his usual smirk.

Cal nodded to his mentor, a brief smile touching his lips. His good spirits were quickly replaced by a worried frown though, as he began scrutinising his figures again. Richard could see over his shoulder that any advantage the conservationists might have had at the beginning of the week was all but gone.

"Solomon Islands?" the Chairman called.

Cal nudged his brother in the ribs. "Don't worry, they'll vote with us too. Before this conference started the Solomons' Government gave a press release announcing they were committed to conservation and looking forward to the sustainable development of marine eco-tourism in their waters."

Richard had a bad feeling though. Something about the way Amimoto was smiling filled him with trepidation. The Solomon Islands' Commissioner jumped to his feet and reached for the microphone, revealing a bright flash at his wrist.

Cal blinked. "Is that a gold watch?"

The Commissioner beamed from ear to ear. "The Solomon Islands is pleased to support this motion."

Cal looked stunned. "Shit! He went against his own government. Now we're really in trouble!"

The remainder of the vote passed in a blur, the pencil gripped in Cal's white-knuckled hand seemingly the only one able to keep track of it.

Richard held his breath as the Chairman stood up to read out the result.

"The vote is 28 votes in favour of the motion, and 28 votes opposed."

There were gasps from around the auditorium.

"In the event of a tied vote, the status quo will stand. The motion to adopt the RMS has been defeated."

Richard let out a relieved sigh.

"Bloody hell," Cal muttered. "That was close. Far too close." He studied his notes with a deep frown. "I wish NGOs got voting rights, then I could add a vote. After Amimoto finished rigging that ballot, the Seychelles is practically the only small country left still voting with us."

"Don't worry," Aurelia said, her voice brimming with confidence. "Amimoto can't bribe or bully any of the big conservation countries that easily, so we're not likely to lose any more votes. The Moratorium vote is only a couple of minutes away. As long as we retain the status quo we can still win that too."

Cal didn't answer straight away, but when he did his voice was strained. "Amimoto won't give up that easily. The cunning bastard will have another trick up his sleeve. I'm sure of it."

The Chairman turned to the Commissioner from Antigua. "As the instigator of this vote, do you wish to add any parting remarks?"

The Antiguan Commissioner stood up, smoothing his hair and flashing an oily smile at the delegates as he prepared for his moment in the spotlight. But before he had a chance to speak, Amimoto got to his feet. "I will speak on his behalf!"

The Antiguan Commissioner immediately dropped his eyes, finding something engrossing on his desk.

The Chairman opened his mouth as if to demur, but Amimoto shot him a vicious look and he snapped it shut again.

Aurelia jumped to her feet. "I object! That's against the rules!" she shouted.

"There is nothing in the rules that forbids it," the Chairman spluttered, but he looked uncomfortable. "You may speak," he said to Amimoto, then plonked himself back on his seat as though eager to relinquish the floor.

The Japanese Commissioner glared at her. "I demand that these activists be removed from the meeting."

Cal laughed. "He's starting to sound like a stuck record."

Richard waited anxiously. Although Amimoto appeared keen to pick up the argument where they'd left off last time, his next attack was a curve ball. "I have direct evidence that these protestors receive money in exchange for carrying out their obstruction stunts!"

Cal looked blank.

"Is he talking about your research funding?" Richard whispered.

"I dunno what the hell he's on about," Cal whispered back loudly. "I think he's talking out of a hole in his arse!"

Amimoto's lip curled at their whispered impertinence, but he didn't let up. "It is quite clear they are waging a deliberate campaign against agents of the Japanese Fisheries Association, a campaign they fund through nefarious misuse of grant money intended for research! Their sinister motives are now revealed! Their attacks against Japan are merely a vehicle for them to drum up more publicity and thereby satisfy their own personal money-making agenda!"

He jabbed a skeletal finger in Cal's direction. "Furthermore, as this man has committed acts of deliberate sabotage and piracy – acts outlawed under the UN

Law of the Sea – I must reiterate my demand he and his colleagues be removed from this delegation and handed over to police to face trial in Japan."

Richard glanced anxiously at his brother.

"Don't worry," Cal reassured him. "He's bluffing. We've already covered this ground; he doesn't have the authority to arrest us. He's just trying to get some mud to stick before the Moratorium vote. He's desperate enough that he'll try anything he can to make us look bad in front of the conference."

Richard looked around the room. There was a buzz of whispered conversation, and many sets of eyes watched them suspiciously. "I-I think it might be working." He glanced at his brother. "Cal, we need to do something…"

***

Cal hesitated. He could see the situation demanded an immediate response, but he was torn.

What do I do?

He dug his cellphone out of his pocket and checked the display.

No messages.

Come on Vicki, I need some hard evidence.

He drummed his fingers on the desk, deliberating. He needed to score some points, and quickly! But with what? Proof the Japanese were killing endangered species would be ideal, but he couldn't afford to delay any longer waiting for it. He needed to respond to the Japanese now.

He rubbed his jaw. He could always present his own research findings, but that was his last chance for a big hit. He knew Amimoto was an exceptionally crafty debater. If he played his own trump card now it wouldn't take the Japanese Commissioner long to come up with some "evidence" of his own to argue it and justify the killing of whales, and regardless of its accuracy that would weaken Cal's point. This close to the Moratorium vote, every argument he delivered needed to do maximum damage to Amimoto's credibility. And timing was everything.

Cal stood up and took a deep breath, still unsure what he was going to say.

Just then a thought came to mind. Actually it was a saying his kickboxing instructor used to impress upon him; "Often the best defence is attack."

Cal smiled and prepared his defence. "My fellow delegates, we have already covered this ground, but if the Commissioner for Japan wants to talk about the UN Law of the Sea, very well then, I accuse him of breaching it!"

He turned to Amimoto, raising his voice so it would carry throughout the auditorium. "A whale is not a fish, so your fleet cannot claim to be fishing. Similarly, UNCLOS is quite clear that the right to fish on the high seas is subject to all other international treaty obligations-"

Amimoto interrupted with a sneer. "Perhaps I should remind the conference that I am fully compliant with all IWC rulings. Scientific Whaling is expressly permitted under the IWC rules. Besides, Japan is only bound by the resolutions we choose to accept."

Cal's jaw muscles clenched. "I was referring to the CITES Convention on International Trade in Endangered Species, the CCAMLR Convention on the

Conservation of Antarctic Marine Living Organisms, and the UN charter," he snapped, "all of which explicitly outlaw this slaughter of endangered species, and have repeatedly condemned your continued violation of international treaties."

Amimoto's eyes glittered, though it was hard to say what angered him more; that Cal had scored a point against him, or that he had failed to realise the direction of Cal's argument in time to counter it. "These treaties are superseded by the jurisdiction of the IWC too," he continued to insist. "It is only logical that the International *Whaling* Commission be the sole body governing the use of whales!"

Aurelia frowned. "Yeah, and the fact that you've bought this commission has nothing to do with that claim, right?" she muttered angrily.

Cal smiled, hoping to wind Amimoto up. An angry enemy was dangerous, but also more likely to make a mistake. "In addition, by your own claims to be 'fishing' you are also in breach of the UNCLOS' own 1996 Agreement on the Conservation of Migratory Fish Stocks," he accused. "Specifically, your failure to protect biodiversity, take preventative measures to prevent overfishing, or collect accurate data concerning your activities."

"Lies!" Amimoto spat back. "There are plenty of whales in the sea. Show me evidence of overfishing!"

Cal ignored the outburst. "As well as causing serious damage to the marine environment, you have violated the Precautionary Approach principle of the Law of the Sea. This agreement, of which Japan is a signatory, requires that states shall be more cautious when information is uncertain, unreliable, or inadequate. The absence of accurate scientific data is no justification for failing to take the appropriate conservation measures."

Amimoto roared like a pressure cooker and puffed out his wizened chest. "Japan has conducted much scientific research!"

Cal threw back his head and laughed scornfully. "Reputable scientific research is published in international, peer-reviewed journals. You publish only in Japanese Fisheries magazines, publications that you personally control. Your 'scientific findings' are propaganda that aren't worth the paper they're printed on!" His sneer left no doubt as to the depth of his contempt.

Amimoto shook with ill-concealed rage at the insult, but Cal wasn't finished yet. "The science behind the Revised Management Strategy is flawed, as are Japan's claims of the potential for sustainable management of whaling. Whale numbers are simply too few, and they reproduce too slowly to support any hunting pressure."

He pressed on, as fast as the thoughts came to him, trying to prevent Amimoto from responding and getting a counter-strike on him. "Minke whales are the commonest rorqual, yet their numbers are not expanding. The population is not stable enough to justify any hunting pressure. They may appear numerous, but only in comparison with the relic populations of the last Great Whales, which are down to a few percent of their historical levels. The history of whaling is a history of serial over-exploitation – one species after another hunted to the brink of extinction. Minke whale populations are no less resilient to a collapse than any of the other whale species were! As the smallest rorqual species, Minkes have not been economical to target directly before now, so they are the only population that hasn't yet been decimated by humans. This is certainly not a justification to do so now!"

"Lies!" Amimoto thundered. "There are millions of whales in the ocean. Our science has proven they can be sustainably harvested on a permanent basis."

Cal turned to sweep his gaze over the delegates, appealing to them directly. "The Japanese claims of over a million Minkes whales in the Pacific are unsound. Recent population surveys have shown there to be a maximum of 750,000 in the entire Southern Hemisphere, and possibly as few as one third of that figure!"

Cal hesitated, wondering whether he should table his own research findings, the last Ace up his sleeve.

Yes, his instincts exclaimed. *Hit them with it now, you won't get a better chance!*

He took a deep breath and began. "Above all though, Japanese pseudo-science is fundamentally flawed. You cannot simply claim there are so many Minkes, therefore so many thousand may be killed per year."

Cal reached down into his backpack and brought out a sheaf of papers that he dropped proudly on the desk. "Genetic profiling work, of which I have the results right here, has shown there are in fact three species of Minke whales in the world, with the Northern and Southern Pacific Minkes falling into two distinct species. When considered with respect to biology, it is clear that we are now talking about separate populations of barely a hundred thousand animals each – not a million!"

He paused for emphasis. "Furthermore, within each of these species the populations are further subdivided into genetically distinct breeding groups, each of different size and conservation status. The smallest units are family groups of up to a few dozen animals, and these all have a distinct local range and feeding ground. There is so little population data on these family units that the quota must be zero! Remember, if there's no interbreeding then these populations are like isolated villages. When one group is hunted out, it's gone forever!"

He stared at the delegates in turn, trying to impress on them the importance of what he was saying. "Each of these units *must* be considered separately for management purposes! Japan would have you believe that the science of hunting whales is as simple as taking meat from a giant supermarket shelf, but that is patently false. The Ocean is not a giant pool they can randomly dip into at will. You cannot lump all Minke whales together into one giant super-population. When you take into account the most basic biology, it is easy to see that even a quota of a *dozen* adult Minkes is excessive. Removing just a few adults from one family unit can destroy its breeding ability, condemning any surviving juveniles to a slow death by starvation, and completely wiping out the local population of that area. The end result is as obvious as it is inevitable: ever-expanding areas of the ocean standing empty. Yet the Japanese stand here before you demanding a quota of *thousands* of Minkes per year!"

Cal raised his voice, trying to project it beyond even the room where he stood. "The only sustainable hunt is no hunt at all! Enough whales have been killed already! I urge you to stand firm against Japanese aggression and wanton destruction of the Earth, before it is too late. Their selfishness is a crime against everything good and reasonable in the world! Their greed is a crime against the future!"

"Hear hear!" Victor Admirante applauded, joined by a scattering of other conservation nations.

Aurelia turned to him, a mixture of triumph and gratitude in her expression, plus a little something else that made his heart jump. She tossed her head and a cascade of bright red hair fell forward, partly obscuring her face. She smiled demurely at him from underneath it. "I've never wanted you more," she whispered, her voice husky with desire.

Cal grinned in reply. Things were definitely looking up!

Don't lose sight of the battle! his subconscious warned.

He reluctantly shelved his excitement, knowing the war was far from over. He had bought some time, but only until the next Japanese counter-attack. Mr Fish knew what he was doing. Regardless of the accuracy of his pseudo-science, he would soon come up with some arbitrary numbers to throw against Cal's claims, and even that implied doubt would be enough to sway some delegates here – if in fact there were any still basing their vote on biology. Cal knew he needed a follow-up to capitalise on this victory, and quickly. He needed a king-hit to blow Amimoto's misinformation right out of the water!

Cal stared again at his silent phone.

"No messages," the screen declared.

He frowned, wondering again what was taking Vicki so long. Was the reception in here bad? Without some hard evidence to discredit the Japanese, the conservationists could kiss the upcoming vote goodbye. Above that however, as time passed with no word he was starting to feel more and more concerned for Vicki's safety.

***

Akogi Yokuke's anger was like a viper coiled in the pit of his stomach. The Kajiki had landed a telling blow with that pile of emotive nonsense. His wild accusations would have no effect on Japan's committed 'allies' of course, but the claims were damaging all the same. There were plenty of minor countries lined up with him and he needed every single one of them on side. This close to the vote he couldn't risk any one of them getting cold feet and going over to the hippies. Yokuke knew he needed time to consolidate his grip on the conference.

He got to his feet and smiled through his teeth. "I request an immediate intermission before the next vote. I must consult with my colleagues."

He turned and began shuffling towards the door, knowing the fat idiot of a Chairman wouldn't dare defy his request.

"V-very well," the Chairman stammered. "The meeting will adjourn for ten minutes."

"Twenty!" Yokuke snapped irritably over his shoulder, as he headed for the side door closest to the private elevator to his suite. Twenty minutes was good. It would give him time to do all he needed. His eyes glazed over, already deep in thought. He would have his aide summon all the Commissioners to him, one at a time. It was time to impress on them the importance of the decision they were about to make!

Yokuke frowned. There was other business to take care of too. He had heard a worrying report of an incident at the Taiyoku Misui Market this morning. Foreigners causing trouble. He bared his teeth. There was only one person that could be.

Yokuke's frown deepened as he wondered what the blonde barbarian was up to. Then he dismissed the problem. It was inconsequential.

Do what you will, Kajiki. You will achieve nothing by running around like a headless chicken trying to cause trouble. It makes no difference to my plans.

Nevertheless however, the intent behind the insult was unforgivable.

"Servant!" he snapped. "Send for the local police chief. I want these meddlesome barbarians placed under constant guard. This type of incident is not to be repeated."

Yokuke's mind moved swiftly back to his scheming. A twenty-minute break was also long enough that people wouldn't want to wait around the chamber. If the meeting disbanded – even temporarily – it would break up the continuity, thereby negating some of the Kajiki's recent advantage.

More to the point though, it would give the Enforcer time to carry out his orders.

Yokuke smiled to himself. Everything was coming together nicely!

As he had exited the conference chamber he'd looked back, pleased to see a blonde head among the crowd hurrying out the main door. He couldn't resist a cruel smile now.

Do you feel the hook in your mouth yet, Kajiki? You are almost caught, my fine swordfish!

***

Kobushi the Enforcer loitered in the corridor, watching, waiting. In his Western-style suit and tie he looked like any other delegate or diplomat from the conference, but in the interests of prudence, he kept to the shadows as much as possible.

A few minutes later, the large double doors to the debating chamber swung open, releasing a wave of conversation from within. The conference was in recess.

Excellent!

Now all he had to do was pick up the target and follow him to a place where he could carry out his orders. He slipped the Polaroid picture into his palm and discretely studied it. He had memorised the target's face, but all Westerners tended to look alike to him and he needed to be sure. One by one, the people filing out of the conference hall were subjected to his surreptitious scrutiny.

Suddenly, a face jumped out of the crowd at him.

That's him!

Kobushi felt a quickening of his pulse, as he always did when the excitement of the job took hold, but no trace of it was revealed in his stony expression.

He returned the photograph to his pocket, satisfied. In this business it was always imperative one was certain before acting. Amimoto-san was not a master forgiving of mistakes.

He took out the newspaper he had collected from a stand – without paying – and pretended to read it. The target walked by him, completely unaware, but Kobushi's eyes were predatory slits as he followed the man's progress over the edge of the paper.

He allowed the target to get a dozen paces ahead before he folded the paper and walked after him.

As he followed, the target broke away from the crowd heading towards the main door, and instead went out a side exit that opened into the Convention Centre's grounds.

Kobushi shoved the newspaper into a trash can and followed him out into the gardens. They were tastefully laid out in the traditional Japanese style, with an emphasis on simplicity of form – the idea being to provide a space where busy conference participants could come for a moment of quiet reflection.

Kobushi didn't mind. The seclusion of the gardens meant no witnesses, and that would make his job easier.

The target didn't seem to be enjoying the solitude though. His head was down, and he was fiddling with the keypad of his mobile phone as he walked.

Kobushi followed him, keeping far enough back to remain undetected. For now.

He carried only his wakizashi sword today. He preferred the length of the full-sized katana, but the short sword was far more discrete. Besides, a true Samurai was equally comfortable with either weapon. It in no way diminished his honour to use the smaller sword.

Kobushi carefully removed his sunglasses and tucked them into his pocket. This was a ritual of his. The main reason was because he liked to look into the eyes of his victims as their life expired, but it also pleased him to know that whoever looked upon his eyes – other than his master, of course – would pay for the privilege with their life.

The target stopped at the edge of a water lily pond to make his phone call. Bright orange koi carp darted beneath the surface and a simple decorative fountain in the centre sent a merry stream of water tinkling into the pond.

Kobushi appreciated the symbolism of it.

It is a beautiful place to die, neh?

He approached cautiously, his soft-soled shoes making no sound. Opening his coat, he withdrew the blade, careful the steel made no sound as he slid it out of the scabbard. Kobushi raised the blade in the air and sprang forward, aiming for a single perfect cut that would remove the head.

The target reacted quicker than he anticipated, spinning around at his approach and flinging up a hand to protect his face. It was a futile gesture, of course, as the steel sliced deep into the bone of his forearm. But the quick kill had been thwarted, and Kobushi felt his annoyance rising. He was proud of his work, and anything less than absolute perfection was unsatisfactory.

The phone slipped from the target's maimed hand and clattered to the path. He moaned softly in a mixture of shock and pain, clutching his injured limb to his chest. Kobushi stepped forward, sword raised. The target suddenly woke up to his fate and scrambled backwards out of range, shouting hoarsely for help.

Kobushi felt his anger rising. His eyebrow twitched rapidly, and he snarled as he lunged forward in pursuit.

The sword flashed as he lowered the tip, then brought it up in a sweeping arc that slashed a ragged gash across the target's throat. A spray of blood burst out, and the screams were silenced, replaced instead by a weak gurgle.

The target clutched at his wounded throat, the shock in his eyes quickly being replaced by morbid fear. He staggered backwards, desperately trying to escape.

Kobushi showed his teeth in a parody of a smile and closed in, wakizashi at the ready. He opened his mouth and spoke for the first time since the frenzied attack began. "My Master, Amimoto-san, sends his regards."

Then he lunged forward, plunging the tip of the sword into the target's chest. He felt the blade catch on the ribcage, then slide within. The target gasped and fell to his knees, mouth working soundlessly. Kobushi smiled again, then twisted the blade. Bracing his foot against the chest, he jerked the sword free, and then in one fluid move he delivered the killing blow that all but severed the head from the body.

Surprisingly, the body remained upright, defying gravity as it balanced like a kneeling Buddha. Kobushi smiled, pleased with the delicate finesse of his coup de grace.

He leaned forward and wiped the blade clean on the target's shirt collar, then with the toe of his shoe, he pushed the body backwards into the pond. It toppled into the water with a splash, where it floated face-down amongst the bright green lily pads.

Kobushi turned and strode away down the path, grinding the unfortunate victim's phone to rubble under his heel as he went.

Chapter 13

The debating chamber was largely empty. Richard Major sat waiting for the conference to resume. A few delegates still milled about, but most had taken advantage of the intermission to step outside for a moment. Richard was alone for now; Aurelia and Summer had popped along to the cafeteria to get a drink, and Cal had left to check up on Vicki.

Richard smiled to himself, his mind wandering. He had originally come into this whole escapade more than a little wary of Cal's 'alternative' lifestyle, but now he felt embarrassed recalling those thoughts. His brother was definitely not the eccentric failure the rest of the family regarded him as. He could see that with absolute certainty now. Cal was a dedicated and capable researcher, just trying to do the right thing in life. The fact that his life might differ from other people's perception of the norm didn't bother him in the slightest. And neither, Richard was proud to realise, did it bother him any more either.

If Cal would rather do this than anything else, then good for him!

Cal would have made a great lawyer, but the fact was he made a better de facto Commissioner!

Richard smiled again as he pondered the changing perception he had towards his brother's work. Cal hadn't changed at all in the last few weeks; therefore the change had to be in his own head. Maybe he was even starting to get a feel for this life himself?

His thoughts turned to Gina again, and for once they weren't the usual negative self-criticism associated with his ex. For the first time since the break-up he was actually pleased his marriage had failed. It was only now with the clarity of distance he was able to see what a sham the relationship had been, and how much better off he was not constantly kowtowing to that manipulative and controlling woman any more.

I wouldn't be here, for a start!

She wouldn't have approved of this escapade, that was for sure! If he had nothing else to show for four years of marriage, the ability to recognise the value of freedom when he saw it made everything worthwhile.

Lost in his thoughts, Richard was surprised when the delegates suddenly began filing back into the chamber en masse and took their seats. He consulted the large wall clock and saw that twenty minutes was indeed up.

The Chairman struggled to his feet, tapping his microphone for silence. "Order. Take your seats please."

Where's Cal? The meeting's about to start!

Richard wanted to shout out, "Wait, my brother's not here!" But he knew the Chairman wouldn't care. Or worse, he might laugh at him.

He wrung his hands, not sure what to do. Suddenly he saw the bright flash of Aurelia's hair as she hurried back to her seat, drink in hand.

"Where's Cal? Have you seen him? He's not back yet!" Richard blurted.

Aurelia blinked in surprise. "I'm sure he'll be ok," she replied. "He's probably just delayed."

But her green eyes revealed a worried expression before she sat down.

The Chairman turned towards Amimoto. "The Commissioner for Japan," he announced.

Richard felt his panic rising as Mr Fish took the floor.

Oh no! Where's Cal? He's not supposed to be missing this!

Amimoto looked directly at him and smirked, as though he not only understood the reason for Richard's anxiety but was also enjoying his distress. Richard suddenly felt sick as a terrible thought dawned.

Does he know what happened to Cal?

He was barely paying attention as Mr Fish began to speak.

Richard sat in stunned disbelief as Amimoto's words flowed over him like a tidal wave, only a few phrases managing to percolate down to his subconscious.

"I refute these false allegations," he was saying. "Japan's Scientific Whaling Program is firmly grounded in science, and enables us to better manage this resource. Our catch is completely sustainable, as is the proposed return to a commercial harvest."

That's not true! Where is Cal to argue these lies?

"This harvest of Minke whales is justified by our findings, and is in fact necessary for the recovery of rarer whale species."

Where the hell is Cal?

Richard was beside himself with worry – not only for his brother, but also for his work. With Cal out of the picture Mr Fish was hijacking the conference, and the last thing the conservationists needed was to lose even more support immediately before the most important vote of the conference.

Amimoto turned to his audience, a half-smile tugging the corners of his lip. "My fellow delegates, the IWC has been held to ransom by the selfish and unreasonable demands of preservationists for far too long. They would have you believe the entire world should be wrapped up in cotton wool and placed on a shelf for fear of breaking it. Well, I am here to tell you that belief is a load of garbage! The purpose of the IWC is supposed to be to facilitate and manage the harvesting of whales! Any ban on taking prolific whale species is a travesty, and a violation of the IWC's own charter! Let us end this tyranny of cultural imperialism once and for all!"

Amimoto sat down to raucous cheers from the High North Alliance. He didn't seem to notice though, so intently was he smirking at Richard.

The Chairman stood up. "It is now time to vote for the Moratorium on Commercial Whaling."

"Where's Cal?" Richard felt the panic beginning to rise in him. "Aurelia, we have to do something!"

She shrugged. "Don't worry, the numbers are all tied up so we've still got the advantage. Besides, we don't get a vote so there's nothing more Cal could do here anyway."

Richard closed his eyes, trying not to think about the damage Mr Fish's speech had just caused them. There had to be something more they could do. It was never too late for the truth!

The Chairman's jowls wobbled as he coughed. "I declare the voting open." He peered though the spectacles perched on the end of his noise, consulting his list. "Antigua?"

The Antiguan Commissioner smiled as he stood up. His gold cufflinks gleamed as he adjusted his tie and prepared to deliver his vote.

Suddenly the double doors burst open.

"Wait! Hold everything!"

The entire conference gasped as one and turned towards the disturbance. A familiar blonde head stood in the doorway.

It's Cal!

Beside him stood Vicki, backpack in hand. Richard felt his spirits soar. His elation was matched only by the relief flooding through him.

Cal flashed his security pass and elbowed his way past the guards who had moved to intercept him. "I have information of grave importance to this conference," he said, his voice calm but filled with authority.

Amimoto glared significantly at the Chairman, but before either of them could intervene, Cal grabbed the nearest microphone.

"We have here a sample of meat from the Taiyoku Misui Fisheries Company, on sale right here at the local Karato Market," he announced.

Vicki reached into her backpack and brought out the sample in its ziplock bag.

"We also have the results of genetic testing carried out on this meat."

Vicki took out the computer printout and held it aloft.

Amimoto's eyes widened, and he must have realised what was coming next. He hissed an order at the Chairman, but he was too late to stop Cal's offensive.

"This meat came from a critically endangered species; a status under which the CITES Convention outlaws the mere possession of animals without a permit, let alone the trade or sale of any body parts," he shouted. "This tissue comes from a Balaenoptera musculus." He paused, evaluating the confused looks he received in response. "Perhaps the Commissioner for Japan can explain to the conference how pieces of a Blue whale came to be for sale by his very own company?"

There were gasps of horror from both sides of the floor, and a buzz of conversation swept the room.

"Yes, that's right. While Amimoto stands up here posturing and bargaining and telling his lies, he does the exact opposite behind his back! Despite his hollow claims to be committed to the long-term survival of whales, he is still killing the most endangered species of all when no one is watching! I think we all agree Amimoto-*san* owes this conference an explanation!" The way Cal spat out the honorific left no doubt as to his true feelings on the matter.

Richard felt his heart surge. This was the proof they so desperately needed!

Vicki caught his eye across the room and winked, silently acknowledging his part in the successful sting to obtain it. Richard gave her a shy smile back, enormously proud but suddenly a little melancholy too. With a sinking heart he realised the meat must have come from the Old Blue he had met face to face in the wild Southern Ocean – the ancient soul who had met a sudden and violent death beneath the hail of harpoons from the Japanese Pelagic Fleet.

Amimoto glared at Cal with enough vehemence to make Richard flinch on the other side of the room. The Japanese Commissioner got to his feet and turned his gaze on the conference, the force of his presence alone was enough to silence the hubbub around him. "These allegations are scandalous!" He snapped. "They are totally baseless and without fact." He sneered at Vicki's DNA profiles. "What proof is this? Anyone can manufacture such flimsy evidence and call it the truth. Japan has made public all scientific findings, including complete and detailed catch statistics. I can promise you there are no Blue whales listed there. That, my fellow Commissioners, is the real truth!"

Richard frowned. Amimoto was cunning. By reminding the conference that Cal wasn't a commissioner of a member country, he was subtly aligning himself with them while at the same time turning their sympathies away from Cal. And once again the delegates seemed to be wavering. It wasn't looking good for the conservationists. Despite the unreliability of Amimoto's denials, the best they could hope for now was damage to Japan's credibility. Killing a Blue whale was illegal under the IWC's rules, but that didn't mean they would, or could, do anything about it. From what he already knew of the IWC and its workings, Richard knew the commission lacked the ability to enforce its own rules. Toothless, Cal had called them. So even if Japan's actions were roundly condemned by all the delegates, there was little anyone could do to stop them.

Judging by the shouted comments from the floor though, it was clear that not everyone was against Japan's stance. Many countries actively supported Amimoto, despite his illegal activities. Or maybe because of them!

The Chairman's silence served to reinforce the point, demonstrating his reluctance to speak out against Mr Fish.

Cal, however, had no such reservations.

"You may deny this until you are blue in the face, but that only makes you a liar!" he challenged the Japanese Commissioner, "Since I have seen – and filmed – your ships committing these acts!" Cal smiled slowly, as if a thought had just occurred to him. "Or perhaps you are ill-informed instead? Perhaps you really do have no idea what is going on? Could it be that you are totally ignorant of the affairs of your own company? The great and powerful Amimoto has lost control of his own men!" he needled. "Or do your crew just see fit to disrespect your orders behind your back?" His lip curled with sarcasm. "What a fine leader that makes you!"

Amimoto's eyes glittered, and Richard could almost see his cold and calculating brain turning over the possibilities in his mind.

Yikes, that one really hit home!

Amimoto's face was contorted with fury at the insult, but his response was completely shocking. "So some rare whales were killed," he snapped. "So what?" He shrugged, laughing humourlessly. "Who cares? They're all rare. I am in the business of making money, not holding hands with whales and long-haired degenerates. Everyone knows whales are finished anyway. Whalers are just trying to extract some value from the resource before it's gone for good. It's only right that we few far-sighted entrepreneurs should make a profit from their passing!"

A stunned silence gripped the chamber. Cal smiled a thin but satisfied smile, perhaps the only person in the room who didn't have to pick his jaw up off the floor.

Richard blinked in surprise.

He admitted it! Amimoto just admitted he doesn't care if he drives whales to extinction!

He was awed by Cal's debating skills in securing the confession, but he didn't have time to marvel at his strategy because Amimoto was not about to let up. The Japanese Commissioner didn't seem at all bothered that he'd just incriminated himself. In fact he was even more defiant than usual. "Who are you to say whales are more important than people anyway?" he raged. "Your perfidious crusade against Japan is plainly obvious, but you will never succeed. No one man can stand in the way of progress, no matter how immature and bigoted his beliefs!" He paused, panting with the exertion of his rant.

Cal glanced at Vicki and shrugged. Their evidence was now on the official record and they had nothing more to add. Mr Fish had dug his own hole to fall into. "No further questions," Cal said.

The Chairman seemed to recover himself. He snorted pompously and waved an irritated hand as he took control of the meeting again. "Very well then. Please take your seats so we can continue with the Moratorium vote."

Many sets of eyes watched Cal and Vicki as they returned to their seats, but Richard couldn't read the mood of the conference. The vote was still too close to call. Cal plonked down in his seat, giving Richard a grim but reassuring pat on the shoulder. "Fingers crossed, Bro. As long as no one else switches sides we'll still hold the status quo, and that's enough for a win."

He didn't look entirely confident though, and Richard could see the doubt in his eyes too.

The Chairman consulted his list and called for the first vote. "Antigua?"

Cal didn't say much as the voting progressed, concentrating on his notebook instead. About three quarters of the way through, he pursed his lips thoughtfully. "Everyone is voting exactly the same so far," he remarked. "If that trend holds out we might just be able to pull this off. With the status quo working in our favour a draw is as good as a win!"

With his head down, Cal didn't notice the spiteful sneer Amimoto shot in their direction. Richard saw it though, and he shivered involuntarily before looking away. Even more concerning than the hate radiating from those slitted black eyes was the triumphant gleam.

Richard swallowed, wondering what evil scheme the Japanese Commissioner would come up with next. He took a deep breath, trying to put it out of his mind and concentrate on the vote.

The Chairman's monotone droned on as he called out the next country. "Seychelles?"

Cal's pen hovered over his notebook, poised to add another tick to their column.

There was no answer.

"Seychelles?" the Chairman prompted again.

Richard looked across to where the Seychelles' Commissioner sat.

His chair was empty.

A sudden prickle of alarm crept up Richard's back. "Where's Victor Admirante?" he whispered.

Cal's head shot up. "What the hell?" he exclaimed.

Amimoto's smile was pure evil. "It would appear the Commissioner has retired from the conference," he said to the Chairman. "Perhaps we should move on?"

The Chairman hesitated.

"Oh shit, this'll put us a vote down!" Cal muttered.

Richard was dumfounded, but Cal managed to gather himself in time to react. He jumped to his feet. "Wait! Let me place his vote."

"I object most strenuously!" Amimoto interrupted. "NGOs do not have voting rights at this conference!"

The Chairman opened his mouth as if to overrule him, but Amimoto glared at him, his face contorted into a snarl. He drew a skeletal finger across his throat in a ragged sawing motion. The meaning was unmistakable.

The Chairman blanched, huffing nervously. "T-the vote is forfeit," he announced. "The Seychelles has withdrawn."

Cal sat down reluctantly, muttering under his breath. "That's it. We're screwed!" He scanned his notebook with a critical eye, shaking his head as he did so. "Only a few countries left – and they're all in Amimoto's pocket. There's not a snowball's chance in hell that any of them will change their vote to us." He knuckled his temples in frustration. "There's no way we can make up one vote…"

Richard was shaken, not the least because his brother was at a loss.

The Chairman called for the next delegate's vote.

Cal appeared to have other things on his mind though. "Victor wouldn't miss this vote," he murmured, deep in thought. "Not even wild horses could drag him away. He dedicated his life to stopping Mr Fish..."

A few minutes later it was all over.

The Chairman did a quick tally of the votes and turned to the conference. "The result is 28 votes to 27. The motion to continue the Moratorium is defeated. I hereby declare a return to commercial whaling, as sanctioned by the charter of the IWC."

Cal shook his head in shocked disbelief. "This is bullshit!" he exclaimed. "How can it be that all the logic and reason in the world counts for nothing? Is everyone here voting purely for their own gain?"

"Not everyone," Vicki reminded him. "Just the ones that Amimoto got to."

Cal seemed not to have heard. "It's bullshit!" he repeated, springing to his feet. He turned to glare at the conference. "This is reprehensible! Japan has one of the highest living standards in the world," he shouted. "They don't need to kill whales to support their economy, or to feed their people. Yet they persist. And their continued defiance in the face of worldwide condemnation, ignoring all evidence to the contrary, while they insist on continuing the slaughter, is the absolute height of stupidity! Not to mention the rest of you short-sighted and greedy countries who rush to join their lolly-scramble!" Cal's voice rang out strong and clear through the hall, holding everyone in his thrall. "This is not about the morality of killing animals, although some people believe that in itself is wrong. This is not about the killing method, although a slow death by harpoon is clearly barbaric and causes unnecessary suffering." He fixed the delegates with a steely gaze. "This is about the fate of entire species and the selfish irresponsibility of killing any whales at all!"

Amimoto shot a murderous look at him, but Cal ignored it. "Governments are not the only powers involved or affected by whaling, and should not have the sole voice at this conference. There are many stakeholders who have a vested interest in the continued survival of live whales in the world's oceans – from eco-tourism operators to far-sighted ecologists – not the least of whom include the whales themselves. Yet none of them got a vote here today."

He glared at Amimoto, as if finding a target for his outrage. "The blatant Japanese abuse of power in hijacking this conference and imposing their will on the world is a breach of those stakeholders' rights! Must I remind Mr Fish that the UN Law of the Sea he is so fond of hiding behind prohibits a nation from subjecting the High Seas to its sovereignty? Yet by trampling our rights in this way that is exactly what he is doing!"

Cal took a deep breath and drew himself up to his full height. "I contend that these silent stakeholders constitute a sovereign community of their own. This Anti-whaling Community is entitled to Rights of Use of unmolested whale populations, and under international law and the charter of this commission our rights must be respected too."

Mr Fish snorted incredulously. "You cannot claim to represent a sovereign state! Only a recognised government can do that, and no government has the right to stop me!"

Cal ignored the outburst. "All species have equal claim to this planet, including its oceans. It is the natural order of things. I refuse to accept that the self-imposed rights of men should outweigh the rights of another species to its very existence!"

Amimoto's smile was cruel. "I can do what I want. The law is clear; this commission is responsible for regulating whaling and it has just given me a mandate to do so!"

Cal stared him down. "The right to existence is the most fundamental principle of nature, and no piece of paper can repeal that!" He turned back to the delegates and spread his arms wide, appealing to them. "I am here to represent the rights of those who cannot speak out or fight back for themselves. I speak for them. I speak for the whales!"

Amimoto tried to interrupt again, but Cal shouted him down, his jaw set. "I refuse to bow to Japanese tyranny, and I call upon the concerned citizens of the world to stand with me! Enough is enough! Whaling must end now!"

Amimoto's laugh was forced and devoid of humour. "Try and stop me!" he sneered, his voice laced with sarcasm.

If he was afraid, Cal didn't show it. He turned back to face his nemesis, icy determination in his eyes. "Furthermore, I consider any whaling vessels to be pirates and aggressors against the Anti-whaling Community, and the continued killing of whales will constitute a state of war between us! You have been warned!"

Richard felt his adrenaline surge. "Yeah! That's telling him!" He punched the air, not caring who witnessed his outburst. For the first time in his life, passion had overtaken his usual shy reservation. He gazed at his brother, standing tall and defiant in the face of injustice, and he knew the respect he felt for him was genuine. Cal's dedication to his work was absolutely sincere. His desire to make a difference promised him far more reward than just making money, but in the face of this monumental injustice his frustration was all the more palpable too.

Richard glanced across at Summer, seated in the public gallery. Her face was flushed with excitement, and she craned her head forward to watch Cal. Richard felt his heart swoop as a lock of golden hair swept forward, hiding her face alluringly. A moment later he blinked in surprise. Her smile was both disarming and unmissable, but for a moment there he thought he caught a glimpse of it.

That would be a trifle odd, given the circumstances…

Then he shrugged it away. It was probably just wishful thinking on his part. Her smile could light up any room and he knew the effect it had on him was electrifying, so it was only natural that his desire might play tricks on him.

Suddenly Summer's expression changed to one of shock. Richard swivelled his head to follow her gaze, and he stared in horror as the main doors crashed open and a squad of police burst into the chamber, batons drawn. A woman screamed, and chairs were knocked over as people seated nearby leaped to their feet in alarm. In the ensuing pandemonium, the police captain made his way over to the Chairman.

"Delegates!" the Chairman called. "Please take your seats. I have just been informed that Victor Admirante, the Commissioner for the Seychelles has been found murdered in the grounds of this convention centre."

The word *murder* had an electrifying effect on the crowd, and they jumped to their feet in mass confusion.

"People, please, remain where you are!"

It was a vain plea though, as the panicked delegates surged towards the entrance.

Cal frowned, assessing the situation. "Everyone back to the ship," he ordered the Team, his voice calm but filled with urgency.

Richard glanced across at Amimoto and saw he was still seated, staring at them. Seeing Richard, he smiled and placed his hands together in a mocking bow. Richard stared back, transfixed, like a fly trapped in a web watching the spider's approach.

What's going on? Did he plan this?

Amimoto continued to smile, and behind him the police closed in towards the remaining delegates.

Richard's feet were rooted to the spot until Cal's urgent shout suddenly broke through his thoughts. "Richard! We need to get out of here. Now!"

***

Akogi Yokuke sat back in his seat, admiring the spectacle. The delegates milled about like sheep, as though confused whether to flee or remain. It was a wonderful demonstration of the psychology of negotiations, and how quickly such arrogant confidence could turn to fear when things went against them, or when the system broke down and the stakes suddenly extended to include their own safety. It was amusing to see the delegates suddenly cowed by fear, especially those who had so vehemently opposed him.

The police moved among them, trying to exert a degree of control and keep everyone in the chamber for questioning – an aim that wasn't entirely successful, he observed.

The Kajiki was hustling his friends towards the door, but Yokuke was unconcerned. They wouldn't get far. If the police didn't pick them up then his men would – and that might even be the more desirable outcome as far as he was concerned. Either way, the entire city was now hostile to the fleeing Westerners. They might be able to buy themselves a little more time by running, but it would do them no good. They were already defeated anyway.

Yokuke snorted at the memory of the foreigner's crazy outburst. What did he think he could accomplish with such an irrational display? Making idle threats like that… His pathetic attempts at intimidation were as empty as the alternatives left to him!

Yokuke smiled to himself.

Those are the desperate politics of a defeated man, neh?

The conference was over and he had won. The Moratorium on whaling was no more, and his Pelagic Fleet was already repaired, refuelled, and ready to set sail for the Southern Ocean again. After twenty years of patient toil, the payoff was finally at hand. He was about to resume commercial whaling at last. The only thing left to do was to rub it in!

Yokuke snatched up his microphone, raising his voice to be heard above the commotion in the chamber.

"On behalf of my Government and the Japan Fisheries Agency, the Taiyoku Misui Fisheries Corporation is pleased to announce our return to commercial whaling," he gloated. "Due to our delayed start this year, I hereby announce an extended season to ensure our new quotas can be met!"

Yokuke kept his gaze fixed on the tall blonde head moving through the crowd. He saw the back stiffen, and the Westerner turned back. For a moment their eyes locked, matching wills across the crowded room.

Yokuke smiled. It was time to exploit his new majority to the fullest. "In addition, I hereby pass a ruling to reinstate the IWC's primary purpose – to manage commercial whale harvesting. From this point on, no motions may be tabled that contradict this purpose. No longer will this commission be hijacked by the selfish and unreasonable demands of conservationists!"

The bright blue eyes stared back, cold with defiance.

Yokuke smiled. The Kajiki was powerless to stop him now, and they both knew it. Not only had the foreigner failed, but he was now in imminent danger himself.

Yokuke held his breath as the police closed in. But the foreigner sensed them and slipped away through the crowd, ushering his team out the side door without a backwards glance.

Yokuke cackled with glee. The look on the Kajiki's face was the reward he craved most of all, though it was but a small fraction of the spoils he was about to receive. Personal satisfaction at besting his adversaries was merely the icing on his cake. A return to commercial whaling promised him much more than just financial gain. He smiled, considering the gratitude the wealthy fishing industry and his coastal prefecture would shower upon their patron.

With that much wealth and political influence I will control the Diet, and the entire government! Like a Shogun of old, the country is mine!

Things had turned out very well indeed, but right now it was time for the final decisive blow! The last loose ends still needed to be tidied away to ensure his victory was complete…

Yokuke's thoughts turned to his Enforcer. He had done his job well. It was a relief to finally have that accursed Admirante out of the way, and Yokuke allowed himself a moment to revel in his victory.

That wretched man has been plaguing me for decades – but no longer!

It was indeed a blessing to be rid of one annoying thorn in his side. Kobushi-san had done very well – but his work was not finished yet! Yokuke smiled slyly as he pondered his next move. He hadn't expected the local police to be so efficient in discovering the body, but it mattered not. He bared his yellow teeth in a savage grin. Perhaps the police captain's zeal could be turned to his advantage. "Servant!" he called.

His aide hurried to his side, head bowed.

"Take this to the Enforcer," Yokuke ordered, handing the man a parcel carefully wrapped in a handkerchief. "Tell him to return to the scene and leave this where the police are sure to find it."

He threw back his head and cackled. "It's time to catch a swordfish!"

***

Dennis Cruikshank sat in the public gallery, careful to keep his expression neutral.

His suspicions surrounding this conference had already proven to be right on the money. The conservation activists fitted the profile of eco-terrorists like a glove, and his background checks had turned up a number of US passport holders in their group – something with obvious concerns for Homeland Security if terrorism became an issue. Right now he could see they were keen to evade the attentions of the local police. A sure sign of guilt if ever he saw one!

He watched the local cops with a trace of sarcasm curling his lip. With their silly white gloves and whistles around their necks they looked more like jumped-up parking wardens than officers of the law, and the way they were handling this situation wasn't much better.

That's no way to conduct an investigation. Especially a homicide!

Cruikshank's eyebrows lowered in a heavy frown. If there really was something going on within the conference, this incompetent lot wouldn't be able to keep a lid on it. If it came to that, they didn't look like they could investigate their way out of a paper bag.

Cruikshank ducked his head, pretending to scratch the hook in his nose as the troublemakers moved in his direction. He was extremely suspicious of the group now, convinced beyond doubt that they were up to no good. The blonde guy in particular had revealed his true colours. That outburst of his was extremely incriminating. Cruikshank had spent his entire working life amongst crims and lowlifes, and he knew a threat when he heard it! Clearly the conference hadn't gone the way the activists hoped, and a little desperation was likely to be all the motivation they needed to switch to terrorism now. Hell, they already had the anger and the anti-social tendencies!

Cruikshank ran a thoughtful hand over his shiny bald pate. His gut told him the protestors would cross the line, and soon. As a law enforcement officer he couldn't allow that course of action to progress. He would stop them because it was the right thing to do. The "global village" theory meant that any terrorist was a potential threat to the US these days, but it was more than just that. His primary motivation was the same as it had always been – he considered it his self-appointed duty to bring law-breakers to justice. Once you had accepted that challenge it was like a pact you made with yourself, and any lowlife who got away became a personal failure.

He twirled the thick bush of his moustache. Failure was not something he did.

Cruikshank watched as the police blundered about, trying to question people in broken English even as they fled towards the doors.

He stifled a chuckle. Luckily for the Keystone Cops here, a real professional was already on the case – even though for the moment all he could do was keep the troublemakers under investigation.

His demand for additional manpower looked more justified every day – although predictably, it hadn't been enough to satisfy his supervisor at first. Cruikshank had insisted though, even going so far as to tell the pompous ass what he thought of him. From the sounds of it he had ruffled a few feathers back at headquarters, but that was ok by him. As long as he got results he didn't care who he pissed off.

His request must have made it right to the top though. They were talking about invoking the joint Japanese-US self-defence treaty, and that was serious. Cruikshank didn't know much about international politics, nor did he care, but the guts of it was that the Jap military was restricted to a self-defence role only. In exchange for them not becoming a military threat to their neighbours in the region, good old Uncle Sam had promised to come to their aid if anyone ever threw more at them than they could take.

Cruikshank grunted with disgust. It sounded like just an excuse to mooch off the US taxpayer to him, although he was forced to concede the point on this case. According to the Japanese Self-Defence Force agreement, US forces would conduct operations to supplement functional areas that exceeded the capacity of the JSDF, and from what he'd seen so far that definitely included any covert investigation and counter-terrorism work!

Besides, the rigorous pursuit of the War on Terror meant it was in America's best interests to hunt down terrorists wherever they were found, regardless of what country's jurisdiction they were currently under.

If you want a job done properly, you gotta see to it yourself!

The powers-that-be evidently thought so too. He had just received word his assignment status had been upgraded from observation to full-scale investigation.

It went higher than that too. He had personally met with a representative from the Japanese Government and promised US support. In return, the Minister had promised him all the resources at his disposal, including a whopping performance bonus when the terrorists were suppressed. Cruikshank was happy to collaborate with the local authorities, as long as they didn't get in his ear and try to do things their way. So far though, the Minister had been very reasonable. Cruikshank grunted to himself. He would keep the Japs in the loop, but the promised performance bonus had nothing to do with it.

He paused thoughtfully. He'd initially found it a little odd that he wasn't dealing with the Minister for Police, but he wasn't about to stick his beak out worrying about local politics.

I s'pose it does make some kind of sense for it to fall under this Minister's jurisdiction – after all, he has the most to lose from it!

Cruikshank glanced across the room to where Fisheries Minister Yokuke sat. Terrorism was terrorism, and a law enforcement officer's responsibility extended to anyone victimised by crime. Yep, he was a cop, but his motivation was the same as any other time when there were perps to be taken down…

This job was about personal satisfaction!

Part III – Direct Action

Chapter 14

Cal Major sat in the Gwendolyn's wheelhouse, watching as the dark shadows of night descended on the harbour. A cold cup of coffee sat untouched beside him. Vicki had gone to the trouble of making it for him but he didn't have the heart to decline, even though he knew he wouldn't drink it. He might have preferred something stronger, but he wanted to keep his head clear. Right now he was too depressed to get drunk.

He stared out across the bay, watching as the water took on the oily blackness of night.

The thoughts that swirled around his head were just as dark.

The loss of Victor Admirante was a severe blow not only to the cause, but also personally. Victor was a friend and mentor, as well as a conservationist.

Cal sighed, tortured to the depths of his soul.

Victor was a good man, and the world has few enough of them.

His thoughts drifted back to a time long ago, when he was still a young environmental lawyer searching for some meaning in his own life. By chance he had attended a marine sciences conference where he heard a visiting lecturer discuss the plight of the world's oceans. His outlook was wise, even visionary, and Cal was intrigued. The words had reached him, striking a chord as though meant for him alone.

Inspired, Cal had approached the podium afterwards, hoping to meet the man. Despite a hectic schedule, Victor had been happy to make time to talk with him, and even had some sage words of advice to offer; "Who knows what you can accomplish if you put your mind to it? One man can always make a difference, my son. Just follow your heart."

The very next day Cal had signed up to do his Master's degree, and during his new career as a marine biologist their paths would cross many more times – and each time Victor would have a warm smile and some fatherly encouragement for him. He was still leading the resistance against Japanese whaling when Cal first attended the Scientific Committee meetings of the IWC, and his patience was as legendary as his determination. Despite his lack of success extinguishing whaling, and the threats against himself, Victor refused to give up. He had pledged his life for the good of the world.

Now he was gone. Murdered.

Cal closed his eyes, surrendering to the pain of grief. "Go in peace, old friend," he whispered. "Your fight is over now." He stared out into the night, blinking as the lights of the bay blurred suddenly. "But ours is not. As much as your life meant something, so too will your death. I swear it."

He blinked furiously, struggling to maintain his composure.

He didn't know how long he sat there, looking out the Gwendolyn's windscreen into the darkness. With the engines silent and the instruments switched off, the ship was more dead than alive. The quiet bridge was a metaphor for how he felt right now; tied up to the rotting wharf pilings of defeat instead of out cruising the wild southern seas, forging through the swells with the wind in his hair.

I'm supposed to be out there, making a difference…

He closed his eyes as old fears returned to crowd in on him in the dark. Thoughts of futility and uselessness. Thoughts of failure.

He had come here with a job to do, and for all his trying, he had accomplished nothing.

His own research was in jeopardy and the whales were doomed. Amimoto had won.

The Japanese Commissioner's evil plans had succeeded.

The only way this can end now is when the Japanese harpoon the last whale.

Cal knuckled his forehead. He had tried to do the right thing. He had tried to follow the book and fight this injustice according to the law. And he had failed. Dismally.

Now a good man was dead, and the whales were worse off than before. The fight was over…

To hell with that! This isn't over until I say it is!

Cal's jaw clenched as his stubborn streak took over. No matter what the problem, there was always another way! If due process had been exhausted, then it was time to look for another approach. He had made a promise, after all! A promise to stop Mr Fish.

He frowned, deliberating. Aurelia had already stormed off to deal with things in her own way, protesting somewhere with her Greenpeace cronies. "I'm not going to sit around here and mope," she'd fired back over her shoulder as she left. "I'm off to get something done!"

Cal was a little annoyed by her attitude. He didn't believe chaining herself to anything would help, nor did he like the unspoken implication that she didn't trust his judgement.

He hadn't given up just yet. Going off half-cocked was no substitute for proper planning, and for any plan to work it would need to be carefully thought out.

The question was what to do. And how soon could they do it.

The local police were still trying to find and interview everyone who'd been at the conference. It would only be a matter of time before they tracked the Team back to the Gwendolyn. Somehow he knew that would spell trouble for them.

There was precious little time left…

"Y'ok, son?"

The gruff voice broke through Cal's thoughts, making him jump. "I-uh… yeah," he mumbled.

The Skipper stepped slowly into the darkened wheelhouse, as though unsure of himself. He hesitated a moment, then reached out a tattooed arm and clapped Cal on the shoulder with his callused hand. "Hell of a thing, that business today…"

Cal nodded.

An awkward silence descended before Cal spoke again. "Skip, can I ask you something?"

"Yup."

"What do you think we should do?"

A relieved grin spread across Duke's whiskery face. "Ah'm all for takin' that motherless bastard down a peg or two," he growled. "He's got it comin' to him, that's fer sure."

Cal grinned back despite himself. He knew he could always count on an old sea dog to put things in perspective. "What did you have in mind?" he said.

Duke shrugged. "Dunno. But it ought t'be painful."

Cal laughed, but the wisdom behind the Skipper's words got him thinking. "Where could we hit him that would hurt the most?" he murmured, pondering out loud.

Neither of them spoke, but as they gazed out the windscreen into the night, understanding flashed between them like a current.

Across the harbour, the mast-lights of the Japanese Pelagic Whaling Fleet twinkled merrily back in the distance.

Cal turned to look at Duke, an eyebrow raised questioningly.

In the darkness, the Skipper's mood was sombre. "They'd crucify us, son. Y'know that?"

Cal nodded, waiting.

"Even if we could pull it off, them bastards'd never let us get away with it. I'm no fan of the law one way or the other, but once we cross that line there ain't no goin' back."

Cal turned to stare back out the window. "Sometimes the ends justify the means," he said quietly.

The Skipper's face registered no emotion. He picked up his bean tin spittoon and spat a wad of tobacco juice into it. "It's bin a long while since I last killed me a gook," he said matter-of-factly.

A wry smile touched the corners of Cal's mouth. Duke was always a good man to have around when you were in a tight spot, despite his partiality. "I don't think that's such a good idea," Cal cautioned. "We can't afford to kill anyone – even if they're whalers who deserve it."

"You sure?" Duke looked disappointed. "A couple of limpet mines in the right place and we could send the whole dang lot of 'em up like the Fourth of July!" He winked. "A man could get hold of such things y'know, as long as he knew the right people to talk to…"

Cal smiled at his enthusiasm. He didn't doubt the Skipper had the skills to bomb the fleet, or that he'd enjoy it immensely.

"Just say the word and I'll get 'em for you…" Duke offered.

Cal shook his head. "No, we should target property only. If we kill someone – even by accident – then we're no better than what we're trying to fight." He frowned. "Besides, we don't have time to wait. This city is crawling with cops. If we're going to do this, we need to do it tonight."

***

Richard sat at the table in the saloon. After the shock of the day's events, everyone had retreated into silence, as though stunned by the enormity of it all. The rest of the Team were all close by, busy with one thing or another, but an air of uncertainty hung over the room, like they were only pretending to be busy. Summer was reading a paperback, but Richard noticed she hadn't turned a page for quite a while. Likewise, Vicki was sitting at her laptop computer, but so far she'd spent most of the evening just staring at the screen. Heath sat in the corner, scowling like usual. Of all of them, he was the one who seemed bothered least by it, but then again, he hadn't actually been there. He was plucking at his guitar – you couldn't really call it playing since he only knew a couple of chords – and the relentless folk songs were starting to become repetitive.

Richard sighed, his head a swirling torrent of emotions mixed with the off-key music.

Suddenly Cal and the Skipper came down the steps from the wheelhouse. Richard watched them. He knew his brother had wanted to be alone for a while, but there was something about the way he held himself now that made Richard pause. Surrounding Cal was an air of silent determination, or was it excitement? Richard knew his brother well enough to know what that look meant. The others sensed it too, and as he and the Skipper sat down at the table, the Team joined them without a word, waiting expectantly.

Cal met their gaze with confidence, and when he spoke his voice was calm but staunch.

"We came here with a mission. A mission to stop whaling. We have suffered a setback today, that is true. But this is not the end. Our task is over only when we decide to relinquish the torch."

Heath's sneer was mocking. "Forget it, man. It's over. We lost already."

Cal glared at him, refusing to be disheartened. "Amimoto has seized the initiative, but we haven't lost yet. We can still fight back, and the place to hurt him the most is in his pocketbook! Whaling is inherently unprofitable – if the Japanese fleet can be incapacitated there's a good chance it'll stay that way. Right now it costs them less to continue whaling than it would to stop, but let's see how the story changes when they have to fish their fleet out from the bottom of the harbour and refloat it first!"

Heath scowled. "Violence is wrong, even against the machines of oppression."

Cal's reply was swift, and decisive. "Sometimes the only way to fight fire is with fire. We are the guardians of the future. The war against whales should have ended decades ago, but it still can now – if we're prepared to step up and do the right thing. There is a time to sit back, but there is also a time to fight."

He stared at each of them in turn, and his voice softened as he continued. "Before us stands a test; one of the most momentous struggles in history – and not just the one we face. At stake is the fate of many whale species. An entire culture hangs in the balance, a culture far older than our own, and one which has committed no wrong against us. Yet our species will annihilate them from the face of the Earth – unless something is done to stop it."

Vicki frowned. "We'll get ourselves in some serious hot water. Those ships are worth a lot of money…"

Cal's response was emphatic. "The Japanese must be stopped. I ask you, all of you, what is the worth of a few ships when measured against the future?"

Vicki nodded, agreeing with him, but her forehead remained creased with worry. "Everyone will be seriously pissed off. The police, the Government, everyone. It'll be like poking a hornet's nest with a stick…"

Cal's smile was reassuring, but tinged with regret. "I won't lie to you. It will be difficult, maybe dangerous. It will be against the law. There is a good chance that even if we succeed, we may go to prison."

Heath fiddled with his lip ring. "It'll be worse than that. They'll label us as eco-terrorists. And they'll be right!"

"One man's terrorist is the next man's freedom fighter," Cal replied without hesitation. "There are criminals and there are people who break the law, but they're not always the same thing. Only your heart can tell you what is right and what is wrong. The choice is not an easy one, especially where the laws of man conflict with the laws of nature. Yet all we can do is what we know is right, regardless of the consequences."

Heath muttered under his breath, shaking his woolly head like a sheepdog. "Violence isn't right though." He stared at Cal, his eyes dark with an unspoken challenge. "Why us, man?"

Cal raised his hands. "Why not us? We are here, standing at the crossroads in history. We have the ability..." He swept his gaze around the rest of the group. "Consider the price of failure. The Fleet will sail for the Southern Ocean in a matter of days. This summer alone will spell the death of hundreds or even thousands of whales, to say nothing of next year, and the one after that. The final battle must be fought. It must be fought now, tonight, and it must be won! Ask yourself this: If not us, who? If not now, when?"

Heath looked down, his eyes hidden behind his beetle-browed frown. "What if we say no?"

Cal shrugged. "Each of you must make your own choice. It is a difficult choice, and one that I cannot make for you. But understand this; once this choice has been made there can be no going back, for any of us. You must be prepared to stay the course, to whatever end."

He gazed around the group, searching their faces. "It's time to make a stand for what you believe in. What do you say?"

The Skipper was like a granite statue next to Cal's shoulder, his arms folded resolutely. He said nothing, but Richard could tell he'd been committed since the moment he came downstairs.

Vicki nodded too. "Count me in. I've been in ever since the Japanese brought this bloody fight to us."

Cal turned to Heath next.

He grunted. "Whatever."

Richard was surprised. Coming from him that was as good as an endorsement – it was about as enthusiastic as he ever got.

Summer looked down, avoiding Cal's eyes. She hadn't said anything the whole time, and now she sat with her hands clasped nervously in her lap. "Okay," she said in a barely audible voice.

Suddenly Richard felt all eyes turn towards him.

He gulped, trying to swallow down the butterflies that swooped in his stomach.

It was true that he'd felt a strong emotional bond with the 'Real World' to which his eyes had been so recently opened. The spirit of the Ocean represented all things wild and free, but the knowledge that it was so fragile for all its raw power came as a cold shock. The realisation that the world was in terrible danger from human greed gripped him like no other tragedy could – an Ocean without whales would be like night without the stars, and it was enough to make his heart burst with grief at such a terrible loss.

Richard had no doubt that the plight of the whales concerned him greatly, but was it enough to become a criminal for?

This was no game they were embarking on. It was dangerous out there. Succeed or not, they could spend the rest of their lives in jail. Cal had said so. People could get hurt, maybe even killed.

Why us? Can't someone else do it?

This was a monumental decision he was being asked to make. Helping Cal with his research was one thing, but this was in a totally different league. This was more than just scary, this was positively dangerous – not to mention downright illegal. It was a premeditated act of criminality. It could ruin his future.

He wrung his hands together. That was the essence of the problem right there. Like it or not, this was a decision on how he wanted to spend the rest of his life. After this point, the choice he spurned would become as distant as a dream. Did he really want to become a fugitive, plagued by guilt and hunted by the authorities wherever he went?

Richard screwed up his face. Where did his loyalties lie? It was a decision that was as agonising as it was critical. He wasn't a biologist like the others, so it could be argued his need to get involved was less than theirs. Besides, how could one man's stand count for anything, especially in the face of such ruthless and determined opposition? Any resistance would be futile without an army to back it up, and all they had was themselves, a half dozen misfits.

How can any one of us possibly make a difference?

Richard was no hero, but at least he was man enough to admit it. He opened his mouth to decline, but the words never made it past his lips.

Something made him hesitate; an image that suddenly popped into his head. It was his brother, standing tall in the speeding Naiad in front of the Kuu-Maru, blocking the harpoons of the Japanese Hunter-Killer boat, shielding the Old Blue with his own body. Cal's words echoed in his ears. "You only get one life, Bro. How you use it is up to you. Me? I'm not here to make money, I'm here to make a difference."

Richard swallowed. At that moment the realisation hit him.

There is no one else.

He sighed, conflicted, searching deep inside himself for answers. The 'Old Richard' would instinctively duck and run for cover, doing anything to avoid conflict. In fact, he realised, he would have been long-gone already – fleeing back to the safety of his comfortable life in the city. He could hear the familiar protests still resounding in his subconscious, "What could I possibly do to save the world? I'm just an electronics engineer. It's not my responsibility!"

Even as the thoughts came to him though, Richard forced them down. He could see them now for what they were. With a sense of shame he recognised the same passive selfishness that was endemic in modern society. Everyone thought things should be different in some way, shape, or form, yet no one was prepared to do anything about it. When push came to shove, everyone cared only for himself.

Not everyone, he realised, looking around him at the Team's expectant faces.

Richard took a deep breath. It was about time the old him changed anyway.

"I'll do it," he said.

***

Dennis Cruikshank sat in his hotel room, binoculars pressed to his eyes as he glassed the quay. The light was fading rapidly, but he kept his attention firmly fixed on the old blue trawler. The lights were burning in the saloon, but he could see people moving around in the darkened wheelhouse too. That was suspicious. Why would people skulk around in the dark unless they had something to hide?

His forehead creased, lowering his bushy brows onto the eyepieces as he frowned. Frustration was not an emotion he did well.

Twenty-five years on the job had finely tuned his cop sense. He could feel its familiar jangling now.

They're up to something down there!

Definitely. He would stake his career on it.

They were planning something, and it bugged him to have to sit up here doing nothing about it.

This may be Japan, but these punks were his self-appointed problem now. It was true he felt no particular sense of duty toward the bumbling local authorities, but cops were the good guys no matter where you were, and any law enforcement officer who could look the other way while a crime was being committed wasn't worth his badge. Besides, he had accepted an official assignment, so these terrorists were now his responsibility too.

The question was, what was he to do about it?

Cruikshank grunted. Predictably, his request for more resources had gone down like a concrete turd back at headquarters, although he had to admit his delivery style would have been as much to blame.

His lip curled with disgust. He told it like it was, that was his way, and if those pencil-pushers back at their desks didn't like that they could take their pencils and shove them up their…

The thought trailed off as he recalled the conversation with Ron Silverman, his supervisor. The old bastard had been as cagey as ever – those damn spooks were all the same – but this time Cruikshank had managed to pry some information out of him. Not surprisingly, the Powers-that-Be hadn't wanted to know about an old street cop's suspicions, or his demands.

Cruikshank had persisted though – it was what he did best – and eventually his supervisor had relented. Not that that meant anything of course. Authorisation still had to come from the top, and the people up there were a long way from the mean streets where the action went down. Even though Silverman had agreed to table the request for a counter-terrorist team to be put on standby, Cruikshank could tell by his tone he was still sceptical. Then the old bastard had let the cat out of the bag.

"I don't want to jeopardise any ongoing investigation by acting prematurely," he'd said, and then Cruikshank knew for certain something was up. He was the one requesting the situation be upgraded, so that had to mean there was already someone else on the case. And that pissed Cruikshank off, big time.

While it was a minor relief to know his appraisal of the situation had been on the money, and was probably being taken seriously, his good mood ended there. "I work my own cases," he growled to himself for the dozenth time that evening, tugging at the corner of his moustache. "Do they think I need a goddamn babysitter or something?"

His supervisor had infuriated him even more by refusing to divulge anything more, and Cruikshank could still feel the vein in his temple pulsing angrily. Eventually he had managed to prise the details out of Silverman, but that only left him in a worse mood.

For him to be in the dark about this meant it had to have been ordered from the very top. And it pissed him off to be left out of the loop.

How the hell am I supposed to get the job done when they go behind my back like that?

It reminded him of a time on the LAPD when the Feds had come marching in and taken over a homicide investigation he'd been working on for eighteen months. It turned out the perpetrator was wanted on felony charges in three states, and that overruled Cruikshank's jurisdiction. He'd had to drop the case and walk away just days from nailing the punk.

Sure, the Feds had gone in all guns blazing and nailed the bastard good and proper – he'd stopped five bullets and had to spend the first year and a half of his sentence in a prison hospital, and he could still piss in three directions at once – but that wasn't the point. The lowlife might have gotten his justice, but Cruikshank hadn't. He'd done all the hard work. That punk was his to take down, and he'd been denied.

He glowered into the night, binoculars trained on the dark shadow of the trawler down at the wharf.

"I'll be damned if I let them take this case off me now," he muttered. "I'm not going to walk away from this one."

The top of Cruikshank's shaved head slid forward into a scowl. There was movement aboard the ship. Something was happening.

His moustache twitched as he snorted his disgust. It went beyond his better judgement to wait for these lowlifes to commit a crime before moving to take them down. He'd been sorely tempted to ignore his orders and take matters into his own hands, but with forced reluctance he decided to stick it out and see what happened.

He reflected on his supervisor's revelation… "So, the suits have assigned an undercover agent to infiltrate the terrorists' inner circle, have they…?" he murmured to himself. "I hope whoever they picked is good enough to handle this case, because my cop sense tells me it'll all hit the fan very soon."

***

Cal Major stood in the Gwendolyn's workshop, deep in thought. Aurelia's absence still bothered him, but he tried to put it out of his head to concentrate on the task at hand. He cast a critical eye over the tool racks, trying to decide what he might need. He hefted a plumber's wrench, weighing it in his hand. It was reassuringly solid, but its head was small. He screwed up his face and replaced it on the rack. They would come across some heavy-duty machinery tonight, and more to the point, since they couldn't risk taking any weapons on board every tool would have to fulfil a dual purpose…

He reached for the largest industrial-sized wrench he could find, stowing it in his canvas duffel bag. He followed it with anything else from the wall rack that might possibly come in handy.

Hacksaw, bolt cutters, mallet…

It was difficult to know what to take since he hadn't had time to prepare. A scouting mission would have been invaluable to know what awaited them, but he couldn't risk it. Time was all but up already.

It has to be done tonight.

Cal didn't even know the layout of the ship he was about to board – hardly the time to discover a locked door or some other obstacle. He racked his brains, trying to think of all possible situations they might encounter, and what tools he might need to deal with them.

Rope, torch, dive mask…

One thing was certain though, once aboard they were committed. They couldn't afford to fail, and they definitely couldn't afford to get caught.

Cal ran a hand through his short blonde hair. The equipment was the least of his worries. Personnel was always the biggest headache for a leader. He wouldn't want to put to sea in the Naiad with an inexperienced crew, and similarly, he knew many of the Team would be totally naive when it came to burglary and sabotage. With a wry smile he realised his own past history with Aurelia and her activist friends wasn't entirely wasted! His amusement was short-lived though. Few of the others had any such grounding, and an inexperienced team could have big problems tonight.

It's not a good thing to go into danger unprepared!

Cal forced his doubts down. There wasn't any other choice.

He'd briefed them as well as he could, and everyone knew what was expected of them. Nevertheless, he resolved to keep Richard with him and Vicki, where he could keep an eye on his brother. He didn't doubt Richard's commitment, but he knew he couldn't expect too much from him when suddenly tossed in the deep end like this. Likewise, he would put Heath and Summer in the second team with Duke. He felt a pang of guilt dumping the two of them on the Skipper like that, but the burly ex-Navy SEAL should be able to handle them, along with any problems they might have. Cal stifled a smile. Besides, the Old Sea Dog would probably have a ball tonight. Covert sabotage was right up his alley!

Cal's thoughts turned back to Aurelia, and his frown returned. He was used to her impetuousness by now, but her absence still bothered him. She had always been a livewire who answered to no one except whatever injustice currently drove her, but deep down a part of him still hoped she would return. The old days were long gone now, but he did miss the togetherness they once shared.

We could have taken on the world…

He couldn't help feeling that her leaving to protest with her Greenpeace cronies was a vote of confidence in his leadership and handling of the campaign so far. Cal closed his eyes, pinching the bridge of his nose with a dejected hand.

It's over. Let her go. You'll only get hurt again.

He sighed. Logic was easy to recognise, but often the easiest resolutions to make were the hardest to keep.

She won't understand. You know that.

Reluctantly, he was forced to agree with the inner voice of reason that spoke in his head. Despite his guilt at not telling her of their plans, he knew in his heart she would never approve. Any kind of protesting would be fine, but direct action fell on the wrong side of her invisible moral line. In his mind's eye he could picture her indignant response. "Violence and aggression never achieved anything," she would say, tossing her hair. "They are the cause of the world's problems, not the solutions."

Cal shook his head sadly. There was no room for half-measures when it came to halting the slaughter. As far as he was concerned it was always the final result that mattered at the end of the day, and a lack of commitment to do what needed to be done wouldn't take them there.

If whales are to survive, the Japanese Fleet must be stopped!

Despite his feelings for Aurelia, Cal knew it was best not to involve her in this. He frowned. In addition to her usual stubbornness he had detected an odd change in her lately. Deception or not, he sensed it would be better for all concerned if the less she knew about this action the better.

Chapter 15

Richard Major waited in silence as they sat around the wardroom table for Cal's final briefing. Everyone was dressed for subterfuge in black, and the tension in the air was electric.

Richard felt as though he would be sick at any moment. There were butterflies doing loops in his stomach, and he'd already broken into a cold sweat under the dark woollen cap he wore. He swallowed and looked up, glancing around the array of faces filled with nervous excitement. Richard managed a watery smile in response. It was too late to back out now. He had agreed to do this and now he damn-well had to go through with it, no matter how terrifying the thought.

Cal was explaining the plan of action. Richard took a deep breath and tried to concentrate on what he was saying.

"The three Hunter-Killer boats are moored alongside the processing factory, but there's too much activity nearby to risk a hit on them now," Cal said. He paused, and Richard could see the conflict within him. "Never mind," he assured them, as if echoing his own thoughts out loud. "If we can take out the support ships that'll be just as good. The Fleet won't get far without a factory ship." He frowned then, his face suddenly grave. "It won't be easy though. Stealth and secrecy will be vital for this to succeed. We can't afford to be discovered before the ships are safely on the bottom of the harbour. That means we have to get on board, do our work, then get away – all without being seen."

His gaze turned thoughtful again. "Who knows, if things quieten down on the wharf and we manage to deal to the support ships without the alarm being raised, we might still get a crack at the Hunter-Killer boats on the way home…"

Heath clicked his tongue stud against his teeth. "Yeah, but what if we get seen, man?"

Cal looked annoyed. "If we're busted, then it's all over. Not only will we be in deep shit, but they'll also have time to pump out the ships before they sink." He looked around the circle of faces. "The first inkling we want the Japanese to have of this is when the sun comes up tomorrow morning and their ships are stuck in the mud at the bottom of the bay – and we're on the open sea headed for home. Anything else and we run a serious risk of failing."

Cal turned back to the group. "Right, everyone knows what to do?"

There was a chorus of assent. Nevertheless, he repeated the plan again; making sure everyone knew their job. Richard nodded. It was simple enough – as long as nothing went wrong. He felt his stomach nose-dive again at the thought. "W-what do we do if something does go wrong?" he stammered, certain the quaver in his voice would betray his fear.

Across the table, Summer suddenly flashed a smile at him; a flirty gesture, and one that was clearly meant to be more lustful than reassuring.

Richard was dumfounded. He blinked, certain he must have hallucinated it.

What's going on?

He stared back at her, unsure how to react.

"If everything turns pear-shaped, get the hell out of there and get back to the Gwendolyn as fast as you can," Cal said.

Richard barely heard him. He was still staring at Summer, and there could be no mistaking her follow-up. The wink she gave him was subtle, but direct. Richard jumped as if slapped, jerking his head away to stare awkwardly at the floor.

What the hell?

Cal appeared not to have noticed the exchange. He patted Richard's shoulder reassuringly, as though mistaking his confusion for plain terror. "Don't worry, Bro. I'll be with you. Nothing will go wrong."

Richard gave a small nod, grateful to him regardless. This would be without a doubt the most dangerous and terrifying thing he had ever faced in his life, and to voluntarily walk into it would take courage he wasn't even sure he had. He sighed. Quite apart from what lay ahead, the anticipation beforehand was sheer torture.

Cal checked his watch briskly and looked around the group. "Right, any more questions?"

There were none.

"Let's do it then!"

Despite Cal's confidence, the group's mood was pensive as they silently trooped outside into the night.

Richard gazed across the strip of water they would have to cross to get to the whaling ships. He would have felt safer walking, but he knew Cal was right, there was too much activity at the Taiyoku Misui Fisheries Company's factory to risk going on foot. He stared across the harbour, the dark expanse of water taking on a sinister appearance in the pale moonlight.

With the Naiad lost, the only other boat on board was the Gwendolyn's little white emergency raft. It was a tiny two-metre inflatable, and compared to the sleek, rigid-hulled Naiad it had more in common with a child's beach toy than a speedboat. It was half the size and a fraction as seaworthy. The raft normally lived behind the wheelhouse where it could float free in an emergency, and Cal and the Skipper jumped up and lifted it down without any effort at all.

Richard eyed it suspiciously. Lying on the wide expanse of the foredeck the little raft looked even more pathetic. It was too small to have a shackle for the crane to hook onto, and in any case it wasn't heavy enough to need it. Cal and the Skipper simply tied a rope to it and lowered it over the side. It settled down onto the water with barely a splash, bobbing merrily next to the Gwendolyn's huge hull like an albino tick on the side of a whale. The Skipper vaulted over the rail and swarmed down the cargo net. He jumped off into the raft, taking up half the space as he stood in the bottom, feet astride. His grizzled face looked back up at them as he beckoned for the gear. Cal lowered the two duffel bags down to him, followed by the tiny ten horsepower outboard motor. Richard was already nervous, and the sight of the motor they were about to put their trust in didn't inspire confidence. The thing looked more like an oversized egg-beater than an engine. Confidence was one thing he had in short supply right now.

Cal's voice suddenly cut through his thoughts. "Down you go!"

Richard gulped. This was the moment of truth, when he had to summon the courage to change the course of his life. Despite promising himself he wouldn't falter, now was the time to make good on his word. He had known this time would come – indeed, he'd been dreading it all evening – but it still took a superhuman effort to goad himself into action. He nodded resignedly to his brother and swung a leg over the rail, reaching for the first rung of the net with a hesitant foot. The rope web swayed in response to his touch. The memory of his last encounter with the cargo net leaped to mind; clinging to it, soaking wet and chilled to the bone, having narrowly escaped death beneath the charging steel hull of a whaling boat. Richard closed his eyes, trying to put such thoughts out of his head. He took a deep breath and started down, clutching the ropes as tightly as a drowning man.

It seemed like an eternity before his foot finally bounced onto the soft rubber of the pontoon below, and he collapsed gratefully into the little boat.

One by one the others came down, and the raft rocked alarmingly as each person stepped in. After a few anxious moments they all managed to get seated without upsetting the little boat, but there was so little room they were jammed in like sardines. With all the weight on board the raft sat low in the water. Richard tried not to look at the black water slopping just a few inches away.

Cal sat in his usual place in the bow, with Vicki next to him, and Heath sat in the stern next to the Skipper. That left Richard and Summer sitting together in the middle with the two canvas bags. Any other time he would have been over the moon being so close to her, but not tonight. He had too many other things on his mind. He stared ahead into the darkness, trying to think about anything except the danger they were about to court.

The Skipper untied the line and they cast off into the night.

It had begun.

It was after midnight, but despite his tiredness Richard knew he would not sleep that night. A cold breeze blew across the harbour, ruffling the inky sea and making him shiver beneath his black woollen fisherman's jersey.

"Let's go," Cal whispered.

"If that piece of junk will start," Heath snorted, curling his lip ring in the direction of the tiny outboard.

Cal's smile was forced as he handed him a paddle. "No motor. We don't want anyone to know we're coming."

"Aw man, it's too far-" the Californian began to protest.

"Shut y' mouth and git y' back into it," the Skipper growled in response.

Heath's grumbling quickly turned into ragged panting as they set off across the bay. Richard shivered as the darkness closed in around them, and he had to force himself to concentrate on pulling the paddle through the dark water as silently as possible. The glow of the moon was muted by the cloud cover, and a light sea fog hung just above the sea surface. The only sound was the splash of paddles dipping into the water.

It was hard work to push the overloaded raft forward, but with six paddles going, their progress was steady. The lights of the processing factory appeared through the fog ahead, wreathed by a ghostly glow. The Skipper steered them away from it, bypassing the Hunter-Killer ships tied up alongside, pointing them instead towards where the darkened support boats lurked further down the wharf. A few minutes later the Nippon-Maru loomed ahead, a malevolent shadow that swallowed up the stars like a black hole.

"There it is…" Vicki's hoarse whisper gave voice to the thought that occupied all their minds.

"Isn't this a kick?" Summer whispered, her voice sounding breathless with pent-up excitement – or maybe something else.

No one replied though, and she lapsed back into an awkward silence. Richard suspected that like him, everyone's attention was fixated on the black ship.

"So far so good," Cal murmured. "This fog should keep us hidden right up to the target." His calm tone was authoritative and reassuring. "As long as it doesn't get too thick to see we'll be sweet."

"Yup." The Skipper's gruff whisper sounded loud in the night air. "This here's a huntin' moon."

Richard felt a chill run through his blood. He wasn't a hunter. Far from it! In fact, they could just as easily become the ones who were hunted tonight! He tore his gaze away from the sinister shadow in the distance, trying to keep his emotions under control.

He glanced at Summer out of the corner of his eye. She sat up straight beside him, her breath coming in excited gasps as she stared ahead into the darkness. Even with her blonde hair tucked under a beanie, she looked stunning under the pale moonlight.

She was so close to him that Richard could feel a tingle of excitement shoot through his body at her presence. She shifted her weight and suddenly their thighs were touching. Richard gulped and tried to move his leg away, but there was no room. Guiltily, he stared ahead, unsure what to do. As much as he was terrified of angering her, he had to admit the feeling was nice.

As if reading his mind, Summer reached out and patted his knee. It was a friendly gesture, but as the seconds passed and she didn't withdraw her hand, Richard felt his pulse surge. He held his breath, too scared to move for fear of spoiling the moment, a confused jumble of thoughts swirling through his head.

What's going on? Does she like me now?

Up ahead, Vicki's ponytail bounced in the dark as she turned her head to the side, watching the lights of the Taiyoku Misui Fisheries Company's factory. Richard blushed, certain she could see what was going on out of the corner of her eye. Suddenly Summer removed her hand, the movement unmistakable even in the dark. Vicki blinked and turned her head away, giving no indication of having seen anything. But as she continued paddling, her gaze fixed firmly straight ahead, Richard thought he saw her shoulders slump ever so slightly.

They paddled the next few minutes in silence, and the enormous black hull slid slowly past, filling the sky like a gigantic apparition that rose threateningly out of the mist.

Richard stared up at it with something approaching superstitious awe, so transfixed by it he even forgot to watch what he was doing. As a result he completely miss-timed his next stroke, driving his paddle straight into Cal's extended blade. The two met with a loud *clunk* that echoed through the still air.

Everyone froze, staring up at the black steel wall, waiting with bated breath to see if a face would appear at the rail, or a warning shout would echo through the mist. But the only sound they heard was the faint hum from the ship's generator. In the darkness, the low but persistent rumble seemed to engulf them, and Richard couldn't tell if he was hearing the sound in the air, or feeling the vibration through the water. Either way, it was an unsettling feeling, as if the great ship was alive – and watching them.

After a full minute, Cal exhaled. "Ok, keep paddling. Let's try to keep it quiet from now on."

"S-sorry," Richard mumbled, feeling his cheeks colour with embarrassment. Neither Vicki nor Summer looked at him this time.

Cal steered them quickly past the huge ship, then cut in a dozen raft-lengths behind its towering rear. Richard could just make out the Nippon-Maru's stern slipway, gaping like a hungry mouth in the darkness.

For a heart-stopping moment he thought that was his brother's goal, but Cal pulled the little inflatable up to the side of the wharf, where a fixed ladder rose up into the mist.

"This is us," Cal whispered, tying the raft to one of the rungs. "We're right under their noses here, so let's keep it quiet."

Cal went up the ladder first, hand over hand like a gymnast, then disappeared over the top. Richard waited, head craned skyward, dreading the thought of what dangers might be waiting at the top.

A moment later Cal's face appeared back over the edge of the wharf. "Ok, coast is clear," he whispered. "Come on up."

Richard reached out a tentative hand and grasped the cold metal of the ladder. The bottom rungs were wet and slippery with weed and sea slime. He jerked his hand back, fumbling in his pocket for his leather work gloves. The last thing he wanted was to slip and fall off half-way up.

"Come on, man. What's the hold-up?" Heath complained.

"J-just getting my gloves…" Richard stammered.

"Quiet y'all!" the Skipper hissed. "You!" he growled at the Californian. "Shut y' mouth." He turned to Richard. "And you, git y' ass up that ladder."

Richard tugged his gloves on and hurried to obey. He gripped the slippery rungs, took a deep breath, and started up.

At the top, he peeped his head over the lip, trying to get his bearings. The wharf was deserted, a few sodium-vapour street lamps casting an eerie orange glow over the scene. Richard peered about, suddenly afraid.

Where's Cal gone?

Then he saw a flash of movement, as a hand beckoned to him from behind a stack of oil drums. Richard clambered onto the edge of the pier and hurried over to crouch in the shadows next to his brother. Cal flashed him a grin in the darkness, then turned back to watch for the others.

Richard was panting slightly, although more from nervousness than exertion. He looked around, finding his gaze inexorably drawn towards the huge bulk of the Nippon-Maru moored further up the pier. From up here he could see the huge steel goalposts that were its deck cranes, rising like skyscrapers out of the mist. He looked away, secretly relieved he wasn't going to have to board the black ship tonight.

As he waited, one by one the others came up the ladder and scampered across to join them in the shadows. When they were all assembled, Cal checked them over. "Everyone ok? No problems?"

They all nodded. All except Heath. "I still say this is terrorism," he muttered under his breath.

Richard gasped, watching Cal's face just in time to see a cryptic look pass between him and the Skipper. His brother's reply was swift, and his tone hard. "You agreed to do this," he snapped. "If you're going to bail, then get the hell out now. Go back and wait for us in the dinghy."

Heath scowled, fiddling with his eyebrow stud, but he didn't reply.

Cal turned to face the rest of them, his face severe. "That goes for the rest of you too. After this point there's no going back. If you're not in, then you'd best leave now. This is your last chance."

The seconds dragged by. No one moved.

This is your chance! Go back and wait on the raft! You don't belong here!

Richard's fears screamed in his ear, but he forced himself not to listen. He crouched lower behind the oil drum, determined not to reveal himself as a coward.

"Ah've heard about enough of this crap," the Skipper growled through his beard. "Ah'm here to sink that there ship, and you two are gonna help me do it, right?" He turned his gaze onto the two field assistants. Even in the darkness, Richard could feel the intensity of his stare. Summer stared at her feet, nodding slowly. A moment later Heath gave his sullen agreement too.

The Skipper spat a wad of tobacco juice onto the wharf plank. "Fine. Let's be off then. All this lolly-gaggin' won't git the job done." He stood up to leave, shouldering the heavy duffel bag full of tools. He hesitated a moment, then turned back and clasped Cal's shoulder with a weather-beaten hand. It was a rare display of emotion. "Take it easy, Son," he growled, a little uncomfortable and clearly unwilling to jinx the mission by being any more specific than that.

Cal flashed a broad grin in the darkness. "See you on the flipside!"

"Yup." The Skipper turned to stare into the darkness. "Good huntin' y'all!" he murmured as the Team divided to go their separate ways.

Richard watched them go through whatever mental preparations they needed. Summer turned to flash him a pulse-quickening grin. He smiled back, suddenly distraught that they were about to be separated, and worried for her safety.

He watched as the Skipper led his group away towards the Nippon-Maru. There was something about that sinister black factory ship that chilled his blood.

Rather them than me!

He knew his turn was about to come though. There was another ship waiting in the darkness, waiting for him…

"You two ok?" Cal whispered.

Vicki smiled thinly, but she had a strange look on her face. Richard could see she was troubled by something. Mindful of the number of times she'd helped him, he offered his best attempt at a reassuring smile. But she didn't look at him.

Cal didn't seem to notice. "Right then, let's do it!" He stood up and led them off in the opposite direction, heading towards the spot where the Fleet's spotter ship lay tied up somewhere in the gloom.

As they crept down the wharf, Richard tried to catch Vicki's eye, but she slipped into line behind him, out of view without stopping or risking a noisy stumble. He let it pass for now.

A moment later the Kyoeishin-Maru suddenly materialised, ghost-like, out of the fog, its long white hull glowing under the pale moonlight. Even at low water the side of the ship still towered above the level of the wharf. Richard stared up towards the rail, heart beating faster. He felt a brief touch of relief when he saw the boarding gantry was still in place – he wasn't sure he could have managed Cal's alternative method of entry; climbing aboard along a mooring line – but any good vibe was short-lived and quickly swamped by trepidation at what they were about to do.

As he followed Cal up the gangplank, Richard felt as though every step was heavier than the last. There were large gaps between the planks, but mercifully, the swirling mist beneath his feet hid the sight of the hungry black water waiting below. Cal paused at the end, scanning the ship for danger. Richard crouched down behind him, trying to see what he was looking at. The deck of the Kyoeishin-Maru was as empty as a graveyard in the moonlight. A moment later, Cal beckoned him to follow then crept forward like a hunting leopard.

This is it!

Richard tried to follow, but his legs baulked. He remained crouched there, rooted to the spot like a bungee-jumper summoning the courage to take the plunge. That single step onto the deck of the ship represented a monumental leap of faith.

Cal wait! Don't leave me!

As he watched his brother's back recede into the shadows before him, Richard could feel the familiar tightness gripping his chest. He had forgotten his inhaler again.

He turned his head away, trying to take deep, calming breaths.

He gazed out across the harbour. At this height he could see clear over the top of the low blanket of mist. In the distance, a familiar mast light twinkled a warm welcome across the water.

The Gwendolyn.

The discomfort of living at sea was long-forgotten now. To Richard, the blue trawler was far more than just another ship moored in the harbour. Her stately lines embodied familiarity, safety, and even the emotional security of an adopted home, of sorts. He was reluctant to turn his back on that and step aboard this ship of danger.

I wish I was back in my cabin right now!

His gaze travelled along the waterfront to the three sharp-nosed Hunter-Killer ships, and the huge whalemeat processing factory dominating an entire city block behind them. The relentless glow from its floodlights challenged the stars above. In the foreground loomed the massive bulk of the Japanese Pelagic Whaling Fleet's factory ship. Richard felt his resolve sink even lower. This was hopeless!

The Taiyoku Misui Fisheries Company was a monstrous entity. Like a gigantic multi-armed octopus, its tentacles reached into all branches of the Japanese Government, and through the boardrooms of international business connections its corrupt influence spread right around the globe.

How can we possibly take on such a huge and powerful organisation?

Picking a fight against such a ruthless and determined enemy was madness. Amimoto's revenge would be swift and decisive. They would stand about as much chance as a whale beneath the Fleet's harpoon cannons.

He stared at the factory, remembering the almost-disastrous finale to their mission to collect some DNA evidence. It made Richard's blood run cold to imagine what might have happened to them if they hadn't managed to escape the mob of angry whalers. And yet here they were again, about to challenge the thuggish whalers in the confines of their own ship. He swallowed nervously, his imagination working overtime as he fretted over the outcome.

You made a promise to Cal! You can't back out now!

Richard gritted his teeth and forced himself to step aboard the Japanese spotter ship, but as soon as his foot touched the deck he was gripped by a fresh wave of panic.

Oh my god! I've crossed the line… I'm a criminal!

As he stood there on rubbery legs he could feel the blood pounding in his ears, and it took all of his willpower not to turn and bolt back down the gangway to the wharf.

I'm not cut out for this! I'm no burglar…

Vicki came up behind him, an eyebrow cocked in a silent question.

Richard found her presence reassuring though, and his mind suddenly cleared. Despite the drama of their previous mission to the Taiyoku Misui Fisheries market, it had been successful, humiliating Mr Fish in the eyes of the world.

Richard closed his eyes, remembering the violent death the Great Whale suffered at the hands of the Japanese Whaling Fleet.

Killing whales was wrong. Of that he was certain.

He turned and stared back at the lights of the whalemeat factory, feeling his anger stirring like a tiny spark of defiance amid the darkness. The murderous industry was driven purely by its own greed for profits, a ruthless desire that would never be satiated as long as there were whales left alive in the oceans of the world.

Cal was right. The slaughter had to be stopped, before it was too late.

Adrenaline coursed through him like a tidal wave. He took a determined step forward, his mind made up. He nodded purposefully to Vicki, to show he wasn't afraid, and together they headed aft. Somewhere below them lay the engineroom, where they had an appointment with Fate.

Ahead of them, Cal had almost disappeared into the gloom and Richard hurried to catch up.

***

Hogei Gyofuku took another swig of saké, belching happily as the fiery liquor hit his stomach. The world tilted drunkenly and he nearly fell off the bed. He grunted. The walls were too far away to hold him up here!

Much bigger than my poky little cabin.

Then again, his flagship the Kuu-Maru was built for a single purpose, and that demanded speed above all else. As a consequence, space and weight were at a premium aboard all the Fleet's catcher ships. Even his captain's quarters were a tiny broom-cupboard compared to this room – but that was why he preferred to bunk here while they were in port. Without the excitement of the hunt to tempt him aboard the Catcher, it was much nicer to reside here.

He flopped back, appreciating the softness of the thick goose-feather duvet and scratched himself contentedly.

Much nicer than the old ship's blanket on my bunk!

He really had come a long way since dropping out of school to take a job on a fishing boat. He had done it the hard way too, rising all the way from deck hand and fish-gutter to Captain and then Master of the Pelagic Whaling Fleet. Quite an achievement for the son of a peasant crab fisherman!

Gyofuku stared up at the ornate gilded ceiling fresco, admiring the opulence factor even if the decoration was much too fancy for his taste. The Executive Suite was Amimoto's private quarters when he deigned to accompany the Fleet. The Old Goat would have an aneurysm to know he was in here, but Gyofuku dismissed the thought with a snort. Amimoto seldom roughed it with the Fleet any more, even when the ships were in port, preferring the comfort of luxury five-star hotel suites on solid ground. It was almost as though the old man was getting soft in his old age.

Gyofuku's smile was self-congratulatory. In the meantime though, it was a shame to let such a fancy facility go to waste, especially since the Executive Suite was perfect for entertaining women.

His thoughts turned to his wife. She had enjoyed the luxury of Amimoto's private quarters on numerous occasions – although the old man didn't know it, of course. One time Gyofuku had even smuggled her aboard during a voyage south – against company policy – although he suspected the other officers had made as much use of the opportunity while his back was turned. He grunted angrily. His wife was a fat ugly whore! No doubt she had already bedded half the men in town during his current absence.

Gyofuku leaned over and slapped the delightful curve of the naked buttock lying next to him, eliciting a squeal of delight. Of all the local working girls, Mintaka was his favourite. She was no geisha, but at least her body was young and firm. Besides, you didn't look at the face when you were getting down to business. He reached his hand higher, groping a dainty breast. With his pudgy fingers he squeezed the nipple hard enough to hurt. The girl's cries of delight turned into a wail of pain. She slapped his hand away and jumped to her feet, snatching up the duvet to cover her nakedness. Her lip quivered with outrage.

"Come on, you little slut," he slurred. "Come over here and show me how much you like it."

He unbuckled his trousers, exposing himself.

Mintaka forgot her indignation. She giggled delightedly, pouncing on the bed like a playful kitten. She curled up next to him, resting her head on the pale flab of his stomach, and reached down to caress his manhood. Gyofuku closed his eyes and lay back, waiting for something to happen.

She persisted for a while, then looked up, bottom lip thrust out in a pout. "He doesn't want to play!" she complained.

Gyofuku opened one eye. "That's 'cause you're doing it wrong, bitch!"

Mintaka sniffed haughtily and sat up, folding her arms across her breasts. A moment later a sly smile spread across her face. "I know just the medicine!" she chirped, rummaging in her purse. She produced a jar of little pink pills, tipping two of them into her hand and offering them to him with a triumphant grin. Gyofuku looked at them and grunted, but he didn't refuse. He knew the potency of those little triangular pills. He struggled up onto one elbow and reached out a podgy hand for them. He threw the pills down his gullet, washing them down with another gulp of saké, then flopped back into the depths of the duvet. He closed his eyes, waiting for the familiar warmth to begin in his loins.

Mintaka resumed her fondling, humming softly.

The minutes passed and the soporific effect of the saké began to creep up on him.

Suddenly Mintaka's hand froze. Gyofuku felt his ecstasy evaporate in an instant. He grunted with irritation and opened one eye. "Keep going!" he ordered.

The girl ignored the command. "What was that? I heard something."

"It was nothing," he slurred. "Just your imagination."

"I heard a noise," she insisted. "You said we were alone on the boat, but I heard a noise."

"What kind of noise?" Gyofuku snapped, struggling to keep his temper in check.

"It was a kind of a thump…"

Gyofuku snorted. "It was just the ship. Keep going!"

Reluctantly, Mintaka returned to her task. He closed his eyes and lay back, groaning with delight as her practised fingers did their work.

Suddenly a metallic clang reverberated through the superstructure of the ship.

Gyofuku's eyes flew open in the same instant.

That wasn't the hull plates contracting! Someone's here!

His first thought was that Amimoto-san had returned to his quarters.

"Iye!" he exclaimed, his voice cracking in fear.

In a blind panic, Gyofuku leaped off the bed, forgetting his pants were still bunched around his ankles. He tripped and sprawled full length on the floor, gibbering in terror. He lay there, naked and prostrate, his whole body quivering with terrified sobs, staring wide-eyed towards the doorway. But as the moments passed and the door remained closed, his composure began to return. He peered at his wristwatch.

It was three in the morning.

Much too late for an old man to be up and about, neh?

But if it wasn't Amimoto, then who was it? Gyofuku had given shore leave to the entire crew to make sure he had some privacy, and the run of the ship during his romp…

His eyes narrowed to slits.

He struggled to his feet, yanking his trousers up over the giant full moon of his buttocks. The girl was still cowering on the far side of the bed. Gyofuku ignored her. He threw on his shirt and reached for the bright red helmet that denoted his rank. If that was a wayward crewman disobeying orders by coming back aboard, he would give him a lesson to remember. He paused, deliberating. The more he thought about it a crewman seemed unlikely though. A trespasser then? But any sane local knew better than to meddle with the Taiyoku Misui Fisheries Company's security. Gyofuku bared his teeth. Any drunk staggering aboard his ship looking for a place to sleep off the evening's stupor would expect to receive a short sharp shock!

What if it's those meddling barbarians?

The thought hit him like a brick.

They wouldn't dare! Would they?

Gyofuku's face contorted into a mask of hatred. Calling the local police was far too easy. He clenched his pudgy hands into ham-sized fists. You didn't get to be the captain of a rough and rebellious whaling crew by taking a soft approach towards discipline. Besides, if it was those accursed foreigners aboard his ship then he would much rather deal with this problem his own way…

As he crept out into the darkened passageway, he could feel his erection starting to bulge against the crotch of his trousers. He drew the skinning knife from the sheath at his belt.

"One way or another, I shall have my pleasure tonight!" he whispered to the blackness that enveloped him.

Chapter 16

Richard Major took a deep breath and followed his brother inside the Kyoeishin-Maru. He ducked his head as he stepped through the white-painted companionway and paused in the darkened passage beyond, waiting tentatively for his eyes to adjust to the gloom.

He shivered, suddenly noticing the loss of the twinkling starlight cover of the night sky from overhead, and unable to escape the growing feeling he was suddenly a prisoner of the ghostly ship.

Vicki joined them a moment later. Richard closed his eyes, wondering if he was imagining the warmth of her breath on his cheek, but feeling somewhat reassured all the same.

Cal clicked on his head torch. The red-filtered lens cast a weak glow down the corridor, barely able to hold the shadows at bay. Richard reached for his light, but Cal forestalled him with a cautionary hand. "Save your batteries. You might need them later."

"It's awful dark down there," Richard observed doubtfully, wishing the single red beam was a little brighter.

"It'll preserve your night vision, and it's less likely to be noticed," Cal replied. "Come on."

He led the way, deeper into the dark and silent ship.

Richard followed, careful to stay close. The darkness crowded in from all sides as they walked, smothering everything except the tiny red circle of light that danced ahead like a will-o'-the-wisp. The shadowy passageway gave way to a staircase, then another passage, then more stairs, leading ever downwards…

"Remember the way," Cal said suddenly. "We'll be in a hurry coming back, and you don't want to take a wrong turn in the dark!"

Richard swallowed at the thought, unconsciously shrinking closer to the comfort of his brother's broad back as they crept deeper into the bowels of the ship.

Finally they could go no further. They stopped in front of the huge steel door that blocked their path. Cal's headlamp picked out the padlock securing the handle.

Richard stared at the lock, a strange mixture of conflicted emotions swirling in his head.

Maybe we'll have to go home now?

He looked down, ashamed of the feelings of relief that started to bubble to the surface.

"Don't worry, that's just a precautionary measure while the ship's in port," Cal observed. "A little lock like that won't slow us down for long."

Richard nodded, wondering if he should be feeling regret, or relief.

Cal reached into the bag for the bolt cutters. One determined snip later, the ruined lock fell clear and clattered to the floor. Cal reached down and picked it up. "Don't want to leave any evidence," he murmured, before dropping it into his pocket. He spun the mechanism then pushed the heavy door open. "Open sesame!" he grinned.

They filed through into the Kyoeishin-Maru's engine-room, greeted by the aroma of diesel fuel and hot lubricating oil, though the rows of pistons stood silently in the darkness.

Richard stared around them, awed by the knowledge of what they were about to do.

Cal wasted no time getting down to business. He shone his torch around, playing the beam across the network of pipes and ducting that festooned the ceiling.

"There!" he announced, pointing to where the thickest one ran down the wall and disappeared into the floor. "The seawater inlet."

"It's a big one," Vicki commented.

Cal nodded. "Yep. That's the source of salt water for use by the ship's marine lab, engine cooling, firefighting… and friendly neighbourhood saboteurs."

He traced the pipe back until it met a huge valve sticking up from the floor. "Ok, let's do it!" He reached out and grasped the wheel atop it, biceps bulging as he strained to move the giant hydrant tap.

Richard was alarmed. "Wh-what are you doing?" he blurted.

"It's ok," Cal grunted in between turns. "Need to shut off the water… before we can get to work."

A few rotations later he stepped back, satisfied. Richard held his breath, waiting for something terrible to happen. But nothing did.

Cal didn't seem concerned. "Right, now comes the fun part!" he said, pointing to the first section of pipe running from the valve to the intake. "This needs to go!"

Richard stared at it. The pipe was almost a foot in diameter and over a metre long. "Looks like they use quite a bit of sea water on board," he laughed, trying to keep the nervous quaver out of his voice.

"Well, they're about to get a whole lot more," Cal said tersely.

He knelt down with his spanner and set to work attacking the bolts that held it in place. Richard scurried over to help him. The pipe section ended in a thick collar at both ends, and each was bolted to a matching flange on the next section.

Richard put his spanner over the first nut and heaved as hard as he could. Nothing happened. He stared at the ring of bolts with dismay. They were as thick as his finger, and there had to be a dozen of them at each end!

We'll never get all those out!

Cal didn't seem bothered though. He rolled up his sleeves and got to work, his tanned forearms bulging with muscle as he gripped the spanner, working patiently and methodically, one nut at a time, separating the stubborn screw threads from each other.

Richard tried a different nut, then another, until finally one relinquished its grip. With a flash of triumph he twisted it off, dropping it into the growing pile around their feet.

As they worked, moisture began to seep from the broken seal between the sections, and the weight of the pipe began to make it difficult to pull the bolts out, even with the nuts gone.

"Hang on, I'll get it." Cal knelt under the section of pipe, supporting it with his knee so the weight didn't jam the bolts in place.

Richard and Vicki hurried to remove the last nuts before his strength gave out.

Richard cursed as his spanner slipped, stripping the skin off his knuckles. He sucked his wounded fingers, then reluctantly retrieved his spanner, struggling to undo the last nut. "It's stuck!" he complained. "I can't shift it!"

Cal's eyes were screwed closed with the effort of lifting the pipe.

Richard felt his panic starting to return.

"Let me help," Vicki said, reaching up to offer her spanner.

With Richard holding the head of the bolt, she heaved against the nut, without success. She muttered under her breath then lifted up her boot to plant a vicious kick on the handle of the wrench. "Take that ya mongrel!" It slipped a little, and with the nut loosened she managed to twist it off with her next swing. Richard couldn't keep the surprise off his face.

Vicki shrugged. "Just like changing a tyre," she murmured.

Cal opened his eyes. "Good job. Ok, help me give it a push," he ordered. Richard knelt down next to him and they leaned their weight against the pipe. With a screech of metal the join parted. A flood of water burst out of the damaged pipe, cascading over them.

Oh my god! It's flooding already!

Richard dropped the spanner and scrambled back in a panic, water swirling around his ankles.

Cal struggled to support the pipe on his own with the weight of water suddenly pressing it down on him. "Richard!"

His brother's shout spurred him into action, and with a guilty start Richard dived back under the torrent to assist. Together they managed to wrestle the pipe section clear of the gushing ends and lower it to the floor without it crashing against the hull.

Richard cast a worried glance at the volume of water still flooding from the breach.

"It's ok," Cal panted. "It's just draining the residual water from the system. It'll stop in a minute."

Cal stood up. His clothes were soaking wet, but he wore an ear-to-ear grin. "That'll do nicely."

He cast a critical eye around. "Make sure you pick up all the tools," he said. "And hide those nuts and bolts somewhere. We don't want to make it easy for anyone trying to replace that section of pipe."

He looked thoughtful for a moment. "We're almost done here", he murmured. "And so far so good. I wonder if I've got time to pay a visit to the bridge on the way out..."

He turned to Vicki. "Can you two handle the valve by yourself?"

She nodded.

Cal's jaw tightened, his mind evidently made up. He rummaged in the tool-bag for a moment, selecting a crowbar for himself, and offering a mallet to Richard. "Go nuts!" he offered, pointing to the dials and switches that lined the engine's control panel. "The more damage the better!"

He checked his dive watch. "Give me a five minute head-start," he said, "That should be enough time. Then crank the water on. All the way."

Vicki nodded. "Be careful."

Cal grinned in reply. "I'll see you on deck. There's a padlock in the bag. Don't forget to secure the door when you leave."

Richard was surprised. Why waste precious escaping time when the ship would be sinking around them?

Cal winked, as though amused by his puzzled look. "It's only fair to replace the lock since we broke theirs getting in. We're not wanton vandals, you know."

Richard frowned. Vicki saw his confusion and came to the rescue. "It'll slow the crew down," she explained. "If their key doesn't work then it'll take them longer to get in here to try and stop the leak."

"By that time hopefully it's too late," Cal added, his tone hard. He crossed the room, his boots sploshing purposefully through the pooled water. At the doorway he paused and looked back. "Look after each other," he said, then he strode through the door and was swallowed up by the darkened ship.

Richard looked across at Vicki, but she was already looking away, working on the intake valve with her spanner.

He bit his lip and headed across to the control panel, hoping she wasn't cross with him for some reason. He stared at the rows of dials and switches, momentarily intimidated. The mallet suddenly felt very heavy in his hand. He stared at it, struggling with the enormity of what he was about to do. He had never intentionally smashed something before – especially something that belonged to someone else. The thought of it seemed somehow wrong. He closed his eyes, wrestling with his conscience.

No! It's whaling that's wrong!

He took a deep breath and raised the mallet over his head. It hovered a moment at the point of balance, as though battling to make up its mind, then plunged downwards. It slammed into the control panel with a crash of breaking glass. Richard cautiously opened one eye. The gauge was broken all right, but the impact still echoed around the room, shockingly loud in the silence. He held his breath, listening.

Oh heck. Please don't let anyone hear that...

Vicki reached into the duffel bag and tossed him an old sack. "Here. Cover the glass with this. It'll make less noise when it breaks."

Richard nodded, chastened. "Sorry."

She didn't reply, turning back to the valve she was working on.

He raised the mallet again, driving it into the face of another dial. It shattered with a muffled crunch. Richard smiled, a perverse satisfaction creeping over him. It felt good to fight back, he realised, and every thump of the mallet was like sweet retribution for what the whalers had done to Old Blue. He lifted the mallet high over his head. Amimoto had a lot to atone for…

A sudden thump broke through his thoughts. He froze in mid-swing, looking around like a naughty child caught in the act. The noise wasn't the discovery he feared though, but Vicki slipping over. She lay sprawled on her back next to the water valve, still clutching the control wheel to her chest. It had evidently been stuck tight, and Richard felt embarrassed he hadn't noticed, let alone offered to help her force it off. He looked down, wincing at the sight of her skinned knuckles. Her dark ponytail hung limply, and with water sloshing around her and soaking her overalls, she looked more vulnerable than he was used to seeing her. Guiltily, he hurried over to help her. She tossed the severed valve handle aside and struggled to her feet before he could assist though, grabbing a large plumber's wrench and turning back to the seawater inlet. Without the wheel to open the valve it stood uselessly, like a giant bathroom tap with no handle to turn it on, but Vicki was prepared.

Richard watched, mesmerised, as the wrench's metal teeth gripped the spindle, then in one determined movement she twisted it open, releasing a deluge of seawater.

Richard's eyes widened in shock, and he stared at the ocean rushing in through the ruined pipe.

It's flooding!

A sudden wave of panic gripped him, the old terror resurfacing to dominate him again. He could see himself trapped in this steel-walled coffin of a room. Drowning in the cold, dark water. It would be a terrible way to die, his corpse white and bloated by the water, fingers raw and bloody from trying vainly to claw his way out, rotting down here for eternity in this watery grave…

"Richard!"

He blinked, torn back to reality. Vicki was looking at him strangely. "Are you ok?"

He nodded, not trusting himself to speak.

"Grab the tools," she ordered. "It's time to go!"

Gratefully, he snatched up the bag and headed for the door, wading through the knee-deep water.

Clang!

A loud metallic crash suddenly split the air. Richard flinched, nearly dropping the bag.

What the hell was that?

He looked back, just in time to see Vicki swing the big wrench like a club, aiming another blow at the naked valve spindle.

Clang!

The sound echoed through the room like the tolling of a bell.

"What are you doing?" he screamed, almost beside himself with panic. They had to get out of here – now – and she was making enough noise to attract half the city!

"Gotta bend this out of alignment," she muttered, lining up for another swing. "Can't let anyone turn this valve off ever again."

He stared at her, surrounded by all the churning water, a sudden vision of horror robbing him of his strength. He could see her in his mind's eye, floating face down in the water, her dark hair swirling around her face like a funeral shroud.

She glanced up at him suddenly, as if sensing his distress. "Go! Grab the tools and get out of here."

Richard shook his head, even though his mind screamed at him to obey.

The water's rising! It's flooding!

"Go!" she repeated. "The bag is heavy, you need a head start. Just leave me the padlock to put on the door..."

She's your friend! You can't leave her here!

He stayed, as though rooted to the spot.

"Hurry!" she urged him. "We've only got a minute before the water pressure forces the door shut and we're trapped down here!"

Richard felt the blood thumping in his head, and a sick sense of dread gripped the pit of his stomach. She was right. He knew it. To dally any longer was to risk drowning. He'd seen it in his worst nightmares.

Still he hesitated though, torn between his fear and chivalry.

"Go!" she insisted, raising the wrench again. "I'll be right behind you."

Reluctantly he turned and stumbled towards the door, black water swirling around his thighs.

***

Hogei Gyofuku crept through the darkened ship, the cuffs of his gumboots slapping quietly against his calves with each step. It was cold below decks, and he was in his shirtsleeves. The night air raised goose bumps where it touched the pale folds of skin on his arms, but Gyofuku didn't notice. He was warmed by the twin fires of alcohol and bravado.

He clumped softly down the rungs of a stairway, heading for the lower level. That was where the noise had originated from, he was sure of it.

He smiled coldly to himself, the warm bulge at his crotch a grim reminder of his purpose.

He was furious that his evening with Mintaka had been interrupted. He had paid the bitch already and she was unlikely to hang around. Fear of being discovered in Amimoto's suite would see to that. He ground his teeth in frustration. He would get no sweet honey tonight.

Gyofuku's eyes glittered like coal seams in the darkness.

Whoever was sneaking around on his ship would pay dearly for ruining his evening. The more his brain grappled with the problem, the more convinced he was it had to be those accursed hippy protesters.

No crew member of mine would dare disobey an order!

In any case, the foreigners had been growing bolder and more troublesome lately. He thought back to their attempts to disrupt his hunt, their publicity-seeking stunts at the conference, and their recent snooping at the local fish market. They were a pain in the backside, that was for certain.

And now they're on my ship!

His lip curled into a snarl at the very thought.

How dare they!

As captain, their mere presence here constituted a personal insult against him, quite apart from their propensity to cause any trouble. He licked his lips nervously. He couldn't afford any more trouble. Amimoto-san would skin him alive if anything happened to delay the Fleet…

Gyofuku's fist tightened around the hilt of his knife, his resolve hardening. The gai-jin would pay the price for meddling. He would see to it!

As Gyofuku prowled down the darkened corridors, a sudden commotion stopped him in his tracks. His eyebrows shot up, revealing his deep-set eyes. He whipped his head towards the sound.

What was that?

The noise was dull and metallic, like two pieces of steel being struck together, and it echoed confusingly through the ship's hull. He cocked his head, listening as it came again. It was loud, and it seemed to be coming from the stern. His jaw hung open as his brain processed the information. That wasn't a reassuring thought.

"The engine-room!" he hissed through clenched teeth. "What the hell are they doing to my ship?"

He spun on his heel and hurried aft, his anger rising with each step. His gumboots clumped loudly on the floor, but as he reached the middle stairway he had the presence of mind to slow down, so that his feet made hardly a sound as he descended down the bare metal rungs. He stepped out into the lower passageway, knife held out in front, searching eagerly for trouble. The corridor was pitch black. He felt for the wall, intending to head towards the engine-room, but a sudden noise made him turn around.

He stared up the corridor, momentarily confused by the dim red glow that suddenly appeared by the forward staircase. Then understanding dawned. It was a red flashlight.

There's someone there! It's the trespasser!

Gyofuku glanced around, checking back down the corridor, but there was no other movement. The trespasser was alone.

He licked his lips in anticipation.

How unfortunate for him!

As he crept forward he slid the knife soundlessly back into its sheath, ready for use at a moment's notice. The blade would be much too quick for what he had in mind!

He interlocked his stubby fingers and flexed them to crack his knuckles. He grinned, showing his teeth in a silent snarl. Bare hands would be much more satisfying, at least to begin with. He would soften this gai-jin up first, before it was time for the knife.

***

Duke Hayward paused outside the door of the Nippon-Maru's engine-room, holding up a callused hand for silence. He cocked his head, listening for any sign of danger. It was a big ship and they'd expended a lot of time getting here. He checked the luminous dial of his dive watch. They were running behind schedule now, but he also knew they couldn't afford to rush.

A scout's time is never wasted.

You couldn't be too careful when operating behind enemy lines, and old lessons died hard. It had been a while, but he still felt the usual exhilaration coursing through his veins – only tonight it was tempered by the fact this wasn't exactly a SEAL mission. The odds were far more dangerous.

"What are we waiting for?" the useless Californian grumbled, brushing his filthy dreadlocks out of his eyes so he could see.

Duke fixed the kid with a cold grey stare, glaring at him until he dropped his gaze. "Keep y' eyes peeled and y' goddamn mouth shut!" he muttered.

These two are a bleedin' liability, that's for sure.

The hippy kid was too impatient and too self-absorbed for this kind of work, and as for the Canadian gal, she made a fetching distraction in that tight top – but that was about all she was good for. Duke shook his head in disgust. The first rule of any op was to make sure you had a trustworthy and reliable team – that was a no-brainer if you wanted to get the job done and get out again in one piece. Having to trust these two to watch his back made him as nervous as a long-tailed cat in a room full of rocking chairs.

Duke made an exasperated noise. Right now, it was his responsibility to watch all their backs, his own included.

The hum of the Nippon-Maru's engines penetrated his thoughts, causing the furrows on his brow to deepen. Even though the din would mask any careless noise they might make, it was still a worrying complication – and one more problem for him to worry about. The fact that the ship was powered-up meant there could be people aboard, and that was a concern. Cal was desperate to avoid any collateral damage with this op. Duke shrugged, considering. The lad was probably right. It did make sense from a strategic point of view, even though on a personal level he might have preferred to send a few of the stab-happy fish-gutters down with their ship.

Mind you, I do have an old score to settle…

He reached out to test the door handle. More importantly though, with any activity on board their chances of discovery jumped like a flea on a hot-plate, and getting caught in the act would bring this op to a sudden crashing halt.

Duke eased open the door to the engine-room and slipped inside. The rattle of the huge engines swelled around him, drowning out his footsteps.

His eyes flickered quickly around the room, sizing up the situation. He pursed his lips in annoyance. There were two crewmen at work on the engine, hunched over with their backs to the door. One of them wore the green plastic crash helmet of a ship's officer. Duke swore under his breath. This was an unwanted complication.

He knew he had to act quickly to avoid the mission being compromised. On silent feet he crept across the room, lining up the green helmet, knowing that at any moment either man could turn around and spot him.

He crossed the room like a shadow and grabbed the officer from behind, his hand automatically clamping tightly across the mouth to prevent a sound.

Duke hesitated. His natural inclination was to twist the head to the side, snapping the neck like a twig. But that would constitute collateral damage, if not outright murder. Outside of a war, you couldn't exactly go taking people out, even if they deserved it.

This damn-well is a war though!

Duke pressed his fingers into the side of the man's neck, feeling for the pulsing, rubbery worm that was his carotid artery.

The Japanese had shown scant concern for his crew after they ran the Naiad down, and even less for the whales.

The captured officer struggled ineffectually in his arms, but Duke held him fast with a bear-like grip.

I ought to choke the life outta you with me bare hands!

Duke's eyes hardened. The Ocean was a generous mistress, but only if you gave her the respect she deserved...

The grizzled old warrior frowned behind his bushy pirate beard. Fishermen were all the same. And these blood-crazed bastards were worse than usual – a blight on the good name of seafarers.

His fingers hardened like railroad spikes as he pressed into the officer's neck, cutting off the flow of blood to the brain. After a moment the man's head lolled forward. Duke released the body and let it slump to the floor, his gaze already fixed on the next target.

At that moment the remaining crewman looked up. He stared at the bearded vision before him, eyes widening in surprise. He blinked, confused, then suddenly he broke and dashed across the room, heading for the control panel.

Duke cursed. "Oh no you don't!" He charged after the fleeing engineer's assistant, angling to cut him off. The man tried to beat him to the gap between two huge turbines, but Duke was quicker. With the full-body check of an American Football blocker, he dropped his shoulder and crashed into the running crewman. At the same time he swung his arm to deliver a vicious roundhouse elbow to the back of his head. The unfortunate man was knocked clean off his feet and he sailed through the air, arms flailing. A second later his flight was cut short as he crashed headlong into an engine mounting block, his helmet bouncing off his head and skittering away. Duke pounced on him and, seizing a handful of the man's overalls, he hauled him up to meet his poised fist. But the crewman's head hung limply, and his eyes were rolled back. Duke snorted with disdain and let him drop. The unconscious man slumped back in a heap on the deck, joining his superior in Fairyland.

Duke straightened and turned to the others standing in the doorway, ignoring the Canadian gal's shocked and accusing stare. "Right, get to work y'all. These bastards' buddies could come lookin' for 'em at any time. We ain't got long."

He glanced around, locating the seawater inlet valve and hurried over to it, wasting no time rolling up his sleeves and getting down to business. He twisted the valve closed, his tattooed forearms bulged with hard knots of muscle as he strained against it. He straightened up, annoyed to see the others standing there gawking.

"What are y' waitin' for? A goddamn written invitation?" He reached in the duffel bag for another spanner and tossed it at the slack-jawed kid, not caring if it clobbered him when he tried to catch it. "Heathcliffe, lose them nuts," he ordered, pointing to the section of the seawater intake pipe that needed removing.

The Californian muttered something inaudible and rolled his eyes. Duke clenched his fists involuntarily. This was no time for the kid's usual shirking. They had a job to get done, and quickly! He had a good mind to lead the little cuss over to the pipe by that damned eyebrow ring of his. Heathcliffe scowled and reluctantly picked up a spanner, temporarily removing the need for Duke to sort him out – even if the little punk still needed a kick up the pants to hurry him along.

Duke began twisting the bolts undone with a little more vehemence than was necessary.

Beside him, the Californian struggled with his first, throwing down the spanner in a fit of frustration.

"Put some muscle into it," Duke snarled.

"I can't. It's stuck," he whined.

"Quit yer snivelling," Duke growled, knuckles whitening as his grip on his own spanner tightened.

Duke glanced up. The blonde hadn't moved. No doubt she wasn't keen to get mixed up with the grease and rust and physical labour required to undo the pipe. He muttered under his breath, his admiration for Miss Vicki increasing. He knew the plucky little Aussie wouldn't have a problem with it. Over on the other ship, she'd be in boots and all, doing whatever needed to be done. She was one tough gal. In fact, Cal's whole team would be doing swell, even his City Slicker of a brother. Duke grunted. Wuss or not, he'd rather have had Richard here right now than either of these two – at least his heart was in the right place. But then again, that was his motive in picking these two… keep the troublemakers as close as possible where they were less likely to screw anything up.

Duke fished the mallet out of the bag for her. "Here. Take that and bust up some of them gauges."

Summer flicked her blonde hair and gaped at him.

"Go on then." He pointed.

She continued to stare at him as though he was mad.

"What's the matter? Cat git y' tongue? Move, Gal!"

She shook her head, defiance written across her face. "I refuse to take an active part in this." she sniffed, folding her arms beneath her bosom.

He swore, partly in frustration, and partly at her.

What the hell did she come here for if she ain't about to get her pretty hands dirty?

"Fine," he growled, jerking his head in the direction of the door. "Git over yonder and keep watch then."

She complied, tossing her hair to show she wasn't cowed, her cheeks coloured with anger and indignation. Duke ignored her, attacking the bolts furiously with his wrench.

Less than a minute later he knocked out the last of his bolts and tossed it aside. Heathcliffe was still struggling with his third, and at that moment his spanner slipped for the umpteenth time. He dropped it and cried out, massaging his skinned knuckles. "I can't do it. It's too hard, man."

Duke couldn't help noticing his reluctance to pick up the spanner again. The kid was a born malingerer. "Quit y' whinin' and put some muscle into it," he growled. "Be quick about it."

Heathcliffe sucked his finger. "Look, Man. I broke a fingernail," he whined.

"Serves you right for not cuttin' 'em," Duke growled.

And that goes double for your hair!

Heathcliffe muttered something under his breath. Duke didn't catch it on account of the kid's lip-ring lisp, but he did make out the words "Fascist pig."

With an effort he curbed his temper. Now wasn't the time, or the place...

He shoved the useless kid aside with barely-disguised impatience, reaching for the remaining bolt. Examining it, he exclaimed in disgust. Heathcliffe had burred the nut so badly that no spanner would grip it now. "Goddamn it. A trained monkey would be more use than you," he muttered, "And it'd likely smell a dang site sweeter too. Ah've a mind to leave y' sorry ass here until it's done."

The Californian glared sullenly back. "Who the hell died and made you Dictator-For-Life?"

Suddenly a klaxon blared.

"What the hell is that?" Heathcliffe blurted, sudden fear showing in his eyes.

Duke had to suppress a smile. The kid looked set to bolt like the dogs was after him, "That'll be thuh ship's alarm," he said. "I expect they've realised we're here."

He stood up, eyeing the last bolt furiously.

It'll take a hacksaw to cut that damn thing loose.

That would take far too long. They were already out of time.

He raised his boot and slammed it into the almost-free section of pipe. The seal split, releasing a spray of water into the air.

The others gasped and backed away towards the safety of the doorway, but Duke ignored them. He lifted his foot and brought it down again, crashing into the stubborn pipe. The rubber seal finally came loose, and the unsecured end of the pipe dropped three inches, dumping a gush of water over the floor. The other end was still held in place by the ruined bolt though, and unless he could get the pipe section out of the way he knew not enough water would spill out when the valve was opened. Duke kicked the pipe a third time, and a fourth, eventually forcing the section far enough aside and bending the last stubborn bolt in the process.

Not perfect, but it'll have to do.

He looked around. The alarm still blared. There was no time to see to the control panel.

"Git them tools outta here," he ordered, hurrying over to the seawater intake valve. He twisted it wide open, releasing a deluge of water into the engine-room. At the first sight of it, the others fled out the engine-room door. Duke cursed, but he was too busy to bother with the likes of them right now. He heaved on the tap as hard as he could, trying to jam the valve open. There wasn't time to bend it, so he tore off the tap and tossed it into the corner, hoping that would suffice. The valve couldn't be closed now without a wrench – with luck that would buy him enough time to ensure the ship filled up. It was a big ship though…

Duke took one last look around. Seawater continued to gush out of the ruptured pipe, already pooling several inches deep on the floor. He grunted with satisfaction, then splashed towards the door, heading for safety. Suddenly he stopped, changing his mind. He hurried back to the prostrate forms of the whalers and grabbed a collar of their blue overalls in each leathery hand.

"Dunno why I'm doin' this," he muttered, as he dragged them roughly out the door and kicked it closed behind him. "Y' can call me a lot'a things, but heartless ain't one of 'em," he remarked to the unconscious heads bumping along the corridor behind him.

Around him, the ship's alarm still wailed.

***

Richard headed up the darkened passageway, lugging the heavy bag of tools over his shoulder. It was awkward, but still easier to carry it that way. He was hurrying, not wishing to get caught by the flooding that was rapidly spreading through the lower decks, but he hesitated too, concerned for Vicki. He didn't want anything to happen to her.

He paused at the bottom of a stairwell and shone his dim red light up, trying to remember if it was the one they'd come down. Nothing looked familiar, and he had to force down the rising sense of panic.

The ship is sinking! There isn't much time!

Vicki was still down there somewhere too. He looked about anxiously, then decided to wait – as much for his safety as hers. She should be following right behind him and she would know the way back up to the deck. The last thing he wanted was to get separated and lost in the innards of a strange and unfriendly ship.

He wasn't alarmed by the sudden furtive scuffling noise behind him. The duffel bag over his shoulder blocked his view down the corridor, but he half-turned, his relief palpable, desperate to ask Vicki for directions. The footsteps crept closer. He waited for her to catch up.

At the last moment he wrinkled his nose, catching a whiff of the rank odour of stale sweat. Suddenly he was seized from behind, arms pinned to his sides in a crushing bear-hug. He tried to shout out but a blubbery hand was clapped firmly across his mouth, stifling his cry.

The tool bag dropped to the deck with a muffled thump.

He struggled, but the arm that encircled him was like an iron barrel stave, pinioning his arms in place. Richard felt himself dragged backwards, his boots scraping uselessly across the floor as he struggled to find purchase on the slick surface. Panic flooded over him like a tidal wave. He was in deep trouble, and he knew it.

He was not a physical person, and he hated the thought of fighting. Even if it came down to a matter of life and death, he had no idea what to do!

His captor dragged him backwards through the darkness. Together they crashed through a door, and into a room. Richard stared longingly at the passageway beyond, but his captor kicked the door closed behind them, sealing off the thoroughfare – and freedom. Richard had no idea where they were, but he knew with a sick sense of certainty that his friends wouldn't find him in here.

He felt the familiar tightness grip his chest.

Oh no, I'm having an asthma attack!

He choked back a terrified sob, suddenly regretting the decision to stick his neck on the line. He had blundered headfirst into this mess, and it wasn't even his fight. Now he was alone and about to face the consequences.

Look where your bravado got you, you fool!

He knew he should have stayed out of this. He should have remained safely on the Gwendolyn, or for that matter, back at his desk. His other life was calm and safe. No one attacked him there!

He gasped for breath, lunging forward in a desperate bid for freedom. But the vice-like grip held him fast. Richard struggled again, determinedly, and suddenly the bear-like arm across his body came away.

I'm free!

His elation was short-lived though, as he was grabbed around the neck instead, and spun around away from the doorway. A blow to the back of his legs knocked his feet out from under him, and then he was on his knees on the floor, staring at a featureless steel bulkhead. The headlamp slipped from his head, falling to the ground where it threw an eerie red glow across the floor. He stared helplessly ahead, unable to turn his head, but the dark cabin offered no solace.

The meaty forearm tightened against his throat, crushing his windpipe.

His captor leaned forward, pressing his stubbly chin next to Richard's cheek. Richard flinched, recognising the red plastic helmet of the whaling captain.

"You are trespasser," he rasped in his ear. "Now you pay punishment!"

His hot breath stank of fish, and alcohol. Richard gagged, his lungs burning with a desperate need for air.

Hogei Gyofuku cackled mercilessly.

A moment later Richard heard the soft scraping of a blade being withdrawn from its sheath. His eyes bulged in terror as the huge knife swam into view. It was nearly a foot long; the blade wide and fat like a machete.

No!

Richard tried to flinch and turn away, but he was held fast. The captain laughed, pressing the edge of the cold steel against his throat. "Now I gut you like a fish!" he chortled. "Sashimi time!"

The knife glinted in the half-light. Richard could see black smears of dried blood darkening its edge. Whale blood.

His throat convulsed in a painful swallow and he felt tears sting his eyes.

So this is how it's going to end…

Chapter 17

Cal Major looked around him. In the moonlight, the darkened bridge of the Kyoeishin-Maru was a veritable Aladdin's Cave of electronics, all bathed in a silvery glow. "Wow," he breathed. The ship was fitted out with sophisticated radar, sonar, and hydrophone, not to mention Differential GPS navigation, an automated computer guidance system, satellite comms, plus a host of other gizmos he couldn't even begin to guess their function… He whistled softly to himself. Amimoto wasn't boasting; this had to be the most well-equipped research vessel in existence!

Just imagine the kind of research you could do with all this hardware at your disposal!

Cal shook his head firmly, knowing it wasn't possible. This ship was dedicated to everything he stood against. He felt a moment of sadness then, as he reflected on his future. His own research career could well be over after tonight. Even if he escaped with his freedom, he might never be able to work as a research scientist again. It was not justice he feared, but retribution. Could a man hide forever? He didn't know, but he held no illusions. Amimoto's tentacles were long, but his anger would last longer. His revenge would be single-minded – and enduring.

Cal could appreciate the irony of it. In order to safeguard the future, he would have to jeopardise his own.

His sigh was deep and heartfelt. It was a hard decision to make. But then, none of the important things in life came easy.

He took one last lingering look at the suite of expensive electronics around him. "It's almost a shame, really," he murmured as he raised the crowbar over his head.

He brought the heavy tool down on the nearest console. The plastic case shattered with a satisfying crunch, sending shards flying in all directions. Cal reversed the crossbar, using the hooked end to rip the case open and expose the wiring inside. Then he raised the heavy bar and struck again and again, pounding the electronics into so much useless junk. His jaw was clenched in concentration, but he gained no pleasure from the destruction.

His thoughts were consumed with Aurelia. Would she approve of this action? Cal sighed again. He didn't know, but reluctantly he had to admit it wasn't likely. She was no stranger when it came to making a stand, but she was also an avowed pacifist. He knew from past experience that acts of deliberate violence didn't go down well with her, especially not destruction on a scale like this. She might understand his motivation but she was a stickler for principles, and she'd already made her beliefs crystal clear.

He hesitated, unsure what to think. There was no denying the feelings for her in his heart, even though his head insisted he'd be a fool to try going down that road again.

He gritted his teeth and brought the crowbar down again, trying not to think about it. He hoped he wasn't also smashing his chances of successfully getting back together with her. He rubbed his temple ruefully. Well, if it came to that, he was no stranger to personal sacrifice…

Cal glanced ahead through the windscreen of the Kyoeishin-Maru's bridge. Out in the night he could see the shadowy bulk of the Japanese Fleet's factory ship. He glanced at his dive watch, wondering if the Skipper's team was on-schedule over there. The radio in his chest harness was silent, which meant the other team hadn't encountered any problems worth breaking radio silence for.

Or something drastic has happened…

Cal grimaced at the thought, but quickly put it out of his mind. The Skipper could take care of anything! He felt a smile come to his lips, despite his concern. This was bread-and-butter stuff for a grizzled ex-Navy SEAL like him. No, *former* Navy SEAL! Cal corrected himself quickly, remembering the Skipper's indignant protest at the term. "There ain't no such thing as an ex-SEAL, Son. Once a man's lived that life, no matter where you take him you can't never take it away from him. A SEAL he is, and a SEAL he'll be, until the day he dies."

Suddenly a klaxon began wailing in the night. Cal froze, arm poised in mid-swing. He lowered the crowbar and stared out the Kyoeishin-Maru's windscreen. The alarm was coming from the Nippon-Maru, and a gang of whalers was already rushing down the dock towards the factory ship. He didn't know what was going on aboard the other ship, but if the Skipper's team hadn't been compromised, they were about to be. He stood for a moment, mind racing.

If it hit the fan his own team were in danger of being discovered too, but Duke was in more immediate danger. Cal reached for the transmit button on his radio. The local police might be able to listen in, but it was too late for that now. The time for stealth had just ended.

"Team Two from Team One, do you copy?"

He waited. There was no response.

"Two from One. Are you there Skip?"

There was still no response. Cal was starting to get worried when the radio suddenly crackled into life.

"Howdy, Son." The connection was distorted by interference, and the Skipper's voice rasped as though he was breathing hard. But his usual candour was instantly recognisable. "Job's done. It ain't pretty, mind you."

Cal wondered what had gone wrong, but knew better than to ask over an unsecured comm channel. It was enough that Duke was finished. "Where are you?"

"On the way out now. Just got me a little baggage t' bring along …"

Cal peered down through the low-lying fog. Their little raft was just visible, bobbing at the end of its mooring rope beneath the towering stern of the factory ship. He frowned. There was no way the Skipper's team could get back to the ladder though. The wharf was swarming with whalers now, like angry wasps roused from a hive, and they were already starting to run up the gangplank aboard the black ship.

"Negative!" Cal shouted into the radio. "Don't go ashore. I repeat, do not go ashore! The dock is compromised."

Cal's eye fell on the huge gaping maw of the factory ship's slipway. That was the perfect escape route, but he couldn't blurt it over the radio. Not when he didn't know who might be listening. "The water! Get down to the water!" he urged, hoping the Skipper would understand.

Looking past the mob of overalls and white gumboots, Cal could see a number of white-gloved security police hurrying to investigate the disturbance too.

"Make it quick, you're going to have company real soon!"

"Ayuh." The Skipper's grunt was non-committal, but Cal knew he would already be weighing up the odds.

Cal's frown deepened. His own team weren't exactly in the clear yet either. He reached for the radio again. "Vicki, you there?"

She replied straight away and he could hear the glow in her voice, a mixture of excitement and satisfaction. "All done, just securing the area."

"Is Richard with you?"

"No. He went on ahead. The water was coming in fast…"

Cal felt his heart sink even as he looked out the window. His brother wasn't on the wharf, and he hadn't emerged on deck yet. That meant he was alone on a doomed ship, without a radio. Even getting lost could prove fatal.

"How long since you last saw him?"

Vicki must have sensed the anxiety in his voice, because her tone became concerned. "A couple of minutes. Why? Is something the matter?"

"I don't know. I hope not. You get topside. I'll go find him."

"Are you sure? I can help…"

"No. This ship is going down. There's no sense all of us risking our lives."

He hurried out of the bridge, annoyed at Richard for not following his order to stay with Vicki.

If anything's happened to him I'll kill him!

He slid down the stair rail to the next level, clicking his head torch on as the darkness closed in around him. The Kyoeishin-Maru was a big ship to search in a short time. He hurried on, deeper into the bowels of the ship. The lowest deck – where the engineroom was located – was the most dangerous part of the ship right now, so that was where he needed to begin his search. If he wasn't already too late!

Suddenly Cal's radio crackled, the burst of static sounding loud in the deserted passageway. He jumped, then grinned at himself, feeling a little foolish.

"Cal, you there Son?"

"Yeah. Go ahead Skip."

"Things are heatin' up out here. Where y'all at?"

Cal swore under his breath. He could hear the Nippon-Maru's alarm still wailing in the distance and he knew the wharf and the black ship would be swarming with bad guys by now. The fog was thin. The Skipper and his team couldn't hope to remain undetected in the little raft for long. They couldn't wait any longer, but Cal couldn't leave the Kyoeishin-Maru without his brother. He swore again, then reached for his radio, the decision made.

"You'll have to leave us, Skip. Go, cast off. We'll meet you back at the Gwendolyn."

"What, you gonna swim home?" the Skipper's voice sounded doubtful.

"Nah, we can make it on foot."

"Bullshit! The whole waterfront's fair crawlin' with trouble by now!"

Cal nodded to himself, knowing it was true. His reply was confident though, belying his own doubts. "We'll be ok. We made it back from the market last time."

There was silence on the other end, and Cal began to worry the Skipper might not agree. Then his gruff answer came back. "Fair enough," he muttered, resigned. "But don't be dawdlin' mind!"

Cal lowered the radio and hurried down the darkened passageway, a sense of desperate urgency creeping into his actions. An inch of water splashed around his feet now. The ship was sinking, and his own team were probably only moments from being discovered too. They had to get clear in time!

As he continued through the deserted ship, his torch beam suddenly picked out a dark shape lying on the ground – an island in the midst of the rapidly pooling water.

Oh hell, please don't let that be him!

With a start, Cal recognised the duffel bag of tools, glad it wasn't his brother lying there, unconscious or dead. He hurried over, but any relief he felt was short-lived.

Richard was carrying those. Why would he drop them… unless something happened to him?

Cal's jaw tensed. He had a bad feeling about this. He reached down and picked up the heavy wrench from the bag, hefting it in his hand.

I knew I brought this for a reason…

Reassured by its solid weight, he hung the crowbar off his belt loop and brandished the wrench instead. Holding it like a club, he crept forward down the corridor, pausing to listen every few steps. Richard was close. Very close. He could feel it.

A faint scraping sound from the other side of a door made him pause.

Sounds of a scuffle?

Cal stared at the door, wondering what might be waiting to confront him on the other side. He gripped the wrench tighter in his hand, then with a grim expression he turned the handle and eased it open.

At that moment a loud siren suddenly shattered the silence. The Kyoeishin-Maru's emergency alarm had been tripped.

***

Richard felt the world growing dim around him. His pulse was pounding in his ears and bright pinwheels of colour starred his vision. He tried to gasp for breath, but the meaty forearm across his throat was unrelenting, choking the life out of him.

There was a strange noise ringing in his ears, but he couldn't identify it. Everything seemed far away, as if down the end of a long tunnel.

He closed his eyes, surrendering to the dizziness, and a dark shroud rose up to engulf him.

Then suddenly, amazingly, he was free. The vice-like grip around his throat relaxed in an instant, and the sweet taste of fresh air flooded back into his lungs. Richard blinked in surprise. He tried to stagger to his feet but his legs buckled and he slumped to the floor on his hands and knees, gasping and retching. Through his distress, he struggled to collect himself, sensing he wasn't out of danger yet.

Where's Gyofuku gone? Why did he let me go?

With an effort he sat up and turned his head, looking for the whaleboat captain.

Gyofuku was still there behind him, but he made no move towards him. Puzzled, Richard stared at him, forcing his addled brain back into life. It took him a moment to realise the beefy Japanese was choking now, clawing at his own throat. It took a while longer to recognise the metal bar of a wrench handle pressed against the saggy folds of the captain's thick neck – and to recognise the hand that held it.

It's Cal!

He sobbed aloud with relief, knowing he was safe now. The gratitude welled up within him, and he felt a tear spring into his eye. Despite being a useless bumbling fool, he had never been forsaken by his brother yet.

Cal saved me! Cal always comes to save me!

Cal flexed, and using his superior height he lifted the portly captain clear of the ground as though he weighed almost nothing. Richard watched as Gyofuku struggled for his life, white gumboots kicking uselessly in the air. Beneath the red plastic helmet his hooded eyes were now round with terror. Richard felt no pity for him. Their gaze met for an instant, and he delighted in the panic he saw in Gyofuku's beady eyes. The tables had been turned, and they both knew it.

In his desperation, the Japanese began to flail about, and Richard's smile suddenly froze. He blinked with horror when he realised what the captain still clutched in his fat fist.

Watch out! He's got a knife!

He opened his mouth to scream a warning, but the only sound that came out was a strangled croak. The knife flashed upwards, slicing into Cal's forearm. He grimaced in pain, and the wrench fell away from the captain's throat. Cal jumped backwards away from the next swing, clutching his wounded arm to his chest.

Gyofuku recovered himself quickly. He advanced forward, brandishing the knife. Cal circled him warily, his own weapon now held tentatively in his injured arm. Gyofuku's smile was cold and triumphant, and he lunged forward, slashing viciously at Cal's face.

Cal dodged awkwardly backwards, avoiding the whistling blade but nearly stumbling. Gyofuku laughed out loud and came forward again.

Cal swung the wrench, keeping him at bay, but Richard could see by his gritted teeth the pain the movement caused him.

Sensing the advantage, the captain came forward again.

Cal swung the wrench over his head like a club, aiming to smash it down on top of the red helmet. But the length of his arm carried the swing too high, and the wrench punched clean through the flimsy fibreboard ceiling panelling above, clanging off a hidden pipe somewhere in the cavity. Cal winced in pain and muttered a curse, struggling to free his weapon.

Gyofuku let out a gleeful snarl and sprang forward, slashing at Cal's eyes with the heavy blade.

Richard held his breath, too terrified to look away.

Cal jerked the wrench free, but was too late to swing it. Instead he flung up his good arm, and Richard was surprised to see the metal hook of a crowbar in his left hand.

Where did that come from?

Gyofuku looked equally shocked as his swing was blocked. He screamed as the crowbar's heavy claw bit into his wrist, then he relinquished his grip on the knife and it was hooked away, spinning across the room to clatter unseen to the floor. Cal's expression hardened and he stepped forward, weapon in each hand.

Suddenly realising his predicament, the captain backed away, gibbering in terror. He raised his hands together, as though praying for mercy. But Cal was already in mid-swing. The wrench smacked into the side of the captain's helmet, knocking him off his feet. He landed heavily on the floor and lay there, groaning.

Cal moved forward to stand over him, raising the wrench to finish him off.

The captain's chin wobbled as he whimpered in terror, helpless to resist.

Cal's jaw tensed, and Richard gasped at the sight of the fire in his eyes. He held his breath.

Then his brother lowered the wrench. "No," he murmured to himself. "You're not worth it."

Suddenly the whole ship lurched and settled over to port.

Richard stumbled, grabbing onto the wall for support. The floor was tilted drunkenly now, and he saw with alarm that water was now squirting around the side of the door. "Cal, what's going on?" he shouted, his voice cracking.

"Time to go," his brother answered matter-of-factly. "Now!"

"W-what about him?" Richard looked at the writhing whaleboat captain, struggling to get to his feet.

Cal was unconcerned. "He'll be all right in a minute or two." He cocked an ear towards the sound of the alarm, still wailing in the night. "Let's get out of here while we still can." He flung open the door, releasing a wave of water into the room. The level was up to their knees now, but Cal strode purposefully out into the corridor. Richard gulped and hurried after him, wading through the dark water.

At the doorway he paused to look back. Gyofuku was on his feet now, and the look he shot Richard was filled with venom and hatred. Richard gulped and hurried after his brother, one hand on the wall for support as he staggered down the slanted passage. A confusion of thoughts jumbled through his head, not the least of which concerned the brutish Japanese captain.

Why didn't Cal kill him when he had the chance?

He was shocked at himself for even entertaining the thought, but somehow he sensed it was the lesser of two evils. His personal aversion towards any kind of violence was tempered by the knowledge of the captain's brutal and vindictive nature, and his ability to nurse a grudge.

They reached the stairway up to the next level and Cal waited to usher Richard up ahead of him. As they passed, Cal looked into his eyes and sighed, as if reading Richard's thoughts. When he spoke, his voice was suddenly philosophical. "Maybe I should have ended it here?" He shrugged helplessly. "I don't know. I have a feeling this feud is far from over though..."

The cool night breeze on deck was a relief after the enclosed claustrophobia in the belly of the sinking ship. Cal threw the tools over the side where they hit the water with a muffled splash and sank out of sight. "That gets rid of the incriminating evidence. Now let's get out of here."

Richard hurried gratefully down the gangplank, pleased to be off the white ship. He cast a dread-filled glance back at the ghostly hull, still wondering how he'd managed to escape from being entombed within the giant watery coffin below its decks.

Vicki was waiting for them, crouched in the shadows on the wharf. "I was starting to think you two had decided to stay aboard to admire your handiwork," she joked, but her smile was forced and the relief was still obvious on her face.

Cal grinned in reply, but she sensed something was wrong, and her gaze flew immediately to the injured arm cradled against his chest.

"You're hurt! You're bleeding!"

"It's ok, I'll live."

"Let me see."

He waved away her attention. "Not now. We haven't got time."

Sirens howled into the night, the ships' alarms joined now by the wail of police cars. Through the mist, they could see the Nippon-Maru's decks were swarming with activity, and already a group of whalers was running down the dock towards the listing Kyoeishin-Maru.

Richard turned his head as the droning of an outboard suddenly reached his ears. The sound was faint across the water and he knew the raft was already far out in the harbour, travelling quickly with only three people aboard it. At least the Skipper and his team were home free.

Richard swallowed, wondering how his team was going to get away. There was no way they could get down the ladder to the water – even if the raft was still waiting – nor could they hope to get along the waterfront without being seen.

"This way. Come on." Cal grabbed his shoulder and led the way up the nearest alley, heading for the back streets that ran behind the Taiyoku Misui Fisheries Co factory. They hurried away from the water, checking each intersection to make sure it was safe to cross. The mist was thinner here, its flow hampered by the buildings crowding over the street, so they had to take more care not to be seen. While Cal paused to check down every cross-street that led to the water, Richard caught another glimpse of the expanding commotion. The ever-present wail of sirens on the night air was a constant reminder of their predicament.

The two cops appeared out of nowhere, stepping around a corner just a few metres in front of them, white-gloved hands raised signalling them to halt. Richard looked around frantically, but there was nowhere to run.

"Damn it," Cal muttered, then whispered an urgent order. "Stay calm. I'll see if we can bluff our way through."

He strode forward confidently, as if to pass by them.

The first cop, clearly in charge, stepped forward to block his way. He held up a hand, speaking in accented English. "Stop please. You come with us."

His companion hung behind to cover him, drawing a Taser gun which he pointed at Cal's chest.

Cal eyed the weapon, but didn't back down. "What's going on? We're just tourists out for a walk."

The cop's eyes registered no emotion. "You are criminal. You under arrest for suspicion of sabotage."

"No, you're mistaken. We're sightseeing."

The cop's expression remained wooden. "You have right to remain silent," he added, reaching for his handcuffs.

Cal muttered something under his breath, and made as if to comply. His sudden lunge was lightning fast, catching even Richard by surprise. While the cop's attention was momentarily distracted with his utility belt, Cal landed a lightning-fast uppercut under his jaw, sending him reeling back on his feet. Before he could fall, Cal jumped forward and grabbed him, spinning the helpless man around like a shield at the exact moment his colleague fired the Taser. The twin barbs ripped through the back of the starched uniform shirt and embedded themselves in the unfortunate policeman's torso. A millisecond later a pulse of high-voltage electricity surged down the cables and into his body. His back arched as the current gripped him, his mouth fixed in a rictus of agony. A high, thin scream escaped from his lips before his legs crumpled and he passed out.

Cal was still holding onto him at the time and the charge flowed briefly into him too, flinging him away with its force. He jerked backwards and sat down heavily on the ground where he struggled to rise, seeming confused and disoriented.

The second cop stared in horror at his fallen partner, mouth working soundlessly as he tried to fathom what he had just done to his superior. Vicki spared him the effort; a quick boot to the groin left him writhing on the ground in agony also. "Come on, let's get out of here," she said, turning to Cal. "You ok?"

Cal got unsteadily to his feet, blinking and shaking his head to clear it. "Man, I feel like I just got hit by the whole front row of a rugby team." He attempted a lopsided grin. "Now I know how the Wallabies must feel every time they play us."

Vicki smiled back, relieved to see he was alright. "It's no wonder the All Blacks are only the second-best team in the world then – you Kiwis don't seem to realise the aim of the game is *not* to get tackled!"

Richard glanced at the writhing cops, then looked around nervously. "That goes double for getting arrested too!"

Vicki laughed, but Richard had only been half joking. His throat still hurt and a kind of shaky weariness had taken over his body. He knew it was the after-effects of the adrenaline that had flooded his system, but right now his legs felt like rubber and all he wanted to do was lie down and rest. The sooner they got out of here and away from danger the better.

At that moment Cal's radio crackled. "Where y'at Son?"

"On the way back now, Skip. ETA maybe ten minutes."

There was a pause, and Richard could almost feel the Skipper's heavy frown. "We got company here already," he muttered.

Cal looked worried. "How many?"

Richard heard the Skipper spit. "Couple dozen cop cars. Headin' right for us."

Cal swore under his breath and Richard felt his panic rising. There were cops everywhere, searching for them. They were cut off!

It's a set-up! It has to be!

He took a deep breath, trying to calm his frazzled nerves. He knew that was impossible, since they had instigated the night's disturbance themselves.

Then why are the cops heading straight for the Gwendolyn? Why do they know exactly where to go?

Richard tried to dispel the thoughts, but they were hard to shake.

Cal's response sent a cold finger of dread down his spine. "Weigh anchor, Skip. Now! Get the hell out to sea before they get you!"

"What about y'all?"

"Never mind us, we'll think of something. Just get the ship to safety or we're all royally screwed!"

The Skipper grunted, as if acknowledging he didn't have a choice, even though he clearly didn't like it. "Watch yer backs out there," he muttered. "Jap-land ain't a safe place for y'all right now."

The radio went silent as he signed off, and Cal and Vicki exchanged a worried look. Richard swallowed. He shared the feeling, and then some! They were abandoned in a hostile city in the dead of night where practically everyone was after them.

What the hell are we going to do now?

He felt the waves of panic rising again, and a familiar tightness crept across his chest.

Chapter 18

The night pressed closer. Richard Major sprinted after the shadowy form of his brother, trying not to lose Cal as he dashed ahead through the darkened streets. Somewhere behind them the two incapacitated cops lay in the gutter, and from the streets all around came the sound of more sirens.

Richard's mind raced. Assault on a police offer. That was a serious crime. They were in big trouble now – as if they hadn't been in deep enough already!

There were armed whalers down on the dock too. Richard shuddered. It would almost be preferable to be caught by the police and locked up, rather than having to face Hogei Gyofuku and his gang of vicious thugs.

Richard's feet pounded along the pavement, his breath rasping in his lungs.

Up ahead, Cal ducked behind a rubbish skip and crouched down. Gratefully, Richard flopped down beside him, puffing like a steam engine. Vicki joined them a moment later, and Richard was mortified to see she was barely even breathing hard.

Cal frowned, collecting his thoughts. "We need to get out of the country. Quickly."

Vicki nodded. "Our first priority is to get away from here though…"

Cal cocked his head, listening to the sirens on the night air. "If the cops know what they're doing they'll be setting up a perimeter to keep us bottled up down here." He knotted his brow, planning. "We need a vehicle," he announced. "And I know just the place to borrow one."

They followed his gaze towards the tall chimneys of the Taiyoku Misui Fisheries Company's processing factory, and Richard felt his stomach lurch.

Oh no, not there!

The last place he wanted to go was back into the lion's den!

"Come on!"

Cal checked the street was clear then hurried toward the imposing factory complex. Reluctantly, Richard followed. It was that or be left behind.

They crept up to the gate at the rear of the factory, looking through the chain-link fence. Outside the loading bay at the rear of the building stood a van and a couple of light trucks.

"What about one of those?" Vicki asked.

Cal frowned. "Maybe, but a white face driving a local delivery truck would look plenty suspicious. We'd have a hell of lot of explaining to do if the cops pulled us over…"

His eye travelled around the side of the building, towards the offices and corporate entrance around the front. "Bingo!"

They all saw it then. A black Mercedes sedan, waiting in the shadows, engine idling. A car thief's dream!

Vicki nodded. "Let's do it!"

Richard said nothing. The fence was a good foot taller than him. He stared at it, his gaze fixated on the vicious-looking razor wire strands running along the top.

"We'll never get over that," he murmured.

Cal grinned. He pulled out his Leatherman tool and began to snip a hole in the fence with the wire cutter.

"Come on Bro." He held open the gap. "Vicki, you wait here."

Richard scrambled through the gap, trespassing for the second time in one night. He swallowed and looked across the compound. The car was parked facing them, so once they left the shadows and crossed the open tarmac there was no chance of approaching it unseen.

"I've got an idea," Cal said, pulling Richard to his feet. "Hold me up. Pretend we're drunk." He draped an arm around Richard's shoulder and began staggering towards the car, singing and slurring.

As they approached, the window rolled down and the driver watched them suspiciously. Richard could see he wore a navy blue jacket and peaked chauffeur's cap. He seemed surprised to see them, but obviously hadn't seen the hole in the fence. Richard mentally crossed his fingers, hoping Cal's plan worked and they'd be mistaken for a couple of drunk fishermen coming back from a night on the town.

The driver stuck his head out the window and muttered something in Japanese, waving them away from the car. Richard hesitated, but Cal winked and nudged him closer, still singing. They could see through the open rear window now, and the back seat was empty.

The driver saw them and reached for the button to roll up the window again. Cal called out something in Japanese and he hesitated, confused. Cal spoke again, more insistent this time.

"Taia, taia," he repeated, pointing to the rear of the car.

"What are you telling him?" Richard whispered under his breath.

"Flat tyre," Cal answered out of the corner of his mouth. "Trust me…"

He staggered forward a few more paces until he was level with the window. Then he leaned forward earnestly, beckoning the driver to take a look. As the man's head came forward, Cal's fist shot out, catching him square on the jaw with a solid punch. Richard flinched, then watched with stunned amazement as the driver's eyes rolled back and his head lolled to the side.

In an instant Cal was standing upright, sober as a judge. He flung open the door and pulled the unconscious driver out, dumping his body on the tarmac. As he straightened up he winced, hugging his injured right arm to his chest. Fresh blood began to ooze out between his fingers. He made as if to get into the driver's seat, but Vicki came hurrying over to join them. She stopped him with a frown. "I don't think so, buster. You're getting in the back with me where I can take a look at that arm."

Cal hesitated, but Vicki's crossed arms brooked no argument. He complied meekly, crawling into the leather-upholstered interior.

"Richard, you drive," he said, holding up a hand to forestall any protest. "Don't worry, it's an automatic. All you have to do is plant your foot and hang on!"

"Grab the cap and jacket off him too," Vicki suggested, pointing at the unconscious driver. "So you look the part."

Richard nodded, but his heart was racing as he knelt down over the inert body, trying to fathom what he was about to do.

We're stealing a car and I'm going to be the getaway driver?

It was madness. Worse than madness. He had no idea what to do.

What if the cops chase us?

High-speed chases only happened in the movies. He couldn't drive like that!

He blinked, forcing himself to move. He stared at the inert form lying at his feet, suddenly nervous. He reached out tentatively, as if half-expecting the man to sit up and grab him at any moment. His hands were shaking as he reached for the buttons, his fingers fumbling over the button-holes.

"Hurry it up," Cal urged from the back seat.

Richard pulled the lapels of the jacket, trying to ease it over the driver's shoulders. But one arm was twisted beneath the unconscious man, and it wouldn't come free.

Vicki laughed. "Don't be shy, he's unconscious!" but her voice was tempered with concern.

"Hurry it up!" Cal shouted. "We're about to have company!"

Richard's pulse was racing as he rolled the body over and yanked the stubborn jacket over the driver's arms. He crammed his arms into the sleeves and struggled into it.

"Quickly!"

Feeling jittery with panic, Richard dived into the driver's seat, slammed the door shut, and planted his foot on the accelerator pedal.

The big engine roared, but the car didn't move.

What the hell is going on?

Richard's panic overtook him and his mind went suddenly blank, forgetting everything he ever knew about cars.

"W-what do I do?" he blurted.

He turned around, desperately looking to Cal for assistance, and his heart missed a beat at the sight that greeted him. He blinked in embarrassment, not knowing where to look.

Vicki had taken off her T-shirt and torn it into strips to bandage Cal's wound, and right now a black sports bra was all she wore on her top half. Richard stared, mouth agape. The shape of her breasts was obvious against the thin fabric. They were perfectly formed, her nipples standing erect in the cold air. Richard stared, unable to tear his eyes away. Up until now he'd only ever seen her in bulky clothes, and he'd never considered what she might look like underneath all those layers.

"Take it out of Park," Cal said, but Richard didn't hear him.

Vicki's belly-button was pierced with a bar set with a simple coloured stone. He stared at it, winking back from her lightly-tanned skin like a secret eye, and he was surprised to find the sight strangely alluring. He could see the muscles of her abdomen tensed beneath her flat stomach, and her biceps flexed as she knotted a bandage. The sight of her fit physique quickened Richard's pulse in a totally different way. She leaned forward then, her cleavage clearly visible, and he suddenly felt his cheeks colouring with embarrassment.

Oh my god, I'm staring like a pervert!

He quickly averted his eyes.

"Take it out of Park! Hurry, they're almost here!" Cal leaned forward and slammed the transmission into Drive. The wheels suddenly found purchase and the big sedan leapt forward in a cloud of scorched rubber. The back end slewed sideways and Richard got such a fright he nearly took his foot off the accelerator.

"Gun it!" Cal ordered as the Mercedes careered across the car park. Richard fought with the steering wheel, trying to hold the charging saloon car in a straight line.

Cal turned to look out the back window. "Come down to watch the fun has he? Hah! That should hold the bastard for a while!"

Richard glanced in the side mirror, wondering how close the pursuers had come. What he saw made his blood run cold. A man in a grey suit was sprinting after the car, samurai sword clutched in his hand. Richard watched with alarm as he kept pace with the car, a few strides behind.

"Persistent bugger, isn't he?" Cal observed wryly.

But that wasn't the worst of it. Not by a long shot.

Behind their grey-suited pursuer the Japanese Commissioner stood under the wash of a street-lamp, hands clenched by his sides, his unblinking stare burning with hatred. Understanding dawned on Richard like a punch to the stomach.

Oh my god, this is Amimoto's car!

Instinctively, he jammed his foot down, pressing the pedal all the way to the floorboards. The big car leaped forward, and gradually the swordsman fell behind.

Richard breathed a sigh of relief.

They rounded the side of the factory, and suddenly the headlights picked out a chain-link fence in front of them. The gates loomed ahead, firmly closed.

Richard's eyes widened in fear, and he began to turn away.

Cal reached forward and laid a hand on his arm, his grip reassuring but firm. "No. Go straight through."

Richard swallowed, trying not to let his trepidation show. "A-are you sure?"

"It's ok, aim for the middle."

Richard took a deep breath as the gate jumped up to meet them, gripping the steering wheel in a white-knuckled grip.

The car crashed into the gates, bursting them open. They hurtled through and out into the street.

"Left turn!" Cal ordered, and the tyres screeched as Richard struggled to comply.

"Ok, ease up now," Cal said. "We don't want to attract any attention."

Richard nodded, not trusting his voice to answer.

As they drove through the sleeping city, he steered like a robot in response to Cal's commands. It was as though his mind had gone blank, and the city flashed by around him in a confusing blur of unfamiliar streets. His brother's calm directions were a lifesaver as they fled out of the waterfront district.

Suddenly Richard saw a flash of red ahead, which he quickly realised came from a car parked across the road.

A police car!

"It's a checkpoint," Vicki murmured. "They've got the whole area surrounded."

As they approached, an officer stepped forward, white glove raised.

"Tomare!" he shouted. "Tomare!"

"He's saying stop," Cal translated.

Richard felt the panic rising in him. They were wanted criminals in a stolen vehicle! Everything hinged on what he did next.

"Cal! W-what do I do?"

"Slow down," Cal said, his confidence almost masking the trace of doubt in his voice. "Slow right down, like you're going to stop."

Richard trod on the brake pedal, and the big car swished to a stop. The cop walked forward toward the window.

"Ok Bro, it's up to you now," Cal reassured him. "Stay calm. Just do what I tell you…"

Richard felt the saliva drain from his mouth.

Oh my god, this is it!

He watched the policeman approach, quivering like a cornered mouse might watch a cat stalking him.

I'm a criminal, and I'm about to get my come-uppance!

He looked down at his grease-stained overalls, saturated from the waist down.

I even look like a saboteur. He'll arrest me in two seconds flat!

He pulled the chauffeur's jacket closed, desperately hoping his legs would be out of sight.

The policeman stepped up to the car and barked an order in Japanese.

Richard stared straight ahead, his mind blocked with fear.

"Tell him; Shizukani. Acchi ni ike," Cal whispered. "It means; Silence! Go away! So say it like you mean it!"

Richard gulped in panic, his mouth suddenly full of cotton wool. The cop came closer.

"Tell him!" Cal hissed. "Shizukani. Acchi ni ike!"

Richard didn't think his voice would work, but he managed to stammer out a response. He copied the words as best he could, certain the officer wouldn't believe his accent.

"Wave him away," Cal ordered. "Look annoyed."

Richard motioned with his hand, trying his best to look impatient, but absolutely certain the policeman could see through his deception. His foot hovered over the accelerator pedal, seconds away from stomping it to the metal.

The cop hesitated, his gaze boring into him.

He's not buying it. Hit the gas! Get out of here!

"It's ok." Cal's whisper was soothing. "Just stay cool."

Richard swallowed guiltily, wondering if his brother could read his thoughts. He reached up to tip the brim of his cap to the policeman, making sure he pulled it down lower, fervently hoping his face was in shadow.

"Tell him again," Cal ordered. "And take your foot off the brake."

As the car inched forward Cal took a deep breath and let loose with a torrent of angry Japanese from the back seat, his voice startlingly deep and commanding.

The policeman blinked in surprise, staring at the tinted glass. Abruptly, he snapped to attention, his white glove coming up in a smart salute. He stepped back and waved them through, eyes firmly on the pavement.

"Ok, let's go," Cal whispered. "Nice and easy."

Richard touched the accelerator and the big car rolled through the checkpoint. He let out his breath with relief, glad he was gripping the steering wheel so the others couldn't see how badly his hands were shaking.

"Nice job!" Cal clapped him on the shoulder.

Vicki added her congratulations too, but Richard could see her smile was a little reserved. He guiltily looked back to the road, wondering if she thought he was staring at her underwear.

"What did you say to the policeman?" he said, anxious to change the subject.

Cal grinned. "I said 'How dare you detain me?' And I told him if he didn't get out of the way this instant I'd make sure he spent the rest of his life writing parking tickets. This is Amimoto's car, after all!"

Richard shook his head in disbelief. That was a gutsy call to impersonate Mr Fish!

He drove on through the financial centre of the city, following Cal's directions.

"That way," Cal pointed, indicating the main highway out of the city. "The whole country will be on the lookout for us in a couple of hours. We need to get the hell out of Dodge!"

"The airport?" Vicki said.

Cal shook his head. "Way too risky. There's bound to be more roadblocks, and once we got to the terminal we'd still have to wait around for a flight." He frowned. "Even if we made it aboard they could still turn the plane around at any time. We'd never make it home without being caught."

Vicki cocked a quizzical eyebrow. "What's the alternative? We can't drive around Japan forever. It won't be long before Mr Fish reports his car stolen and then we're up the creek." She rolled her eyes. "It's not like we can blend in with the locals!"

Cal nodded, agreeing with her. "I've got a plan." He signalled to Richard. "Get off the expressway at the first exit outside the city."

"The coast road?"

"Trust me." Cal's voice sounded thoughtful though, and he was already gazing across the city towards the eastern horizon, where the first touch of dawn was lightening the sky. "We'll have to hurry," he murmured. "It'll be daylight in an hour or two."

The coast road was narrower and winding, wending its way over the hills and headlands that rose up from the sea. The city quickly gave way to a patchwork of farmland and scattered dwellings, but the darkness hid them from prying eyes. Richard found himself concentrating hard to keep the headlights following the centreline. The big car swished around the curves though, handling them effortlessly, and Cal kept urging him to drive faster.

Richard tried to oblige, even though his natural instinct was to slow down.

I'm no rally driver!

Compared to his little Toyota hatchback at home, driving this roaring monster was a nerve-wracking experience.

Every so often Richard caught a glimpse of the surf crashing against the dark rocks, or breakers rolling up onto the sand of a deserted beach, glittering like quicksilver in the moonlight. He gripped the steering wheel tighter, dreading the thought of the car plunging off the road and down onto the rocks.

They drove in relative silence for nearly fifteen minutes.

When Cal finally spoke, there was a worried edge to his voice, and the glow of the dawn was already wiping away the stars. "This'll have to do. Pull over here."

Richard steered the big car onto the shoulder. It slid to a stop, and Richard saw they were at the edge of a gently-sloping beach. The waves growled angrily in the darkness, tumbling onto the sand with a dull roar.

Cal sat forward, wincing as his newly-bandaged arm bumped the seat. "Ok, this is the end of the line. Make sure you take everything with you 'cause we won't be coming back," he cautioned, using the sleeve of his jacket to wipe down the door handles and other surfaces they might have touched.

Richard climbed out of the car, watching as Cal gave it the once over. A steady breeze was blowing in off the sea and Richard felt its chill as it ruffled his damp clothes. Vicki shivered in her sports bra, and he suddenly felt sorry for her. He took off the chauffeur's jacket he was wearing and held it out for her. She looked surprised, then took it with a grateful smile. There was just enough light for Richard to see the dimples in her cheeks, and the sight made him feel warm inside.

"This is no good," Cal muttered, shaking his head. "The first person along this road will spot the car. How can we hide it?"

Richard looked around, but the shortening shadows revealed no suitable concealment anywhere nearby. The few scraggly bushes were barely big enough to hide behind themselves, if it came to that.

"There was a cliff about a mile back. We could torch it and push it over the edge," Vicki suggested. "That'd deal to the fingerprints too."

Cal raised an amused eyebrow but shook his head. "No time. Besides, the flames would be visible for miles…" Then he grinned suddenly. "I've got it! You two head down to the beach, I'll join you in a sec."

He got back into the car, pulling his cuffs over his hands so he wouldn't leave any fingerprints on the freshly-rubbed-down steering wheel.

Vicki shrugged and headed off. Richard followed her down onto the beach. His feet sank into the soft sand as he walked, increasing the trepidation he felt with each step. He wasn't sure what Cal was planning, but looking across the deserted beach towards the waiting sea gave him a rising sense of disquiet.

A moment later he heard the engine rev, and the headlights swung around to illuminate the beach. Richard held up a hand to shield his eyes from the glare, then with a start he realised the lights were bearing down on him. He jumped aside as the big car barrelled past him onto the sand. Its momentum carried it right down the beach until it bogged in the soft sand by the water. The engine revved, spraying sand behind the wheels. The big car settled lower, digging itself into the soft beach.

"It's stuck!" Richard called, not quite sure if he should offer to push – or if this had been Cal's intention all along.

Cal jumped out, leaving the door open. "Never mind, that's far enough." He grinned impishly. "The tide's coming in. That'll hide it for the next six hours or so – plenty of time!"

Vicki rolled her eyes. "Strewth, Amimoto's gonna be pissed!"

Cal laughed. "Who cares? We're aiming to cause him as much financial damage as we can, right?"

Richard said nothing. At the mention of the Commissioner's name, he had subconsciously looked back the way they had come, but the road remained empty. Dawn was beginning to colour the eastern sky though, and the shadows of night were steadily being replaced by the grey murk that heralded the first sign of daybreak.

Cal frowned. "We need to hurry. We should be off this beach before it gets light enough to see."

Richard glanced around, wondering what he had in mind. The world was still fuzzy and indistinct, but he couldn't see anywhere for them to hide here.

Cal spoke quickly into the radio, then turned to Richard. "Still got your head-torch?"

Richard reached up, but all he felt was the brim of the chauffeur's hat. He shook his head. "I must have lost it. Sorry Cal…"

Cal flashed a brief smile. "It's ok. Just stick close to me." He turned and splashed into the sea.

Richard felt his stomach sink into his boots at the thought and panic flooded through him.

Oh no! Please, no!

He'd only just managed to escape from drowning once tonight, and now Cal wanted him to go back in the water again!

"It's ok," Cal called back. "Come on."

Richard could tell from his brother's tone that he was anxious to get away from there. He sighed, knowing they had little other choice now. He shot a glance at the stranded car. They certainly weren't going anywhere in that.

Reluctantly, he stepped forward, hesitating in the shallows, feeling the icy coldness of the water creep higher on his legs. He took a few more steps, then a wave washed around his legs. His overalls were soaked again now, and the wet material flapped with the current, tugging at him as though eager to pull him out into deep water and drown him. He shivered, trying not to think about what he was about to do. To think about it was to admit that he had no idea what might be out of sight below him, all around him. There could be anything waiting out there in the silent water.

Cal turned back and beckoned him. "Come on."

Richard took a deep breath and began to wade out. The dark water swirled around his waist. A wave crashed into him, slapping him in the chest hard enough to knock him over. He stumbled, then regained his balance. The wave swept on past, but suddenly the water level was up around his neck, lifting him up. Richard found himself on tiptoes, his feet barely skittering across the bottom as he sought a firm footing.

"Swim!" Cal called, turning to duck under the next breaker that came thundering down on them. Richard stared at the breaker towering over his head, transfixed by the wall of water rushing straight towards his face. At the last moment he flinched away, just as the churning water engulfed him, swirling over his head and knocking him backwards.

He came up gasping and spluttering, alarmed to see the others were out of reach now. Panic lent him urgency, and he flailed his arms like a windmill, trying to catch up.

Cal turned back to wait for him. "Nothing like a night swim to wash out the cobwebs, eh?" Richard was too terrified to reply, or even attempt to return his grin, but Cal's confidence did bolster his nerves. Richard took a deep breath to calm himself and tried to regulate his arm strokes.

Finally they were out beyond the breakers, bobbing at the edge of a seemingly endless expanse of cold water that stretched away into the darkness. They were over deep water now, and Richard forced himself to think happy thoughts, rather than letting his mind dwell on what might be lurking below the surface this far out.

He didn't want to know, he decided, suspecting that the knowledge might well tip him over the edge. He trod water, panting slightly, the first twinges of muscle cramp beginning to tighten its grip on his calves in the cold water.

They huddled together for warmth and Richard lowered his head, drifting off with the motion of the swells. He wasn't sure how long he floated like that – it could have been five minutes, or fifteen – but suddenly he became aware of a sinister presence.

He lifted his head and looked around, holding his breath with trepidation. Then he saw it. A tall, triangular fin slicing through the water towards them.

Richard felt an icicle of terror seize his bowels.

Oh my god!

His mouth goldfished silently as he struggled to get the word out. Finally he managed a strangled croak. "Shark!"

The others were instantly alert, watching the fin as it circled around their tight little group.

"It's probably nothing to worry about," Cal tried to reassure them. "Sharks aren't mindless killers like in the movies. He's probably just curious." But his voice betrayed a trace of concern as he cautioned them. "No sudden movements, though… No one's bleeding, are they?"

Richard felt as though his heart had stopped. He stared at Cal, aghast, pointing at his blood-soaked bandage. "Y-your arm!"

Vicki had bound it well, but the battering from the surf must have reopened the knife wound he'd received from the whaleboat captain. The gash was bleeding again, and dark tendrils of blood trailed into the sea.

Cal muttered a curse under his breath.

Suddenly another dorsal fin broke the surface only a few body lengths away. It was quickly followed by another, and another. Richard gasped, feeling the panic seize him. His worst nightmare was coming true. He flailed his arms and tried to lunge backwards, recoiling in horror as he waited for a huge body to crash into him and bury its fangs in his flesh.

"It's alright!" Cal's calm voice broke through his terror. "They're dolphins. See, their dorsal fins are smaller, more rounded."

Richard gulped air, trying to contain his fear. He felt like a condemned man who'd just cheated death, and his heart still raced wildly. He craned his neck, trying to spot the shark, wondering how long their reprieve might last. The dolphins surfaced again, on their other side. "T-they're coming back."

"They do that," Cal explained matter-of-factly. "Dolphins will never leave a sick or injured family member. They always stay to protect them."

Richard stared into the gloom, puzzled. "But we're not their family…"

The dolphins continued to circle around them in the dark, right at the edge of Richard's vision. Whether they were just curious, or were truly concerned for the swimmers, he couldn't tell. But their presence definitely gave him some comfort.

At least we're not entirely alone out here.

After a while he realised the shark had indeed gone, although just how far away he didn't know. He peered apprehensively down into the black water, feeling as helpless as a baby in the woods despite the patrolling dolphins.

Please don't let it come back…

Cal took out the radio again, but the usual welcoming green glow of the backlit display was absent; replaced instead by a lifeless blank screen. He held the clear plastic dry-bag higher, peering into it. Several inches of water sloshed around in the bottom, courtesy of the dousing it received beneath the waves. Richard stared at it in horror, but Cal just muttered under his breath and stuffed the useless radio back into the pocket of his jacket.

"W-what now?" Richard spluttered, stammering partly through fear and partly because his teeth were beginning to chatter.

"We wait," Cal replied grimly. He reached for the strap of his head-torch still looped around his neck, and pulled it back onto his head.

"Wait for what?"

Cal frowned in concentration and began clicking the torch on and off. The light reflected off the water, over and over, illuminating their faces in a pale red glow each time.

"A passing fishing boat," Cal murmured absently, still looking out to sea.

Richard followed his gaze, but the horizon was empty. He looked back behind them, but the shore was out of sight too; the safety of dry land little more than a vague shadow beyond the surf line.

He shivered and huddled closer to the others for warmth. The dolphins had gone.

Chapter 19

Akogi Yokuke had been fast asleep in bed when his aide had awoken him – trembling in anticipation of his master's anger – to bring him the bad news.

"Baka ie!" Yokuke snapped. "Muri desu." He roused himself irritably, waving away his servant. "Nonsense! That's impossible!" His first reaction had been one of disbelief, then as the enormity of it sank in, helpless fury in anticipation of the loss. In business, as in life, a certain amount of bad fortune was unavoidable, and it was a measure of the truly great businessmen that they were able to rise above it. But even so, he knew the implications of this accident could be enormous.

Bad fortune of this magnitude could cripple me!

However, he could not sit idly by ignoring the problem until morning. A lifetime of honing his business acumen had taught him the best place to be in a crisis was right in the middle of it, if only to prevent the situation becoming even worse. So he had summoned his driver and ordered him to head at once for the waterfront.

The disaster that greeted his eyes there was indeed real, and even more shocking than he could have imagined; his great factory ship listing at her moorings like a common town drunk.

"Ariemasen!" he whispered. "It's not possible!"

How could something like this happen?

He looked around. Crewmen and factory staff milled about on the dock, shocked and confused, but uncertain what to do. There was no sign of Hogei Gyofuku.

Yokuke felt his anger rising. He had left strict instructions for the Captain to maintain an extra-vigilant watch over the Fleet, but he had evidently deserted his post – or was asleep at it.

Probably drunk too, neh?

Yokuke's anger flared at the thought, and he turned to take it out on the nearest sailors. "What the hell are you waiting for?" he snarled. "Get aboard and start the pumps! I forbid you to return to shore until the ship is afloat!"

Without the Nippon-Maru, his highly-trained whalers would be little more than common fishermen, and worth about the same to him. To Yokuke, the huge factory ship was more than just an innovative industrial stratagem and a technical marvel – it was the very heart of his Fleet. So much more than just a multi-billion Yen investment, it was the link that allowed his company to extend its reach all the way across the globe to the frigid waters of the Antarctic. True, each voyage was a long and expensive sojourn, but through his political connections the generous government subsidies more than covered his costs, and every kilogram of meat the Nippon-Maru was able to deliver back to the high-class restaurants of Japan was pure profit. Every whale the Fleet brought back was worth over a million US dollars each, and the lion's share went straight into his private coffers.

He paced up and down the wharf, wondering how bad the leak was, and whether the ship could be saved.

Then came a panicked shout that the Kyoeishin-Maru was taking on water too.

Yokuke turned and stared down the wharf in disbelief. Through the mist he could just make out his fine research ship, wallowing like a dead whale at the end of her mooring ropes.

"Don't just stand there!" he roared at the nearest men. "Get over there and see to it!"

At once the situation became clear to him. This was no random accident. This was a deliberate act of sabotage, and with a sudden burst of anger he knew who was responsible.

He turned to his aide, hovering nearby. "Servant! Wake up the police chief. Tell him to dispatch every police officer he can muster! I want every koban emptied and the city searched from top to bottom. The perpetrators of this crime must be apprehended!"

Yokuke's brow wrinkled like a wizened old prune as he frowned. Money could buy a great deal of power and political influence in Japan, but there was a far more important commodity when commanding the respect of already-powerful men: one's reputation. Yokuke knew this incident was a serious embarrassment to him, and a blow to his standing in the eyes of the Diet. The fact his underlings were largely responsible for the poor security was immaterial, the mistakes of peasants were always answerable by their lord. Was he not in charge of them, after all? And in a land where hard work and success were respected above all else, an accident caused by laziness or ineptitude would be bad enough. But to have someone else take advantage of you because of your own failings – and a dirty gai-jin at that – was absolutely unforgivable!

My honour must be restored!

Yokuke turned on his heel and shuffled purposefully towards the wide entrance of the Taiyoku Misui Fisheries Company's massive complex. He had done all he could down on the wharf, and there was a more urgent crisis developing. His office was where he needed to be now. He had more important business to take care of, the business of politics.

He was shaking with rage at the audacity of these pirates who had dared to sabotage his Fleet, but the first step towards ameliorating the consequences was to apprehend the criminals. They must still be in the country, and that meant they were still within his grasp.

He knew he would get no more sleep that night.

Yokuke sat behind the large Western-style desk in his private office on the top floor of the Taiyoku Misui Fisheries Company's office building. Through the large windows he could look out over the moonlit bay. The scene that greeted him refreshed his anger every time he looked at it. The red glow from the lights of dozens of police cars lit the sorry spectacle of his sunken ships, although Yokuke noted with disgust that the perpetrators of this heinous crime would be long gone in the fifteen minutes it had taken them to arrive. While the local police's response had been slow, his was characteristically swift, beginning the moment he stepped into his office.

Since this was a personal attack against me, it is only right that I should take care of it myself, neh?

It was true that he had now been forced into damage-control to protect his career, but there was never a setback so great that it could not be turned to some advantage.

His temper worsened as he considered the wider implications of this perfidious act though. Such an embarrassing humiliation could have grave implications for his standing in the Diet. To lose face was to lose respect, and to lose respect was to lose power.

Prime Minister Takahashi was easily manipulated, but Yokuke was not the only senior minister to manoeuvre him for his own ends, and he knew it.

He frowned, turning the problem over in his mind. Forty years in politics had not dimmed his intuition, nor his desire to cling to power whenever a new challenge arose to threaten it.

The Japanese mining and logging sectors in particular, were his greatest rivals. They had a strong power base from their lucrative off-shore investments – operations in Papua New Guinea and other Southeast Asian countries where labour was cheap and permits easily bought from naïve and broke local governments. They would undoubtedly seek to expand their financial empires, and their profits. For that they needed political influence.

Yokuke considered the relative strengths of his enemies. They were extractive industries too, similar to his own, and that meant they would always have an edge over the more slower-growing and market-driven economics of the electronics and heavy industry sectors that were their other competition for power. But the other extractive industry competitors all had something he did not, and that was peace of mind. The sea was a much more difficult location to make a profit from. It was hard enough sometimes just finding the fish, especially the rarer and more lucrative stocks like whales, but even then you could not claim ownership. There was no such thing as a mining concession for him. The only way to claim his rightful ownership of a stock was to make sure it was caught and hauled aboard one of his ships first. That always made it a continual race to fish out a new area first, an unseemly scramble where he was forced to compete with other fishing industrialists, especially the Korean pirates, the rapacious Taiwanese, and the filthy Filipino savages.

Yokuke exclaimed in annoyance. Why was it his political enemies seemed to have such an easy time of it? After they had negotiated their cutting rights or obtained their prospecting licence – even if they paid a pittance for it – no one bothered them any further. They could make money as fast as they could chop it down or dig it out of the ground, but no one was going to come and take their profits off them in the meantime. They definitely had no troublemaking foreign hippies causing them grief!

Yokuke frowned.

Nor would any of his enemies – political or competitive – be likely to sit on their hands and do nothing in the face of his setback.

"I have been away from the Diet for too long," he murmured to the silent office. "Every day I am away from the halls of power is another day my enemies have to work against me unopposed, undoing my own plans and furthering their own interests."

He stood, his mind made up. Nothing must be allowed to stand in the way of his success, no matter what the cost. If it was to be a race to secure both his rightful profits and political position, then it was a race he was determined to win. Failure led to extinction. To survive in business – as in life – there could be no room for second place.

Extinction is for the weak, since they deserve their Fate!

Yokuke clenched his shrunken fist into a bird-like claw. It was time to do what he did best!

His thoughts were interrupted by a polite knock at the wood-panelled door.

He turned to acknowledge his Enforcer. "Greetings Kobushi-san. Your timing is impeccable."

Kobushi bowed in response, removing his dark glasses and waiting respectfully.

"I have another task for you," Yokuke announced. The Enforcer stood impassively, but Yokuke was pleased to detect a greedy glint flicker in the depths of his soulless black eyes.

"I must return to the capital immediately. Come, Walk me to my car and I will explain what I need you to do."

On the way to his transport, Yokuke gazed out the window of the building's glass elevator. How ironic it was that he was right now standing in a marvel of human architectural and industrial achievement, yet looking down on an equivalent testament to human destructiveness.

"You have seen the results of this scurrilous and cowardly attack against me tonight?" he said, gesturing to the disaster playing out below them on the waterfront.

"Yes Master."

"What should an appropriate response be?" he asked, watching the Enforcer's face intently.

"Your honour requires this insult against you be avenged."

Yokuke smiled, pleased at the unquestioning loyalty he saw. "Kobushi-san, my faithful samurai, I have an important task for you. Find the stinking gai-jin dog who has committed this unspeakable act. Hunt him down wherever he flees, and bring me his head on a platter."

"Hai, Oyaban!"

The Enforcer bowed and replaced his dark glasses.

The elevator reached the ground floor and the doors slid open. Yokuke stepped out into the glass-fronted lobby of the building, pleased to see his car waiting for him outside. His private jet was standing by to take him to Tokyo, and he needed to get to the airport as soon as possible.

Suddenly he came to a surprised halt. Something about the scene in front of him was not right. He could see his driver was not at the wheel of the car. The door stood open though, and someone was crouched down next to it. Then the person straightened up, and Yokuke saw at once it wasn't his driver. The features were not even Japanese. With a sharp intake of breath he recognised one of the meddling barbarians.

"Iye!" he hissed in surprise. Their audacity knew no bounds!

The troublemaker was clutching a familiar uniform jacket, and it was only when he began putting it on that Yokuke noticed the prostrate form of his driver still on the ground. Wearing the misappropriated jacket now, the thief jumped into the driver's seat.

"Kobushi-san, kill that man!"

The Enforcer drew his katana and sprang forward, the moonlight glinting on the wicked curve of the long blade.

The engine revved, then with a squeal of rubber the car accelerated away.

Yokuke stared after the speeding car. He was certain he'd seen a blonde head lean over from the back seat – a head that was unmistakably the Kajiki. His fists clenched helplessly.

The theft of his private limousine added a personal touch to an already unforgivable insult, but it was more than that which so enraged him.

What devilry was he planning with my vehicle? Was this to be an assassination attempt on me?

Yokuke's eyes narrowed. This was one mistake the Kajiki would not live long enough to regret.

He would see to it. Right now though, all he could do was stand there and watch as the Westerners sped away in his own car.

Kobushi's speed was impressive as he sprinted after the fleeing car, katana held high in a two-handed grip over his shoulder. It was the classic killing pose, but Yokuke could see the samurai would not have time to deliver the fluid poetry of a beheading stroke. Yokuke's lip curled involuntarily as the Mercedes' expensive grille became a battering ram, the car crashing through the gates and skidding into the street with a squeal of tortured tyres.

You will pay for this, Kajiki. Mark my words.

Kobushi's pursuit slowed, then stopped. He looked up the street after the speeding car, knowing he had been outclassed. Then he sheathed his sword, returning with his head bowed. "Forgive me, Master. I have failed you."

Yokuke said nothing, neither agreeing nor disagreeing. His rage was white-hot, flooding through him with the intensity of a burning flare. It took a supreme effort to maintain his composure, reminding himself firmly that revenge was always best served cold. When he finally did speak, his voice was as hard and lifeless as a gravestone. "Find the Kajiki, no matter where the rat-hole he flees to." He turned his gaze on the Enforcer, impressing on him the seriousness of what he was about to say. "Killing will be too quick for this gai-jin scum. First I want you to utterly destroy his life and everything he holds dear. Then I want you to sabotage everything he stands for. Only then will you kill him. As slowly and painfully as possible." Yokuke's smile was cold. "You shall have whatever you require to accomplish this task."

"Hai!" The Enforcer removed his glasses and bowed deeply in acknowledgement, at the same time expressing gratitude for this opportunity to redeem himself. He had not been so quick though, that Yokuke was unable to see his eyes – and particularly the glint of greedy anticipation that flickered across the otherwise expressionless mask of his face.

Yokuke's lips tightened into a thin line. "For the sake of both our honours, do not fail me!"

***

Dennis Cruikshank sat in his hotel room chain-smoking. The TV was on, tuned to a local Japanese news channel, although he was only half-watching it. He couldn't understand any of the commentary, and besides, he could see most of what was going on down at the waterfront anyway. He looked out of the window with a mounting sense of frustration.

"This is bullshit!" he muttered under his breath.

He could tell by the commotion that something major had gone down, although he couldn't say he was altogether surprised. Through the mist across the harbour he could see the flickering glow from dozens of police lights.

They must have half the bloody force down there.

Yet the eco-terrorists had still managed to elude them. He'd seen them himself as they slipped back aboard their fishing boat, then made a run for it with no navigation lights. The ship had slipped out of the harbour undetected, while a few minutes later the Shimonoseki Police had attempted to shut down roads around the waterfront district. Not only was it too little too late, but they hadn't even managed to close the barn door after the horse had bolted!

How could the local Keystone Cops have let themselves get caught with their pants down like that?

I could have told them these perps were gonna pull something tonight. He tugged at the corner of his moustache angrily. *In fact, I did!*

The vein in Cruikshank's temple began to pulse as he recalled the conversation. Minister Yokuke had given him a contact in the local force, but the guy was just a lowly lieutenant, the lowest rung on the command hierarchy. Apparently, not many of the top brass spoke English. That was the line he'd been fed anyway. Cruikshank wondered if he was being sidelined and ignored deliberately. The lieutenant certainly hadn't seemed that interested in his telephoned warning.

"Ah, so sorry, no policeman is avairable," he'd replied in accented English, his voice fuzzy as though he'd just been woken up.

Cruikshank had no sympathy for the man's interrupted sleep, especially given it was his own all-night surveillance that had picked up the protestors lowering their boat in the early hours of stupid o'clock. He had told him in no uncertain terms that he had witnessed the preparations for a crime about to be committed, and suggested as politely as he could manage that the lieutenant should get off his backside and do something about it.

"Yes, yes. I have someone investigate," the officer promised, sounding more like he wanted to get off the phone so he could go straight back to bed.

Cruikshank hung up in disgust. He had continued to maintain his surveillance, but he hadn't seen any cops do a drive-by of the protestors' fishing boat, let alone go aboard to investigate. They'd probably decided their nice warm police station was more inviting than the chill of an autumn night – although by that stage there wouldn't have been much to see aboard the ship anyway. The crime was already underway on the other side of the harbour.

Cruikshank was watching the carnage now, still disgusted that the perpetrators had gotten clean away, apparently successful. He glassed the far side of the harbour with his binoculars. He could make out at least two of the whaling ships sunk at their moorings, and the sight riled him. Despite predicting funny business was afoot, he hadn't been able to prevent this crime.

How the hell did those punks manage to pull this off?

Surely there should have been too much security for them to get aboard, and for that matter he hadn't heard any bombs go off…

Cruikshank scratched the hook of his broken nose, contemplating. As if on cue, the sudden buzzing of his cellular phone made him look away from the window. He glanced down at the little screen, its backlight filling the room with a weak glow.

It was an encrypted text message. With an anticipatory frown already tightening his brow, he entered his password to decode it.

"Agent confirms suspects are planning illegal activity. Probable sabotage planned for tonight. Recommend extreme vigilance," he read.

Cruikshank stared incredulously at the screen, cracking his knuckles in frustration.

"No shit!" he exploded, furious at the damned Mickey Mouse operation those spooks back at HQ were running. "This is a goddamn joke!"

What the hell was the point in having an undercover agent if the info wasn't passed on in time for him to do something about it? He hurled the phone across the room where it bounced off the bed and onto the floor. Changing his mind in a flash, he stormed across the room to retrieve the phone, snatching it up and punching the Reply button.

The blood pounded in his head as he waited for a connection. The two rings it took his supervisor to pick up the phone only intensified his frustration.

"This is Ron Silverman."

"What the hell is going on?" Cruikshank demanded.

The voice at the other end was calm and unruffled. "A report from our undercover agent."

"I know that. Why the hell wasn't I told sooner?"

"Pull your head in, Cruikshank. This is still on a need-to-know basis, and right now, you don't."

"It's too late for that. It's already done and dusted and the punks got clean away!" Cruikshank snorted. "This whole setup is bullshit," he muttered. He could picture the bastard sitting behind his desk, with that pompous little half-smile that so infuriated him plastered across his mug. Suddenly he'd had a gutsful of the whole Secret Squirrel bullshit.

The damned terrorists had managed to outwit everyone so far, despite all the background work and all the danger flags he'd raised. He was the only one who seemed to have taken the threat seriously, but his hands were so tied up with bureaucratic tape he might as well be out here playing with himself.

This case needed to be busted wide open. It was time for some good old-fashioned police work. "I say we move now," he said. "Let's arrest these low-life punks and pack them off to Guantanamo where they can't cause any more trouble!"

Silverman's reply was immediate and emphatic. "No. All you have against them so far is suspicion. There's no hard evidence linking them to any crime."

"Bullshit! I saw them leave their ship and paddle across the harbour in the middle of the night!" Cruikshank insisted.

"Yes, but did you see them interfere with these Japanese ships? Did you actually see them commit any crime? Do you have any hard evidence proving they were involved?"

Cruikshank muttered angrily, knowing his superior had a point, but also knowing that was the root of the problem. Watching and waiting might be a spook's specialty, but that didn't stop crimes being committed. All this pussyfooting around played right into the terrorists' hands. They needed to be stopped before they did anything really bad.

Five minutes alone in an interview room with them and I'd have them confessing!

His supervisor's voice softened. "I believe what you're telling me, but we need hard evidence before we can move. The most we could get them on right now is destruction of property. That's not even an extraditable offence. We need to catch them in the act of planning or carrying out a terrorist act." He paused thoughtfully. "Threatening lives would be even better – preferably Americans, but Japanese will do."

"What about the agent?"

"What do you mean?"

"What are his orders?"

Silverman's laugh was maddening. "You know I can't tell you that."

"Give me control of him then," Cruikshank demanded.

"That's not possible."

Cruikshank swore under his breath. "Why the hell not?"

His supervisor's tone turned conciliatory. "It's crucial the agent's identity remains secret. But rest assured you will be kept in the loop. All relevant info will be filtered back to you as soon as it's declassified."

Cruikshank snorted. He knew what that meant. "An agent I can't make use of is no damn good to me," he growled.

"That's not true-" Silverman started to spin more of his usual placatory bullshit, but Cruikshank cut him off.

"Here's the deal. These punks have already crossed the line, so it's too late to nip this in the bud. They'll be looking over their shoulder now – guilt does that to people – so we've missed our chance to pick them up without any fuss."

He frowned, tugging his moustache. "They'll more than likely scatter for a while, like cockroaches when you turn on the light, but they ain't done yet. I'll stake my reputation on it. Problem is, we got nothing on their whereabouts now, so stopping their next crime will be twice as hard."

The smooth dome of his forehead furrowed. He would have to start from square one again, and quickly. The next attack could be directed against US interests. "The punks have more than likely fled Japan, and aren't likely to return. It's gonna take a lot more effort to get them now."

"Rest assured, the agent is close enough to keep them under surveillance," Silverman promised.

"That ain't good enough!" Cruikshank fumed. "Don't you get it? If we want to stop these guys before they pull something else then your agent is gonna have to push harder. He's gonna have to take some risks in order to uncover any incriminating evidence. We need to set up a trap for them!"

The phone was silent for a long time, and Cruikshank began to hope he'd finally gotten through to his supervisor.

"Very well," Silverman said at last. "I'll see what I can arrange."

***

Richard stood at the Gwendolyn's bow rail, riding the light swells as they dipped beneath her hull. Dawn had broken already and the golden sky wiped away the blackness of the previous night, along with his doubts.

It had seemed like the three of them waited for an eternity in the dark sea, floating together in waterlogged silence out beyond the breakers. Then finally a dark shadow had disengaged itself from the night, and as it rose up before them, Richard had recognised the friendly sweep of the Gwendolyn's hull silhouetted against the stars, cargo net already in place. He had scrambled gratefully up to the deck, aware that this was the second time the gallant little ship had rescued him from a watery grave.

Richard closed his eyes now, enjoying the feel of the wind as it ruffled his hair. It was a sunny autumn morning and it felt good to be aboard again and underway, freed from the confines of the noisy, smelly fishing port and the city of Shimonoseki pressing in on all sides. The salty tang of the open sea filled his nostrils, and the waves sighed softly as they slipped past beneath the bow. The Gwendolyn was more than just a ship to him now, more even than a home; she was his salvation.

His thoughts drifted back to the previous night. It had definitely been a terrifying ordeal.

No, it was an experience.

Richard smiled faintly to himself, aware that the terror he'd felt just a few hours ago was already fading in the rays of the warm morning sun. Nevertheless, it was a relief to have escaped, and Richard felt his elation rise as he watched the coast of Japan steadily recede in their wake. His worries were dispelled, to be quickly replaced by a warm glow of satisfaction. Not only had he survived, but the Team had succeeded!

They had heard the news bulletin earlier on BBC World, all of them crowded together around the shortwave radio in the Gwendolyn's cramped wheelhouse. Richard manoeuvred himself next to Summer, pleased to see her again after the enforced separation, and enjoying the excuse to be close to her. Standing in front of Heath, he could smell the hippy's stale body odour, and the faint wafts of perfume from her freshly-washed hair were far more tantalising. As he inched forward though, he unintentionally jostled her.

Oh my god, I touched her bum!

She turned, an annoyed frown already creasing her features. Richard held his breath, terrified of earning her displeasure. Incredibly though, when she saw it was him she simply gave a terse smile and turned back to the radio. He blinked in surprise, his confused emotions making it a battle to concentrate on the radio.

The announcer's voice was faint and distorted with static, and despite his deadpan British accent his message was uplifting. Richard knew they had done well. The grins on the faces around him said it all.

The Kyoeishin-Maru wouldn't be spotting any more whales. It was reported sunk, lying in the silt on the bottom of the harbour.

Where it belongs!

Richard was proud of the spark of defiance he was able to muster.

Cal had reckoned the damage would be too great to salvage the white ship, even if they had to refloat it to unblock the berth. "Seawater is as corrosive as battery acid to machinery and electronics. With the amount of damage we did, it'll be far cheaper for them to start again with a new ship – if they can afford it."

The Nippon-Maru was badly damaged too. It had suffered a lot of flooding, but the great black factory ship also needed a lot of water to sink it, and the crew had managed to get the pumps started in time.

Duke spat disgustedly into his tin at that news, refusing to look at the two field assistants who'd been with him.

Cal, always leading by example, tried to settle the air with a positive spin. "Hey that's great," he said clapping the Skipper on the back. "With any luck you managed to put that bloody ship out of action for the rest of the season. Add a year's loss of productivity to the repair bill and that might be enough to tip the whaling industry over the edge."

The Skipper just cursed and muttered something inaudible.

But when the radio reporter announced that the Japanese Pelagic Whaling Fleet would be delayed in port indefinitely for repairs, even he joined the jubilation that erupted aboard the Gwendolyn, managing a whiskery grin as a spontaneous cheer broke out on the bridge. "That'll teach them dirty bastards a lesson!" he growled.

Richard smiled at the memory, reliving his own sense of satisfaction at the Team's achievement. They really had done it! They'd taken on an evil giant and won!

For the first time in his life he had accomplished something he actually felt proud of. It wasn't the sort of thing you could go bragging to people about, of course, and his parents weren't likely to approve… But even so, in the grand scheme of things he actually had helped make a difference! This was something that would stay with him forever, he realised, and recalling his earlier hesitation to get involved made him feel mildly embarrassed now. Perhaps even a little ashamed. He frowned beneath his closed eyelids.

For better or for worse, he was involved now. There would be no backing out. But as he stood there enjoying the warmth of the sun on his skin, he realised the knowledge didn't bother him nearly as much as he'd feared it would. In fact, quite the opposite was true. He had begun a new journey in life, one he was compelled to see through to the end. And as long as he followed in his brother's broad shadow, Richard knew he had nothing to fear.

When he opened his eyes again, a pod of dolphins was cavorting around the boat, surfing in the bow waves and leaping playfully out of the water alongside. He wondered if it was the same pod of dolphins that had visited them in the night, keeping a vigil over the swimmers. Had their presence deterred any predator that stalked them from the shadows? He didn't know, but he felt an unspoken bond with them all the same.

Their lithe grey backs glistened as they arched through the air, turning to look directly at him, before splashing back below. Richard was stunned at first, then gladdened by the tacit acknowledgement from wild creatures. They leaped closer, as if to include him in their game. He stared at them, fascinated, as though looking upon the world for the very first time. He wondered what it would be like to be a dolphin, spending your life swimming and frolicking in the water with your friends.

He laughed out loud at their antics, delighting at these precious shared moments with such carefree spirits. The fact that they were wild animals, jumping so close he could almost touch them, only added to his sense of wonder as he watched them play. And as he continued to watch, Richard realised this moment was indeed a rare gift – and something he never would have experienced sitting at his desk in his old life.

He smiled, watching as the morning sun glittered on the water, lighting every ripple and splash like liquid gold.

In his heart, he knew now he had made the right decision. The wild places of the world held a simple and unique beauty all their own. The wilderness and the creatures who lived in it *deserved* protection, and he resolved to do whatever he could to help them.

***

Cal Major stood in the Gwendolyn's wheelhouse, his attention alternating between the chart spread in front of him and the sea outside.

Duke snored softly nearby, asleep in the sea-chair in front of the ship's wheel. Cal grinned to himself. The poor bloke was exhausted. He'd been at the helm all night, first searching for the three of them in the water, then steering the Gwendolyn safely through the darkness as they made their escape. When dawn broke Cal had offered to relieve him, and it was a measure of the Skipper's trust in him that he'd agreed – and a measure of his dedication to his duty that he refused to go below to his cabin. "Ah'll stay right where ah'm needed," he'd drawled. "Wake me thuh instant anything happens." Then he'd lowered his voice to a harsh whisper. "Them blood-crazed fish-heads won't take this lyin' down, Son. Mark my words, they'll send a posse after us, as sure as day follows night."

Cal frowned, checking the radar for the hundredth time that morning, and the GPS, then forced himself to relax for the moment. He turned his gaze towards Richard, standing at the bow, and his frown softened momentarily. His brother actually seemed to be enjoying himself at the rail, laughing as he watched the playful spectacle of the dolphins bow-riding their wake. They were Pacific White-sided dolphins, a large pod travelling between feeding grounds. Cal smiled to himself. Just a few short weeks ago Richard would have been a picture of abject misery. He would have been hanging over the side puking instead, the motion of the ship as alien to him as the life of a biologist.

He really had come a long way in that time.

Cal sighed then, troubled by his conscience. He hoped he'd managed to take Richard's mind off his troubles by bringing him here. It seemed like a lifetime ago that his brother had phoned him, but he'd recognised the pain and desperation in his voice. He'd guessed at the depths of the depression Richard was mired in when he called, what with the break-up of his marriage and all, and he just couldn't turn his back on him. It was a tough decision to make though. The Gwendolyn had been scheduled to depart for his spring research voyage in a few days time, and time and tide waited for nobody. The only option had been to bring Richard along, so he'd thrown caution to the wind and bought him an air ticket to Christchurch, telling him to meet them at the dock.

Up until this moment he hadn't been sure if he'd made the right decision though. He'd intended to give his brother a break from it all, a chance to get away from his troubles, and maybe gain a different perspective on things – but what he'd dragged him into the middle of went far beyond that.

Cal shook his head guiltily. He certainly hadn't meant for Richard to get mixed up in all this strife over whaling – or any of the crew for that matter – but Fate had a funny way of intervening in even the best-laid plans sometimes.

He pursed his lips thoughtfully. Then again, Richard had managed to rise to the challenge. He was still terrified most of the time – Cal could see it in his eyes – but the fact he managed to overcome his fears spoke volumes for his character.

Richard had done well last night. The ordeal was a difficult ask of anyone, but he had acquitted himself well.

He's stronger than I realised. He could make a good biologist if that's the path he chooses.

Cal nodded to himself. From the Skipper's grumbled report, Richard had performed better than the two field assistants he'd hired at great expense. True, sabotage wasn't entirely within their job description, but integrity was, and if they agreed to do a job he expected them to give it a hundred percent.

According to Duke, neither of them had.

Heath, in particular, was a source of concern. He was dirty, bad-tempered, and lazy, but there was just something about him that set off a warning in Cal's head…

He was open with his insubordination, and that kind of attitude was dangerous, especially aboard a ship. In a confined living environment it was easy for any negativity to fester, spreading amongst the rest of the crew like a cancer, until it finally boiled over.

Cal rubbed his face with his hands, feeling suddenly tired. He was in charge of the voyage, and the Skipper was in charge of the ship. Together, their word had to be law at sea, and it had to be obeyed – not because they enjoyed being dictatorial, but because it was dangerous out here. Any insubordination, even hesitation at the wrong time, could kill them all. It was that simple.

Heath's bad temper was a source of constant friction since the moment he'd arrived. In fact, it almost seemed worse lately. Cal wondered if the stress of the recent action was getting to the Californian. Would he be dumb enough to actually try something mutinous?

I'll have to keep a close eye on him.

Cal frowned. As if the dreadlocked activist wasn't enough to deal with, he wasn't the only worry.

Summer was a more specific problem for harmony aboard ship.

She was definitely eye-catching, but that wasn't something he could hold against her, even if she liked to flaunt it to get out of the messy, boring, or physical jobs, or to get anything else she wanted. Cal's worries were more explicit than that. He had noticed her recent attention towards Richard, and the knowledge sat uneasily. She was the kind of overly-confident woman who had 'tease' and 'man-eater' written all over her. She was quite capable of treating his brother like a doormat, just for sport.

Cal sighed. To be fair, she might actually like Richard… His brow creased. Then again, she might be just playing games. And the last thing he wanted to see was his brother getting hurt by a woman, again. Richard's ex was a nasty piece of work too, and Cal had never liked her. Gina was as fake as her feelings for Richard – and as far as Cal was concerned his brother was well rid of her. The saddest thing about their break-up was that it had taken so long, and that Richard seemed to have taken it so hard. Well, that was why he'd brought him out here, to get his mind off all that. The last thing his brother needed was to trade one grasping predatory woman for another.

He's too nice to cope with that kind of crap.

Cal turned to look out the windscreen again, watching Richard. He was in another world. He was completely engrossed, watching the dolphins as though they were alone together in the universe.

Cal's smile was sad, recognising the blossoming idealism he had once felt too. His own carefree naivety had long ago been replaced by the weight of responsibility; responsibility for his crew, his research, and even for the Ocean itself. It was a sobering thought to realise something as wild and powerful as the Ocean could be threatened by a creature as puny as man, but the evidence was all around to see…

Cal ran a hand absently through his blonde hair. Any pleasure he got from watching the dolphins was tempered by his knowledge of the harsh realities of the world. They were still in Japanese waters here, and in all likelihood these dolphins were marked for death. Japanese whaling didn't begin or end with their Pelagic Fleet.

For years the IWC had ignored pleas by scientists and remained silent on the issue of killing dolphins and smaller cetaceans – and coastal Japanese fishermen exploited that complicity to the fullest. Their local dolphin drives resulted in entire pods of hundreds of dolphins being corralled into bays and butchered, ostensively to supply dolphin meat to local restaurants, but mainly because they were seen as unwanted competition for already over-exploited fisheries.

Cal shook his head sadly. Wherever you looked, people were destroying the natural order of the world as if there was no tomorrow.

It was only right to do what he could to stop it before it was too late, even though sometimes it seemed like a hopeless cause. No matter what anybody did, the relentless march of human civilisation continued to sweep across the globe, obliterating everything in its path. It was definitely a sobering thought.

One thing at a time.

They had won a small victory last night. The War for the Whales was by no means over, but this opening skirmish was a good start.

It could have gone better though…

Cal stared down at the chart without seeing it. In truth, he was mostly pleased with the night's results, although success was always a relative measure, he reminded himself. 'If onlys' were fine to ponder, but compared to failure the cause was still well ahead. It would have been nice to sink the factory ship, of course, and they hadn't been able to target any of the Hunter-Killer boats at all… but it was a good start.

He frowned suddenly. He would have a far greater problem justifying his actions to Aurelia. Successful or not, she was unlikely to approve.

He hastily put the thoughts out of his mind, knowing he couldn't afford to worry about that now. The wheels were already in motion and it would take all his wits to stay ahead of the game.

Cal hoped the Japanese people and their government saw this act for what it was – an attack against an unsound environmental practice, not a personal attack against them or their culture. He was forced to concede that was unlikely.

The Japanese authorities would be spitting tacks, and Mr Fish's propaganda mill would have a field day with this. He rolled his eyes, imagining the headlines in the morning's papers. No doubt they would be filled with references to illegal aggression, terrorism, out of control extremists, and irrefutable evidence of piracy.

Cal sighed, still troubled by conflicting emotions. Perhaps it was because of his subconscious desire to do the right thing, to conduct this battle with some sort of honour – even though in the end he knew that mattered little. It was impossible to make an omelette without breaking some eggs along the way. If people's livelihoods were affected by his actions, well that was unfortunate, but it was only a minor issue in the grand scheme of things. If people hated him because of this, well, that was to be expected too. At the end of the day he knew he could concern himself only with the greater good. The end result was all that mattered.

He checked the radar again, then turned to look aft. Past the leaping dolphins in their wake, the coast of Japan was just a fuzzy smear on the horizon now, but Cal knew better than to assume the Team were home and hosed yet. Their sudden illegal departure from port without the harbourmaster's clearance had caught the local authorities on the hop, but the element of surprise wouldn't last forever.

Somewhere out there was a Japanese destroyer, shadowing them. He had first picked it up on the scope an hour ago, but it hadn't closed with them in that time. He wondered if the Gwendolyn was too quick to catch, or if the pursuers were content just to follow them for now.

Why? Are they planning something?

Cal's tactician's brain jumped into action, already working out his next move. The quickest route home took them southeast past the island of Honshu, but also kept them close to the Japanese coast for far too long – much too risky with a warship stalking them. He had decided to head due west instead. It was the quickest route out of Japanese-controlled waters; taking them straight towards Korea. Of course he wasn't sure he could count on a warm welcome from the Koreans, but that wasn't exactly part of the plan either. He intended to hit Korean waters then head due south, keeping just inside their maritime border – that would slow up any pursuers who would have to seek permission to chase and intercept any shipping within a foreign government's jurisdiction. It was a risk of course, since they didn't have clearance to enter the Korean-controlled zone, but it was the quickest way to reach international waters.

We should be safe if we can make it to the High Seas.

While not exactly lawless, international waters weren't subject to the laws of any individual country, and right now that would work in their favour. He knew the Team had committed relatively minor crimes by international standards – destruction of property, maybe assault – even if the Japanese authorities begged to differ. That meant the Team couldn't be extradited or apprehended outside Japanese jurisdiction, not without an official Interpol arrest warrant anyway, and that would take time. On the open sea there would be no cosy deal-making between governments to hand them over.

He checked the chart again, his blue eyes squinting with suspicion. Then again, it wouldn't pay to take anything for granted. Amimoto was a crafty and dangerous adversary – and no doubt bent on revenge. He also wasn't renowned for following the rules.

Cal stared wistfully at his brother, standing at the bow watching the dolphins. He wished he could share his carefree mood, but his own thoughts remained troubled.

Cal's jaw clenched involuntarily. It was a pity they hadn't managed to put the Japanese Whaling Fleet out of action for good. Even though the Nippon-Maru was laid up for repairs, the fact that the factory ship had survived meant sooner or later the Fleet would put to sea again, and the slaughter would continue.

This war is far from over yet.

He kept his thoughts to himself for now, but they continued to swirl in his head like storm clouds gathering on the horizon. He faced the knowledge with grim acceptance.

Sooner or later they would have to confront the whalers again, this time on the High Seas.

***

Kobushi the Enforcer stood in the harbourmaster's office. The building overlooked the waterfront, and further down the wharf he could see the damage wrought on the Fleet by the previous night's sabotage. The sight of the sunken ships was unmissable, especially with the crowd of police and incredulous onlookers still milling around the site.

He wondered briefly how much was the financial cost. This was bad for his master, and bad for his clan's dealings with the Taiyoku Misui Fisheries Company. By far the worst result of this atrocity though, was the insult to his master's honour.

"Kangaerarenai koto da!" he growled to himself.

That these criminals would dare attack Amimoto-san! It is unthinkable!

His master had been shown to the world as a victim, a weak man who would let himself be taken advantage of by common criminals – and dirty foreigners at that! The loss of honour was monumental!

Kobushi's mouth tightened. The shame automatically transferred to him. As a loyal vassal he had sworn to serve and protect Amimoto, and his master's fate was his own. His thoughts turned back to the incident in the early hours of that same morning. The dirty gai-jin dogs had stolen Amimoto-san's private vehicle right in front of him, and he – Kobushi – had failed to stop them. He had returned to his master's side in shame, offering to commit seppuku on the spot to atone for his uselessness.

Amimoto-san had frowned, as if considering, then shaken his head. In his great wisdom and compassion he had granted Kobushi another chance. An opportunity to redeem himself. An opportunity to find the foreign criminals and make them pay for their crimes. Kobushi adjusted his dark glasses. He would enjoy carrying out that order.

First things first though.

Kobushi turned away from the window, fixing his attention back onto the be-spectacled harbourmaster standing defiantly in front of him.

"Answer my question!" he snapped, his frustration beginning to get the better of him. "The ship that was moored over there. Where did it go?"

"So sorry," the man repeated, shaking his head maddeningly. "I cannot give out that information."

Kobushi's eyes narrowed to compassionless fissures behind his glasses.

I ought to slit your impertinent throat like a common peasant for disrespecting me like that.

On the outside, his half-smile remained frozen in place. "I am samurai, and you will kindly address me as Lord when I speak to you."

The man said nothing.

Kobushi's hand, which had been around the harbourmaster's throat the whole time, began to tighten.

"Y-yes, Lord," the man gasped at last, fear beginning to show in his eyes.

Kobushi grunted. Cooperation at last. "The ship?" he prompted.

The harbourmaster couldn't meet his gaze. "S-so sorry, Lord," he choked. "I cannot give out this information. I could lose my job. That would bring dishonour to my family," he added pitifully.

Kobushi frowned, his eyebrow already beginning to twitch. With his free hand he reached up and slowly undid the top button on his shirt. The harbourmaster's gaze followed him curiously, then suddenly his eyes widened in fear as he caught sight of the dragon tattoo.

"You know what this is don't you?"

The man nodded, too afraid to speak.

Kobushi gave a thin smile. "Then you know that I will kill you without hesitation if you continue to defy me." It was a statement, not a question, and he paused to let his words sink in.

The harbourmaster writhed in his grip, then suddenly his gaze flickered to a paper on the desk behind him. He looked away guiltily.

Kobushi smiled.

Ah, your eyes betray you.

Leading the unfortunate man by the throat, he strode across to the desk and picked it up.

It was a computer printout detailing the vessels in port that day. Kobushi scanned it quickly, his eye drawn inexorably to the Western name near the bottom: *Gwendolyn.* That was it!

The information was sparse though, and even the home port meant nothing to him.

"Where is Ritter-ton?" he asked, stumbling over the pronunciation of the foreign name.

Silence.

The hand around the harbourmaster's throat tightened until it began to cut off his air. Still smiling into the insolent face, Kobushi reached down to untuck his shirt, revealing the hilt of his wakizashi sword stuck into his belt.

The harbourmaster's eyes bulged white with fear. "Lyttleton, Lord. It's in New Zealand," he gasped.

Kobushi's smile was serpentine.

Ah, so that finally loosened your tongue! What a pity I cannot trust you to hold it now!

With his free hand he took off his dark glasses, folded them carefully, then placed them in the pocket of his shirt.

Abruptly, he released the man. The harbour master stood there, surprised, his hand reaching up to massage his bruised throat. Then he regained his wits and began to back away, feet pattering on the carpet in his haste to flee.

The soft scrape as Kobushi loosened his sword in its scabbard carried across the room. The man immediately fell to his knees, hands clasped together in supplication. "Onegai!" he wailed, begging pitifully for his life. "Please!"

The smile never left Kobushi's face. In a single fluid motion the wakizashi flashed out of its scabbard, inscribed a perfect arc through the air, then slid back into the confines of its sheath.

The harbourmaster stared at him in shock. Then, almost in slow motion, his head lolled forward and toppled to the floor, releasing a fountain of blood.

Kobushi reached into his shirt pocket and casually replaced his sunglasses. The police were unlikely to come here asking questions, but even if they did, no one would speak of his visit now. Tidying up all possible loose ends was not only the mark of an expert, but also his guarantee of silence.

I am going to New Zealand, and no one must know I am coming.

Part IV – Desperation

Chapter 20

Cal Major felt a glow of satisfaction as the little islands slid into view on the horizon, the low-lying coral atolls as familiar to him as the neighbourhood he grew up in, or perhaps even more so. He had spent many tropical winters here in the warm waters around the Vava'u Island group in northern Tonga, studying the great Humpback whales in their secret calving grounds. After crossing thousands of kilometres of open ocean, it was good to be back in friendly waters again.

It was not just familiarity that warmed his heart though, but the knowledge that they had made it here safely. The week-long voyage from Japan had been an anxious time for him, with the responsibility for the crew's safety resting squarely on his shoulders. In truth, he was still concerned about pursuit, even though there had been no sign of the Japanese warship since their first night on the run from Shimonoseki. Duke had done a good job of losing them in the dark, and Cal smiled at the memory of the Gwendolyn's daring night-time dash, running without lights, and dodging around the Ryukyu Islands and through the narrow shoals of the East China Sea where the huge destroyer couldn't follow. "Ah'd like to see them sorry starched-shirt bastards round us up now," the Skipper had growled through a jawful of tobacco. "Them useless Navy squids are all thuh same – all hat and no cattle. It'll take nothin' short of another SEAL t' ketch this ole soldier!"

Cal suspected the Japanese Navy had given up the pursuit that first night when they'd left Japanese waters, although he wasn't taking any chances. Even though it had barely been five minutes since his last check, he scrutinised the radar again, an action that was becoming almost habitual while he was on watch and even a regular obsession when he wasn't. The screen was blank, except for the shadow of the island lying ahead off the port bow. Cal wasn't reassured though. His mind still grappled with the death of Victor Admirante, the state of the Japanese pelagic Whaling Fleet, and the wrath of Amimoto that would surely follow him. With a rueful shake of the head he realised he would be looking over his shoulder for a long time to come now. He glanced back out the window, trying to take his mind off things. It was another beautiful day under the hot tropical sun, and the warm trade winds blowing in through the open window ruffled his hair gently.

He wondered if the Team was still bothered by the events of the past few weeks, but he had to admit it didn't look like it. He had noticed Duke occasionally staring out to sea the way they had come, and sometimes Vicki, but not the others. The trauma seemed to have receded behind them as soon as Japan slipped below the horizon. They were going about their duties with an almost festive air lately, particularly Summer who was out sunbathing on deck in her bright pink bikini any chance she got. Cal supposed this was as good as a holiday for them, especially those who hadn't been to the tropics before. A Canadian like Summer was probably more used to ice and snow than 30 degree Celsius temperatures, especially in November, so this was better than a cruise!

Richard and Heath were on the fore-deck below him, monitoring the data sent back by the towed sonar array which followed in their wake like a torpedo. Richard was concentrating on the laptop screen in front of him, busy sending minute calibration corrections to the datalogger. Cal smiled. His brother had taken to the gadgets like a duck to water – just like he'd hoped.

He really could make a good research biologist…

Cal was pleased with the results they'd collected so far too. The towed sonar was a highly-sensitive, omni-directional receiver, and out beyond the shadow of the ship it could detect whales from a considerable distance – as long as you knew where to start looking. The sheltered coastal waters of the Polynesian islands were alive with whalesong, and all indications were that the Humpback breeding season was in full swing. Cal smiled happily, already planning the data collection he wanted done when they reached the calving grounds just a few kilometres away.

The Gwendolyn steamed on through the sparkling water.

Cal's gaze drifted across to the radio and his smile faded. He closed his eyes in thought, wrestling with a problem that had nagged him for the past few days.

He knew he ought to call up and report the Gwendolyn's position. Since fleeing Shimonoseki without the harbourmaster's permission they had been travelling in secret for the best part of a week. Without filing a destination or route plan no one knew where the hell they were. That suited his cautious nature just fine right now – if no one knew where they were they were less likely to wake up one day and find a Japanese warship blocking their path. But it was also a double-edged sword. The sea was an unforgiving place. Tropical cyclones were common in this area, and if anything happened out here no one would even begin to know where to look for them.

Cal weighed his options. Since the Team was ostensively a Greenpeace delegation at the conference that had given him a convenient out. He could use Greenpeace as an intermediary, reporting their position directly to Greenpeace New Zealand's headquarters. They could be relied on to maintain secrecy, but be ready to pass on the relevant information in the event of an emergency. But it sat uneasily with him to have to align himself with an environmental organisation. As a scientist, he dealt in properly-acquired experimental data, not the kind of hype and sensational stories that were more likely to grab headlines. He could see that there was sometimes a need for that kind of approach, but it was not his way, nor would it do his professional reputation any good to be linked with a group that used those tactics as its preferred campaigning method. Cal sighed. Greenpeace was a funny outfit. Though he agreed with what they were trying to do, often their approach left him shaking his head. It made him cringe to see their protests sometimes, especially the ones where they tried to use simplistic and idealistic emotion to convince people, rather than facts. That kind of quasi-religious approach to the environment was more likely to turn moderate people away, just like even a committed Christian might ignore a rabid street preacher haranguing him as he walked past. Solutions were never as simple as the zealots liked to make out, especially without taking any direct action – and all the publicity in the world could only ever take you so far.

Cal pulled a face. Though their end goals may be similar, their methods couldn't be more different, and that thought brought him back to his single biggest quandary of all.

Aurelia.

As Greenpeace's campaign manager against whaling that meant there was a better-than-even chance she would be responsible for monitoring the position data he provided. The voyage had reported only to Greenpeace while they were at the conference, and for now it was probably best to keep it that way. Telling any authorities where they were was inviting trouble.

Cal chewed his lip while he considered. Aurelia had already flown back to New Zealand – eager to stir up public opinion – which also made it more than likely she would be the one who answered the radio and received his sit-reps in person. He tried to tell himself it was concern for her safety that made him hesitate – Amimoto was a powerful man, and if she was in possession of information he wanted then her life could be in danger.

But in truth it was more than that. Cal knew she would disapprove of what he had done, and right now he couldn't face her condemnation. He had loved her once, and despite everything that had happened since, somewhere deep in his heart he knew he still did. Perhaps it was a fool's hope, but he wondered if maybe, just maybe, they might still be able to patch things up and rediscover the feelings they once shared…

He sighed as he remembered how it used to be, their love so unrestrained and intense, fuelled by the heady and intoxicating passion of their shared idealism. He had never loved anyone else that much – neither before nor afterwards – and he knew he could search the whole world without ever finding another girl like his feisty red-headed livewire.

It would be so good just to hear the sound of her voice again…

Cal reached for the radio mic, and before he knew it he was transmitting his callsign.

The response came almost immediately, before he could change his mind. "Receiving you loud and clear, Gwendolyn."

Though distorted by the high-frequency radio waves, her voice was unmistakable. It gave him a boost to hear her again, and he felt the warm glow of her presence despite the fact the signal had travelled all the way across the largest ocean in the world and bounced off the upper layers of the atmosphere to get there.

He smiled and gave her his position report.

"Tonga eh?" She remarked. "What are you doing there?"

Cal blinked in surprise. She must have had an atlas open next to her to look up the coordinates that quickly.

"When are you due home?" she pressed him.

"How do you know I'm not staying out here?"

"Just a hunch." She laughed airily, but Cal was still troubled.

"What news of the Japanese Whaling Fleet?" he said, avoiding her question.

Her voice turned serious. "The Kyoeishin-Maru is written-off, and the Nippon-Maru is still laid up in dry dock for repairs."

"That's good news!" Cal enthused.

"No it's not. The Japanese were furious. Amimoto vowed the factory ship would be repaired in time to accompany the Fleet south again this summer. He's not going to take this lying down and I fail to see how you hope to accomplish anything by deliberately antagonising him."

"He wasn't that taken with your protesting either," Cal pointed out.

She ignored the jibe. "He's going to retaliate now, it's a matter of honour for the Japanese. They're stubborn like that."

"What can he do with no support ships?" Cal laughed dismissively.

Aurelia's reply was icy. "The three Hunter-Killer boats left port the day after you did."

Cal's smile died and he felt a prickle of alarm at the back of his neck.

So Gyofuku is back at sea already. That's bad news.

Again he cursed himself for not being able to finish off the Japanese Whaling Fleet in one go. "Where were they headed?" he demanded.

"How the hell should I know? Out to prove they can still kill whales I expect!" She turned on him then, her tone bitter and accusing. "It *was* you, wasn't it? You're the one who attacked those two ships. I hope you realise you've only made things worse!"

Cal opened his mouth to defend his position, to explain what had really happened, but she didn't give him a chance to speak.

"You had no right to do a thing like that! You were representing Greenpeace and you had no right to take the law into your own hands!"

He tried to reason with her. "The Gwendolyn is not a Greenpeace ship, nor was this an official Greenpeace voyage. We were only representing Greenpeace while we were at the conference. Besides, since when do you care about the law?"

"Since when it comes asking questions of me!" she snapped. "Do you realise what you've done? Not only have you ruined years of hard work we've done lobbying against whaling, but you've also dragged Greenpeace's name through the mud!" Her voice was shrill with anger now. "The cops are sniffing around, the media are circling like vultures. Everyone is blaming us for the attack. They're painting us as the villains, like we're some kind of eco-terrorist group or something!"

"Well, consider it a bit of free publicity," Cal chuckled, then he cringed, forced to turn down the radio as a tirade burst out of the speaker. "Okay, okay.

I'm sorry you copped the heat, but I'm not sorry for what happened," he added defiantly. "It had to be done. It was the only way to stop them."

"That's a load of rubbish. Violence never solved anything!"

Cal felt the glow from their success evaporate. "What violence? We didn't hurt anyone."

Aurelia sucked in her breath. "Only because you were lucky. What if you had killed a fisherman? What then? The world would have vilified us! All of us. And you would have just handed the whalers their victory on a plate!"

"Yeah, but I didn't-"

She cut him off. "Why take the risk? Violence only leads to escalation and more violence. It's inevitable that someone will eventually get hurt. Can't you see that?" Her sigh was deep, her exasperation plain. "You always were so infuriatingly stubborn. Why won't you give up the violence and return to peaceful protest?"

It was Cal's turn to be angry now, as the familiar argument reared its ugly head between them. "Don't be so naïve, Aurelia. Can't you see that all the protests in the world won't ever make any difference in the end? Greenpeace can't change the world. I'm sorry, but that's the way it is. Non-violent protest can show people what's going on, but that's all it can do. Ultimately people must change the world for themselves. That means someone has to take action!"

She exhaled sharply. "I pity you, and your lack of faith."

Cal laughed, but it was a hollow sound. "Faith is for religion, I deal in fact. And the facts are plain – we're out of time. Whaling must be stopped, immediately, or it will be too late. We haven't got time to wait for the greedy businessmen of the world to suddenly grow a conscience, or the self-absorbed politicians to realise there might be votes in it for them to protect a few whales on the other side of the world. Whales need protection, now."

"Victory at any cost is too high a price," she countered.

"It's a price I'm willing to pay. Failure would be far worse."

"Damn it Cal, why won't you stop? For all our sakes!"

He laughed sadly. "I'm not one of those fawning puppy-dog boys who follow you around at Greenpeace. You can't bend me to your will just by smiling and batting your eyelids."

"Cal, please! I'm begging you to stop. What if you kill someone? You'll undo years of hard work gaining public support for our cause."

Cal didn't answer, but his silence was telling. Public opinion didn't matter to him, only results. This was a war, and you had to expect casualties in a war. No one deserved to die – not even a whaler – but his resolve was hardened. The whalers certainly showed no respect for life. Not for the whales, and certainly not for his Team. Several times Gyofuku had nearly killed them already, whether through recklessness or outright malice, and Cal held no illusions that he would try again as soon as he got the chance. He rubbed his temples wearily. "I'm not out to kill anyone, Aurelia. Just to stop them."

"But the risk is always there!"

Cal smiled sadly at the irony. "Risk is how great things are accomplished…"

***

Richard sat on deck, watching the Gwendolyn's progress towards the two uninhabited islands. They were about a kilometre apart, and they lay ahead like sparkling jewels in the turquoise sea, the dark green of their jungle-clad backs contrasting with the brilliant white of the coral sand beaches fringing their edges. Richard glanced up, watching the seabirds wheeling overhead. He recognised many of them now; terns, noddys, long-tailed tropicbirds, and the streamlined black silhouettes of the frigate birds. Below, shoals of silvery fish scattered in choreographed chaos at their approach. The sun shone down, and a warm breeze danced on his bare arms. If ever there was a paradise on Earth, this peaceful tropical haven was it.

After the wintry hostility and negativity of Japan, it was a welcome change.

Richard sat on the Gwendolyn's gently-rolling deck, bare legs crossed underneath him, although in truth he was so attuned to the ship now that he barely noticed the motion. He'd become used to life at sea. In fact, in some ways he'd grown to enjoy it. He had even managed to catch up with his journal entries from the start of the voyage – although the funny thing was they weren't nearly as negative as he'd intended. Writing them down now, some time after first coming aboard ship, his early experiences at sea didn't seem so bad any more. And as he put his thoughts to paper he found himself appreciating the experiences he'd had, rather than lamenting them.

During the crossing from Japan he'd been able to manage a shift balanced in the galley during rough weather, not once running to the head – the correct sailing term for a toilet – to be sick, even though he was looking down the whole time. He wasn't sure if his simple meal was up to the standard of the Skipper's chilli, or one of Vicki's legendary 'shrimp' stir-fries, but everyone had praised his efforts and he was beginning to feel accepted as part of the crew now.

He had volunteered to help out with the sonar tow again this morning, even though it meant working with Heath, the one depressing spot aboard. But Richard liked to work with the electronics, plus it was a nice opportunity to work outside. He'd found that if he could ignore the Californian's constant griping and sour moods that the scenery more than made up for it. Accordingly, his arms and legs were already browned by the sun, a testament to a pleasant past week.

Richard crouched on the deck now, trying hard to concentrate on the laptop screen in front of him. He was embarrassed for Cal that he and Heath had overheard his private radio conversation through the window, especially Aurelia's criticism, but he was even more shocked by Heath's muttered assent.

"She's right," the Californian said, fiddling with his lip ring. "Violence is wrong. It's against the karma of the World." His scowl deepened. "This is bullshit. It's all bullshit. Cal's crazy. He's going to get us all killed, man."

Richard stared at him, flabbergasted that he could even think so, let alone say it out loud. It was against his nature to argue with anyone, but the urge to defend his brother was strong. He took a deep breath and met his eye. "Cal knows what he's doing," he said in a small but resolute voice. Heath glared back at him, and Richard felt uncomfortable. He looked away to defuse the tension.

Suddenly he heard a splash and a blast of air like an escaping steam vent. It was a sound he had learned to recognise, and his heart surged with excitement as he sprang to the rail.

"Whale!" he shouted.

A knobbly and barnacle-encrusted head broke the surface a hundred metres from the boat, followed by the whale's wide, stocky body. Richard watched as the dark blue back rolled forward as the whale prepared to dive again, revealing a low stubby dorsal fin atop a wide hump.

Cal slid down the outside stairway from the bridge and hurried to stand at Richard's shoulder. "Humpback," he announced. "It's a male." He raised his binoculars as the whale raised his tail to dive. "Hey, I know this whale!" Cal said. "It's Mana! He's from New Zealand!"

Richard didn't question his identification. He knew that every humpback had a unique pattern of markings on their bodies, although researchers usually used their tail flukes for identification because they were the most visible at sea. His brother had been studying whales for years and it was a measure of his experience that he could recognise individuals by sight.

"I tagged Mana at Kaikoura a couple of years ago." Cal grinned, his pleasure as plain as if he'd run into an old friend.

Richard smiled happily as he watched the whale swim. "Did you name him?"

Cal nodded. "The Maori concept of mana means not only power or prestige, but also a kind of spiritual life force. I thought it was a good comparison since he was a future herd bull."

Richard nodded, understanding completely.

"Every winter the Humpbacks migrate up the East Coast of New Zealand and through Cook Strait on their way up here to breed," Cal continued. "Then every summer they head back south to feed in the Southern Ocean." He winked at Richard. "This whale's a travelling Kiwi, just like you!"

Richard smiled back, feeling a sudden bond of kinship with the whale.

"Keep watching," Cal urged.

Puzzled, Richard turned back to the rail, but there was nothing to see. The whale had dived, and the surface of the sea was undisturbed, like deep blue glass. A minute passed and Richard looked quizzically at Cal again, but his brother said nothing, merely gesturing out to sea again.

Suddenly the surface erupted in an explosion of flying spray. Richard gasped as a huge dark shape rocketed clear of the water, long fore-flippers extended like enormous wings. It was the whale, standing vertically on his tail as he leaped clear of the water, as if trying to take to the air and fly away. The Humpback towered to the height of a three-storey building and hung motionless for a moment at the point of balance. Then he arched his broad back and rolled onto his side as he fell back towards the sea. He plunged beneath the waves with a tremendous smack, and a splash big enough to overturn a small boat.

"Holy cow!" Richard whispered. Though the Humpback was a little over half the size of the enormous Blue, he was still easily as long as a bus, and the agility with which he threw his enormous bulk out of the water was breathtaking.

"He's showing off," Cal smiled. "There must be ladies around." His grin broadened. "We're in the right place then, eh!"

He pointed between the two islands that lay ahead. "A few seasons ago we discovered a breeding spot in the channel there."

His face took on a wistful look, and Richard wondered if he was reminiscing.

"Humpback whales have been breeding in these same waters since time began – but there's so few of them left now." Cal's face creased with sadness. "People have killed over a quarter of a million of them over the last century or so. No one knows how many Humpbacks there once were, but right now the population is under one fifth of the numbers estimated in the 1960s, and the population was already seriously depleted by then. Even that census was done during the period of massive illegal and unreported hunting carried out by the Soviets. In just twenty years they killed an extra 40,000 Humpbacks on top of the already-generous quotas they'd allocated themselves – part of the 90,000 kills they never reported."

He pursed his lips, his disgust plain. "Yet the Humpbacks are still not to be left in peace. Just when they're beginning to show signs of recovering, Amimoto is about to target them again. The historic slaughter by the Soviets is about to be superseded by a new Japanese slaughter in the present."

Richard watched as the whale spouted again, the twin spouts of vapour charged with vibrancy in contrast to the placid water around. "Why is it so hard to protect whales?" he said.

"International cooperation is difficult at the best of times," Cal admitted. "It's extremely hard to conserve migratory species, especially when they cross through so many different governments' territorial waters – or the open sea where absolutely everyone can claim a right to them."

Richard stared out to sea, hoping for another view of their fellow Kiwi. It struck him then how arbitrarily the world of today had been divided up – based entirely on the boundaries of human conquest. While a whale might be safe in New Zealand waters, as soon as he ventured out his life was threatened by Japanese whalers with their harpoon cannons. This whale's ancestors had been swimming the same oceans for millennia, and now he and his kind suddenly found their vast migration route had been carved up into areas of exclusive ownership by people. Despite taking the land as their personal property, people weren't satisfied with that. They wanted the seas for themselves as well, claiming not only all the fish for themselves, but also the right to hunt and kill the last great travellers themselves.

Richard hung his head, feeling suddenly ashamed for the plight of the whales, and all the other species of the planet. He turned to his brother, his mind brimming over with questions.

"People have such a great power over the world. Why don't we care more about what we're doing to it?"

Cal shrugged. "Power does not create greatness. True greatness comes from how you wield power. Unfortunately, most people are interested only in making money." He waved his hand in an expression of futility. "Practically every aspect of modern society is unsustainable, yet people cannot comprehend that fact because they can't, or won't, look beyond their own lifetimes. They think that because their forefathers always did things this way that they can too, without considering the fact that the Earth's vast capacity to absorb damage will eventually run out. No one is prepared to heed the warning signs because it's too hard to change. Modern man has been on this Earth for just a few hundred generations since we started in our caves – barely a blink of an eye in an evolutionary timescale – so how can we possibly think we've got a winning formula for success? All we are doing is mortgaging our future, or more likely, that of our grandchildren.

The Industrial Revolution was barely 200 years ago, yet already things have changed beyond recognition in that short time; the human population is sky-rocketing, wilderness is disappearing, demand for resources outstrips supply, extinctions are climbing, and our rampage is even altering the climate of the planet itself." He laughed hollowly. "No one is around to remember how clean the air was before the factories, or how many more fish were in the sea before the commercial fleets began plundering them, so the perception is that how it is now is normal." He shrugged. "If you ignore the overall picture and just concentrate on one person's lifetime, maybe you can explain away the degradation as a minor symptom of 'progress', but that doesn't alter the fact that it cannot go on forever."

The lines on his face deepened as he spoke, and Richard felt himself moved by his brother's words, and by his conviction.

"The laws of man are arbitrary, but no species can afford to break the laws of nature," Cal continued. "People cannot afford to continue living outside the natural order of things. It can only end in disaster." He shrugged helplessly. "Societies have collapsed before. It will happen to us too, probably sooner rather than later at the rate we're going. Technology won't save us from a fundamental flaw in attitude – all it will mean is that this time the collapse will be global when it hits, and probably severe enough that we'll destroy ourselves and the whole planet along with us."

He turned his head to look into Richard's eyes, his gaze intense and penetrating. With a start, Richard saw sadness in his brother's eyes.

Cal's sigh was heartfelt. "Whales have been living peacefully in the oceans for 80 million years. My only hope is that somehow they're still here to inherit the world back from us when we've destroyed ourselves…"

The Skipper steered them toward the narrow gap between the islands, and Richard caught sight of two more blows in the channel, one of them a diminutive but perfect imitation of the other. "Look, more whales!" he shouted.

"It's a mother and baby." Cal smiled protectively. He turned to Richard. "Ready to get some DNA samples for the database?"

His tone was matter-of-fact, and Richard stared back, searching his brother's face for any trace of humour.

"How can we get close to them without the Naiad? Won't the Gwendolyn's engines scare them off?"

Cal nodded in agreement, but he hadn't been joking. He stripped off his shirt, revealing his broad chest, rippling with muscle and tanned by working outdoors. "Fancy a swim?" he grinned.

Richard looked down, not wanting to meet his eye. How to explain how he felt about deep water? He found himself looking instead at the greenstone carving hung around his brother's neck. It was odd, he realised, that he'd never really seen it closely before. Though the pendant was beautiful and intricately-carved, Cal always wore it under his shirt where it couldn't be seen – almost as if it was a private thing.

Cal waited expectantly, and the sun twinkled off the New Zealand jade, illuminating the carved spiral with the same deep green hue as the tropical lagoon that waited invitingly below.

But Richard was unable to answer. And before he could find the words to explain himself it was too late. At that moment Summer had appeared around the corner of the wheelhouse, holding her towel. Her tiny pink bikini accentuated every curve of her body, leaving very little to the imagination. Richard had been mesmerized by her confident display of her body ever since they sailed into the tropics, and when she was lying out on the deck he found it impossible to concentrate on his duties. As she sauntered towards them now, he swallowed, unbidden thoughts tumbling into his head – wondering what it would be like to hold her close, to feel that wonderful body pressed against his own. His pulse quickened, as much from nervousness as anything else.

He knew it was rude to stare, but he couldn't help himself. She noticed him looking at her, and a satisfied smile flickered across her lips. Richard felt his cheeks colouring and he stared down at the deck beneath his bare feet. Though the sun was warm on his back, he didn't want to remove his own shirt, embarrassed by his pale desk-bound body.

Cal hadn't seemed to notice their unspoken exchange though, nor the appreciative glance Summer gave his chiselled pectoral muscles and hard, flat stomach. Richard frowned though, as if an invisible cloud had passed across the clear blue sky overhead.

Just then they felt the sudden stillness as the Gwendolyn's engines fell silent.

"That's our signal," Cal grinned. Before Richard could say anything more he climbed onto the rail and launched himself over the side. Richard gasped and ran to look over, just in time to see his brother tuck into a graceful dive, plunging deep into the crystal blue water. Summer smiled seductively at Richard and swung her leg over the rail, climbing down the cargo net to join Cal in the water.

"Ready with the gear!" he called up.

Richard turned. Vicki had come up behind him, carrying several waterproof boxes of equipment which she lowered over the side to the others waiting below. Richard hurried to help, and as they leaned together holding the rope, he was suddenly aware of how close they were standing. Unlike Summer, she didn't wear lots of perfume, but he could smell the clean freshness of her hair. She was wearing a pair of khaki shorts, and an old denim shirt with the sleeves rolled up. As they worked, her bare leg brushed his own, and he felt a tingle at the light but accidental contact. Her thigh was bronzed and strong; not a stick-thin and shapely model's leg, but instead hard with muscle and toned like an athlete's. He glanced down as they lowered the rope. Her tan was not perfect like that of a beauty queen either, but marred by several small white scars, a legacy of an active life and a gung ho attitude towards it. Richard stared at her legs, mesmerised by the tiny imperfections. Rather than seeing blemishes though, he found them strangely appealing.

They finished lowering the last box and Vicki stepped back, breaking the spell. She smiled her thanks for his assistance, and began unbuttoning her shirt to reveal a glossy black bikini bra the same colour as her hair. "Are you joining us?"

Richard kept his eyes on the water, suddenly embarrassed and mindful of his earlier indiscretion while she was changing.

Vicki's smile was friendly though. "The water's warm here," she said, misunderstanding his apprehension. "Once you get in you'll feel fine." She slipped off her shorts and dived over the side, long legs flashing in the sun before she splashed down next to the others.

Richard stared after her. It was a long way down. The rail was a good four metres above the water but it seemed a lot higher from up here. He felt his apprehension mount. He didn't want to miss this opportunity to swim with whales, but the alternatives were daunting. Climb slowly down the cargo net, shirtless, with everyone watching – or jump off the rail.

Richard took a deep breath and – before he could change his mind – he whipped off his shirt and hastily tumbled over the rail towards the waiting water. Suddenly he was airborne, and there was no going back. He felt his stomach leap into his throat as he fell through the air, arms pin-wheeling madly for balance.

Oh blimey! What have I done?

It was too late for recriminations now though, all he had time to worry about was the water rushing up to meet him like a wide green wall.

Splash!

He hit the water hard enough to knock the breath from his lungs, plunging deep beneath the surface. He felt the water tear at his clothes with unseen hands, and an explosion of bubbles tried to force its way up his nose until he was sure his head would explode. Through his closed eyelids, he could feel the darkness of the deep water close in around him. His chest tightened involuntarily, and he tried not to think about how deep the water was, or how far they were from land. Instead, he kept his eyes screwed tightly shut and clawed for the surface.

He came up spluttering, greeted by Cal's approval. "Yeah! Nice one, Bro!"

Richard rubbed the water from his eyes, managing a weak smile.

Cal handed him a mask and snorkel. "Come on, we've got to swim for a bit to get close."

Richard was apprehensive as he pulled the mask strap over his head. The tight rubber seal pressed against his face unnaturally, making him feel slightly claustrophobic.

"It's ok," Vicki said, treading water opposite him. "Just remember only to breathe through your mouth, otherwise the mask will suck onto your face and you won't get any air."

Richard nodded, grateful for the advice, and he clamped the rubber mouthpiece of the snorkel beneath his teeth. He could hear each panicked breath rasping through the plastic tube, knowing the worst was still to come. The nearest shore was several hundred metres away – much further than he could swim. He dreaded the thought of putting his face underwater; terrified of how it might feel, terrified of what he might see down there, terrified he might somehow swallow water and drown – in fact he was terrified of the whole idea.

Suddenly he felt something grab his left bum cheek.

What the hell was that?

He squeaked in alarm, spinning around to see what it was. His jaw dropped when he saw Summer there, her hand still extended. He stared at her, lost for words.

Did she just pinch me?

He felt his cheeks colouring, although this time the embarrassment was not self-inflicted. Summer seemed to delight in the power she wielded over him though. She raised her hand to trace a finger across his chest. "Hey stud," she purred. "That was a macho jump you did back there."

Richard blinked in shock. He tried to reply, but his throat closed up. In truth, he didn't really have any idea what to say anyway.

Out of the corner of his eye he saw Vicki turn away, a strange look on her face. Cal was frowning, but he turned away too without saying anything and began swimming.

Richard glanced after them, but Summer didn't give him any time to think. She winked at him then paddled away too, leaving him alone. He watched her go, his thoughts a jumble of confusion.

Was she just hitting on me?

As he struggled to make sense of it one thing was certain though, with the other three all swimming away now, Richard knew he would have to put his face in the water or be left behind.

He took a last look around at the warm tropical day, as if to postpone the inevitable. A white tern circled overhead as it searched for fish, the sun shone down, sparkling on the surface of the water, and Richard was even more reluctant to put his head underwater into the cold, silent world below.

He glanced back towards the Gwendolyn. The Skipper had stayed aboard to mind the ship, and Heath had too – for reasons known only to him. Richard could see his scowling face watching them from the rail and he suddenly felt apprehensive.

He took a deep breath, trying to force all the negative thoughts out of his head.

It's just like a swimming pool, he told himself. *Nothing scary about that.*

He tried not to think about the vicious sharks and sea monsters that lived in it and might even now be lurking in the dark depths just below him.

He took a deep breath and by sheer force of willpower he plunged his face into the water, gritting his teeth as it closed over his head. Snorkel or not, it was the most unnatural feeling he could think of to breathe with his face underwater though, and he instinctively held his breath for as long as he could. When he could hold out no longer he finally succumbed, taking a tiny panicked sip of air through his clenched teeth. Weird sensation or not, the air coming through the curved tube was real enough, and his lungs weren't about to argue. With his eyes still tightly closed, Richard was able to regulate his breathing, convincing himself he was actually lying on his bed at home rather than floating face down over the blue abyss.

It took a supreme effort to force himself to open his eyes.

Yet when he finally did, all his worries were forgotten in an instant. The world that greeted him underwater was unlike anything he had ever seen before. About twenty metres below him lay the sandy bottom, sculpted into miniature dunes by current and tide. It glowed in the sunlight, flickering and shimmering with the wave lines shining down from the surface.

"It's beautiful," he whispered, though there was no one around to hear him.

A school of fish swam by, each as large as his head, their silvery sides glittering with every movement. He reached out to them, but with a flick of their forked tails they were gone.

All around him the water was green and clear as glass. He hung suspended in space, and the sensation was akin to flying – or, more precisely, hovering – over the sandy bottom. He paddled with his arms, testing his new wings, and the distant dunes slid slowly past as he glided overhead.

Then with a sudden start, he realised he was dallying. He kicked his feet, hurrying to catch up to Cal and the others.

The bottom fell away as the water deepened, and Richard felt the chill of the depths groping up toward him. He shivered involuntarily and kicked harder, trying to catch up to the others.

Richard was panting for breath when Cal finally stopped at his chosen spot; the narrowest point between the two islands.

"This is the place," he said. "There's a deep-water channel between these two islands, so the water is nice and sheltered but plenty deep enough for whales. It's the perfect spot for a mother Humpback to have her baby."

Richard tried not to think about how far they were from the ship, alone in the deep water with its denizens. He jumped as the sudden blast of a whale spout hissed behind him. "A-are you sure it's ok for us to be this close?"

"It's ok," Cal grinned, misunderstanding the question. "I have a permit to approach marine mammals."

He passed one of the Velcro scratch-poles to Vicki. "Can you try for the little guy?"

She nodded.

He turned to Richard. "You stick with me. We'll see if Mum wants a belly-rub."

Richard felt his heart skip a beat. The mother whale was a massive, dark shadow in the water. She looked huge, even from this far away.

You want us to swim up to her?

His chest began to tighten at the thought, but it was too late to back out. Cal had already turned away to Summer and he passed her the video camera in its underwater housing. "Reckon you can get some footage for the database?"

"This is so exciting!" she gushed in response. "I just love whales! I've always wondered what their skin would feel like to touch. Do you think we'll be able to pet them? What about riding on their backs?"

Cal's brow furrowed, and Richard could see he disapproved of the idea – to say nothing of the danger. Summer didn't seem to notice though, and she continued chattering. "This is such an amazing experience to swim with them. You know, I've always thought it's so sad about them almost going extinct and all. It's such a pity they can't keep whales in zoos for future generations of people to enjoy too."

Cal's frown deepened. "Whales belong out here," he muttered, then turned to swim away.

Richard hurried after him, kicking hard to keep up. Underwater, the deep indigo-blue void spread out ahead of them forever. As he watched, a dark shadow disengaged itself and Richard felt himself holding his breath as it moved toward them. His heart hammered in his chest as the whale swam closer, and he felt a nameless primeval terror when confronted with so huge a creature. From the tip of her barnacle-encrusted chin to the ends of her broad black tail flukes, the Humpback whale dwarfed him. She was as big as a semi-trailer, but far swifter and more graceful than he – an awkward alien in her underwater world. The white undersides of her flippers and belly shone with a strange, almost ethereal glow through the gloom.

With a ponderous grace, she gave a great sweep of her wing-like pectoral fins and swam towards them, soaring like a great bird underwater.

"Megaptera novaeangliae," Cal said, releasing a cloud of bubbles as he spoke through his snorkel. "Some call them the angels of the sea."

Richard nodded, awestruck. The mother whale certainly did look like a flying angel.

She turned her great head slightly, as if studying them, then swam closer.

Richard's eyes were saucers behind his mask. Just one of her enormous pectoral flippers was larger than he was. He was face to face with one the largest race of beings ever to live, and this meeting was in her element, on her terms. One flick of her tail and she could swat him like an insect. Richard held his breath, trying to remain invisible. He had never felt so insignificant in all his life.

The whale's tail undulated lazily, propelling her forward with effortless ease, straight towards the two swimmers in her path.

If she wants to, she could swallow us both – whole!

Richard felt his nerve failing. He shrank behind Cal, knowing that without his brother's reassuring confidence he would have bolted for the ship already.

Cal turned back and flashed a broad grin, his eyes sparkling behind his mask.

Buoyed by his brother's example, Richard managed a smile in return.

He didn't follow as Cal dived down though, the long pole extended in front of him. He stayed floating at the surface, watching the trail of bubbles from Cal's snorkel as it filled with water, suddenly feeling very apprehensive. His brother looked so vulnerable down there. He was dwarfed by the whale, and completely at the mercy of the gigantic creature.

Richard had no idea if it was standard practice for researchers to get a skin sample while swimming next to a whale, or if it had only ever been done from boats before. He knew enough about his brother to know that wouldn't stop him trying now though.

Cal didn't swim towards the whale for fear of scaring her, instead hovering motionless underwater, waiting. She swam towards him, unconcerned. As she passed he reached out with the long Velcro scraper, rubbing it gently along her flank.

Richard held his breath. One swat with a gigantic flipper could knock him unconscious – or kill him! Would she panic or lash out?

But the mother whale didn't seem bothered by the scraper at all. Richard could sense a peaceful serenity in her that he found amazing. Despite the long history of human aggression towards her kind, she was completely unconcerned by their presence. Then, incredibly, she rolled over, exposing her white-patterned belly and allowing Cal to scratch it gently for her. She slid by, a gentle leviathan of the deep, and Richard saw her eye swivel towards him as she passed. Her gaze was trusting, even inquisitive, and he was thankful that she and her baby hadn't met any of the bad humans he knew were out there.

Cal stayed down as long as his lungs would allow, then surfaced again, giving the whale her space as soon as he had obtained his sample. He quickly transferred the scraper head to the plastic bag at his waist. "She just let me rub her belly!" he exclaimed. "That's the most vulnerable part of her body. What other wild creature is so friendly and trusting towards people – especially one so endangered?"

The whale circled back towards them, intrigued by their presence, and it was at that moment Richard got his first good look at her calf. Swimming shyly close to his mother, he had until now been obscured on her far side. He was longer than a man, but still a tiny baby next to his mother's broad flank. He was a perfect imitation of her, right down to his little snub-nosed baby face, and his little baleen plates were still feathery and bright with newness.

"He's only a few days old," Cal whispered. "He was probably born right here."

Vicki was on the other side of the mother Humpback, and as they watched, she swam slowly up to the pair, reaching out towards the calf.

The little whale shrank closer to his mother, seeking reassurance from her great presence. She rumbled softly to him, and laid her huge flipper protectively across his back, hugging him close. Richard couldn't help his smile. She was a good mother. She would keep him safe from danger, loving and nurturing while teaching him the ways of the sea. The little calf was only a few days old, but he had been constantly surrounded by the love and companionship of his mother from the very moment of his birth.

Vicki withdrew her hand and began to back away, not wishing to frighten the baby whale. But at that moment something amazing happened. As though sensing she meant no harm to them, the mother whale stopped and turned, offering a full broadside view of her and her calf. As they watched, she nuzzled her youngster, reassuring him with her touch, then nudged him closer so Vicki might scratch his back too.

"Wow," Cal whispered. "Would you look at that! She's showing off her baby to us. What a proud mum!"

Richard stared, feeling suddenly humble. Despite what the 'elitists' among human society liked to claim, here was another undeniably intelligent creature, and even more significantly, the mother whale had recognised that same awareness in them. Despite the all-but insurmountable language and cultural differences that separated their two species, she had managed to reach out across the huge gulf between them.

Richard couldn't keep the happy smile off his face.

The flash of the camera lit the water as Summer collected photos for the database.

Cal turned to Richard. "I think we have this female on file already, but her little one needs a name." He grinned. "Would you like to have the honour, Bro?"

Richard blinked in surprise, suddenly choked up with emotion.

What a privilege, to name my own baby whale!

He swallowed, feeling suddenly self-conscious.

"I'd like to name him Ohana," he said tentatively. "It's Hawaiian for family. I thought it's a nice name, and since we're in the Pacific and all…" he trailed off uncertainly.

Cal smiled. "That's a beautiful name. And fitting. Ohana it is!"

Richard smiled back happily. As he floated in the deep blue of the channel, he suddenly felt as close to paradise as it was possible to get on Earth.

All around them the water was filled with the haunting melody of whalesong. Richard could actually feel the notes vibrating through his body, from his chest right down to his feet. He kept his head underwater, transfixed by the encounter. This was a much livelier aria than the deep bass song of the Old Blue, the notes rising and falling in a complicated musical score. In addition to the soft sounds of the mother whale crooning to her child, they could hear another song filling the channel.

Cal saw him listening and winked. "It's a love song," he explained. "Mana, the male we saw before, is courting her. More than likely, the genetics will confirm he's little Ohana's father."

Vicki smiled. "Humpback whale songs consist of complex repeated patterns, each one unique and evolving over time. They learn the melody from their parents and the dialect varies between groups in different geographical areas, and at different times of the year. They have different songs to say different things. There's recent evidence that whales and dolphins each have a unique sound pattern that others can identify them with – just like a name. They can introduce themselves to strangers, respond when their name is called, and even use an identifier to discuss another individual who isn't present… Although we've got a long way to go before we can work out what they're saying about him!" She smiled, gesturing towards the open sea from where Mana's song flooded into the channel. "It's an intricate symphony that fits every human criteria for language – and the requirements for genuine intelligence."

Richard closed his eyes, letting the ageless beauty of the music carry him away. He felt as though time itself had stopped and he was witnessing the same peaceful serenity as at the beginning of life itself – or at least from a time far beyond the memory of his own history.

Suddenly a long sombre note drowned out everything else, shattering the mood. The sound was too harsh for a whale, and it took Richard a while to realise it was coming from the world above. As he poked his head above the surface he realised it was a blast from the Gwendolyn's foghorn.

That's odd.

Then he felt the distant rumble as her engines started up, and he felt a sudden rush of alarm.

What's going on? Don't leave us behind!

The peace was shattered, the moment lost. The mother whale shied away from the sudden metallic noise in the water, and Cal pulled him clear of the powerful sweep of her flukes.

"W-what's going on?" Richard spluttered.

Just then Cal swore and punched his fist in the water. "You've got to be fucking kidding me!"

Richard followed his gaze, and the sight that greeted him made his heart seize in his chest. Charging around the side of the closest island were three sleek grey ships, their profiles sinister and unmistakable. Each hull swept forward to a tall scythe-like prow, and all were topped with a menacing black harpoon cannon. Three Japanese Hunter-Killer ships, led by the Kuu-Maru.

"Oh no," Richard whispered, feeling a wave of helpless fear sweep over him. "Please, no."

Chapter 21

Time stood still.

Richard Major hung suspended in the water, deep in the middle of the unfolding nightmare. He and his brother watched, powerless to intervene, as the Japanese whaling ships raced towards them.

The nearby islands were uninhabited. There was no one else around for hundreds of kilometres.

No witnesses!

Below them in the channel the mother Humpback and her calf milled around, confused and agitated by the approaching noise.

Richard glanced back toward the Gwendolyn and saw the Skipper talking frantically into the radio. A moment later his lips moved in a silent curse and he hurled the mic aside. Gyofuku was ignoring all transmissions. A blue and white 'Alpha' flag shot up the Gwendolyn's mast, the international symbol for 'Keep clear, divers in the water.' There was no response from the Kuu-Maru or its escorts. Quickly, the Skipper hoisted a second flag, the black and yellow chequered 'Lima' flag. Its meaning was blunt; 'Stop your vessel immediately!'

Still the Hunter-Killer ships charged towards them.

The Gwendolyn's engines roared as the Skipper opened up the throttles. He sped past the group in the water, temporarily ignoring them as he raced to head off the whalers.

Richard suddenly felt very alone floating there.

The Hunter-Killer boats fanned out like a pack of hunting dogs, forcing the Skipper to choose which of them to confront. If there was any doubt as to their intentions, it was dispelled now.

The Gwendolyn headed straight for the lead whaler, and with a sick feeling in the pit of his stomach, Richard recognised a familiar red-helmeted face leering back through the windscreen as the two boats charged toward each other.

Gyofuku wasn't game enough to play chicken though. The Kuu-Maru changed course ever so slightly to avoid the impending collision, and the other two Hunter-Killers swung wide, aiming to bypass the gallant research trawler.

Richard could almost feel the Skipper's frustration – there was no way he could stop all of them at once. Whichever ship he blocked, the others would get past him.

Recognising the danger, the Skipper swung the Gwendolyn in a hard turn to port without slowing, intending to come about. Her bow lunged directly toward the Tosho-Maru, forcing it to yield and swerve away. But as the trawler turned the other two whalers sped past, led by Captain Gyofuku in the Kuu-Maru.

The Gwendolyn's engines screamed as she turned to charge in pursuit, racing to cut off the whalers before they could reach the helpless group in the water.

Richard swallowed as he saw the gunners standing behind their menacing black cannons. It was going to be a close-fought race!

The ships were barely a boat length away now, and still charging at full speed towards them.

Vicki and Summer floated a little off to the side, and Cal called urgently to them. "You girls get out of here. Now!"

Summer needed no convincing. She turned and fled, arms windmilling in panic, but Vicki hesitated.

"What about you two?"

Cal's tone brooked no argument. "I said go!" he shouted.

Reluctantly she obeyed, stroking clear of the danger.

Richard watched like a cornered mouse as the whalers continued to bear down on them.

The Gwendolyn hadn't managed to pull ahead of the speeding Hunter-Killers yet, but the Skipper swung her nose sideways anyway, veering towards the nearest grey hull in an attempt to cut them off. The Kuu-Maru swerved away, forced to take evasive action or be physically barged out of the way.

The Tosho-Maru steamed on though, and the Skipper's defence was desperate now. He swung the Gwendolyn broadside in front of it, stopping directly in the way in an attempt to shield the group in the water.

It worked, sending the Hunter-Killer straining to a stop as its engines went to full reverse. Water foamed behind its stern as its props spun backwards, fighting to check its momentum.

Richard exhaled with relief. The whales were below and behind him now. Any attempt to harpoon them would have brought the whalers right on top of him and Cal.

His relief was short-lived though, as a tall grey prow swerved around the Gwendolyn's stern. The Kuu-Maru hadn't slowed, and now that the Gwendolyn was stationary she was caught at a disadvantage. The Skipper threw the engines into reverse, and though her props thrashed valiantly against the water, the Gwendolyn wasn't quick enough to block the speeding Japanese ship. The Kuu-Maru side-stepped neatly around her, charging straight for the whales – and the helpless swimmers in the water.

Richard felt his bowels turn to ice. He gaped powerlessly, as though trapped in a waking nightmare.

Cal waved an arm over his head. "Clear off, you mongrel!" he yelled. "You can't come through here." He raised his voice as the ship kept coming. "Hey! HEY!"

His shout was lost in the roar of the Kuu-Maru's engines, and the breakers foaming at its bow.

The charging Hunter-Killer ship was close enough now that Richard could see the expression on Gyofuku's face, and the murderous glint in the whaler's eye sent a chill down his spine.

"He's seen us, Cal. Oh god, he's seen us and he's not going to stop!"

The grey prow towered over them, blocking out the sun.

"Dive!" Cal shouted. "Now!"

Richard swallowed a panic-stricken breath and ducked his head under water.

The whaling ship was close enough that he could already see it underwater, a dark shadow slicing towards them. With his heart hammering in his chest, he began swimming down, towards the dim blue depths of the channel. But his progress was ineffectual. The water resisted his passage, enveloping him like treacle and slowing his movements. He kicked out desperately with his legs, fighting against the buoyancy which tried to pull him back towards the surface.

He looked back. The shadow was practically upon him now.

I'm not going to make it!

Richard closed his eyes, waiting for the impact that would crush his body, driving the breath from his lungs.

Suddenly he felt a strong hand encircle his wrist. Richard opened his eyes and looked into Cal's worried face. His brother pointed downwards, towards the silent depths.

Richard shook his head.

I can't!

Cal ignored his protest and struck out strongly towards the seabed, still holding Richard's arm, dragging him down with him. As they descended, Richard felt the dark blue depths close in around them, and the pressure sent knives of crushing pain into his eardrums. He closed his eyes again, waiting for the vice-like grip to cave his skull in.

Then the Kuu-Maru thundered overhead, a tumult of deadly noise, its props thrashing through the water only metres from them.

Richard's lungs screamed for air, and he felt himself growing weak.

Suddenly he felt the grip on his wrist release, and a strong arm pushed him towards the light. He looked up, towards the mirrored blanket that was the surface. The sunlight sparkled on the water high above, enticing, tantalising, but so far away. Down here, surrounded by the chill of the deep water, he knew it was too far away. He would never make it back.

Then just as he was about to give up, Cal's strong arm encircled his waist, and he felt himself propelled upwards. Together, the brothers shot upwards like a torpedo fired from a tube, driven by Cal's strong scissor-like kicks. The darkness and pressure fell away, until finally Richard's head broke through the surface again. He surfaced like a porpoise, gasping for breath as he shot clear of the water. Then he fell back, and as he floated beneath the warm sun he sobbed with relief, sucking in deep lungfuls of sweet air.

Beside him, Cal was already looking around for the girls. When he saw they were safely treading water out of harm's way, he turned his attention back to Hogei Gyofuku, glaring at the grey stern of his speeding flagship as it pursued the fleeing whales. "That son-of-a-bitch tried to kill us," he said through clenched teeth. "He'll pay for that, I promise you, Bro."

With a sick sense of certainty, Richard knew that they weren't the only thing Gyofuku would attempt to kill that day. The mother whale and her calf were already in mortal danger. He watched with mounting apprehension as the ship bore down on them, feeling protective of the tiny whale he had named – but powerless to do anything. The sense of helplessness was overwhelming.

Swim, little Ohana, he willed silently. *Swim for your life!*

***

Enjoy your bath!

Hogei Gyofuku smirked as the dirty hippies receded in his wake. If they had survived at least they would respect him next time!

He cackled and lifted his saké flask in an ironic toast.

He had triumphed over them and their efforts to ruin his season. Now, to top off his victory he would have their precious whale too!

"Gunner!" he roared. "Make ready!"

Just then Gyofuku saw a second spout, in miniature, from behind the mother's broad back.

A cruel smile broke across his lips. So, this sea-pig had a piglet with her! That should make the job easier – and more pleasurable!

A moment later the mother whale's pointed snout broke the surface as it breached in front of the ship, leaping clear of the water as it surfaced for air, desperately trying to shield its calf from the danger.

Gyofuku's pock-marked face twisted into a gleeful snarl. He liked it when they put up a fight.

The gunner crouched behind the gun, trying to get a bead on the panicked animal.

The mother whale swerved again, throwing off his aim.

The gunner sweated as he swung the heavy cannon around, trying to keep the huge flank in his sights.

"Idiot!" the Captain swore at his gunner. "Not that one." His eyes narrowed. "A wise man exploits his enemy's greatest weakness."

***

Richard looked on in disbelief.

The chase was short. In the narrow channel there was little chance for the whales to escape. The little calf surfaced first, his newborn lungs unable to cope with a protracted dive underwater. That was the moment the whalers had been waiting for, and the Hunter-Killer swooped on him.

Richard stared in horror as the gunner swivelled his weapon towards the tiny back.

"Nooo!"

It was all over in a few terrible seconds. The crash of the Kuu-Maru's harpoon gun shattered the still air, and little Ohana's squeal of terror was cut short almost as soon as it began. The untethered harpoon stuck out of his tiny body like a lance, and his head slipped beneath the waves.

Panic-stricken, his mother turned back and raced to his side, gently lifting her unresponsive youngster to the surface with her snout, urging him to breathe.

But he would never breathe again.

A moment later, the Kuu-Maru's cannon thundered again, reverberating through the narrow confines of the channel. The mother whale shuddered in agony as the grenade-tipped harpoon tore deeply into her back, blasting her insides away.

Richard felt the thud of the blast through the water, the concussion wave pummelling his own chest like a sledgehammer. The mother whale rolled over onto her side, raising her large wing-like fluke as if to cradle the lifeless body of her calf to her.

Richard shook his head in shocked disbelief. All around him the water echoed with her final song; a sad, mournful cry of pain as her life slipped away.

"No," he whispered. "No…"

But there was nothing they could do. The scene played out in front of them like some terrible horror film. Cal gritted his teeth, his greenstone pendant clenched in a white-knuckled fist.

Richard gaped, transfixed, as the fatter of the three whaling ships pulled alongside the whale and swung its large black stern crane over her.

"It's the Shushu-Maru," Cal spat. "They're using it as a temporary processing-ship."

Defeated in her frantic race, the Gwendolyn slowed and turned back towards the swimmers in the water, the Skipper's responsibility now for the safety of his crew.

Working quickly and unopposed, the Japanese whalers transferred the harpoon lines to the Shushu-Maru's crane and the mother whale was dragged aboard over the side, still struggling weakly. She was longer than the width of the deck and her tail overhung one side, her head the other.

"They'll cut her up at their leisure," Cal spat, his disgust plain. "This ship is their newest Hunter-Killer boat. It was launched in 1998 – nearly fifteen years *after* the Moratorium began – and it was specifically designed to include a killing deck and freezers so it could operate away from the factory ship for short periods."

Richard could see the blue-overalled crew running about on deck with their long knives. He looked away, his heart heavy with sadness.

"Come on," Cal said quietly, and they began swimming towards the Gwendolyn, leaving the whalers to their brutal work.

The Skipper slowed the Gwendolyn's engines to an idle and threw the cargo net over the side for them to clamber aboard again. His face was lined with worry beneath his whiskers as he helped them aboard. "By Jeezus," he muttered as they flopped gratefully onto the deck. "I thought that dirty bastard had killed y'all."

"Not this time," Cal muttered, his teeth clenched with quiet fury.

They looked across to see that the whalers had finished securing the mother Humpback to the deck of the Shushu-Maru. The calf was ignored, his tiny carcass too small for them to bother hauling aboard. His lifeless body floated forlornly in the swells, alone in the deep channel for the first time in his short existence.

"He was so little," Vicki murmured, her voice catching. "He never even got a chance at life…"

Richard felt tears pricking his eyes, and the sudden and brutal sense of loss made him feel sick to his stomach.

The whaling boats opened their throttles, and in a cloud of diesel exhaust they sped out towards the vast expanses of the Pacific Ocean again.

"Look at them cowards run!" The Skipper spat pointedly over the side. "They know they're not s'posed to be here."

"Quick! We have to follow them!" Cal exclaimed, but the Skipper shook his head.

"We ain't got enough fuel left for a wild goose chase t' god knows where. Besides, the damage is already done."

Cal's eyes blazed with anger. "They're killing mothers and babies!" he fumed. "We have to stop them!

"They're murdering bastards!" Vicki agreed. "Out for easy pickings in the breeding grounds to make up for lost time!"

The Skipper rubbed his whiskery chin and looked away. "Yep, and ah'm real sorry 'bout that. 'Twas a hell of a thing they did, make no mistake. But there ain't nothin' we can do right now. We've been at sea for too long. We gotta get t' port and resupply before we can go after 'em."

"We can't run away," Cal insisted. "With no opposition Gyofuku will have free reign to kill as many whales as he likes out here. And if he's still around when the migration begins he'll discover their migration path. He'll be able to follow the whales all the way to the Antarctic, killing all the way."

The Skipper shrugged helplessly. "We ain't got enough fuel for that."

"The Nippon-Maru might be repaired in a few weeks too," Vicki pointed out. "If their factory ship is able to join them, the Japanese Fleet will be able to hunt continuously. They'll turn this into the most productive season they've had yet."

Cal's eyes shone with conviction. "Like hell they will!" He turned to the Skipper. "What's the nearest port?"

"Nuku'alofa, the capital of Tonga. We can be there by evenin' tomorrow."

"How long to refuel?"

"Not long, mebbe a couple hours." He paused, then looked down, avoiding Cal's scrutiny. "Make it overnight though – ah've some other things to organise while we're ashore." Under his breath he added, "And the darkness will hide 'em from prying eyes."

Cal's eyebrows flickered and he hesitated a moment, deliberating, but he didn't question the Skipper's recommendation – or his unspoken plot. "Very well," he agreed, his eyes taking on a dangerous glint. "Make it happen."

***

The headlights picked out the jungle beside the road as Duke Hayward threw the battered van around another corner, speeding back towards town amid a cloud of dust and exhaust fumes. He glanced at his watch, frowned, then planted his foot to the rust-pitted floorboards.

A few minutes later the lights of Nuku'alofa appeared on the skyline ahead.

As he entered the outskirts of the capital, a skinny mongrel dog scampered clear of his approach, its eyes glowing in the headlights as it glared balefully back at him from the safety of the verge. Duke sped through the darkened streets without slowing. Around him, the town of Nuku'alofa slumbered on in the warm night air.

Duke wasn't interested in enjoying the tropical atmosphere. He had a lot to do that night.

The van belonged to a former SEAL buddy of his. Mad-Dog was another of Uncle Sam's misguided children who hadn't gone back Stateside after the war, preferring instead to explore local business opportunities in the Pacific – although in Mad-Dog's case Duke suspected it was mainly a case of avoiding the MPs. A particularly large consignment of ammunition had mysteriously disappeared in the confusion after the fall of Saigon, and rumour had it Mad-Dog knew more than he was letting on. He lived in Tonga now, and had done so ever since the authorities in American Samoa began to take a dim view of his activities a few years back.

Mad-Dog was pleased to see him, and they'd spent a few minutes reminiscing and catching up on news of mutual friends. But Duke had gotten down to business first. The night was wearing on, and this wasn't a social call.

Mad-Dog was happy to oblige, being a businessman at heart. With a couple of days notice, and for the right price, he would offer his services anywhere in the Pacific, so he was only too happy to help out an old buddy who came asking. Duke wondered if that was at least partially because the civil wars in East Timor and the Solomons had quietened down for the moment, making work a bit thin on the ground. Even Fiji hadn't had a military coup for a while. Yep, Mad-Dog was always a good buddy to have. He was a supplier – and the best there was.

Duke's weathered face creased into a grin as the van rumbled down towards the harbour.

Under the moonlight he saw the Gwendolyn riding at anchor out in the bay, refuelled, reprovisioned and ready to sail on the early morning tide. Duke felt his mood soften ever so slightly as his gaze settled on her familiar lines. His Old Gal was always a welcome sight, and for an old sea dog like himself there were few enough pleasures left in life.

His face hardened as he contemplated the situation they were in though. This time when they left port they would be sailing straight into the teeth of danger. The Japanese Whaling Fleet was somewhere nearby, hunting unopposed, and he knew there was only one way they would ever quit. He curled his lip, spitting a wad of tobacco juice out the open window. The prospect of danger didn't faze him – nor death. He had faced those fears and conquered them long ago, in the tropical hellhole of Vietnam.

Duke touched the scar at his throat, staring out into the balmy night. The steamy jungles of 'Nam suddenly didn't seem all that distant…

It was more than his own memories weighing on his mind though. His father had been killed in the Pacific, not that far from here. Hayward senior had served in the Marine Corps, shot to death by the Japs at Guadalcanal while he tried to protect the free world from their crazed and unprovoked imperialism. Duke was just five years old at the time, but he was old enough to understand that his Pop was never coming home. He was old enough now that he wouldn't ever forget, either.

He spat again. Now it seemed he had his own battle to fight against Japanese imperialism. Their arrogance was outclassed only by their greed. And their savagery.

He'd seen it before on the battlefield – men so taken by battle lust they went stir-crazy. Becoming so desensitised to the blood and killing it became a way of life for them – or even a necessity.

He shook his head. Fishermen were all the same, and whalers the worst of all. It wasn't right to disrespect the Sea like those damn fish-heads did. She was the only mistress he'd ever truly belonged to, and as a sailor he knew it was his duty to protect her.

Duke gripped the van's steering wheel harder. As if he didn't already have reason enough to settle the score, the Jap captain Gyofuku had made this personal.

"This time he's gone too far. I ain't gonna put up with crap from him forever," he promised himself. He preferred to deal with his problems directly, but lately he'd felt about as useful as a one-legged man at a butt-kicking contest. It just wasn't in his nature to keep turning the other cheek, and that dirty bastard Gyofuku had made sure he rubbed salt in the wound good and proper this time. Duke had been forced to watch, powerless to intervene, as Cal and his brother disappeared beneath the prop of that stinking cess-pit whaling ship, convinced he was witnessing their sudden and violent death.

Duke's grey eyes turned as steely as his resolve. His crew were his responsibility, and he didn't intend to lose any of them to the rubber-booted butcher and his persistent attacks. The blasted Jap just didn't know when to give up.

Well, he's pushed me a mite too far this time. If it's a showdown he wants then it's a showdown he'll git!

Duke pulled up next to the wharf. The stakes were critical now, and a prudent man was always prepared… and that meant you sure as hell didn't want to be taking a knife along to a gunfight. He glanced back towards the tarp-covered cargo in the back of the van.

Just give me one chance…I'll thrash him like a rented mule!

At that moment a red light blinked out of the darkness. Duke's hand slid to the .45 at his waistband. The light shone twice more, both long flashes this time.

W – Whiskey.

Duke relaxed. That was his call-signal. He flashed a response with the van's headlights then jumped out of the driver's seat and slid open the side door. A moment later he was joined by Cal.

"You took your sweet time," the Kiwi muttered. "Where have you been?"

Duke grunted noncommittally in response. "Y' found the new boat ok?"

Cal nodded. "Yeah, a brand new Naiad, right where you said to pick her up. She's a beaut!" He rolled his eyes. "I don't even want to know what kind of strings you had to pull to get hold of her – especially so cheap."

Duke ignored the unspoken question. "Let's git this lot out t' the ship then."

Cal saw the timber and cement bags in the back. "You planning a little DIY building work?" he laughed.

Duke ignored the joke. "We need to stow it all aboard before thuh tide turns."

Cal opened a waterproof case and whistled as he saw the new radios to replace the walkie-talkies that sank with their old inflatable. Then his eye fell on the black canvas dive bags. "You got SCUBA gear there too?"

Duke nodded. Technically that was true, although only one of the waterproof bags actually contained dive gear. The rest was hardware of a different kind…

Cal whistled appreciatively as he examined a dive regulator. "How the hell did you manage to get all this stuff?"

Duke's tattooed forearms knotted as he dragged a bag of cement towards him and hefted it onto his shoulder. "Saved a buddy's life when we stumbled into a goddamn VC ambush."

They loaded the rest of the cargo in silence.

A few minutes later they were ready to cast off. The new inflatable accommodated the cargo easily, even the large sheets of plywood. Duke regarded it with satisfaction. He might even owe his old buddy a favour after this one.

He left the keys in the van where Mad-Dog's man would find them in the morning, then jumped aboard.

"Ah'll drive," he said, pleased to see the Naiad's steering controls were on a central console, allowing him to stand at the helm rather than having to crouch in the stern like an ape. The new Naiad was bigger than her predecessor too. She was six metres long, with a rigid hull and twin 70 horsepower outboards. She would be a quick one, Duke thought, silently grateful to Mad-dog for parting with her. He resisted the temptation to open the throttle up though, and the engines burbled quietly as they stole across the dark harbour, leaving no wake behind them.

The water glittered like obsidian beneath their hull and Duke was reminded of the eyes of the pit viper that nearly had him one time in the jungles of 'Nam. It had lain at face height, silently coiled in a tree, waiting to ambush him…

Duke frowned. He wasn't a worrier by nature, but all the same he couldn't help fretting about what lay ahead. After witnessing the horrors of Vietnam, he had resolved long ago to fight only for the right reasons if he was ever going to fight again. Putting Hogei Gyofuku in his place definitely qualified on that score, but there were other problems to consider too.

"The next time we cross paths with that crazy Japper it's gonna be all on. Y' know that, right?"

Cal nodded, but he didn't answer straight away.

"D'ya think that Heathcliffe kid's got what it takes?" Duke blurted out, determined to speak his mind. "I don't trust that stupid hippy not t' lose it if things get hairy. That Canadian gal too. They're both about as much use as hip pockets on a hog."

Cal shrugged helplessly. "What choice do we have? We can't leave them here, and we definitely can't do it without them."

Duke spat pointedly over the side. "When the shit hits the fan there won't be no room for doubt, that's fer sure."

Cal was silent for a long time, as if chewing that over. He turned back to stare at Duke, a strange look in his eye. "Skip, what are you planning?" he asked. "What else did your mate give you?"

Duke glanced guiltily at the black duffel bags – his insurance policy against Japanese aggression. He looked away, not liking lying to the lad, but knowing Cal wasn't ready to know yet. The time might come when he could be persuaded to use extreme force, but it wasn't now.

"Nuthin' much. Just some supplies that might come in handy is all." He stroked his beard, muttering a curse under his breath. "Plus a special delivery for Gyofuku and his goddamn Fleet," he growled to himself.

***

Richard stood at the bow rail as the darkened Gwendolyn slipped out of the harbour. The hour was early, and the morning was still blanketed with the veil of night. He was tired but he hadn't been able to sleep. It was hot and claustrophobic below decks, although the worst contributor to his insomnia came from within.

Richard's stomach was tied in knots. They were heading out into the dark unknown again, and this time he knew only too well what danger awaited them. He closed his eyes, trying to clear his mind, but he couldn't shake the image of the Kuu-Maru's murderously spinning props as it nearly ran them down. Hogei Gyofuku was a madman. He had nearly killed them today, and there was no doubt he would try to finish the job if they ever crossed paths again.

Richard stared out into the night. Gyofuku was out there now, somewhere nearby, waiting for them, daring them to try and stop him.

Why don't we just sail home?

Richard sighed. In his heart he already knew the answer.

He'd seen the look in Cal's eye. His brother had been pushed too far. The Skipper too. This time the Gwendolyn would be searching not for whales, but for the Japanese Whaling Fleet. And when they found them a confrontation was certain.

Richard shook his head. The very thought made his knees feel weak. This was definitely the 'big league' all right, but even though every instinct screamed at him to back out now while he still could, something held him back. He was upset at witnessing the violent death of more whales, especially the little calf. In fact, he was angry. He had felt a special bond with them. The shared experience with the mother Humpback whale and her calf was not only exhilarating but almost unfathomable by everyday standards, and he knew it would stay with him for the remainder of his lifetime.

It's just not right what the Japanese are doing...

At that moment Richard heard a furtive noise behind him. He jumped as someone came up behind him.

"Couldn't sleep either, eh?" Cal asked.

Richard nodded, slightly embarrassed.

Cal joined him at the rail, his presence reassuring. "At times like this I try to remember what it is we're here for," he said quietly, as though sensing Richard's consternation.

Richard continued to stare out to sea, still worried, and a little confused too. They were here to do research, weren't they?

Cal was silent for a while as he stared out to sea. "Only about six hundred Humpbacks breed here in Tonga," he said suddenly. "They won't stand up to more than five or six years of hunting before they're exterminated. That'll mean no more Humpbacks migrating through New Zealand waters either."

Richard didn't answer. He knew it was a terrible thing but he was reluctant to get involved again.

Haven't we done enough already?

Cal sighed. "You know the Japan Fisheries Agency is already leaning on the Tongan government to open up their territorial waters to whaling," he said, without looking around. "They're pressing for permission to hunt here legally instead of having to skulk around like thieves in the night."

"Surely Tonga wouldn't give in to Amimoto's bullying?"

Cal shrugged. "He's offering a lot of money, and this isn't exactly a rich country..."

Richard felt his frustration growing. It was the same old story repeating itself anew. "But there's money in whale tourism too," he exclaimed. "Much more money. Sustainable money. And the profits would benefit the local economy instead of going straight offshore into the Taiyoku Misui Fisheries Company's pockets!"

Cal nodded. "That's true, but tourism takes time to develop, and it requires an investment of capital first. Selling whale quotas to Japan is easy money now, and lucrative."

Richard shook his head. "Only until the whales are all gone! Surely the locals can see how dumb that is?"

Cal shrugged. "The older generation here used to eat whalemeat too. They remember the taste with nostalgia for the old days. They see nothing wrong with eating whales, and they are the people who are in positions of power in government."

Richard felt a little spark of anger begin to burn within him again. "But cultural history is no excuse! There simply aren't enough whales any more. The Earth has reached a point now where attitudes have to change. People can't keep going with their same old ways."

He clenched his fists, angry now. "These whales don't belong to anyone. Why should either country have the right to decide their fate?" he demanded.

Cal didn't answer, and when Richard looked over he saw his brother was smiling at him, his eyes filled with pride.

Richard blinked, suddenly aware of the passion that had awoken within himself. Passion that went against everything he had learned to accept about life.

Well, you've come this far. Why not see it through to the end?

Although he was terrified of where it might take him, he knew this path was one he needed to follow. He was starting to see that everyone had a contribution to offer, regardless of their experience. Himself included.

The breeze freshened as they headed out to sea, and Richard shivered at the sudden goose-bumps on his bare arms. With a rising sense of foreboding he knew the golden weather was about to turn.

This was the big league, he realised, in more ways than one.

Cal frowned as though he too sensed the change in the sea's mood.

"It's time for us to finish this, Bro," he murmured. "I'll be damned if I'm going to let that bloodthirsty bastard slaughter another whale in front of me! What do you say?"

Richard took a deep breath and nodded, not trusting his voice to answer.

Chapter 22

Richard Major stood at the bow rail, hypnotised as he watched the endless blue wavetops disappear beneath the Gwendolyn's hull. They were almost a full day's sailing from Tonga, and the land had already slipped far below the horizon behind them. On all sides, only the bright blue spread of the tropical ocean surrounded them, shining in the sun.

It was hard to know what to feel. He had just witnessed a terrible act, but now he was surrounded by beauty on all sides – evidence perhaps of Nature's capacity to endure.

Richard turned his head to take it all in, no longer quite so intimidated by the vast openness. A large pod of dolphins swam off their starboard side, churning the water to foam with their passage. They weren't bow-riding, and paid little attention to the ship. As he watched them though, a lithe grey body suddenly shot clear of the water, twisting like a corkscrew. It twirled over and over like a spinning top, then splashed back into the water on its side. Richard blinked in surprise. He'd seen dolphins jump before, but never like that. Another followed just as exuberantly, pirouetting with the grace of a ballerina. They were about the size of Bottlenose dolphins, but sleeker and more streamlined. He watched them, fascinated.

"Spinner dolphins," Cal said from his elbow.

Richard jumped. He'd been so absorbed watching their acrobatics he hadn't heard his brother's approach.

"They're the only species of dolphin that spins like that when they jump."

Richard felt his curiosity piqued. "Why do they do it?"

Cal shrugged "Social display most likely. No one really knows. Maybe they've discovered it's a good way to have fun!"

Richard nodded. It did look like fun. If he were a dolphin he would love to be able to twirl like that.

With a sudden thump, a flying fish landed on the deck next to them. It lay there, gasping, having fled from the path of the dolphins. Richard stared at it in wonder. He'd never seen a flying fish before. Its elongated fins were extended to form two sets of gossamer wings, one large, one smaller, shimmering in the sunlight.

He reached down and scooped it up, gently tossing it over the rail and back into the sea.

"Isn't it amazing what can live out here, far from the sight of land?" Cal said.

Richard nodded, appreciating now that this huge empty landscape was far from the barren waste it had first seemed to him.

"It's one of the last unspoiled places on Earth," Cal said wistfully, "One of the few places we haven't ruined yet." He rolled his eyes. "Although it's not for want of trying. Nowhere is untouched by humans any more, not even here. The commercial fishing fleets of the world have raked the oceans clean in just a few decades, and pollution spreads like a creeping cancer across the globe to poison what is left. Even in the pristine wilderness of the polar seas, whales and other marine mammals accumulate so much toxic heavy metal poisoning through the food chain that they qualify as hazardous waste when they die. And the shredded ozone layer over the Antarctic bombards them with massive doses of UV radiation." He laughed hollowly. "Where do you start? She's a hard road trying to change the world. Gotta pick your battles to fight, eh Bro?"

Richard nodded, his thoughts suddenly turning, unbidden, back to Hogei Gyofuku and his Fleet.

It seemed there would be no escaping being reminded of the inevitable conflict. The fate that awaited them, somewhere over the horizon, brooded over Richard's thoughts with all the subtlety of a gathering stormcloud. The fact that the Japanese whalers were no longer hanging around the island breeding grounds meant they were already heading south, searching for the great migration path down to the Antarctic. He swallowed, trying to force his anxiety down.

"How will we find them out here? We could search for weeks."

Cal nodded. "True, but we don't need to find the Fleet. There's only one route south from here. Find the Humpbacks and we'll find the whalers." He turned away from the rail. "Come on," he said, leading the way up the outside ladder to the wheelhouse.

The Skipper didn't look up as they entered the bridge. His steely grey eyes were riveted on the horizon.

Cal gestured at the laptop on the console next to him, and Richard recognised the rows of numbers on the screen.

"My last active sat-tag," Cal confirmed. "It's on a female Humpback I tagged last season, right here near Tonga."

"Where is she?"

"Heading south. She's about a day ahead of us, but we're catching up.

Richard was silent for a long time, wondering who else might be gaining on the migrating whale. Finally he spoke.

"Cal?"

"Yeah?"

"What are we going to do when we find the Whaling Fleet?"

Cal looked away, avoiding his eyes, although Richard couldn't help noticing the brief glance that passed between him and the Skipper.

"Something that should have been done a long time ago," Cal muttered under his breath. Then he smiled a little too broadly, as though forcing a jovial expression. "Don't worry yourself about it, Bro. Everything will be ok."

Later that day though, Richard's thoughts were still troubled as he tried to focus on his duties. He was in the galley with Heath, preparing the day's dinner. It was actually Heath who was rostered to cook, but he always needed an assistant since, unlike everyone else, he refused to cater for those with different dietary preferences to his own.

The Skipper particularly detested the dry lentil loaf he made virtually every time he was on chef duty, and he made his feelings plain.

"A fellah can't do an honest day's work an' survive on this stuff," the old sailor would grumble to himself. "Ah gotta have me some protein, dang it!"

Being a total vegan, Heath even refused to cook with cheese. Rather than argue with him, those who wanted something else found it easier to organise their own cooking roster for the nights he was chef, hence the reason Richard found himself elbow-to-elbow sharing the tiny galley tonight. He was actually quite proud of his own culinary efforts to date. Despite being at sea, the meals he managed were far more adventurous than the microwaved TV dinners he used to cook for himself at home whenever his wife was out socialising.

Ex-wife, he reminded himself, surprised at how little emotion thoughts of Gina and her treachery now evoked in him. He shrugged, wondering if that was the sign he was finally over her, and returned to his cooking.

Tonight he had whipped up a stir-fry of chicken, fresh vegetables, and some sweet potatoes that Vicki had picked up from the local market while they were ashore in Tonga. He was feeling proud of himself, and even Heath's constant grumbling failed to dampen his mood.

He got out a carton of long-life milk and reached for a saucepan to make a white sauce – the finishing touch to his creation. The dish was different, but he hoped the others would like it. Now that his confidence was building he enjoyed trying out new things – even cooking.

"Don't use that pan!" Heath screamed at him suddenly.

Richard jumped so high he nearly banged his head. "W-what's wrong?" he stammered.

"That's a vegan pan. You'll contaminate it."

"It's ok, it's just for the white sauce. I'll wash it when I'm done."

"There's milk in that recipe," Heath sniffed disdainfully. "If you want to be a blood-thirsty carnivore that's your bad karma, but you've got no right to ram your fascist beliefs down my throat!"

Richard hesitated. Normally he would go along with Heath when he was in one of his moods – it was easier than trying to argue with him. And Heath did seem to delight in complaining around him, probably because Richard was the only one on the ship who didn't tell him to shut up and pull his head in. All of a sudden though, Richard had finally had enough. Maybe it was because he was already on edge, but tonight he didn't feel like keeping his mouth shut and tolerating the usual crap.

"It's not blood, only milk," he pointed out reasonably. "And I said I'll wash the pan afterwards."

Heath brushed the matted wool out of his eyes to glare at him. "Just in case you're too thick to realise, I'll spell it out for you… Milk is an animal product too!" He stuck his tongue behind his bottom lip, imitating a retard.

Richard looked down at the bench, rattled but not cowed yet. "I don't see what's so bad about drinking milk anyway," he muttered.

Heath loomed over him, his lip ring glinting like some distorted fang.

Richard slid off his stool and drew back, a little intimidated despite the fact he was bigger than the weedy Californian.

"Animal rights is about more than just not murdering them," Heath spat. "It's also about animal welfare. Do you know what that is?" he sneered. "No, I guess you don't. You're just like that trigger-happy brother of yours… Hey, let's have some fun by shooting little holes into some poor defenceless creatures!" he mocked.

Richard stared at him, aghast. Where on Earth had that outburst come from? "The biopsy sample doesn't hurt the whales," he protested. "And it's not for fun. It's for research."

Heath snorted. "Yeah right! Like it's got nothing to do with your dumb-ass jock brother getting his jollies. He's just trying to compensate for his small penis and prove what a big man he is!" He leaned forward, close enough to make Richard recoil from his body odour. "Terrorising whales is no better than killing them – it's extreme psychological abuse." He curled his lip ring. "You're as bad as the fucking Japanese, all of you."

Richard was completely lost for words. How could Heath manage to be so bad tempered that he could find fault with anything? Richard shook his head. "Why did you even come on this trip?" he asked finally.

Heath grunted. "Sometimes I wonder myself," he said, then stomped out to the mess with his food.

Richard watched him go.

Later, during the meal, Richard kept to himself. He was still smarting from Heath's outburst, and given the Californian's thunderous scowl he had no wish to reopen the wound. He kept his mouth closed and his eyes on his food, trying to avoid giving Heath any provocation.

The Skipper clearly had no such reservations though.

"You've been smokin' weed in y' cabin again," he announced, glaring straight at the insolent activist. It was a statement, not a question.

"So what?" Heath challenged him. "You're not my mother." He rolled his eyes skyward. "Or are you going to play Chief Dictator of this fascist little police-state of yours and arrest me for independent thought?"

"Smokin's a fire hazard," the Skipper growled, "And there will be no lightin' up below decks – of anything. You git me?"

Heath fired up immediately. "So much for living in a free and democratic society," he sneered. He fixed his beady gaze on the Skipper. "This is a violation of my basic human rights. Tell me something Pops, does it make you feel like a big man to order people around?"

"Ok, everyone calm down," Cal cut in, trying to mollify the situation before it turned ugly. "We're not trying to repress anybody's rights, but the

Skipper has a point. Fire is a big danger aboard ship. If you want to smoke you can always go to the rear deck," he offered reasonably.

Heath was past listening to reason though. "I don't have to put up with this crap from the likes of you lot! You're not going to burden my life with your pedantic rules!"

His eyes had an almost crazed look as he glared at them. "You fascists won't control things forever. You better watch your step. The revolution is coming!"

The Skipper didn't reply to the implied threat, but his gaze was intense and unblinking and his eyes were flinty and dangerous, the same colour as a storm-tossed sea.

Even Heath knew better than to provoke him any further, and he hurriedly scooped up his plate to leave.

As he walked past Summer, she wrinkled her nose. "Would it kill you to take a shower once in a while?" she sniffed disdainfully.

Richard saw Heath's shoulder blades stiffen as the barb struck home. He said nothing though and stalked huffily from the room, but she didn't even seem to notice. Her attention had shifted already – to Richard. She sidled closer to him, smiling like a temptress.

Richard blinked at the swiftness of the change, but her seductive smile was disarming.

"Mmm, this food is good," Summer purred, leaning closer. "My compliments to the chef."

He suddenly noticed she was eating the main dish and flushed with embarrassment. "W-wait," he stammered. "I made a non-chicken version for you."

Summer blinked, looking confused. "Oh. I thought vegetarians can eat chicken… Can't they?"

Richard shrugged helplessly, wishing he could disappear. Around the table the others seemed suddenly engrossed with their food.

"Oh, no matter. It's not like I'll go to Hell or anything!" Summer laughed gaily to cover the awkwardness, then sidled even closer to him. Her singlet was already tight across her chest, but as she lent across it slipped forward revealing the curve of her breasts.

Richard kept his eyes on his food so he couldn't be accused of staring down her top. Across the table he noticed Vicki was doing the same thing.

Summer leaned even closer. "What's for desert?" she continued, smiling wistfully. "I'd kill for a flat white and a donut. We've been at sea for so long I've almost forgotten what they taste like."

Richard held his breath as her bare foot caressed his leg under the table, and he tried desperately not to blush.

Cal hadn't seen the hidden contact, and he laughed innocently. "I promise we'll stop at Tim Horan's – just as soon as we can find a 'sail-thru'."

Summer didn't laugh with him. She had a blank look on her face.

Richard was confused too. "Tim Horan's? What's that?"

"It's a Canadian donut store chain," Cal explained. "They're really proud of it over there. It's kind of a patriotic thing." He was frowning, although his expression was hard to read. He waved a hand absently. "It's ok, Bro, I wouldn't expect you to know that if you've never been to Canada…"

Abruptly, Summer stood up. "It's such a lovely evening I think I'll go eat on deck," she announced. Cal was watching her intently, but she ignored him. Her face was staid and completely unreadable, but suddenly, as though on the spur of the moment, she bent down and kissed Richard full on the mouth. His eyes flew open in shock, scarcely able to believe what was happening. Then just as quickly as it began, it was over.

Summer straightened up, a self-satisfied little smile at the corners of her mouth. As she turned to go she winked her mascara-tinted lashes at Richard. He stared after her, too shocked to respond, watching her long tanned legs as she walked towards the door, and hanging on every sway of her hips beneath her ripped denim shorts.

Vicki inhaled sharply and stood up too. "I've got some stats to run in the computer lab," she muttered, then turned to leave in the opposite direction. She kept her eyes downcast the whole time, refusing to meet Richard's gaze.

He stared down at his food. Only Cal and the Skipper remained at the table with him now. He shot a quick glance at them, but neither spoke.

An uncomfortable silence settled over the room.

Finally, the Skipper stood up and cleared his throat noisily. "Don't git blinded by a nice rack," he muttered, frowning at Richard, then stomped down the staircase towards the hold, shaking his head as he went.

Richard watched him go, ears burning with embarrassment. But inside he was still angry from his earlier fight with Heath and he quickly felt his indignation rising to match it.

It's none of his business what I do! And how dare he talk that way about Summer?

He glanced back at Cal, hoping for some kind of support from his brother.

Cal coughed self-consciously. "He's right, Bro. I don't reckon she's being genuine with you."

Richard blinked. He had been expecting congratulations, man-to-man. A blokey pat on the back, 'Good score mate!', that kind of thing. Anything but this.

"W-what?" he managed to splutter.

"Summer's a man-eater, Richard. She'll chew you up and spit you out when she's done."

Richard stared at him, lost for words. Cal continued, misinterpreting the reason for his silence.

"All I'm saying is you could do a lot better…"

Richard had heard enough. He jumped to his feet, cutting him off. "Why can't you be happy for me?"

Cal rolled his eyes, avoiding his gaze. "I just don't want to see you get hurt. I brought you out here to get away from all that." He shrugged helplessly.

Richard glared at him, feeling his anger boil to the surface. "Yeah? Well maybe you shouldn't have bothered. I can take care of myself!"

Inside, he was seething.

It's just like when we were kids! Cal's so used to always getting the best of everything that he can't bear it now when his loser of a brother suddenly does better than him!

He shook his head, wondering if Cal had a secret inferiority complex.

Well this time he'll just have to deal with it!

He marched towards the door.

"I'm just trying to help you," Cal protested.

Richard whirled around, his anger raw. "Bullshit! You're just jealous!"

He slammed the door behind him as he left.

***

Later that evening Cal sat in the wheelhouse by himself. The blaze of the sunset was brief, as it always was in the tropics. The sullen orange ball of the sun seemed to hang suspended for a moment, briefly igniting the sea, then it plunged below the horizon without a backwards glance.

Cal sighed, his own thoughts mirrored by the swiftly advancing shadows. The Team's morale was the worst it had been since they set out. They had initially pulled together well, but the strain was starting to tell now. It was as though the weeks at sea had served to drive a wedge between everyone, shortening tolerance levels and inflaming every trifling annoyance. Little niggles that might normally be laughed off suddenly compounded until personalities began to grate and the inevitable flare-ups occurred.

Heath's outburst at dinner had been a perfect example. He was becoming more and more difficult lately, and his attitude was starting to affect morale aboard. Cal wondered how he could have overlooked such obnoxious and confrontational tendencies when he hired the loser. It was obvious the Californian had more than a few issues going on, but it was too late for recriminations now. Cal knew he had to try and make the best of the bad situation.

The outcome of that depended largely on Heath though, and Cal didn't hold huge hopes of him pulling his head in for the remainder. He was just too outspoken. The idiot was probably feeding his own paranoia by smoking too much pot, but telling him to lay off the stuff for a while wasn't exactly advice he was likely to heed – even if he did follow the Skipper's instructions not to smoke it below decks – and if he didn't, Duke's response would be to offer him a long walk off a short plank.

Cal rubbed his temples wearily.

I'm gonna need kid gloves to keep order aboard – and to keep the Team from each others' throats.

The situation promised to get worse before it got better though. Prolonged periods confined together in close quarters only brought out the worst in people. Normally he planned his research voyages to stay under six weeks for precisely this reason, but then, this wasn't exactly a normal situation. He couldn't put anyone ashore, much less call a halt to the expedition. They had only one choice out here; put their differences aside and work together.

Otherwise Amimoto wins automatically, without so much as a challenge.

Cal shook his head, although it was more out of dismay than denial. He was still worried by Richard's flare-up, but not sorry for warning against his burgeoning relationship with Summer.

I was only trying to watch out for him. Can't he see that?

Cal stared out into the night, wondering if he was in danger of losing his own brother too.

His thoughts drifted to Duke, usually a bulwark of support – especially when it came to maintaining the orderly flow of life aboard ship.

Lately even he had been acting strangely, opting out of watches so he could go below for hours at a time, where he got up to who knows what. Cal had asked him what he was doing down in the hold, hour after hour, and he found the Skipper's evasive answers difficult to stomach – especially from someone he considered a partner in command, if not a mate.

Why is he lying? I thought we were a team?

Cal struggled with his suspicions. If he was honest with himself he might even consider the grizzled old sea-dog as something akin to a replacement for a missing father figure in his life. That made the Skipper's apparent withdrawal even harder to accept.

I'm on my own. Everything's threatening to go belly-up, and there's no one I can turn to…

The loneliness of command was one thing, but Cal knew he faced an even bigger challenge in keeping his Team together. Things were at their lowest ebb now, right at the most critical time. He sighed. Maybe it wasn't fair to expect the Team to cope with such a big ask, after all, it wasn't what they'd signed on for.

Then again, he thought bitterly, *everyone agreed to go through with it.*

It might be natural for them to get cold feet as the intensity ratcheted up a few notches, but he'd warned them there could be no backing out once the die was cast.

It's too late for anyone to turn back now!

Cal checked the ship's course on the compass, then glanced up to the stars for confirmation. But there was no reassuring twinkle overhead. The night sky was obscured by a veil of high cloud, just like their future.

He sighed again, recognising he was on edge too. The strain was starting to tell all around, and it couldn't have surfaced at a worse time. A deadly showdown was looming, and everyone would need to pull together if they were going to get through it.

He stared at his hands, feeling suddenly helpless.

All I can do is try to keep the peace.

Several hours passed as Cal sat alone in the dark, staring sightlessly ahead while the Gwendolyn steamed on through the night.

As his mind came back to the reality of the present, he realised what had disturbed him – a small noise from the radio room behind the bridge.

Was that the Skipper coming to relieve him and take the next watch? Cal glanced at the luminous dial of his watch. If so, he was nearly late, and that was unlike him. Aboard ship Duke ran things with military precision, particularly the duty watches. His orders were plain; "If you think you're tired getting' outta bed to go on watch, how d'ya think the poor bastard who's been sittin' there for hours feels?" he would say. "All watch personnel will report five minutes before their start time t' be briefed by the outgoing watch. That way the poor bastard can git straight back to bed when his time's up, without having to stay up on account of your lazy ass, see?"

Even Heath had eventually gotten the hang of it, although Cal and Duke had decided between them that Heath and Summer would only do daylight watches. That way they were never in sole charge of the ship, and there was always someone else around to keep half an eye on things.

Which was why it was strange that Duke hadn't arrived yet. Cal checked his watch again. It was 12:58; two minutes to go before his shift was over. He frowned.

What the hell is he up to down in the hold, anyway?

At that moment he heard the noise again, a furtive scuff on the floor.

"That you, Skip?" he called.

There was no answer.

Cal got up and walked back into the radio room, leaving the light off since his eyes were already adjusted to the dark.

The room was empty, but without the strip lights overhead to drown it out he could see the light shining up the companionway from the passage on the level below. As he watched he saw it flicker, as though a shadow had just crossed in front of it.

Someone's down there!

He dived through the hatch and slid down the handrails, taking the entire staircase in one leap. He landed in a crouch, catlike, at the bottom, ready to surprise whoever was sneaking around at this time of night.

But the passageway was empty, and the doors to all the bunkrooms were closed. Cal frowned, poking his head through the doorway into the mess. It was dark and deserted, as was the galley behind it.

Maybe someone wanted a midnight snack. Or maybe I'm just imagining things.

He shrugged and hurried back upstairs.

As he passed though the radio room, a sudden beep made him pause. The fax machine blinked twice, then the 'Ready' light came on.

That's weird. Did it just finish sending a message?

He jabbed the redial button, but he didn't need a phone book to recognise the number that came up – it was the fax at the Greenpeace Head Office in Auckland. He frowned.

Nothing unusual about that – except that I've been using the radio to send our position reports…

Cal shrugged, dismissing it. The number was probably in there since the last time he'd sent a fax to Aurelia.

He went back to the bridge, checking the ship's position on the GPS's display as he passed it. He sat down in the wheelhouse and glanced at his watch again.

Thirty seconds to go. Where the hell is Duke?

At that moment he heard heavy footsteps coming up the stairs behind him.

The Skipper looked contrite. "Sorry ah'm late. Thought I heard someone creepin' about in thuh passageway," he muttered. "Went to check it out."

Cal raised an eyebrow. "Who was it?"

"Didn't see nobody. He must've took off."

Cal frowned, wondering if it was an excuse, but knowing better than to press the Skipper for details on what he himself had been doing.

"You finished down there, or what?" he asked, trying to keep the accusation out of his voice.

Duke studied his sandals, looking almost sheepish. "Yup," he murmured, but his face clouded over and Cal knew he would get nothing out of him about what he'd been doing down below.

"Your watch," Cal said curtly, "Nothing to report." Then he stomped downstairs to his bunk, trying to curb his irritation.

***

The next day Richard sat on watch in the wheelhouse, watching as the lines of position data slowly marched across the laptop screen beside him. It was a grey overcast day outside, and the mood of the sea had changed. The light seemed to have left the water, rendering it a dull grey-blue. The wind had picked up too, and flecks of white began to dot the sea, all the way to the horizon.

He cast his gaze over the rolling swells, absently looking for a tell-tale cloud of vapour that would indicate a whale – even though they were still twenty nautical miles behind their target. They were tracking another female Humpback – the last equipped with a sat-tag – and she was already half-way to the Kermadecs. The island group lay just above New Zealand and he knew it would take them over a day's sailing to catch up.

Not much to do in the meantime…

The waiting was the worst part. There was only so long he could keep his anxiety in check.

Richard looked enviously at the polished wooden spokes of the ship's wheel, itching to hold it. There wasn't much for him to do on the bridge. The Skipper had programmed the autopilot with the most recent data sent from the sat-tag which would automatically steer the ship towards the whale's last known position. All he had to do was monitor the instruments and keep a collision watch for other shipping – which was few and far between since they were steaming far outside any shipping lanes here.

The dreary weather was a perfect match for his mood. Though Richard was a little bored and frustrated sitting on watch, he had plenty of time to think, and that was part of the problem. He was feeling more than a little contrite this morning, his behaviour last night still weighing on his mind. It wasn't like him to snap at anybody, least of all his own brother. Cal had only been watching out for him. That was what brothers were supposed to do, wasn't it?

He felt like he should apologise, but something still held him back. He couldn't quite tell if it was stubborn pride, or anxiousness.

He sneaked a glance at his brother, working down on the fore-deck below him. Cal was deploying the large TV-like antenna he used for tracking the signals from the VHF tags. It was much more labour intensive than receiving a nice sat-tag position via the satellite downlink, and positioning had to be done manually. Cal was frowning as he concentrated, cupping his free hand to the headphones while he listened for the barely-perceptible changes in beep volume that would indicate signal strength from the distant transmitter.

Richard suspected he was trying to pinpoint Mana, the male Humpback he'd met the previous day and the one Cal remembered from Kaikoura all those years ago. Richard was interested, but too afraid to ask given his brother's serious mood. Cal had worn a permanent frown all morning, obviously deeply immersed in his own problems. Richard knew from past experience not to bother him when he was in that kind of mood, especially since he might be to blame for it. The response would only be sharp – or he might get his head bitten right off.

Richard sighed, wondering how it had come to this, an angry wall of silence between him and his own brother.

With a heavy heart he turned his attention back to the laptop screen, staring at the position data from the sat-tag. As the lines of data marched across the screen he suddenly noticed something strange. The continuous data output meant the whale was still at the surface, and had been for some time, whereas the usual surface interval was just a few minutes. He stared at the figures, mentally computing the coordinates into real-world locations. With a start, he realised the whale had been virtually stationary at the surface for the last ten minutes. He felt his stomach contract into a hard knot as understanding dawned.

He hurried to the side window and flung it open. "Cal, I think you'll want to take a look at this," he shouted down, unable to keep the foreboding out of his voice.

Cal came at a run, without even stopping to put down the antenna in his hand, and he burst into the wheelhouse just as the transmission failed altogether.

The last line of numbers hung on the screen, blinking futilely, the data incomplete.

Cal swore under his breath, sizing up the situation in an instant. "That sat-tag didn't stop transmitting on its own," he muttered. "The bastards have got another one!"

"What are we going to do?" Richard blurted, giving voice to his fears. "How will we find the migration path now?"

Cal looked grim. "We've still got a couple of VHF tagged Humpbacks out there somewhere… but they could be anywhere between here and Antarctica by now."

"How will we know which one of them to go to though?"

Cal rubbed his temples, clearly frustrated by the situation. "We won't. We'll have to pick one and hope for the best."

"Which one is the closest?"

"Don't know. We can't tell the distance from the VHF signal, just direction."

"How do you normally find whales with it then?"

He shrugged. "Sail blindly towards it and hope for the best, I guess."

Richard's brow furrowed. "But out here with nothing to block the signal it could be coming from hundreds of kilometres away!"

Cal nodded sadly. "Yeah. That's why we don't normally use VHF to locate whales, since it isn't as good for tracking a target. We use it mainly to confirm an identification of a whale we're looking at, or we set up a datalogger and the presence of a signal tells us which whales are passing through an area…" He shrugged helplessly. "But if you want a precise position, well, that's what sat-tags are for!"

Richard frowned, frustrated that they were apparently thwarted by technology. In his experience radio signals were just like electric currents, they followed a predictable and well-defined set of rules…

"There has to be a way!" he murmured, closing his eyes in concentration. He put aside everything else that was bothering him, and in a moment it was all forgotten as he dedicated his mind to the problem at hand.

Here was an electronics problem, and that was what he knew best.

A few moments later he smiled slowly as the beginnings of an idea formed. "Wait," he said breathlessly, and a grin broke across his face. "There's a directional VHF antenna mounted permanently on the mast, right?"

Cal nodded.

Richard pointed to the portable antenna still in Cal's hand. "Can you mount that one too, somewhere back near the stern."

Cal shrugged. "Sure, but I don't see how-"

Richard held up a hand to forestall questions. "If you route the feed back here I can plug them both into the laptop," he said, grinning like a Cheshire cat now. "Once you have two signals it's a simple matter to compute the stronger one in relation to the ship's axis." He used a whiteboard marker to sketch a diagram on the Perspex plotting board on top of the chart. "And if we have two independent bearings to the target then it's simple trigonometry to plot them both and do a biangulation."

A smile broke across Cal's face as he caught on. "And the point of intersection gives us the exact location of the source!" he finished triumphantly. "Nice going, Bro!" he said, clapping Richard heartily on the back. "I knew there's a reason we brought an engineer on board!"

Richard beamed, heartened by the praise.

Suddenly he remembered Cal's speech the night they sank the White Ship. "One man can always make a difference. No matter what your experience, everyone has something to offer."

Richard smiled proudly, pleased he was able to help where no one else aboard could. He turned back to Cal, hoping to bask in his brother's approval.

Cal was already heading for the door though, deep in thought. His frown had returned, his good mood as fleeting as the sun on this grey day. Richard's smile died.

Is he still mad at me? Am I a disappointment to him?

That was the one thing that could shake his new resolve.

How could he carry on if his own brother secretly hated him? Richard knew he had to find out for sure. He took a deep breath, determined to keep the stammer out of his voice. "C-Cal, are you mad at me?"

Cal stopped and turned to stare at him, looking surprised. "No, of course not," he said, and his blue eyes softened. "I'm sorry Bro, it's just… I've had a lot on my mind lately." He sighed then, a weary sound that seemed to come from some untapped place within. "And it's not over yet, not by a long shot. The Japanese Fleet is still out there somewhere and we're running out of time." He looked away, almost apologetically, as though not wanting to burden Richard with his problems. "We've still got a lot of ocean to cover, and every hour we spend looking could equal another dead whale… I just hope we can locate the Fleet before it's too late."

***

Dennis Cruikshank sat at the desk in his hotel room. He was sick of the incompetent local police force, sick of being thwarted again, sick of this whole goddamned city, in fact.

He picked up his cell phone again, frowning as he punched his access code into the keypad. The message had come this morning, and his lip curled as he re-read it on the little screen; "Agent reports minor incident with Japanese Fleet at sea. Suspects reportedly planning further confrontation, violence likely."

Cruikshank swore under his breath. "What the hell am I supposed to do about that?" he muttered. It was bullshit. It was worse than bullshit – not least because that was all he had to go on. He had called his supervisor the moment it arrived, demanding answers, determined to extract the truth out of him.

"I'm sorry Agent Cruikshank, but that's all the information I have to give you at present," came the predictable response.

"All the information you have, or the information you'll give me?" Cruikshank snapped.

Silverman avoided the question, spinning him the usual crap about 'levels of involvement', and his inability to release 'un-vetted information'.

Cruikshank swore and hung up the phone, even more frustrated than ever.

That was this morning, and he was still seething inside.

He had called the Fisheries Minister's office next, hoping to be tossed a bone, but determined not to sit around on his ass like a piece of meat until Silverman jerked his chain. The whole time he was gritting his teeth and sneering inwardly at how pathetic the chain of command in his own department was.

Minister Yokuke was disarmingly civil, even making time for a personal meeting despite his busy schedule. He was visibly pissed off though, and as he recounted details of the latest incident at sea, Cruikshank could feel the anger like a cold chill in the room. He was ranting in Japanese, but his translator dutifully translated. "Not content with their recent acts of violence, these troublemakers have resumed their usual showboating and harassment of my vessels and their crews at sea, attempting to interfere and prevent them fishing for whales in international waters. An activity which is entirely legal under all applicable laws and conventions!" the Minister added, his eyes glittering with malice.

Cruikshank nodded. "We have a common interest in bringing these criminals to justice," he said.

The Minister lowered his voice, and even though he couldn't understand the language, Cruikshank could feel the ice in his words. "These terrorists have violated Japan's territorial sovereignty with their cowardly attacks on our citizens," the aide dutifully translated. "The Japanese Government would be extremely appreciative if this band of troublemakers were apprehended and returned here to face justice for their crimes." Minister Yokuke smiled like a cobra, and Cruikshank blinked despite his composure.

He'd come across many attitudes in his time, and most were only skin-deep. He sensed this one was different however, this was not for show. In front of him was a truly dangerous man.

Yokuke inclined his head in a bow, his voice dripping with honey. "May I take this opportunity to express my pleasure at working with my United States allies on this matter. Rest assured, you will receive the complete support of my department and my government for your investigation."

Cruikshank had nodded his thanks as he left, pleased he was working with this guy and not against him.

Minister Yokuke had been true to his word. In fact, he had been very helpful, providing classified dossiers his own security people had compiled on all of the perpetrators – which was certainly more information than the local police had.

Cruikshank drummed his fingers on the edge of the cheap hotel desk now. The dossier lay open in front of him. With a frown, he flicked through it again, his forgotten cigarette already burning low in the ashtray.

The information it contained was a goldmine, vital intelligence on the enemy he hunted.

For instance, it revealed the Skipper of the vessel was ex-military – a former Navy SEAL no less! Cruikshank frowned as he flicked through the bio on him. The guy had seen action in Vietnam, which raised the stakes somewhat. In addition to his Special Forces training, he'd also faced the disciplinary committee on several occasions, ranging from insubordination to striking an officer. Only minor trouble with the law since then, mostly bar fights and common assault, although he was believed to be a part-time smuggler and arms dealer when the notion took him. Cruikshank grunted. *All in all a fine citizen!*

He wondered how easy it would be to take this lot by force.

It wasn't the Skipper's bio that held his attention though, but the blonde kid he recognised from the conference. His rap-sheet was squeaky clean – which made him an even bigger security threat from the point-of-view of US border security. Cruikshank stared at the grainy photo paper-clipped to the page. It had been taken surreptitiously in Japan, probably outside the conference, but the subject seemed to have sensed the presence of the covert cameraman. He was looking straight at the lens, jaw clenched as though in an unspoken challenge.

Cruikshank frowned at the picture in front of him. This one was trouble. He'd seen evidence of it at the conference already, and he could see it now in the eyes. A man's eyes always betrayed his intentions, and the eyes staring back from the photo seemed to lock with his own, confident and fearless. Cruikshank knew the type well. This was not a man to give up easily. Even without the confirmation of more violence at sea, he would have predicted this one would head straight into the thick of things.

Cruikshank twirled his moustache distractedly. It wouldn't be easy bringing this lot down, and he knew he was already behind the play again.

The suspects had quit Japan. The local authorities knew that much at least. They'd upped and left, sailing away like thieves in the night, although exactly where they'd gone was apparently beyond the Shimonoseki Police Department's powers of deduction.

Cruikshank didn't need to hazard a guess though. Even without the latest report from the Pacific to confirm it he knew the most likely place was right in the middle of trouble – in other words, wherever the Japanese Fleet was headed.

Cruikshank knew his intel had to improve if he was going to nail these bastards. The agent needed to stop all this pussyfooting around and get closer to the suspects' plans, regardless of the risks. He shook his head, wishing again for one of his own undercover operatives from the LAPD instead of this damned spook-trained pussy.

Without timely information I can act on, that agent is next to useless!

Cruikshank shook his head in disgust. He held out little hope that either suggestion would be acted upon though, despite his strongly-worded attempts to persuade his supervisor to the contrary… The whole thing was doubly frustrating since he could see these punks posed a bigger threat to US interests than any Japanese nationalist groups, or Middle Eastern hijackers for that matter. With the War on Terror in full cry, it wasn't about whether these militant environmentalists *had* targeted US interests, but whether they *could*.

Cruikshank tugged his moustache angrily. The CIA were so obsessed with Al Qaeda these days they were practically blind to any other threat lurking on the horizon. The fact that US citizens were involved in this made it not only a gigantic diplomatic embarrassment, but also a dangerous security risk. He knew these punks' attack on the Japanese ships was just the tip of the iceberg now they'd moved to deliberate acts of sabotage and violence. And who knew where that path might lead them?

"Well I damn-well don't intend to wait around to find out," Cruikshank muttered. Homeland Security was his responsibility now, and terrorists were terrorists as far as he was concerned. His fists clenched in sympathy. "We just can't have terrorist groups running free and causing mayhem!"

The problem was, what could he do about it?

His anger bubbled like a cauldron, hot enough to make the vein at his temple pulse angrily. He snatched up the phone again, punching up Silverman's details. He resisted the temptation to call his supervisor in person though, knowing he would be too tempted to tell the old bastard what he thought of his detective abilities.

That, and he had a plane to catch.

Instead, he typed a quick text message; "Have acquired new intel on subjects. Believe they pose an immediate risk to national interests. Request direct action to intervene. Extreme force recommended."

He stabbed the 'Send' button, then dropped the phone into his pocket.

He stood, scooping up the dossier and slid it into his holdall. As he did so, a piece of paper slid out onto the floor. He picked it up, and the blonde terrorist stared back at him.

Cruikshank's eyes narrowed until they were almost hidden behind his bushy brows.

He glared at the photo. "I'm onto you," he muttered. "You may think you're invincible, but I'm after you now. Sooner or later you'll slip up. And then your ass is mine!"

Then he slid the photo into his back pocket, picked up his bag, and turned to leave the room.

Chapter 23

The next day dawned even greyer than the last. After breakfast Richard Major surreptitiously checked the weather radar in the bridge, and was alarmed to discover a tropical storm was poised to sweep across the South Pacific.

Cal was at the helm, but didn't seem too bothered by the dire forecast. "It's ok, Bro," he said. "It'll pass to the north of us. We'll just get a bit of a blow for a day or two."

Richard wasn't altogether convinced though, and as he went back aft he cast a worried look towards the leaden sky, searching unsuccessfully for the sun. Without it the sea was rendered a dull lifeless grey, the colour of weathered asphalt. Whitecaps spread across the dark water as far as he could see, more numerous than galaxies in the night sky.

Richard tried to put his apprehension aside and concentrate on his duties.

Vicki had organised him and the two field assistants to help her with some plankton surveys off the rear deck this morning. He wasn't sure how much of her motivation was purely science-based though, because he couldn't shake the nagging feeling it was just to give them something to do to take their mind off things…

Though the Gwendolyn sailed alone on the storm-roughened sea, it was common but undiscussed knowledge that the Japanese Whaling Fleet was also out here, lurking somewhere just over the dark line of the horizon. And under the gathering thunderclouds, everyone realised the coming storm's fury could be deadly.

Richard lowered his eyes, forcing himself to concentrate on his job.

Much to his consternation he'd been assigned to work with Heath, which did nothing to improve his mood. The Californian was already scowling and muttering under his breath, scratching furiously at his sunburned neck. Despite his background, his pasty skin was evidently no match for the tropical sun. Tiny flakes of dead skin rained down like snow. Richard looked away. He didn't want to get into another conversation with Heath, knowing it would only end in another one-sided bitching session. He kept his eyes down and tried to make himself invisible – anything to avoid becoming embroiled in another conflict with the surly activist. He glanced towards the girls, wishing he was working with them instead. Though the air was cooler today, the wind was cold, so there were no bikinis on show. He might as well have been invisible today though. Neither of the girls paid any attention to him, as though the chill in the air was catching.

Richard tried to concentrate on his job. The plankton trawls were carried out using large conical nets with a small collecting jar mounted onto the bottom. This could be unscrewed to retrieve the seawater it contained, complete with plankton sample. It took careful concentration to get a sample and bring it back aboard without tipping it and upending the collection jar. Vicki wanted samples from different depths as well as different locations, which required some skill to open the net at the right time. If you opened it too early, or closed it too late, the jar might include critters taken from the wrong depth and that would confound the sample.

They worked in relays, two people to a net, lowering it over the side with a gentle splash.

Richard quickly found it was even harder to get a good sample with the ship steaming along at cruising speed, but no one questioned the need to find the migrating Humpbacks as soon as possible, so he made do as best he could.

He smiled to himself, still feeling the warm glow of satisfaction from being able to put his electronics skills to good use for the mission. His mind went back to the previous night when he and Cal had been testing the new system he'd come up with. Richard had set up his new directional antenna array to automatically scan through the frequencies of all remaining VHF-tagged whales, but Cal insisted on manual control whenever he was on the bridge, which was how they'd found themselves together on the bridge under a moonless sky. As Richard obediently stepped through one frequency after another, the lines of data flickered across the screen.

Richard remembered stifling a yawn. It was late, and he was tired. Then suddenly his brother exclaimed, "Wait, go back!"

Richard obliged, raising a questioning eyebrow. Cal was busy concentrating on the computer screen though. "That's Mana's frequency," he murmured to himself, as if thinking hard. "Can you plot the last ten position estimates we've got on him?"

Richard nodded, and a vertical line began to draw itself on the screen, segment by segment, representing the whale's voyage south. As the last section flashed up though, both brothers shot a worried look at each other.

"Is that right?" Cal said.

Richard was confident his program's algorithm was correct, but he hastily double-checked the calculations on a piece of paper. After a moment he nodded, still not sure what to say.

The last vector was nearly sixty degrees out. The whale had veered sharply away from his southerly course, abandoning the migration path.

Cal swore under his breath. "Something's spooked him good," he muttered, but the hard glint in his eye revealed he already knew what. He smacked the table with his closed fist. "Damn it!" Then he turned to Richard. "Set a course to intercept him on the new vector. We need to get there as soon as we can!"

Richard hurriedly fed the coordinates into the Gwendolyn's autopilot, and the deck canted beneath them as she responded.

The Skipper must have sensed the change in the ship's course because he stuck his head up out of the companionway to see what was up. He said nothing as Cal briefed him on the situation, but his scowl deepened until his bushy eyebrows nearly covered his eyes.

Then he had spat over the side and stomped back below to return to his mysterious work in the hold.

That was the previous night, and the Gwendolyn couldn't be more than a few hours away now. Across thousands of miles of ocean they had managed to detect the whale's course change, predict his movements, and were now about to arrive on the scene. Richard smiled to himself, secretly proud of his own efforts, even though the butterflies in his stomach increased with every passing moment.

"What's got you so happy?" the Californian complained petulantly.

Richard suddenly realised he'd been smiling. "I… uh… nothing," he stammered, the smile wiped from his face in an instant.

"You looking forward to some more piracy?" Heath sneered, curling his lip ring in disgust.

Richard lowered his eyes and shook his head. He was telling the truth too. The anticipation was almost as terrifying as the inevitable conflict itself. But being around Heath was enough to dampen his mood as well.

"Violence is wrong, Man," Heath lectured him.

Richard said nothing, trying to will him to shut up and leave him alone.

Heath must have been immune to telepathy though, his voice becoming even more whiny as he continued. "Your brother is crazy. I didn't sign up to fight nobody. Especially not on the orders of some fascist megalomaniac out to satisfy his dirty little private vendetta. What the hell's he trying to do anyway? Start a war with Japan?"

He lowered his voice. "Well I ain't getting involved. I'm not risking my neck for no one. I say we tell him to get bent, him and his tame gorilla."

Richard gasped and snuck a glance at the girls. Despite Heath's conspiratorial whisper, they weren't standing all that far away. They said nothing, but Richard could tell by Vicki's terse frown that she'd overheard. Suddenly he felt his colour rising, and his embarrassment was almost as strong as his shame at being implicated in this smelly hippy's crazy plans for mutiny. Vicki caught his eye, her face unreadable. Richard opened his mouth to try to protest his innocence but his voice wouldn't work.

Heath looked momentarily guilty too, like a stray dog caught raiding a rubbish bin, and he flicked his tongue stud anxiously against his teeth with an annoying click.

Then his bravado seemed to return. He raised his voice, loud enough to include the girls as well. "What the hell, we're all victims here! I say the lot of us should march up to the bridge right now and demand an end to this madness. Tell the both of them we've had enough. Make them turn the ship around right now and take us back to port. We could sit under a palm tree drinking piña coladas. Who's with me?"

There was silence for several long moments as the others stared at him.

"You'd do well to keep your mouth shut and your idiotic ideas to yourself," Vicki said icily, turning her back on him.

Heath's whine became shriller as he sensed failure. "What's with you people? This isn't our problem! We've no business perpetrating acts of violence against anyone."

Richard took a deep breath and challenged him. "What about the whales?" he demanded, pleased his voice sounded more confident than he felt. "Whose problem is that?"

Heath looked incredulous. "Are you all war-mongering fascists? We're not the goddam world police!"

Vicki smiled thinly. "Why don't you think of us as the World's conscience then? We're just going to put right an illegal and immoral wrong being committed in the name of Science."

Heath glared then stomped away, refusing to look at any of them. As he left, he muttered over his shoulder, "Violence is wrong, Man. In the words of the Creator, the most high Rasta-far-i; no act of violence ever goes unpunished."

Vicki watched him go, her expression unreadable. "You two finish up this tow," she said quietly, gesturing to the plankton net still in the water. "Then you can break for lunch. I need a word with Cal."

While Vicki hurried away Summer laughed cattily and gestured towards Heath's retreating back. "Shit, is he psycho or what?"

Richard nodded politely, still struggling with the bulky net on his own. She didn't offer to help.

"Do you think Heath might have a point though?" she was saying.

Richard stopped and turned to stare at her. "What? Mutiny?"

"No, silly. That maybe it's time to go home. After all, we've been out here for ages..." She flashed a disarming smile to reassure him of her motives. "It's been such a long time since I last had a facial, and I can't even remember what a mall looks like!" She pouted theatrically for emphasis. "It's exciting saving the world and everything, but don't you think it would be nice to get back to civilisation soon? I mean, like, we don't want to overdo it out here!"

Richard made a non-committal noise, somewhat concerned by what he was hearing. He felt like he should be defending Cal and his work, but he was mesmerised by her smile, and those full, kissable lips…

Summer grinned as if sharing some private joke with herself, then with the suddenness of a pouncing cat she leant over and kissed him again.

Richard froze, unsure what to do, but terrified of spoiling the moment. She broke off and regarded him thoughtfully, an amused little half-smile tugging the corners of her mouth.

"Want to go somewhere more private?" she purred.

Richard's mouth was so dry he knew he would never get any words out. He nodded from somewhere far away, barely in command of his body. She led the way, hips swaying provocatively through her tight shorts. He gazed after her, the plankton sample forgotten in his hand. Then he stumbled along behind like a dazed sleepwalker, although the blood was pounding in his head.

As they reached the rear companionway he glanced up and saw Vicki watching from the side door of the bridge. Their gaze met for an instant, locking together, and her cobalt blue eyes were earnest but downcast. Richard could almost believe she was trying to tell him something. Then abruptly she hung her head and turned away.

"Come along, sweet thing," Summer called from the bottom of the stairs.

Meekly, he obeyed. She took his arm and led him purposefully toward the cabins. As they walked down the deserted passageway, she leaned closer.

Richard closed his eyes, waiting for the delicious touch of her lips on his own. But it didn't come, and suddenly she was whispering in his ear instead. "What does your brother intend to do if we find the Japanese?"

He shrugged, surprised at the question.

"How far do you think he's prepared to go?" she insisted.

He shrugged again. "How should I know?"

They were outside the door to her cabin now, and she swept it open with a flourish, revealing her neatly-made bunk. Then she turned back and kissed him briefly on the mouth again. Richard felt his breath catch in his chest.

"Perhaps you could find out?" she suggested, then before he even had time to blink, the door closed in his face.

Richard didn't know how long he stood outside her cabin for, but he was thoroughly bewildered by what had happened. She had seemed like she was about to ask him in, so why would she suddenly change her mind?

Did I do something wrong?

He felt dreadfully hurt and confused.

Maybe I should apologise?

He reached out his arm and almost summoned the courage to knock on her door, ready to ask for another chance. Then his hand dropped limply to his side.

Forget it. You're a born loser.

He turned and shuffled slowly away, head bowed like a monk at prayer. He was turning the exchange over and over in his mind, worrying at it like a dog with a slipper. What had happened? She had definitely acted like she was interested in him. She did kiss him after all!

Maybe I was being too forward?

Yes, that must be it. He nodded slowly, already half-believing himself. You couldn't expect a lady to move too quickly, after all. He would just have to be patient. A faint smile touched his face. She would be worth the wait though. Whatever it took, he was determined to win her over…

Suddenly a shrill bell jolted Richard out of his brooding. It took a moment for him to collect his thoughts and work out what was going on. It was the ship's alarm.

"Oh dear," he whispered to himself. "That can't be good."

Then Cal's shout carried down the companionway. "All hands on deck! Prepare for action!"

Richard gulped and forced his feet to respond. He hurried up to the bridge, feeling a sense of foreboding hanging over him like some evil presence, and it grew stronger with every step.

In the wheelhouse Cal and Vicki were standing next to the laptop, their faces grim. Richard saw at a glance that the screen was blank. The VHF transmitter had gone offline, the signal terminated.

Duke was at the helm now, summoned from below by the alarm. He ignored them all, his face contorted into a snarl of hatred as he glared out the windscreen.

Richard followed the direction of his gaze.

There was the Japanese Fleet; the three Hunter-Killer boats crowded together like grey vultures at a corpse. He stared at them, feeling a sudden loathing of his own for the hateful ships – and everything they stood for.

The Shushu-Maru was in the centre, and a host of blue-overalled crew waited impatiently on the deck. There was an air of murderous anticipation about them as they laughed and joked together, their long knives at the ready.

With a heavy heart Richard saw the huge tail flukes sticking up out of the water, the chain already biting cruelly into the whale's skin as his lifeless body was winched aboard the Shushu-Maru.

Cal glassed the scene with binoculars, his face wooden. But Richard heard his small intake of breath and knew he had recognised the whale. With a sense of despair he realised it had to be Mana, the VHF whale they had been following all the way from Tonga – little Ohana's father. He was dead now, or dying; his insides blasted away by a Japanese harpoon. He would never again sing his beautiful song, sire any baby whales, nor return to the underwater canyons of New Zealand's Kaikoura coast. He had swum the World's oceans, but now his long journey was over.

Richard closed his eyes in a silent goodbye, hoping that the Great Whale was now reunited with his family in a better place.

"We're too late," he whispered, a great sadness weighing on him.

"The hell we are!" Cal lowered the binoculars, his jaw set.

Richard blinked with apprehension. He knew that look.

"Stand by to lower the Naiad," Cal ordered, turning to leave the bridge. "Vicki, Richard, you're with me. The rest of you get on the crane."

Richard felt his stomach plunge towards the pitching floor. It was to be the little inflatable versus the deadly Hunter-Killer ships again.

Oh hell. This is it!

The promise of conflict hung in the air like electricity around a lightning storm. This was the showdown he had been dreading. Richard's legs felt as though they would hardly hold him up.

Suddenly he became aware of the defiance in the room. Heath was standing by the door, and he hadn't moved yet.

"Problem?" Cal enquired.

The Californian clicked his tongue stud against his teeth. "I'm not doing it," he announced.

Cal's regarded him carefully. "I'm not asking you to do anything scary. Just lower the boat for us – like you were hired to do."

Heath snorted. "Doubtful! I was hired to help with research, not terrorism. I'm not doing it!" he insisted. Then he turned on his heel and stalked away.

Cal turned to Summer, also standing by the door, hands folded defiantly across her chest. "And you're siding with him?" The accusation hung bitterly in the air.

She avoided his eye. "No. It's just… I don't want to get involved. It's illegal, you know, and people could get hurt. I can't be part of that."

Cal's eyes blazed furiously, but he held his temper. "Fine, wait below. I'll deal with you two when this is over." He turned to the Skipper. "Come about, I'll man the crane myself."

The Gwendolyn didn't slow though, continuing to shoulder her way through the swells.

"Skip, we'll need to come about to lower the boat," Cal said again.

The Skipper turned slowly to face them, then shook his head. "Nope. Can't let y' do that, Son."

Richard gaped at him, and even Cal was taken aback. "What's going on, Skip?" he said slowly, the wariness evident in his measured tone. "Are you against me too?"

The Skipper turned back to stare out the windscreen, as though his concentration was elsewhere.

Richard felt his unease growing.

What the hell is going on here?

He was glad Heath was out of the room, but suddenly the thought rang ominously. What was the treacherous hippy up to? Had he somehow managed to persuade the Skipper over to his side?

Richard felt cold fingers of dread slide down his back.

Is this a mutiny?

The Skipper held up a callused hand. "I can't let y'all go out there in that little boat. That murdering Jap bastard'd have y' innards this time, for sure."

Cal somehow managed to look relieved and frustrated at the same time. He opened his mouth to argue, but Duke cut him off, his voice gruff with authority. "It ain't worth the risk to my crew. Besides, what would you hope t' do?" He shook his head angrily, gesturing at the dead whale. "It's done with already. Ah'm sorry Son, but we're too dang late."

"It's never too late," Cal muttered angrily, but Richard could see he was wavering.

"It's never too late t' even the score," Duke corrected him. "And that's what I intend t' do now."

Cal watched him thoughtfully. "Skip, what were you doing down below these past few days?"

Duke turned to grin at him, and his glittering grey eyes and wild beard gave him the air of a battle-hungry pirate. "Fillin' the bow with concrete," he answered matter-of-factly.

Then with a smirk he reached forward to open the throttles right up. "It's long past time to open a can o'whoop ass!"

The Gwendolyn surged forward in response, and Richard was forced to grab for the ceiling rail to steady himself. His terror was equalled only by his excitement.

At full power, the Gwendolyn swept down on the stationary whalers like a diving bird of prey. The Japanese ships were huddled furtively together while they carried out their grisly and iniquitous work, and the Gwendolyn's dark bow was almost upon them before a crewman finally noticed and screamed an urgent warning.

"Brace!" the Skipper warned. Then he threw back his head and laughed. "See you bastards in hell!"

The whalers looked up, startled, caught in the act of hauling Mana's bleeding carcass aboard.

The two ships collided with a grinding crash and an impact that flung Richard to the floor, along with everything on the chart table. From the deck below he heard an avalanche of pots and pans in the galley, but it was almost drowned out by the terrible screech of tearing metal that filled the air around him.

The ship finally came to a halt and he sat up, dazed. The silence was ominous, like the aftermath of a tornado, and he carefully extracted himself from the pile of charts and debris on the floor. His eyes widened as he saw the dent on the bulkhead where it had been hit by a flying paperweight – only inches away from his head.

He stood up slowly, checking his limbs to make sure everything still worked. Around him he could hear groans and muttered curses as the others did likewise.

Incredibly, the Skipper was still standing at the wheel, hands gripping it as though sculpted from marble. He snorted like an angry bison. "Take that y' blood-thirsty bastards," he muttered, reaching forward to throw the engines into reverse.

With a scream of tortured metal, the two ships parted again, revealing the full extent of the damage.

Incredibly, the Gwendolyn's stout hull panels were all in place, although she was missing plenty of her handsome blue paint and there was a long tear high up on her bow.

The Shushu-Maru had not fared so well though. The reinforced concrete ram in the Gwendolyn's bow had plunged deep into the weaker panels of its side, crushing them like an aluminium can. Richard's eyes widened in horror as he stared at the gaping hole in the grey hull. The steel plates had been torn open as though made of tinfoil, and the deadly sea already boiled and foamed in the breach. The grey ship settled in the water then listed on its side, mortally wounded, the dead-weight of the attached whale now acting as a giant anchor to pull it over. The deck canted steeply and yellow helmets scrambled to and fro like headless chickens, but the ship was doomed. It tipped further over, tossing several blue-overalled bodies into the water. The deck was already too steep to walk on, the ship beyond saving as Mana's posthumous revenge dragged it down in a final act of irony.

"That's for the Sea," Duke growled under his breath. "You bastards can take those imperial ambitions back to y' own empty waters."

Richard watched, mesmerised as more blue-overalled whalers jumped over the side, throwing themselves at the mercy of the ocean.

The grey ship settled lower, claimed by the hungry waves.

The Skipper swore suddenly, breaking the spell at last. Richard glanced up and his bowels were instantly turned to ice as he saw the towering prow of the Kuu-Maru slicing towards them.

The Skipper spun the wheel away and the Gwendolyn's engines throbbed as he opened up the throttles. She picked up speed, gamely avoiding the charging grey ship.

Richard exhaled with relief, but at that moment the Tosho-Maru accelerated forward in front of them, aiming to block their escape. From astern, the Kuu-Maru lunged at them again, and again the Skipper turned away, denying Gyofuku their vulnerable broadside.

Vicki frowned. "We have to get out of here! We can't outmanoeuvre two ships at once. They'll trap us!"

The Skipper shook his head. "It's a bluff. They won't leave their shipmates to drown."

But despite his efforts to get away from the scene of the sinking Shushu-Maru, the remaining two Hunter-Killers continued to harry the Gwendolyn. They closed in remorselessly, heedless of their crewmates floundering in the water behind them.

With every turn, the Tosho-Maru manoeuvred in front, still blocking their path, and the Kuu-Maru circled behind like a hungry shark waiting for the chance to charge at them.

Richard watched the grey ships anxiously, hating the sight of them. He looked back, mesmerised, picking out Captain Gyofuku's snarling face on the bridge. With a trace of fear he noticed the white-helmeted gunner standing behind his harpoon cannon, high on the Kuu-Maru's prow.

The Skipper looked grim but his attention was focused on the Tosho-Maru ahead. He feinted to port, then spun the wheel hard to starboard, aiming to get past the grey ship before the Kuu-Maru hit them from behind.

They almost made it past, but the Tosho-Maru responded quickly and seconds later the sleek grey hull slid back across their path again.

"Hit him," Cal muttered. "It's our only chance to get clear."

Richard glanced behind. The Kuu-Maru was close behind them. Very close. If they rammed the Tosho-Maru broadside they'd be stopped dead in their tracks, and that would be all the delay Gyofuku needed to catch them.

The Tosho-Maru was blocking their path in a lethal game of chicken. Richard held his breath as they bore down on it.

Grimly, the Skipper held his line. At the last moment the Hunter-Killer swerved away, the Tosho-Maru's captain apparently changing his mind, unwilling to sacrifice his ship. It was still in their path but offering only its narrow stern as a target now as its captain desperately tried to get his ship clear of the Gwendolyn's reinforced bow.

"Damn it. Can't get a clear shot at the side," the Skipper muttered.

"Hit the bugger anyway!" Cal shouted. "Go for the stern! Try to put the keel bulb into their rudder!"

The Skipper patted the wheel gently. "Here we go Old Gal, you can do it!"

Richard flinched as the collision reverberated through the hull, ringing in his ears like a giant cymbal. The Gwendolyn struck a glancing blow on the Tosho-Maru's stern, driving low and hard like a rugby forward. The grey ship spun sideways as the Gwendolyn crashed against it, her improvised battering ram stoving in the stern beneath it. Then with a grinding screech of metal they were shouldering past.

Cal glanced back, lines of worry creasing his forehead. Richard looked too. The Kuu-Maru's blade-like prow was still questing for them, barely a boat-length away.

Richard swallowed nervously. The bow of the Hunter-Killer was ice-strengthened and reinforced to handle the recoil of the heavy cannon mounted atop it, and the thick steel plates came to a knife-edge that promised to split them like a log of wood if it hit. The dull grey paintwork glistened with sea spray as the ship thundered towards them.

"We're not out of the woods yet," Cal murmured. "Give it full power Skip. We've got to get clear."

***

Hogei Gyofuku gripped the wheel as the Kuu-Maru crashed over another wave. His rage was as tempestuous as the hurricane building to the North, and it spurred him on. Not only had those accursed Western protestors dared to interfere with his hunt again, but this time they had actually sunk one of his ships! Before his stunned gaze they had deliberately rammed the Shushu-Maru, and now it was sinking!

He could feel the vein pulsing in his neck, writhing beneath the rolls of fat like an enraged slug. Blind rage was the overriding motivation driving him now. Revenge was obligatory, both for his own honour and that of his master!

Gyofuku gulped instinctively. Amimoto-san would not be pleased. Not at all.

He glared out the window, his gaze fixed on the fleeing blue ship ahead. He ignored the Shushu-Maru's crew, floundering in the water behind. After all, they deserved their fate. It served them right for being so stupid! In fact, when this was all over he might well send a few of his own crew overboard to join them – his radar operator first of all!

How the hell had the filthy barbarians managed to get so close before anyone noticed?

Incompetence!

It was the only explanation. And Gyofuku refused to tolerate such ineptitude aboard his ship.

First things first though, he promised himself. *I will not be denied my revenge!*

His almond eyes pinched together as he glared out of the windscreen. He was gaining on the hippy scum, but not fast enough for his liking, and definitely not fast enough to inflict enough damage when he hit them. He intended to cut them clean in half with his two-storey-high reinforced bow, just like a giant meat cleaver! But for that to happen he needed them slowed down a little first.

His eye fell on the Tosho-Maru, still steaming ahead of the fleeing trawler, and a cold smile spread across his face. It was time for the junior captain to prove his worth at last!

Tosho-Maru!" he barked into the radio. "Can you hear me?"

"Hai!" came the reply.

"Captain, I order you to block that ship. Do not allow the terrorists to get away!"

The junior captain's voice came back, sounding shaky with fear. "But Captain Gyofuku-san, if we slow they will hit us also!"

Gyofuku slammed his meaty fist against the bulkhead in frustration. "I want those criminals apprehended!" he shouted. "You are ordered to block that ship at all costs! Do I make myself clear?"

He threw the handpiece aside without waiting for a reply, and turned forward to stare hungrily out the windscreen.

The Kuu-Maru charged forward at his bidding, lunging for the Blue Ship's unprotected stern, while ahead, the Tosho-Maru attempted to block the hippies' escape.

Gyofuku enjoyed the spectacle as his prey fled before him, just like a doomed whale. The trawler turned first one way, then the other, trying to deceive him, seeking a way out of the trap. Each time he was pleased to see the Tosho-Maru respond quickly, blocking the way while keeping its vulnerable broadside away from danger. The Kuu-Maru bore down remorselessly. Revenge was imminent, and it would be sweet!

"I have you now," Gyofuku gloated as the collision loomed.

Then incredibly, the Tosho-Maru turned away, trying to flee. In one swift movement the Blue Ship crashed into the catcher's stern and managed to barge its way past without slowing. Gyofuku stared in disbelief as it burst through his trap and accelerated away, out of reach.

He stared after it impotently for several long moments, his jaw slack with disbelief. Then his rage returned, even hotter than before.

These filthy terrorists will not make a fool out of me! I will not be denied my revenge!

He jammed the throttles right forward into the red line, and the Kuu-Maru's twin screws bit into the ocean. Gyofuku's eyes glowed with malice as he glared at his prey. "Gunner, load a harpoon!"

The gunner bowed and hastened to obey. Gyofuku saw with annoyance that he selected one of the barbed lances for securing a whale to the boat.

"Iye! Not that one!" he exclaimed. "Load an explosive head – and remove the cable. I want this one to fly like an angel!"

The gunner swallowed nervously but did as he was ordered.

Just then the High Frequency radio crackled in the Kuu-Maru's bridge. Gyofuku snorted with irritation, but ignored it – he had no time to listen to whichever of his useless captains was snivelling now.

Then the radio burst into life. The transmission was distorted by static and atmospheric disturbance after travelling across thousands of miles of ocean, but the voice was unmistakable, and the fury in it quenched Gyofuku's ardour like a bucket of ice water.

"Gyofuku! Where the hell are you?"

Gyofuku bowed low, forgetting he could not be seen. "Y-yes master?" he managed to reply.

Amimoto cut him off brusquely. "I have just been informed that the Shushu-Maru's distress beacon has been activated. What in the name of the Kami is going on out there?"

Gyofuku's voice bleated with obsequiousness. "So sorry master, it is just a minor setback. I am about to deal with the aggressors now. The Western scum will pay dearly for their crimes."

"No!" Amimoto snapped. "Your primary responsibility is the safety of the Fleet. Cease this nonsense at once!"

"But master, they are within my grasp-"

"I said no! You will not lose any more of my ships!" Amimoto thundered. "Take whatever is left of the Fleet and make for the nearest port for repairs, at once! If you risk any more of my ships I will personally cut off your testicles and watch you eat them!" Then his voice lowered to a cruel hiss. "Do not trouble yourself with the filthy gai-jin. I have my own plans for them. They will be dealt with in good time."

The radio fell silent and Gyofuku glowered at it, sulking with the indignant outrage of a whipped schoolboy. He knew better than to defy Amimoto though.

Reluctantly he reached forward and eased the throttles back. The Kuu-Maru slowed to an idle, and it took all of his self-control to watch the hippies sail away.

I could have caught them! I could have run them down like the cowardly dogs they are!

His pudgy hand went unbidden to the skinning knife sheathed at his belt, and he toyed absently with the handle.

This is not over. They have not bested me, I swear it!

His hand still trembled with anger as he reached for the radio. "Tosho-Maru. I order you to return to the Shushu-Maru and rescue all survivors, then come to my position at top speed."

"So sorry Captain Gyofuku-san, they have damaged one of our propellers. We can travel at half-speed only."

Gyofuku cursed and slammed his fist against the bulkhead.

A sudden flash of lightning split the darkening sky, and then the heavens opened. He stared out through the rain-lashed windscreen as the storm enveloped his ship. The distant Blue trawler was only just visible now past the silhouette of the harpoon cannon.

Gyofuku snarled with frustration as he watched them slip out of his grasp.

With an effort he managed to control his rage. "I will have my revenge," he muttered, shaking his fist at the sky. "Rest assured, you foreign devils, our paths will cross again. You are a long way from safety yet." His gaze settled on the harpoon cannon and he bared his teeth in a mirthless smile. "And when we meet again, this little surprise will be waiting for you!"

Gyofuku's smile hardened as a plan took shape in his mind. Amimoto had ordered the Fleet to port for repairs, but he hadn't specified which port!

Triumphantly, he turned to bark an order at his First Mate. "Set a course for New Zealand!"

***

Richard hung on to a bulkhead as the Gwendolyn pitched and rolled. She was battling at full speed through steadily rising seas, and he could feel her struggling. The waves rolled in from behind them, at times threatening to break over the stern. The weather radar had confirmed the storm's shift. It was now heading due south – directly towards them. Richard stared aft, but he ignored the menacing dark clouds. All his attention was riveted on the grey shadow lurking below them.

The Kuu-Maru had been pursuing them since the collision. It had fallen back somewhat, but was still following slowly, tracking them like a bloodhound. Its hull was long and narrow, and it sliced through the waves like a spear pointed unerringly at them.

Richard scarcely dared to breathe, and the tension in the bridge was palpable. The Skipper alone was his usual unruffled self. He reached for his tobacco tin and crammed a wad of the dark leaf behind his bottom lip.

"Not to worry. This old gal's got a few surprises in her."

He grasped the throttles with a weather-beaten hand and opened them wider, pushing the engine revs past the red line. The Gwendolyn's diesels roared in response, and she forged ahead gamely.

Gradually they began to pull away, and the Kuu-Maru slipped back beyond the line of the wake. Time dragged by, but Richard didn't let himself relax, knowing they weren't out of danger yet. With Gyofuku still behind them they wouldn't be safe until they stepped ashore on New Zealand soil again. They would never escape with their lives if he caught them after this insult to his honour – the psychotic whaleboat captain had already tried to kill them for less.

Richard shivered, suddenly noticing the chill in the air.

Then, as if to answer his dire predictions, a red light suddenly glowed on the dash.

"What's that?" Richard pointed, aware how shrill his voice sounded.

The Skipper's frown told him all he needed to know. "Water in thuh bilge," he muttered as he reached across to flick on all the pump switches. "Must've forced a weld back there."

Richard held his breath, waiting for the pumps to work their magic, but the light stubbornly refused to go out.

"Goddamn it all to hell," the Skipper cursed. "Cal, you and y' Bro git below and see to that, will ya!"

Richard was stunned. "Y-you mean we've got a leak?" he stammered, visions of the drowning Shushu-Maru already permanently etched into his memory, the dark water boiling malevolently up through the rents in her hull.

"Yup," the Skipper answered laconically. "Best not to dally in case it floods thuh pumps."

Richard closed his eyes, and suddenly he was in the White Ship's engineroom again, rooted to the spot in terror, watching the water gush from the broken pipe and flood the room. Despite what people said, he knew drowning would be far from peaceful. It would be a cold, lonely, and terrifying way to go, floundering helpless and panic-stricken as the water rose up to claim the last precious pockets of air – and last of all would be the air from your own lungs…

What if we're sinking too? I don't want to die like that! Oh god, I don't want to drown!

"Richard! Are you ok?"

Cal's voice broke through his thoughts. Richard blinked, looking around. The only other ships out here were hostile. The Tosho-Maru had abandoned the chase after they hit it. It had limped back to the Shushu-Maru and had just been visible in the distance, rescuing the crew of its stricken sister ship. But Richard knew there would be no one to help the Gwendolyn. If they sank they would go down with all hands. He felt his panic rising, flooding him like a deluge.

"I-I don't think I can do it, Cal," he croaked. Then his legs gave way and he sat down heavily.

"I'll go," Vicki said.

She glanced at Richard, her lips pursed contemplatively. Then she and Cal headed below.

Richard watched them leave, trying not to think about the danger that awaited them in the bowels of the ship. Suddenly he felt queasy. The waves had been steadily growing all day and finally the motion made his stomach turn over. He lunged for the side door of the wheelhouse and staggered down the outside ladder to the deck, barely making it to the rail in time. As he hung there retching over the side, he heard a familiar whiny voice behind him.

"Hey, I don't blame you for chickening out, Man," Heath said. "Let the fascist bastard do his own dirty work!"

Richard said nothing.

He leaned over the side and retched again, suddenly afraid. He was ashamed of his own cowardice, and desperately anxious for Cal and Vicki, knowing that if anything happened down there in the flooded hold he would never be able to live with his guilt.

With an effort he lifted his head to look back the way they had come. The sky was dark and foreboding as the tropical storm bore down out of the North. Towards the horizon he could just make out the dirty grey smudge of the Kuu-Maru, almost hidden by the huge slate-grey breakers, but still unmistakably stalking them.

He shivered. Gyofuku's cold-blooded determination was chilling. They were a long way from home, and it would be dangerous to get caught in rough weather with a leaking hull – let alone if the grey Hunter-Killer ship was to catch them. He shuddered to think what might happen out here in the middle of nowhere, with no one to help them, nor even any witnesses…

Richard silently hoped the Skipper's seamanship was up to the task.

***

Akogi Yokuke sat in his expansive Tokyo office, but even these extravagant surroundings did nothing to improve his mood. He stared into space, not even seeing the elaborately-carved antiques that lined the walls, treasures that had taken him a lifetime to accumulate. Priceless artefacts alone could not restore a man's slighted honour.

His gaze settled on the display case containing a battered leather flying helmet and a yellowing Japanese flag of the old style. The rays of the Rising Sun were inked with many tiny characters – messages of love and support from a proud family. The items had once belonged to his father, just a humble clerk before the war, but honoured forever afterwards as a hero. Before his last flight he had given his helmet and flag to his young son to remember him by, and then had given his life in glorious service to Japan. In the spirit of Kamikaze – the divine wind that destroyed the ships of Khan's invading Mongol Hordes – he had crashed his Zero in flames onto the deck of the American carrier Yorktown during the Battle of Midway Island. Yokuke nodded thoughtfully, old enough now to appreciate the beauty of his father's sacrifice.

He opened the case and took out his father's silver hip flask, inscribed with the characters representing luck and fortune, and still containing the sake from his last toast to the Kami, the protective gods who would watch over his family in his absence. Yokuke lifted the stopper and savoured the aroma of the sixty-five-year-old liquor. He felt no sadness at the loss of his father, only bitterness that his sacrifice had been in vain.

"You fought for the glory of Japan and our emperor, yet still we find ourselves under the heel of the West," he whispered, clutching the flask in his clawed hand.

Yokuke felt nothing but disgust as he contemplated the world today. Japan had regained her deserved greatness among the world's economies, but it was a hollow victory devoid of real power. It had been many long years since his nation dared to defy the West, and few of his countrymen still felt the pride of nationalism. Yokuke's lip curled, disgusted at their duplicity.

"History has shown us it can be done," he whispered. "The celebrated attack on Pearl Harbour proved without doubt that Japan could be master of her own destiny... and still can."

Yokuke's face hardened as his thoughts came back to the present and his fury returned as fresh as ever. It was an absolute outrage that these Western terrorists could dare to damage his assets, and their naked aggression was an affront to his honour. Their continued attacks against his Fleet represented a grave business threat, but more than that, they made his blood boil!

With an effort, he controlled his emotions, slipping into the detached machination with which he analysed all his business crises. It was clear from such reckless acts that his enemy was becoming increasingly desperate, and the thought gave him a brief flash of satisfaction in the midst of his anger.

Do you feel the hook in your mouth yet Kajiki? Because I am slowly but surely reeling you in!

He cackled to himself, gloating over his imminent success. Everything was falling into place at long last. His bold plan had paid off. The IWC was now under his direct control, and he would ensure it once again honoured its true purpose – to facilitate the orderly development of the whaling industry – as had been agreed by the original signatories nearly half a century ago. He allowed himself a smile. The Moratorium on Whaling was about to be consigned to history. The detestable environmentalists' stranglehold over the IWC was over, and their selfish and self-serving policies of the previous few decades were finally about to be dismantled.

Yokuke poured himself a celebratory drink from his father's silver flask. "A man's honour is a reflection of his achievements," he said, raising his glass in a toast to his own success. His father may have failed to win his war, but being the better man, Yokuke would not. "The skill of a master kuromaku is the ultimate embodiment of harmony between the two-fold ways of the pen and sword."

He would restore Japan's honour. His Fleet's activities in the Southern Ocean were now legitimised, and with a return to full-scale commercial whaling his already-vast fortune was set to skyrocket, along with his political power. Those who opposed him in the Diet's halls of power would soon be humbled. In fact, little remained for him to do except to mop up the last of the resistance.

He clapped his hands, beckoning for his private secretary to approach.

"Call the Minister of Defence. Tell him I want a Naval force prepared for immediate departure, to include as many destroyers as possible."

The secretary's eyes widened. "So sorry, my lord. This is to be a combat mission? The Armed Forces' charter expressly forbids offensive operations."

Yokuke frowned with annoyance. The man was clearly suffering from shock to speak out of turn like that. Given his long and exemplary service he chose to ignore the indiscretion though – this time.

"I have a damaged vessel – the victim of a terrorist act – and it must be escorted safely to port. If the aggressors are still around and foolish enough to attempt to intervene, well, that will be their bad karma, neh?"

Yokuke smiled coldly and continued without waiting for an answer. "Send a message to our American allies too. Inform them that I am declaring this terrorist threat a danger to Japan's national security. Under terms of the Joint Self-Defence Treaty I formally request an American commando unit assist our navy to arrest these criminals." His smile turned cruel. "I've heard the US Navy SEALs have a reputation for efficiency."

Yokuke paused thoughtfully. "The Fleet is heading to New Zealand for repairs. The government there must publicly condemn this act of piracy at once, and surrender these criminals to us the minute they enter their jurisdiction."

His secretary coughed politely behind his hand.

Yokuke cocked his head like a fighting rooster, fixing an unblinking eye on the man. "Yes? You have something to say?" he snapped.

His secretary bowed deeply. "Please excuse me, my lord, but the New Zealanders are a proud people. They have a reputation for standing their ground in the face of extreme diplomatic pressure. At the height of the Cold War they banned the ships of America and Britain – their allies – from entering their waters because the superpowers refused to accommodate their country's new anti-nuclear stance."

Yokuke's lip curled at the thought of a government displaying such a naïve and immature attitude, but he waved a dismissive hand. "If they refuse, you are authorised to use whatever threats and sanctions are necessary to change their minds. Cut all trade if needed. We'll see how proud they can remain whilst living in the Stone Age, neh?"

He turned away. "That will be all."

The secretary hesitated for a fraction of a second. Then he bowed deeply and backed out of the room, hurrying to do his bidding.

Out of the corner of his eye Yokuke watched him go, annoyed by the open display of impertinence. Then he bared his yellowing teeth as his mind snapped back to the most pressing problem at hand; the problem of the Kajiki. He had already made plans to deal with him, and they were good, but there was no harm in making sure.

A wise man leaves nothing to chance, neh?

He picked up the phone and dialled a long-distance number known to him alone. "Kobushi-san, I have an urgent job for you to do in New Zealand."

Chapter 24

Dennis Cruikshank sat in his rental car, shifting uncomfortably in the seat. He had taken a big Holden, the largest car they had available, but it still felt confining compared to his trusty old Chevy pickup back home – although he had to admit it was a huge advance over the claustrophobic little toy he'd put up with in Japan.

He picked at the upholstery with frustration. Crossing the Equator to get here meant he'd gone from early winter back to summer again, and he was having trouble adjusting. It was a hot day out, but with the engine off he had to rely on the open window rather than the air conditioning, and his legs were already sticking uncomfortably to the fake leather seats.

He sighed and looked again at the newspaper spread across the steering wheel.

"Conflict on the High Seas!" the headlines screamed, and that alone told him most everything he needed to know. He tugged his moustache aggressively as he skimmed the article.

Another whaling ship sunk!

This time the conflict had happened at sea. The reporter had not been exaggerating. And nor had he. These punks were trouble, and the sooner his idiot superiors running this investigation wised up the better!

He was furious that he hadn't been able to do anything to stop crime, and more to the point, that his supervisor overruled his request for direct action.

Cruikshank rubbed his head absently, as if perfecting the shine on a bowling ball, but on the inside he was seething.

What pissed him off most of all was Silverman's goddamn cautiousness. The old fool was so concerned with doing everything by the book and covering his own ass no matter what, that he'd damn near let the punks get away with murder!

"You should have stayed in retirement, Pops," Cruikshank muttered angrily. "You're a washed-up old dinosaur."

It was infuriating to see an opportunity wasted, and he was even more disgusted that these long-haired, unwashed scum were still walking around free.

They might have gotten the best of him once, but they wouldn't again. He would damn well make sure of that!

Cruikshank shook his head, annoyed as much by the knowledge that he still didn't know what was going on with this case. He was unable to contact the undercover agent directly, and his superiors were dithering as usual. He snorted with disgust.

Spooks are like goddamn politicians: they're a bunch of old women when decisive action is required!

He did know that the criminals had already returned to their home port the previous morning, followed half a day later by a storm-damaged Japanese whaling ship. According to the harbourmaster the remaining catcher boat was due to arrive in the next day or two – sporting evidence of a collision at sea – and escorted by the Japanese Navy.

He grunted.

That should ruffle a few feathers!

Cruikshank folded the newspaper and reached for his binoculars.

New Zealand was definitely at ground zero for whatever confrontation might happen next.

He propped his binoculars on the steering wheel, frowning absently. Despite coming straight from Japan, he still wasn't used to the driver's seat being on the wrong side of the car. To add insult to injury, the fancy digital thermometer on the dash read 32 degrees outside. The beads of sweat running off his bald head told him that had to be metric – like the damned speedometer – since it felt damn near a hundred to him!

The browned grass and hot dry breeze blowing in the open window reminded him of LA's Santa Ana wind – always guaranteed to turn the crazies crazier and send the murder rate spiralling! – Although the imposing line of snowy mountain peaks to the West looked more like they belonged in the lawless wilds of Alaska…

From his vantage point high on the Port Hills' Summit Road, Cruikshank could see the whole of Christchurch's Lyttleton harbour stretched out below him like a postcard. He wasn't interested in the view though, and as he glassed the area past the fuel tanks and container yards of the port, the wharves slid into sight, jutting into the sparkling turquoise waters of the bay like dark fingers.

He smiled to himself as a familiar blue trawler jumped into focus, tied up alongside the pier. "Aha! Got you, you bastards! Let's see you get away from me this time!"

***

Richard carried his morning cup of coffee from the galley, hurrying up the stairs to join the voices he could hear in the wheelhouse.

He was happy. Vicki and Duke had just re-provisioned the stores, which meant the coffee was real. And as he took the steps two at a time, Richard marvelled at how placid the ship's motion was compared to the wild rollercoaster ride of the previous day. Despite its name, the Pacific Ocean could be anything but, and running before the tropical storm yesterday the Gwendolyn had been tossed around like a cork.

As he stepped into the sunlight streaming through the big front windscreen, Richard said another silent thank you to the valiant little ship, and the skill of her grizzled Skipper who had brought them safely to port away from the clutches of the storm.

"Morning," Vicki greeted him.

Richard smiled a response as he looked out over the sparkling waters of Lyttleton Harbour, fascinated by the deep green colour of the water. It looked like milky Pounamu – the precious jade that came from the West Coast – and the water was never that colour up north…

Richard sipped his coffee thoughtfully. He had always liked the South Island. The sight of its tall mountains and rugged landscapes brought back happy memories of childhood camping holidays, and promised far more freedom and adventure than he would ever know at his desk in the heart of the city.

Instinctively, he turned to look for the Southern Alps, but they were hidden by the steep ring of hills surrounding Lyttleton – the crater rim of a massive ancient volcano.

White weatherboard houses clung to the hillside behind him, shimmering in the heat of the summer sun overhead. Below them, Richard could just make out the black mouth of the road tunnel emerging at the base of the Port Hills, linking the harbour with the city of Christchurch. The historic timeball was visible atop the harbourmaster's building, and a blue ensign fluttered from the flagpole next to it – the Union Jack in the corner contrasting with the four bright red stars of the Southern Cross.

It was good to be back in New Zealand.

Cal walked in, shirtless, towelling his wet hair. Richard was relieved to see he hadn't overslept much longer than his brother.

"How's it look?" the Skipper asked.

"Hull plates look fine," Cal answered. "You're right, it must be just a stretched seam."

With a guilty start, Richard realised his brother hadn't just gotten out of the shower but had actually been up at first light diving below the ship to inspect the collision damage.

The Skipper dropped a newspaper on the chart table in front of Cal. "Picked this up for ya. Goddamn media's been having a field day with thuh whole business," he muttered.

Cal frowned as he picked up the paper, and his expression darkened even more as he skimmed the article. "The Japanese Government is already jumping up and down shouting about piracy and terrorism at sea," he explained to Richard. "They've lodged an official protest with the New Zealand Government demanding they hand us over to face trial in Japan." He laughed. "Sounds like Amimoto has been throwing his weight around alright."

The Skipper spat a wad of tobacco juice into his tin. "If y' ask me those dirty bastards deserved what they got," he growled. "Considerin' the number of times that fat captain has tried to run y'all down he's lucky I didn't decide to harpoon his ass fer good measure!"

Cal's frown remained. "All the same, I think it would be best if we kept a low profile while we're in port. How soon can we sail again, Skip?"

"Hmm. Gotta double check those hull welds… but I'd say a day. Two at most."

Cal nodded. "Okay, in the meantime everyone is to stay aboard ship. No one goes ashore without my say-so – it's too risky."

"Whatever! That's a load of crypto-fascist bullshit, man!"

Richard looked around to see Heath standing in the doorway.

"You can't order us around," he whined. "In case you hadn't noticed, this is a free country!"

Cal didn't turn. "We can't afford to have any trouble with the authorities while we're here… or the media. Just stay in your cabin and keep out of trouble eh?"

"No way, man. This is your trouble, not mine. You can't keep me here against my will, that's kidnapping! I'm going ashore, and you can't stop me!"

Richard couldn't see Cal's face, but he saw his jaw muscles clench below his ear.

"I'm giving you an order," Cal said through gritted teeth. "Stay aboard the ship. If you're not going to obey it then don't bother coming back."

"This is bullshit! Are the rest of you gonna put up with this crap?" Heath flicked his tongue stud nervously against his teeth. He looked around for support, but there was none. Richard studied the floor, careful not to catch his eye.

"Screw you, Man. Screw the lot of you!" Heath's voice became shriller and he backed towards the door. "I'm going. And if anyone asks I'm gonna tell them everything… how you kept us here against our will, how you forced us to take part in this madness, how you deliberately planned to attack those ships, everything!"

The Skipper moved to intercept him, but Cal put up an arm. "Nah, let him go," he murmured.

Duke snorted. "The little punk is more trouble than a rattler in the britches. We can't let him squeal – he'll cause us no end of strife."

"He'll do worse if we try to keep him here," Cal said under his breath. "It's probably for the best if we part ways now."

Duke's fists clenched and unclenched. "At least let me knock some sense into his head!" he growled, loud enough for all to hear.

Cal shook his head, but Richard could tell by his brother's faint smile that he was at least partially taken with the idea.

Heath fled.

Cal ignored him and walked over to turn on the transistor radio.

Richard let out a sigh of relief, suddenly aware he'd been holding his breath. The confrontation between his brother and Heath had been a long time coming though, and he'd fully expected a violent showdown. But Cal was remarkably restrained, even though Heath's departure would cause a lot of problems aboard ship – and potentially even more when he got ashore! Richard couldn't help wondering how far the outspoken activist might take his threats, and if the inevitable had only been postponed.

The chatter of the radio broke through his thoughts. It was tuned to a talkback radio station, and the DJ was already worked up.

"...What do you think about the Japanese killing whales? And what do you think about them doing it here, in our backyard – bringing warships with them for protection, no less? Is it breathtaking arrogance, or just a lot of fuss over nothing?"

The announcer paused for breath, and Richard could almost see the cheesy smirk on his face. Controversy was a goldmine for talkback shows.

"And what do you think of the people trying to stop them?" the host continued. "Are they dedicated heroes? Or are they dangerous radicals damaging our country's reputation and risking World War III? You decide! And be sure to call us up to have your say on air!"

Cal looked furious, but he reached over to turn the volume up.

"Here's our next caller. Hello, you're on the air!"

"Yeah gidday. About this whaling business, I'm in favour of it!"

The host chuckled. "Oh? Why's that?" he said, deliberately leading the caller on.

"Yeah, well this whole thing sounds like a bloody conspiracy to me!"

"Do tell me about it," the host invited, prompting shamelessly.

"Well, there's this bunch of Greenies trying to tell us them whales are endangered and all that, but there's actually tons of 'em. Every summer there's hundreds of the buggers washed up on the beaches, suiciding themselves!"

"I see," said the host. He sounded amused, as though he could already see his ratings climbing.

"And what's more, if whales are really as smart as them bunny-huggers reckon, then why don't they just swim away from the Jappers' boats eh?"

There was a moment's stunned silence as everyone – the host included – digested what the guy had said.

"Idiot!" Vicki was first to react. She flicked her ponytail with annoyance. "What a fine bunch of intellectuals your fellow countrymen are!" she sniffed.

Cal rolled his eyes, managing to look sheepish and annoyed at the same time. "There's lots of farmers and fishermen around, you can't expect them to understand. Whales are all the same to them. Ignorance is the natural state until you are shown or taught otherwise." He gave a helpless shrug. "It's just like the fishermen wanting to cull fur seals; it's only those people involved in the tourism industry – the ones whose livelihoods are directly tied into marine mammal tourism – whose eyes are open to the issue. The rest just base their response on bigoted hearsay they get down at the pub, or jump to conclusions without any grasp of the facts."

He gestured at the radio. "This idiot's a perfect example! Proper scientific research is crucial to understanding what's really going on. For starters, it's pilot whales that usually strand, and they're actually more closely-related to orcas and dolphins than baleen whales. No one is claiming they're critically endangered – yet – and they're definitely not as endangered as the big rorquals the Japanese whalers target. But there's no evidence they intend to kill themselves when they strand either. They get stuck mainly around the sandbars and shallow tidal waters like in Golden Bay, probably when the pod's leaders become disoriented or sick. The others stay with them because of their strong family bonds. They all die because they don't want to leave their loved ones!"

He paused, then shook his head, obviously frustrated. "Besides, what the hell kind of logic is it to kill even more of them just because they strand? Naturally-occurring mass mortality events are bad enough without adding human-induced pressure too. That's a sure way to drive any species to extinction!"

The radio host chuckled gleefully. "Well, that sure lit up the switchboard! Let's see how many of you we can fit in before the next commercial break…"

Richard listened, desperately hoping someone would call up to argue with the last caller's opinion. It was almost a matter of national pride in front of Vicki.

There were the predictable outraged responses amongst the callers, but there was a worrying amount of indifference too, and even some support for the Japanese whalers. He was saddened and a little disappointed in the country, but he thought about what Cal had said, hoping it was a case of people not knowing any better rather than simply not caring. After all, wasn't it true that he knew next to nothing about the plight of whales himself just a few short months ago?

Then came the last caller of the session.

"Hello, you're on the air!" the host announced.

"Yeah, about those people trying to stop the whaling… they're a bunch of losers! I reckon they should all grow up and get a life. They bloody well need to get a haircut and a real job!"

Cal reached over and snapped the radio off. "Yeah, of course," he muttered, his voice dripping with sarcasm. "How silly of me. The real aim in life is to see how much money you can make!"

Vicki laughed in sympathy, but then her eyes turned serious.

"What can we do now?" she asked quietly. "Is the whole world against us?"

"Well, the Green Party wants to send a frigate to protect the whale sanctuary – which is ironic since they're usually the ones agitating to cut defence spending and dispense with the military altogether!" Cal paused, as if considering the likelihood. "They're only a minor coalition partner, so they'll likely be overruled by the others who are more right-wing. The National Party has been pretty vocal from the opposition benches. They'd rather send a frigate to arrest us! But then, that's hardly a surprise. They're a right-wing party so they'll have their trade and business interests to safeguard above all else."

Vicki smiled thinly at his sarcasm. "So who'll get their way? What's going to happen?"

Cal shrugged. "Hopefully nothing. The Labour Government is sitting on the fence. For now."

"Any chance they'll go in to bat for us?"

Cal shook his head. "Not if Amimoto's started piling the pressure on them. I think they're quietly hoping the whole thing will just go away!"

"Like hell!" the Skipper growled. "I ain't goin' nowhere. Except back to sea. I say we put a stop to this bullshit once and for all!" He frowned beneath his bushy eyebrows. "That Mr Fish is a dirty crook. He acts like the goddamn king of England just because he's got a bit of money. He thinks he can snap his fingers and he'll have the world lick his boots an' call it ice cream. Well, not me. I ain't kowtowing to nobody." The steely glint returned to his eyes. "And I've a mind to take 'im down a peg or two."

Cal hesitated for a long time. When he finally spoke his tone was distant, as though giving voice to his innermost deliberations. "The Tosho-Maru is due in port tomorrow – along with its escort. We'll have a couple of days while they make temporary repairs here, then they'll aim to put to sea again to finish killing their quota for the season. After that the window of opportunity closes, maybe for good. With that Japanese Navy destroyer running escort we won't get near them at sea, and we're not exactly welcome in Japan any more so we're unlikely to get anywhere near Shimonoseki to get another crack at them in their usual port."

Cal fell silent then, staring into space. At length he nodded slowly. "I think you're right, Skip," he said. "There's only one way Amimoto will stop, and that's if we stop him."

Vicki nodded too, adding her agreement.

Richard gulped, feeling the familiar surge of alarm course through him at the thought of what might happen. He took a deep breath, determined not to let it show. The guilt of the previous day had returned to gnaw at his insides. This time he was determined to pull his weight though, no matter what!

He glanced anxiously across the water. The port spanned a small bay, and the sinister-looking Kuu-Maru was tied up on the far side of it, separated from them by several hundred metres of open channel. Despite being significantly smaller than the bulk tankers and container ships moored alongside, the Kuu-Maru's sharp lines gave it a predatory air, like a grey wasp amongst a crowd of docile giant locusts.

Cal swung the binoculars towards the base of the distant pier – where several port security guards and a hastily-erected fence were doing their best to keep a crowd of placard-wielding protesters at bay. At that distance Richard could hear nothing though, and the banners waved silently like grass in the wind.

Richard heard his brother inhale sharply, and at the same time he caught sight of a fiery red mane in the front ranks. He didn't need binoculars to recognise Aurelia, or the angry confidence that surrounded her.

"What the hell does she think she's doing?" Cal muttered.

No one answered him.

Cal clicked his tongue with a mixture of frustration and annoyance, then handed over the binoculars for Richard to look.

The protestors seemed content just to make their presence felt for now, so Richard panned to the right, searching for the Kuu-Maru. The menacing grey bow suddenly jumped into view, and below it he caught sight of a posse of blue-overalled whalers lining the wharf, ready to protect their ship if the protestors broke through the cordon. From their plastic helmets and batons, and the severe looks on their unsmiling faces, they were ready and willing to crack some heads despite being in a country that officially opposed whaling.

Richard swallowed and looked back towards the Hunter-Killer ship's bridge, searching for a familiar pock-marked face and red helmet. Gyofuku wasn't there, but another man was standing next to the wheel, staring down the wharf towards the demonstrators.

He was taller than the fat captain, but Richard could sense the aura of danger surrounding him.

Despite the heat, the man was wearing a suit and a long trench coat, and his face was mysterious behind dark glasses. The Japanese turned suddenly and looked up, raising his shades for a moment to stare directly at him. Richard felt his blood run cold as their eyes seemed to meet, even though he knew it was impossible for the man to have seen him from that distance.

"W-who's that guy on the bridge?" he blurted. "He looks mean."

Cal snatched up the binoculars to look. "Where? I don't see anyone. Was it Gyofuku, the captain?"

Richard shook his head. When he looked again the bridge was empty, but the image of the man's black eyes still stuck in his mind. "No. This guy looked even meaner..."

With a sudden chill, Richard realised he had seen the man before. It was dark at the time, but there could be no mistaking the menacing air that hung over the man.

"I-I think it's the sword guy. The one who chased us when we stole Amimoto's car."

Cal looked suddenly concerned, but he said nothing.

Richard shivered, suddenly feeling the need to go below, out of sight, and he picked up his coffee cup to return to his bunk.

The Skipper coughed, then cleared his throat noisily. "I say we blow the dirty bastards out of the water – the whole dang lot of 'em!"

Cal looked up and grinned indulgently, but shook his head.

The Skipper grunted. "I know, I know. No bombs and no dead gooks, right?" His shaggy head shook in mock despair.

"No, Skip. I've got a better plan…"

"I s'pose it's too much to ask that y' let us in on it?"

Cal winked mysteriously, but he was giving nothing away for now.

"Can you keep an eye on the ship?" he said, pretending to change the subject. "I need to go ashore for a bit…"

***

Later that morning, Cal sat at a now-familiar battered orange Formica table watching the world rush by outside on Colombo Street. He was somewhat leery about returning to the vegan café, and the waitress' suspicious stare didn't help his mood any.

Small though Christchurch was, he always felt claustrophobic in any city, and today he felt even more on edge than usual.

A modified sports car rolled past on shiny mag wheels, its exhaust rumbling. The driver's face was hidden behind tinted windows.

Cal watched with a strange sense of detachment.

The contrast between this world and the Real World couldn't be more striking. Instead of a great expanse of sea and sky – the domain of whales and seabirds, here the landscape was concrete and steel – a barren waste populated only by hordes of people and noisy vehicles belching exhaust fumes into the atmosphere.

Cal sighed. Today he had even more to occupy his mind that usual.

He reached for the dandelion coffee he'd felt compelled to order – mainly to alleviate the sullen stare the dreadlocked waitress kept levelling at him. It hadn't worked though, and she still watched him suspiciously from behind the counter.

With an attitude like that I wonder if she knows Heath?

He coughed to cover his sudden laugh, then it turned into a real cough as he took a sip of his drink. The stuff was horrible! It tasted worse than real coffee!

He pushed the cup aside, wondering again what the hell he was doing here.

Just then the bell over the door jangled, and he turned, catching his breath at the sight of her. Her bright auburn hair framed her face like a flaming halo, and he was aware of the old flutter in his chest. It had only been a few weeks, but it felt like an eternity since he'd last been in the same room as her.

He allowed his gaze to slip lower. She wore a little green singlet and her nipples were clearly visible through the thin fabric, as hypnotising as those of a goddess. The sarong she wore knotted at her waist was tantalisingly see-though, and beneath its seductive folds, her long shapely legs might have been carved from marble.

Damn, she's beautiful!

He felt the familiar desire for her welling up within him, but realising instinctively it wasn't a good thing to give in to it.

She hadn't noticed him sitting in the corner, and she nodded to the waitress, receiving a conspiratorial smile in return.

"Aurelia!" he called.

She jumped, then looked slightly relieved as she recognised him, but she still didn't relax.

"Cal. What are you doing here?" she accused.

"Looking for you."

"How did you know I was here?" she blurted, looking worriedly over her shoulder.

"You mean Christchurch, or this café?"

"Both."

He shrugged, grinning at her. "There are protestors everywhere down at the wharf. I figured you wouldn't be too far away!"

She didn't return his smile.

He tried to start again. "Aurelia, we need to talk."

"I think we've already said everything," she replied, with just a touch of sadness.

Cal took a deep breath, determined to say what he came here to say. "You know this protesting will never change Amimoto's mind," he said slowly. "It's a matter of honour for the Japanese – he'll never back down."

"Then it's up to us to tell the world what he's doing. Turning public opinion against him, against this slaughter, is the only way to stop him."

Cal rolled his eyes. "You can't link this to your 'Meat is Murder' campaign," he persisted. "Animal rights is a separate issue."

"Not to me it's not," she said stiffly.

Cal threw up his hands in exasperation. "But it is to the general public! Can't you see that? All you're doing is alienating the average person."

"And you're insulting their principles," she shot back. "How do you know they don't have love in their hearts for the whales?"

He dropped a copy of the local newspaper onto the table between them. She eyed it but made no move to pick it up.

"Have you read this?" he demanded. "It says here that you're calling on the people of New Zealand to join you for a day of mass spiritual telepathy with the whales! That you're going to join hands and send a silent message of love and harmony to the whales – along with a warning to stay away from the Japanese ships!"

"So?"

"So it makes you sound crazy."

"Is that what you think?"

He rolled his eyes skyward. "You know I don't. But this isn't about what I think. The average person in the street will write you off as a crackpot if they hear that kind of stuff."

"That kind of stuff," she sniffed, "Happens to be what I believe in."

Cal sighed. "But it doesn't help us. We need to educate people, not convert them."

"You make it sound like I'm trying to recruit them into some kind of cult," she replied, a dangerous edge creeping into her voice.

Cal laughed, knowing instantly it was the wrong thing to do.

She bristled with anger. "Who are you to pass judgement on my beliefs?" she snapped. "It's not like you're so saintly yourself…"

Cal held up a hand to forestall her, but it was too late to back up now. The old argument had reared its ugly head again.

"Your invasive research is almost as bad as what the whalers do to them!" she hissed.

Cal kept his voice calm, trying to reason with her. "The tags don't do the whales any long-term harm. And they're necessary to learn more about them-"

"You're violating the spiritual sanctity of their bodies! They deserve to live in peaceful, unmolested harmony."

Cal opened his mouth to remind her that whales were animals, not some kind of magical totem, but he managed to restrain himself. This argument had already spiralled well out of control.

He tried a different tack instead. "Aurelia, please! Your protests down at the wharf have got the Japanese all riled up about security here. The port is swarming with their goons – they've even got warships on the way!"

"That's your doing!" she snapped. Then she stared at him for a moment, her face flushing with anger as understanding dawned. "So that's what this is about!" she exploded. "You're worried I'm going to spoil your chances to attack them again!"

Cal looked away, but it was too late. She must have read the guilt on his face.

Her eyes sparkled with anger. "How dare you!" she hissed, shaking with fury. "How dare you demand I ignore my principles and look the other way so you can undermine everything I stand for?"

"Shh. Calm down," Cal pleaded, looking around to see frosty glares from the other patrons. "I'm not telling you to look the other way. We're on the same side here, can't you see that? We need to work together on this."

"My principles also include non-violence," she said icily. "Which puts me squarely in conflict with you as well."

Cal tried his friendliest smile. "Come on Aurelia, let's not fight again. Please. We have enough problems as it is."

She didn't smile back. "I don't know what you're up to now, and I don't really want to. But violence is never the answer!"

"It's not violence. It's just direct action."

"Until someone gets hurt! You need to stop. Please Cal. I'm asking you to stop. For me?"

Cal's sigh was heartfelt. "You know I can't do that. It's the only thing Amimoto understands. It's the only way to stop him, the only way to save the Great Whales from extinction."

A shadow seemed to pass across her face, and her eyes lost their impish twinkle. "Then I'm sorry, but I have nothing more to say to you."

"Aurelia, be reasonable…" he began, but seeing the determined look on her face he let the sentence trail away. A lock of her red hair hung forward, partially screening her face, but behind it her eyes blazed green with fury.

She's even more beautiful when she's angry.

He fell silent, knowing from bitter experience that he would get nowhere if he persisted.

Reluctantly, he checked his watch and stood up to leave. He needed to get back to the ship now if he was to get his gear ready in time. He still had to refill his SCUBA tank from this morning…

"I have to go now," he said lamely, knowing she would see that as the cop-out it was. He was never any good at dissuading her once her mind was made up, and in his heart he knew they would never agree on the need for direct action.

"Friends?" he ventured, by way of a peace offering.

She said nothing, and he thought she was planning to ignore him. He turned sadly to leave, but just as he was about to step into the street she spoke up.

"The manner of a victory matters as much as the result," she called after him.

He looked back. "Huh? What's that supposed to mean?"

She shrugged, refusing to meet his eye. "Just that if you continue down this path you've chosen I can't have anything more to do with you."

***

Kobushi crept down the corridor, keeping to the strip of carpet where his soft-soled shoes made no sound. The steel deck above him boomed suddenly, and he froze, hand flashing to the sword-hilt at his belt. He carried only his wakizashi for this mission, his katana left behind aboard the whaler. Speed and concealment were paramount to avoid discovery, and should he have to draw a sword down here, the big katana blade would prove too long to wield effectively in the confines of a ship.

He cocked his head, listening. It sounded like someone had just jumped onto the deck above him. Though it was still mid-afternoon, Kobushi had assumed the Westerners' ship would be deserted. They should all be down at the far pier, protesting the arrival of the crippled Tosho-Maru with her military escort.

After all, protesting is what they do, neh?

The sound of footsteps overhead confirmed his suspicions. Someone had just returned to the ship. His eyes narrowed behind his dark glasses. Amimoto's instructions to him had been clear; "Carry out your orders in secrecy. The Western scum must not discover the little surprise you have left for them until they are well out to sea!"

It was time to go.

He turned and headed aft towards the stern ladder. It was the more secluded of the two, and once on deck he could slip silently over the side and swim clear if necessary to avoid detection.

His lip curled involuntarily at the thought though. He was almost sorry his sword was to remain sheathed for this mission. It would be far more satisfying to challenge and defeat his enemies in combat than to sneak around like a thief and sabotage their boat. His honour as a warrior demanded no less! He controlled his impulses with an effort though, Amimoto's orders to him had been clear!

Just then, as if the gods had heard him – or sought to mock him – a door opened barely half a dozen paces ahead of him and a man came out.

Kobushi froze, waiting.

A moment later the man saw him. He stopped dead, gaping at him. A coffee cup slipped from his grasp to spill, unseen, across the floor.

Kobushi recognised the man instantly. He was one of the criminals who had been at the conference. His brown hair was thinning at his temples, and his body looked skinny and weak. He had the look of a clerk or an office-worker, not a warrior.

No matter, an enemy is an enemy. And what better opportunity to test my blade?

Kobushi paused a moment longer, evaluating his options. It was too late to avoid detection. His only recourse was to silence this witness. Permanently.

His decision made, he turned the full power of his gaze on the man, like a cobra stalking a mouse, aiming to hypnotise him to the spot with the force of his will. He glided forward on silent feet, the movement all-but invisible beneath the folds of his long coat. As he stole forward, wraith-like, narrowing the range, his hand drifted ever so slowly towards his sword-hilt.

His prey remained transfixed, eyes wide with terror.

But then a sudden flurry of footsteps from the other end of the ship broke the spell.

Someone was coming down one of the forward stairways.

His prey came to his senses at last. He yelped in terror and fled back into the room, slamming the door behind him.

Kobushi cursed his luck, wakizashi flashing into his hand as he started forward at a run.

A second later he reached the door. A flying kick burst it open before the bolt could be slid, and then he was in the room.

His enemy had not gone far.

The bunkroom was a dead-end, and he was trapped like the filthy vermin he was.

The man backed up, naked terror on his face, eyes never leaving the wicked curve of the blade. Then he stumbled, falling to the floor. He tried to back up, but the wall was behind him.

Kobushi felt nothing but derision. This was almost too easy. Only a lowly peasant lacked the honour to fight for his life.

The man's mouth worked silently, as though trying to beg for mercy, and he stretched out a hand as if to ward off the blade.

Kobushi smiled coldly. His prey was totally at his mercy. He reached up to remove his dark glasses, folded them carefully and placed them in his shirt pocket. Then, still smiling, he raised the wakizashi over his head to deliver the killing blow.

Chapter 25

Dennis Cruikshank glanced at the road map he'd spread over the Holden's large steering wheel, pretending to read it. His eyes darted shiftily beneath his heavy brows though, his attention actually directed towards the small café a block further down the street. The suspect had been inside for the past hour now, out of sight, and Cruikshank wondered again if he might have been given the slip.

Had the punk slipped unseen out a rear door, leaving him watching the front entrance like a dolt until some neighbour got suspicious and called the local cops on him?

That was always a risk with a lone stakeout…

Next to the car a banner of flags flapped in the breeze. Cruikshank looked around surreptitiously, alert for any undue interest directed at him. Luckily there was none so far. He'd been illegally parked outside this second-hand car yard since the perp entered the café, but so far no one had bothered him, although one little old lady had looked like she wanted to come over and give him directions. He grunted. This was New Zealand after all!

Just then a hot young broad grabbed his attention as she sauntered up the street. She was definitely eye-catching with her bright red hair and a flimsy scrap of cloth tied around her waist in place of a skirt. But that wasn't the source of Cruikshank's interest though, he'd recognised her in a heartbeat. She was the firebrand protestor from the whaling conference.

"Hello sugar," he murmured. "Welcome to my stake-out!" He chuckled to himself, gloating. "Looks like something's about to go down after all!" In an instant his decision to tail the blonde kid here was vindicated. He smirked in the direction of the café. "I knew you were the chief troublemaker, and I knew you'd be up to your usual mischief if I hung around long enough!"

The bell over the door jingled as the redhead disappeared into the café as well.

Cruikshank craned his neck trying to see through the glass, but the light was wrong. All he could see was the reflection of the street. He swore, tempted to use his binoculars, but knowing that would ruin his cover as a lost tourist.

Not that he suspected anyone here would notice, but it was better to be safe than sorry. Years on stakeout as a beat cop had taught him to always play it safe. The day you took a chance was the day it came back to bite you on the ass!

What were they discussing? Cruikshank wished he had a mic on the pair, and wondered again if it was worth risking moving the big car closer to get a view of them.

Those two are up to no good in there, I'll bet the farm on it!

There was nothing he could do for now though but wait and watch. As the minutes dragged by, he wondered again if he should try to get within earshot… but that would mean gaining access to the building, something that would blow his cover for sure.

Then abruptly the door opened and the blonde kid came out. He was alone, and he headed off down the street without a backwards glance. He was frowning though, and Cruikshank could tell by his expression that he was still deep in thought. The kid aimed a kick at a stray cola can, sending it bouncing off a storefront into the gutter. He didn't even look up as a passer-by glared at him. Cruikshank chuckled to himself. The meeting definitely hadn't been a social call – and it didn't look like it had gone well.

Interesting!

He waited a minute more, but the redhead didn't emerge. He hesitated, at odds over what to do next. He sensed she wasn't a primary offender, but she definitely knew something…

Maybe I can use her to get to the others?

Cruikshank didn't have a whole lot to go on right now, but that was precisely the time when good old-fashioned policing could scare up a break. Those damn spooks he worked for now would have a fit at the thought of breaking cover and confronting a suspect – even a minor one – but sometimes a cop had to trust his gut and act on an impulse. And his instincts hadn't failed him yet.

He opened the car door and stepped out into the heat. As he sauntered past the café windows he tried to peer in, but was thwarted by the reflection again. He could make out a collage of papers taped to the inside of the glass though. A closer inspection revealed they were fliers and articles clipped from badly-printed newspapers. Headline banners jumped out at him; "Meat is Murder!", "Communist Party Broadsheet", "Anarchists for Anti-globalisation!", and "Why the WTO is Evil!"

Cruikshank ignored the rest, wrinkling his nose with distaste. He'd seen it all before. It seemed crazies were the same the world over.

The windows were actually dusty display cases jutting forward into the street, either side of the door, the building obviously having started life as some kind of store before its present incarnation.

Cruikshank frowned. Anyone in there would have seen him by now though, and he didn't want to look more suspicious by walking away again.

Before he could change his mind he strode up the single step to the door and pushed it open. A bell jangled as he stepped inside, his nose assailed immediately by the twin odours of coffee and incense.

Wouldn't be surprised if there's a little marijuana smoke in the air too…

The redhead was sitting at a table in the far corner. She was by herself, and apart from a brief glance when he walked in, she paid him no mind.

Cruikshank checked her out. She was even more good-looking up close. Quite a dish, in fact. He smiled to himself as he approached. Despite their respective positions, there was no harm in a guy admiring a nice pair of tits.

"This seat taken?"

She didn't look up. "Piss off buddy, I'm not in the mood."

Cruikshank bristled at the latent hostility, but was careful to keep his expression neutral. Even though this one was a terrorist associate he couldn't afford to scare her off. Knowing her background he also knew she wouldn't be overly keen to open up to a law enforcement officer, or to anyone representing governmental authority for that matter. Unfortunately he didn't have much choice if he was going to get her to talk, she'd already made it clear she wasn't interested in idle chitchat. He weighed up his options, then shrugged. There was no substitute for good old-fashioned policing, and he always backed himself when it came to interviewing difficult suspects. In fact, he prided himself on being able to read just how far he could push each one to get results.

He sat down, laying his badge on the table between them. "I'd just like to ask you a few questions, Miss."

"What are you? Some kind of cop?"

Cruikshank put on his friendliest smile, neither confirming nor denying the accusation.

She glowered back. "Are you going to arrest me for free speech or free association?" she snapped, her chin jutting defiantly. "Where's your snout, Pig?"

Cruikshank ignored the jibe. His suspicions had been right on the money.

"You're not under arrest for anything, Miss, although I think we both know you're involved in a lot of trouble."

Her head snapped up then, eyes instantly wary as they searched his face. He held her gaze and smiled inwardly, sensing her suspicion. He'd found the nerve easily enough, but this next bit would have to be played just right…

"I'm not here to violate anyone's rights," he assured her, palms held out to placate any hostility. "I'm just asking for your help is all."

"What do you need my help for?"

Cruikshank smiled and shrugged, playing the bumbling 'Good Cop' role. Inwardly, he was relieved.

I've got her talking. So far, so good.

It was time to cut to the chase.

"What do you know about the whaling ships that were destroyed two weeks ago in Shimonoseki harbour?"

He was watching her eyes and he saw the wall go up. "Where?" she replied levelly. "I don't know what you're talking about."

Cruikshank hesitated. They both knew she was lying, but how to get her to admit it? Every interview subject could be turned, as long as you knew what angle to use. There had to be a key to unlocking this one, but he would have to tread very carefully or he'd lose her. He had no authority to question her, so if she got up and walked out that would be it. He would only get one crack at it so he'd have to rely on experience and intuition alone…

"Do you know that three crew members were severely hurt during the latest escapade at sea? One of them required hospitalisation."

"No," she said, then hastily corrected herself. "I-I don't know what you're talking about." She looked down at the table, avoiding his gaze, but the brief flicker of concern on her face had been enough.

Bingo!

Cruikshank allowed himself a moment to gloat.

Then he put on his friendliest smile. "I'm sure that wasn't the intent," he soothed, "but you have to realise this is a dangerous game your friends are playing. Someone could easily get hurt next time. Badly. Maybe even killed. Is that something you'd want to live with on your conscience?"

She said nothing, but he could tell his words were having an effect. She was no longer denying knowledge of the incident or the perpetrators any more.

"I'm just trying to stop the saboteurs from making a big mistake," he continued. "As a mature and responsible member of society yourself, I'm sure you'd agree we can't have people lashing out with violence simply because they disagree with someone else. That's hardly very civilised, is it?"

She shook her head slowly, still staring at the table.

Cruikshank smiled to himself. It was time to drive the wedge.

"I'm not here to persecute anybody, but the saboteurs brought this trouble on themselves. They crossed the line. It's one thing to protest peacefully, but the law is there to protect everybody. You just can't go breaking it willy-nilly and putting people's lives at risk."

He watched her eyes, reassured by the emotion he saw mirrored there. His instincts hadn't failed him. He'd found the key to taming her. Now it was time to reel her in.

"This group has committed some serious crimes already, and I think we both know they're capable of doing it again. Next time they might not be so lucky. They need to be stopped before someone gets hurt, including themselves. What do you say?"

She looked at him, conflicted. But then her eyes hardened again and she folded her arms across her chest.

"I'm sorry. You've come to the wrong person. I can't help you."

Cruikshank's brow furrowed.

So she's a feisty one after all!

Maybe it was time to stop pussy-footing around?

"Now look," he said, his tone suddenly hard. "These people are terrorists. As far as the law is concerned you're either part of the solution, or you're part of the problem. Now which is it to be?"

"Are you threatening me?" She glared at him, her fire returning. "I don't have to sit here and listen to this bullshit. I know my rights."

She made as if to rise, but Cruikshank put a hand on her wrist to restrain her. She bristled at his touch, outrage written across her face.

Cruikshank removed his hand, but used the force of his gaze to delay her a moment longer. "I apologise if I've come on a little strong," he said carefully,

"But you have to understand the importance of this. Time is short, and these people must be stopped. For their own sakes as well as anybody else's."

He placed his business card on the table. "My mobile number's on the bottom. Please call me if you have any information that might be of use… where these people are headed, what they're planning next, anything."

She stared back at him, chin jutting defiantly. "I don't know who you think I am, but I'm not a bloody informant!"

Cruikshank smiled, amused by the fire in her green eyes. She was a handful alright! He wondered briefly if he might even have started to slip under her spell, because he did feel a little sorry for her predicament.

It was time to close this interview now though, while he still had a semblance of control.

"Thank you for your time, Miss." He stood up, leaving the card on the table.

She made no attempt to pick it up.

He needed to leave her something to stew over.

"Remember," he said over his shoulder. "Someone could get killed next time. By not speaking out you'll be equally to blame. Is that something you can live with for the rest of your life?"

He headed for the door, confident he'd planted the seed of doubt in her mind.

With a little time and a lot of patience she might yet be persuaded…

At the door, Cruikshank glanced back over his shoulder, pleased to see she had picked up his card.

***

Cal Major jammed his foot on the brake pedal and skidded to a stop in a spray of flying gravel. He jumped out, leaving his car at the far end of the compound and banged the door closed, not really caring if the dodgy lock had caught or not. The long-term parking yard at the port was relatively secure, and no one was likely to steal his battered old Subaru anyway.

It was a necessary evil for him to own a car. He only used it when he was in town – and every time he came back here he felt even less compulsion to return. He couldn't stand the oppressive feeling of having so many people around him. He hated suburbia and the contrived, artificial existence that went with it. It just felt so… false. The whole time he was here, surrounded by concrete and steel, he was longing instead for the wide open spaces of the real world.

He took a deep breath to clear his thoughts, delighting in the salty tang of the sea that enlivened the air. Then he grimaced as he caught a waft of diesel exhaust and the harsh chemical fumes of antifouling paint wafting across from the dry-dock nearby.

I can't wait until we're back at sea again, far from the sight of land.

On top of everything else he was still angry at Aurelia's stubborn refusal to budge. Hell, he was angry at her! Couldn't she see how counter-productive her protesting down at the wharf was?

She can be so bloody pig-headed sometimes!

He sighed, knowing that her unshakable conviction was one of the things he found so alluring about her. Yet how was it possible to be in love with and totally infuriated by someone at the same time?

He shook his head disgustedly.

Women!

His mood darkened even more when he looked out to sea and saw the approaching commotion heading into the harbour. The sea was streaked by the wakes of hundreds of small boats, and there in the centre of it all was the familiar grey hull of the Tosho-Maru. Cal watched the Hunter-Killer ship, flanked by the even larger bulk of the Japanese warship escorting it.

The collision damage was plainly visible on the Tosho-Maru's stern, along with some additional damage from the storm it had been forced to sail straight through.

"A pity that storm didn't sink you," he muttered under his breath. "Because now I'll have to finish the job!"

The Japanese ships crept into port, trying to negotiate a path through the throng of small craft. A foghorn blared, but no one took any notice. Cal smiled briefly as he saw kayakers and jet skis amongst the flotilla. It was good to know at least some of his countrymen had their hearts in the right place – even if it made his plan that much more difficult…

Shaking his head philosophically, he hurried along the dock towards the Gwendolyn.

As he approached though, he could see through the window that no one was on watch on the bridge.

That was unusual.

He jumped aboard, already beginning to feel annoyed.

Where the hell is everyone. Surely they didn't all go down to watch the Tosho-Maru circus berthing?

He hurried up the ladder to the bridge, but his suspicions were confirmed when he stepped through the door into the wheelhouse. It was deserted.

"Hey Skip!" he called.

There was no answer.

Cal felt his frustration rising. He'd asked the Skipper to maintain the watch while they were in port – you couldn't be too careful!

Then a thought came to him.

It's not like Duke to be slack about security…

Worried now, he turned to leave. Then a sudden impulse made him turn back and reach under the dash behind the ship's wheel. His hand came away empty.

The Skipper's shotgun was missing.

"Oh shit!"

Truly alarmed now, Cal slid down the ladder to the saloon. It too was deserted.

Where the hell is everyone?

He hurried down the centre companionway to the lower deck. He looked around briefly, wondering where in the ship to begin searching, then ran forward to the workshop. It was empty, but he paused long enough to snatch a plumber's wrench off the wall rack before hurrying on with his search.

The laboratory was empty too, but something caught his eye. A microscope was sitting out on the bench though, a slide still clipped under the eyepiece as if someone had been using it only moments before.

"Oh no," he whispered, hoping like hell he wasn't too late.

He hurried through into the computer room, bursting through the door like a tornado.

A familiar black ponytail was seated at the desk ahead of him.

"Vicki!" he exclaimed gratefully, but his relief was short-lived.

She didn't respond.

Her back was to him as she sat at her laptop, the screen filled with numbers where she had been working on her data. She swayed slightly in her chair, then he realised she was twitching, as though she was having a fit – or being electrocuted!

"Vicki?" he called urgently. "Can you hear me?"

She still didn't respond.

He rushed forward, ready to intervene. It was only then that he realised she was wearing headphones, the volume turned up loud enough he could hear the music from several metres away, her ponytail bobbing merrily in time to the beat.

He marched over and yanked the headphones away from her head. "Vicki!" he shouted in her ear.

She jumped out of her seat, fists coming up as she whirled around to face him. "What the hell?" Recognising him then, she relaxed, aiming a playful punch at his arm. "Strewth Cal, you scared the bejeezus outta me…" She trailed off as she saw the look on his face. "What is it?"

"Dunno. Something's wrong." He was already halfway to the door again by then but he turned back, his face as grim as he felt. "Find a weapon."

He didn't wait for her but hurried aft, checking rooms as he went.

The corridor was still deserted, but he felt the silent tension in the air, as though the ship herself was holding her breath.

There was no time to lose!

The next door led to the bathroom and ablutions block, but just as he was about to enter something made him hesitate with his hand still on the handle.

What was that?

He cocked his head, listening, then turned and looked back down the corridor. The door to the last bunkroom was ajar – something that was potentially dangerous aboard a ship where you could hit rough seas without warning.

Cal felt his trepidation mounting.

"That's Richard's bunkroom!"

The rules aboard ship were simple, but firm. Safety depended on them. And the rules said doors were never left free to swing unsecured.

Cal frowned. At the start of the voyage he might have written an oversight like that off to his brother's inexperience, or plain forgetfulness. But not now. Not when Richard had found his sea-legs at last.

Something's not right.

He hefted the heavy wrench and hurried down the corridor.

Cal ran swiftly and silently down the passageway. Just outside the bunkroom he noticed a puddle of spilled coffee, the cup lying discarded next to it. He was certain something was wrong now.

He bent down, touching a finger to the liquid. It was still hot.

No time to lose!

Grimly, Cal reached for the door.

He was alert for trouble, but the sight that greeted him when he pushed the door open floored even him.

His brother was sprawled on the floor, back to the wall, fear in his eyes. Standing over him was a tall assailant in a long coat. The man raised his hand and Cal's eyes widened as he saw the naked blade glinting.

Holy shit!

"Please!" Richard croaked in a hoarse whisper, and to Cal, his brother's desperate plea seemed meant for him.

Spurred into action, he lunged silently forward, bringing the heavy wrench down on the man's forearm. The blow elicited a grunt of pain, and the sword clattered onto the floor.

Cal raised the wrench for another swing, but the man was too quick for him. He twisted around, catlike, avoiding the blow. Then without even pausing he launched forward again, hands chopping for Cal's throat in a vicious attack of his own, seemingly unperturbed at the loss of his weapon.

Richard hadn't moved, his eyes still wide with fear. "Get out of here!" Cal yelled to his brother. He backed away and found himself looking into the face of a Japanese man, with close-cropped hair and a wicked-looking scar beside his right eye.

A sword cut? Who the hell fights with swords now?

He racked his brains. This was the swordsman who'd chased them alright. But who the hell was he?

As he looked into the Japanese's hooded eyes, he thought he detected a flicker of amusement. Then suddenly the man came at him again. With the element of surprise gone, Cal suddenly felt himself struggling to hold his ground. His assailant was good. Very good.

It took all of his kickboxing training just to defend himself. As he warded off strike after strike, he knew it was only a matter of time before the man had him. His assailant was much too quick to risk trying a big swing of the wrench, but his guard was too strong to get through with a jab.

Cal glanced down and felt a flash of despair he realised Richard hadn't moved. He knew he couldn't protect both of them from this man. "Get out of here Bro!" he shouted. "Now!"

He was relieved to see Richard obey finally, scrambling for the open door.

The man came forward again, launching a flurry of blows at his head, most too fast even to see. Cal blocked frantically, relying on instinct alone, searching desperately for an opening.

He lashed out with the wrench, but his assailant had been expecting the ill-timed attack and he caught Cal's arm, twisting his elbow. Cal cursed with pain and the wrench slipped from his grasp, but he didn't have time to worry about it.

He jerked his head to the side just as a fist pounded against the bulkhead – the spot where his face had been only moments ago. It was the same arm he'd clobbered with the wrench, but his assailant's face remained wooden, showing no sign of pain, or even discomfort.

The only exception to the man's emotionless determination was his eyes. They were black, soulless slits that glittered with hatred. And anticipation.

Cal knew he was fighting a killer.

He backed away, until he felt the dresser behind him. He was out of space.

His attacker smirked. He knew it too.

Cal knew he had to do something, and quickly.

He reached behind him, groping for something – anything – he could use for a weapon. His hand closed over a small hard-backed notebook.

Richard's diary!

Cal hurled it at the assailant's head.

The Japanese flinched, raising a hand to ward off the missile.

That was all the time Cal needed. He dived to the side, snatching up his wrench and turning to meet the retaliation that was already on the way.

As the man advanced, Cal let fly with a spinning kick at his assailant's head. His attacker saw it coming and – as Cal had anticipated – he scorned a block, electing instead to land a quicker technique of his own while Cal was still turning. Even though he was expecting it, Cal was still surprised at the speed of the counter-attack as the man's foot flashed towards his chest. Desperately, he swung the wrench. His assailant clearly hadn't expected the second attack and his response was a fraction too slow. As he turned away, the wrench caught him on the side of the shoulder – at the same moment as his foot connected with Cal's chest – knocking them both off their feet.

But the Japanese still managed to turn the situation to his advantage. He twisted away as he fell, lunging towards where his sword lay. He somersaulted, snatching it up from the deck and rolling to his feet in one sinuous movement.

As soon as Cal hit the deck he knew he was in deep trouble. The impact knocked the wrench from his grip and sent it spinning away. He scrambled to his feet, looking around for respite. This time the wrench lay well out of reach.

Oh shit!

Cal's jaw tightened as he realised the seriousness of his predicament. Without a weapon he was screwed.

The Japanese advanced menacingly on him. He brandished the sword, gloating as he pointed it at Cal's heart.

Time slowed. Cal saw the elaborate scrollwork etched onto the blade, and the attacker's white-knuckled grip on the hilt.

Strange! He's missing a finger!

Then the Japanese raised the sword over his head to deliver the killing strike.

This is it! I'm done for!

Cal looked around desperately, trying to gauge how he could dodge the swing, but knowing in his heart that he couldn't.

Then a sudden shout stopped them both in their tracks.

There stood Richard, brandishing a fire axe he'd ripped from the wall in the corridor. "G-get away from my brother!" he challenged.

Cal felt a rush of pride at Richard's newfound courage, but he knew it was foolish bravado. His brother didn't know how to fight, much less with a weapon he'd never even picked up before. The seasoned killer would have him in an instant.

"Richard, get out of here!" he ordered.

Richard shook his head bravely. "No. I'm going to protect you."

Cal felt as though his heart would burst, but he knew he had to make his brother obey.

"Richard, do it! You can't help me!"

Richard stubbornly stood his ground, though Cal could see the terror on his face.

The attacker turned on Richard, sword still held high.

Cal knew it would be suicide to try and tackle the man without a weapon, but he also knew he couldn't watch his only brother die in front of him.

He readied himself to charge, just as a shadow appeared in the doorway. It was Vicki.

"Freeze Sucker!" she yelled, pointing a handgun at the assailant's chest.

The Japanese hesitated, his attention focused on the gun.

Cal's eyes widened as he saw it was a flare pistol, and it was unloaded.

Vicki was bluffing.

The assailant's eyes flickered briefly. He had seen it too.

He bared his teeth in what might have been a smile, then he headed forward again, sword held high. Vicki refused to back down. She stood shoulder to shoulder with Richard, and neither of them moved.

Cal knew he had to act quickly.

"No you don't! Over here! Hey!"

He lunged for the Japanese, aiming a kick at his head.

His assailant turned and swung at him, and it took all of Cal's agility to dive clear of the scything blade. He landed heavily on the deck, at the same moment relieved and dismayed to see the man coming to finish him off. He struggled to his feet, determined not to die on the ground.

The sudden roar of the shotgun was deafening in the enclosed space. Cal flinched as the sound battered his eardrums, and he felt the heat of the blast on his cheek. The shock hammered his senses but he forced himself to react, jumping back away from the danger of the flashing blade.

The smoke cleared and he steadied himself against the wall, shaking his head to clear the ringing in his ears.

The Skipper stood like a statue next to the others, shotgun aimed directly at the trespasser's head. His warning shot had passed directly between him and Cal – missing their heads by inches – to shred the ceiling panel, but Cal could tell from the furious look on his grizzled features that he was done playing games. The next shot would be aimed to kill.

The Skipper worked the pump, ejecting the still-smoking cartridge and loading another, his aim never wavering from the man's head. "Thought I smelled me a rat," he growled. "What the fuck are y' doin' on my ship?

The Japanese straightened up, still clutching his sword. Cal saw the hatred glittering in his eyes, and he knew the man was sizing up his new adversary.

The Skipper knew it too, and he wasn't giving an inch. "Don't move Charlie!" he hissed. "Next one's gonna be right between y' slanty eyes. You git me?"

The black eyes glittered like obsidian, then the man smiled and sheathed his sword. He took a step forward, inviting the Skipper to spar, hand-to-hand.

Duke ignored the challenge, his finger tightening on the trigger.

"Don't kill him," Vicki whispered. "That'd ruin us!"

"The bastard tried to stick y'all. He deserves a first class ticket to hell."

Cal shook his head, trying to clear his mind. The concussion from the blast had addled his wits. His head still felt like it was full of cotton wool.

"No. She's right," he murmured, managing to find his voice. "The authorities would come down on us like a ton of bricks. They'd arrest us, seize the ship. We'd never leave port again. Amimoto would win…"

"Only if they found a body…"

"No Skip, it's too risky."

The Skipper hesitated, deliberating. Finally he curled his lip, obviously not entirely happy with his choice. He motioned at his prisoner with the barrel. "Alright you, get the fuck off my ship before I decorate that there wall with y' innards."

As the Skipper escorted the man away at gunpoint, the others lapsed into stunned silence, still in shock from the sudden violence.

Cal stared after the man, his mind working overtime.

Who the hell was that guy?

The Japanese definitely knew how to fight – with or without that sword of his. He had been well-trained.

Cal's mind went back to the missing finger. Wasn't that a hallmark of the Yakuza – the Japanese mafia? He pursed his lips as a nasty thought occurred to him. Could Amimoto have sent a professional assassin against them?

Either way, Cal knew they had been very lucky just now. He had seen the single-minded homicidal urge in the depths of those eyes. He also knew that he had not seen the last of that man…

Cal rubbed his aching temples. There was unfinished business between them now, and next time they crossed paths he was certain someone would not walk away… and the odds were definitely in the vicious samurai assassin's favour.

Maybe we should have killed him when we had the chance?

Chapter 26

Richard Major sat in the Gwendolyn's wheelhouse. He felt like he was in the way as the others bustled around him, but he knew he couldn't be alone right now. He couldn't face going below to his deserted quarters… not after what had just happened down there.

He was still badly shaken up by his near-death experience. Night had already fallen, and with it came the creeping shadows that only intensified his unease.

He told himself such an attack was to be expected, given the conflict he was mixed up in now. And though he didn't relish the prospect, he did expect to have to face violence on the high seas. But not here. Not in his own cabin aboard the Gwendolyn, and not while safely berthed in a friendly port in his own country.

He felt the anxiety grip him. Mr Fish's reach was long indeed.

What the hell have I gotten myself into?

Richard tried to put it out of his mind, even though his heart was still pattering like a tap-dancer in his chest.

Every vague shape he saw in the darkness brought with it the promise of more lurking danger – the sword-wielding killer come to finish him off…

Richard shook his head to clear it, but the images kept repeating themselves in his mind like an endlessly looping tape; the blade, long and wickedly sharp, glinting in the shadows; the killer, silent and deadly, rushing out of the darkness toward him; and his eyes, cold and dead-looking like those of a snake.

Richard shivered again, grateful to Cal for rescuing him in time. He knew, without a doubt, that without his brother's quick action he would be dead.

"I owe him my life," he murmured.

That made it all the more significant that Cal had gone straight into action again. As soon as night fell he'd pulled on his wetsuit and slipped into the dark water, armed only with a crescent wrench and the puny dive knife strapped to his leg.

The others had tried to persuade him not to go, that it was too dangerous. But he'd refused to listen.

"I have to strike back!" he insisted as he donned his SCUBA tank. "Don't you see? Otherwise Amimoto has won already. We can't let ourselves be intimidated, no matter what he does. If we don't keep fighting back then we've already lost."

Then he inserted the regulator between his teeth and slipped beneath the water. A faint trail of bubbles marked his passage as he headed across the harbour.

Richard stared into the night, awed by his brother's bravery, and his conviction.

The crippled Tosho-Maru was moored directly alongside the Japanese warship, creating a virtually impassable barrier from the wharf. Even if it was possible to run the gauntlet and avoid the various security personnel guarding the pier, a would-be saboteur still had to board and cross a Navy ship to get to it. No one in their right mind would even attempt such madness… yet what Cal was planning wasn't much better.

Richard stared at the huge bulk of the warship that dominated the wharf and the mid-sized ships clustered around it. A huge number '101' was painted on the hull, and the white numbers glowed in the moonlight – in contrast to the rest of the ship. Though larger than the whaling ships, the warship was equally sleek, and painted the same sinister grey.

Richard's eye was drawn to the bow, where in the shadows a huge deck gun hunched ominously, and behind that a forest of missile tubes threatened the sky. It looked every bit as menacing as the two whaling ships tied up next to it, but Richard felt his blood run cold. This ship too was a Hunter-Killer, only it was designed to kill other ships. Ships like theirs.

"Them bastards sure are playin' for keeps now."

Richard jumped, startled out of his thoughts.

The Skipper didn't lower his night vision scope. "It's a Murasame-class destroyer," he observed.

"It's got a lot of g-guns," Richard said.

"Yup. Worst of all is that there helipad on the rear deck though. We cain't outrun no damn chopper if they decide to send the whore after us."

Richard stared at the helipad with some trepidation, and the conversation lapsed into silence again, the two of them alone with their brooding thoughts.

The chugging of a small petrol engine drew Richard's attention to the lighter moored alongside the Tosho-Maru's stern. The flat-bottomed raft contained a salvage pump, and a thick drain hose snaked its way aboard to keep the seawater from flooding the damaged ship.

As he listened, Richard was suddenly aware of a change in the engine note of the pump.

"That's our boy," the Skipper announced confidently.

Richard peered into the darkness, but couldn't make out anything unusual. "Are you sure?"

"Yup. The load just went off that engine. That means he's disconnected the hoses."

A moment later the engine revved again, struggling to pump water uphill.

"That's it, he's connected 'em up again. Good job, Son!" He lowered his voice to a hoarse whisper. "Now get thuh hell outta there before they wise up…"

Richard closed his eyes. He could only imagine what Cal might be feeling now as he slipped away, swimming back through the gloom with the black waters of the harbour closed in overhead. The mere thought elicited a shudder, and he willed his brother to hurry back. The dangers of the dark water were nothing compared to what the Japanese would do if they caught him sneaking around and interfering with their ships again.

Hurry up, Cal!

Richard held his breath, waiting for a warning shout from the deck of the Japanese ships or a searchlight beam to cut through the darkness.

The wait was excruciating.

Just then, a sudden noise behind made him jump. He spun around as Vicki appeared up the stairway, carrying two cups. The comforting aroma of freshly-brewed coffee filled the narrow room.

"Are you feeling better?" she asked, her cheeks dimpling with a concerned smile as she offered him a steaming cup.

Richard nodded, managing a grateful smile in return, but his hands were still shaking so much he couldn't take the mug.

She put it down next to him, then sat down. After a moment's silence, she turned to him.

"You know, that was a brave thing you did tonight…"

Richard stared at her. "What? Nearly getting myself killed?"

She held his gaze and her eyes were unusually intense, the same brilliant blue as a cloudless summer sky.

"No. Going back to stand by your brother. Not everyone would have been so brave."

Richard looked down at the chart table, feeling suddenly sheepish. "A lot of good I managed to do him…" he muttered.

Vicki placed her hand on his, silencing his protest. "You're a good man, Richard," she said earnestly.

Richard felt his colour rise. He felt he ought to compliment her back, but his throat seized up with embarrassment.

Then a sudden commotion on the deck snatched the moment away.

"Halt! Who goes there?" the Skipper challenged, hurrying down the outside ladder to confront the trespasser. "Identify y'self!"

"We should get down there," Vicki said, her tone grave now. "He might need help."

As they hurried down the outside stairway they heard a contrite voice call back. "It's ok. It's just me, Summer."

As they joined him at the rail Richard could see the Skipper was not amused. "Summer?" he growled. "Where thuh hell you been, Gal? I thought you was in y' cabin?"

"No. I-I had to go out for a bit. I had some errands to run while we're in port."

"It's the middle of thuh goddamn night!" The Skipper frowned, and Richard knew he was debating whether or not to chew her ear off for disobeying Cal's orders. Finally, he cleared his throat. "Hurry up and get y'self aboard then. We may have to cast off real soon, and if so we'll most likely be runnin' for it like a jailbreaker over the wall."

At that moment Cal's face appeared over the rail. He leaned over and dropped his weight-belt onto the deck with a thump, then slid over to join it. Richard rushed to help him take off his heavy SCUBA tank.

"Cheers, Bro," Cal said, running a hand through his wet and tousled hair. "Jeez, it's darker than a storm drain down there. I could've done with some light."

"Yeah?" the Skipper laughed. "And why not a loud hailer t' tell the Jappers you're coming too?" He shook his head, frowning good-naturedly. "Nice work. Best get y'self ready though, Son. I'd just as soon get thuh hell outta Dodge quick-smart. That lot're bound to discover your little surprise any moment now."

Cal grinned in response, unzipping his wetsuit. At that moment he paused, and Richard knew he'd just noticed Summer – still dolled up in her city clothes – trying to slip past the group.

"What's going on? Where have you been?"

Summer looked momentarily guilty, then she suddenly grabbed Richard's hand and led him out towards the companionway that led below.

"Where are you two off to?"

Summer winked in reply, then before Richard could answer she turned and kissed him forcefully, propelling him down the steps. Out of the corner of his eye he saw Cal raise an eyebrow and Vicki turn away.

Summer had a victorious smile on her face as she led him down the corridor, and this time she pulled him into her cabin before kicking the door closed.

Richard's heart was beating even harder than before, and he scarcely dared to believe his luck.

Summer loosened the tie that held her hair back, and it fell over her shoulders in a golden wave. She wore a sleeveless top, and as she tossed her head he could see an intoxicating glimpse of her cleavage. She smiled seductively then sat down on the bed, crossing one long tanned leg over the other.

Richard found he could hardly breathe, but he knew he would have to do without his inhaler. He couldn't miss this – it was a dream come true!

She patted the bed, beckoning him to sit next to her. "Come over here and let's have some fun."

He obeyed, his feet moving of their own accord, as if in a trance.

As he sat down, Richard found he could hardly tear his eyes away from her. She was a sight to die for.

"Why don't you lie down and make yourself comfortable?" she invited.

He nodded and lay back, his mouth dry. Suddenly his hand brushed against something cold under her pillow. Something metal.

He turned to see what it was, then blinked in surprise, shocked to discover he was looking at a patterned metal handgrip. Though he'd never seen one before, he knew there was only one thing it could be.

"What the hell's that?" he whispered hoarsely. "Is it a gun?"

Summer reacted like she'd been stung, hurriedly shoving it back under her pillow, her face a picture of guilt. She looked like a teenager caught smoking by her parents.

"It's just for self protection," she said defensively. Then she smiled, turning on the charm at once. "Surely you know how dangerous it is what we're doing?"

She turned suddenly, pushing him onto his back, then lay on top of him. He lay still, not daring to move. He could feel her chest pressed against his, separated only by a layer of cotton, and the knowledge made his pulse race.

"Cal's got us mixed up in a whole heap of trouble," she murmured. "I'm just taking the necessary precautions."

She leaned down and kissed him, a light brush on the lips, then paused to trace his chest with a finger. "Do you know what Cal's planning next?" she asked. "Where was he going just now, with his SCUBA gear?"

She watched him, waiting for an answer.

Richard leaned up and tried to kiss her again, but she pushed him away and sat up, frowning distractedly. "Don't you think I have a right to know what's going on?" she sniffed. "After all, it's my safety that's on the line too!"

Richard looked at her, a little hurt by the rebuff. He shrugged. "Cal knows what he's doing. I don't know what he's planning, but I'm sure we can rely on him to do the right thing."

"Whatever that is."

Richard frowned, a little put out by her tone. "Don't you think this cause is important enough to take a few risks for? Amimoto's probably got it in for us now no matter what we do. Don't you think protecting the last whales should be our primary concern?"

She shrugged, disinterested. "So how far do you think Cal's prepared to go?"

Richard hesitated, raising himself up on his elbow to look at her.

What did she bring me here for?

She met his gaze, then suddenly her demeanour softened again. She smiled warmly, lips parting in a sensual pout. Then without warning she reached for the hem of her singlet and pulled it over her head. She wore a bright red satin brassiere, and when she leaned forward provocatively Richard felt as though his eyes would bulge out of their sockets.

"I'm sure you'd like to play with these, wouldn't you?" she purred huskily.

Richard swallowed and nodded, not trusting his voice.

She smiled again. "First I need to know exactly what Cal's been up to since we docked here…"

***

Cal Major stood dripping on the deck, a pool of water quickly forming around his feet as he watched Summer lead his brother away. He was annoyed with her for disobeying his orders not to leave the ship – for it was obvious she had – but he was also suspicious. Where had she gone, and why?

He frowned, not liking her brazen relationship with Richard either, nor the way she publicly claimed him.

That girl is trouble…

He sighed, wrestling his arms out of the wetsuit and peeling it off. He had more important things to worry about now.

He hurried up the outside stairway to the bridge, his mood already brightening slightly at the memory of the mission. He was still buzzing with success and the after-effects of adrenaline.

That should hold the bastards for a while!

He was pleased with his accomplishments. He'd succeeded in his plan without being spotted. The pump was now actively filling the Tosho-Maru's hold with water, and the longer his subterfuge went undiscovered the greater the damage that would result. He grinned to himself. The flooding might even send the Hunter-Killer to the bottom if no one discovered it in time.

As he hurried onto the Gwendolyn's bridge though, his frown had returned. There was still one whaling ship remaining – Gyofuku's flagship. He stared across the water at the Kuu-Maru, the grey silhouette all but camouflaged by the night, and he knew any success was far from secure, or complete.

"Oi! You're drippin' on my floor!"

Cal turned to grin at the Skipper. "Yeah, but doesn't it have the sweet taste of victory to it?"

Duke clapped him heartily on the back. "Dunno 'bout that, and I sure ain't gonna taste it t' find out!" His weathered features split into a craggy grin. "Nice job, Son. You done good!"

Cal nodded thoughtfully. "Maybe. We'll see."

He reached up to turn on the HF radio, tuning it to the frequency the Japanese Fleet used. It was silent, but for the regular hiss of static.

He reached for the Skipper's night vision goggles, but the green-tinged view also revealed no unusual activity aboard any of the ships.

So far so good.

He sat down to wait.

The hours crept by. Midnight came and went. As the night wore on, Cal glanced across at the Skipper, slumped in his chair behind the wheel. He looked so peaceful sitting there, as though the worry lines of the world had been lifted from his face, leaving just a tired old man. Suddenly Cal felt protective. Despite his gruff exterior, the Skipper was getting old, and Cal knew the new day would bring its share of trials. They all needed their rest.

"Skip, why don't you go to bed?" he whispered.

Duke opened one eye. "Nope. I'm gonna stay right here and keep an eye on things – there's trouble in the air tonight." His eye closed. "Why don't you get t' bed?"

Cal laughed sleepily. "I'm going to keep an eye on things too."

It was two hours later when he finally heard the transmission, a sudden burst of Japanese amidst the static. He blinked, wondering if he'd dozed off and dreamed it. Then the voice came again, angry and insistent, and Cal felt his adrenaline surge. There was no mistaking the speaker, or his mood.

Amimoto!

"They've found it," Cal murmured. "And they're not happy. Tosho-Maru is sunk at its moorings." The transmission continued, and his eyes widened.

"What is it?" the Skipper growled.

Cal held up a hand for silence as he listened, then he swore under his breath. "The Nippon-Maru is repaired. It set sail from Japan this morning." His shoulders slumped. "And it gets worse. Amimoto just ordered the Kuu-Maru to sea tonight, immediately. They're going to rendezvous at their hunting grounds in the Southern Ocean…"

Duke didn't reply.

"Damn it! What will it take to stop him once and for all…?" Cal muttered, thinking aloud. "We'll have to hurry if we're going to beat him this time!"

Duke still didn't reply.

Cal turned to look at him, suddenly aware of what he was asking, and the implicit danger to the Gwendolyn and her Skipper, as well as her crew. This ship was all the old Sea-dog had in the world, and he was asking him to put all that on the line. This wasn't Duke's fight, nor was it part of the contract they'd signed – Cal had chartered the ship to carry out his scientific research only.

The Skipper paused thoughtfully, adjusting the wad of tobacco behind his lip. "Dang," he said. "That'll give them dirty bastards at least a day's head-start on us."

Cal's smile was as grateful as it was relieved. "Like hell it will," he promised, his jaw tightening with resolve. "Get the crew up, and prep the ship for departure."

"It's two in the morning," the Skipper reminded him.

"I don't care. Get them up. This isn't a bloody holiday camp. I want everything ready to leave the minute I get back."

"Where are y' goin'?"

"I've got some urgent business to attend to!"

He hurried below, sliding down the stairway in a single jump. He hurried to the lab, then through into the equipment storeroom beyond. It took a moment's worried search before he saw what he was after, then another moment to wrestle the big duffel bag out from under the bench.

As he hurried back into the corridor with the bulky bag slung over his shoulder, Vicki's door opened. She was dressed in boxer shorts and an old t-shirt, her hair tousled with sleep. "What is it?" she murmured sleepily. "What's going on?"

"No time to explain!" Cal shot back over his shoulder. "We have to sail immediately."

As he hurried up to the deck, he was reassured as he heard her run back into her room and flick the light on. Vicki could always be relied on in a crisis.

He took the stairs two at a time, barely pausing to vault over the rail onto the wharf.

His feet pounded down the planks as he ran, and the bag bumped awkwardly on his shoulder.

From across the harbour came the throb of a heavy diesel engine.

"Oh shit," he whispered to himself. "Gotta hurry!"

At the end of the wharf he turned left, following the shoreline. He ran past the car park, then the giant petrochemical silos.

As he ran, his mind churned over the latest developments. Heath was still AWOL. That meant they would have to leave without him. He felt a flash of anger.

I paid him up front for six months!

The principle mattered more to him than the money though. A man's reputation was only as good as his word – and Heath had reneged on both.

Cal pursed his lips, his frustration remaining. Still, he had to admit it wasn't the end of the world. Deep down he was pleased to see the back of the bad-tempered Californian. Though Heath's heart seemed to be in the right place, some of his views were much too extreme to be compatible with a scientific research programme, and Cal didn't entirely trust him. It was his quarrelsome and outspoken nature that really clinched it though. He was bad for morale aboard ship, and at least this removed the need for an ugly confrontation to fire him. He wouldn't be missed much either. Cal didn't need the troublesome activist to help run the ship – it could be handled by just two if it came to that. What he did need him for was help with his research, but with a disgusted shake of his head Cal knew he wouldn't be doing much more of that for the remainder of the season.

He ran on.

The ship was closer now, the engine rumbling just over his shoulder, out in the centre of the small bay. Cal risked a glance behind, but could see nothing. It was running without lights, invisible in the darkness.

He reached the harbour breakwater at a dead run, and he jumped up and hurried out along the top of it without slowing. It was treacherous footing in the dark, but he hopped from boulder to boulder, trusting his feet wouldn't fail him. Luckily his career as a marine biologist made him well used to boulder jumping, and the rocks were dry, allowing his practiced feet to find a safe path of their own accord.

Cal ran determinedly, still angry at the disruption to his research, and that all his efforts to save the whales – scientific and otherwise – seemed to count for nothing. But as he thought about it now, a sudden thought made his blood run cold.

What if my research is actually helping the Japanese kill more whales?

He had been losing a hell of a lot of tags lately. Could it be that Gyofuku and his Fleet were using the transmitters he had put on the whales to track them? The VHF transmitter signals were unencrypted, and even if the Japanese didn't have the same direction-finding ability as the Gwendolyn did – thanks to Richard – if they possessed a scanner that could be tuned to the right frequency range they could at least get an idea if there were any whales in the area. And any small advantage available to the lookout and gunner aboard the Hunter-Killer ships stacked the odds even more heavily in their favour.

Damn it! Why didn't I think of that before?

The very idea made Cal madder still, but it was with a touch of sadness that he decided he must abandon his research program completely for now. He had sworn to use his work to help the gentle giants of the sea. Despite his reluctance to admit defeat, he knew he couldn't tag any more whales until he was sure – one way or another – that he wasn't aiding in their deaths.

Well, there's more than one way to stop the Fleet!

Suddenly, the breakwater came to an end. Cal skidded to a stop, panting. This was as close as he could get to the harbour mouth. He crouched down, swinging the bulky bag off his shoulder and struggling with the zipper. The engine was louder now, closer.

Not much time!

Cal struggled to control his adrenaline, knowing that success now depended on a steady hand. He reached into the bag and lifted out his crossbow, bracing the shoulder stock against his chest as he strained to cock the heavy bowstring.

It locked with a satisfying click, and he loaded it and settled into a crouch with the weapon hugged against his cheek, the elbow of his supporting hand balanced on his knee for stability. His breathing was still ragged from the run, and the crossbow seemed heavier than usual. His aim wavered each time his chest rose and fell.

It was a moonless night. That had helped him when he needed concealment earlier, but now it would be a hindrance. He squinted, barely able to see the fore-sight in the darkness.

Cal took a deep breath and steadied his aim, waiting for his target to materialise out of the blackness.

One shot, and I can't afford to miss…

***

Akogi Yokuke slammed down the telephone, frustrated rage gnawing at his insides like a live thing. It was after 11pm in Tokyo and he was still working at his office in the Halls of Parliament, but now he knew he would not get home at all that night.

Another ship lost.

This time it was the Tosho-Maru – in addition to the loss of the Shushu-Maru, the newest asset in his Fleet. The combined catcher-processing ship had been his own brainchild, and now it was at the bottom of the sea. Along with his second-remaining catcher.

An aide in Shimonoseki had patched the call through to him from the Taiyoku Misui Fisheries Company's radio network the moment they had received the bad news.

Yokuke slammed a wizened fist onto the desk. "Damn that useless fool Gyofuku! How in the name of the Kami did he manage to lose another ship?"

This new attack on the Fleet, and his corresponding loss of face, would be a serious setback to his plans. In four decades of politics he had learned a lot, including how to sense trouble. His enemies in the Diet were already circling like vultures, waiting to seize the power he had so carefully accumulated. Which of them would make the first move? The mining industrialists? The loggers? It mattered not. He would never willingly resign, nor would he give up his power.

"I will do whatever it takes to fight off this threat to usurp my power – beginning with the wretched foreigners who brought this upon me!"

Yokuke's lip curled into a snarl as his anger coalesced to a focus. That accursed blonde Kajiki was the root of all his problems. He was proving to be as dangerous as a scorpion in the boot.

But what was he really after?

It was clear to Yokuke that the whole anti-whaling movement was nothing more than an insincere fabrication – a convenient barrow for Western politicians to push to buy them some votes from their immature and ignorant populace. No one could possibly be that fanatical about a bunch of dull-witted animals! And whales were obviously just dumb animals. They had no culture, and no inherent worth other than as a resource to be harvested. Could whales possibly match the thousands of years of language, arts, and culture that Japan had amassed? Of course not! Could a whale ever comprehend the sense of glory and honour with which a samurai views death? Never! Such a notion was inconceivable! He'd seen it himself, thousands of times – they died like animals!

Yokuke's brow wrinkled. The anti-whaling movement must be a conspiracy then. A plot by the New Zealand Government to end all whaling, supported by the Australians and the perfidious Americans too.

What better way to dominate the world than by forcing other countries to become dependent on their agricultural exports?

Yokuke snorted with a mixture of anger and disgust. The attacks against Japan's Whaling Programme were nothing more than politically-correct racism to further their secret agenda. "These Western imperialists are too cowardly to come right out and attack the Japanese race itself, so they attack our culture instead," he muttered. "Well, it is time Japan stood up for herself!"

To him, the situation was simple. The superior rights of people over other animals was undeniable, and the rights of Japanese to maintain their cultural diversity was paramount. The only question was how best to see it done.

As he pondered his options, Yokuke's thoughts came back to the brash American cop. His lip curled with involuntary distaste. Like all round-eyes, the big man stank of body odour and cheap fried food. Plus, Yokuke found him brusque and arrogant to deal with, an altogether distasteful man.

Nevertheless, as a master Kuromaku such things didn't concern him, nor would his personal feelings get in the way of him using the American any way he could to further his own purpose. He smiled like a fox.

The man was an uncivilised barbarian, but perhaps a useful one.

Yes, the bull-like American could prove very useful. His overconfident impetuousness could be turned into a valuable asset, but how best to use it…?

Yokuke smiled again and put the thought aside for now. He had more pressing business to attend to.

"Servant!" he shouted.

An aide instantly appeared in the doorway, bowing low.

Yokuke waved a hand impatiently. "Tell me, have I received a reply from the New Zealand Police yet? Will they extradite these criminals to face justice here in Japan?"

The aide kept his eyes on the floor. "So sorry, Master, they have refused. They say there is not enough evidence to charge them with any crime."

"We'll see about that," Yokuke muttered darkly, his face contorting with hatred. "The Kajiki is on borrowed time now."

Then his temper got the better of him. "Enough! This insult to my honour has continued long enough. I will not negotiate with these police like they are my equals. Get me the New Zealand Ambassador on the phone."

"Master, it is the middle of the night. He will be at home, in bed."

"Then wake him!" Yokuke snapped. "And be quick about it!" He held out his hand waiting for the receiver to be placed into it.

"Hello?" The voice on the line was blurry with sleep.

Yokuke smiled to himself. New Zealand's ambassador to Japan was well-known to him, as were all foreign diplomats in Tokyo. He found it was always easier to deal with people when they were already aware of his reputation.

"Mr Ambassador," he began, his tone treacherously congenial. "Let's talk about your country's trade debt to my country…"

The New Zealand diplomat was astute enough to realise he hadn't been woken in the middle of the night to exchange pleasantries, nor to talk about trade. Either that or he was too sleep-addled to try. He respectfully waited for Yokuke to come to the point.

And once the Japanese Fisheries Minister had an entire country bent to his will with the threat of trade sanctions, he was only too happy to oblige.

"Mr Ambassador, my demands are simple – and let me make it clear to you this is not a request you can refuse…"

Chapter 27

Dennis Cruikshank pulled into the motel parking lot, hurrying to his room before his dinner got cold.

He still felt naked walking around without his gun, but local laws were local laws – even if they were small-time and out of touch with reality. He grunted to himself, pleased he'd managed to smuggle his piece into the country anyway. How the hell the local cops managed to fight crime when no one carried guns was beyond him.

He let himself into his motel room and sat down on the bed, sparing a withering look for the stove in the corner.

"What the hell do I want with that thing?" he had asked the manager when he was shown into the room. "Even making Ramen noodles in the microwave is too much effort for me!"

He was met with a blank look. Evidently they had some cheap knock-off instant noodle brand here instead – and more annoyingly, the motel didn't have a restaurant.

Luckily he'd managed to find a McDonald's amongst all the vendors at the food court down the road. He opened the brown paper bag and reached for the familiar red carton that held his burger.

"Ah, the staple stake-out food! At least they've got some civilisation in this backwards little country," he muttered to himself.

His cellphone rang suddenly before he could take the first bite.

Cruikshank lowered his burger and picked it up, frowning as he studied the screen. It was a local number, and one he didn't recognise.

"Yes?" he snapped, answering it, annoyed at having his meal interrupted.

"Are you the American anti-terrorist guy?"

Cruikshank was immediately alert. "Who wants to know?"

"A friend told me about you," the speaker replied, carefully avoiding the question. "I have some information you might be interested in…"

The voice sounded muffled, as though the telephone receiver was wrapped in a cloth, provoking Cruikshank's suspicions even more. The more worried an informant was about being identified, the bigger the mess they usually turned out to be involved in.

"What kind of information?"

"Are you interested in the Gwendolyn and her crew?"

It sounded like a woman – or maybe a man speaking in falsetto to disguise his voice.

Cruikshank smiled to himself. "What about them?"

The speaker continued, almost tripping over the words in haste to get them out. "It might interest you to know they're planning more attacks against the Japanese. They will put to sea again very soon, with the aim of confronting the Fleet in the Southern Ocean. They're planning to stop them using violence."

"What kind of violence?"

"How should I know? You're going to arrest them or something, aren't you?"

"I'll look into it. How did you come by this information?"

"I already told you everything I know," the voice whined. "Look, I have to go now."

"Wait! Who are you?" he insisted. "How can I get in contact with you again?"

"I have to go, Man!"

The line went dead.

Cruikshank frowned thoughtfully as he mulled over the call, but he couldn't keep the satisfied smirk off his face. His efforts here on the ground had yielded up results already.

Things were starting to fall into place.

But he knew he had to hurry to spring the trap before the troublemakers got away again. The situation called for immediate apprehension of the suspects – using extreme force if necessary!

He picked up his phone and dialled his supervisor's secure line. Despite the time difference it was still late Stateside, but Silverman picked up within two rings.

"Ah, Agent Cruikshank. What do you have to report?"

"No time to explain now. Where's that SEAL team I requested?"

"They're on standby at Pago Pago, in American Samoa."

Cruikshank swore. "That's hours away! What are they doing there?"

"It's the nearest active military base."

"The US Antarctic Program has a staging post in Christchurch…" he suggested.

"That could take days to arrange," Silverman demurred. "We don't have an agreement in place with the New Zealand Government to stage combat operations from their territory."

Cruikshank rubbed his shiny head with frustration. "I don't care what it takes – dress them up as scientists if you have to! Just get them on a plane!"

Silverman hesitated, and Cruikshank could tell he was dithering again. Sure enough, the old goat tried to argue his call. "I'm sorry Agent Cruikshank. I don't see how this is a US problem. I agree this group are troublemakers, but so far they haven't directly threatened our country's interests. On those grounds I'm not sure I can justify to the Defence Department why we should be committing US assets against them."

Cruikshank bit off the curse that leapt to his tongue. "It's all in my field brief," he said through clenched teeth. "You'll get your justification soon. Just get me that SEAL team!"

He ended the call, his mind already racing ahead to the next problem. The protestors were troublemakers, all right, and the only way to combat trouble was with an even bigger stick! But what was he going to do in the meantime? As much as he was loathe to do so, it looked as though he would have to rely on local law enforcement resources to pick up the slack.

He clenched a fist angrily, already anticipating the lack of competent support he could expect to receive. It was one thing for the US to take on the leading role of global law enforcer in the fight against terrorism, but it was still staggering how many of these two-bit sponging countries refused to pull their weight even in their own territorial jurisdiction. Did they think they could bury their heads in the sand and pretend terrorism would go away?

Cruikshank muttered another oath, shaking his head in disgust.

He took a savage bite out of his burger and gulped it, pausing only to lick the juice off his wrist.

There are always ways to get things done.

Still chewing, he reached for his phone again.

***

Cal Major hurried back towards the Gwendolyn, eager to get back aboard and cast off.

The Kuu-Maru was already heading south again, and he knew Gyofuku would waste no time trying to kill Japan's new self-determined quota of whales.

As he ran back down the pier towards the Gwendolyn, he was pleased to see her bridge spotlight lance briefly out of the darkness to illuminate him. The Skipper was on the ball. He was taking no chances with any suspicious activity near his ship.

Cal could hear the soft hum of her engines as she waited for him, eager to depart. He kept running, holding up a hand to shield his face and closing one eye to preserve his night vision as best he could. A moment later the searchlight blinked out again, Duke evidently satisfied it was him.

Cal rubbed his eyes as he ran, still seeing spots from the glare of the powerful beam. Suddenly he heard a noise behind him, the crunching of tyres on gravel. Cal spun around, peering myopically, in time to see a police car enter the port complex. It came without lights or sirens, cruising slowly but purposefully through the darkened lot – and it was heading directly towards him.

"Shit!"

He sprinted the last twenty metres to the ship and leaped down onto the deck.

"Skip, time to cast off! We're about to have company!"

Cal tossed the bulky duffel bag through the nearest hatch and hurried aft. The police car was already nosing along the pier. What the hell did they want at this time of night?

Have we been betrayed?

There wasn't a moment to lose. He untied the stern mooring line and dropped the thick hawser onto the deck.

Hurry up!

Without bothering to coil up the rope he sprinted straight to the bow, reaching for the second mooring line.

"Ahoy there aboard ship!"

Cal hesitated, his hand resting on the rope. The cops were already out of the car, heading towards the ship. They were unarmed, which would make a getaway relatively straightforward. But it also meant they weren't expecting any trouble. He frowned, wondering what they wanted, but knowing that running from the New Zealand police now would only confirm whatever suspicions they had – not to mention causing much bigger problems later.

Can I bluff my way through this?

At that moment one of the cops spotted him crouched on the deck. "You there! This is the police. Stand up where we can see you."

Cal straightened up. "Yes? What can I do for you?"

One of the cops came forward. He had a goatee beard shaved to a severe point, and three sergeant's stripes on his shoulder. "We'd like a word with the master of this vessel. May we come aboard?"

"What's this about?" Cal prompted, stalling for time.

"We have papers to serve on the master of this ship."

"What kind of papers? What's this about? Can't it wait until morning?"

The sergeant wasn't about to be diverted though. "This vessel is alleged to have been involved in an incident at sea – a breach of maritime law." He reached into his shirt pocket and brought out a folded letter. "I have here a warrant to seize this ship pending an investigation."

"That's ridiculous. This is a research ship. We have all the necessary permits for our work."

"I'm sure you do. But that's not what this is about."

Cal feigned confusion, playing for time. "Eh? What do you mean?"

"This ship was allegedly involved in a collision at sea…" The sergeant frowned, becoming frustrated. "Now look, where's the skipper? If we don't start getting some answers soon we're going to have to start making arrests," he added ominously. "Is that what you want?"

Cal ignored the question. He could tell he'd pushed his luck about as far as he could. He put out his hand for the document, reaching across the narrow strip of water that separated them. "Let me see that."

He skimmed its contents with a lawyer's eye for detail. "This isn't a search warrant!" he exclaimed. "You can't board the ship."

The sergeant smirked at him. "We weren't planning to search the ship… unless you have something to hide?"

Cal cursed himself. He'd walked into that one. He knew he was going to have to play this cool.

"I'm going to need to see all the crew up here," the sergeant said flatly.

"Why?"

"They can't stay aboard. The ship is being impounded until the Maritime Authority representative arrives to investigate the allegations."

Cal hesitated, deliberating.

"If you don't call them up here we'll have no choice but to arrest the lot of you," the sergeant warned.

Reluctantly, Cal called for the others. If the police's responsibility was just to seize the ship and hand it over to the Maritime Authority then maybe they wouldn't treat the job all that seriously, so long as he didn't give them a reason to. And maybe that still left him a little room to manoeuvre…

"Who's the skipper?" the second cop repeated.

"I'm in charge." Cal stepped forward quickly, before anyone else could speak.

The sergeant looked momentarily surprised, but didn't argue. "Will you please accompany us down to the station. We have a few questions we'd like to ask you."

Cal noticed the second officer surreptitiously looking over the Gwendolyn's bow, no doubt looking for fresh scrapes or evidence of a recent impact. At least they hadn't mentioned anything about Shimonoseki harbour – yet.

"Am I under arrest?"

"Not at this time."

"Then I can refuse?"

"Only if you want to be arrested."

Cal pursed his lips, trying not to think about how much time this would waste. Gyofuku was even now steaming south, unopposed. Cal sighed. It seemed he had little alternative but to comply.

"What about my crew?" he demanded.

"They cannot remain aboard, but at this time they are free to go. They may have five minutes to collect what belongings they need."

Cal shot a look at the others, silently willing them not to interfere for now – but to get the ship ready to sail, without him if necessary. His gaze briefly met with Duke's, and the Skipper inclined his head ever so slightly. That would be plenty of time for him to hide anything incriminating. Being a part-time smuggler and a cagey old bastard, Cal didn't doubt he would have hiding places aboard the ship where things would never be found – short of tearing the whole ship apart. He grimaced immediately, hoping it wouldn't come to that.

He knew if he didn't cooperate with the police this could take a very long time. The authorities held all the cards right now, and they had all the time in the world.

"What about the security of my ship?" he said.

"It will be placed under guard."

Cal frowned, wondering if Amimoto might try something. But he didn't press the issue, wondering too if the person most likely to be breaking and entering the ship might turn out to be him.

"Fine. Let's get this over with then."

He reluctantly allowed himself to be led away and placed in the back of the police car.

The Central Police Station was a large multi-storey tower in the heart of the Christchurch CBD. The interview room was a cramped, fluorescent-lit dungeon somewhere deep in its basement.

Cal sat in a hard-backed plastic chair, faced down by the sergeant who had brought him in. There was no sign of the other cop, but Cal suspected he wasn't too far away – probably recording the interview. He glanced briefly at the CCTV camera mounted on the wall then shifted in the chair, trying not to let his frustration show.

"Please keep your hands on the table where I can see them," the sergeant instructed curtly.

Cal rolled his eyes. "What's the big deal" You've already searched me for weapons? What am I gonna do – scratch myself?"

The interview was equally exasperating as the cop went over and over his story with a fine-tooth comb, searching for any inconsistencies or contradictions. Cal tried to stick to the facts, describing his research and his legitimate purpose for being close to whales, how the Japanese ships had interfered with his tagging program, and how eventually they'd become frustrated trying to get to the whales and lashed out at his team. He played up the incident where Gyofuku had run down the Naiad, and played down the collision with the Shushu-Maru, blaming it on the confusion of the melee as the Japanese ships harassed the Gwendolyn – careful to mention it was three against one.

But once the first spin began then it was always harder and harder to keep it going, and as the questions became more and more direct he was left with little room to manoeuvre. It was late, and he was tired. As the interview wore on, Cal found himself working harder and harder to maintain his story. He could feel the beginnings of a headache coming on too.

"What about the sinking of those ships at Shimonoseki Harbour in Japan?" the sergeant challenged suddenly.

It was a curveball, designed to unsettle him, but Cal had been expecting the question all evening so managed to keep his expression neutral. "What about it?" he challenged.

"Ships blown up at their moorings? Sounds like terrorism to me! What would you know about that?"

Cal shrugged. "There weren't any bombs. I heard it was just a mechanical misadventure aboard. Maybe the crew did something they shouldn't have?"

"On *both* ships?"

Cal offered a faint smile. "Maybe Japanese sailors are exceptionally clumsy."

"You seem to know a lot about it," the sergeant said.

Cal shrugged. "I read the papers. Doesn't mean I had anything to do with it."

"What about the whaling ship that sank at its moorings at Lyttleton this evening?"

"It was leaking when it sailed in here. Besides, I have an alibi. I never set foot on shore all evening."

"How convenient! In fact, this was all very convenient for you, wasn't it? " the cop pressed. "And revenge would be a pretty obvious motive for you, wouldn't it?"

Cal's half-smile returned. "Ditto for them."

He knew it wasn't worth the trouble trying to tell the police about what really happened at sea. With no independent witnesses such claims would always be treated as hearsay, and with no proof of Gyofuku's murderous actions at sea Cal had no evidence in his own defence. And Amimoto was even craftier. Cal knew he would have covered his tracks scrupulously. Of his more sinister involvement; bribery, murder, and assassination, there would be no trace.

Cal sighed. Besides, he was guilty of retaliation too.

No, he would never be able to convince the police of what was really going on, although he could waste plenty of time trying. Time he did not have.

For now, his best defence was denial and silence. He needed to get the hell out of here and back to his ship!

At that moment a loud buzzer sounded in the room, and a bulb lit up on the wall. The sergeant looked annoyed. "Excuse me a moment," he said stiffly, then got up and strode out of the room. The heavy door swung shut behind him, drawn by the hydraulic strut atop it. It locked with a loud *click*.

After the cop stepped out, Cal wearily rubbed his temples. About the only consolation was that he wasn't handcuffed.

What a night!

This was too good an opportunity to pass up though, so he stood up, feigning a stretch. He glanced at the camera mounted on the wall, waiting to be ordered to return to his seat, but nothing happened. Cal sidled over to check the door handle. It wouldn't budge.

"Damn!" he muttered.

The interview room had an internal window that looked out into the corridor. Peering through the corner of the vertical blind, Cal could see the sergeant standing down the end of the passageway.

Thinking quickly, he grabbed his plastic drinking tumbler off the table and drained the water from it, then held it up to the window. With the open end pressed to the glass and the base against his ear it became an eavesdropping device, channelling sounds from outside the room.

"What is it?" he heard the sergeant asked irritably, from down the hall. "Can't you see I'm in the middle of an interview?"

Cal had no trouble hearing the reply. "This here's a load of horseshit! Can't you see this punk is guilty as sin?"

It was an American accent – and delivered at typically unrestrained volume.

Intrigued, Cal edged the blind open and peered out the window again. He could see the sergeant's back further down the corridor; outside what he guessed was the control room for monitoring the various interview rooms on the floor. It seemed the second policeman wasn't the only one keeping an eye on progress.

At that moment the second speaker took a step forward, and Cal could see the voice belonged to a big bruiser of a man. With his bald head and broken nose he had the look of a prison guard or a particularly street-wise cop – not a bad assumption given the current location – but Cal could tell from his attitude that this guy was something more than just a regular beat cop.

It was his eyes that gave him away. They revealed a hard and arrogant edge. This guy was dangerous.

The man looked vaguely familiar, but it took Cal several moments to work out where he'd seen him before. With a sudden flash of adrenaline the memory returned – this guy had been in the Press gallery at the IWC conference.

Cal frowned, momentarily confused.

What's going on here?

Then he noticed the oversized silver badge sticking out of the pocket of the guy's jeans, and everything fell into place. The showy emblem bore the crest of the US Homeland Security Agency. Terrorist-hunters.

This was bad.

"What the hell is this Mickey Mouse police department of yours playing at?" the Yank shouted.

Cal carefully edged the blind wider.

The Kiwi sergeant was glaring at the big man, but managed to maintain his composure. "Agent Cruikshank," he said stiffly. "International cooperation agreements don't give you the right to walk in here and take over. It'd be best if you accept that we do things differently in this part of the world…"

"I still can't believe you let his punk friends walk!" the agent fumed.

"Don't worry, we haven't let them go. Our department has been keeping them under constant surveillance from the moment they stepped off the ship."

The agent snorted, clearly disparaging of their ability to do so. "Well this perp is the ringleader! You can't let him out of your sight!"

"We don't have enough evidence to charge him with anything, so we can't continue to hold him here."

"Who's in charge of this two-bit operation?" the agent snapped. "Where's your superior?"

The sergeant struggled to maintain his demeanour. "It's the middle of the night. He's home in bed."

The American muttered a curse under his breath, then he eyeballed the sergeant. "What about suspicion of terrorism? Can't you hold a suspect for 72 hours without charge under anti-terrorism laws?"

The sergeant's voice was strained. "This isn't America, mate. Our citizens have rights. We can't detain anyone unless we have enough evidence to charge them with a crime."

Cal breathed his silent thanks at that, glad he lived in a country that hadn't yet bowed to the same knee-jerk and heavy-handed response to the threat of terrorism that was steadily eroding the rights of citizens overseas.

No one even knows what a terrorist is any more anyway!

That was the craziest irony of all. The authorities were ready to label him and his team as terrorists and throw everything they had against them, yet they'd never hurt a single person!

What about Amimoto? What he and his Fleet are doing is nothing short of global terrorism!

Cal suppressed his anger. Apparently money and power was enough of a defence against justice.

The American agent was equally unimpressed as he faced down the Kiwi cops, and he clearly wasn't willing to let the matter drop. "What a load of crap!" he spat. "Fine, if you won't hold him on suspicion of terrorism, how about murder?"

"Murder?"

"That's right. He's wanted by the Japanese police on charges of murdering Dr Victor Admirante, a Seychelles national who was killed at the IWC conference a few weeks back."

"You have evidence?"

The bull-headed Yank lowered his voice to a conspiratorial whisper, forcing Cal to strain to pick up his next words.

"Apparently his DNA was found at the crime scene…" he paused dramatically, "…on a pen."

"A pen?"

The American agent shrugged. "As far as I know it wasn't used in the actual crime, but it links our man to the crime scene – which is good enough for me!"

Cal felt his blood run cold at the sudden mention of Victor's name. He was angry enough about his friend's murder to begin with, but to suddenly find the finger of blame pointing his way was enough to floor him temporarily.

What the hell is going on here?

Why would anyone think he had anything to do with it? The whole situation was tragically ironic… perhaps even a little too ironic for belief!

Cal's eyes widened as understanding dawned. Only one man was capable of dreaming up such a devious and plainly evil scheme, let alone pulling it off.

Amimoto!

It had to be.

The bastard set me up!

The knowledge that a good man had been murdered was bad enough, but the sudden thought that he himself might have been the reason for it was enough to fill Cal with fresh anger – anger that was quickly replaced by grim determination.

At that moment he knew he would not rest until Amimoto was brought to justice and his corrupt and avaricious empire destroyed. The evil megalomaniac had already profited from murder and killing for long enough. It was time to put the world right.

Cal looked around the interview room, searching for a way to escape, but also knowing that to do so would be tantamount to admitting guilt.

In the next room the American agent delivered his ultimatum.

"This punk is a wanted criminal. The Japanese Government want him extradited to face justice in Japan. Turn him over to me and I'll personally escort him there. Will you comply?"

The Kiwi sergeant nodded, reaching for a phone. "I'll have to check with my superior, but if what you say is true then, yes. Evidence linking him to a murder is good enough to satisfy the conditions for an extradition."

At that moment the agent looked his way. Cal ducked back out of sight.

He looked around the room desperately. There was very little time left.

The Kuu-Maru was even now steaming south towards the Japanese hunting grounds, unopposed, and Gyofuku would waste no time making use of this advantage. Amimoto had trapped him nicely.

His enemy held all the cards, and Cal held none. His only recourse was to get away as soon as possible. Consequences could wait.

He cast a critical eye around the room. This was a public interview room in the low-security part of the building. There had to be a way out of here!

His eye settled on the security camera.

First things first – better make sure no one's watching.

He crossed the room and jumped at it, grabbing the cable and yanking it out of the back.

That should give me a few moments…

He reached into his pocket, but with a sinking heart he remembered they'd taken his pocket knife during the search. All he had left was his wallet and cellphone.

On a sudden hunch, Cal pulled out a credit card and crossed to the door. He crouched down next to the lock and tried to slip it into the door crack, but the card was too fat to fit. He swapped it for a thinner card, his laminated University ID card. Wiggling it into the gap, he lined it up with the lock mechanism and pushed gently. The angled bar slid back under the pressure until…

Click

Success! He eased the door open and glanced out.

The cops were still down the corridor, their backs turned. It was now or never!

He slipped his cellphone out of his pocket and dialled quickly.

It was nearly four in the morning, but it was answered on the second ring.

"Hey Vicki," he whispered.

"Cal! What's going on? Where are you?"

"Listen, I can't talk for long," he cautioned. "Is Duke with you?"

"Yeah. We're all at my flat. Is everything ok?"

He ignored the question. "Can you get back to the ship?"

"Just a minute." He heard a whispered conversation with someone nearby before she came back on the line. "Yeah, I think so. There was one Port security guard watching it but Skip will take care of him. Shouldn't be a problem."

Cal nodded to himself, a plan already taking shape in his mind. "Ok, now listen carefully. The cops are watching you so make sure you lose them before you head back to Lyttleton."

"We're busting the ship out?"

"Yep. It's not safe for us to stay in the country any longer. And you need to hurry. I've got to get away from here now, and I'll probably be in a bit of a hurry – especially if I have to borrow a vehicle from the police station."

"But you're all the way across town. It's a half hour drive!"

"I know. You'll have to cast off without me. Head for New Brighton Beach. I'll meet you at the pier." He paused. "If I'm not there I want you to keep sailing. Head south. Find Gyofuku. You know what to do."

She was silent for a moment, and he wondered if she'd heard. Then she spoke, her voice sounding sad. "Ok. But you know we need you here…"

"I'll do my best," he grinned, touched by her faith in him. "See you on the flip-side."

"Ok. And Cal?"

"What?"

"Be careful!"

Cal smiled grimly as he hung up the phone, then turned back to the door.

The cops were still down the corridor. For now. He edged the door open.

It was time to leave!

Part V – The Frozen Sea

Chapter 28

Feeling a sick sense of déjà vu in the pit of his stomach, Richard Major crouched on the wharf. Ahead, the dark shape of the Gwendolyn waited in the darkness, impounded at her moorings.

He was sweating. He fiddled with the hem of his rough woollen balaclava, wondering again what the hell he was doing here. He hated the thought of violence, and breaking the law certainly wasn't something he was comfortable with – even if it was starting to become commonplace. Desperate situations did call for desperate measures, after all!

He swallowed, trying to dispel the butterflies swooping in his stomach.

Just then his eyes caught movement in the darkness.

Oh no, something's happening!

The security guard stepped out of his kiosk, stifling a yawn, and trudged out on his hourly rounds. He clicked on his torch, shining it over the Gwendolyn's side rail, checking the mooring lines. Satisfied everything was in order he continued down the length of her hull.

His pace was slow and methodical, although Richard suspected that was more from fatigue than meticulousness given it was the middle of the night.

Richard held his breath as the guard passed by the stack of fuel drums further down the dock. Even knowing what was about to happen didn't prepare him for the swiftness of it. With sudden violence a shadow came alive and launched itself at the guard – the thud of the blow carrying clearly in the night air.

The man slumped to the ground like a puppet whose strings had been cut. Richard clapped a hand over his mouth, stifling the instinctive gasp of horror that sprang to his lips.

The Skipper – dressed entirely in black – bent over and nudged the inert form with the toe of his boot, then turned to beckon the rest of them forward.

"Ok, let's go!" Vicki whispered from somewhere nearby.

Richard forced himself to his feet, running woodenly to the Gwendolyn's rail. He tried not to look at the guard's body as he passed it.

"Oh my God," Summer gasped from somewhere behind him. "He's not dead is he?"

No one answered her.

Richard jumped aboard the Gwendolyn, feeling a brief thrill as his feet landed on the familiar deck. He hurried up the ladder to join the others in the wheelhouse.

"Where's that bit of Canadian crumpet got to?" Duke asked.

Vicki shrugged. "Gone down to her cabin."

Duke grunted. "Any sign of that weaselly hippy? Jumped ship for good, has he?"

"I guess."

"Hmph. Good riddance."

The Skipper turned back to the ship's wheel. "Stand by to cast off. We need t' get the hell outta here," he growled, flicking on the power switches that lit up the Gwendolyn's bridge. "Miss Vicki. You know how t' prime the engines for a cold start?"

She nodded, already on her way below.

"Richard. See t' the mooring lines will ya?"

"What about Cal?" Richard protested. "We can't leave him behind!"

"We can't afford to wait neither. If he ain't here, then he ain't here. This place'll be fair crawlin' with coppers any moment…"

Richard hesitated, unwilling to give up on his brother, but too afraid to challenge the Skipper's order.

Duke turned to him, his voice gruff but not unkind. "We gotta leave now, Son. Cal wouldn't want us t' fail on account of him, now would he?"

Richard shook his head. "No, I guess not."

Of course Cal would want them to carry on without him, but that didn't make it any easier.

I don't know if I can do this without Cal…

He forced his feet to carry him out into the night, where he struggled to untie the heavy stern lines. He was terrified, and his hands shook uncontrollably. But somehow he managed to get the thick ropes loose.

The deck rumbled beneath his feet as the Gwendolyn's engines burst into life. Richard jumped with alarm and scrambled forward, almost tripping in his haste to free the bow lines. A moment later the engines began to throb and he felt the surge as the propeller drove against the water.

The Gwendolyn accelerated away from the wharf, slipping away into the night. Richard leaned over the bow rail to help keep a lookout since they were running without lights. As the night closed in around the ship, he could feel the light breeze ruffling his hair. It was an eerie – and unsettling – feeling to be speeding across the slick black water without knowing what might lie ahead in the darkness. Vicki came up from below to join him and together they kept watch for danger ahead. He strained his eyes searching for the breakwater at the harbour entrance, and then for the dark fingers of rock that might mark a reef ahead. The harbour entrance was at the end of a long channel, between two massive ancient lava flows that ran out to sea. Richard tried not to look at the sharp volcanic rocks flashing by alongside them.

He felt empty and lost without Cal there.

Ten minutes later they were passing the ghostly abandoned gun emplacements at the end of Godley Head, and then the land fell away on either side and the wide expanse of the Pacific Ocean lay before them. Richard relaxed, suddenly aware how long he had been holding his breath.

The Skipper began to swing the wheel to starboard, aiming for Antarctica.

"Wait!" Vicki called up to him. "Head up the coast for a bit. We have to see if Cal made it out."

Duke shrugged doubtfully, but did as he was told. The Gwendolyn swung close to the dark cliffs again, hugging the coastline.

No one spoke.

Eventually they came to the lights of Christchurch. First was the seaside suburb of Sumner, then Southshore, twinkling in the darkness. Richard saw the wide river mouth of the Heathcote Estuary, a dark void between them. A few minutes later the sound of surf reached their ears. Then the New Brighton Pier finally slid into view – projecting out into the waves like a defiant bridge to nowhere.

The Gwendolyn throttled back to a throaty idle, and three pairs of eyes silently scanned the shore.

"I don't see nothin'," the Skipper said at last, shrugging apologetically. "And we cain't afford to hang around here for long neither."

Vicki sighed, then nodded.

Duke reached for the throttle.

"Wait!" Richard called. "Listen!"

They paused, craning their necks towards the distant shore. Then the sound he'd heard came again; the faint wail of sirens on the air.

Vicki broke into a wide grin. "That's gotta be Cal!"

"Clear the deck for action! Get that cargo net ready!" the Skipper shouted, and Richard hurried to obey, suddenly terrified for his brother.

The sirens rose in volume then the first police car appeared, speeding along the waterfront. On squealing tyres it skidded around the roundabout at the base of the pier, then screeched to a stop further up the street, blocking one lane. A policeman jumped out and tossed a metal strip across the road, the spikes atop it glinting wickedly. Both lanes were now blocked.

More sirens approached from the west.

For several long moments they could see nothing but the deserted street, bathed in the eerie blue and red flicker of the police lights. Then the white truck burst into view down the street. It was a prison wagon, and its engine roared as it thundered towards them. Its armoured windscreen was already starred by some impact. Richard gasped.

Is that a bullet hole?

The truck careered down the street, swerving wildly to prevent the pursuing police cars from getting alongside it.

The truck bore down on the parked police car, as if to ram it out of the way. At the last moment it veered aside – straight over the spike strip. The spikes tore into the tyres, shredding them with a loud hiss. The truck swayed as the driver fought for control, then the ruined tyres began to disintegrate under the weight of the vehicle. Strips of rubber tore loose, and sparks flew from the wheel rims.

The end of the street arrived quickly and the truck attempted to negotiate the roundabout at speed. But its destroyed wheels refused to obey and it skidded out of control, slamming straight into the concrete traffic bollard in the centre.

The sudden impact brought it to a bone-jarring halt, and the silence that followed was ominous.

Steam hissed from the crumpled grille, and a cloud of concrete dust hung in the air.

Suddenly the truck's door opened and a figure clambered out, looking dazed and disoriented from the crash.

There was no mistaking the tall athletic physique though, or the blonde hair.

"It's Cal!" Richard whispered.

The pursuing police cars screeched to a halt behind the crashed truck, and officers spilled out. Richard saw guns.

Oh no! Run Cal!

They would be on him in moments!

Cal's shoulders sagged, defeated. He began to raise his hands.

Just then the Skipper let out a long blast on the Gwendolyn's air horn.

Cal's head snapped around at the sound, and he began to run, slowly at first, painfully, then gradually picking up speed.

The police followed, shouting for him to stop.

Cal ignored them, feet pounding on the pier's wooden slats as he ran.

Moments later came several loud cracks as they opened fire.

Cal flinched and stumbled, but kept running.

The Skipper wrung his hands helplessly, but there was nothing he could do to help. There was no way the Gwendolyn could approach any closer to the pier. The swells quickly rose to breaking surf that would dash the ship against the piles.

"Run, Son," he breathed. "Run like the dogs was after ya."

Cal reached the end of the pier and the police hesitated, waiting to see if he would surrender or turn and charge them. But he did neither.

Without even wavering, Cal leaped off the end into the darkness, towards the water waiting far below.

The Gwendolyn's engines thundered in response, and she surged forward before he'd even hit the water.

As they fled down the coast, Richard sneaked a glance at Cal, still dripping wet as he sat on the Gwendolyn's chart table, unwilling to go below and miss any of the action.

"Are they following us?" Cal asked.

The Skipper glanced at the radar. "No sign yet."

"Hold still!" Vicki muttered as Cal leaned forward again, trying to peer out the darkened windscreen.

The Skipper was heading south at full throttle, and all spare eyes on the bridge were searching the night for danger – in front and behind.

Cal grimaced as Vicki finished stitching the gash on his shoulder.

"Couldn't see a bullet in there," she said. "Must have just grazed you."

"Maybe it bounced off?" he said with a cheeky grin.

"Not funny," she replied, slapping a gauze pad on his back hard enough to make him wince. "Next time you go pulling a stunt like that don't come crying to me to patch you up!"

Cal nodded sagely, as though recognising the concern in her voice. "Yes Mum."

Vicki stared at him, then she laughed. "Don't get cheeky with me, buster, or you'll get my thong across your legs!"

"Thong?" The Skipper was horrified.

Cal laughed. "She means a jandal. That's a flip-flop to you, Skip. It's apparently what they discipline kids with in Oz." He grinned wickedly. "Must be casual Friday every day if they don't wear shoes or belts over there!"

He ducked as she aimed a playful punch at his arm.

Duke just shook his head. "Still sounds more like X-rated Friday t' me," he muttered.

Richard smiled at their banter, knowing they were just blowing off steam. It was their way of dealing with the stress of the job – although he felt more like throwing up. He'd been scared to death the whole time, and he knew his hands were still shaking.

He stared ahead into the night. It had to be a miracle they'd made it this far, and at any moment he expected to see police lights come swooping out of the darkness. They had police boats didn't they?

The thought of what lay ahead was even more daunting, and Richard allowed himself a guilty moment to wonder if they might never catch up with the Japanese Fleet. They were searching blind now that Gyofuku had a head-start on them.

How can we possibly stop him from killing more whales?

The Gwendolyn needed to get there as soon as possible. But where exactly was that? They were definitely too far away to try tracking down a specific whale – and in any case, the pods would be too spread out for that strategy to work. Without knowing which one the Kuu-Maru was heading for they could end up hundreds of kilometres away from where they were needed.

Plus, there was no time for a lengthy search by trial and error. The Southern Ocean was vast. And as Cal had pointed out earlier, the season would last for just another few weeks while the weather held – time that could easily be spent searching fruitlessly. Gyofuku would waste no time killing as many whales as his ship could hold, whereupon he would immediately sail back to Japan to sell his ill-gotten booty.

They would have to predict his likely hunting ground and head straight there to have any chance of intervening.

Richard sneaked a glance at his brother, but Cal was deep in concentration, his frown giving nothing away. The Gwendolyn's bridge had fallen silent now, everyone alone with their private thoughts. It was very late and there were more than a few stifled yawns, but nobody left the room.

Though they had made good their escape, they all seemed to feel the shared tension that still hung over the wheelhouse. Everyone knew what lay ahead. Tonight had been just the beginning.

Richard looked around the room. It was a comfort to be with the others at a time like this, however small. Their presence alone was reassuring and it was good to know that – except for Summer who was below in her bunk – the Team's solidarity was resolute. That, and no one wanted to risk being caught out if something did happen.

Richard felt his heart waver at the thought of the conflict that still hung on the horizon, a monstrous black fear that hovered over him like a circling vulture. He sighed deeply, knowing Captain Gyofuku and his thugs were only the beginning of their worries though. They had to get there first.

Richard stared at the weather fax pinned to the wall. It was barely six hours old but it told a forbidding story. Two massive low pressure systems had collided in the Southern Ocean, the isobaric pressure lines converging until they were almost touching at a point south of New Zealand.

Gale force winds.

There was a massive storm out that way, and this time there would be no running ahead of the weather. This storm lay right across their path. They were headed at full speed right for it.

Richard remembered the storm-battered Tosho-Maru as it limped into port in Lyttleton, and he fervently hoped the Gwendolyn would see them safely through their trial

"What's on the radar?" Cal blurted, breaking the silence.

"Nuthin'…" the Skipper replied. "Which is kinda weird, since we should at least be able to see the shadow of the coastline."

Cal frowned, looking suddenly concerned. "What about the VHF receiver?"

Duke reached forward to switch it on, but only loud static filled the room as he scanned through the frequencies.

"Radio? GPS?"

Duke shook his head.

"Something's wrong," Cal muttered, jumping off the table. "They don't all go down at once!" He ducked out the wheelhouse door and clambered up onto the roof, favouring his injured shoulder slightly, though it didn't slow him down.

Vicki looked after him and shook her head resignedly.

A moment later Cal uttered a string of obscenities. His face appeared over the side again. "Here's the problem," he said darkly, proffering the severed end of a cable for them all to see.

It had been cut cleanly with a knife.

"All our antennas are like that!" Cal said. "Someone's sabotaged our electronics!"

"I'll wager that was your Japper friend from before," the Skipper muttered. "I knew that bastard was up t' no good!"

Richard stared at the sliced cables, suddenly feeling the assassin's cold blade pressed against his throat again. He gulped, glad to have escaped that fate, but wondering what else might go wrong. They were alone out here in the dark, with no radio and no navigational equipment.

At that moment both the Gwendolyn's engines spluttered and died.

***

Hogei Gyofuku swayed on his sea-chair as the Kuu-Maru lurched over another huge swell. He gazed impatiently through the spray-lashed windscreen.

The wind was picking up again. In this wild and windswept ocean the next storm was never too far away. It would take more than a storm to deter him though.

Things were looking up now he was finally rid of the meddling protestors. He grunted with amusement. Their interference was over for the season. Amimoto-san had arranged everything nicely! Even if they managed to escape jail and break their ship out of impound, they would never find him in time. The Southern Ocean was a huge place, and where he was going they would never find him. Never!

Holding the wheel one-handed, he groped for his saké flask to toast his success.

The Kuu-Maru crashed down into a trough, but his grip on the wheel was firm, as was his destination. South. All the way to Antarctica.

Let's see those wretched barbarians try to stop me there!

He was heading for the Balleny Islands and Cape Adare, right to the very edge of the Ross Sea itself – the Antarctic territory claimed by New Zealand.

He chuckled to himself, amused by his brilliance.

No one would even know he was there! It was the perfect crime!

How ironic that his glorious finale to the whaling season would take place right in the very waters claimed by his enemy's nation!

And how fitting!

He knocked back another draught of the fiery saké.

The stupid Westerners would never think to look for him there. And even if they did, what could they do? They wouldn't dare follow him that far south without an ice-strengthened ship. He laughed savagely.

I've got a quota to fill!

But that was only the beginning…

Gyofuku's eyes took on a predatory gleam. He'd had enough of taking measly Minkes this season. Even the massive Humpbacks were too slow to put up much sport. He smiled to himself.

It was time to prove the extent of his manhood. It was time to hunt Blues! As many as he could find!

He licked his lips with anticipation, gazing ahead out the windscreen.

Gyofuku smiled as he stared out at the cold grey sea, absently searching for the telltale double cloud of vapour amidst the spray.

At that moment something bright orange caught his eye. It was lying on the deck, partially hidden in the scuppers that drained the water away. He blinked with surprise.

What is that thing?

Ordering his First Mate to take the wheel, Gyofuku hurried down to the deck as fast as his portly frame would allow. He got there just in time, moments before the object was washed out through a drain hole and over the side.

He picked it up, turning it over in his hands. It was small, plastic, and orange, but that was all he could fathom. He stared at it, scratching the stubble at the back of his neck. The thing lay in his hand, thin and graceful in his sausage-like fingers. It was hollow at one end, with plastic fins at the other… but he had no idea what it was or how it came to be on his ship.

He squinted into the hollow tube, screwing up his face at it, but the answer still eluded him. "Bah! It's nothing but rubbish!" he spluttered, hurling the object over the side. The wind caught it, tumbling the thing into the sea where it was quickly lost in the wake.

Gyofuku stomped back up to the bridge, eager to return to the shelter of the cabin. The wind was definitely getting colder as the Kuu-Maru forged southwards.

All the better to catch some whales! he gloated.

Why the wretched creatures had to swim all the way down here to satisfy their hunger was beyond him though – but it did mean less competition from the pirate vessels run by the Korean, Taiwanese and Filipino captains. Only the might of Japanese industry was capable of sending a Fleet to follow the whales all the way to the windswept ocean at the bottom of the world!

Only real men dare to hunt this far south!

Gyofuku was looking forward to continuing his hunt in the Antarctic feeding grounds. The dense concentration of whales down here would allow him to meet his quota, or perhaps even exceed it! And with the greedy whales concentrating on filling their bellies, harpooning them would be as easy as shooting fish in a barrel!

He snorted disparagingly. It was clear to him whales were not intelligent since the beasts had no ability to comprehend the significance of the Kuu-Maru stalking them, and no concept of danger until it was much too late.

How stupid of them, neh?

He smirked to himself. Amimoto-san would be pleased with his haul this season. Perhaps a promotion would even be in order? Gyofuku felt his excitement building.

But it was more than thoughts of success that did it. Much more.

"Now the meddling barbarians are out of the way I can afford to kill some sea-pigs slower," he promised himself.

There was nothing to compare with the thrill of hauling one of the brutes aboard alive, and butchering it while still struggling…

Gyofuku reached down to adjust his overalls, his hand lingering at his crotch.

He gazed ahead out the windscreen, searching for the familiar burst of spray that would indicate a whale, his saliva already beginning to run with anticipation.

***

Richard hung on to the sloping roof of the Gwendolyn's wheelhouse, his heart in his mouth every time the ship crested over a wave.

"Why, oh why, did I volunteer to do this?" he whispered to himself.

The grey pre-dawn light gave enough light to work by now, and the soldering iron smoked in his hand as he fumbled for another cut cable. He could see down into the bridge through the skylight, and though he wished he was safely down there with the others, he knew he had an important job to do up here. After much cursing at the top of his lungs, the Skipper had managed to fix whatever was wrong with the engines, so now everyone was counting on him.

"Electronics is what you do," he reminded himself.

He took a deep breath and relaxed his hold on the roof. Though it was terrifying to let go his grip, he needed both hands to work. His elbows were already skinned raw from trying to stay on the pitching roof while he worked, but he tried to close his mind to the discomfort.

A few minutes earlier he had nearly fallen off the roof as the engines rumbled back into life, but his adrenaline had quickly turned into grateful relief. Duke was a miracle worker with that engine – but that put the pressure squarely on his shoulders now! They were no longer stranded, but they still needed their electronics!

Richard glanced down through the skylight now as the Skipper reappeared from below, wiping his greasy hands on his overalls. "Dirty bastard cut me fuel line," he growled. "Boy, I'd love t' get my hands around his neck. No one messes with my Old Gal!"

"Lucky there was enough fuel in the system to run the engines for a while," Vicki said. "Otherwise we'd have had a hell of a job escaping."

The Skipper frowned. "Maybe that was his plan? T' let us get aways offshore so we'd be stranded out here?"

Everyone went silent, thinking.

Richard swallowed at the thought. Sweating with fear, he eased the wire cutters from his pocket and tried to expose the core of the next cable.

To the east, the dawn broke in a fiery red blaze, lighting up the edge of the cloudbank ahead like it was on fire. It was a beautiful, but foreboding sight.

"Red sky in the morning…" Cal murmured from just over his shoulder. "Sailor's warning!"

Richard jumped, nearly falling off the roof. He hadn't heard his brother climb up behind him.

"H-huh?"

"Oh, nothing. Just an old superstition." Cal crouched down next to him. "Need a hand?"

Richard nodded, pleased and grateful. This was a devil of a job to do by himself. "Hold here," he directed as he soldered the cable back onto the VHF antenna. Several neat joins later their tracking system was operational again. Richard reached for the next cable.

"Pity we don't know which whale to track," he said.

Cal grinned suddenly. "Who says we need to track a whale?"

Richard was puzzled. "Well, how else are we going to find the Japanese Fleet?"

Cal winked at him, his eyes taking on an amused gleam. "It just so happens that the Kuu-Maru came within crossbow range on the way out of Lyttleton harbour. The wooden flagstaff on its foremast has acquired a brand new VHF tag, transmitting on our usual frequency band."

Richard shook his head in wonder. Cal had a plan for everything!

Now if I can just get the electronics back online…

The dawn's fire faded as they worked, and the huge cloudbank on the horizon darkened to the colour of gunmetal. A solitary Wandering Albatross skimmed across the wavetops on his lonely journey across the featureless wastes of the Southern Ocean. He had been following the ship for several hours now, as though surprised and curious to find other travellers out here on the waves.

Richard had never felt more alone though. But for the rest of the Team, it seemed like there was no one else in the world willing to support his stand – but plenty to oppose it. He sighed. His conscience was troubling him too.

His and Cal's parents had passed away several years ago, and even though he still missed them he was glad they couldn't see him now. He knew they'd be disappointed and angry with him for running foul of the law. They had strict beliefs on what constituted a successful life too. Richard didn't like disrespecting his parents' wishes, but for once in his memory he disagreed with them. He was glad he'd made this stand, even though it had come to this… fleeing from the authorities like a common criminal.

He glanced at his brother, working silently next to him. Cal never seemed to mind what people thought of him – or his self-appointed crusade out here.

Richard opened his mouth, then hesitated, searching for the right words. "Cal. Do you ever regret giving up your career to do this?"

Cal paused and looked up. He shrugged, but his eyes were probing. "I don't miss the corporate world, if that's what you mean." He thought a moment, then added, "This is my life now. Research science is a legitimate career, and don't let anyone tell you differently!"

Richard nodded, believing it, but he was still troubled. "I know, but it's just that… Mum and Dad wanted us to be successful and… well… I don't want to disappoint them."

Cal smiled sadly. "What's the definition of success?" he said. "It should be about your achievements in life, not how much stuff you have." He frowned. "It sure as hell shouldn't be based on what other people think of you. Not your parents, your neighbours, or anyone else in society. Who are they to judge anyway?"

He shrugged, emphasising his disdain. "Why is it that the magical badge of 'Success' always seems to come back to how much money you make? Most people these days are more selfish than ever! They only care about themselves and their own shallow lives. But what's the purpose of devoting your life to business and the pursuit of money? What a hollow existence that is! You can't take money with you, it doesn't make you a better person while you're alive, and it definitely doesn't make the world a better place – far from it in fact!"

He looked out to sea, staring at the dark clouds on the horizon as though lost in thought.

"Consumerism is the biggest blight on the Earth. Not only does it turn everyone into desk-bound slaves as they struggle to stay in the race, but it's ruining the planet!"

He shook his head sadly. "All those billions of consumers place insatiable demands on the Earth's resources; power, water, food, space, and raw materials to build all the useless junk you could ever want down at your local mall – along with plenty of stuff you will never need. And does anyone ever reuse any of those materials? No. You use something once and throw it away. Everything is disposable – except for the giant landfill needed to bury it all in as soon as people are finished with it! How many trees are cut down just so Western burger joints can put every burger in a cardboard box? Millions! And it costs the planet another 25 million trees every year just so Asians can have a fresh set of chopsticks with every meal! And what about all the raw materials that went into making the mountains of old car tyres, computers, and cellphones that we don't want any more? It all ends up at the dump! The whole of human society is unsustainable!"

He threw up his hands in frustration. "Everyone knows burning fossil fuels is destroying the Earth's climate, yet how many give up their cars? Together they all still contribute tonnes of pollutants into the atmosphere every day while sitting in endless traffic jams just to get to work and back. But does anyone care? No! City planners want to build more roads, gas-guzzling SUVs are the fastest-growing car market in America, and the US Government is willing to go to war to protect their right to cheap oil. What a stupid setup! It's completely unsustainable!"

He turned back to Richard, looking angry. "Just like hunting whales!"

Richard nodded guiltily. Up until a few months ago he had been one of those selfish consumers. Not because he thought it was the right way to live – in fact he could see now it wasn't – and not even because he'd made a conscious decision to live like that… It was just the way society worked. Everyone did it.

Cal's eyes took on a dangerous glint. "The giant corporations behind consumer society are the worst offenders. Taiyoku Misui Fisheries Co is already one of the largest and richest companies on Earth – and most definitely at the expense of it! They're responsible for wiping out whole fishing grounds – even whole fisheries – in pursuit of a quick profit. Yet Mr Fish's desire for ever more power and riches remains insatiable. All that devastation and destruction, just so one man can make a few more billions than he already has. What a waste!"

Cal shook his head sadly. "In reality, consumerism is responsible for the worst excesses upon the planet. In order to be successful, big businesses have to be as ruthless as possible. They share all the same hallmarks as psychopaths."

He held Richard's gaze, his eyes suddenly taking on a hidden depth. "The Cree Indians have an ancient prophecy: Only after the last tree has been cut down, only after the last river has been poisoned, only after the last fish has been caught, only then will you find money cannot be eaten…"

Cal sighed pensively. "Definitely gives pause for thought, eh?" He blinked then, as though embarrassed to be talking about something so personal to him. But when he continued, his expression was still earnest. "For what it's worth, I don't intend to let the likes of Amimoto put that prophecy to the test. Money isn't the only thing that makes the world go round. Not the Real World, anyway."

Richard nodded, understanding at last what had motivated Cal to give up his old life – why he did what he did now. It was still a hard choice for anyone to make though.

Richard looked out to the horizon. The albatross had gone. They were all alone on the grey sea.

Cal turned to him. "You're a good person Richard. Don't be afraid to follow your heart – there's more to life than making money for some company. Do the right thing, be true to yourself, and you will always be a success."

Richard nodded, grateful to his brother, but unable to find the words to express it.

Cal smiled and patted his shoulder, as though he understood perfectly.

Richard reached for the last cable and soldered it in place with a neat join, his thoughts still far away.

A sudden shout from below made him jump, and he nearly fell off the roof again.

"Radar's back online!" Duke called up from the bridge. "Y' might want to come have a look at this…"

"What is it Skip?" Cal called back.

"Trouble!"

They scrambled down off the roof and hurried back into the wheelhouse.

Richard looked at the large sinister-looking blob on the radar display. "Is that the Fleet?" he asked, puzzled. "It's behind us!"

"Nope." The Skipper tugged his beard thoughtfully. "Wrong shape. I'll wager it's that Jap destroyer we seen in Lyttleton."

"Closing speed?" Cal asked.

"None. Once they found us they slowed right up. Just shadowin' us. For now." He spat a wad of brown tobacco juice into his tin. "That ain't the worst of it…" he muttered.

Everyone turned to look at him, their faces registering sudden concern.

"Ah've had us on a zigzag course since we passed Stewart Island. Ain't no way they could blunder onto our tail."

Cal frowned. "What are you saying Skip?"

"Them bastards made right for us from well beyond radar range – even allowin' for their fancy military radar!"

"You mean…?"

"Yep!" Duke spat again, pointedly. "It means they already knew right where t' find us!"

***

Dennis Cruikshank stood at the empty dock, fists bunched angrily at his sides. He glared at the vacant berth in front of him. The dirty punks had given him the slip again – breaking out of police custody, no less!

He was furious that the local cops had dragged their feet long enough for the terrorists to slip through the net he was tightening around them, but he saved his anger for the perps themselves.

This time I'll make them pay, he promised himself.

The water slopped irritatingly around the wharf piles, mocking him.

He'd heard no word of this action before it happened. No warning from the undercover agent supposedly watching their every move.

Grinding his teeth with frustration, Cruikshank fished out his cellphone and stabbed the 'Call' button.

"What is it, Agent Cruikshank?" His supervisor answered on the second ring, his voice sounding strained.

"Have you read my report yet?" Cruikshank snapped.

"It's under consideration," Silverman assured him. "I've had more important issues demanding my attention."

"Such as?"

Silverman hesitated, and for a second Cruikshank thought he was going to get the traditional brush-off. But then the old man surprised him. "There have been... uh... difficulties with the flow of information from the field."

"Really? So what's the word from your good-for-nothing undercover agent then?"

"No word for 24 hours. At the last report they were in port and everything was normal."

Cruikshank swore. "Well let me tell you something, I'm standing here looking at the spot where they *were* in port and I can assure you the situation here ain't fucking normal! The ringleader busted out of police custody last night and they took off!"

"Yes, yes, I'm aware of last night's sudden developments," Silverman said, sounding exasperated. "Let me assure you we're working to re-establish contact-"

"Forget that," Cruikshank interrupted. "Just tell me where the bastards are headed and I'll sort this out myself!"

"We have difficulty getting up to date intelligence while the ship is at sea, but I've committed extra resources to the case..."

"Hope your agent hasn't been sprung!" Cruikshank grunted, in no mood to listen to Silverman's spin. "We're gonna need pinpoint intelligence from now on. All I can say is, he better be up to the task!"

"Yes, yes. I've got everyone I can spare at this end working on it."

Cruikshank snorted.

Better late than never!

"I don't think I need to remind you this situation is escalating – just like I warned you!" he said.

"Indeed it is – along with every other terrorist threat I have to monitor!" Silverman snapped. "Al Qaeda has been a far more immediate problem until now!"

"Until now," Cruikshank repeated. "Now this has really hit the fan though, hasn't it?" He laughed humourlessly. "Three separate attacks on friendly shipping, and we've been caught sitting on our hands the whole time! Quite an embarrassment isn't it?"

Silverman exhaled deeply. "Yes. Yes it is. The whole world's gone mad these days. There's more damned terrorists popping out of the woodwork than I can shake a stick at!"

Cruikshank rubbed his head with impatience. "Yeah, and now this lot are at it again, with no assets within hundreds of miles who can stop them – except this agent of yours! Might be about time to switch him to an active law enforcement role, I reckon. Think he can handle it?"

Silverman coughed. "I... uh... it would be best not to rely on that eventuality."

Cruikshank felt his anger rising. "What? Why the hell not?"

There was a telling pause at the other end. Finally his supervisor spoke. "This is the agent's first assignment."

"What? For Christ's sake! Tell me you're kidding!"

"This was a low priority case," Silverman retorted defensively. "It was classed as low-risk. The agent's task was to be intelligence-gathering only. We weren't to know things would escalate so quickly."

"You could have listened to me!" Cruikshank growled, adding a curse for emphasis. "Well I hope you're listening now. This situation is rapidly going from fucked-up to worse, and that agent is the only resource we have on the spot so he damn-well better be prepared to earn his keep!"

He kicked blindly out at a wharf pile in front of him, struggling to keep a lid on to his temper.

The one consolation he had was that Washington was finally starting to sit up and take notice of the situation here. He'd been hollering at them until he was blue in the face, but there was nothing like a little action with the police to finally grab those pen-pushing bureaucrats' attention.

Last night's chaos had achieved what he could not. Gunfights and high-speed pursuits got people's attention. The perfect environment to submit his report.

The timing couldn't have been better!

His moustache twitched as he smiled to himself. Not only did he have a captive audience in the Government, but he knew his report could not be ignored now.

Although he hadn't actually done anything against the rules, by a stroke of devious cunning he had managed to subvert the usual processes. Activating the Joint US-Japanese defence treaty was brilliant – even though the Japanese Fisheries minister had to claim some of the credit for the idea – and it had given his request a fast-track straight to the President's desk in the Oval Office, all-but guaranteeing Cruikshank an immediate mandate to act.

He twirled his moustache. "Well, have you read my report yet?"

"Yes. I think it's safe to say everyone here in Washington has been alarmed at the rapid deterioration of this situation. The Government is concerned about the implications and is anxious for it to disappear as quickly and quietly as possible."

"Meaning…?"

Silverman hesitated as though reluctant to continue. "The Defence Department has approved your request. I've been given full authority to authorise whatever immediate preparations you need." He sighed, as though still not sure this was the best decision. "The SEAL team is already en route. Get ready to rendezvous with them at sea. You have a Green Light for armed intervention."

Cruikshank punched the air with ill-concealed glee. "Alright! About fucking time!"

Chapter 29

The Roaring 40s gave way to Furious 50s as the Gwendolyn gamely forged her way deeper into the Southern Ocean. Richard Major lay on his bunk and groaned weakly as his alarm went off. He was still strapped into bed so he let it ring. He didn't need a wake-up call, since he'd barely slept a wink all night due to the constant rolling.

He grimaced, transported back to his first week at sea. He had thought he was finally used to the motion of a ship, but he'd never experienced anything quite like this before. He was covered in new bruises where he'd been mercilessly pummelled against the walls. Then again, he'd never been this far south before – where the sea heaved like an angry giant. The waves here were mountainous cliffs of angry water, and the wind had the icy bite of Antarctica behind it.

Just then the Gwendolyn surged over another wave crest the height of a small building, before pitching down the other side with a dizzying drop. Richard fumbled with his straps and rolled over, reaching for his bucket as his stomach churned threateningly.

He was seasick and miserable, and missing land.

"What am I doing here?" he whispered to no one in particular. "I'm not cut out for this."

His determination was starting to fail him, and he wondered – not for the first time since the previous night – what the hell he was thinking when he'd agreed to return to sea. "Who am I kidding? I'm no marine biologist!"

At that moment he would have given almost anything to be back at his nice safe desk working on a circuit board. Or for that matter, almost anywhere other than this perpetually-moving roller coaster from hell. His head felt like it would continue to spin for weeks afterward.

He felt decidedly wretched.

He knew without looking that the vast seascape outside would be empty and devoid of life. The albatross had been absent for days now. It seemed the Veteran Mariner knew better than to hang around in the path of a storm.

We're the crazy idiots heading straight into it.

Richard sighed.

We're also the ones with no choice…

Right now though, he cared far less about stopping Gyofuku than he did about stopping the world from spinning so crazily around him.

He struggled out of bed, pulled on some clothes, and staggered out into the wildly pitching corridor.

He skipped breakfast since he was feeling so queasy already, heading straight up to the bridge instead. Well, as straight as he could manage at any rate. He felt like he was taking his life in his hands as he clung to the rungs halfway up the stairway, resisting its determined effort to buck him off.

Vicki was at the helm, and her dark ponytail bobbed merrily as she turned back to greet him. "Don't worry. You'll get used to it in a day or so." She smiled. "Just remember to hang on to the wall when you walk around. And don't put anything down without tying it to something or it won't stay put for long!"

She pointed to a sipper cup firmly anchored in a cup-holder. "I made you a coffee."

"T-thanks," he murmured, feeling suddenly embarrassed by her show of kindness.

He took the drink and hastened to the map table – desperate to get away from the lurching, spinning view of the world visible out the windscreen.

He tried to think about something – anything – to keep his mind off how seasick he felt. Summer wasn't around, but that was hardly surprising. Lately she'd been spending just about every spare moment holed up in her cabin.

The notion entered his head to go down and see how she was feeling, and maybe offer some joint sympathy – misery loved company after all. He dismissed the idea out of hand. He was too shy to impose on her uninvited, and besides, he was feeling much too grotty to impress her with scintillating conversation skills.

His gaze travelled unbidden to the radar screen, and the sinister-looking blob still trailing the Gwendolyn, lurking somewhere below the horizon behind them.

Richard looked away, not wanting to think about the looming showdown.

Something the Skipper had said continued to nag at him though, hovering at the edge of his thoughts like a phantom. Suddenly he realised what it was. The Skipper was suspicious how easily their pursuers had been able to find them. Heath was the obvious suspect if they had indeed been betrayed, but how were the warships able to know where they were if the dreadlocked Californian was no longer aboard?

Did he plant some kind of bug?

Suddenly Richard was in his element. He hurried over to the computer where the data from the VHF antennas was analysed. After a moment to crack his knuckles and order his thoughts he got to work, fingers flying over the keys. He reconfigured the receiver to scan the entire bandwidth, not just the frequencies of Cal's tags. But as the minutes dragged by his enthusiasm dissipated into the relentless hiss of static.

No signals. There's nothing out here. Not even a whale!

One thing was certain though, Heath definitely hadn't planted any bug that was broadcasting their position.

On a sudden hunch, Richard widened his search to include satellite uplink frequencies. The results were predictable though – any signals conspicuous by their absence. A sudden burst of distortion made his heart race, but his excitement was quickly dispelled as he scanned back through the frequency. There was no signal, and whatever it was had gone.

"Probably just some kind of interference," he told himself.

He saved the worthless scan results anyway, as if to prove the morning wasn't wasted.

It was hard to accept his hunch had been proven wrong. He realised then how desperately he'd wanted to find some evidence for Cal, knowing this was probably the one area where he could prove his worth. Not only did he feel like a failure now, but each sweep of the radar reinforced the presence of the dark shadow behind them.

He looked away from the display, determined to think about something else.

Richard needed to clear his head. He stood, heading towards the outside door before he could change his mind. "I'm going to take a walk on deck," he said.

"Be careful," Vicki warned. "It's rough out there."

She was right.

The wind threatened to tear the door out of his hands, and Richard was glad he'd put on his parka. He dug in the pockets for his gloves and beanie, holding the rail in a double-handed death-grip as he started tentatively down the ladder.

What the hell am I doing!

Richard forced himself down the ladder and onto the deck, swaying towards the next rail like a drunk. Out on deck, surrounded by the wind and pounding seas, he was suddenly exposed to the raw power of nature – and the storm was still a day's sail ahead of them yet!

He gritted his teeth and hung onto the rail, determined not to retreat inside like a coward.

And after a few minutes he surprised himself. Though it was definitely cold and blustery out here, it was actually easier to cope! He found he could see the waves coming so he could predict the ship's movement. Although he still had to time his steps to be able to make any progress along the deck, his stomach actually felt better than when he was inside.

He made his way forward, surprised to see the wide open space of the foredeck was gone.

Cal looked up from where he was working, grinning when he saw him. "Morning Bro! Tie yourself off with a deck line!" he shouted over the wind. "We don't wanna lose you overboard!"

Cal and the Skipper had been working on deck all night with hammer and saw. The nights were getting shorter the further south they went, and the extra hours of daylight had been put to good use. The two of them had erected sheets of plywood to make sheds enclosing the Gwendolyn's front and rear decks.

"It'll protect the Naiad," Cal explained, "And us. The seas down here can get massive. Wouldn't want anyone out for a stroll getting washed over the side."

He and the Skipper were working with paintbrushes and rollers now, painting the new covered decks the same dark navy blue as the hull.

Richard picked up a brush and began to help out, the regular gale-force blasts of fresh air and splash of flying spray quickly driving away his nausea.

Soon the bare plywood was covered in blue, making the new constructions look like mini shipping containers stacked in front and behind the white bridge.

The painting didn't stop there though. At Cal's behest they moved onto the ship's superstructure itself next, laying down dark stripes with each brush stroke.

"Sorry 'bout this, Old Gal," the Skipper muttered. "Best t' consider it a makeover!"

Richard stifled a giggle. Duke's beard was flecked with blue, and he looked more like a hairy clown talking to his ship than a fearsome pirate.

Just before lunch the Gwendolyn's entire handsome white upper was covered under an all-over coat of sombre blue.

"Why the new paint?" Richard wanted to know.

Cal looked uncomfortable. "Camouflage," he said finally. "It's the same colour as the sea. The new deck profile will change the Gwendolyn's appearance too. Hopefully her new silhouette will make her look more like a longliner. It's not much of a disguise," he admitted, "But it might buy us some precious time when we go into action…"

Richard swallowed, turning to stare at the grey horizon behind where the warship stalked them. Ahead, the whitecaps stretched all the way to the dark mass of stormclouds boiling ominously in the gunmetal sky. Somewhere beyond them, Gyofuku was already prowling the seas, looking for whales to kill.

We have to stop him!

But they would have to head straight into the teeth of the storm to get there in time.

That night the storm hit. With a vengeance.

A furious gale swept out of the south – making the pre-storm seas seem positively tame by comparison. Richard had thought he'd experienced rough weather already, but nothing could have prepared him for this.

On all sides rose twenty metre high breaking waves – walls of foaming white water taller than a multi-storey office tower – and the windows were lashed by horizontal driving rain, mixed with blinding spray whipped up by the shrill wind.

The waves were breaking over the Gwendolyn's bow as she drove through them, sending torrents of hungry water swirling across the forward deck – threatening to sweep away the new deck covering at any moment.

To venture outside would be madness.

Even walking anywhere was all-but impossible on the wildly-pitching floor, and despite clinging to a bulkhead rail Richard had to fight to stay on his feet.

Each shuddering wave tried to tear his grasp loose and send him flying into the wall behind.

Richard sneaked a glance at his brother, and even Cal wore a worried frown. Only the Skipper seemed unfazed – or perhaps resigned to their fate?

Everyone was crowded together on the bridge, huddled around the heater, while outside the wind howled like a demon. It seemed strangely surreal to be this cold in the middle of summer, but summer was far behind them now. The warmth of the sun was just a distant memory in this place.

Even Summer herself had emerged from her cabin, looking wide-eyed and terrified. Sleep would have been impossible anyway – especially given that anyone risked a concussion just by remaining in their bunk – and it made sense for all hands to gather where they might be needed. It was also the closest place to the life-raft, Richard observed. Although there was no way in hell he even wanted to contemplate braving this storm in that little thing.

It was a blessing when the long grey twilight finally gave way to the blackness of night – if only because the terrifying mountains of water were no longer visible. It was a mixed blessing though, not being able to see the waves. The thundering breakers continued to lunge out of the night, pouncing on the Gwendolyn without warning now, flinging her around like a cork in a whirlpool.

At times the rough seas even hampered their forward progress, and Richard began to wonder if the vicious storm might spell failure for their mission. Regardless of whether they survived it unscathed or not, they were making slow progress and still too far away from the Fleet to beat them to the Antarctic now.

The one consolation was that for as long as the storm lasted, Gyofuku and his Fleet couldn't hunt any whales in weather like this. Right now it didn't seem like much of a consolation though.

Richard flinched as the Gwendolyn was battered by a particularly savage wave. "A-are you sure we're gonna be ok?" he stammered, aware of how small his voice sounded amidst the din of the storm.

The Skipper stared at him, and Richard suddenly felt foolish. But then Duke's laugh boomed like a concrete mixer full of gravel. "Don't you worry 'bout a thing. This old gal's weathered more storms than you've had hot dinners!" His beard twitched into a whiskery grin. "This here's the finest damn ship on thuh waves! She used to brave Arctic storms by the dozen trawlin' the North Sea, and she ain't gonna be bothered by our quick little jaunt south!"

Richard nodded politely, still not convinced.

Duke stared ahead into the heart of the storm, and his voice turned suddenly wistful. "Let me tell you something…" he began. "Gwendolyn – the real Gwendolyn – was a very special gal. She was my high school sweetheart. We was gonna get married, y' know… just as soon as I got back from 'Nam." He paused, and his shoulders slumped suddenly as though a light went out within him.

"She passed away not two months b'fore my tour was up. Killed in a car wreck. Drunk driver ran a stop sign…"

He sighed deeply. "She was my entire reason for staying sane in that hellhole of a country, and without her I didn't have nothin' t' live for no more.

So I signed up for another tour, figurin' 'What'd I have to lose?' Maybe I was ready to join her? I dunno. But Death couldn't find me. I stayed in that place until the war was lost – until Charlie took over the entire goddamn country. Then I became a drifter."

He sighed again. "I was just a young buck then, but I ain't never been back t' the States since. Too many painful memories, see?"

He gestured out the windscreen into the dark night. "After my discharge I made me a new home, here on the Sea."

Richard stared at the Skipper's tattoos, which seemed suddenly fainter against the leathery skin on his forearms. Richard wondered how he could have ever found the gruff old sailor so terrifying.

"I started out as a deckhand," Duke continued, "Crewing on freighters and fishin' boats and whatnot. Some of 'em were a rough lot; smugglers, gun-runners, and worse. But I got by. Took many a year b'fore I could afford me own ship though, but I ain't never looked back. She became my life instead."

He gazed out into the darkness. "The Sea's a good Mistress," he said wistfully. "But all ah've left of me sweetheart now is the ship I named in memory of her."

His shaggy eyebrows dropped in a sudden frown. "What I'm gettin' round t' saying is this: I ain't about to let anything happen to this Gwendolyn, and I reckon nor is the real Gwendolyn. Sometimes I feel her presence, like mebbe her spirit is with me, watching over her namesake…"

He coughed awkwardly, as though embarrassed for revealing too much of himself.

Then he turned to Richard, patting the ship's wheel tenderly with a calloused hand. "Don't y'all fret, now. Ah've complete faith in this old gal. She's seen me through plenty o' blue weather before, and I ain't got no reason to doubt her now." He offered a whiskery grin that was as near to friendly as he could manage. "She'll take us all thuh way t' the gates of hell, Son."

"That's what I'm afraid of," Richard whispered.

No one said anything on the bridge for a long time after that.

The night lasted barely an hour or two before the sky began to lighten, and the world was dominated by the mountainous churning waves again.

It was Cal who finally broke the silence. He wore a deep frown on his face, as though lost in thought. "Skip," he murmured at last. "What are we gonna do when we get there?"

"Knock a few heads t'gether, I imagine," came the droll reply.

A brief flicker of amusement crossed Cal's face, then he was serious again. "How do we get the job done though? We have to finish it once and for all this time, whatever it takes. But we can't use lethal force."

Duke raised a bushy eyebrow. "That'd be like picking a fight with the biggest outlaw in town – with both hands tied behind y' back!"

Cal didn't meet his eye. "No lethal force," he insisted. "I'm sorry, but we can't give them any excuse to hang us out to dry."

The Skipper didn't argue any further, but his disgusted expression made it plain what his own thoughts on the matter were.

"How can we stop Gyofuku without using lethal force?" Vicki asked quietly. "He's not about to listen to reason!"

"You let me worry 'bout that, Miss Vicki," the Skipper insisted, immediately assuming responsibility. "I got more than a few tricks up me sleeves. And one or two surprises hidden away for a rainy day."

He thumped a brick-like fist on the dash for emphasis. "Them Jappers're gonna wish they'd'a gone home thuh first time we asked 'em nicely! B'sides, me and that damned knife-happy captain got our own unfinished business to attend to," he added under his breath.

Cal said nothing.

Richard wasn't sure if his brother had heard the last bit or not, but he felt his own heart start to race. The thought of conflict alone was enough to bring him out in a cold sweat, but knowing there was going to be deliberate and unavoidable personal violence gave him the shakes.

Suddenly he wasn't sure if he was ready for the showdown with the Japanese Fleet.

"C-Cal, we're doing the right thing, aren't we?"

Cal turned to lay a reassuring hand on his shoulder, looking searchingly into his face. "What does your heart tell you Bro?"

Richard nodded, understanding, but still terrified.

Cal smiled at him, in a forlorn way. "In the whole of the universe scientists haven't found a single other planet with life aboard. There are no liquid water oceans, let alone whales. In the context of the entire universe, what is the continued existence of an entire race of unique life forms worth? What is that value when compared to a bit more cash in the hand for a man or an economy that doesn't even need it?"

Richard looked at the floor. He knew without a doubt that something needed to be done, but he still hadn't entirely shaken the vain hope that someone else might arrive to relieve him of the responsibility.

Cal continued, speaking softly, choosing his words with care. "As a biologist, I believe we all have a duty to protect every species in the world, or at least question the right to annihilate them. Humans are the most indiscriminate killers on the planet. Every other species – even much-maligned sharks and other predators – kill only when they are hungry, and take only as much as they need for their next meal. Humans are the exception. The only exception. We relentlessly pursue our prey whenever we find it – even to the point of extermination – and we wage a ruthless war on any competitors or perceived threats."

Cal blinked suddenly, and Richard could see a deep sadness in his eyes.

He wasn't finished though. "If the entire age of the Earth was compressed into a single calendar year, then we have been here only since 2 minutes to midnight on December 31st – yet we act as though everything belongs to us. Even life itself."

Cal shook his head, his disbelief clearly heartfelt. "Mass Extinction is inevitable with that attitude. In fact, it's already happening. We're facing the Sixth Mass Extinction Event in the history of the world – the greatest loss of life since the dinosaurs died out – and this time it's our fault. Direct interference, habitat loss, and then human-induced climate change will spell the end for hundreds of species. Nearly a quarter of all mammals alive today are in imminent danger of extinction – many of those have already been reduced to tiny relic populations of thousands or even just a few hundred individuals left. And even those are still under constant pressure from humans. There simply isn't anywhere safe for them to get away from us any more. Many mammal species will disappear from the wild for good in just a few decades if something isn't done now."

Summer spoke up from the back of the room, surprising Richard with her sudden interjection. "But isn't extinction a normal process? Doesn't it just mean these species aren't suited to survive any more?"

Cal's smile remained tolerant. "Sure, extinction is a 'natural' process – in fact, three quarters of all known species are already extinct – but it's not normal at the rate we're causing it. It's definitely not good for the world's biodiversity if everything dies off at once! The IUCN Redlist predicts that human-induced extinctions will soon reach a hundred to a thousand times normal extinction rates – and that's based only on documented and confirmed extinctions to date, so it's a conservative estimate. Some scientists predict fifty percent of species on Earth could be gone in a hundred years." He turned to look at Summer, his smile fading. "Those extinctions are occurring not because of natural selection processes, but because we've changed the world so much and so fast that we've pulled the rug from under these animals. The world they evolved to live in is rapidly diminishing and they can't adapt fast enough. Pretty soon the only species left will be those capable of surviving in the degraded and polluted 'humanised' environment that's left."

"Supposing God gave us dominion over the Earth?" Summer sneered.

"Then we're doing a piss-poor job of taking care of it!" Cal replied. He held up a hand to forestall her next question, clearly not wanting to get drawn into a theological debate with her now. "Moral arguments aside, it's plain stupid to decimate the same planet we have to live on too. Nature might be able to cope with a few extra extinctions here and there, but if we keep wiping out species then sooner or later entire natural systems will begin failing. We just can't keep removing links without the chain eventually breaking. And as much as people like to think we don't need nature, we all still need air to breathe, food to eat, decomposers to clean up after us, and a favourable climate to live in."

"How many species can we afford to lose before that breakdown happens?" Richard whispered.

Cal shrugged. "How many rivets can you remove from a plane before it's no longer safe to fly in?"

He turned his attention back to Richard, and his expression was set. Determined. "Humans have effectively declared war on the whales," he said quietly. "Over the past century we have used our intelligence and technology to decimate their once-great populations. Even now, with their survival hanging in the balance, people continue to pursue the last survivors relentlessly to the ends of the Earth, killing them on sight. Why? What justification could people possibly have for annihilating whales? They're no competition to us, no threat." He sighed. "The reason is as shameful as the unprovoked slaughter itself. It is greed, pure and simple."

Cal flicked a potent look at Summer, as though daring her to try and challenge him.

She studied her fingernails though, and he continued. "We are just one species on this planet. I don't believe we have the right to choose the fate of any of the others. The whales are the largest animals to ever live on Earth, and the world would definitely be the poorer for their passing. They have become a symbol for those far-sighted people trying to stem the tide of human destruction. This is our line in the sand, and we must succeed. If we can't save the largest species, what hope is there for the rest of the planet?"

Cal glanced in Summer's direction again. "To most people the relentless spread of human influence across the planet symbolises progress, the triumph of man against nature! We've created the unique illusion for ourselves that we're somehow separate from the laws of nature. The average person on the street doesn't even know how the Real World is supposed to work, let alone care about it. But we cannot defy natural laws forever. We are just one strand in the web of life; whatever we do to the web, we will ultimately do to ourselves."

Richard closed his eyes, remembering the joy and exhilaration he'd felt when he met Old Blue, the gentle giant of the ocean, face to face in the wild free seascape of his own realm. Cal was right. The freedom to live your life was the single most important right of any species. Whales' right to exist should be paramount, far outweighing any Japanese aspirations to make a quick buck at their expense. The balance of the world needed to be redressed, urgently. Apathy by the current generation would certainly doom whales forever, not only denying them a future, but also denying all future generations of children the chance to meet one as he had. Whales would be just a memory… a few photographs consigned to history books or a collection of old bones displayed in museums – for the rest of eternity. Richard gritted his teeth, knowing such a tragedy could not be ignored. It was time the greedy and grasping whaling business got a taste of its own medicine.

Someone must step up and do what needs to be done. Now!

Richard was conflicted however, knowing he couldn't expect anyone else to fight a battle he wasn't prepared to himself. It was a difficult decision to make too, knowing there was the certainty of violent conflict at the end.

But he also knew he couldn't bear to watch another whale die. He had seen it too many times already, and each time was worse than the last.

Watching whales killed day after day starts to do things to you – it tears out a part of your soul.

And now he'd seen it with his own eyes, whaling was not something he could ever forget – nor stand by and allow to continue.

Human greed will destroy the World if left unchecked.

Richard opened his eyes, staring out at the wild and windswept vista of the Southern Ocean. The sky was dark, blotted out by the storm that raged around them.

Cal followed his gaze. "Ironic, isn't it?" he said. "Life began in the oceans long before people were around. Our own distant ancestors would once have swum here alongside the whales. Even today, over two thirds of the planet's surface is covered by water – yet we still insist on calling it Earth! That pretty much sums us up as a species – we just don't have a clue!"

Vicki had been silent the whole time, pensive, but she spoke up suddenly as if to echo Richard's own thoughts. "My father taught me another proverb once. It goes like this: Treat the Earth well for it was not given to you by your parents, it was loaned to you by your children."

Richard stared into the storm. "Is there a future for us on this planet? People, I mean…"

Cal sighed. "I don't know, Bro. I honestly don't know if we deserve one."

***

Cal Major was thoughtful as he made his way back to the radio room. He'd never seen Duke open up to anyone like that before. Even he didn't know much about the grizzled old sea-dog's past.

Skip must really be taking a shine to Richard!

His own thoughts were still troubled though. Despite Duke's confident reassurance, Cal had enough experience at sea to know the Skipper was deliberately glossing over the danger so as not to alarm the others. He didn't want to worry the Team, but he was anxious about the storm. It would be all but impossible for them to turn around and run before it now – not without presenting the ship's vulnerable broadside and stern to the waves.

That'd be asking for trouble… she'd founder in minutes!

But what was the alternative?

Valiant though she was, the Gwendolyn couldn't cope with the relentless pounding of the waves forever. Sooner or later her hull would begin to weaken under the onslaught. And if the storm worsened in any way…

Cal rubbed his face in his hands.

The complications of command!

He bore the responsibility of his Team's safety squarely on his shoulders, and it was not a burden he carried lightly. Help would be a long time coming if they got into trouble out here. If at all.

He cast a worried gaze over the navigation equipment.

Everything was on-line and working fine. For now.

But all it would take to isolate them would be one freak wave, or an extra-big gust of wind that tore off the radar dome. Or the radio antenna…

Cal debated with himself. He knew he ought to send a position update while he still could, just in case.

"I'm not calling for help," he told himself.

They didn't need it, yet, and there was no point anyway, since the only ships for miles around belonged to the enemy. "I'm just giving a position report so someone knows where we are…"

He picked up the radio and transmitted his callsign.

Aurelia answered almost immediately – leading him to wonder if she'd been sleeping by the radio back in New Zealand.

He felt the familiar tingle run through him at the sound of her voice, but the feeling didn't seem to be reciprocated.

"Greenpeace receiving. What is your message Gwendolyn?" she replied, talking to the callsign rather than him. She sounded relieved at his call rather than pleased, and her tone remained brisk and businesslike.

Cal forced down his emotions and gave his position report. After a pause he added mention of the warships stalking them.

Aurelia sucked in her breath, revealing her mood in an instant. "Your own violence is escalating the situation!" she snapped irritably. "I warned you. Your actions are the reason the Japanese are getting more aggressive! Don't you realise the damage you're doing to the Cause?"

Cal flinched, surprised at her sudden vehemence. But his own hackles quickly rose in defence. He was in no mood to put up with her preaching at him again.

"It's your campaign that's naive," he accused. "What exactly are you trying to prove, anyway?"

"We need to raise public awareness," she insisted. "We need graphic pictures of what's going on out there to show to the World. If people are confronted with the slaughter in their own living rooms then they'll be less able to ignore the issue!"

Cal rolled his eyes. "Who's really ignoring the issue? I'm out here to protect whales. If Greenpeace ships are prepared to sit by and watch whale after whale killed in front of you, it just proves you're more interested in posing for your own cameras. What you do is just publicity stunts. Nothing more."

"You sound like Amimoto!" she spat viciously. "Whose side are you on, anyway?"

"I'm on no one's side but the whales," he said simply.

"Obviously! You're sure as hell not a team player! We're trying to retain the moral high ground out there and you're stabbing us in the back! You've got no understanding of the theory of non-violent protest action!"

"I understand it perfectly," he replied, careful to keep his voice even. "I've seen Greenpeace's campaign with my own eyes. And I've seen it fail for the last twenty years. How many whales have been killed in that time? Tens of thousands! Your way will not work on the Japanese. Amimoto simply will not stop killing whales unless he is made to stop."

"Your approach is endangering the Cause, as is your attitude!"

"At least I'm doing something," Cal replied, more sad than angry. "In two decades Greenpeace hasn't saved a single whale from the harpoon!"

There was a sharp intake of breath down the radio, then a furious pause. When Aurelia finally spoke, her voice was tight with barely-suppressed rage. "The game is up, Cal. It's time to turn yourself in."

He sensed something else in her tone too, an ominous edge of finality.

"Aurelia," he said carefully. "What's going on?"

Her laugh was hollow. "I never could lie to you, Cal." She paused, as if gathering herself for a confession. "Alright then, you might as well hear it from me… I cannot countenance your actions, and my conscience won't allow me to be an accomplice to your violence any longer."

"What are you saying?"

"I passed on your position reports to the Authorities. They're on their way to bring you in. It's over, Cal."

Suddenly he felt the walls pressing in on him. He grabbed onto the edge of the chart table to steady himself, shuddering as a sick sense of despair gripped his insides. Through the confusion of thoughts swirling through his mind, one jumped to the fore: vindication.

"I've been giving you false position reports since Tonga," he blurted, still a little shocked that his foresight had proven necessary.

Of all the people against me, how could Aurelia be the one to betray me?

Aurelia laughed cruelly. "I know about your little game with the numbers. All your position reports have been out by exactly twenty nautical miles – close enough to narrow down a search area should it come to that, but not close enough for anyone to find you quickly." She pretended to applaud. "Very clever, Cal. But not clever enough!"

Cal blinked, his mind reeling. "But how did you…?"

She laughed again. "You underestimate my influence. I have many sources."

Son of a bitch!

Understanding flashed in an instant. Cal's expression hardened with barely-suppressed anger. "Heath!" he hissed, furious with himself for not having suspected what was up. He'd seen the way the hippy fawned after her – how had he not guessed Heath had been passing on secret position reports?

He shook his head, momentarily overwhelmed.

Once Aurelia knew what he was doing with the numbers it would be a simple matter to deduce the Gwendolyn's correct position now, even with Heath no longer aboard to provide his deceitful updates. Cal knuckled his temples with frustration. He had to hand it to her; she was devious!

If anything, that made the betrayal even harder to take.

"You're never happy unless you're manipulating men, myself included!" he exploded. "Does what we had together count for nothing? Do you have any feelings at all for me?"

"Cal, don't take it like that," she said, her voice sounding pained. "I never meant to hurt you, or to betray your trust. I just had to stop you before you hurt someone. You know I love you! My feelings for you are real, and just as strong as they always were."

"Oh please!" Cal interrupted. "Save your breath. If you really loved me, you'd love me *because* of who I am, not in spite of it. Love is supposed to be about mutual respect and understanding between two people – not abstract ideals. You've made it plain where your loyalties lie. And I can't love someone I don't trust."

"I'm sorry you feel that way Cal, but please don't take this personally. It doesn't change how I feel about you."

"Forget it Aurelia. It's over between us."

"Please, Cal. Give yourself up," she repeated, sounding desperate now. "You'll only make things worse!"

"I thought you knew me better than that?"

"Cal, please! Don't do this! You know it will only end badly. Are you prepared to die for your cause?"

Cal laughed, but it was completely devoid of humour. "Everybody dies…"

He reached up and snapped the HF radio off, ending the conversation. Then without a pause he reached behind and tore out the wires.

"So be it," he muttered grimly.

There would be no more position reports. The Gwendolyn would be operating entirely alone now. If anything went wrong then no one would be coming to look for them.

***

The storm finally blew itself out on the morning of the third day. Richard felt weak with relief. It wasn't just his body that was exhausted from fighting against the storm, but his entire being. He'd just been subjected to the worst experience of his life. It had been like being trapped inside a washing machine on spin cycle – for three whole days! Though the ship cruised sedately now, his head still spun with dizziness, and his stomach felt as though it was permanently upended.

He staggered to his feet, wondering how he'd managed to fall asleep on the low bench seat in the chart room. There was no sign of Summer, but Cal and the Skipper were on the bridge, staring fixedly ahead.

Richard took a few steps forward, and the view he saw out the Gwendolyn's windscreen made him gasp.

The sky was still overcast, but the world was eerily still. The heavy black storm blanket had been replaced by a misty layer of cloud settling right down low, as if reaching for the Gwendolyn's mast. But it was the view below the swirling cloudbank that took his breath away. The dull turquoise sea was filled with huge white shapes the size of rocky islands.

Icebergs!

The brilliant white ice was dazzling against the dark backdrop of the sea. Some of the bergs were enormous, rising higher than the height of the ship, their centres tinged bright blue with age.

"Wow," Richard breathed. "Look at that!"

Neither Cal nor the Skipper answered, busy navigating a safe passage through. The Gwendolyn crept forward at half-speed, as if tiptoeing through a field of sleeping giants.

Richard stared silently up as the massive icebergs slid by, floating all around them like sentinels.

"Strewth, how's that for a sight to wake up to!" Vicki jogged up the stairs to join them, a secretive little smile tugging at her dimples. "We crossed the Antarctic Circle during the storm," she announced.

Then she brought her hand out from behind her back where she had been hiding a small bottle of champagne. "I was saving it for a special occasion," she said sheepishly. She popped the cork and poured some into their mugs – now sitting sedately on the table. The Skipper shook his head when she came to him though, and with a sly wink he reached under the dash and brought out a bottle of whiskey. "This here's a real man's drop. Guaranteed to put hair on y' chest!"

Vicki chuckled in response, then turned to Richard. "This is further south than most people ever go in their lifetime, and you survived one hell of a crossing to get here!"

She raised her mug. "Welcome to the Land of the Midnight Sun! In Antarctica the sun never goes below the horizon for the entire summer!"

"Wow, the whole summer?" Richard was suddenly taken by the concept. "We should be able to find plenty of whales to study if it never gets dark."

"It's also good for Gyofuku to kill plenty of them," Cal said grimly. "We have until this autumn to stop him – after that we'll have to wait until summer comes around again next season." He raised his mug in a toast. "To the first sunset of the year. May the sun not set until we've ended the old world order!"

Richard swallowed nervously. The end of summer was still a couple of months away, but he had a sneaking suspicion they had only days to go until the showdown.

He glanced at his watch, suddenly realising it would be Christmas in a few days too. Richard normally liked Christmas, but this time he felt a strange sense of detachment towards the whole festive season. While the rest of the world celebrated and holidayed, the Team still had a job to do out here. A dangerous and thankless job. He sighed. Although his sense of celebration was tempered by the knowledge of the looming conflict, he also knew his outlook towards everything in life had changed irrecoverably now. He knew he wasn't missing anything at home but an empty house, and the more he thought about it he couldn't think of anywhere else he'd rather be. Or people he'd rather be with.

"To friends," he whispered, taking a small sip of his champagne.

The Gwendolyn continued south at a cautious pace, wending her way ever deeper into the ice-laden seas under the Skipper's watchful eye. Richard stared at the giant bergs as they slid by, dwarfing the ship with their immense bulk, and he felt very small below them.

The sea was as smooth as glass, and after the fury of the past few days the change was striking. Richard could almost feel the suspense in the air, as if the Ocean itself was holding its breath.

He sneaked a glance at his brother. Cal seemed to have no time for admiring the view though. He spent every waking moment on the bridge, watching the radar, monitoring Richard's radio-frequency tracker, or listening to the hydrophone. He took all his meals there, refusing even to go below to sleep. On the few occasions when he had snatched a quick rest while sitting in the chair, he invariably had a pair of headphones clamped tightly over his ears, ready to wake the moment something happened.

Richard was concerned, so single-minded was his brother's obsession. He tried to not to fret too much though, knowing Cal had a lot of responsibility to worry about.

The sudden shout startled him back to reality.

"Hot damn!"

Richard jumped and looked back.

Cal was on his feet, headphones clasped to his ears with both hands.

"What is it?" Richard asked.

In response, Cal leaned across and flicked on the speakers. Suddenly Richard found himself in the middle of the strange unearthly melody of whalesong again.

"It's a Blue!" Cal whispered excitedly. "About a day further south of us."

He screwed his face up, deep in contemplation. Suddenly his eyes flew open. "No way!" he whispered. "It couldn't be… not after all these years. Could it?"

He turned to Vicki. "Have you got the Vocalisation Database handy?" he said, his voice almost breathless with excitement.

She nodded, passing over her laptop. Cal plugged in the cable from the hydrophone, letting the computer analyse the signal. A moment later his face split in a broad grin. "Oh my god! It is her! It's Koru – the first blue whale I ever met!"

He jumped up and clapped Richard on the back, laughing happily.

"I didn't think I'd ever see her again."

Richard smiled, listening to the otherworldly music, and he could almost feel the hope in her uplifting song.

Cal's voice turned wistful. "I wonder what she's been up to all this time? I haven't seen her for so many years. I even wondered if she might be dead…"

He couldn't keep the smile off his face for long though. It was as if he'd just run into a long-lost friend. "It's good that our paths have finally crossed again," he grinned.

Abruptly his smile faded, and he swore. A moment later Richard realised that the signal from the hydrophone had changed. All heads snapped towards the speakers as a far more sinister sound filled the room. It was the shrill whine of high-speed propellers.

Chapter 30

Captain Hogei Gyofuku's face was taut with excitement, and he panted breathlessly. He gripped the Kuu-Maru's wheel with both pudgy hands as it sped in pursuit of the whale.

Ahead, a twin cloud of vapour shot high into the air, moments before a broad back broke the surface. It was a blue whale!

Gyofuku's smile was ugly with greed.

Karma, he thought jubilantly. *I will make my quota after all this season. And then some!*

As the charging Kuu-Maru bore down on its victim, he reached for the intercom.

"Gunner! Load a harpoon! An iron harpoon!"

He chuckled to himself. "I'm going to keep this sea-pig alive as long as possible!"

The whale sounded immediately its lungs were replenished with air, desperate to get away, but Gyofuku sneered after it. "Swim all you want, it only prolongs the inevitable! You cannot get away from me!" He laughed mockingly. "You can flee, but you will only die tired, neh?" His smile turned into a sinister smirk. "And you will only intensify the thrill of the chase!" he whispered thickly, his excitement mounting.

"Captain Gyofuku-san!" his First Officer interrupted suddenly.

Gyofuku spun around, furious at the interruption. "What is it?" he demanded, a gob of spittle flying from his mouth.

"There is a ship on the radar!"

"Of course there is," Gyofuku snapped irritably. "It's the Nippon-Maru coming to rendezvous with us."

The green helmet twitched as the officer shook his head vehemently. "No, Captain-san. It's too fast…"

"Then it's one of the warships, come to escort us."

The officer shook his head again, proffering the binoculars he was holding. "The ship is blue."

"Blue? Let me see!" Gyofuku snatched up the binoculars and pushed past him to stare out the window behind them.

A sudden trepidation lodged in the pit of his gut, but as the mystery vessel jumped into focus he felt relief. He didn't recognise it.

"It's just a long-liner," he said, waving a dismissive hand. "Probably even one of our own."

"So sorry, Captain-san, but please be repeating your observation."

Gyofuku frowned angrily, ready to cuff the officer for wasting his precious time.

Against his better judgement he raised the binoculars to stare at the mystery ship again, wondering what there was to be concerned about. He could see nothing amiss.

Slowly it dawned on him that it was heading directly for them, and it was a long way south for a long-liner to be operating…

Suddenly the radio crackled into life. Gyofuku cringed instinctively, expecting an ear-lashing from Amimoto. But it wasn't the long-range ship-to-shore HF radio, it was the VHF radio – short range, ship to ship, line of sight only.

The voice was clear and commanding – and speaking in English! "Attention Whaling Vessel Kuu-Maru, you are engaged in illegal hunting activities in a protected area. Please desist and leave this area immediately!"

Gyofuku's sunken eyes bulged in surprise.

"Furthermore, you are violating the sovereign rights of the Anti-Whaling Community. Continued aggression on your part will be interpreted as an act of war. You have been warned!"

Gyofuku found his voice at last. "Iye," he hissed. "It's the dirty hippies!"

How was this possible? They were supposed to be locked in a New Zealand jail cell!

How in the name of the Kami did they manage to find me?

He blinked in surprise, his mouth working soundlessly like a beached fish. He lowered the binoculars, still shocked at the sight of the red-suited eco-warriors uncovering the high-speed inflatable from its hiding place at the stern of the blue ship.

The ship is disguised! They tricked me!

It was them alright, and they were about to interfere with his hunt yet again!

Beneath the loose folds of his throat, the vein in his neck began pulsing angrily.

How dare they continually impinge my right to kill whales?

Gyofuku felt the spiteful anger flood through him and his eyes narrowed with malice.

This is the last time they will interrupt my sport. I swear it!

He reached up to sound the ship's alarm. "Clear the decks!" he shouted into the intercom. "Prepare for battle!"

Then he called for his destroyer escort.

It's time to teach these meddling protestors a lesson they won't ever forget!

***

Richard stood at the Gwendolyn's stern, staring forward at the ice-laden ocean.

Visibility was down to around half normal. The damp blanket of cloud pressed down almost to mast-height, as if to suffocate the sea. Underneath it, the air was still clear enough, but the scattered icebergs had grown denser now, mixed with ice floes on the surface like giant white lily pads. The sea-ice floes broke apart beneath the Gwendolyn's concrete-lined bow, but the Skipper steered well clear of the huge bergs, their tops hidden in the mist. Some of the taller ones began to block their way, forcing the Gwendolyn to zigzag through them.

Richard stared ahead, trying to ignore the clearly audible cracks that came from the ice cliffs towering over them. The huge bergs crowded so closely around the ship now that if one broke apart the tidal wave would surely hit them, even if the icefall didn't.

Richard felt the cold despite his survival suit.

All around, the air was silent and still, crisp with the smell of ice.

He stared at the harsh, yet hauntingly beautiful scenery. As beautiful and unforgiving as the seascape was though, the environment wasn't nearly as hostile as what lay ahead.

With a heavy heart Richard allowed his gaze to settle on the sinister yet familiar shapes trespassing here, unable to tear his eyes away from the terrible sight of the intruders in this wild and free place.

The sinister grey Kuu-Maru was less than a kilometre away now – close enough for Richard to hear the warning klaxon blaring at their approach.

The Black ship had arrived behind it, still several kilometres distant, but hurrying greedily after its ruthless Hunter-Killer. It dominated the low horizon like a dark hulking giant, ramming smaller bergs out of the way as it impatiently forged a path through the ice-laden seas.

The grey Hunter-Killer ship was no longer slinking stealthily through the ice. Knowing he had been discovered, and with his prey now in plain sight, Gyofuku charged forward with predatory eagerness.

Richard looked ahead, to where he'd last seen the broad blue back. The fleeing whale had submerged again, the sea clear now except for a last panicked gasp hanging in the still air.

Etched into his memory though, was the vivid white scar he'd seen running across the whale's tail – unmistakable evidence of an encounter with a driftnet long ago.

It was definitely Koru, the first Blue Cal had met when he saved her all those years before. And she was swimming for her life.

Richard felt his heart go out to her.

She was an intelligent, sentient being just like himself. He could only imagine the terror of being hunted, pursued relentlessly, desperate to escape, until finally able to swim no longer. Then, exhausted, forced to face a violent end, before being slowly and brutally despatched at the point of a blunt iron spear.

The thought was enough to make his blood run cold.

Koru was one of the last free spirits of the Earth, a lonely reminder of how empty the wild places had become – yet even now she was remorselessly hunted down in her own domain.

Richard felt his anger rising.

It's not right!

This was supposed to be a safe place for her! The sea belonged to whales, not people. Since 1994 the Southern Ocean had even been declared a whale sanctuary!

But out here on the last windswept frontier of the globe, the law was just a technicality, and the eyes of the world couldn't see what really went on. The only law that held any weight was the Law of the Gun. The harpoon gun.

Richard clenched his fists as he glared at the menacing black weapon high atop the Kuu-Maru's tall prow.

"Stand by to lower the Naiad!" Cal called.

Richard jumped as Cal's shout cut through his thoughts, and a surge of adrenaline swept through him.

This is it!

As the deck crane whirred into life, for the first time ever Richard felt more excitement than fear.

Earlier that day, Richard had been out de-icing the deck. Wherever it touched the ship, the sea spray turned immediately to ice, and soon the Gwendolyn had been covered with a layer of white frosting.

As pretty as it looked though, the fairy-dust ice crystals had a far more dangerous potential. If left to build up, their weight could eventually capsize the ship. And so Richard and Cal were out on the deck, wrapped in their bright red survival suits, knocking off icicles with a wooden club.

They worked slowly but methodically, trying not to raise a sweat – since any moisture would turn to a freezing layer of ice inside their clothes.

Richard's mind wandered as he worked, ranging from the upcoming showdown with Gyofuku to concern for Summer, still holed up in her cabin.

Suddenly the silence was shattered as a huge grey four-engined plane swooped out of the low sky. It found them, zooming so low overhead that the rumble from its four propellers had rattled the windows. Richard watched as the pilot turned his head to stare at them as it thundered past. He had been so used to the solitude out here it was a shock when their privacy was so suddenly and noisily violated.

Cal immediately headed for the bridge. Richard dropped his ice-club and sprinted after him, greatly alarmed.

"P-3 Orion," the Skipper announced, peering up at it. "Armed maritime surveillance… and anti-shipping."

"And it's got RNZAF markings," Cal added with a frown. "Looks like the New Zealand Government has finally chosen sides."

The plane banked around in a wide turn then returned for another pass. It roared by again, then was gone, its exhaust leaving four dirty brown smudges behind it in the sky. Richard watched until it was swallowed in the cloud. It made no attempt to contact them on the radio. That was an ominous sign.

"Well, we're committed then," Cal said with a frown. "That was a recon flight. You can bet the welcoming committee won't be too far behind." He sighed. "Our own government has denounced us. We can't go back, so we might as well go forward!"

They steamed on in silence towards the speeding grey Kuu-Maru. Everyone held their breath as the Gwendolyn crept up on the Japanese Hunter-Killer ship, waiting and hoping their disguise would hold.

As the Kuu-Maru headed ever deeper into the ice-field, the Skipper voiced his displeasure. "That dirty bastard knows what he's doin'. He's a cunning one, that's fer sure." He tugged at his beard with annoyance. "We ain't ice-strengthened. If these bergs start closin' in we're in big trouble. And if the Old Gal gets trapped in the ice it'll crush her hull like an eggshell!"

The Skipper had spent part of the voyage down labouring in the hold to fix timber reinforcing beams inside the hull – but all aboard knew it was just a temporary measure. If the Ice managed to trap them in its vice-like grip, they were done for.

The big grey Hunter-Killer ship continued to bear down on Koru, and Richard found he was holding his breath, willing the frightened whale to swim faster. He sneaked a glance at Cal, and could tell from his brother's tight-lipped frown that he felt the same way. Cal had a personal bond with this whale, and seeing her in danger now would be like seeing an old friend in peril. And the worst part of all would be having to stand by and watch her killed before your eyes, unable to prevent it.

Richard held his breath as the nightmare continued to unfold, silently begging Cal to stop it.

"Right, I've had enough of this bullshit. It's time to play our hand!" Cal grabbed the VHF radio and angrily ordered the Kuu-Maru off.

Predictably, there was no response from Captain Gyofuku.

The Hunter-Killer continued to charge in pursuit of the fleeing whale, the gunner already standing behind his loaded cannon. It wouldn't be long now before the Kuu-Maru got within harpoon range.

Richard could see the frustration written on Cal's face, and the deep emotion swirling behind it as he watched Koru swim for her life.

"Son of a bitch!" Cal muttered, eyes locked on Koru and her desperate attempts to escape. "What did she ever do wrong? She deserves the right to live her life out here without interference. Once, many years ago, I hoped she might represent hope for the recovery of her kind, but I guess some things never change!" He clenched his fists helplessly. "Gyofuku has gone too far this time! I won't let him take her! I won't!" He swore under his breath. "Whales don't belong to Japan – or to any country – and he has no right to be down here killing them in the middle of a bloody sanctuary!" His tone turned hard. "It's time to put a stop to this slaughter!"

Duke coughed awkwardly. "Y' know, if it's a scrap you're plannin', ah've got some… uh… supplies hidden away. Thought it prudent to make some preparations while visitin' with Mad-Dog," he explained with a sheepish grin. "That, and he had some nice toys layin' round…"

Cal offered a brief smile, but shook his head. "We can't risk any casualties. Any legal defence we have left will be shot right through if we make a hostile move – we can't afford to appear heavy-handed."

"Can we afford not to?" Vicki said quietly. "We're already well outnumbered, and Gyofuku isn't going to take any more interference lightly…"

"It'd be suicide pickin' a fight with that lot unarmed," the Skipper added darkly.

Cal nodded, his expression troubled. "I know," he said reluctantly. "That's why we'll have to carry weapons. But we can at least save force for a last resort."

"Then how do y' plan to stop 'em?" Duke asked. "Coz my Old Gal is much too light t' ram that fat-assed factory ship. That thing's too goddamned big to make a dent in!"

"Damaging the Nippon-Maru's propulsion or steering won't be enough," Vicki mused aloud. "We'll need to damage the freezers and processing equipment to put it out of action for good."

Richard swallowed, wondering how they could do that.

Cal looked around at the faces assembled before him. "Ok, here's what we're going to do…"

The bridge fell silent as he spoke. They listened attentively, no one commenting even when he suggested boarding the dreaded Factory Ship. Richard felt sick to his stomach, even though he'd had a nasty suspicion it would come to that.

When Cal had finished, no one moved. It was as though they were all frozen in thought.

He cocked a questioning eyebrow at Duke and the Skipper nodded slowly.

Cal turned to Vicki next. She would be the one in the thick of it with him. "Are you up for it?" he said.

She nodded bravely.

"What about that good-fer-nuthin' Canadian gal?" the Skipper asked.

Summer was still holed-up in her cabin. She had been there all day – ever since the likelihood of catching up with the Fleet had dawned – and she had already refused point blank to have any part in challenging Gyofuku, much to Richard's consternation.

"Forget it, we don't need her." Cal turned to look at Richard next.

Richard suddenly felt his knees go weak, but he forced himself to stay on his feet and take his orders like a man. "W-what about me, Cal?" he whispered, already dreading the reply.

"You stay here. Help the Skipper with the ship."

Stay here where it's safe! Richard's mind immediately filled in the unspoken caveat.

It was a reprieve, but it felt like a coward's way out.

But he didn't protest. In fact, it took all of his composure not to sob out loud with relief.

The Skipper tugged his beard, muttering under his breath. "I still don't like it," he said. "The odds ain't good. Not good at all."

"The price of failure is worse," Cal replied. "True, we'll be up against it. But what choice do we have? The only option we have left is to fight, even if it means we go down fighting."

Richard's eyes widened in alarm, but Cal smiled gently. "Don't worry, Bro. It won't come to that. I promise."

"What if they try to stop us?" Vicki said quietly. "You have to decide. Are you prepared to go all the way?"

Cal looked grim, and he was silent for a long time. Finally he spoke. "What are a few human lives when compared against the continued survival of an entire species?"

She held his gaze, then nodded, accepting the conditions.

Richard was worried though. It sounded like Cal might be planning deliberate violence against the Japanese after all!

He turned to look behind them. The Japanese destroyer was already close enough to see now, a dark blot on the horizon behind them. He hastily averted his eyes. He felt like a condemned man being forced to watch as the masked and faceless executioner sharpened his axe in plain view.

Duke glared at their pursuer, but made no direct comment. "There's more ships showin' on thuh radar," he muttered grimly. "Probably your navy," he said to Cal. "And mine. Looks like thuh whole damn world wants a piece of us!"

Richard took the news like a punch to the stomach. "Oh no," he whispered aloud. "A-are we going to die?"

The Skipper shrugged. "Who knows? A soldier's always ready to die," he added. He stared ahead, his eyes glazing slightly. "Me? I ought t' be dead already. Dunno how I walked away from that goddamned VC ambush in thuh jungle – not when all me buddies were getting' shot up all around me. Ah've asked m'self that same question ever since..."

The Skipper stared ahead into the grey of the fog, his voice trailing off. "So many wasted deaths…" he whispered. Then he blinked suddenly, snapping back to the present. "If I learned nothin' else in them godforsaken jungles in 'Nam, I learned this: It was a hell of a war to be fightin'. We ought'a never been there in thuh first place – it weren't our battle to fight."

He shook his shaggy head morosely. "Ain't no one can know what thuh outcome of a contact might be, so there's only one way to make sure y' don't die a wasted death – and that's pickin' thuh right battle to fight in!"

The Skipper shrugged, then turned his weather-beaten face towards Richard. "Life's in the hands of Fate," he said simply. "But if time's finally up now, at least Death will be for a noble cause this time. We're all Soldiers for thuh Earth now."

Richard shot a glance at his brother. Cal's face was grim. Determined.

He noticed Richard looking at him and smiled. "Don't worry, Bro. Everything will be ok." His tone was warm, compassionate almost. "Any success, no matter how small, is still a success. And success is the beginning of victory." He smiled. "Just remember what I told you and everything will be fine." Then he patted Richard on the shoulder and turned to leave.

Richard felt his heart sink at the enormity of his brother's words. "Wait, Cal. Don't go! There has to be another way!"

Cal looked back over his shoulder. "I'm sorry Bro. There's no other way."

"But it's too dangerous! What if you get killed?"

Cal smiled sadly. "The only thing worse than dying is never having lived. If I don't achieve something with my life then I might as well never have been born."

Then he turned and headed aft, to where the Naiad lay waiting on the rear deck.

Richard watched him go, his head spinning. Just because Cal had pledged not to use lethal force didn't mean the Japanese wouldn't. Hogei Gyofuku had already made it perfectly clear he would rather kill them than see his hunt interrupted – and he had already tried! And the combined US-Japanese military force bearing down on them definitely weren't here to seek a diplomatic solution either!

Richard knew he was facing the challenge of a lifetime.

He took a deep breath and shouted after his brother. "Wait! If you're going then I'm coming too!"

Now Richard found himself holding on for dear life as the Naiad skimmed across the ice-choked sea. The frozen slush was as thick as soup, and chunks as big as his fist clattered against the hull. He closed his mind to the sound, trying not to think about what a larger piece might do.

His earlier excitement was gone, whipped away by the stinging wind to be replaced with the familiar nervous flutter in the pit of his stomach. The ever-present anxiety was compounded by the presence of danger – real and immediate now – in the form of the menacing Japanese ships. While it was a release to finally have the suspense over, the reality was even more chilling.

Richard blinked, eyes watering in the frigid slipstream.

The sinister black bulk of the Nippon-Maru loomed on the horizon like an evil omen. He stared at it, transfixed.

Somehow he sensed his destiny was inextricably linked with the gigantic factory ship.

A sudden image jumped into his head – dark water trapped within coffin-like steel walls, rising to smother any precious pockets of air that might remain…

Richard felt a cold chill seize him.

He shook his head before the images of drowned bodies came, desperate to avoid the irrational terror he knew would accompany them. He knew he would have to conquer his fears and go aboard the Nippon-Maru. He had volunteered for this mission and it was too late to back out now!

He tore his eyes away, forcing himself to concentrate instead on the immediate danger posed by the charging Hunter-Killer ship. The Kuu-Maru was rapidly gaining on its prey, and Koru was clearly tiring. Her breaths were becoming noisier and more frequent as she gasped for air.

She wore no transmitter, so they had to judge her passage underwater by experience alone. Aboard the speeding inflatable everyone was silent, concentrating. Cal stood in the bow, scanning the frigid waves ahead. Vicki stood at the Naiad's centre console, driving hard, an occasional hand signal from Cal the only communication that passed between them.

Richard sat in the stern, alone with his thoughts. The new Naiad was larger, and with the steering console now amidships he felt more isolated from the others. He gazed at the red backs in front of him. Shared companionship was important when you were scared stiff!

Richard tried not to let his mind wander.

He had one job to do and when the time came he knew he had to be ready!

The Naiad swerved suddenly, flinging Richard sideways. He hadn't noticed Cal's hand signal. He steadied himself, heart thumping in his chest.

The Kuu-Maru was dead ahead now, still charging single-mindedly in pursuit of its victim. Vicki gunned the throttle and the Naiad's twin engines roared. In a blast of icy spray they swept past the Hunter-Killer's stern, overtaking close enough that Richard could see the expressions on the sullen faces glaring at them over the rail.

Suddenly the grey hull veered towards them, cutting right across their path. The wall of steel loomed overhead, threatening to wipe them out. Richard gasped, but Cal pointed straight ahead, indicating for Vicki to hold their line.

Moments later the Kuu-Maru corrected its course again, turning away as it headed directly for the fleeing whale.

It was a bluff!

Richard felt weak with relief, wondering how Cal had known Gyofuku wouldn't give up his pursuit for anything.

Then with a sudden spurt, the Naiad shot ahead of the speeding ship, crashing over the bow wave and shooting out into the clear water in front.

The Kuu-Maru accelerated immediately, sending its blade-like prow scything towards them.

Richard's eyes widened in horror, and he clutched at the pontoon he was sitting on, unable to speak or look away.

Vicki swerved clear, juggling the throttle to keep them just out of reach of the thundering juggernaut.

Richard closed his eyes for a moment, trying to calm his nerves. At least they were too close under the grey ship's bow here to see the bridge – and the evil pockmarked face he knew would be up there.

Richard turned to look ahead.

Cal was already standing in the bow, trusting Vicki's seamanship while he scanned the sea ahead.

"There!" he shouted.

Richard followed the direction of his outstretched hand. Moments later, Koru surfaced again in a cloud of exhaled vapour. She blew again, gasping with panic and exhaustion.

As he watched the magnificent creature and listened to her laboured breathing, Richard was struck by how similar they really were. Despite the obvious differences, when you got down to the simple biology people and whales were not that different from each other. And that knowledge crystallised his resolve.

We have to save her!

High on the Hunter-Killer's tall prow, the harpoon gunner crouched over his squat, ugly weapon.

"Quickly!" Cal shouted over the wind. "He's lining up the shot!"

Richard felt his heart catch in his chest.

Please no! We can't lose Koru to them. We can't!

After all he had been through, he knew he wouldn't be able to cope if the brutal Japanese captain killed another whale in front of them.

As though in response to his silent entreaty, Vicki revved the engines and the Naiad sped forward, crowding as close behind the whale as possible – putting them right in the path of the gunner's aim.

Richard held his breath, waiting for the boom as the cannon fired.

It didn't come.

Instead, an enraged voice bellowed an order in Japanese.

With a sigh of relief Richard looked up at the Kuu-Maru's foredeck, puzzled by the sudden activity he saw there. The gunner was standing at the front of his gun!

Then Richard felt a sudden surge of victory flood through him as he realised what was happening. The gunner was unloading the harpoon gun!

They're giving up! We've won!

He felt like laughing out loud with relief.

But what happened next made his voice catch in his throat. The harpoon gun didn't stand empty for long. No sooner had the gunner finished unloading it than he hurried forward with another projectile and slid it down the cannon's eager mouth. Richard could clearly see the bright orange tip on the end. With a sudden spike of fear he realised he was looking at the warhead of a grenade harpoon.

And as he looked on in horror, the gunner jumped back behind his weapon and traversed the barrel steeply down – pointing it directly at them!

Richard tried to shout a warning, but his voice came out as a strangled croak.

The gunner braced himself behind the cannon, locking eyes with Richard as he took aim.

Richard felt as though he was staring into the Abyss.

"L-Look out!" he managed to gasp.

The cannon discharged with an explosive thud, sending the untethered harpoon streaking towards them like a missile.

Vicki reacted in the same instant, swerving hard to port.

The harpoon flew low and straight, unencumbered by a cable.

Richard's eyes were wide with horror as he watched it streak towards them, helpless to do anything.

The harpoon slammed into the sea barely a metre behind the Naiad, at the very spot they had been only moments before. It detonated with a dull roar. A huge eruption of water flung spray high into the air, and the inflatable's stern was lifted right out of the water. What seemed like an eternity later, the outboards finally splashed back down again – the sudden impact jarring the speeding boat and threatening to flip it.

Vicki wrestled with the wheel, somehow managing to keep the Naiad under control without slowing, and keep them clear of the Kuu-Maru's blade-like bow lunging hungrily behind them.

Richard's breath came in short gasps, and he felt the waves of panic wash over him as spray continued to rain down all around.

"Son of a bitch!" Cal spluttered. "That psychotic bastard nearly killed us!" He stared back at the grey ship in disbelief. "Those harpoon heads are supposed to have a safety detonator on them – they won't go off until the trigger hooks catch in the whale's flesh, when the warhead is already buried inside the animal…" He shook his head, still mildly stunned. "Gyofuku must have rigged that one to blow immediately! The bastard *tried* to kill us!"

High on the foredeck of the speeding Hunter-Killer ship they saw the white-helmeted gunner run forward to load another harpoon into his cannon.

Three pairs of eyes instantly gravitated to the evil-looking orange tip.

"Strewth," Vicki whispered. "They're playing for keeps now! There's no way we can dodge those forever – we'll have to give up!"

Richard stared back at the Kuu-Maru in shell-shocked silence. He wanted to crawl into a hole and hide until this was over. Never had Death felt so near before.

"Like hell we're giving up!" Cal muttered.

The gunner crouched behind the cannon and took aim again.

"Hard to starboard!" Cal ordered, the sudden manoeuvre forcing Richard to flail for balance, as he clutched the pontoon for dear life.

"Ok Richard… Now! Do your thing!"

Richard felt the helplessness surge within him.

Oh no! I can't do it! Why the hell did I volunteer for this?

He forced it down as determinedly as he could manage.

I can't let Cal down!

He rolled off the pontoon and crawled on his hands and knees to the back of the boat. With shaking hands he reached into the plastic bin and grabbed hold of the contents. Cal's secret plan. A fishing net.

It was a reinforced nylon gillnet, the kind marine biologists hate because they never break down. If lost at sea the ghost nets will float in the ocean forever, continuing their indiscriminate kill, ensnaring and drowning anything they encounter. Richard knew his brother hadn't made the decision to jettison it lightly, but right now they had an urgent need for its sinister abilities.

His fingers refused to work properly in the bulky gloves of the survival suit, but he managed to pick up the invisible filaments – each strong enough to support many times his own weight. He threw the end of the net over the stern, making sure to keep it clear of the motors.

Vicki immediately swung the Naiad in a sweeping turn to starboard, the net paying out in a huge arc behind them.

The Kuu-Maru thundered forward without check, straight over the top of it. There was a sudden muffled bang and it shuddered to a halt.

A furious tirade of Japanese carried down to them from the bridge.

Cal's grin was huge. "Nice one! That ought to hold the bastard for a while!"

Koru swam clear, heading south as fast as she could. Cal watched her go for a moment, then turned his gaze towards the monstrous factory ship.

"Right," he said softly. "It's time for the main event."

Vicki pointed the Naiad's bow straight at the Nippon-Maru, and the wind whistled as they sped to intercept it.

As they skimmed across the icy expanse of water that separated them, Cal turned and began rummaging in the duffel bag behind him. Richard caught sight of the contents – large blocks of what looked like grey Plasticine, each with a kitchen timer attached.

The Skipper's supplies!

Richard gulped, knowing it was not Plasticine at all, but plastic explosive!

The explosive power contained in each bundle was enough to cause major damage to the hated factory ship… or kill if planted carelessly. The responsibility weighed heavily.

Next to the charges were the cans of kerosene that would form the incendiary parts of the bombs.

"A mild toasting'll give them dirty bastards one more thing to think about!" Duke had chuckled.

Fire was indiscriminate and unmanageable once started though, but Cal had finally agreed, knowing they would need a sizeable diversion to allow them to get away again. Because in order to be any use, the demolition charges needed to be planted *inside* the black ship!

Richard felt the familiar tightness grip his chest. He looked up as the huge black monster loomed ahead, right on cue.

His heart raced out of control. He closed his eyes to the menacing sight, trying to steel himself for what was to come next.

An image of the whales he had met came to him then; first the Minke mother and her calf in the Southern Ocean, then Mana the Humpback and his family in Tonga – including little Ohana who had been so innocent and defenceless against the evil of the world. And of course, there was Old Blue himself. Richard screwed his eyes tighter, feeling a deep sadness as he thought about the whales. He had seen them all alive, swimming wild and free in their Ocean realm. And now they were dead. All of them. Killed and butchered right in front of him. And he hadn't been able to stop it.

He opened his eyes, focusing on Koru's broad back as she swam away toward the distant pack ice. He knew her reprieve would only be short-lived. The Japanese Hunter-Killer ship was disabled temporarily, but her life wasn't out of danger yet. Her future still hung in the balance. Richard took a deep breath.

Ok. I'm ready to do this!

He turned to look ahead, grimly determined as they sped up to the huge bulk of the Nippon-Maru.

Vicki took them around to the rear where the huge stern slipway yawned like a hungry mouth. High above, the deck rail was lined with hostile pairs of eyes, peering balefully down at them. Richard held the stares, eyeing them defiantly back. He cast his eyes up to the huge goal-post-like cranes, which reached up into the mist as if to challenge the sky. Beneath them the ship's infectious yellow superstructure ringed a crowd of angry whalers waiting on the deck – clubs and long-handled knives in hand.

"Ready?" Vicki shouted over the wind.

"Take us in!" Cal yelled back.

The twin outboards roared and the Naiad shot forward, heading straight for the massive slipway ramp. Right on cue the water cannons blasted down to meet them.

***

A black-shrouded figure stepped out onto the Nippon-Maru's deck, trench coat flapping in the chill breeze.

Kobushi glared out from beneath the tinted lenses of his sunglasses.

The enemy approaches!

He smiled to himself, pleased with his decision to transfer across to the Nippon-Maru. He had sailed on Captain Gyofuku's whaler from New Zealand, but when they rendezvoused with the factory ship in the Southern Ocean he had gone across to the larger ship. He was pleased to be away from the sight of the loud-mouthed peasant of a captain, but his decision was driven purely by a suspicion his skills would be more likely utilised here. And his prediction had proven right!

Now the enemy was on the way. He need do nothing more than wait, and their own rashness would bring them right too him. It was the perfect setup.

He sat down, cross-legged on the deck.

The advantage will be mine!

As he waited he prepared himself, clearing his mind for battle.

He took out his katana and laid it deliberately on the deck beside him.

There will be plenty of room to swing a long sword here, neh?

Nearby, the gang of ruffian whalers shouted impatiently, crowding forward to meet the enemy. But Kobushi didn't move. He smiled to himself as he waited, knowing the waiting would soon be over.

Chapter 31

As the Naiad skimmed towards their destination, Cal Major turned to look back, checking on his Team. Vicki gave a quick thumbs-up, and Richard managed a brave smile.

Cal grinned back at them, pleased to see Richard had donned his air tank without any help. The few instruction sessions they'd had time for had really soaked in.

Cal nodded to himself. His bro had come a long way in just a few months. Richard was a true biologist-in-the-making now – but he still had one final test to go!

Cal turned forward again to stare at the huge bulk of the Nippon-Maru that towered ahead of them.

This is it! The point of no return!

He had agonised over this moment for weeks, but he knew in his heart it had to be done. There was no other way. And as much as he didn't want to lead his colleagues and friends into harm's way, he knew they had volunteered of their own free will.

They're a good Team!

Cal felt his heart burst with pride as he looked at them, particularly his brother. Richard had proven his courage by volunteering for this mission. He had come so far in such a short time!

Cal's hand went to the greenstone pendant that hung at his neck, seeking the familiar touch of the cool stone. It possessed a strength that had given him reassurance before in times of need. But he didn't need it any more. It had come to him long ago, at a time in his life when he needed guidance. But now it was time to pass it on. In a spur-of-the-moment decision, Cal reached up and slipped it off. "Here," he said, leaning across to hang the leather cord around Richard's neck. "This'll bring you good luck." Richard stared at the green spiral of carved stone, eyes wide with surprise. Cal watched him marvel at it just like he'd done the first time he saw it. The polished detail of the carving was mesmerising, as was the way the stone seemed both translucent and mysteriously opaque at the same time – almost as if it was imbued with a spirit of its own.

Richard shook his head, perhaps sensing that such a finely-crafted artefact must be expensive. "I can't take this, Cal. It's yours."

Cal waved a hand. "I'm giving it to you. Wear it with pride."

He grinned at his Team.

They were as committed as he was – even though that didn't make his job any easier. He was responsible for their safety, and the burden weighed heavily.

Cal gritted his teeth.

It's time!

Then he raised his arm and pointed directly at the ship.

Vicki gunned the engines in response, lining the Naiad up with the gaping wide door of the stern slipway. Above the huge opening, yellow-helmeted deckhands lined the stern rail, glaring down at them.

The bow lifted higher as Vicki raised the outboards, trimming them until the props were only just below the surface, clear of any danger.

The heavy jets from the stern-mounted water cannons played across the water ahead, but Vicki was not to be deterred. She held their course unwaveringly and the water jets slammed into them with the force of multiple fire hoses. But her determined charge took the hose operators by surprise and the water jets fell behind. Moments later the Naiad burst clear in a cascade of flying spray.

"Brace!" Cal yelled as the slipway suddenly loomed.

They hit it at full speed. He had a moment of concern that the angle was too steep and the Naiad's hull would be ripped out. Then with a surge of adrenaline they were blasting up the slick ramp like a giant water-ski jump.

Cal hung onto the pontoon for dear life, clutching the grapnel anchor in his free hand. If they didn't have enough momentum to get to the top of the ramp he would have to throw it, aiming to secure the inflatable in place on the slipway so they could get out and scramble the rest of the way up.

Hopefully there was something at the top the grapnel could catch on, and hopefully he could hook it – because he would only get one attempt!

He needn't have worried though. Vicki had judged the incline perfectly. The Naiad had just enough momentum to carry them over the lip at the top, then they shot out into the open and slid to a stop on the Nippon-Maru's huge flensing deck. This was the huge wood-planked area where the whales were butchered after being hauled aboard, and the gaps between the boards were still clotted with dried blood. Cal felt his anger swell as he caught sight of the huge cranes and processing equipment ahead. But he didn't have time to dwell on it as a crowd of angry Japanese whalers surged toward them. Whatever surprise they might have had at seeing the inflatable shoot up the ramp onto their ship was quickly dispelled. They were clearly spoiling for a fight. Cal knew the whalers must have been looking forward to this showdown for some time, and he had no doubts they intended to settle the issue right here and now!

They came forward in a tight mob, brandishing clubs and long-handled flensing knives.

Vicki and Richard were still in the boat, and Cal knew he couldn't let the gang of blue-overalled thugs trap them there. In a matter of seconds it might be too late. Someone had to hold the whalers off before the inflatable was surrounded on the deck.

He glanced back, but knew he couldn't get to his duffel bag in time.

There's only one thing for it!

Unhooking the grapnel chain from the anchor rope, he jumped down to the deck and stepped forward, swinging the improvised weapon at his side.

"Hurry! Get the gear and stay behind me. I'll clear a path!"

He glanced back, but Vicki was still crouched over in the bottom of the boat.

Cal swore, knowing it was down to him to keep the whalers at bay.

He strode forward, his anchor chain whistling a challenge as it spun through the air.

Despite their overwhelming numbers the whalers hesitated, uncertainty in their eyes.

Then a green-helmeted officer stepped forward, urging them on.

Growling with malice the whalers pressed forward, surrounding Cal.

He swung the chain faster, spinning the grapnel over his head now, using the whole length of the chain to keep them at bay.

Again they stopped, just out of reach of the spinning hook.

Again the officer ordered them to attack.

Cal turned continually, trying to keep them all in view, wondering where the first attack would come from.

Then suddenly a burly whaler in a stained apron rushed forward, club raised.

In a flash, Cal knew his future was now in the balance. If he couldn't hold off the charge he would be swamped in seconds. He had to prevent this attack immediately!

Take this, you bastard!

Cal lunged forward with his front hand, swinging the chain at full reach. The sudden movement caught the whaler by surprise. The heavy weighted grapnel head crashed into the side of his yellow crash helmet, knocking him off his feet.

Cal grunted with satisfaction, ignoring the man even as he stumbled. That one would be too stunned to cause any more problems for a while – unlike the rest of them!

Cal yanked the chain back before the grapnel could fall to the deck, already turning to swing it in a defensive arc behind him.

He wasn't a moment too soon!

From behind, another one lunged forward with a long-handled flensing knife held like a spear, meaning to stab him in the back. Cal had just enough time to direct his flying grapnel towards the blade as it flashed towards him. The two weapons collided with a clash of steel, the momentum of Cal's swing knocking the blade wide. The grapnel's prongs caught then, hooking behind the other weapon's shaft and locking them together. Seizing the opportunity, Cal yanked the chain back, pulling the flensing knife out of its surprised owner's hands.

That was all he had time for though, as the surly throng pressed forward on all sides. He tried to swing the grapnel at them, but it was still caught on the long knife and the extra weight was too much. Locked together, the weapons just skittered uselessly across the deck.

Shit!

Cal knew he absolutely had to keep the whalers at bay. There was no way in hell he could fight that many of them hand-to-hand, and if they reached him now he would be swamped.

Still clutching the chain, he tried to swing the free end. But it was too short and his movements were hampered by the weight on the other end.

The whalers pressed in.

A club flew at his head.

Cal dodged it, swinging the chain to sweep out the attackers legs. The whaler went down, screaming as the bones in his ankle cracked beneath the heavy links. But another club was already following the first. Cal caught that one with the chain, turning the weapon aside long enough to kick its owner in the groin. But out of the corner of his eye he saw another attack flash toward him from behind. He tried to turn, already knowing he wouldn't make it in time. The steel tank on his back seemed to double in weight as he moved, and he raised an arm in a vain attempt to protect his face. But there would be no escaping the blow. Cal gritted his teeth, waiting for the impact.

Suddenly a boom rang out across the water.

Something hit his attacker square in the chest, lifting him off his feet and hurling him backwards.

Cal blinked, momentarily stunned.

What the…?

Then he heard the unmistakable sound of a shotgun slide being pumped.

It's Duke!

He looked across the deck to see the Gwendolyn alongside.

From the wheelhouse door the Skipper raised his shotgun and fired again.

Directly behind Cal another attacker went down, writhing in agony.

He's been killed!

Cal felt a moment of alarm that his plan was unravelling already. Dead Japanese whalers would surely condemn them all in the eyes of the Law.

With a surge of relief he saw the white plastic object lying on the deck. It was a baton round – non-lethal shotgun ammunition developed for law enforcement. The Skipper must have deliberately sought some out in anticipation of this day!

Cal laughed out loud with relief, knowing the 'moral sacrifice' the grizzled old former-SEAL had gone to on his behalf.

Around him, the whalers hesitated, weighing the odds.

Cal knew there were still more of them than the Skipper could shoot in time. If they rushed him again he would still be in trouble. He yanked the grapnel free and began to swing it again, thankful for the reprieve.

The green-helmeted officer barked more orders, sending the whalers on the attack again.

Cal turned warily, waiting for the next charge, knowing he might not survive it.

Suddenly a female shout cut through the hubbub of angry voices. "Put your mask on!"

Cal couldn't take his eyes off the circling mob, but with his free hand he yanked his full-face dive mask down over his head, barely having time to check the regulator was firmly attached and the air turned on.

Seconds later, a small metal cylinder bounced through the circle and landed at his feet.

He stared at it, his eyes drawn to the lettering on its side: 'CS'.

Vicki got to my bag!

It was a tear gas grenade!

Suddenly a billowing cloud of gas erupted, and the effect on the whalers was immediate. They doubled over, eyes streaming, gagging and retching where they stood. The fight went out of them in an instant, and with a few swift kicks Cal was able to clear a path out of the circle.

At that moment Vicki and Richard appeared at his side through the haze, their breathing sounding harsh and mechanical through their air tanks. Vicki handed him his crossbow bag, and he could see Richard was holding the other with the charges.

The pride he felt in his Team was real.

"Thanks for that," he said, meaning it. "I promise I'll never hassle Aussies again!"

Vicki laughed behind her mask. "Bullshit! You will too!"

Cal laughed with her. "Yeah, ok, maybe I will. But you know I won't really mean it."

She punched him playfully on the arm. "I already know that – mainly 'cause you're full of crap!"

The gas cloud parted for a moment, revealing the Kuu-Maru off in the distance, its engines still stopped. Cal knew it wouldn't take long before Gyofuku got rid of that net though, and then it would be all on. Time was short.

"Right, let's get on with it," he muttered grimly. "We've got a job to do."

He strode forward and the cloud swirled around, engulfing him again. Vicki and Richard fell in step behind him and he led them towards the door to the inside of the factory ship.

The attack came suddenly and without warning.

Cal caught a glimpse of a black shape out of the corner of his eye, then suddenly a blade was flashing towards his back. He reacted in an instant, dropping the bag he was carrying and swinging the chain to meet it. At the same time he lunged with his free hand pushing Richard clear of the danger.

His brother fell heavily but Cal didn't have time to worry as he whipped the chain around to block another strike.

Out of the gas loomed a figure in a black trench coat and dark glasses, long katana sword held aloft.

Cal felt a finger of ice seize his heart.

"Oh shit. Not you!" he whispered.

It was Amimoto's assassin, and he had a cloth tied ninja-style across his face to keep out the gas. The assassin stepped forward then dropped the point of his sword, pointing it directly at Cal's heart. The meaning was plain.

Cal's thoughts immediately went to the crossbow in the bag at his feet, but there was no way he could get to it in time. It might as well have been on the moon. He was committed already – locked in a fight for his life.

He shot a glance over his shoulder. Richard was still sprawled on the deck where he'd fallen, Vicki behind him.

"You two, get out of here! Now!" Cal ordered.

"What about you?" Vicki shouted back, her voice muffled by her mask.

At that instant the sword flashed towards his face. Cal swung the grapnel desperately, forcing his attacker back for a brief moment.

"I said go!" In his heart he knew there was nothing she and Richard could do here. This guy was too vicious. Too dangerous. If they stayed then all three of them risked their lives. He couldn't allow that.

"I'll take care of this! You two get below and do what you need to do. Quickly!"

Vicki hesitated a moment longer, clearly torn. Then she grabbed Richard and they headed through the doorway and disappeared.

The assassin came at him again, feinting low, then slashing down at his head with a two-handed chop.

Cal grabbed the chain in both hands and raised it over his head, frantically trying to ward off the killing blow. The blade clashed against it, sending off sparks and jarring his whole body with the force of the impact. Before he could recover, the assassin swung the blade again, and Cal knew what was coming.

Desperately he swung the grapnel at his attacker's legs, hoping to trip him.

The assassin saw it coming though, and jumped nimbly out of the way.

Cal turned to keep him in sight, swinging the grapnel close to his body. He couldn't risk a bigger swing to keep his adversary further away – that would take too much time. The assassin was good. Too good. And the tiniest opening was all his sword-arm would need...

They circled each other, each hunting for an opening.

Cal knew it would take all his skill and cunning just to hold the assassin off.

He willed the Skipper to blast the bastard, but the shot didn't come.

With a sinking heart, Cal realised Duke couldn't see him through the cloud of gas – and probably wouldn't have a clear shot anyway. He would have to finish this fight himself.

They continued to circle each other, feinting, probing, looking for a weakness in the other's defence.

Cal's mask began to fog up with the exertion, and sweat stung his eyes. The sound of his own breathing was loud in his ears, rasping through the regulator.

He knew he couldn't keep this up forever. But he also knew he had to hold the assassin off long enough for Vicki and Richard to complete their task. Otherwise the mission was over.

We must not fail!

Then, with explosive violence the assassin lunged at him again.

***

Richard stumbled down the steel gantry ladder, his footsteps echoing through the tomb-like corridor. He clutched the duffel bag awkwardly to his chest, keenly aware of the importance – and potency – of its contents. The charges Duke had prepared for them would cripple the factory ship's processing ability – and therefore its usefulness to the Fleet – so long as they could get to the vulnerable machinery to set them off.

Richard felt his heart in his throat. This was much worse than burglary and sabotage – this was a full-on frontal assault!

There's no one else who can do it though!

He tried to calm his breathing, aware of the air-management skills Cal had taught him.

Ahead, Vicki's red-suited back led the way, her wooden ice-club ready to deal with any resistance.

Abruptly, the corridor opened out into a cavernous room. It was two stories high, and easily as big as a basketball court. A stationary conveyor belt snaked downwards from the ceiling, leading from the flensing deck. The floor was lined with stainless steel tables stretching the entire length of it, and the overhead fluorescent strip lighting glinted back from the polished surfaces.

But despite its hospital-like cleanliness the room seemed somehow sinister – like there was a hidden depth of feeling in the shadows that crowded around the edges, barely held at bay by the lights.

It was like being in a gigantic morgue. Richard stopped, feeling suddenly uneasy.

"The processing room," Vicki whispered. "This is where they cut up the whales into portions. They package the meat for sale right here on the ship, so when they return to port it's ready for immediate delivery to market."

Richard shuddered, suddenly realising it was the aura of death that hung over everything.

He shook his head sadly, wondering how many whales could be processed here at once.

The room is so big!

He could only imagine the sight when the huge tables were piled high with butchered meat, and the floor was slick with whale blood…

They walked forward slowly, their footsteps loud in his ears.

At the far end of the room sat rows of machinery, squat and menacing in the shadows. Richard recognised giant industrial-sized mincers, slicers, saws, and other contraptions he could only guess at. The machines sat silently in the half-light, waiting.

Though his head told him they were just inanimate objects, Richard suddenly felt like he was in the presence of pure evil. These machines were designed for just a single purpose, and they were tainted with the blood of thousands of innocent lives.

This whole ship was a giant floating monument to the dark side of human excesses.

The grand scale of this industry of death was almost beyond comprehension.

Locked in his thoughts, Richard was slow to hear the furtive footsteps creeping up behind him.

"Look out!"

Vicki's warning shout cut through his trance.

Richard spun around, just as three whalers brandishing curved meat cleavers rushed at him. The first one, an ugly thick-set man in a blood-stained apron, grinned toothlessly and hacked at his head.

Richard panicked, trying to duck the blow, but was hampered by the bag in his arms. As the blade whistled towards him he knew in a moment of crystal clarity that it would catch him on the side of the head. His heart seized in his chest.

"Nooo!" With a primal shout, Vicki jumped in the way, swinging her ice-club to meet it. The blade bit into the wood with a solid *thunk*!

The whaler pulled back his lips in a surprised snarl. With his missing front teeth and bulging biceps he had the look of a veteran brawler, but he didn't know quite what to make of a feisty Aussie chick armed with a club. Vicki swung again, driving him back.

But the other two surged forward then, coming at her from both sides.

"Throw a grenade!" she called urgently, her voice muffled by her mouthpiece. "Quick!"

Richard dropped the duffel bag and fumbled with the zip.

Ratting through the bag, he wished he'd had the foresight to put one in his pocket for immediate use. Finally his gloved fingers found what they were searching for and he yanked a gas grenade out of the bag. Fumbling, he clawed at the pin, eventually managing to hook it away. In a flash, the spring-loaded metal flange flicked clear, arming the detonator.

But then he hesitated, still panicking.

Vicki was surrounded now, and he didn't know where to throw it.

Would it explode and injure her too?

The grenade continued its silent countdown though – it would go off at any second!

"Oh hell," he muttered, close to tears now.

The first whaler suddenly realised what he was doing and broke away from the group, lunging toward him with his knife outstretched.

Richard dropped the grenade and snatched up his club. With trembling hands he prepared to fight.

At that moment the grenade went off between them, engulfing his attacker in a cloud of choking white smoke. The man dropped the knife and fell to his knees, retching and clawing at his eyes.

Richard hurriedly stepped forward into the cloud and kicked the grenade towards Vicki, helping to spread the gas towards her two assailants.

"Whew, that was close! Thanks!" she called as the whalers went down. "Now let's get this job done before any more of them show up."

Richard bent down to pick up the duffel bag again, thankful for the opportunity to hide how badly he was shaking.

"The freezers are in there." Vicki pointed to a heavy door with an oversized lever-action handle on it.

Richard nodded, not trusting his voice to speak. Air hissed around the rubber seal as he pulled the heavy door open and he felt the blast of frigid air even through his insulated survival suit. He felt anxious going into the unknown by himself, but he gripped his club tightly and forced himself to step through before his nerve could fail. He tried not to think about what he was doing. It was earlier that same morning that he'd been using the club to clear ice off the ship, but now he had to be ready to crack someone's head open with it!

The calm morning already seemed a lifetime away now.

Inside, the huge freezer room was packed to the ceiling with rows of portable shelving, and every shelf was piled high with cardboard boxes. He went over to the nearest one, brushing the ice crystals away with a gloved hand. Underneath was a drawing of a cartoon whale – the Taiyoku Misui Fisheries Company's logo. These were boxes of whalemeat, just like the ones he'd seen in Shimonoseki. Except that there were enough boxes here to fill *three* of the tents he'd seen at the Karato Fish Market.

Richard made his way slowly down the rows, past thousands of boxes. He was glad his full-face mask covered his nose, because the sight of all the congealed blood on the boxes told him the room would have the nostril-clogging reek of a slaughterhouse.

He walked on, keeping his eyes ahead. The sight of all that whalemeat was enough to take his breath away.

But it also hardened his resolve.

At the far end of the room he stopped. In front of him were giant cooling plates of the freezer, and next to them the compressor unit and circulation fan.

He opened the duffel bag and took out one of the Skipper's demolition charges.

How can you go through with this? It's so far outside the law!

Pausing just long enough to silence the last voice of protest in his head, Richard placed the charge against the machinery like he'd been shown.

"This here's C4 plastic explosive," the Skipper had explained to him. "There's enough bang there t' cut clean through six inches of solid steel!" Richard must have looked alarmed at the prospect, but Duke had been quick to reassure him. "Not t' worry. It's a shaped charge so it'll blast inwards. It's perfectly safe so long as you get y' face outta the way after you set it! Perfect for destroyin' machinery without loss of life," he'd growled, clearly disgusted at the very notion.

Remembering his instructions, Richard placed the bomb, checked the detonator was firmly embedded in it, then twisted the dial of the timer.

He felt his pulse race as it began to tick.

Time to get out of here!

But he wasn't done yet. He still had to set an incendiary bomb to destroy the whalemeat so it could never be sold.

He knew he had to hurry. Vicki was alone out in the processing room and more whalers could show up at any time. And they sure didn't share the Team's reservations about unnecessary violence. Or killing!

***

Cal fought for his life.

He could feel the burden of the tank weighing on his back, the straps already beginning to bite into his shoulders. Every movement was an effort. It was like trying to fight underwater. He was tiring quickly and he knew he was at a distinct disadvantage, but he dared not try to ditch his air supply, heavy though it was. Right now, the debilitating gas cloud was the only advantage he had.

The assassin came at him again, sword flashing, but then his attack faltered and he stumbled.

Cal realised his adversary was coughing, clearly affected by the gas – although the wrap-around sunglasses and bandanna tied across his face afforded some protection from the worst of it.

Cal redoubled his efforts, determined to exploit the meagre advantage the gas gave him. The assassin avoided the flying grapnel though, and stepped forward, closing the range before he could swing it again. The katana came up, as if in slow motion.

Desperate now, Cal grabbed the assassin's sword arm, determined to stop him using it.

Then they crashed together, chest to chest, locked in a clinch.

Too close for either fighter to use his weapon, they wrestled with each other instead, both trying to control the other's weapon or throw him off balance long enough to free their own.

Cal stared back into the expressionless face, all-but hidden behind the dark shades and ninja mask.

Suddenly the assassin let go his sword hilt with one hand and lunged at Cal's face, trying to claw his mask away.

Cal twisted his head clear, then rammed his forehead into his adversary's nose in a vicious head butt. He felt the crunch of cartilage breaking, and the assassin's grip loosened. The Japanese stumbled backwards, reeling, taken by surprise by this unorthodox method of fighting.

Blood ran down the front of the white business shirt under his coat.

Cal moved forward, but the assassin was still as dangerous as a pit viper. The long katana stabbed towards his thigh, aiming for a crippling blow.

Cal stepped aside, swinging the grapnel to meet it. The long prongs caught the sword blade, locking the two weapons together. He immediately jerked the chain back, yanking the weapon out of his surprised adversary's hand.

Cal swung the grapnel up. The sword wasn't as awkward as the long-handled flensing knife had been, and with a triumphant swing of the chain it flew around his head. Almost instantaneously, the sword came loose and sailed into the air where it was lost over the side.

Cal stepped forward, ready to deliver the final blow. But the assassin wasn't beaten yet.

He smoothly back-pedalled out of the way, then reached up and yanked the bandanna away from his face. Touching his gloved hand to his shattered nose, he held the blood-smeared fingers up for inspection.

His lip curled in a vicious snarl at the sight.

Then with a gleam of cold rage on his face he reached under his coat and drew a second, shorter sword.

Oh shit! Now he's pissed!

Cal gritted his teeth and waited, prepared to meet the fury that was about to be unleashed.

Then with a sinking heart he felt a breeze on his face.

Wind!

The gas was already dissipating quickly. Soon the protective cloud would be gone – along with any slight advantage he might have over this trained killer.

Cal knew he was in serious trouble.

He spun the chain as wide as he dared, trying to keep the circling attacker out of range.

Just then a low rumbling sound reached his ears. It sounded like distant thunder, but it kept growing, rolling and swelling around him as the source approached.

Oh shit! Helicopters!

Cal looked around, but he couldn't see anything through the haze of tear gas. He anxiously keyed his radio. "Skip, do you hear that?"

A familiar laconic voice answered in his ear. "Yep. Cavalry's on the way – but it ain't ours!"

Cal felt the shadow of failure threatening to engulf him.

"Bugger it all to hell! Where are they?"

"I see 'em. Two Seahawks, and a Sea Stallion flying escort. They're comin' in fast from thuh north. And there's a half dozen warships behind that. They're gonna hit us, and they're gonna hit us hard!"

"Can you hold them off?"

Duke sighed. "I don't think so, Son. It's the SEALs."

Cal swore under his breath. Everything was turning to custard. The weight of command pressed down on him, and he knew the decisions he made in the next frantic seconds could make or break this mission – and the lives of his Team.

The Gwendolyn was outnumbered and outgunned. But as long as the New Zealand Government hadn't issued an international arrest warrant, no foreign power could touch a vessel under Kiwi jurisdiction. She ought to be safe in New Zealand waters – if Duke could get there in time. Making a run for it was a gamble, but it was their best hope. Getting caught out here in international waters would be tantamount to suicide.

"Skip, head for the Ross Sea! The ship will be safe there!"

There was no answer. Cal tried again, desperately.

"Get out of here while you still can! We'll catch up in the Naiad. Skip, can you hear me?"

Duke's voice suddenly roared in his earpiece, coarse with displeasure. "Horse shit!" he spluttered. "I ain't leavin' my crew, or a job half-done! I told y' already, Son, ain't nobody can take on a SEAL e'cept another SEAL!"

Just then Cal heard the hissing exhalation of a whale blowing nearby and his heart sank. He knew it was Koru. And she was still in mortal danger.

All of a sudden, his resolve hardened. Seven years of painstaking scientific research counted for nothing if he couldn't protect any whales. Documenting the plight of whales was a waste of time without the courage to back it up with action. Koru had become the Cause. She was once his hope for the survival of her species, and he couldn't afford to let that hope die.

"I won't let them kill you," he murmured. "So help me, I won't."

But right now there was nothing he could do. He faced off against Amimoto's assassin, locked in a fight for his own life.

At that moment Cal heard the rumble of the Gwendolyn's diesels as she wheeled around, and just before she raced away the smoke cleared briefly. He caught sight of Duke standing at the wheelhouse door, ready to face the threat head-on, his shotgun firmly grasped in his hands.

Cal felt his heart miss a beat as he realised what his friend intended.

The Gwendolyn was on a collision course with the speeding Hunter-Killer!

Oh hell, be careful Skip!

Suddenly Cal's thoughts were interrupted by a blood-curdling yell. The assassin launched himself forward with a full battle cry, his short sword a blur of flashing light.

Cal was forced to grab his chain with both hands and parry for his life.

***

Richard grabbed the duffel bag and hurried out of the freezer and back into the processing room. Through the swirling gas filling the room he was relieved to see Vicki crouched down beside the mincing machine, her respirator hissing as she worked.

She barely looked up as he came through the door. "Ok?"

He nodded, looking at his watch.

Not much time!

"Almost done," she said. "Put a fire bomb over there – just to make sure."

Richard hurried to comply, placing the device where it would engulf the machinery after the main disabling charges went off.

He checked the components as he rigged it, making sure the timer was securely wired to the flare that served as the detonator, then fitting that into the top of the fuel container where it could reach the flammable vapours inside. The fireball would be big, and there was always a chance it could spread out of control and threaten the whole ship.

His hands were unsteady as he reached for the timer, but he steeled his resolve and twisted the dial with determination, arming the incendiary bomb.

It's done!

Vicki was almost finished rigging the processing machinery when a sudden crackle of radio static brought both their heads up in unison.

"Attention, crew of the Gwendolyn! This is an urgent message to you!"

Richard's jaw hung open in surprise. He would have recognised that sultry voice anywhere.

"It's Summer!" he whispered.

Vicki cocked her head quizzically. "What the hell?" she muttered. She reached for her radio mike, sounding annoyed. "Summer, what's going on? We're supposed to maintain radio silence unless it's an emergency!"

Summer laughed humourlessly. "This is an emergency – for you! This business has gone far enough. It's time to give yourselves up."

"What's going on?"

"Give yourselves up now, before it's too late!"

Vicki's reply was level, but delivered through gritted teeth. "Summer, what the hell are you doing?"

Summer laughed again, but her next words had a chilling effect. "I'm an undercover agent for the US Department of Homeland Security. You're all under arrest for terrorism!"

Richard's eyes widened in alarm and he felt the words hit him like a punch to the stomach.

Oh no! It can't be true, can it?

Vicki's eyebrows shot up, but she maintained her composure. "I don't think you're in any position to lay down the law to us. What are you going to do, come over here and put the cuffs on us yourself?"

Summer ignored the unspoken challenge in Vicki's tone. She laughed again. "Oh, but I don't need to! You see, my backup is already on the way. I directed them here myself."

"You're lying!"

"Am I?"

"Yeah, Cal disabled the ship-to-shore radio."

"Yes, wasn't that clever of him? Nevertheless I've been keeping the authorities informed for some time now with the Sat-phone in my cabin."

Vicki sucked in her breath. "You backstabbing little slapper!"

"Same to you, you stuck-up Aussie bitch!" Summer shot back. Then she laughed gleefully. "The Navy SEALs will be here at any moment so I strongly advise you to drop your weapons and surrender to me. You're about to get justice one way or another!"

"I hope you rot in hell!"

Summer laughed again. "Now now, anything you say may be used in evidence against you!"

Richard slumped against the nearest machine, feeling sick to his stomach. His insides ached as though he'd just been eviscerated.

The person he loved – or thought he loved – had just betrayed him! He struggled to make sense of the emotions that flooded through him. His first response was outright denial, but he couldn't deny what he'd just heard, and somewhere deep inside he knew she wasn't joking.

He found his voice at last. "S-Summer, what are you doing?" he whispered.

The voice that answered him was cold and emotionless. "Isn't it obvious? I'm shutting down your little crime spree."

Richard reeled back in shock. "But you can't! What about the whales? I thought you believed in the cause?"

Summer sniffed disdainfully. "I let you believe what I needed you to in order to get my job done."

"But we have to save the whales!" he persisted. "What about the Ocean? Don't you care about the future of the planet?"

Summer's laugh was callous. "I don't have to fake that hippy bullshit any more, and you'd do well to drop it too. It won't get you anywhere when they send you to Guantanamo with the rest of the terrorists!"

Richard felt his heart rip in half. He'd believed she was someone else. Someone who cared about the world. Someone who he would have been happy to spend his life alongside. Now he found out he was wrong. She had deceived him.

"Was any of it true?" he whispered sadly.

Summer chuckled again, proud of herself. "No. I'm not even Canadian! I'm a Valley Girl – born and bred in West Hollywood!"

"You used me," Richard whispered, still swamped by disbelief. "How could you do that to me?"

"I'm a professional. It's my job."

"But you said you loved me!"

"I lied. Get over it."

"What about that night in your cabin? The time we kissed?"

"Oh, that!" She sneered disdainfully. "Every job has its cringe factor!"

Richard hung his head, crushed.

"Don't listen to her!" Vicki hissed. "We've still got a job to finish!"

He stared vacantly at her, emotionless. Then he noticed the genuine concern on Vicki's face.

She held his gaze, her blue eyes hard, determined. "You can do better than her, trust me."

Abruptly she turned her anger toward Summer. "How did you get to the Gwendolyn's radio? And where's the Skipper?"

***

Duke Hayward stood outside on the wheelhouse ladder, scanning the grey sky. The clatter of the helicopters was closer now, but an even more immediate danger presented itself dead ahead. The sinister grey bow of the Kuu-Maru cut through the ice-laden sea, making straight for its factory ship.

Ahead of it was the she-whale, her spouting desperate now as the Japanese catcher boat herded her mercilessly back towards her doom.

With a frown, Duke sized up the situation. Gyofuku must have freed the net from his ship, and now he was racing back to the fight, driving the whale ahead of him at the same time.

Duke regarded the boarding party assembled on the catcher's fore-deck, clutching their knives and clubs, ready to jump aboard the Nippon-Maru and cause trouble for his crew! He quickly realised the Japanese captain's plan in herding his prey back this way – kill the whale and seize back control of the factory ship at the same time! And victory was very nearly within his grasp.

"Oh yeah? Not on my watch!" Duke muttered to the wind.

He hefted his trusty Remington, shaggy brows already beetling in frustration. The non-lethal baton rounds would be hard-pressed to stop that many angry whalers, and the gang heavily outnumbered the Gwendolyn's small boarding party.

"Ain't no cause for restraint now – gotta to keep them reinforcements away, no matter what!"

His crew's lives depended on it.

He pumped the shotgun's slide rapidly, ejecting the useless plastic rounds. "A goddamn riot gun'll be no use to me now," he muttered, cramming the tubular magazine full with lethal lead-filled buckshot cartridges instead.

On the Kuu-Maru's prow, the gunner took aim behind his harpoon cannon, lining up the fleeing whale in his sights.

Duke knew at that moment he was the only thing standing in the way of another senseless death at sea. He spat contemptuously over the side. Enough was enough. He'd seen the Sea disrespected enough times already to let these imperialistic bastards get their hooks into another whale in front of him.

The gunner gripped his trigger and prepared to fire.

Like hell! You ain't getting' this one without a fight!

The Gwendolyn's autopilot was already bearing him on an interception course and Duke raised his Remington as they sped straight at the catcher's bow.

Abruptly the Kuu-Maru swerved away, Gyofuku chickening out of the test of wills.

Duke's lip curled in a contemptuous sneer, and his attention switched to the gunner.

Then the white helmet suddenly jerked up in surprise as the man saw him. He swiftly swung the big cannon around, pointing the orange-tipped grenade harpoon directly at the Gwendolyn.

Duke's rage boiled furiously.

Oh no you don't!

He quickly adjusted his shotgun's choke to keep the shot spread as tight as possible. This was long range for a scattergun, but he only needed a few pellets to hit their target…

He squinted along the sights, taking careful aim.

The shotgun thundered in his hand.

The gunner immediately dived for cover as the blast hit the front of the cannon, and he lost his white plastic helmet in his haste to cower behind it. But Duke wasn't aiming at him.

He worked the pump to reload without dropping his aim, firing again almost immediately.

Another swarm of pellets clattered off the front of the harpoon gun, but the spread was too wide. Duke cursed, beginning to wonder if the range was just too far to be effective.

Come on, you son of a whore!

He fired again.

This time the main blast of pellets was concentrated dead on target. The orange harpoon head exploded in a blast of smoke, bursting open the cannon's muzzle in the process.

Sweet music to the ears! They won't be usin' that thing again in a hurry!

Pleased with his efforts, Duke began feeding more shotgun shells into the magazine.

Suddenly the radio crackled in the wheelhouse behind him. Duke's response was immediate, and contrite.

Oh Christ, Cal! I've left the boy alone!

The crazy Kiwi was still busy fighting that sword-wielding Japper on the factory ship! Alone!

Duke looked back but the Nippon-Maru was astern of him now, and he couldn't even see what was happening aboard. He hurried back to the wheelhouse to turn the Gwendolyn around.

Bursting through the door he suddenly found himself face-to-face with a Glock 9mm pistol. He stopped in surprise. Though outwardly calm, his mind raced with long-forgotten survival skills, taking him a moment to realise it was held by the blonde Canadian gal.

"'Bout time you emerged from that cabin," he quipped. "Come to make y'self useful, huh? Well get to it then, there's plenty more of 'em out there."

The pistol never wavered from his face.

"Very funny," she said. "Now drop the gun."

Duke raised a bushy eyebrow, stalling for time. He didn't know where the hell that pistol had come from, but he knew none of the possibilities were good. "You wanna watch where you're pointing that thing, Missy. Guns are dangerous."

He tightened his grip on the shotgun held across his chest, wondering if he could bring it to bear before she could fire a bullet off.

She motioned with the barrel of her pistol. "Drop it!"

Duke knew he didn't have time to waste playing silly games. His crew needed him.

He took a step forward.

She thumbed back the hammer of the pistol. "That's far enough! I'm taking control of this ship. You're under arrest."

He squinted suspiciously at her. "What thuh hell are you playin' at, Missy?"

"I said drop it!"

He stood impassively, ignoring the order.

I ain't givin' up my ship to nobody – least of all you!

As much as he didn't want to believe this situation, he suddenly knew it made sense. He cussed himself for not figuring her out earlier. "I reckoned you might actually care 'bout what we're tryin' t'do out here," he muttered aloud. "Guess I had y' wrong then."

"I guess you did," she affirmed. "This cause of yours is nothing but a load of ideological extremism. You're all violent criminals and I'm here to personally see you go down for it."

"Oh yeah? And maybe I ought to blast you good!" Duke muttered, still clutching the shotgun to his chest.

"You won't do it," she sneered. "I'm an agent of the United States Government. Your government. Besides, you ain't got the stones, pops!"

Duke sagged, knowing Summer was right, but not for the reasons she thought. He could never bring himself to point a gun at a woman, much less pull the trigger. It just wasn't right.

He swiftly evaluated his options. She was standing a good three metres away, but even if he could reach her he knew there wasn't much he could do. Pistol-whipping her with the butt of his gun was out of the question, as was punching her lights out. His misguided sense of chivalry wouldn't let him lay a hand on a woman. And she seemed to know it.

"What are you going to do, old man?" she sneered. "Give it up!"

Duke hung his head, knowing she had him over a barrel. He lowered the shotgun, letting it slip from his fingers. "You're a sorry excuse for a biologist, ain't ya?" he growled, mightily pissed off but powerless to act.

Summer laughed casually. "I'm not a biologist. I'm a Homeland Security agent."

"Oh yeah? What did they pay y' to rat out y' friends?"

She wrinkled her nose disdainfully, and her next words had an electrifying effect on him.

"They're not my friends. They never were. I just used them to get inside this terrorist cell of yours."

The thought of her cruelly and shamelessly stringing poor Richard along made Duke's thermostat rise almost as much as her deception had. Women weren't supposed to use their wiles that way.

"You evil little hussy!"

Something snapped inside him and before he could stop himself he was charging forward across the room.

Her eyes widened, the sudden move catching her by surprise. All of a sudden the brazen cockiness on her face was replaced by uncertainty, swiftly turning to outright fear.

She fumbled for the trigger and the pistol roared twice, echoing in the narrow confines of the room.

But her aim was high.

The first shot whistled over Duke's head to clang off the wall behind. The second struck him in the shoulder, barely slowing his charge.

Two shots were all she had time for as he lunged at her.

He grabbed for the weapon with both hands and tore it from her grasp. Then his momentum carried him into her, his shoulder crashing into her chest, and she sprawled backwards. Her head hit the bulkhead behind and she went out like a light, slumping to the floor with her blonde locks spilling over her face.

Even through his anger, Duke felt a moment of concern for her. "Now look what y've gone and made me do," he muttered, shaking his head.

He straightened up, thumbing the safety and shoving the pistol down his waistband. He had more important matters to attend to now.

Ignoring the gunshot wound in his shoulder, he spun the Gwendolyn's wheel hard to port, bringing her around.

The Kuu-Maru was already lining up alongside the factory ship, boarding party at the ready. Time was short.

Duke glanced down at his pump-action shotgun on the floor and frowned.

It would take two hands to use the weapon effectively, and his shoulder was already beginning to stiffen up…

B'sides, it's long past time to open up a can' o' whoop ass!

The decision made, he reached up and lifted one of the ceiling panels, feeling around in the concealed alcove above it. Then his hand touched what he sought and he lifted the weapon down carefully, almost reverently, turning it over in his hands.

It had a distinctive upturned wooden stock and a gaping wide muzzle.

It was an M-79 grenade launcher – the weapon that had saved his life many times in 'Nam.

Duke smiled to himself as he clicked open the breech and tipped the barrel forward like a giant single-barrelled shotgun. He ran his hand thoughtfully over the fat 40mm grenades tucked into the bandolier on the shoulder strap. His eye fell on the gold-painted heads of the High-Explosive projectiles.

His lip curled in anticipation. "That bleedin' homicidal Jap captain deserves an HE round, right in thuh kisser!"

Then he thought of Cal. He sighed and took out a grey-tipped grenade with a red band and loaded it into the oversized breech instead. The black lettering on it read 'M651 Tactical CS gas'. "Ain't nobody can say ah'm heartless," he muttered.

Duke opened the wheelhouse door and stepped out into the watery Antarctic sun.

He hadn't used a thump-gun in over thirty-five years, but he didn't hesitate. He could send a grenade through a foot-square pillbox window from two hundred yards. His accuracy had saved his life before. It wasn't a skill a good soldier ever forgot.

He flipped up the graduated foresight and took aim at the Kuu-Maru's bridge.

"Chew on this you bastard!" he growled.

The familiar hollow *thunk* as the weapon discharged evoked a powerful rush of nostalgia, and for a moment Duke almost felt as though he was back in the steamy tropical jungles of 'Nam again.

The grenade hit one of the little side windows of the Kuu-Maru's bridge dead-centre and smashed through in a shower of glass. Moments later it exploded, filling the room with tear gas. The choking white cloud billowed out the broken window and around the edge of the door frame. Duke's lip curled with satisfaction.

Just like postin' a letter!

Anybody inside would be incapacitated and puking his guts out for the next little while!

He smiled at the thought of Gyofuku gagging and retching.

Just then the clatter of rotor blades alongside rose to a crescendo, and the downdraught sent stinging spray into his face.

"Dang it all to hell!" he muttered angrily. "Why don't y' tend to your own rat killin'."

But the helicopters swept overhead on their way to the Nippon-Maru.

The game was nearly up.

Duke hurried back inside to the radio.

"Naiad from Gwendolyn," he called. "You there Son?"

Cal's voice came back faintly, panting with exertion. "Yeah… Barely… Having some trouble with Amimoto's personal attack dog though."

"Y' need a hand?"

"No… I'll manage…. Need you to keep those helos off my back."

Duke squinted up at the sky. "They're almost to ya."

"I know… Can hear the racket," Cal replied, desperation beginning to creep into his voice. "We're not done with the charges yet… Need more time to finish the job." He paused, as if knowing what he was about to ask. "Can you delay them?"

Duke sighed as he spun the Gwendolyn's wheel, knowing that was no small ask. "Ah'll see what we can do," he said, patting the polished wooden spokes beneath his fingers. "Don't worry, Son. We'll buy y' some time."

With his free hand Duke clicked open the M-79's mechanism and flicked away the empty and still-smoking cartridge case. He hurriedly fed another grenade into the mechanism and snapped it closed. The tip of this round was not grey, but gold.

As he leaned out the door to fire, Duke knew that for him and his Old Gal time was already up.

Chapter 32

Last one!

Richard Major finished setting the charge and straightened up, shouldering the now half-empty duffel bag.

Vicki grinned and stood up. She was done too.

Suddenly there was a thunderous clatter outside. It rose to a crescendo, rattling the high windows and seeming to vibrate through the black hull of the ship.

They both froze, looking up fearfully.

The helicopters were here.

"Bloody hell!" Vicki exclaimed. "We're almost out of time!"

She beckoned him over urgently, then unzipped the duffel bag and reached inside. With a determined expression she grabbed three charges and shoved them down the front of her jacket, followed by a couple of the tear gas grenades.

"What are you doing?" Richard asked, feeling suddenly uneasy.

She didn't look at him.

"Take the rest of the charges back to Cal," she ordered. "He'll need them to use on the bridge."

"What about you?"

"I'm heading to the engineroom."

Richard felt his heart stop. "But you can't! Not by yourself. It's too dangerous!"

She paused suddenly, looking him in the eye. Her face was resolute, but wistful. "Someone has to do it!" she replied.

"Let me go with you then!"

Vicki shook her head. "No. Cal needs that bag…"

Richard hesitated, not wanting to leave her alone.

A sudden vision sprang into his mind, and Richard gasped as the familiar nightmare seized him. He saw a drowned body, hanging suspended in a flooded room, its skin pale and lifeless in the dark water. Even before he saw the dark tendrils of hair framing the face – serene and beautiful in death – he knew without a doubt it was Vicki.

Richard choked back the sob that tried forced its way out. "No," he whispered. "You can't go down there. Vicki, please…"

She smiled sadly. "I have to do it Richard."

She crouched down next to the bombs they'd just set, her actions hidden by her back.

"What are you doing?" Richard demanded.

She didn't reply, but when she stepped away he saw the timers had been twisted forward. Only sixty seconds now remained!

"Vicki, what the hell are you doing? How will you get back?"

She grinned, showing her dimples. "I'll find another way out. I'm a resourceful girl." Then her smile faded. "We can't afford to give the SEALs time to get aboard and disarm the charges."

"Vicki please, don't do it! You could get killed down there!"

She looked back at him one last time, her expression unreadable. "I'm not doing this for me."

Then she headed for the stairs.

"Go Richard! Get out of here!" She called over her shoulder. As she disappeared down into the bowels of the ship her voice floated back up to him. "I'll see you on the flip side!"

Richard watched her go, suddenly overwhelmed at the thought of losing her.

The timers ticked relentlessly, counting down the seconds.

He blinked, the awful realisation finally galvanising him into action.

Numbly, he shouldered the duffel bag and stumbled towards the exit.

The long corridor seemed endless as he blundered along it, heading for the oblong rectangle of light at the end.

Just as he emerged into the weak sunlight of the Antarctic day, the deck shuddered beneath him, throwing him to his knees. The first explosions had gone off inside the factory ship.

***

Cal Major held the chain taut and whipped it across his body, managing to parry the assassin's savage charge.

His mind raced, knowing he couldn't afford to be delayed here. While he was preoccupied fighting this evil black-coated samurai, the plan was falling apart. His Team needed him.

He was furious at Summer's betrayal, but at the same time he found he wasn't surprised. He snorted contemptuously. "I knew she was no biologist!"

His thoughts turned to his brother. Richard had sounded devastated by her scathing rejection of him, and Cal knew his brother's fragile self-esteem had just been crushed. But he also knew that was the least of his worries right now.

Just then he heard a sudden crash of gunfire from the direction of the Gwendolyn. Worriedly, he snatched a quick glance over his shoulder, but she remained obscured by the pall of gas.

He had to hope the Skipper was ok. He certainly couldn't offer him any help. He was stuck fighting for his own life. For better or for worse, each of them would have to take care of themselves for the time being.

Cal was suddenly jerked back to reality as the assassin chopped viciously at his chest. He jumped back out of range, searching for an opportunity to counterattack. But the silent black-masked samurai was good. Too good. He lunged forward again, sword flashing in a blur of movement – almost too fast to see.

The chain jarred and tore at Cal's hands with each sword stroke he caught on it, but he was still losing ground. Every attack drove him backwards, and he knew he couldn't hold out forever. It was only a matter of time.

The assassin swung at him again, feinting low then swinging high. Cal dodged just in time, the blade whistling within inches of his face. He shuddered at the thought of the maiming blow it would have inflicted, mentally cursing himself for letting it get that close.

Come on! Wake up!

He was tiring quickly though. His arms felt like lead, and every movement seemed slower than the last. He eyed his attacker warily, shuffling continually backwards to stay out of reach of that sword.

All of a sudden Cal felt something solid at his back. With a sense of dismay he realised it was a wall behind him. He had reached the end of the deck. There was nowhere else to retreat to.

Behind his black mask, the assassin's eyes glittered. He knew it too.

Cal sidestepped immediately, but the sword was already whistling towards him. He flung himself away from it, and would have made it clear in time – except for the fateful hazard underfoot. It was an abandoned whaler's helmet – white – the same colour as the gas cloud and difficult to see. Cal tripped over it and stumbled, his momentum carrying him into the side of a huge cable drum. He crashed against it hard enough to lose his grip on the grapnel chain, and his balance. Grabbing onto the lip of the drum to stop himself falling, he found his eyes two inches from the same puke-coloured paint as the ship's superstructure. This drum held a huge winch, wound with the massive steel cables used to haul the whale carcasses up the slipway and onto the deck for dismembering. The symbolism was not lost on him…

Move! You are not going to die like this!

The sword was already coming down though, humming as it cut through the air.

There was nowhere to go.

In desperation, Cal did the only thing he could do – and the one thing he had been taught never to do. He turned his back on his opponent.

The sword hit him square in the back, driving him forward with the momentum of the blow. A huge crash rang out as the tempered blade glanced off the solid steel air tank on his back.

Before the assassin could swing again, Cal lashed out with a fierce rear thrust kick, catching his opponent off guard. His heel drove straight into the man's sternum, winding him and sending him staggering backwards.

Cal snatched up his grapnel chain and spun to face his attacker, whirling the grapnel to press home his counterattack.

Incredibly, the assassin's sword was still up, stunned though he was.

Knowing the samurai was still as dangerous as a cornered rattlesnake, Cal hesitated for just a fraction longer. Searching with his foot, he found the abandoned helmet and kicked it up at his opponent's face.

The assassin flinched and dropped his shoulder in defence as the hard plastic missile hit him and bounced away. But that was all the opening Cal required. He stepped forward, swinging the grapnel in a two-handed strike over his head.

The sword went up to block it, but Cal had judged the swing perfectly. The blade clashed onto the middle of the flying chain, but at the end of the weapon the grapnel continued its swing unchecked, pivoting over the upraised sword to catch the samurai in the upper back.

He grunted with pain, and Cal yanked the chain to drive the grapnel's claws deeper into his shoulder. Jerked forward off balance, the assassin made one last half-hearted attempt to catch Cal on his sword-point.

Stepping smoothly to the side, Cal pulled him directly onto the huge drum.

The assassin hit the immobile machinery face-first, his head snapping backwards with the impact before he collapsed in a heap.

Cal wrapped several turns of the chain around his adversary's neck then yanked the lolling head up to meet the finishing strike. With his fingers tucked underneath his hand, he tensed it into the iron-hard weapon of a martial artist, preparing to drive the heel of his palm into the nose. The blow would drive the shattered cartilage up through the nasal cavity and into the brain. It was a killing move.

"Time to finish this once and for all," he muttered, aiming for the trickle of blood already running onto the upper lip

But behind the assassin's mask his eyes were closed and his breathing laboured, hampered no doubt, by the gas still surrounding them.

Cal hesitated, then reluctantly lowered his hand. Though he felt no pity for this soulless killer, he knew he couldn't bring himself to kill a defenceless man – evil or not.

He let go of the assassin and stood up, allowing the head to slump back onto the deck with a thud. The body lay motionless. "You're not worth the effort."

There was more important business to take care of. He needed to finish setting the charges, find the rest of his Team, then get the hell off this ship.

Cal looked around, knowing he might already be out of time.

At that moment the roar of rotor blades built up to a thundering crescendo overhead.

Oh shit! The helicopters are here!

The downdraught from the spinning rotors blew away what remained of the gas cloud, leaving the Nippon-Maru's flensing deck suddenly exposed.

The helicopters buzzed overhead, wheeling around like predatory insects in the sky. Cal shaded his eyes with his hand and looked up, just in time to see the nearest machine open fire on the Gwendolyn's bridge.

The rattle of gunfire and breaking glass jolted home the perilous reality of their situation. Cal knew the Skipper couldn't hold out forever. He had to finish the job and get his Team back to the Gwendolyn before the net closed around them.

He turned his gaze up to the rear of the Nippon-Maru's bridge, settled atop the pus-yellow superstructure at the far end of the ship – and the high windows situated where they could look down over everything like dark sightless eyes.

The control room!

Cal glared back, knowing he had to get in there.

Through the windows he could see at least three green-helmeted officers on the bridge.

Three against one. It would be a tough fight. The captain and his deputies would never surrender control of the ship willingly.

Cal's jaw clenched as he steeled himself for action. Force was the only way.

He hurriedly retrieved his crossbow from the bag and slung it across his back by its carrying strap. He hoped he wouldn't have to use it, but he wasn't about to come this far and fail now. That, and three against one was hardly fair odds.

He had one CS grenade and one demolition charge on him. Not much, but it would have to do.

Cal started forward, determined.

Suddenly Richard burst through the doorway ahead and staggered out onto the deck – just as a sequence of explosions rocked the Nippon-Maru.

They both struggled for balance as the ship pitched violently beneath them. A plume of black smoke rose from the ventilator pipes at the edge of the deck.

That'll be the end of the processing room!

Cal grinned at his brother, proud of his efforts. "Nice job!" he called, giving a thumbs-up.

Richard didn't respond. In fact, he seemed dazed and confused.

Cal felt a sudden premonition as he realised Richard was alone. He ran over to him, grabbing his shoulders to look into his face.

"Richard, what's going on? Where's Vicki?"

"D-Down in the engineroom. She went to plant more bombs."

Cal shook his head in dismay, hoping she would be alright. She was so headstrong!

He pursed his lips. The plan was going to hell with all of them separated!

But it was too late to worry about that though. He had to get to the bridge!

He grabbed the duffel bag off Richard, along with the wooden ice-club.

"Back to the Naiad," he ordered, propelling his brother towards the far end of the deck with a gentle push. "Get ready to leave the moment we return."

Richard nodded distantly and shuffled away.

Cal watched him for a moment, concerned, and feeling another pang of guilt at getting his brother mixed up in all of this.

Then, thrusting aside his misgivings, he turned and hurried forward, searching for a way up to the bridge. He moved quickly, conscious of the need to hurry.

He was half-way up a steel companionway leading up the outside of the bridge when the ship lurched again, a ferocious double explosion booming somewhere deep below his feet.

He swayed on the ladder, grabbing at the handrail for balance.

That was a big one!

On a sudden impulse, he keyed his radio mike. "Nice going Vicki, head back to the Naiad now," he called. "I'll be there soon."

There was no answer.

"Vicki, are you there?"

Silence.

Cal swore under his breath.

Can anything else go wrong?

At that moment he heard the clatter of rotor blades as the helicopters wheeled overhead again. With a sense of dismay he watched them pounce on the Gwendolyn, dropping into a hover over her forward deck and uncoiling abseil ropes as they prepared to drop an assault team on board.

"Oh shit!" he whispered.

He was about to tell Duke to get the hell away from here when he saw a familiar shaggy silhouette outside the wheelhouse. It was the Skipper, and he wasn't about to surrender his ship without a fight. Cal caught sight of the shotgun in his mate's hand, and with a sick sense of certainty he knew what the Skipper was planning to do.

"You can't take them all on, Skip. Get out of here!" he called urgently.

But Duke either couldn't hear the radio or was ignoring it.

As he looked on helplessly, Cal saw him raise the shotgun.

"Jeezus, Skip! No! They'll kill you!"

Cal stared in horror.

At that moment the side door of the Nippon-Maru's bridge opened above him and a green helmet appeared at the top of the ladder, shouting and pointing down at him.

Shit! I've been spotted!

There was no time to waste!

Go! Go! Go!

Gripping the club tightly in his fist, Cal charged up the ladder.

***

Richard stood beside the Naiad, puffing from the exertion of pushing it. It was half turned-around now, but still needed to be closer to the edge of the slipway ready for launching. Richard remained frozen in place though, his heart racing.

He'd heard Cal's urgent radio call go unanswered, and he knew with absolute certainty that something terrible had happened to Vicki.

Someone needs to go and look for her!

His pulse raced at the thought, because the realisation that hit him was immediate and momentous.

There is no one else!

Cal was up on the black ship's bridge, and the Skipper was over on the Gwendolyn.

He blanched at the thought of Vicki lying down in the dark depths of the ship, imprisoned within the steel sarcophagus, alone, and probably hurt.

I can't do it. I can't go down there!

His conscience protested, refusing to listen.

You have to go!

Still he hesitated, searching for any available excuse.

Cal said to wait here, he reminded himself.

But that was before Vicki was in trouble!

Richard closed his eyes, ashamed of his own cowardice. He knew Vicki wouldn't hesitate to intervene if he was in trouble – indeed, she had stepped up for him many times already...

The nightmare vision leaped into his head again – Vicki's drowned body, floating in the dark water. He felt the strength go out of his legs and he slumped down, petrified of sharing the same fate.

But he knew he couldn't abandon her, not when there was still hope, however small. She needed his help.

You have to do it!

All of a sudden something Cal had once said to him popped into his head. "You can accomplish anything if you put your mind to it… I believe in you, Bro!"

Inspired, Richard took a deep breath, steeling himself for action before he could change his mind. He checked his air supply, his mind racing.

Ok, I'll need a weapon!

Reaching into the Naiad, he drew out the largest spanner in the toolkit. It felt unwieldy in his hands and he didn't know how to use it effectively as a weapon. But it would have to do. He slipped it into his back pocket, making sure the protruding handle was within easy reach.

Richard turned away from the safety of the Naiad and started forward, heading back toward the black ship's hold.

Just outside the doorway he discovered the motionless body of Amimoto's assassin, the anchor chain still wrapped around his neck. Richard remembered the murderous gleam in the assassin's eyes when he attacked him on the Gwendolyn. He shivered with dread, even though the black eyes were safely closed now. At any moment though, Richard expected the killer to wake up and make a sudden lunge toward him. With his heart thumping he stepped forward, skirting warily around the body.

The eyes remained closed.

With newfound respect for his brother's skills, Richard hurried past the defeated killer, heading back down the corridor to the destroyed processing room.

Once there, he was shocked at the amount of thick black smoke now filling the cavernous room, obscuring everything behind a hot, choking blanket. In the gloom, he could just make out the hungry orange flicker of the flames as they devoured the butchering machines.

He was glad of his air supply, but time was short. He had only enough air for a brief search. He had to find Vicki and get her out before the fire took hold.

Last chance to back out!

Richard ignored the thought and started forward defiantly, surprising himself with the force of his resolve.

I've got to find her!

With each breath rasping mechanically in his ears he headed down the darkened companionway to the lower decks, where he'd last seen Vicki.

At the bottom the shadows closed around him like a shroud, and the lower passageway stretched away into darkness ahead of him. Fumbling in the chest pocket of his survival suit, he found his little head torch and clicked it on. By the light of the pale red beam he could just make out the detail of the floor in front of him. It wasn't much of a confidence booster, but it was enough. He took a brave step forward into the unknown, then another, feeling his way along the wall. His breathing sounded loud in his ears now.

Richard made his way down the passage for what seemed like an eternity, before a handrail suddenly loomed in front of him like an apparition. He gasped, taking a moment to recognise the shadowy form. It stood there like a sentinel, silently guarding the staircase beyond. He stared down into the dark pit in the floor, knowing that was the way Vicki would have gone – the way down to the engineroom.

The darkness down there was even more pervasive. With the power out, natural light was the only illumination below-decks, and it couldn't penetrate this deep inside the black ship's hold.

Richard slowly descended the stairs, feeling for each step like a blind man.

Suddenly he felt an icy touch on his ankle. He recoiled in horror, a strangled cry escaping his lips. Shining the torch beam down, he saw the floor rippling in the weak light.

With a crushing sense of despair, he realised he was looking at water.

Insidious, black water.

The bottom of the stairwell was flooded.

Richard felt his courage falter.

Not that! Please, anything but that!

The water lapped greedily at the stairs, and Richard managed to choke back the anguished moan that rose to his lips. He touched Cal's greenstone carving around his neck.

If ever I need good luck, it's now!

Just the thought of Cal seemed to give him strength though. He knew his brother would never hesitate.

You can't quit now! Vicki's down there!

Fighting back the waves of panic, Richard took a deep breath and lowered his foot into the unknown depths. The step was there, just under the surface, and reassuringly solid beneath his boot. He swallowed and took another step down, gasping as the water rose hungrily around him. Even through the insulated survival suit he could feel the creeping cold gnawing into his bones, and he knew without a doubt that the frigid water promised a slow death for any who dared to brave it too long.

Vicki is somewhere down here!

He continued down the unseen steps, wincing in anticipation as the water rose around him, compressing the rubber lining of the suit against his body.

He held his breath as the dark water finally closed over his head, his heart thudding like a jackhammer in his chest. The cold water swirled all around him, and he couldn't see more than two feet in front of his face. Richard choked back the panic, knowing this was what it would feel like to be trapped underwater and drowning!

His chest tightened in response and it took a supreme effort to force himself to breathe again. But the relief as the dry bottled air continued to flood into his lungs was cathartic.

Ok, I'm not drowning. I can do this!

With his torch beam barely penetrating through the dark water, Richard swam along the flooded corridor, feeling ahead for any obstructions.

Suddenly his outstretched hand encountered a solid object. He flinched in alarm, jerking his hand away from whatever danger might be lurking. Moments later the relief flooded through him as he realised it was an immobile steel bulkhead. In the weak red glow of his torch he saw a hinge.

A door!

He turned the handle and pushed against it, heaving against the weight of water on the other side. It swung slowly open, revealing a dark and flooded chamber.

Richard bit his lip as he recognised the terror of his nightmare. Forcing his fear down, he pulled himself through the submerged doorway. The room was large, perhaps two stories high, and dominated by several massive turbines filling its entire height.

The engineroom!

He was near the top of the room, but the water level had already reached the ceiling, completely engulfing everything. He peered down, searching for the floor, but saw nothing but blackness. The catwalk leading down from the door disappeared into the depths below him, but the feeble torchlight wasn't strong enough to penetrate the murk.

Richard fought the instinct to flee, knowing Vicki had to be down there somewhere.

Taking a deep breath, he let go the door frame and paddled out over the blackness. It waited below him like a bottomless pit, ready to swallow him up.

He ignored the wild thoughts conjured up by his mind, forcing himself to breathe slowly and methodically. An asthma attack down here could be fatal since there was no way he could use his inhaler with his mask on, if he could even get to it.

He swam using a clumsy dog-paddle, making his way down the channel between two of the huge turbines.

Suddenly something caught his eye in the depths below, a lighter-coloured object against the blackness.

He ducked his head lower, shining the feeble torchlight down.

Then he recoiled in horror as a ghostly shape materialised out of the gloom, limbs sprawled like a spectre reaching up to drag him down to a watery death.

An instant later he realised it was a body, dressed in a familiar red survival suit.

It's Vicki!

Her eyes were closed and it took Richard a moment to realise her leg was trapped beneath the wreckage of a twisted pipe. She must have set off her explosives while still in the room, then been trapped there when it flooded around her.

He choked back the emotion that threatened to overwhelm him.

Oh please, don't let her be dead!

***

Duke Hayward raised his grenade launcher, knowing he had only seconds left to act! While the larger Sea Stallion held off to provide fire support, the two smaller helicopters darted in and flared into a hover over the Nippon-Maru's bow. Duke recognised them with a frown. They were HH-60 Seahawks – the highly-modified combat rescue version favoured for fast deployment by the US Navy SEALs. He could see the black-clad and heavily-armed soldiers in the open doorways, preparing their abseil equipment. He knew he had to stop them before they roped down and stormed onto the factory ship.

It's time to finish this!

Duke squinted through the M-79's foresight. The grey fuselage of the lead helicopter leapt into view. He took aim, knowing the High-Explosive grenade would punch straight through the thin-skinned aluminium fuselage, and the blast would tear through the closely-packed troops inside…

Somehow it almost didn't seem fair.

Duke lowered the weapon. He couldn't bring himself to do it.

The men aboard that chopper were just soldiers carrying out their orders. He had no quarrel with them. He had even been in their shoes once.

He dropped his aim and squeezed the trigger, sending the grenade into the side of the nearby Kuu-Maru instead. The clang as the projectile struck the hull was instantly engulfed by the roar of the explosion.

The helicopters veered away, startled by the sudden appearance of a heavy weapon below them. They retreated away from the Gwendolyn and buzzed around like agitated bees.

Ignoring them, Duke reloaded and sent another grenade into the drifting catcher boat, just above the waterline.

"You might live t' see another day," he muttered at the unseen Japanese captain, "But you're damn well gonna have t' swim home!"

The big Sea Stallion rushed forward then, loudspeaker blaring. "Attention unidentified trawler. Lay down your weapons immediately! This is your final warning!"

Duke could see the door gunner crouched behind his multi-barrelled Gatling gun, ready to back up the threat.

"Surrender your ship or you will be fired on!"

Duke glared at the hovering huge gun platform.

Like hell you're getting' my Old Gal without a fight!

The helicopter swept in for a high-speed pass, the huge rotors throwing up a curtain of spray.

Knowing what was coming, Duke threw himself to the floor just as the door gunner opened up with his Gatling gun. The spinning barrels sent a stream of bullets into the Gwendolyn's wheelhouse, shattering the windows, stitching across the floor, then tearing huge chunks out of the wood-panelled rear wall. Despite his better judgement, Duke pulled the unconscious Summer to safety with him. He hugged the edge of the steel bulkhead, covering his face with his heads as glass and splinters swept the room, waiting for the maelstrom to cease.

Then the helicopter swept past, rotors clattering as it banked around for another pass.

Oh no y' don't!

Duke snatched up his grenade launcher and jammed a grey-tipped projectile into the breech. Crouching next to the dash, he took aim through a shattered side window.

The big helicopter roared in at the same height as the bridge, giving the door gunner an uninterrupted field of fire.

Duke pulled the trigger, then rolled aside as the bullets began to rain down around him.

The grenade flew cleanly through the open door, detonating inside the fuselage. The minigun immediately fell silent and the helicopter veered sharply away, white smoke pouring out of it.

Duke stood up, brushing shards of glass out of his beard.

"You jackasses asked for that," he muttered darkly. "Smash my boat up and see what happens to y'all!"

He shook his head in disgust, incredulous that he had just been fired on by his own country – and by Navy SEALs no less!

He touched the old scar at his throat, contemplating the irony of life. He had been gravely wounded fighting a dirty little war in his country's name and they gave him a damn medal for it. Now he was out here doing the right thing and fighting the good fight and they sent his own SEAL boys out to kill him!

He spat angrily, frustrated by the whole goddamned situation.

"We ain't the bleedin' enemy," he cursed, shaking his fist at the circling helicopters. "Y'all should be shootin' up them dirty gooks over there. They're the ones doin' wrong out here!"

Suddenly the two Seahawks swooped in, the lead machine flaring over the Gwendolyn's foredeck. The abseil ropes tumbled out. Duke raised an eyebrow, surprised they had committed without their fire support.

"So, comin' for me now are y'?"

Duke grunted. He knew the odds. The SEALs would come in hard and fast, guns blazing. They would hit with everything they had, subdue all resistance, then worry about picking up whatever pieces might remain.

He stooped to pick up his shotgun off the floor, wincing at the tightness in his shoulder. But his hands were steady. Determined.

He was damn well going to defend his ship and his crew. Come what may.

"I'm a soldier for the Earth now," he muttered.

Holding the shotgun's slide in his good hand he jerked his arm, cocking the weapon one-handed.

Duke glanced through the shattered windscreen, his mind racing.

SEALs were tough bastards – wolverine mean and hard as nails. They wouldn't take no nonsense. How the hell was he going to prevent them boarding?

He scowled as he looked around the bullet-riddled room. He knew they wouldn't hesitate to take him out and he was mad enough now to shoot back if they had another go at him. But he also remembered the promise he'd made to Cal.

He sighed, shaking his head pessimistically.

"Ok then, Son," he whispered. "We'll do it your way. I'll hold 'em off as long as I can – just be sure y' finish the job!"

Chapter 33

Richard Major stared in horror at the motionless form of his friend.
"Oh my god, Vicki," he whispered. "You can't be dead. You can't!"
Silently, he willed her to wake up, imagining the smile of recognition that would light up her face. But her eyes remained closed and she didn't move.
Richard felt the tears pricking his eyes as he gazed down at her pretty face, suspended in the water below him. She looked so serene and peaceful, as if only asleep, and her skin was so pale and innocent against the creeping blackness all around. He knew it was the pallor of death though – the stealthy creeping touch of the freezing water.
I'm too late!
He gazed forlornly at her, his heart filled with despair. It was just as he'd foreseen. A few wisps of raven-black hair had escaped from under her hood, and they floated gently in the water, framing her face. Below them he could make out a large bump on her forehead, evidence no doubt, of a blow that had stunned her long enough for the water to seize her in its clutches.
I was too slow. I failed you…
Then suddenly he noticed a faint flurry of bubbles escaped from her respirator, rising toward him.
Richard felt his pulse surge immediately.
She's breathing! She's alive!
With panic spurring him forward, he dived down to her, clawing his way through the black water. Ignoring the pain that pressed in on his eardrums, he seized Vicki under the arms and tried to lift her to safety.
Nothing happened.
He pulled again, harder, but she remained firmly anchored in the darkness.
Her eyelids fluttered briefly and he brushed the hair away from her mask, waiting to see if she would wake.
Suddenly the ship lurched as a distant explosion reverberated through the hull.
"Hold on!" Richard exclaimed. "I'll get you out of here. I promise!"
He pulled himself down into the darkness, feeling it press in closer around him.

Ignoring the discomfort, he followed the cuff of her trousers until it disappeared from view.

His torch glow revealed a pipe bent across her foot, trapping it in place. It was a seawater intake pipe, with a large diameter and reinforced sides.

Oh Vicki, what have you done?

She must have blown the intake pipes instead of the engines, relying on the corrosive action of the seawater to do the damage for her. But she had misjudged the force of the explosion, and the broken section of pipe had landed on her foot, trapping her as the water rose all around.

Richard's courage nearly deserted him at the thought, knowing how terrible it would feel. He wrestled frantically with the heavy pipe, pulling at the metal with both hands. But it wouldn't budge. Panting with exertion and frustration, he tried again. Still it wouldn't move.

I can't do it! his mind screamed.

You have to do it!

Desperate now, he remembered the spanner in his back pocket. Wedging it underneath the pipe he braced his feet against the side of the turbine and pushed with all his might, levering against the immovable object.

Slowly, almost imperceptibly, it began to move. One millimetre. Then two.

Suddenly his hands slipped and the spanner dropped from his grasp, sinking out of sight like a stone.

Oh no!

He felt around for it, searching desperately in the dim light of his torch. But it was gone, swallowed up by the darkness.

Distraught, he hammered against the metal with his fists, but the blows were softened by the water and bounced ineffectually off. He grabbed the pipe with both hands and pulled with all his might. Suddenly it shifted, and he realised his efforts with the spanner had succeeded in bending the pipe a fraction, permitting some movement.

Please let it be enough!

Grabbing Vicki's foot with both hands he pulled and twisted, almost insensitive in his haste, until he finally managed to wiggle it free. Then, almost weak with relief, he hugged her body to him and paddled upwards toward the submerged door.

They were not out of danger yet though. Not by a long shot!

As they entered the flooded corridor the ship shuddered again – another explosion booming through the hull.

Richard swam faster, fear driving him onwards as he bore his precious burden towards safety.

The minutes seemed like hours before his head finally broke the surface, and he wondered dimly if the ship was still filling up with water.

Got to get out of here!

Vicki's body seemed to double in weight as he pulled her clear of the water, but giving up was not an option. Placing her arm across his shoulders he half lifted, half dragged her up the stairs to safety.

But the ordeal was not over yet.

The blaze had fully engulfed the processing room now. It was hotter than a furnace, and the searing heat forced him down to his knees. Surprisingly though, everything was dark, and he couldn't see more than a foot in front of his face. Steam rose in clouds from his wet survival suit, and he knew they couldn't survive long in this heat. He dropped to his knees and crawled forward, dragging the unconscious Vicki with him through the thick smoke, groping blindly for the doorway to the corridor that led back to the deck.

Knowing that to become lost and disoriented would mean certain death, he followed the wall, feeling his way through the smoke, inch by inch, his breath rasping in his ears.

What seemed like an eternity later the wall opened out into the corridor. Gratefully he scrabbled down it, still on all fours, dragging his precious burden.

His knees were already battered and bruised from crawling, but he didn't slow down.

Vicki was a dead-weight draped across his shoulder, and she kept slipping off, forcing him to crawl one-handed while he held onto her. But he would not leave her behind. He dragged her as respectfully as he could, going as fast as he could towards the waiting rectangle of light, trying not to bump her head along the way.

Richard was panting and drenched in sweat when they finally emerged into the world again. After the claustrophobic darkness of the hold it was like being born again, and he pulled off his mask gratefully – the air tank all but spent – and sucked in a huge lungful of fresh air.

He gently lowered Vicki down, laying her next to an old chain on the deck. She murmured softly, and he leaned over her to remove her mask.

Her eyes flickered open. "Richard!" she exclaimed, trying to look around. "Where are we?"

"It's ok," he whispered, heaving a huge sigh of relief. "You're safe now. We're up on the deck. We just have to get back to the Naiad."

"You saved me!" she said, and it was a statement, not a question. "I knew you wouldn't leave me there!" She leaned up and kissed him on the cheek.

Richard blushed immediately but she smiled up at him, dimpling her cheeks, and the sight was enough to make his heart somersault with joy.

He helped her up to a sitting position. The Naiad sat nearly thirty metres away, but the deck was empty, offering a clear run to it.

"Can you make it?" he asked.

She nodded, struggling to her feet.

Richard kicked the abandoned anchor chain out of the way and helped her up. He felt his pulse quicken as she embraced his shoulder for support, but the feeling couldn't mask the nagging worry in the back of his mind. He couldn't help thinking there was something he had forgotten. Something important!

He cast a worried glance over his shoulder. The Kuu-Maru drifted nearby, with several large smoking holes blasted in its side. Richard's attention was drawn to the Gwendolyn though, with bullet holes riddling her superstructure and her bridge windows smashed like broken teeth.

The battle had well and truly begun!

Just then a sudden clatter of rotors signalled the arrival of a helicopter off the factory ship's bow – the one place where there was deck space not completely overshadowed by the huge steel girders of the deck cranes.

Oh no, they're here for us!

Richard turned back to look, and with a sinking heart he saw the black-clad warriors aboard it preparing to rope down onto the deck.

Cal's still on the bridge!

Richard knew his brother was in big trouble. It was too late to go and help him now – if in fact there was anything he could do to help.

Richard knew there was nothing he could do but flee.

But a sudden deep rumble of diesel engines made him turn his head. A familiar navy blue hull swept past, heading straight towards the danger.

The Gwendolyn!

The Skipper came out on deck, and with a lump in his throat Richard saw the shotgun in his hands. He raised it and a sudden puff of smoke spurted from the muzzle. Richard blinked in disbelief, realising Duke was drawing the commandoes' attention – but at the expense of his own chance of escape.

Richard stared in horror, unable to look away.

It was a full second later before the crack of the gunshot reached his ears, like watching a slow motion film.

The Skipper fired again.

Suddenly the helicopter lurched and began to pull away from the deck.

Like a bad dream, Richard was forced to watch the nightmare unfold.

He saw the soldier in the open doorway of the chopper raise his assault rifle. The faint *pop-pop-pop* sounded tinny and toy-like, almost swallowed up by the roar of the hovering helicopter's engine. But by the time the sound reached his ears, it was already too late. The Skipper had fallen to his knees, clutching his chest.

"No..." Richard whispered, shocked by what he'd just witnessed. "No!"

The Skipper lunged back inside the wheelhouse, shotgun in one hand, the other clutching his chest. Blood welled out between his fingers.

Richard craned his neck, trying to see if the Skipper was alright.

Suddenly a running figure burst out the wheelhouse door and leaped off the top rail into space. For a moment he thought it was Duke making good his escape. But then he saw the blonde hair trailing behind.

"Summer!" he whispered, suddenly conscious of his feelings for her. Though it was true he had cared about her once, the pain of betrayal was fresh in his mind. She had manipulated him, callously deceiving him for her own ends.

She never loved me...

He closed his eyes briefly, wrestling with his emotions.

Below him, Summer plunged into the icy water with a splash.

Richard opened his eyes and looked away, suddenly indifferent to her fate. There were enough warships around them now. One of them would pick her up...

The helicopter wheeled overhead, closing in on the Gwendolyn. But more puffs of gunsmoke through the shattered windscreen forced it away again.

"Go Skip!" Richard urged, so caught up in the show he was forgetting his own predicament. "Show them who's boss!"

Just then a strange whistling sound reached his ears.

Puzzled, Richard cocked his head to listen.

The whistle intensified into a dull shriek, and suddenly a huge geyser of water erupted off the Gwendolyn's bow.

"What the hell was that!" he exclaimed

Vicki's whisper was soft, but ominously compelling. "Guns. Big guns."

Richard looked out toward the horizon. What he saw made his courage falter. It was the Japanese destroyer that had been shadowing them since they left New Zealand. The red and white Rising Sun flag fluttered arrogantly at its pennant, the only splash of colour amid the intimidating grey.

With a heavy heart he knew there could be no escape any more. The sleek and sinister destroyer was designed for just a single purpose – and now it had finally caught up with them…

As he watched, a smudge of smoke suddenly puffed out of the barrel of the huge deck gun. Richard stared, oblivious to the impending danger. Suddenly the shriek of the next incoming round reached him, and the reality of the situation dawned.

Oh no, the Gwendolyn's a sitting duck!

It hit with an inky-black explosion down by the waterline. The brave little ship shivered as the shell tore into her hull, and Richard felt the savage heat and the shockwave of the blast from where he was.

He waited for the Duke's answering salvo, but none came. Smoke rose from the hull, and the shattered bridge. With a sinking realisation he realised the destroyer was far out of range of any weapon the Skipper possessed – if he was even in a state to fire back any more.

Another massive shell rocketed in – the gunners having found their mark at last – and the Gwendolyn shuddered beneath the onslaught, beginning to founder. The new deck covering splintered like matchsticks, the thin plywood no match for high explosives.

"Come on. We can't help him from here!"

Richard blinked, then nodded gravely. He and Vicki were definitely not out of danger yet themselves.

But before they could move, the helicopter returned with a thunderous roar, hovering over the black ship's forward deck again in a tornado of wind and noise.

This time it met no resistance. The black-garbed commandos roped down purposefully, disappearing out of sight behind the bridge superstructure. Then the helicopter climbed away again just as swiftly.

The soldiers were aboard. There was very little time left.

At that moment a lone figure emerged through the bridge's side door, standing high on the external companionway. He was dressed in red, and he held a crossbow in his hands.

It's Cal!

Richard felt his heart soar, even though he saw Cal was limping slightly, and had a cut above his eye. Despite that, he walked with determination, and black smoke poured out the doorway of the bridge behind him.

As he watched, Richard saw his brother crouch and adopt a firing position. He pointed the crossbow down at the deck below him, aiming at the hidden soldiers. It was loaded with a triangular broadhead point. A hunting bolt.

Richard felt the desperation seize him. Cal didn't know the two of them were out! He was going to take on the soldiers when they should all be escaping together!

Richard mentally computed the odds, and they weren't good. Eight SEALs had roped aboard the ship, but Cal's crossbow had only one shot at a time. He was courting certain death, and Richard knew he had to stop him.

He reached for his radio mic, then realised his head was bare. He had taken off his headset when he removed his mask!

Desperate now, he shouted to Cal, waving his arms, beckoning him to return to the Naiad with them.

Incredibly, Cal heard him over the racket. He looked back, waved, then shook his head. He pointed towards the Naiad, ordering Richard to leave. Then he smiled sadly, hefted his crossbow again, and turned away. The message was plain. He couldn't get there before the assault force now, so he had to ensure their escape.

Richard's stomach sank with dread for his brother, but he knew his first responsibility was to Vicki. Reluctantly he turned away, determined to get her back to the inflatable, then return to help him.

But as he turned, he was forced to a sudden halt, eyes widening as he stared at the sword tip held to his throat.

Vicki inhaled sharply as she recognised the trench-coated figure. "You!"

The assassin turned to leer at her, gloating, but the sword never wavered.

Richard stared at the killer, feeling numb with fear.

Oh no. We're dead!

But then he saw the blood on the man's shoulder, and the red marks on his throat. The knowledge that this evil samurai assassin was not invincible emboldened him.

"Cal should have killed you when he had the chance!"

The assassin gave no sign of comprehension, but his black eyes flicked back to lock on Richard's face and he glared menacingly along the length of the steel blade at him.

Then, slowly and deliberately, he brought out his left hand from under his coat. In it he held a familiar headset.

Richard felt his indignation rise. "Hey, that's mine!"

The sword point pricked his throat, and he gulped.

The assassin raised the stolen radio and spoke for the first time.

"Herro, bronde Westerner," he said in correct, but heavily-accented English. "My master, Yokuke-san, sends his regards."

Cal's head snapped around at the sound of the voice in his earpiece, the sudden anguish plainly visible on his face.

The assassin's lips drew back in a gleeful snarl as he surveyed his prisoners. "My master wishes you to know that your friends are about to die by his order, and by the same weapon that slew the Commissioner of the Seychelles."

His dark glasses were gone now and his eyes glittered with triumph at the look of helpless torment that passed across Cal's face. "Yes, your friend Admirante died on his knees in front of me also," he hissed, in a voice as cold and hypnotic as a serpent. "And know this – he died badly!"

Then he dropped the radio and raised the sword over his shoulder in the classic two-handed killing stance. "It is my honour to carry out this order!" he hissed, his voice carrying easily in the shocked silence.

Cal, still waiting to ambush the advancing SEALs, could only look on in horror.

At that same moment the heavily-armed commandos caught sight of Cal high above them, and a confused volley of shouting rang out as they dived for cover – warnings to each other followed immediately by orders for him to surrender.

Richard knew it would take super-human shooting for Cal to hold them all off now.

But Cal didn't hesitate. Before anyone could react he raised the crossbow to his shoulder in one fluid movement and fired.

The swish of the sword snapped Richard's focus back to the assassin, and he knew he was staring Death in the face. As the blade flashed towards them he tried to duck and cover Vicki's body with his own. But even as he did so he realised it was a futile gesture. This was it. The moment of final reckoning.

He turned his face to the assassin, determined to meet his death like a man.

But the blow never hit.

The sword froze abruptly in mid swing, then clattered to the deck.

Cal's voice crackled through the abandoned radio at their feet. "That's for Victor."

The assassin gargled, clutching at the crossbow bolt that had just sprouted from his throat. Blood pumped from the severed carotid artery, bright red and steaming in the cold air. Richard stared, wide-eyed with shock.

The killer sank to his knees, still clawing uselessly at his neck.

Before he could stop her, Vicki sprang forward launching a solid kick to the side of his head. "And that's from the rest of us!" she exclaimed.

The assassin toppled over and lay writhing on the deck, his blood staining the boards that had already seen plenty.

At that moment Richard became aware of the gunshots echoing from the front of the ship.

Whirling around, he was just in time to see a red form tumble over the rail and plummet down to the sea below.

"Cal! No!"

But it was too late. He wasn't sure if his brother had slipped or jumped, but the bright smear of blood left on the sickly yellow paintwork proved the bullets had hit home.

"Nooo!"

Richard looked over the rail, searching the waves for his brother. But Cal was gone, swallowed up by the frigid water.

Distraught, he began to run to the spot he'd last seen him. Vicki caught his sleeve.

"No! We have to go! Now!"

"B-but I have to get to Cal…" he stammered weakly.

"The Naiad! We need to get to the Naiad!"

Reluctantly, Richard allowed himself to be led away. Vicki was right.

If we can just get to the Naiad we can pick him up!

He avoided the assassin thrashing weakly on the ground, heading for the inflatable sitting at the far end of the deck.

As she passed, Vicki stomped on the killer's forearm, kicking his sword out of reach with her foot.

Richard turned back. "What are you doing?"

"This is evidence," she replied, glaring at the prostrate form of the assassin, and the rapidly-growing pool of blood around him. She stooped to pick up the weapon. "If this sword did kill Victor Admirante then DNA testing will prove the link. It will not only clear Cal of the murder, it will incriminate this bastard. And his master!"

The assassin slumped into unconsciousness, his life-blood draining away.

At that moment the first SEAL came into view, assault rifle held threateningly at his shoulder as he stalked along the side deck. He hadn't seen them yet, but Richard knew that couldn't last much longer.

"Come on, let's go!" he urged.

They sprinted down the deck, dropping their shoulders to charge at the Naiad's pontoons like a rugby forward pack. The inflatable resisted their efforts at first, stubbornly remaining where it was.

"Heave!"

Richard pushed against the rubber bumper with all his might. Finally it began to move towards the waiting slipway.

"It's going! Jump in!"

Vicki vaulted over the pontoon and into the boat, just as it tipped over the edge of the slipway and began to slide. At the stern, Richard stumbled as the boat slid away from him, then fell headlong. In a few terrible moments the pontoon slipped from his grasp and the boat slid away down the ramp, leaving him stranded.

Behind him, he could already hear heavy booted feet pounding on the deck planks. The SEALs were coming!

Oh no. I'm done for.

He raised his head to look down the slipway, taking one last lingering look at freedom.

Floating down in the swells behind the factory ship's giant stern, Vicki beckoned him frantically.

"Richard, come on!" she shouted up at him.

He closed his eyes, listening to the stampede behind him. They would be on him in moments.

It's too late!

"RICHARD!"

His eyes flew open at the desperation in her tone. Suddenly he realised the selfishness of surrender.

It's not too late! It's never too late!

He looked down at the ice-laden sea waiting hungrily below. Then taking a deep breath, he threw himself headfirst down the slipway.

His stomach leaped into his mouth as he plunged straight down the slick ramp, struggling to twist his body around and sit upright. He didn't manage it. He hit the water hard, plunging deep under the surface. A lump of ice struck him on the temple, dazing him. The cold seized his chest tightly enough to make him want to gasp, but he had no air tank any more. He opened his eyes, fascinated by the faint glow reflected off the icebergs in the water all around. He floated for a moment, hanging in space, unexpectedly peaceful.

Maybe drowning wouldn't be so bad after all?

At least he could go with no regrets. He had tried his damnedest to make a difference! This would be a release…

Suddenly he felt strong hands lifting him up.

His head broke the surface, and he wheezed for air. He clung to the rubber pontoon, too weak to climb over it.

"Come on!"

Vicki grabbed him by the armpits, hauling him aboard.

Richard lay panting in the scuppers, water pouring off him. He was exhausted. Physically and mentally.

A sudden booming explosion brought him scrabbling to his feet.

He looked out towards the Gwendolyn, and the sight that met his eyes was sickening.

The plucky ship – his home for the past few months – was barely recognisable. Her handsome blue paintwork was scarred and blackened, and Cal and Duke's new deck coverings lay in shredded piles of kindling wood. Huge holes had been blasted in her hull and superstructure, and she sagged, mortally wounded.

Fires were burning out of control below decks, and a huge pall of black smoke rose into the sky, marking her demise like a funeral pyre.

A final shell shrieked in, and the entire ship shuddered as it blasted home.

She settled lower into the water, the end coming quickly as her back broke.

Richard watched silently as the brave little ship went down, claimed by the sea.

As the bridge slipped beneath the waves, he thought he saw the Skipper's shaggy pirate beard behind the wheel, defiant to the end.

The sight brought his anguish to the fore.

"Skip, no!"

Why hadn't he got clear? Richard closed his eyes, trying to blot out the grief.

This can't be happening! It's not supposed to end like this!

His thoughts turned to his brother, injured and now lost at sea.

We've got to do something!

"Quick, we have to find Cal!" he implored. "It's not too late!"

Vicki said nothing.

"Vicki?"

He followed her sombre gaze up to the stern rail of the black ship. It bristled with gun-toting commandos, all aiming down at them. He stared at the row of muzzles, lined up with the menacing promise of a sudden and violent death.

They were trapped. There was no escape.

A warning shot cracked over their heads, buzzing like an enraged hornet.

Richard stared out to sea, searching vainly for any sign of his brother. There was none.

He sighed, defeated at last, and raised his hands in surrender.

It was over.

***

Dennis Cruikshank jumped out of the tender and hurried up the hastily-erected gangway on the side of the whaling ship, eager to supervise the processing of his prisoners.

His adrenaline was still buzzing with the usual high he got in anticipation of a bust, only this time he wouldn't be able to blow off any steam by cracking some heads. He was still annoyed that he hadn't been able to join in for this sting, but the Navy had jurisdiction and rules were rules…

He emerged onto the deck of the giant factory ship, momentarily put off by the size of the destruction evident. It looked as though there were huge fires below decks. They'd probably take days to extinguish.

Then his customary anger returned.

I'll see these perps put away for a long time for this!

His prisoners were lying on the deck, their hands trussed behind their backs with plastic flex-cuffs, covered by a gun-toting SEAL in mirrored sunglasses.

Cruikshank's forehead beetled immediately. "There's only two of them," he snapped at the soldier. "What happened to the rest?"

He was met with a blank shrug. "Over the side."

The commander sauntered over then, grinning like a quarterback who'd just thrown a game-winning touchdown pass. He was obviously well pleased with his efforts. "Agent Cruikshank," he greeted him, forced to raise his voice over the din of circling helicopters. "Seems your intel was spot on." He gestured towards the thick smoke cloud still billowing up from the fire in the hold. "This gang were up to plenty of mischief when we dropped in on them."

"Dirty hippies," Cruikshank muttered, shaking his head. "What the fuck goes on in those pot-smoking heads of theirs?"

"Beats me." The commander gestured at the prisoners. "But they're all yours now. Not bad for a morning's work, wouldn't you say?"

"Nice bust," Cruikshank agreed. "This is what law enforcement is all about. Guys like you and me at the sharp end of it, doing the hard yards to make the world a better place!"

Just then another soldier hurried over to speak to his commander. "They're ready to take the captured inflatable aboard the destroyer now."

Cruikshank was scathing. "What the hell do ya want to do that for?" he demanded. "Cut it loose!" He pointed at the nearest soldier. "You! Shoot out the pontoons!"

He turned back to the commander, his lip curling with disgust. "I'm not carting that piece of junk all the way back home. Tell the captain of the destroyer his gunners can use it for target practice."

"What about the missing terrorists?" the commander asked. "Want us to organise a sweep for them?"

Cruikshank's reply was immediate – and definite. "Hell no! Let the scum swim home!"

The SEAL team leader raised a surprised eyebrow. "You sure? Abandoning them out here probably counts as a war crime or something…"

"This is a civil matter, not a war. They don't have any rights. And it's about time they learned crime doesn't pay."

The commander shrugged. "You're the boss."

***

Richard shuffled awkwardly up the gangplank to the American warship, chains clinking at his wrists and ankles. It was a small consolation, but at least he and Vicki didn't have to suffer the indignity of being imprisoned by the Japanese.

He turned to look back, feeling the spark of defiance still burning within him. The last two whaling ships in the Fleet were crippled now, both pouring black smoke into the steely sky. He watched as the Japanese Navy tried to get towlines on their drifting vessels.

Good riddance!

Richard's pleasure was savage, but the feeling was short-lived.

He flinched as the destroyer's heavy machine-gun opened up next to him, its roar seeming to tear apart the very air itself.

The large calibre bullets tore into the Naiad, puncturing the pontoons and shattering the fibreglass steering console. The little boat deflated with a sad sigh, settling on the water like a strip of abandoned sailcloth.

Richard bit his lip as he watched the gunfire destroy the last link to Cal's research.

It's over. They've won.

Vicki stood silently next to him, her head bowed.

Together they looked out to sea.

Richard wondered what had become of Koru. There was no sign of the great blue whale but it was his fervent desire that she had escaped. As he gazed across the featureless expanse of water, he found himself hoping that somewhere in those mysterious blue depths the haunting echo of whalesong might still endure.

"Swim, Koru," he whispered, his voice lost to the wind. "Swim free."

Though he was uplifted by the thought she was still alive and able to travel the vast oceans of the world, he knew the Team had paid a heavy price to secure her freedom.

"All right, move along," a guard growled, prodding him in the back with a gun barrel.

Reluctantly, Richard turned away.

He felt the deck rumble beneath his feet as the destroyer accelerated, and the bow swung north, towards the civilised world.

Richard felt the melancholy settle over him. He knew this was the end of the line. He and Vicki were in serious trouble, but fears about their fate were not foremost in his mind right now.

I am not sorry! We did what had to be done!

What saddened him more was leaving the Real World he had come to regard as home.

Richard turned his back on their heading, facing south instead, towards Antarctica.

He stared at the distant pile of debris floating on the water, watching it recede. It marked the last remnants of the Team's valiant stand, and the Gwendolyn's final resting place at sea.

There was no sign of Cal. Or Duke.

And as he watched the Southern Ocean fall away behind the stern, Richard was conscious of how ephemeral their wake was. In the distance it was already beginning to fade, along with any evidence they were ever there. The ship left just a tenuous white mark behind as evidence of their passage – before the endless ocean wiped away the past behind them.

Richard continued to stare into the distance, gazing at the forlorn wreckage of Cal's Naiad, bullet-riddled and partially sunk, abandoned to the sea.

Suddenly, just before it disappeared from view for good, he thought he caught a glimpse of a red shape bobbing in the waves next to it.

He blinked in surprise, rubbing his eyes with a manacled hand. But when he looked again there was nothing there.

Just the timeless ocean stretching all the way to the horizon.

Epilogue

One year later…

The grey stormclouds scudded across the sky, darkening the sun.

The bottlenose dolphin bull was worried. He was used to the sounds of fishing boats as he led his pod up and down the coast, but something troubled him today. He had worked hard to find this school of silvery sprats, searching backwards and forwards across the shallow waters of the bays, all the time listening for the fuzzy echo return that indicated a darting school of fish. The fish were scarcer these days, and the dolphins had to travel further, searching harder to find them. The Pod had been blessed with two dozen new calves that spring, playful and mischievous. But that made the search for food all the more imperative. For the youngsters to thrive their mothers needed a good supply of food or their milk would dry up. And that was what made him hesitate today, reluctant to order the Pod to abandon the meal he had worked so hard to find.

A female swam up, offering him a juicy fish head from the sprat she'd just caught. But the bull ignored the delicacy. It wasn't that he didn't appreciate her thoughtful offering, just that his attention was focused instead out into the dark water.

He was used to the presence of fishing boats in the bay – indeed, there were more of them than ever before, searching relentlessly for the elusive shoals. Sometimes they even followed the dolphins, exploiting the Pod's superior skill at finding fish, then laying out their own nets instead to sweep the oceans clean.

But something seemed different this time. Wrong.

While his Pod fed at the mouth of the bay, the fishing boats circled closer than normal, and more numerous. And under the leaden sky they drew still closer. Uncertain now, the bull began to sense danger. Whistling to his Pod, he commanded them to follow and led them out towards the safety of the open sea. But the boats crowded closer, ringing the entrance to the bay, cutting off their escape. The bull dived, preparing to look for a way under the obstacle, but as he approached the boats a horrible metallic clanging rang out through the water. He shied away, the harsh din ringing in his sensitive ears. He tried again, but a wall of noise blocked the way to the open sea, hemming the dolphins in. The bull hesitated. Behind him the Pod milled around, uncertain, all thoughts of food forgotten. He turned back to them, swimming away from the boats. Whistling for the Pod to follow, he led them towards the shore.

The boats followed.

Fear spread quickly through the Pod as the water ran out. Some dolphins beached themselves in the shallows, panicking at the touch of the sand beneath them. Others remained in the deeper water just beyond the waves, still trying to dive away from the source of the terrible noise. But there was no escape. Eventually they gave up trying to get away and lay on the surface, overwhelmed.

The bull surveyed his stricken Pod. He raised his head out of the water.

A light rain had begun to fall, blanketing the world above in a silent mist.

He gazed up at the dark sky, seeking deliverance that would not come. The fishing boats had drawn closer still now, crowding into the bay, forcing the dolphins onto the beach.

A female surfaced by his side. It was his mate. She clicked softly, afraid. He replied confidently, reassuring her – but not convinced himself.

He dived again, knowing the Pod was in terrible danger, and determined to find a way out. The bull headed straight for the open sea again. He swam with his sonar off, a silent bullet streaking through the darkness. Ignoring the painful cacophony of metal on metal, he charged straight towards the line of boats, desperately seeking an escape route for his pod.

Beneath the boats the din reached a crescendo, but he gritted his teeth against it, determined to find a way out of the bay. As he shot through the gap beneath their hulls, his spirit soared. He had found an escape!

But suddenly he found himself ensnared, caught as if by unseen hands. The fishermen had strung their nets across the entire width of the bay, and there was no escaping their insidious grasp. The touch of the nylon filaments was as light as a gentle kelp frond, but as merciless and unyielding as the death grip of a Kraken, snaking up like invisible tentacles to ensnare him. The bull battled to free himself, but the more he struggled, the more he was enveloped in the treacherous nylon folds.

Eventually he lay still, suspended in the water, exhausted from his struggles. His lungs screamed out for air, but the surface – though tantalisingly near – was out of reach.

Just beyond him lay the path to open water, and freedom. Enticingly close, beckoning. But even if he could have escaped, he would not. He would never abandon his Pod. They were his family, as well as his responsibility. And he would share their fate.

He closed his eyes, weak from lack of oxygen.

Just before the world went black, the bull's sensitive hearing caught the first splash of booted feet in the shallows, followed by a familiar dolphin voice screaming in panic.

***

Richard blinked, massaging his temples with frustration. He rubbed his eyes and stared at the flickering computer screen, wondering for the millionth time why he'd gone with such a complicated circuit design for this project. He was running out of time. He needed to get this prototype working before the final deadline.

He traced the layout with one finger, at the same time peering at the mess of wires on the table next to him.

"Whoever said the life of an electronics engineer was easy," he muttered under his breath.

He stared at the blank wall of his office in front of him, thinking back to his time on the Southern Ocean – back to another time, in another world. A world that was far-removed from the life of an Electronics Engineer. He sighed wistfully, wondering if it had all been worth it.

Did we actually achieve anything?

That depended on your point of view. They had managed to put the Japanese Whaling Fleet out of action.

But for how long? The voice in his head demanded. *The War for the Whales is not won that easily!*

It had been a small victory, that was true, though it was just one battle in a long and bitter war. A war that had not ended yet. And the Team had definitely paid a high price for it. The price for fighting on was almost too much to bear thinking about.

Richard felt the grief well up in him again. He closed his eyes for a moment as his thoughts turned back to Cal. Not a day went past that he didn't think about him – and Duke too. That his brother was missing at sea was the hardest part to deal with. Without a body to mourn and say goodbye to he'd had no closure. And the faint hope that stubbornly refused to die only made things worse. The 'what ifs' that plagued him each day were a form of emotional torture in themselves.

Richard sighed again, remembering some of the last words Cal had said to him, spoken that day aboard the Gwendolyn before they made their stand. "What are a few human lives when measured against the continued survival of an entire species?" With a heavy heart he realised Cal was not talking about whalers. He had been foretelling his own sacrifice. His brother had already made his decision. When they went aboard the black ship Cal would have already known that he would go as far as he had to for what he believed in. "The greatest use of a life is to spend it for something that will outlast it," he used to say.

And he didn't flinch when the final test came!

Richard screwed his eyes shut to force back the tears, that fateful day on the frozen sea still vivid in his mind. Cal had faced the end without hesitation, and he had traded himself so that the Team might escape.

He gave his life for me.

Richard's guilt returned afresh to haunt him.

Why? I don't deserve it!

He rubbed his eyes, knowing he could never hope to fill his brother's shoes – nor even live up to his expectations.

He stared vacantly at the computer screen, not even seeing the circuit diagram through his blurry eyes.

Whatever made Cal think I could be a biologist?

Cal had been right about one thing though; and that was knowing the best way to get public support. The uproar surrounding the whale conservationists lost at sea had focused both national and international scrutiny and public opinion against the Japanese whaling like never before. Mr Fish had gone into the trial already on the defensive, vilified by the news media and forced to publicly defend himself under the accusing glare of the cameras before the investigation had even begun.

Richard allowed himself a sad smile, struck by the providential way things had turned out.

On account of Cal's escape from custody, the New Zealand police had intercepted the prisoners as soon as the US-led flotilla had returned to Lyttleton – much to the Yanks' annoyance. Agent Cruikshank in particular, had been reluctant to give up his prisoners. But almost as though he had planned in advance what would happen, Cal's actions had ensured a local jurisdiction over the fugitives, and the New Zealand Government was keen to prosecute its citizens under its own laws.

Like a bad penny, Heath had turned up at the trial, turning 'Crown Witness' to testify against them on behalf of the prosecution. He was offered witness protection and name suppression, but even hiding behind a screen like a coward it was obvious who it was. Richard would have recognised his personal brand of belligerence anywhere!

He hadn't seen the dreadlocked hippy since the trial was over, except for one time on the nightly news. Heath and Aurelia were filmed chaining themselves to the front door of a supermarket, while they protested against what they alleged was the sale of Genetically-Modified food products.

Richard surprised himself at his indifference. He hadn't even known the two of them were an item – if in fact she was actually giving him any kind of recompense for dutifully following her around – but he was sure she was only using the Californian to further her own agenda. As soon as he was no longer useful to her she would toss him aside.

Women are all the same!

Richard shook his head, knowing he was allowing his recently-created cynicism to get the better of him.

Summer had testified against them too, of course. He had ignored her for the duration of the trial, surprised at how easy he found that now. Betrayal had a uniquely sobering effect – especially on cases of purely superficial attraction! It was amazing how obvious the signs pointing to her true nature were now, given the wisdom of hindsight.

In any case he hadn't had to put up with her for long. The trial was conspicuous by its brevity – almost as if the judge was embarrassed by the whole affair and eager to see the end of it. Cal was missing, so as far as His Honour was concerned there was no case to answer in the eyes of the New Zealand Government. Since the others hadn't breached New Zealand law those charges were dismissed, and the accusations of international terrorism couldn't be upheld through lack of evidence. In his closing address the judge was loudly critical of Agent Cruikshank and his actions, even going so far as to imply he used excessive force with the barest mandate to act. Of course the issue of US national security was raised in defence, but the judge would have none of it. He accused the American agent of over-reaction, pointing out that the biologists had done nothing against America, and nothing to warrant an arrest by them. He even went so far as to suggest that the joint American-Japanese Navy force's heavy-handedness on the High Seas constituted an act of piracy in itself.

On that note the judge had cautioned the defendants on their future conduct and dismissed the case. Richard and Vicki were as delighted as they were surprised, but they hadn't had time to sit around and congratulate each other. Both America and Japan still had outstanding warrants for their arrest, and Interpol had a long reach. As did some of the other players involved. The last place they wanted to end up was in a Japanese prison facing charges of terrorism and attempted murder. So they had been forced to go to ground for a while – Vicki back to Australia, and Richard back to his electronics. Their only contact during that time had been via brief and heavily-encrypted emails.

Richard felt the pressures of those past months threaten to weigh down on him again. The life of a fugitive definitely wasn't easy.

Even though Amimoto had been arrested and jailed in Japan for his part in the corruption and murder at the heart of the IWC scandal, his influence was still strong. And his anger was as ardent as ever.

Richard turned back to his circuit diagram, wondering if he would ever be able to go back to his life without looking over his shoulder.

***

Akogi Yokuke stared at the display cabinet housing his precious antiques, though they did nothing to improve his mood. Despite the fact that he had been permitted to furnish this room to his own tastes and he still enjoyed unrestricted contact with the outside world, there was no mistaking this room for what it was…

He shuffled around the confines of it, squinting angrily. There were no bars on the windows, but the door was locked and a guard stood out in the corridor to vet all visitors.

Though luxurious, the fact remained this was still a prison cell.

That knowledge alone was enough to raise his ire.

How dare they keep me here!

It was ironic that after all the shady dealings he had instigated over the years, it was taking care of that wretched Victor Admirante that had landed him here!

Ironic, yes, but still gravely insulting!

Yokuke clenched a wizened fist, already scheming about how to get himself out of jail and take his revenge on the people who had put him there.

The Kajiki had met with a fitting end, and he allowed himself a smile to savour that victory. But there were still others to feel the force of his wrath…

The remaining protestors for a start. Along with his enemies in the Diet who had betrayed him.

He curled his lip at the memory of his peers in parliament, crowding greedily around like vultures at a carcass, climbing over themselves in their eagerness to seize his power and carve it up for themselves.

They will not rest on their ill-gotten laurels for long! I will take back what is rightfully mine!

Japan's fishing industry could not be allowed to falter – there was far too much at stake.

Not that he would ever allow that to happen, however.

Even though his influence was undiminished from this jail cell – well appointed as it was – his first priority was to cast aside this ridiculous incarceration as soon as possible.

After all, it is a matter of honour, neh?

Following that, his focus would be to get back his Fleet and rebuild Taiyoku Misui Fisheries Company's fortunes. He still had a controlling interest in dozens of fishing and food production companies around the globe – including New Zealand, Canada, and the lucrative American domestic market – and in today's society that was more power than most word leaders possessed. And more permanent.

If I cannot control the Western barbarians by force, then I shall do it by stealth!

He smiled. When it came to international influence, money spoke its own language!

Yokuke bared his yellowing teeth as he reflected on the lack of respect that accompanied modern American capitalism though. Respect that a great man like himself deserved.

How dare they call me to account?

In days of old, none would have dared challenge his authority, yet here he was, shamed and caged up like a common criminal!

His anger burned at the injustice of the situation.

Privilege and fortune belonged to those who earned it! Predatory behaviour was the natural order of things. Peace was merely an illusion – and a dream of the weak.

Real men make their own destiny!

Yet in this aberrant age of human rights, common men of inferior races were still taught they were the equal of their betters, and the world was led by the cultural imperialism of Western barbarians, who forced their will upon the rest. They were undeserving, decadent scum, yet they controlled the world with breathtaking arrogance.

Yokuke shook with silent rage.

Japan had been shamed before the world, the Government forced to apologise.

Yet Japan's reputation had been tarnished through no fault of his. He had tried to lead the Land of the Rising Sun to greatness.

And I will yet!

Yokuke's eyes glittered with malice towards the enemies of Japan, and he resolved to restore his country's sullied honour.

After all, a nation without pride has no reason to exist!

His mind turned automatically to business again, evaluating his options. What remained of his great pelagic whaling fleet was tied up at Shimonoseki, awaiting a near rebuild. He had already transferred ownership of the severely damaged vessels to Kyoubou Seppuku, a holding company of which he held the controlling interest. And for the time being, Kyoubou Seppuku would be officially chartered by the Government-run Institute of Cetacean Research for the purposes of scientific research. That should direct some of the international condemnation away from his commercial operation!

Kyoubou Seppuku would also be the company that bore the cost of salvage and repair – along with the risk. A holding company could safely go bankrupt with no threat to him, and the associated dishonour if Kyoubou Seppuku folded would affect neither his, nor Taiyoku Misui's good name.

I will rebuild my empire yet!

The Japanese whalemeat markets were still open, providing the means. It was a huge incentive for local fishermen and pirate whalers alike, and a golden opportunity for a shrewd business backer like himself to control the supply and make even more money. It was also a financial incentive to repair the whaling Fleet as soon as possible.

Yokuke's grin was vulpine as he laid out his plans.

In the medium term he would sponsor pirate whalers to meet the shortfall until the Fleet was repaired. There were plenty of mercenary fishing captains out there whose ships were available to anyone with a little money. It was easy enough to mount a harpoon gun on the bow and convert any old tub into a whaler! And by flying flags of convenience from some random country they would never be traced back to Japan, let alone to Taiyoku Misui Fisheries. Yokuke smiled. He already had plenty of Third-World governments on his payroll and eager to do his bidding…

His eyes glittered with greed as he reached for his telephone.

In the shorter term there were other means to ensure the market's demand for whalemeat was met. Means that were right on Japan's doorstep.

Dolphins.

***

Hogei Gyofuku stamped his feet against the morning chill, irritated by the delay. He looked out into the darkness of Taiji Bay. He could hear the dolphins puffing out beyond the waves, and he was impatient to get started.

He fished out his flask from the pocket of his coat and knocked back a draught of saké, spluttering as the warmth of the liquor spread down to his belly.

It would be light soon. Then it could begin.

As he waited, his thoughts turned to his own fortunes, and the bad karma that saw him confined to land now. He was a whaleboat captain without a ship, forced to join the common fishermen in their dolphin drive.

His disgust was palpable, and it brought the bile to the very tip of his throat. He snorted and spat a gob of phlegm onto the sand.

At least there was some honour in hunting down and killing the bigger brutes in the distant Southern Ocean. These little ones were nothing more than vermin to be exterminated.

It is an insult to my honour, neh?

He was under no illusions as to the source of this dishonour to him, however.

Bad karma it was not! It was those meddling protestors that ruined my boat!

Not only had they shut down the Fleet, they had also had the honourable Amimoto-san arrested!

Gyofuku chuckled suddenly, amused that the Westerners thought they could stop his master that easily.

Amimoto had many contacts within the industry, and despite being in jail his influence had not lessened. After all, he had been the one who organised this dolphin drive.

Gyofuku could appreciate the business skill of his master. The unscrupulous dolphinaria owners in the cities always needed more specimens for their circuses, since it was not an easy thing to keep dolphins alive and doing tricks in captivity for long. And without live animals there would be no income for the owners, so they were willing to pay handsomely for a few unblemished animals delivered alive to their waiting trucks – usually young females whose spirits were more easily broken. That money would easily cover the costs of the drive, and then the rest of the pod belonged solely to Taiyoku Misui Fisheries Company. The fishermen could earn a handsome bonus for a day's work, and the "whalemeat" markets in the cities wouldn't have to close down for lack of meat. And of course, the company's shareholders could reap a tidy profit.

Though he grumbled about his loss of station, Gyofuku had to admit he didn't really mind being here. As lowly as it was, he did enjoy this work.

Dolphins angered him. They ate too many fish. Taiji was a fishing town, not unlike his own, and the fishermen depended on fishing for their livelihoods. Lately the catches had been smaller and smaller, the fish harder to find than ever.

And that was clearly the fault of the dolphins. They were too greedy. They took too many fish. Sometimes they even took the fish right off the hooks – all but the head. They left that useless scrap behind for the fishermen!

Such an insult! It's like they deliberately taunt us, neh?

Gyofuku's pockmarked face tightened into a sneer. How fitting that the meat of these dolphins could now help the fishermen pay their bills. He would enjoy punishing the sea-pigs for their greed!

He gazed out to sea, at the ring of fishing boats that encircled the bay. The dolphins' only escape route had been tightly sealed off! He bared his lips in a greedy smile, feeling his excitement building with the knowledge the whole pod was at his mercy.

I will kill them all – but slowly, at my leisure!

***

Stricken by the cries of distress from his pod, the bull dolphin redoubled his efforts, battling to free himself from the net. But his desperate struggles were to no avail, and gradually they grew weaker again. The knotted nylon bound him tightly, a prisoner of a watery grave.

Directly above him shone the mirror of light that was the surface. Tantalising. Vital. But out of reach. Already his chest was beginning to tighten with the urgent need to breathe. The prospect of a slow, unnatural death by drowning filled him with dread. But the bull controlled the waves of terror that threatened to engulf him, knowing he needed to be strong.

Around him, the fishermen continued to make their terrible noise, forcing the rest of the pod into the shallows.

The bull hung suspended, an unwilling witness to the looming annihilation of his pod. He called out, trying to reassure his friends. But it was a futile effort. All now realised the dreadful fate that awaited them.

Some of the young males attempted to charge the net too, but the bull warned them off, already trapped in its fatal embrace.

The Pod huddled protectively together, the calves in the centre, their tiny dorsal fins tucked close to their mothers.

Suddenly an alpha female left the group, serene and determined. His mate. She headed toward the beach without looking back. Whether in a moment of bravery, or sad acceptance, she launched herself down the crest of a wave towards the sand.

She seemed to hesitate a moment as the wave began to retreat around her, then she turned away from the sea, choosing to remain behind. The water hissed on the sand as it washed out, leaving her stranded on the shore. The light sparkled on her body, water drops glistening like jewels on her smooth skin – a final memory of the ocean whose gentle caress she would never feel again.

Perhaps she hoped her sacrifice might deliver her friends, or perhaps she was just impatient to get the horrible business over with before her courage failed.

The pod bull whistled a frantic warning to her, but she was beyond his help.

A fisherman walked down the sand, and she stopped struggling as he loomed over her. She lay still as he raised his harpoon, closing her eyes as the blade plunged down.

As the first scent of blood tainted the water, the dolphins panicked. Wide-eyed with terror, they rushed to get away. Confused and leaderless, the Pod darted chaotically, thrashing the water to foam in their attempts to flee.

But there was no escape, and as the butchery continued a sense of grim finality descended over the bay. Under the softly falling rain, the dolphins lingered at the surface, awaiting their fate.

Some willingly entered the shallows where the harpoons flashed. Others, whimpering softly, had to be forced to meet the spear.

The blades came down again and again, falling on adult and infant alike. The fishermen would spare none.

Gradually the sea began to run red with blood.

The pod bull felt his lungs begin to burn, and the greyness pressed in on him. He had failed in his duty. Not only could he not save his pod, he could not even share their fate. Defeated, he surrendered himself to the embrace of the Deep. Just as he closed his eyes for what would be the last time, a dark shape slipped into the edge of his vision.

***

Richard blew softly to clear the tendril of smoke that rose from the circuit board then lowered his soldering iron, satisfied with his handiwork at last.

He fiddled with the mess of cables running into the back of his laptop then turned back to the screen.

Bingo!

He reached across to flick on the speaker, and a confused babble of clicks and whistles flooded out.

Dolphins! And they sound distressed!

In the blue glow of the screen he saw what he had been hoping for – the incoming data from the array of remote hydrophones he had deployed across the coast.

He poked his head out the doorway and called up to the deck. "Ok, it's showtime! I've got a large pod, maybe a hundred all up. They're heading straight for the shore in a bay about two kilometres ahead of us. I'm picking up the noise from multiple propellers all around them!"

The floor vibrated beneath him as the boat's engine roared into life, and he hurried gratefully out of his cramped workroom down in the hold. The chartered launch was designed as a big-game-fishing boat and it was small. Much smaller than the Gwendolyn. But then again, this was only supposed to be a temporary mission.

Richard opened the door and stepped out into the pale early morning light, turning to look towards Taiji Bay. The sea was slate grey under a squally sky, and he felt a chill in the air that had nothing to do with the crisp October morning. Even with false passports he knew they were taking a huge risk coming back to Japan.

He sniffed, forcing the doubts out of his mind.

One man can always make a difference, he reminded himself.

The shore was a dark shadow in the half-light, and he raised the night vision scope with grim resolve, already prepared for the sight that awaited him.

The fishermen were shadowy figures in the gloom, wearing wetsuits and long coats against the misty rain that had begun to fall. But even as the beach lightened with the dawn of a new day, they waded out into the water to begin their grisly work.

The first dolphins were dragged alive onto the beach, where their throats were slashed and they were left to bleed to death. They gasped for breath, struggling and thrashing around in pain, as though trying to swim away from the horror. But none would escape. Their only release was to be a slow and painful death.

Impassionate to their suffering, the fishermen moved on without a backwards glance, their knives rising and falling methodically.

As the beach became crowded with bodies the fishermen moved into the shallows where the dolphins waited, despatching them with jabs and thrusts of their long spears. The waves began to darken, and the sand was stained with blood. A river of it ran down the beach, dark and ominous in the pale morning light, flowing towards the water as though seeking the solace of the ocean one final time.

Under the stormy grey sky, Richard remembered Old Blue. He remembered the peaceful serenity that seemed to emanate from the huge creature, and the ageless wisdom reflected in the depths of his great eye as they had looked at each other. They were two individuals connecting for the briefest instant, despite the wide and uncrossable void of understanding that separated them. Richard knew the whales embodied a sanguine and timeless knowledge almost as old as the Ocean itself, but they spoke a language people could never hope to understand.

And that made Old Blue's brutal death all the more tragic.

How can a culture so ancient be destroyed so easily?

Richard shook his head in despair, finding it almost beyond comprehension that people could be so short-sighted in their greed for money and power. They would stop at nothing to have their way!

Is a dead whale really that important to them?

At the rate the whaling nations of the world continued killing, the day would soon come when there were no more whales to kill!

Would they learn their lesson then? Somehow he doubted it.

Richard closed his eyes, suddenly weary of the slaughter, wishing the horror would go away. But he knew that when he opened his eyes it would still be happening, stark and brutal in its efficiency.

"Only your heart can tell you what is right and what is wrong," Cal had said to him once, and he felt the wisdom behind those words now. His heart ached with sorrow.

Richard sighed as his thoughts drifted again to his brother. The official verdict was he was lost at sea, presumed drowned, but Richard couldn't accept that. After everything that Cal had strived for, he couldn't believe it could be over just like that. Despite the pain and uncertainty it caused him, he preferred to think of his brother as simply 'missing'.

Where are you Cal? I need you here!

Wherever he was, Richard was sure his brother was still fighting the good fight. And he hoped he could find the strength to live up to Cal's expectations too.

Richard turned his attention back to his hydrophone array. With a heavy heart he listened to the underwater sounds, amplified through his sensitive equipment. They were cries of panic and distress from intelligent and self-aware creatures, just like himself.

As the slaughter intensified he was forced to turn the volume down.

Standing there in the early morning twilight, with the sound of the dolphins' distress still ringing in his ears, he suddenly knew he couldn't stand by any longer.

Taking a deep breath he stared out to sea, looking towards the promise of dawn lightening the Eastern sky. With more determination than he had ever felt in his life before, he vowed he would never let the vast ocean fall silent. Without the songs of whales and dolphins it was just a cold, lifeless void below the waves. Without life in the seas it would be a dead world… the hauntingly beautiful notes that had echoed down through the millennia would gradually fade from existence, until they became just a memory – a faint and ghostly whisper lingering on in the darkness.

Richard's heart thudded with the significance of his decision.

He reached a hand up to his chest. Nestled next to his skin was the hard outline of a greenstone pendant underneath his shirt. Cal's pendant. It was all he had left of his brother now, other than the memories, and he found it reassuring to touch the physical reminder that seemed imbued with his brother's spirit. He brought it out and stared at the cool green stone in the dawn light, tracing the spiral with his finger, drawn to the mystery in its hidden depths. Yet it wasn't until that moment, surrounded by the last of the night, that he fully appreciated the symbolism of the design. Though it might bring him luck, it wasn't supposed to be a good luck charm. It was carved in the shape of a spiral, a stylistic representation of an unfurling fern frond. In Maori lore, the design was known as a Koru, and it symbolised a new beginning…

He closed his eyes, remembering Duke's last whispered words he'd overheard on the radio.

I'm a soldier for the Earth now.

Richard clenched his jaw, and when he spoke his voice quivered slightly – but not from fear.

"Dive team, stand by! Two minutes to contact!"

A silhouette suddenly disengaged from the shadows at the bow, and the outline of a figure-hugging black wetsuit appeared before him in the last of the moonlight, dive tank already strapped in place.

A mane of raven-black hair – the colour of the night sky – fell forward, hiding her face.

Richard stared at her, mesmerised by her beauty, and his heart swelled to bursting point. "Be careful out there!" he whispered. "Promise me!"

Vicki didn't answer, but came to him, sweeping him into a fierce embrace.

She kissed him hurriedly, passionately, as though the sense of danger that hung over them lent an urgency to their love.

Richard gazed down at her fondly, shaking his head. "I still don't know why I agreed to let you do this…"

"Because you know you couldn't stop me!" Vicki sniffed defiantly, and she reached up, businesslike again, to tie her hair back into its customary ponytail. She pulled her facemask over her head and adjusted the strap.

Richard sighed and abruptly the set of her jaw softened again.

"We're doing the right thing," she whispered, as if reading his innermost thoughts.

Richard smiled back at her, and understanding flashed between them without the need for words. "I know your father would have been proud of you," he said quietly. "I am."

She lowered her eyes, looking down towards where the dark water waited. "Thanks Richard. That means a lot to me."

Richard's smile was tinged with sadness. "I'm not Richard any more. The old Richard is gone. Call me Rich."

She grinned in approval, showing her dimples. "See you on the flip-side, Rich!"

Then she turned and slipped over the side into the blackness.

Richard took a deep breath and turned away, refusing to watch as the dark water closed over her head.

He raised the binoculars, listening for the splashes as the rest of the dive team entered the water.

His attention was already focused miles away though – on the distant shoreline. That was where his trial waited.

He felt the familiar tightness beginning in his chest, and without even looking away from the binoculars he reached into his pocket for his inhaler. But as he drew it out, something made him hesitate.

I don't need this any more!

Richard opened his fingers and let the inhaler fall to the deck, his attention still riveted on the shadowy figures moving around on shore. As he watched the fishermen going about their gruesome work, his fingers holding the binoculars turned white with the force of his grip. But his breathing remained calm and measured.

The shadows moved meticulously among the helpless dolphins, stony-faced and impassionate, impervious to their cries, their purpose as grim as reapers.

Suddenly, Richard sucked in his breath as he recognised a burly figure striding amongst the beached dolphins, bloody knife in hand. Though it was still too dark to make out the face, the portly silhouette alone was enough to recognise him. That, and the red plastic crash helmet perched on the fat rolls of his neck.

Hogei Gyofuku!

As the whaleboat captain's knife came down on another innocent victim, Richard's eyes narrowed. He hefted the wooden club at his side, feeling the anger flow through him. In a flash he realised that cameras were no use here. Nor was protesting. Documenting the slaughter would not save these lives.

"Take us in!" he called out to the helmsman. "I've seen enough dolphins killed for one morning. It's time to bust up this little party!"

As the launch sped towards shore, Richard's thoughts went to the dive knife strapped to his thigh. When he had buckled it on this morning he had intended it for emergency use only. Now he wasn't so sure.

Whatever will be, will be…

Richard knew he had a score to settle on that beach, and not just for himself.

I'm ready take on the world if I have to!

He felt the adrenaline surge through him in anticipation – a feeling that no longer filled him with terror.

He was a biologist now.

And a soldier for the Earth.

Richard stared wistfully at the dark water slipping under the bow. Cal's repeated lament drifted back to him as the wind ruffled his hair; "It's tough to change the world, Bro. You can't force people to change the way they think, just like you can't force them to care. They need a reason to change their ways, but if they can't see the right way for themselves already, well, I sure don't know how to show them…"

Richard nodded contemplatively to himself as he thought of the notebook in his pocket – in which he had written down everything that had happened over the past months.

He turned back to the shore, just as the first golden rays of dawn lit the wave-tops.

The world could indeed be a jaded and uncaring place, but if Cal's words couldn't sway people then maybe his story could…

THE END

Author's Note

Sadly, the facts and figures presented in this story are accurate, and the central conflict described here is inspired by real life circumstances.

The dolphin slaughter at Taiji Bay in Japan is real – and takes place every year. The Japanese Pelagic Whaling Fleet is also real, as is their complete defiance of the IWC's Moratorium on commercial whaling and the Southern Ocean Whale Sanctuary. Every year they continue to slaughter hundreds of whales in the Southern and North Pacific Oceans under the guise of "scientific" research – the kill taking place perhaps even as you read these lines.

At the time of writing, other nations are beginning to follow the example set by Japan and are reinstating commercial whaling operations of their own – Norway and Iceland already setting themselves similar quotas in the northern hemisphere. Other countries, while not actually undertaking whaling themselves, nevertheless use their vote in the IWC to support the continuation of whaling in the oceans around the world.

What can I do to stop it?

- Buy additional copies of *Echoes in the Blue.* For every book sold at normal retail price I will make a donation to save the whales. See www.cgeorgemuller.com for details.
- Write letters to the Japan Fisheries Association, and the governments of Japan, Norway, Iceland, and every other pro-whaling nation, expressing your displeasure at their continued defiance of international opinion.
- Petition your Member of Parliament or local representative to put diplomatic pressure on Japan and other pro-whaling nations to end this senseless kill, once and for all.
- Donate money to conservation organisations committed to saving whales.
- Think carefully where you spend your consumer dollar. Don't buy whalemeat or any other product derived from endangered species (Visit www.CITES.org for more information). Don't support any of the parent companies making money from whaling.
- Consider what you personally can do to help. Whales need all the allies they can get! Besides, the life of a marine biologist can be its own reward!

Legitimate science has shown that the larger whale species have never recovered from the over-exploitation of last century. Many other cetacean species are still hunted today – including smaller whales and dolphins whose population biology remains poorly understood – but are even now threatened or teetering on the brink of extinction.

If the wanton slaughter continues it is only a matter of time before more species join those already on the Red-list, and cetaceans may be exterminated, one by one, from the oceans of our planet.
Forever...

The future is in our hands.
C. George Muller, 2006